D0866481

Doctor Zhivago

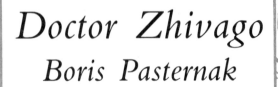

Doctor Zhivago
Boris Pasternak

Translated from the Russian by
Max Hayward and Manya Harari

BANTAM BOOKS
TORONTO · NEW YORK · LONDON · SYDNEY · AUCKLAND

CONTENTS

THE PRINCIPAL CHARACTERS
IN THIS BOOK

Yurii Andreievich Zhivago (as a child, called *Yura;* affectionately, *Yurochka)* is the son of Andrei Zhivago, a profligate, and Maria Nikolaievna Zhivago.
Evgraf Andreievich Zhivago, his half brother, is the son of his father and Princess Stolbunova-Enrici.
Nikolai Nikolaievich Vedeniapin (Uncle Kolia) is his maternal uncle.

Antonina Alexandrovna Gromeko (Tonia) is the daughter of *Alexander Alexandrovich Gromeko,* a professor of chemistry, and his wife *Anna Ivanovna,* whose father was the landowner and ironmaster Ivan Ernestovich Krueger.
As young people, Yurii Andreievich Zhivago and *Misha Gordon,* son of a lawyer, live with the Gromekos.

Larisa Feodorovna Guishar (Lara) is the daughter of a Russianized, widowed Frenchwoman, Amalia Karlovna Guishar. Rodion (Rodia) is her younger brother.

Victor Ippolitovich Komarovsky was Andrei Zhivago's lawyer and is Madame Guishar's lover and adviser.

Lavrentii Mikhailovich Kologrivov is a rich industrialist; his wife, Serafima Filippovna; their daughters, Nadia and Lipa.

Pavel Pavlovich Antipov (Pasha, Pashenka) is the son of a railway worker, Pavel Ferapontovich Antipov. After his father's exile to Siberia, he lives with the Tiverzins (Kuprian Savelievich and his mother, Marfa Gavrilovna), another revolutionary family of railway workers.

Osip Gimazetdinovich Galiullin (Yusupka), son of Gimazetdin, the janitor at the Tiverzins' tenement; he is a Moslem.

Innokentii Dudorov (Nika), son of Dementii Dudorov, a revolutionary terrorist, and a Georgian princess.

Markel Shchapov, porter at the Gromekos' house, and his daughter *Marina (Marinka).*

PART ONE

CHAPTER ONE

The Five-O'Clock Express

1

On they went, singing "Rest Eternal," and whenever they stopped, their feet, the horses, and the gusts of wind seemed to carry on their singing.

Passersby made way for the procession, counted the wreaths, and crossed themselves. Some joined in out of curiosity and asked: "Who is being buried?"—"Zhivago," they were told.— "Oh, I see. That's what it is."—"It isn't him. It's his wife."— "Well, it comes to the same thing. May her soul rest in peace. It's a fine funeral."

The last moments slipped by, one by one, irretrievable. "The earth is the Lord's and the fullness thereof, the earth and everything that dwells therein." The priest, with the gesture of a cross, scattered earth over the body of Maria Nikolaievna. They sang "The souls of the righteous." Then a fearful bustle began. The coffin was closed, nailed, and lowered into the ground. Clods of earth rained on the lid as the grave was hurriedly filled by four spades. A little mound formed. A ten-year-old boy climbed on it. Only the state of stupor and insensibility which is gradually induced by all big funerals could have created the impression that he intended to speak over his mother's grave.

He raised his head and from his vantage point absently glanced about the bare autumn landscape and the domes of the monastery. His snub-nosed face became contorted and he stretched out his neck. If a wolf cub had done this, everyone would have thought that it was about to howl. The boy covered his face with his hands and burst into sobs. The wind bearing down on him lashed his hands and face with cold gusts of rain. A man in black with tightly fitting sleeves went up to the grave. This was Nikolai Nikolaievich Vedeniapin, the dead woman's brother and the uncle of the weeping boy; a former priest, he had been unfrocked at his own request.

He went up to the boy and led him out of the graveyard.

2

They spent the night at the monastery, where Uncle Nikolai was given a room for old times' sake. It was on the eve of the Feast of the Intercession of the Holy Virgin. The next day they were supposed to travel south to a provincial town on the Volga where Uncle Nikolai worked for the publisher of the local progressive newspaper. They had bought their tickets and their things stood packed in the cell. The station was nearby, and they could hear the plaintive hooting of engines shunting in the distance.

It grew very cold that evening. The two windows of the cell were at ground level and looked out on a corner of the neglected kitchen garden, a stretch of the main road with frozen puddles on it, and the part of the churchyard where Maria Nikolaievna had been buried earlier in the day. There was nothing in the kitchen garden except acacia bushes around the walls and a few beds of cabbages, wrinkled and blue with cold. With each blast of wind the leafless acacias danced as if possessed and then lay flat on the path.

During the night the boy, Yura, was wakened by a knocking at the window. The dark cell was mysteriously lit up by a flickering whiteness. With nothing on but his shirt, he ran to the window and pressed his face against the cold glass.

Outside there was no trace of the road, the graveyard, or the kitchen garden, nothing but the blizzard, the air smoking with snow. It was almost as if the snowstorm had caught sight of

Yura and, conscious of its power to terrify, roared and howled, doing everything possible to impress him. Turning over and over in the sky, length after length of whiteness unwound over the earth and shrouded it. The blizzard was alone in the world; it had no rival.

When he climbed down from the window sill Yura's first impulse was to dress, run outside, and start doing something. He was afraid that the cabbage patch would be buried so that no one could dig it out and that his mother would helplessly sink deeper and deeper away from him into the ground.

Once more it ended in tears. His uncle woke up, spoke to him of Christ, and tried to comfort him, then yawned and stood thoughtfully by the window. Day was breaking. They began to dress.

3

While his mother was alive Yura did not know that his father had abandoned them long ago, leading a dissolute life in Siberia and abroad and squandering the family millions. He was always told that his father was away on business in Petersburg or at one of the big fairs, usually at Irbit.

His mother had always been sickly. When she was found to have consumption she began to go to southern France and northern Italy for treatment. On two occasions Yura went with her. He was often left with strangers, different ones each time. He became accustomed to such changes, and against this untidy background, surrounded with continual mysteries, he took his father's absence for granted.

He could remember a time in his early childhood when a large number of things were still known by his family name. There was a Zhivago factory, a Zhivago bank, Zhivago buildings, a Zhivago necktie pin, even a Zhivago cake which was a kind of *baba au rhum*, and at one time if you said "Zhivago" to your sleigh driver in Moscow, it was as if you had said: "Take me to Timbuctoo!" and he carried you off to a fairy-tale kingdom. You would find yourself transported to a vast, quiet park. Crows settled on the heavy branches of firs, scattering the hoarfrost; their cawing echoed and re-echoed like crackling wood. Purebred dogs came running across the road out of the clearing from the recently constructed house. Farther on, lights appeared in the gathering dusk.

And then suddenly all that was gone. They were poor.

4

One day in the summer of 1903, Yura was driving across fields in a two-horse open carriage with his Uncle Nikolai. They were on their way to see Ivan Ivanovich Voskoboinikov, a teacher and author of popular textbooks, who lived at Duplyanka, the estate of Kologrivov, a silk manufacturer, and a great patron of the arts.

It was the Feast of the Virgin of Kazan. The harvest was in full swing but, whether because of the feast or because of the midday break, there was not a soul in sight. The half-reaped fields under the glaring sun looked like the half-shorn heads of convicts. Birds were circling overhead. In the hot stillness the heavy-eared wheat stood straight. Neat sheaves rose above the stubble in the distance; if you stared at them long enough they seemed to move, walking along on the horizon like land surveyors taking notes.

"Whose fields are these?" Nikolai Nikolaievich asked Pavel, the publisher's odd-job man who sat sideways on the box, shoulders hunched and legs crossed to show that driving was not his regular job. "The landlord's or the peasants'?"

"These are the master's." Pavel, who was smoking, after a long silence jabbed with the end of his whip in another direction: "And those are the peasants'!—Get along," he shouted at the horses, keeping an eye on their tails and haunches like an engineer watching his pressure gauge. The horses were like horses the world over: the shaft horse pulled with the innate honesty of a simple soul while the off horse arched its neck like a swan and seemed to the uninitiated to be an inveterate idler who thought only of prancing in time to the jangling bells.

Nikolai Nikolaievich had with him the proofs of Voskoboinikov's book on the land question; the publisher had asked the author to revise it in view of the increasingly strict censorship.

"The people are getting out of hand here," he told Pavel. "A merchant in a nearby village has had his throat slit and the county stud farm has been burned down. What do you make of it? Any talk of it in your village?"

But evidently Pavel took an even gloomier view than the censor who urged Voskoboinikov to moderate his passionate views on the agrarian problem. "Talk of it? The peasants have been spoiled—treated too well. That's no good for the likes of us. Give the peasants rope and God knows we'll all be at each other's throats in no time.—Get along, there!"

This was Yura's second trip with his uncle to Duplyanka. He thought he remembered the way, and every time the fields spread out, forming a narrow border around the woods, it seemed to him he recognized the place where the road would turn right and disclose briefly a view of the six-mile-long Kologrivov estate, with the river gleaming in the distance and the railway beyond it. But each time he was mistaken. Fields followed fields and were in turn lost in woods. These vast expanses gave him a feeling of freedom and elation. They made him think and dream of the future.

Not one of the books that later made Nikolai Nikolaievich famous was yet written. Although his ideas had taken shape, he did not know how close was their expression. Soon he was to take his place among contemporary writers, university professors, and philosophers of the revolution, a man who shared their ideological concern but had nothing in common with them except their terminology. All of them, without exception, clung to some dogma or other, satisfied with words and superficialities, but Father Nikolai had gone through Tolstoyism and revolutionary idealism and was still moving forward. He passionately sought an idea, inspired, graspable, which in its movement would clearly point the way toward change, an idea like a flash of lightning or a roll of thunder capable of speaking even to a child or an illiterate. He thirsted for something new.

Yura enjoyed being with his uncle. He reminded him of his mother. Like hers, his mind moved with freedom and welcomed the unfamiliar. He had the same aristocratic sense of equality with all living creatures and the same gift of taking in everything at a glance and of expressing his thoughts as they first came to him and before they had lost their meaning and vitality.

Yura was glad that his uncle was taking him to Duplyanka. It was a beautiful place, and this too reminded him of his mother, who had been fond of nature and had often taken him for country walks.

He also looked forward to seeing Nika Dudorov again, though Nika, being two years older, probably despised him. Nika was a schoolboy who lived at the Voskoboinikovs'; when he shook hands with Yura, he jerked his arm downwards with all his might and bowed his head so low that his hair flopped over his forehead and hid half his face.

5

"The vital nerve of the problem of pauperism," Nikolai Nikolaievich read from the revised manuscript.

"Essence would be better, I think," said Ivan Ivanovich, making the correction on the galleys.

They were working in the half-darkness of the glassed-in veranda. Watering cans and gardening tools lay about, a raincoat was flung over the back of a broken chair, mud-caked hip boots stood in a corner, their uppers collapsed on the floor.

"On the other hand, the statistics of births and deaths show," dictated Nikolai Nikolaievich.

"Insert 'for the year under review,'" said Ivan Ivanovich and made a note. There was a slight draft. Pieces of granite lay on the sheets as paperweights.

When they finished Nikolai Nikolaievich wanted to leave at once.

"There's a storm coming. We must be off."

"Nothing of the sort. I won't let you. We're going to have tea now."

"But I must be back in town by night."

"It's no use arguing. I won't hear of it."

From the garden, a whiff of charcoal smoke from the samovar drifted in, smothering the smell of tobacco plant and heliotrope. A maid carried out a tray with clotted cream, berries, and cheese cakes. Then they were told that Pavel had gone off to bathe in the river and had taken the horses with him. Nikolai Nikolaievich had to resign himself to staying.

"Let's go down to the river while they're getting tea ready," suggested Ivan Ivanovich.

On the strength of his friendship with Kologrivov, he had the use of two rooms in the manager's house. The cottage with its own small garden stood in a neglected corner of the park, near the old drive, now thickly overgrown with grass and no longer used except for carting rubbish to the gully, which served as a dump. Kologrivov, a man of advanced views and a millionaire who sympathized with the revolution, was abroad with his wife. Only his two daughters, Nadia and Lipa, with their governess and a small staff of servants, were on the estate.

A thick hedge of blackthorn separated the manager's house and garden from the park with its lawns and artificial lakes which surrounded the main house. As Ivan Ivanovich and Nikolai Nikolaievich skirted the hedge, small flocks of sparrows flew out at regular intervals. The blackthorn swarmed with them, and their even chatter accompanied them like water flowing in a pipe.

They passed the hothouses, the gardener's cottage, and the ruins of some stone structure. They were talking about new talent in science and literature.

"Yes, there are gifted men," said Nikolai Nikolaievich; "but the fashion nowadays is all for groups and societies of every sort. Gregariousness is always the refuge of mediocrities, whether they swear by Soloviëv or Kant or Marx. Only individuals seek the truth, and they shun those whose sole concern is not the truth. How many things in the world deserve our loyalty? Very few indeed. I think one should be loyal to immortality, which is another word for life, a stronger word for it. One must be true to immortality—true to Christ! Ah, you're turning up your nose, my poor man. As ususal, you haven't understood a thing."

"Hmm," said Ivan Ivanovich. Thin, fair-haired, restless as an eel, he had a mocking little beard that made him look like an American of Lincoln's time: he was always bunching it up in his hand and nibbling the tip. "I say nothing, of course. As you know, I look at these things rather differently. But while we're at it, tell me, what was it like when they unfrocked you? I bet you were scared. They didn't anathematize you, did they?"

"You're trying to change the subject. However, why not. . . . Anathematize me? No, they don't do that anymore. It was unpleasant, and there are certain consequences. For instance, one is banned from the civil service for quite a long time, and I was forbidden to go to Moscow or Petersburg. But these are trifles. As I was saying, one stand is that it is possible to be an atheist, it is possible not to know whether God exists, or

why, and yet believe that man does not live in a state of nature
but in history, and that history as we know it now began with
Christ, and that Christ's Gospel is its foundation. Now what is
history? It is the centuries of systematic explorations of the
riddle of death, with a view to overcoming death. That's why
people discover mathematical infinity and electromagnetic
waves, that's why they write symphonies. Now, you can't
advance in this direction without a certain faith. You can't make
such discoveries without spiritual equipment. And the basic
elements of this equipment are in the Gospels. What are they?
To begin with, love of one's neighbor, which is the supreme
form of vital energy. Once it fills the heart of man it has to
overflow and spend itself. And then the two basic ideals of
modern man—without them he is unthinkable—the idea of free
personality and the idea of life as sacrifice. Mind you, all this is
still extraordinarily new. There was no history in this sense
among the ancients. They had blood and beastliness and cruelty
and pockmarked Caligulas who do not suspect how untalented
every enslaver is. They had the boastful dead eternity of bronze
monuments and marble columns. It was not until after the
coming of Christ that time and man could breathe freely. It was
not until after Him that men began to live toward the future.
Man does not die in a ditch like a dog—but at home in history,
while the work toward the conquest of death is in full swing; he
dies sharing in this work. Ouf! I got quite worked up, didn't I?
But I might as well be talking to a blank wall."

"That's metaphysics, my dear fellow. It's forbidden by my
doctors, my stomach won't take it."

"Oh well, you're hopeless. Let's leave it. Goodness, what a
view, you lucky devil. Though I suppose as you live with it
every day you don't see it."

It was hard to keep one's eyes on the shimmering river,
which, like a sheet of polished metal, reflected the glare of the
sun. Suddenly its surface parted in waves. A big ferry loaded
with carts, horses, and peasants and their women started for the
other shore.

"Just think, it's only a little after five," said Ivan Ivanovich.
"There's the express from Syzran. It passes here at five past
five."

Far out on the plain, crossing it from right to left, came a neat
little yellow and blue train, tiny in the distance. Suddenly they
noticed that it had stopped. White puffs of steam flurried over
the engine, and then came a prolonged whistle.

"That's strange," said Voskoboinikov. "Something's wrong. It has no business to stop in the middle of the marsh out there. Something must have happened. Let's go and have tea."

6

Nika was neither in the garden nor in the house. Yura guessed that he was hiding because they bored him, and because Yura was too young for him. When his uncle and Ivan Ivanovich went on the veranda to work, Yura was left to wander aimlessly about the grounds.

How enchanting this place was! Orioles kept making their clear three-note calls, stopping each time just long enough to let the countryside suck in the moist fluting sounds down to the last vibration. A heavy fragrance, motionless, as though having lost its way in the air, was fixed by the heat above the flower beds. This brought back memories of Antibes and Bordighera. Yura turned this way and that. The ghost of his mother's voice was hallucinatingly present in the meadows. He heard it in the musical phrases of the birds and the buzzing of the bees. Now and then he imagined with a start that his mother was calling him, asking him to join her somewhere.

He walked to the gully and climbed from the clear coppice at its edge into the alder thicket that covered its bottom.

Down there among the litter of fallen branches it was dark and dank; flowers were few, and the notched stalks of horsetail looked like the staffs with Egyptian ornaments in his illustrated Bible.

Yura felt more and more lonely. He wanted to cry. He slumped to his knees and burst into tears.

"Angel of God, my holy guardian," he prayed, "keep me firmly on the path of truth and tell Mother I'm all right, she's not to worry. If there is a life after death, O Lord, receive Mother into Your heavenly mansions where the faces of the saints and of the just shine like stars. Mother was so good, she couldn't have been a sinner, have mercy on her, Lord, and please don't let her suffer. Mother!"—in his heartrending anguish he called to her as though she were another patron saint, and suddenly, unable to bear any more, fell down unconscious.

He was not unconscious for long. When he came to, he heard

his uncle calling him from above. He answered and began to climb. Suddenly he remembered that he had not prayed for his missing father, as Maria Nikolaievna had taught him to.

But his fainting spell had left him with a sense of lightness and well-being that he was unwilling to lose. He thought that nothing terrible would happen if he prayed for his father some other time, as if saying to himself, "Let him wait." Yura did not remember him at all.

7

In a second-class compartment of the train sat Misha Gordon, who was travelling with his father, a lawyer from Orenburg. Misha was a boy of eleven with a thoughtful face and big dark eyes; he was in his second year of gymnasium. His father, Grigory Osipovich Gordon, was being transferred to a new post in Moscow. His mother and sisters had gone on some time before to get their apartment ready.

Father and son had been travelling for three days.

Russia, with its fields, steppes, villages, and towns, bleached lime-white by the sun, flew past them wrapped in hot clouds of dust. Lines of carts rolled along the highways, occasionally lumbering off the road to cross the tracks; from the furiously speeding train it seemed that the carts stood still and the horses were marking time.

At big stations passengers jumped out and ran to the buffet; the sun setting behind the station garden lit their feet and shone under the wheels of the train.

Every motion in the world taken separately was calculated and purposeful, but, taken together, they were spontaneously intoxicated with the general stream of life which united them all. People worked and struggled, each set in motion by the mechanism of his own cares. But the mechanisms would not have worked properly had they not been regulated and governed by a higher sense of an ultimate freedom from care. This freedom came from the feeling that all human lives were interrelated, a certainty that they flowed into each other—a happy feeling that all events took place not only on the earth, in which the dead are buried, but also in some other region which some called the Kingdom of God, others history, and still others by some other name.

To this general rule Misha was an unhappy, bitter exception. A feeling of care remained his ultimate mainspring and was not relieved and ennobled by a sense of security. He knew this hereditary trait in himself and watched morbidly and self-consciously for symptoms of it in himself. It distressed him. Its presence humiliated him.

For as long as he could remember he had never ceased to wonder why, having arms and legs like everyone else, and a language and way of life common to all, one could be different from the others, liked only by few and, moreover, loved by no one. He could not understand a situation in which if you were worse than other people you could not make an effort to improve yourself. What did it mean to be a Jew? What was the purpose of it? What was the reward or the justification of this impotent challenge, which brought nothing but grief?

When Misha took the problem to his father he was told that his premises were absurd, and that such reasonings were wrong, but he was offered no solution deep enough to attract him or to make him bow silently to the inevitable.

And making an exception only for his parents, he gradually became contemptuous of all grownups who had made this mess and were unable to clear it up. He was sure that when he was big he would straighten it all out.

Now, for instance, no one had the courage to say that his father should not have run after that madman when he had rushed out onto the platform, and should not have stopped the train when, pushing Grigory Osipovich aside, and flinging open the door, he had thrown himself head first out of the express like a diver from a springboard into a swimming pool.

But since it was his father who had pulled the emergency release, it looked as if the train had stopped for such an inexplicably long time because of them.

No one knew the exact cause of the delay. Some said that the sudden stop had damaged the air brakes, others that they were on a steep gradient and the engine could not make it. A third view was that as the suicide was a prominent person, his lawyer, who had been with him on the train, insisted on officials being called from the nearest station, Kologrivovka, to draw up a statement. This was why the assistant engineer had climbed up the telegraph pole: the inspection handcar must be on its way.

There was a faint stench from the lavatories, not quite

dispelled by eau de cologne, and a smell of fried chicken, a little high and wrapped in dirty wax paper. As though nothing had happened, graying Petersburg ladies with creaking chesty voices, turned into gypsies by the combination of soot and cosmetics, powdered their faces and wiped their fingers on their handkerchiefs. When they passed the door of the Gordons' compartment, adjusting their shawls and anxious about their appearance even while squeezing themselves through the narrow corridor, their pursed lips seemed to Misha to hiss: "Aren't we sensitive! We're something special. We're intellectuals. It's too much for us."

The body of the suicide lay on the grass by the embankment. A little stream of blood had run across his forehead, and, having dried, it looked like a cancel mark crossing out his face. It did not look like his blood, which had come from his body, but like a foreign appendage, a piece of plaster or a splatter of mud or a wet birch leaf.

Curious onlookers and sympathizers surrounded the body in a constantly changing cluster, while his friend and travelling companion, a thickset, arrogant-looking lawyer, a purebred animal in a sweaty shirt, stood over him sullenly with an expressionless face. Overcome by the heat, he was fanning himself with his hat. In answer to all questions he shrugged his shoulders and said crossly without even turning around: "He was an alcoholic. Can't you understand? He did it in a fit of D.T.'s."

Once or twice a thin old woman in a woollen dress and lace kerchief went up to the body. She was the widow Tiverzina, mother of two engineers, who was travelling third class on a pass with her two daughters-in-law. Like nuns with their mother superior, the two quiet women, their shawls pulled low over their foreheads, followed her in silence. The crowd made way for them.

Tiverzina's husband had been burned alive in a railway accident. She stood a little away from the body, where she could see it through the crowd, and sighed as if comparing the two cases. "Each according to his fate," she seemed to say. "Some die by the Lord's will—and look what's happened to him—to die of rich living and mental illness."

All the passengers came out and had a look at the corpse and went back to their compartments only for fear that something might be stolen.

When they jumped out onto the track and picked flowers or

took a short walk to stretch their legs, they felt as if the whole place owed its existence to the accident, and that without it neither the swampy meadow with hillocks, the broad river, nor the fine house and church on the steep opposite side would have been there. Even the diffident evening sun seemed to be a purely local feature. Its light probed the scene of the accident timidly, like a cow from a nearby herd come for a moment to take a look at the crowd.

Misha had been deeply shaken by the event and had at first wept with grief and fright. In the course of the long journey the suicide had come several times to their compartment and had talked with Misha's father for hours on end. He had said that he found relief in the moral decency, peace, and understanding which he discovered in him and had asked him endless questions about fine points in law concerning bills of exchange, deeds of settlement, bankruptcy, and fraud. "Is that so?" he exclaimed at Gordon's answers. "Can the law be as lenient as that? My lawyer takes a much gloomier view."

Each time that this nervous man calmed down, his travelling companion came from their first-class coach to drag him off to the restaurant to drink champagne. He was the thickset, arrogant, clean-shaven, well-dressed lawyer who now stood over his body, showing not the least surprise. It was hard to escape the feeling that his client's ceaseless agitation had somehow been to his advantage.

Misha's father described him as a well-known millionaire, Zhivago, a good-natured profligate, not quite responsible for his actions. When he had come to their compartment, he would, unrestrained by Misha's presence, talk about his son, a boy of Misha's age, and about his late wife; then he would go on about his second family, whom he had deserted as he had the first. At this point he would remember something else, grow pale with terror, and begin to lose the thread of his story.

To Misha he had shown an unaccountable affection, which probably reflected a feeling for someone else. He had showered him with presents, jumping out to buy them at the big stations, where the bookstalls in the first-class waiting rooms also sold toys and local souvenirs.

He had drunk incessantly and complained that he had not slept for three months and that as soon as he sobered up for however short a time he suffered torments unimaginable to any normal human being.

At the end, he rushed into their compartment, grasped

Gordon by the hand, tried to tell him something but found he could not, and dashing out onto the platform threw himself from the train.

Now Misha sat examining the small wooden box of minerals from the Urals that had been his last gift. Suddenly there was a general stir. A handcar rolled up on the parallel track. A doctor, two policemen, and a magistrate with a cockade in his hat jumped out. Questions were asked in cold businesslike voices, and notes taken. The policemen and the guards, slipping and sliding awkwardly in the gravel, dragged the corpse up the embankment. A peasant woman began to wail. The passengers were asked to go back to their seats, the guard blew his whistle, and the train started on.

8

"Here's old Holy Oil," Nika thought savagely, looking around the room for a way of escape. The voices of the guests were outside the door, and retreat was cut off. The room had two beds, his own and Voskoboinikov's. With scarcely a moment's thought he crept under the first.

He could hear them calling and looking for him in other rooms, surprised at his absence. Finally they entered the bedroom.

"Well, it can't be helped," said Nikolai Nikolaievich. "Run along, Yura. Perhaps your friend will turn up later and you can play with him then." They sat talking about the student riots in Petersburg and Moscow, keeping Nika in his absurd and undignified confinement for about twenty minutes. At last they went out onto the veranda. Nika quietly opened the window, jumped out, and went off into the park.

He had had no sleep the night before and was out of sorts. He was in his fourteenth year and was sick and tired of being a child. He had stayed awake all night and had gone out at dawn. The rising sun had cast the long dewy shadows of trees in loops over the park grounds. The shadow was not black but dark gray like wet felt. The heady fragrance of the morning seemed to come from this damp shadow on the ground, with strips of light in it like a girl's fingers.

Suddenly a streak of quicksilver, as shiny as the dew on the grass, flowed by him a few paces away. It flowed on and on and the ground did not absorb it. Then, with an unexpectedly sharp movement, it swerved aside and vanished. It was a grass snake. Nika shuddered.

He was a strange boy. When he was excited he talked aloud to himself, imitating his mother's predilection for lofty subjects and paradox.

"How wonderful to be alive," he thought. "But why does it always hurt? God exists, of course. But if He exists, then it's me." He looked up at an aspen shaking from top to bottom, its wet leaves like bits of tinfoil. "I'll order it to stop." With an insane intensity of effort, he willed silently with his whole being, with every ounce of his flesh and blood: "Be still," and the tree at once obediently froze into immobility. Nika laughed with joy and ran off to the river to bathe.

His father, the terrorist Dementii Dudorov, condemned to death by hanging but reprieved by the Tsar, was now doing forced labor. His mother was a Georgian princess of the Eristov family, a spoiled and beautiful woman, still young and always infatuated with one thing or another—rebellions, rebels, extremist theories, famous actors, unhappy failures.

She adored Nika, turning his name, Innokentii, into a thousand impossibly tender and silly nicknames such as Inochek or Nochenka, and took him to Tiflis to show him off to her family. There, what struck him most was a straggly tree in the courtyard of their house. It was a clumsy, tropical giant, with leaves like elephant's ears which sheltered the yard from the scorching southern sky. Nika could not get used to the idea that it was a plant and not an animal.

It was dangerous for the boy to bear his father's terrible name. Ivan Ivanovich wished him to adopt his mother's and intended, with her consent, to petition the Tsar for permission to make the change. When lying under the bed, indignant at all the world, he had thought among other things of this. Who did Voskoboinikov think he was to meddle so outrageously with his life? He'd teach him where he got off.

And that Nadia! Just because she was fifteen, did that give her the right to turn up her nose and talk down to him as if he were a child? He'd show her! "I hate her," he said several times to himself. "I'll kill her. I'll take her out in the boat and drown her."

His mother was a fine one, too. Of course she'd lied to him and Voskoboinikov when she went away. She hadn't gone anywhere near the Caucasus, she had simply turned around at the nearest junction and gone north to Petersburg, and was now having a lovely time with the students shooting at the police, while he was supposed to rot alive in this silly dump. But he'd outsmart them all. He'd kill Nadia, quit school, run away to his father in Siberia, and start a rebellion.

The pond had water lilies all around the edge. The boat cut into this growth with a dry rustle; the pond water showed through like juice in a watermelon where a sample wedge has been cut out.

Nika and Nadia were picking the lilies. They both took hold of the same tough rubbery stem; it pulled them together, so that their heads bumped, and the boat was dragged in to shore as by a boathook. There the stems were shorter and more tangled; the white flowers, with their glowing centers looking like blood-specked egg yolks, sank and emerged dripping with water.

Nadia and Nika kept on picking flowers, tipping the boat more and more, lying in it almost side by side.

"I'm sick of school," said Nika. "It's time I began my life—time I went out into the world and earned my living."

"And I meant to ask you about square root equations. My algebra is so bad I nearly had to take another exam."

Nika thought there was a hidden barb in those words. Naturally, she was putting him in his place, reminding him he was a baby. Square root equations! Why, he hadn't even begun algebra.

Feigning indifference to conceal his feelings, he asked, realizing at the same moment how silly it was: "Whom will you marry when you're grown up?"

"That's a very long way off. Probably no one. I haven't thought about it."

"I hope you don't think I'm interested."

"Then why do you ask?"

"You're stupid."

They began to quarrel. Nika remembered his early morning misogyny. He threatened to drown her if she didn't stop calling him names. "Just try," said Nadia. He grabbed her around the waist. They fought, lost their balance, and fell in.

They could both swim, but the lilies caught at their arms and legs and they were out of their depth. Finally, wading through the sticky mud, they climbed out, water streaming from their shoes and pockets. Nika was the more exhausted of the two.

They were sitting side by side, drenched to the skin. No later than last spring, after such an adventure, they would have shouted, cursed, or laughed. But now they were silent, catching their breath, overcome by the absurdity of the whole thing. Nadia seethed with inner indignation, and Nika ached all over, as if someone had beaten him with a club and cracked his ribs.

In the end Nadia said quietly, like an adult: "You really are mad," and Nika said in an equally adult tone: "I'm sorry."

They walked home dripping water like two water carts. Their way took them up the dusty slope swarming with snakes near the place where Nika had seen the grass snake that morning.

He remembered the magic elation that had filled him in the night, and his omnipotence at dawn when nature obeyed his will. What order should he give it now, he wondered. What was his dearest wish? It struck him that what he wanted most was to fall into the pond again with Nadia, and he would have given much to know if this would ever happen.

CHAPTER TWO

A Girl from a Different World

1

The war with Japan was not yet over when it was unexpectedly overshadowed by other events. Waves of revolution swept across Russia, each greater and more extraordinary than the last.

It was at this time that Amalia Karlovna Guishar, the widow of a Belgian engineer and herself a Russianized Frenchwoman, arrived in Moscow from the Urals with her two children—her son Rodion and her daughter Larisa. She placed her son in the military academy and her daughter in a girls' gymnasium, where, as it happened, Nadia Kologrivova was her classmate.

Madame Guishar's husband had left her his savings, stocks which had been rising and were now beginning to fall. To stop the drain on her resources and to have something to do she bought a small business; this was Levitskaia's dressmaking establishment near the Triumphal Arch; she took it over from Levitskaia's heirs together with the firm's good will, its clientele, and all its seamstresses and apprentices.

This she did on the advice of Komarovsky, a lawyer who had been a friend of her husband's and was now the man to whom she turned for counsel and help, a cold-blooded businessman who knew the Russian business world like the back of his hand.

It was with him that she had arranged her move by correspondence; he had met her and the children at the station and had driven them to the other end of Moscow, to the Montenegro Hotel in Oruzheiny Pereulok, where he had booked their room. He had also persuaded her to send Rodia to the military academy and Lara to the school of his choice. He joked carelessly with the boy and stared at the girl so that he made her blush.

2

They stayed about a month at the Montenegro before moving into the small three-room apartment adjoining the workshop.

This was the most disreputable part of Moscow—slums, cheap bars frequented by cabmen,* whole streets devoted to vice, dens of "fallen women."

The children were not surprised by the dirt in the rooms, the bedbugs, and the wretchedness of the furniture. Since their father's death their mother had lived in constant fear of destitution. Rodia and Lara were used to being told that they were on the verge of ruin. They realized that they were different from the children of the street, but, like children brought up in an orphanage, they had a deep-seated fear of the rich.

Their mother was a living example of this fear. Madame Guishar was a plump blonde of about thirty-five subject to spells of palpitation alternating with her fits of silliness. She was a dreadful coward and was terrified of men. For this very reason, out of fear and confusion, she drifted continually from lover to lover.

At the Montenegro the family lived in Room 23: Room 24, ever since the Montenegro had been founded, had been occupied by the cellist Tyshkevich, a bald, sweaty, kindly man in a wig who joined his hands prayerfully and pressed them to his breast when he was trying to be persuasive, and who threw back his head and rolled his eyes in ecstasy when he played at fashionable parties and concert halls. He was rarely in, spending whole days at the Bolshoi Theater or the Conservatory. As

---

*Cabmen: The Russian expression here is *likhachi*—fashionable cab drivers who had an unsavory reputation as a class.

neighbors they helped each other out, and this brought them together.

Since the presence of the children sometimes embarrassed Madame Guishar during Komarovsky's visits, Tyshkevich would leave her his key so that she could receive her friend in his room. Soon she took his altruism so much for granted that on several occasions she knocked on his door asking him in tears to protect her from her benefactor.

3

The workshop was in a one-story house near the corner of Tverskaia Street. Nearby was the Brest railway with its engine depots, warehouses, and lodgings for the employees.

In one of them lived Olia Demina, a clever girl who worked at Madame Guishar's and whose uncle was employed at the freight yard.

She was a quick apprentice. She had been singled out by the former owner of the workshop and was now beginning to be favored by the new one. Olia had a great liking for Lara Guishar.

Nothing had changed since Levitskaia's day. The sewing machines whirred frantically under the tread of tired seamstresses or their flitting hands. Here and there a woman sat at a table sewing quietly with a broad sweep of the arm as she pulled the needle and long thread. The floor was littered with scraps. You had to raise your voice to make yourself heard above the clatter of the machines and the modulated trills of Kirill Modestovich, the canary in its cage in the window (the former owner had carried with her to the grave the secret of the bird's improbable name).

In the reception room the customers clustered in a picturesque group around a table heaped with fashion magazines. Standing, sitting, or bending over the table in the poses they had seen in the pictures, they discussed models and patterns. In the manager's chair at another table sat Faina Silantievna Fetisova, Madame Guishar's assistant and senior cutter, a bony woman with warts in the hollows of her flabby cheeks. A cigarette in a bone holder clamped between her yellowed teeth, squinting her yellowish eyes and blowing a stream of yellow smoke from her nose and mouth, she jotted in a notebook the measurements, orders and addresses, and requests of the thronging clients. Madame Guishar had no experience of running a workshop. She felt that she was not quite the boss, but the staff were honest and Fetisova was reliable. All the same, these were troubled times and she was afraid to think of the future; she had moments of paralyzing despair.

Komarovsky often went to see them. As he walked through the workshop on his way to their apartment, startling the fashionable ladies at their fittings so that they darted behind the screens playfully parrying his ambiguous jokes, the seamstresses, disapproving, muttered sneeringly: "Here comes his lordship," "Amalia's heartache," "old goat," "lady-killer."

An object of even greater hatred was his bulldog Jack; he sometimes took it with him on a lead on which it pulled with such violent jerks that Komarovsky followed stumbling and lurching with outstretched hands like a blind man after his guide.

One spring day Jack sank his teeth in Lara's leg and tore her stocking.

"I'll kill that demon," Olia whispered hoarsely into Lara's ear.

"Yes, it really is a horrid dog; but how can you do that, silly?"

"Ssh, don't talk so loud, I'll tell you. You know those stone Easter eggs—the ones on your Mama's chest of drawers. . . ."

"Well, yes, they're made of glass and marble."

"That's it. Bend down and I'll whisper. You take them and dip them in lard—the filthy beast will guzzle them and choke himself, the devil. That'll do it."

Lara laughed and thought of Olia with envy. Here was a working girl who lived in poverty. Such children were precocious. Yet how unspoiled and childlike she was! Jack, the eggs— where on earth did she get all her ideas? "And why is it," thought Lara, "that my fate is to see everything and take it all so much to heart?"

4

"Mother is his—what's the word . . . He's Mother's . . . They're bad words, I won't say them. Then why does he look at me like that? I'm her daughter, after all."

Lara was only a little over sixteen but she was well developed. People thought she was eighteen or more. She had a good mind and was easy to get along with. She was very good-looking. She and Rodia realized that nothing in life would come to them without a struggle. Unlike the idle and well-to-do, they did not have the leisure for premature curiosity and theorizing about things that were not yet practical concerns. Only the superfluous is sordid. Lara was the purest being in the world.

Brother and sister knew the value of things and appreciated what they had achieved so far. People had to think well of you if you were to get on. Lara worked well at school, not because she had an abstract love of learning but because only the best pupils were given scholarships. She was just as good at washing dishes, helping out in the workshop, and doing her mother's errands. She moved with a silent grace, and all her features— voice, figure, gestures, her gray eyes and her fair hair—formed a harmonious whole.

It was a Sunday in the middle of July. On holidays you could stay in bed a little longer. Lara lay on her back, her hands clasped behind her head.

The workshop was quiet. The window looking out on the street was open. Lara heard the rattle of a droshki in the distance turn into a smooth glide as the wheels left the cobbles for the groove of a trolley track. "I'll sleep a bit more," she thought. The rumble of the town was like a lullaby and made her sleepy.

Lara felt her size and her position in the bed with two points of her body—the salient of her left shoulder and the big toe of her right foot. Everything else was more or less herself, her soul or inner being, harmoniously fitted into her contours and impatiently straining toward the future.

"I must go to sleep," thought Lara, and conjured up in her imagination the sunny side of Coachmakers' Row as it must be at this hour—the enormous carriages displayed on the cleanly swept floors of the coachmakers' sheds, the lanterns of cut glass, the stuffed bears, the rich life. And a little farther down the street, the dragoons exercising in the yard of the Znamensky barracks—the chargers mincing in a circle, the men vaulting into the saddles and riding past, at a walk, at a trot, and at a gallop, and outside, the row of children with nurses and wet-nurses gaping through the railings.

And a little farther still, thought Lara, Petrovka Street. "Good heavens, Lara, what an idea! I just wanted to show you my apartment. We're so near."

It was the name day of Olga, the small daughter of some friends of Komarovsky's who lived in Coachmakers' Row. The grown-ups were celebrating the occasion with dancing and champagne. He had invited Mother, but Mother couldn't go, she wasn't feeling well. Mother said: "Take Lara. You're always telling me to look after Lara. Well, now you look after her." And look after her he did—what a joke!

It was all this waltzing that had started it. What a crazy business it was! You spun round and round, thinking of nothing. While the music played, a whole eternity went by like life in a novel. But as soon as it stopped you had a feeling of shock, as if a bucket of cold water were splashed over you or somebody had found you undressed. Of course, one reason why you allowed anyone to be so familiar was just to show how grown-up you were.

She could never have imagined that he danced so well. What clever hands he had, what assurance as he gripped you by the waist! But never again would she allow anyone to kiss her like that. She could never have dreamed there could be so much affrontery in anyone's lips when they were pressed for such a long time against your own.

She must stop all this nonsense. Once and for all. Stop playing at being shy, simpering and lowering her eyes—or it would end in disaster. There loomed an imperceptible, a terrifying border-line. One step and you would be hurtled into an abyss. She must stop thinking about dancing. That was the root of the evil. She must boldly refuse—pretend that she had never learned to dance or that she'd broken her leg.

5

That autumn there was unrest among the railway workers on the Moscow network. The men on the Moscow-Kazan line went on strike, and those of the Moscow-Brest line were expected to join them. The decision to strike had been taken, but the strike committee was still arguing about the date. Everyone on the railway knew that a strike was coming and only a pretext was needed for it to begin.

It was a cold overcast morning at the beginning of October, and on that day the wages were due. For a long time nothing was heard from the bookkeeping department; then a boy came into the office with a pay sheet and a pile of records that had been consulted for the deduction of fines. The cashier began handing out the pay. In an endless line, conductors, switchmen, mechanics and their assistants, scrubwomen from the depot, moved across the ground between the wooden buildings of the management and the station with its workshops, warehouses, engine sheds, and tracks.

The air smelled of early winter in town—of trampled maple leaves, melted snow, engine soot, and warm rye bread just out of the oven (it was baked in the basement of the station buffet). Trains came and went. They were shunted, coupled, and uncoupled to the waving of furled and unfurled signal flags. Locomotives hooted, guards tooted their horns, and shunters blew their whistles. Smoke rose in endless ladders to the sky. Hissing engines scalded the cold winter clouds with clouds of boiling steam.

Fuflygin, the Divisional Manager, and Pavel Ferapontovich Antipov, the Track Overseer of the station area, walked up and down along the edge of the tracks. Antipov had been pestering the repair shops about the quality of the spare parts for mending the tracks. The steel was not sufficiently tensile, the rails failed the test for strains, and Antipov thought that they would crack in the frosty weather. The management merely shelved his complaints. Someone was making money on the contracts.

Fuflygin wore an expensive fur coat on which the piping of the railway uniform had been sewn; it was unbuttoned, showing his new civilian serge suit. He stepped cautiously on the embankment, glancing down with pleasure at the line of his lapels, the straight creases on his trousers, and his elegant shoes. What Antipov was saying came in one ear and went out the other. Fuflygin had his own thoughts; he kept taking out his watch and looking at it; he was in a hurry to be off.

"Quite right, quite right, my dear fellow," he broke in impatiently, "but that's only dangerous on the main lines with a lot of traffic. But just look at what you've got. Sidings and dead ends, nettles and dandelions. And the traffic—at most an old shunting engine for sorting the empties. What more do you want? You must be out of your mind! Talk about steel— wooden rails would do here!"

Fuflygin looked at his watch, snapped the lid, and gazed into the distance where a road ran toward the railway. A carriage came into sight at a bend of the road. This was Fuflygin's own turnout. His wife had come for him. The coachman drew in the horses almost at the edge of the tracks, talking to them in a high-pitched womanish voice, like a nursemaid scolding fretful children; they were frightened of trains. In a corner of the carriage sat a pretty woman negligently leaning against the cushions.

"Well, my good fellow, some other time," said the Divisional Manager with a wave of the hand, as much as to say, "I've got more important things than rails to think about." The couple drove off.

6

Three or four hours later, almost at dusk, in a field some distance from the track, where no one had been visible until then, two figures rose out of the ground and, looking back over their shoulders, quickly walked away.

"Let's walk faster," said Tiverzin. "I'm not worried about spies following us, but the moment those slowpokes in their hole in the ground have finished they'll come out and catch up with us. I can't bear the sight of them. What's the point of having a committee if you drag things out like that? You play with fire and then you duck for shelter. You're a fine one yourself—siding with that lot."

"My Daria's got typhus. I ought to be taking her to the hospital. Until I've done that I can't think about anything else."

"They say the wages are being paid today. I'll go around to the office. It it wasn't payday I'd chuck the lot of you, honest to God I would. I'd stop all this myself, I wouldn't wait a minute."

"And how would you do that, if I may ask?"

"Nothing to it. I'd go down to the boiler room and blow the whistle. That's all."

They said goodbye and went off in different directions.

Tiverzin walked across the tracks toward the town. He ran into people coming from the office with their pay. There were a great many of them. By the look of it he reckoned that nearly all the station workers had been paid.

It was getting dark, the lights were on in the office. Idle workers crowded in the square outside it. In the driveway stood Fuflygin's carriage and in it sat Fuflygin's wife, still in the same pose as though she had not moved since morning. She was waiting for her husband, who was getting his money. Suddenly sleet began to fall. The coachman climbed down from his box to put up the leather hood. While he tugged at the stiff struts, one leg braced against the back of the carriage, Fuflygina sat admiring the silver beads of sleet glittering in the light of the office lamps; her unblinking dreamy eyes were fixed on a point above the heads of the workers in a manner suggesting that her glance could, in case of need, go through them as through sleet or mist.

Tiverzin caught sight of her expression. It gave him a turn. He walked past without greeting her and decided to call for his wages later, so as not to run into her husband at the office. He crossed over to the darker side of the square, toward the workshops and the black shape of the turntable with tracks fanning out from it toward the depot.

"Tiverzin! Kuprik!" Several voices called out of the darkness. There was a little crowd outside the workshops. Inside, someone was yelling and a boy was crying. "Do go in and help that boy, Kuprian Savelievich," said a woman in the crowd.

As usual, the old foreman, Piotr Khudoleiev, was walloping his young apprentice Yusupka.

Khudoleiev had not always been a tormentor of apprentices and a brawling drunkard. There had been a time when, as a dashing young workman, he had attracted the admiring glances of merchants' and priests' daughters in Moscow's industrial suburbs. But the girl he courted, Marfa, who had graduated that year from the diocesan convent school, had turned him down and had married his comrade, the mechanic Savelii Nikitich, Tiverzin's father.

Five years after Savelii's horrible end (he was burned to death in the sensational railway crash of 1888) Khudoleiev renewed his suit, but again Marfa Gavrilovna rejected him. So Khudoleiev took to drink and rowdiness, trying to get even with a world which was to blame, so he believed, for all his misfortunes.

Yusupka was the son of Gimazetdin, the janitor at the block of tenements where Tiverzin lived. Tiverzin had taken the boy under his wing, and this added fuel to Khudoleiev's hostility.

"Is that the way to hold a file, you Asiatic?" bellowed Khudoleiev, dragging Yusupka by the hair and pummelling the back of his neck. "Is that the way to strip down a casting, you slit-eyed Tartar?"

"Ouch, I won't do it anymore, little uncle, ow, I won't do it anymore, ouch, it hurts!"

"He's been told a thousand times: first adjust the mandrel and then screw up the chuck, but no, he must do it his own way! Nearly broke the spindle, the bastard."

"I didn't touch the spindle, honest I didn't."

"Why do you tyrannize the boy?" asked Tiverzin, elbowing his way through the crowd.

"It's none of your business," Khudoleiev snapped.

"I'm asking you why you tyrannize the boy."

"And I'm telling you to move off before there's trouble, you socialist meddler. Killing's too good for him, such scum, he nearly broke my spindle. He should thank his lucky stars he's still alive, the slit-eyed devil—all I did was tweak his ears and pull his hair a bit."

"So you think he should be beheaded for this. You ought to be ashamed of yourself, really, an old foreman like you—you've got gray hair but you still haven't learned sense."

"Move on, move on, I tell you, while you're still in one piece. I'll knock the stuffing out of you, preaching at me, you dog's arse. You were made on the tracks, you jellyfish, under your father's very nose. I know your mother, the slut, the mangy cat, the crumpled skirt!"

What happened next was over in a minute. Both men seized the first thing that came to hand on the lathe benches where heavy tools and pieces of iron were lying about, and would have killed each other if the crowd had not rushed in to separate them. Khudoleiev and Tiverzin stood with their heads bent down, their foreheads almost touching, pale, with bloodshot eyes. They were so angry that they could not utter a word. They were held firmly, their arms gripped from behind. Once or twice they tried to break free, twisting their bodies and dragging their comrades who were hanging on to them. Hooks and buttons went flying, their jackets and shirts slipped off, baring their shoulders. Around them was a ceaseless uproar.

"The chisel! Take the chisel away from him, he'll smash his head in. Easy now, easy now, Piotr old man, or we'll break your arm! What are we playing around with them for! Drag them apart and put them under lock and key and there's an end to it."

With a superhuman effort Tiverzin suddenly shook off the men who clung to him and, breaking loose, dashed to the door.

They started after him but, seeing that he had changed his mind, left him alone. He went out, slamming the door, and marched off without turning around. The damp autumn night closed in on him. "You try to help them and they come at you with a knife," he muttered, striding on unconscious of his direction. This world of ignominy and fraud, in which an overfed lady had the impertinence to stare right through a crowd of workingmen and where a drink-sodden victim of such an order found pleasure in torturing his comrades—this world was now more hateful to him than ever before. He hurried on as though his pace might hasten the time when everything on earth would be as rational and harmonious as it was now inside his feverish head. He knew that all their struggles in the last few days, the troubles on the line, the speeches at meetings, the decision to strike—not carried out yet but at least not cancelled—were separate stages on the great road lying ahead of them.

But at the moment he was so worked up that he wanted to run all the way without stopping to draw breath. He did not realize where he was going with his long strides, but his feet knew very well where they were taking him.

It was not until much later that Tiverzin learned of the decision, taken by the strike committee after he had left the underground shelter with Antipov, to begin the strike that very night. They decided then and there which of them was to go where and which men would be called out. At the moment when the whistle of the engine repair shop blew, as though coming from the very depths of Tiverzin's soul, hoarsely at first and then gradually clearing, a crowd was already moving from the depot and the freight yard. Soon it was joined by the men from the boiler room, who had downed tools at Tiverzin's signal.

For many years Tiverzin thought that it was he alone who had stopped work and traffic on the line that night. Only much later, at the trial, when he was charged with complicity in the strike but not with inciting it, did he learn the truth.

People ran out asking: "Where is everybody going? What's the signal for?"—"You're not deaf," came from the darkness. "It's a fire. They're sounding the alarm. They want us to put it out."—"Where's the fire?"—"There must be a fire or they wouldn't be sounding the alarm."

Doors banged, more people came out. Other voices were heard. "Fire? Listen to the ignorant lout! It's a strike, that's what

it is, see? Let them get some other fools to do their dirty work.
Let's go, boys."

More and more people joined the crowd. The railway
workers were on strike.

7

Tiverzin went home two days later, unshaven, drawn with lack
of sleep, and chilled to the bone. Frost, unusual at this time of
year, had set in the night before, and Tiverzin was not dressed
for winter. The janitor, Gimazetdin, met him at the gate.

"Thank you, Mr. Tiverzin," he babbled in broken Russian.
"You didn't let Yusupka come to harm. I will always pray for
you."

"You're crazy, Gimazetdin, who're you calling Mister? Cut it
out and say what you have to say quickly, you see how cold it
is."

"Why should you be cold? You will soon be warm, Kuprian
Savelich. Me and your mother Marfa Gavrilovna brought a
whole shedful of wood from the freight station yesterday—all
birch—good, dry wood."

"Thanks, Gimazetdin. If there's something else you want to
tell me let's have it quickly. I'm frozen."

"I wanted to tell you not to spend the night at home,
Savelich. You must hide. The police have been here asking who
comes to the house. Nobody comes, I said, my relief comes, I
said, the people from the railway but no strangers come, I said,
not on your life."

Tiverzin was unmarried and lived with his mother and his
younger married brother. The tenements belonged to the
neighboring Church of the Holy Trinity. Among the lodgers
were some of the clergy and two *artels*, or associations, of street
hawkers—one of butchers, the other of greengrocers—but most
of them were workers on the Moscow-Brest railway.

It was a stone house. All around the dirty and unpaved
courtyard ran a wooden passageway. Out of it rose a number of
dirty, slippery outside staircases, reeking of cats and cabbage.
On the landings were privies and padlocked storerooms.

Tiverzin's brother had fought as a conscript in the war and
had been wounded at Wafangkou. Now he was convalescing at

the military hospital in Krasnoyarsk, and his wife and two daughters had gone there to see him and to bring him home (the Tiverzins, hereditary railway workers, travelled all over Russia on official passes). The flat was quiet; only Tiverzin and his mother lived in it at present.

It was on the second floor. On the landing outside there was a water butt, filled regularly by the water carrier. Tiverzin noticed as he came up that the lid of the butt had been pushed sideways and a tin mug stood on the frozen surface of the water. "Prov must have been here," he thought, grinning. "The way that man drinks, his guts must be on fire." Prov Afanasievich Sokolov, the church psalmist, was a relative of Tiverzin's mother.

Tiverzin jerked the mug out of the ice and pulled the handle of the doorbell. A wave of warm air and appetizing vapors from the kitchen came out to him.

"You've got a good fire going, Mother. It's nice and warm in here."

His mother flung herself on his neck and burst into tears. He stroked her head and, after a while, gently pushed her aside.

"Nothing ventured, nothing won, Mother," he said softly. "The line's struck from Moscow to Warsaw."

"I know, that's why I'm crying. They'll be after you, Kuprinka, you've got to get away."

"That nice boyfriend of yours, Piotr, nearly broke my head!" He meant to make her laugh but she said earnestly: "It's a sin to laugh at him, Kuprinka. You should be sorry for him, the poor wretch, the drunkard."

"Antipov's been arrested. They came in the night, searched his flat, turned everything upside down, and took him away this morning. And his wife Daria's in hospital with the typhus. And their kid, Pasha, who's at the *Realgymnasium*, is alone in the house with his deaf aunt. And they're going to be evicted. I think we should have the boy to stay with us. What did Prov want?"

"How did you know he came?"

"I saw the water butt was uncovered and the mug on the ice— sure to have been Prov guzzling water, I said to myself."

"How sharp you are, Kuprinka. Yes, he's been here. Prov— Prov Afanasievich. Came to borrow some logs—I gave him some. But what am I talking about, fool that I am. It went clean out of my head—the news Prov brought. Think of it, Kuprinka! The Tsar has signed a manifesto and everything's to be

changed—everybody's to be treated right, the peasants are to
have land, and we're all going to be equal with the gentry! It's
actually signed, he says, it's only got to be made public. The
Synod's sent something to be put into the Church service, a
prayer of thanks or something. He told me what it was, but I've
forgotten."

8

Pasha Antipov, whose father had been arrested as one of the
organizers of the strike, went to live with the Tiverzins. He was
a clean, tidy boy with regular features and red hair parted in the
middle: he was always slicking it down with a brush and
straightening his tunic or the school buckle on his belt. He had a
great sense of humor and an unusual gift of observation and
kept everyone in fits with his clever imitations of everything he
heard and saw.

Soon after the manifesto of October 17th several revolutionary organizations called for a big demonstration. The route
was from the Tver Gate to the Kaluga Gate at the other end of
the town. But this was a case of too many cooks spoiling the
broth. The planners quarrelled and one after the other withdrew
from participation. Then, learning that crowds had nevertheless
gathered on the appointed morning, they hastily sent representatives to lead the demonstrators.

In spite of Tiverzin's efforts to dissuade her, his mother joined
the demonstrators, and the gay and sociable Pasha went with
her.

It was a dry frosty November day with a still, leaden sky and
a few snowflakes coming down one by one. They spun slowly
and hesitantly before settling on the pavement like fluffy gray
dust.

Down the street people came pouring in a torrent—faces,
faces, faces, quilted winter coats and sheepskin hats, men and
women students, old men, children, railwaymen in uniform,
workers from the trolley depot and the telephone exchange in
knee boots and leather jackets, girls and schoolboys.

For some time they sang the "Marseillaise," the "Varshavian-
ka," and "Victims You Fell." Then a man who had been
walking backwards at the head of the procession, singing and

conducting with his cap, which he used as a baton, turned around, put his cap on his head, and listened to what the other leaders around him were saying. The singing broke off in disorder. Now you could hear the crunch of innumerable footsteps on the frozen pavement.

The leaders had received a message from sympathizers that Cossacks were waiting to ambush the procession farther down the street. The warning had been given by telephone to a nearby pharmacy.

"What of it?" said the organizers. "We must keep calm and not lose our heads, that's the main thing. We must occupy the first public building we come to, warn the people, and scatter."

An argument began about the best building to go to. Some suggested the Society of Commercial Employees, others the Technical School, and still others the School of Foreign Correspondence.

While they were still arguing they reached the corner of a school building, which offered shelter every bit as good as those that had been mentioned.

When they drew level with the entrance the leaders turned aside, climbed the steps of the semicircular porch, and motioned the head of the procession to halt. The doors opened and the procession—coat to coat and cap to cap—moved into the entrance hall and up the stairs.

"The auditorium, the auditorium," shouted a few voices in the rear, but the crowd continued to press forward, scattering down corridors and straying into the classrooms. When the leaders at last succeeded in shepherding it into the auditorium, they tried several times to warn it of the ambush, but no one listened to them. Stopping and going inside a building were taken as an invitation to an impromptu meeting, which in fact began at once.

After all the walking and singing, people were glad to sit quietly for a while and let others do their work for them, shouting themselves hoarse. The crowd, welcoming the rest, overlooked the minor differences between the speakers, who agreed on all essential points. In the end it was the worst orator of the lot who received the most applause. People made no effort to follow him and merely roared approval at his every word, no one minding the interruptions and everyone agreeing out of impatience to everything he said. There were shouts of "Shame," a telegram of protest was drafted, and suddenly the crowd, bored with the speaker's droning voice, stood up as one man and forgetting all about him poured out in a body—cap to cap and row after row—down the stairs and out into the street. The procession was resumed.

While the meeting was on, it had begun to snow. The street was white. The snow fell thicker and thicker.

When the dragoons charged, the marchers at the rear first knew nothing of it. A swelling noise rolled back to them as of great crowds shouting "Hurrah," and individual screams of "Help!" and "Murder" were lost in the uproar. Almost at the same moment, and borne, as it were, on this wave of sound along the narrow corridor that formed as the crowd divided, the heads and manes of horses, and their saber-swinging riders, rode by swiftly and silently.

Half a platoon galloped through, turned, re-formed, and cut into the tail of the procession. The massacre began.

A few minutes later the avenue was almost deserted. People were scattering down the side streets. The snow was lighter. The afternoon was dry like a charcoal sketch. Then the sun, setting behind the houses, pointed as though with a finger at everything red in the street—the red tops of the dragoons' caps, a red flag trailing on the ground, and the red specks and threads of blood on the snow.

A groaning man with a split skull was crawling along the curb. From the far end of the street to which the chase had taken them, several dragoons were riding back abreast at a walk. Almost at the horses' feet Marfa Tiverzina, her shawl knocked to the back of her head, was running from side to side screaming wildly: "Pasha! Pasha!"

Pasha had been with her all along, amusing her by cleverly mimicking the last speaker at the meeting, but had vanished suddenly in the confusion when the dragoons charged.

A blow from a nagaika had fallen on her back, and though she had hardly felt it through her thickly quilted coat she swore and shook her fist at the retreating horsemen, indignant that they had dared to strike an old woman like herself, and in public at that.

Looking anxiously from side to side, she had the luck finally to spot the boy across the street. He stood in a recess between a grocer's shop and a private stone house, where a group of chance passersby had been hemmed in by a horseman who had mounted the sidewalk. Amused by their terror, the dragoon was making his horse perform volts and pirouettes, backing it into the crowd and making it rear slowly as in a circus turn.

Suddenly he saw his comrades riding back, spurred his mount, and in a couple of bounds took his place in the file.

The crowd dispersed and Pasha, who had been too frightened to utter a sound, rushed to Marfa Gavrilovna.

The old woman grumbled all the way home. "Accursed murderers! People are happy because the Tsar has given them freedom, but these damned killers can't stand it. They must spoil everything, twist every word inside out."

She was furious with the dragoons, furious with the whole world, and at the moment even with her own son. When she was in a temper it seemed to her that all the recent troubles were the fault of "Kuprinka's bunglers and fumblers," as she called them.

"What do they want, the half-wits? They don't know themselves, just so long as they can make mischief, the vipers. Like that chatterbox. Pasha dear, show me again how he went on, show me, darling. Oh! I'll die laughing. You've got him to the life. Buzz, buzz, buzz—a real bumblebee!"

At home she fell to scolding her son. Was she of an age to have a curly-headed oaf on a horse belt her on her behind?

"Really, Mother, who d'you take me for? You'd think I was the Cossack captain or the Chief of Police."

9

Nikolai Nikolaievich saw the fleeing demonstrators from his window. He realized who they were and watched to see if Yura were among them. But none of his friends seemed to be there though he thought that he had caught sight of the Dudorov boy—he could not quite remember his name—that desperado who had so recently had a bullet extracted from his shoulder and who was again hanging about in places where he had no business to be.

Nikolai Nikolaievich had arrived from Petersburg that autumn. He had no apartment in Moscow and he did not wish to go to a hotel, so he had put up with some distant relatives of his, the Sventitskys. They had given him the corner room on the second floor.

The Sventitskys were childless, and the two-story house that their late parents had rented from time immemorial from the

Princes Dolgoruky was too big for them. It was part of the
untidy cluster of buildings in various styles with three court-
yards and a garden that stood on the Dolgorukys' property,
bounded by three narrow side streets and known by the ancient
name of Flour Town.

In spite of its four windows, the study was darkish. It was
cluttered up with books, papers, rugs, and prints. It had a
balcony forming a semicircle around the corner of the house.
The double glass door of the balcony was hermetically sealed
for the winter.

The balcony door and two of the windows looked out on an
alley that ran into the distance with its sleigh tracks and the
irregular line of its houses and fences.

Purple shadows reached into the room from the garden. The
trees, laden with hoarfrost, their branches like smoky streaks of
candle wax, looked in as if they wished to rest their burden on
the floor of the study.

Nikolai Nikolaievich stood gazing into the distance. He
thought of his last winter in Petersburg—Gapon,* Gorky, the
visit to Prime Minister Witte, modern, fashionable writers.
From that bedlam he had fled to the peace and quiet of the
ancient capital to write the book he had in mind. But he had
jumped out of the frying pan into the fire. Lectures every day—
University Courses for Women, the Religious Philosophical
Society, the Red Cross and the Strike Fund—not a moment to
himself. What he needed was to get away to Switzerland, to
some remote canton in the woods, to the peace of lakes,
mountains, sky, and the echoing, ever-responsive air.

Nikolai Nikolaievich turned away from the window. He felt
like going out to call on someone or just to walk about the
streets, but he remembered that Vyvolochnov, the Tolstoyan,
was coming to see him about some business or other. He paced
up and down the room, his thoughts turning to his nephew.

When Nikolai Nikolaievich had moved from his retreat on
the Volga to Petersburg he had left Yura in Moscow, where he
had many relatives—the Vedeniapins, the Ostromyslenskys, the
Seliavins, the Mikhaelises, the Sventitskys, and the Gromekos.
At first Yura was foisted on the slovenly old chatterbox
Ostromyslensky, known among the clan as Fedka. Fedka lived
in sin with his ward Motia and therefore saw himself as a
disrupter of the established order and a champion of progressive

---

*A priest who was thought to be a revolutionary leader but also was suspected of
being an *agent provocateur.*

thought. He did not justify his kinsman's confidence, and even took the money given him for Yura's upkeep and spent it on himself. Yura was transferred to the professorial family of the Gromekos and was still with them. The atmosphere at the Gromekos' was eminently suitable, Nikolai Nikolaievich thought. They had their daughter, Tonia, who was Yura's age, and Misha Gordon, who was Yura's friend and classmate, living with them.

"And a comical triumvirate they make," thought Nikolai Nikolaievich. The three of them had soaked themselves in *The Meaning of Love* and *The Kreutzer Sonata* and had a mania for preaching chastity. It was right, of course, for adolescents to go through a frenzy of purity, but they were overdoing it a bit, they had lost all sense of proportion.

How childish and eccentric they were! For some reason, they called the domain of the sensual, which disturbed them so much, "vulgar," and used the expression in and out of place. A most ineptly chosen term! "Vulgar" was applied to instinct, to pornography, to exploitation of women, and almost to the whole physical world. They blushed or grew pale when they pronounced the word.

"If I had been in Moscow," thought Nikolai Nikolaievich, "I would not have let it go so far. Modesty is necessary, but within limits . . . Ah! Nil Feoktistovich, come in!" he exclaimed, going out to meet his visitor.

10

A fat man in a gray Tolstoyan shirt with a broad leather belt, felt boots, and trousers bagging at the knees entered the room. He looked like a good soul with his head in the clouds. A pince-nez on a wide black ribbon quivered angrily on his nose. He had begun to take his things off in the hall but had not removed his scarf and came in with it trailing on the floor and his round felt hat still in his hand. These encumbrances prevented him from shaking hands with Nikolai Nikolaievich and even from saying How-do-you-do.

"Um-m-m," he mooed helplessly, looking around the room.

"Put them down anywhere," said Nikolai Nikolaievich, restoring Vyvolochnov's power of speech and self-possession.

Here was one of those followers of Tolstoy in whom the ideas of the genius who had never known peace had settled down to enjoy a long, unclouded rest, growing hopelessly shallow in the process. He had come to ask Nikolai Nikolaievich to speak at a meeting in aid of political deportees that was to be held at some school or other.

"I've spoken at that school already."

"In aid of our exiles?"

"Yes."

"You'll have to do it again."

Nikolai Nikolaievich balked a little and then gave in.

The business dealt with, Nikolai Nikolaievich did not attempt to delay his guest. Nil Feoktistovich could have left at once but he evidently felt that it would be unseemly and was looking for something lively and natural to say by way of parting. The conversation became strained and awkward.

"So you've become a Decadent? Going in for mysticism?"

"What do you mean?"

"It's a waste, you know. Do you remember the county council?"

"Of course. Didn't we canvass for it together?"

"And we did some good work fighting for the village schools and teachers' colleges. Remember?"

"Of course. It was a splendid battle."

"And then you became interested in public health and social welfare, didn't you?"

"For a time, yes."

"Hmm. And now it's all this highbrow stuff—fauns and nenuphars and ephebes and 'Let's be like the sun.' I can't believe it, bless me if I can—an intelligent man like you, and with your sense of humor and your knowledge of the people. . . . Come, now. . . . Or am I intruding into the holy of holies?"

"Why all this talk? What are we arguing about? You don't know my ideas."

"Russia needs schools and hospitals, not fauns and nenuphars."

"No one denies it."

"The peasants are in rags and famished. . . ."

So the conversation dragged on. Knowing how useless it was, Nikolai Nikolaievich tried nevertheless to explain what attracted him to some of the writers of the Symbolist school. Then, turning to Tolstoyan doctrines, he said:

"Up to a point I am with you, but Tolstoy says that the more a man devotes himself to beauty the further he moves away from goodness. . . ."

"And you think it's the other way round—the world will be saved by beauty, is that it? Dostoievsky, Rozanov,* mystery plays, and what not?"

"Wait, let me tell you what I think. I think that if the beast who sleeps in man could be held down by threats—any kind of threat, whether of jail or of retribution after death—then the highest emblem of humanity would be the lion tamer in the circus with his whip, not the prophet who sacrificed himself. But don't you see, this is just the point—what has for centuries raised man above the beast is not the cudgel but an inward music: the irresistible power of unarmed truth, the powerful attraction of its example. It has always been assumed that the most important things in the Gospels are the ethical maxims and commandments. But for me the most important thing is that Christ speaks in parables taken from life, that He explains the truth in terms of everyday reality. The idea that underlies this is that communion between mortals is immortal, and that the whole of life is symbolic because it is meaningful."

"I haven't understood a word. You should write a book about it!"

After Vyvolochnov had left, Nikolai Nikolaievich felt extremely cross. He was angry with himself for having blurted out some of his most intimate thoughts to that fool, without impressing him in the least. Then his annoyance, as sometimes happens, changed its target. He recalled another incident.

He did not keep a diary, but once or twice a year he would record in a thick notebook some thought which struck him particularly. He got out the notebook now and began to write in a large, legible hand. This is what he wrote.

"Upset all day by that silly Shlesinger woman. She came in the morning, stayed till lunchtime, and for two solid hours bored me reading out that gibberish—a libretto in verse by the Symbolist A—to the cosmogonic symphony by the composer B—with the spirits of the planets, voices of the four elements, etc., etc. I listened with impatience, then I couldn't stand it and begged her to stop.

"And suddenly I understood everything. I understood why this stuff is so deadly, so insufferably false, even in *Faust*. The whole thing is artificial, no one is genuinely interested in it. Modern man has no need of it. When he is overcome by the

---

*A writer of the period who was an exceptional stylist.

mysteries of the universe he turns to physics, not to Hesiod's hexameters.

"And it isn't just that the form is an anachronism, or that these spirits of earth and air only confuse what science has unravelled. The fact is that this type of art is wholly out of keeping with the spirit, the essence, the motivating force of contemporary art.

"These cosmogonies were natural in the ancient world—a world settled so sparsely that nature was not yet eclipsed by man. Mammoths still walked the earth, dragons and dinosaurs were still fresh in people's memory. Nature hit you in the eye so plainly and grabbed you so fiercely and so tangibly by the scruff of the neck that perhaps it really was still full of gods. Those were the first pages of the chronicle of mankind, it was only just beginning.

"This ancient world ended with Rome, because of over-population.

"Rome was a flea market of borrowed gods and conquered peoples, a bargain basement on two floors, earth and heaven, a mass of filth convoluted in a triple knot as in an intestinal obstruction. Dacians, Herulians, Scythians, Sarmatians, Hyperboreans, heavy wheels without spokes, eyes sunk in fat, sodomy, double chins, illiterate emperors, fish fed on the flesh of learned slaves. There were more people in the world than there have ever been since, all crammed into the passages of the Coliseum, and all wretched.

"And then, into this tasteless heap of gold and marble, He came, light and clothed in an aura, emphatically human, deliberately provincial, Galilean, and at that moment gods and nations ceased to be and man came into being—man the carpenter, man the plowman, man the shepherd with his flock of sheep at sunset, man who does not sound in the least proud, man thankfully celebrated in all the cradle songs of mothers and in all the picture galleries the world over."

11

The Petrovka looked like a corner of Petersburg in Moscow, with its matching houses on both sides of the street, the tastefully sculptured house entrances, the bookshop, the library,

the cartographer's, the elegant tobacco shop, the excellent
restaurant, its front door flanked by two gaslights in round
frosted shades on massive brackets.

In winter the street frowned with a forbidding surliness. Its
inhabitants were solid, self-respecting, prosperous members of
the liberal professions.

Here Victor Ippolitovich Komarovsky rented his magnificent
third-floor apartment, reached by a wide staircase with massive
oak banisters. His housekeeper, or rather the châtelaine of his
quiet retreat, Emma Ernestovna, took care of everything
without meddling in his private life; she ran the place unseen
and unheard. He repaid her with the knightly delicacy to be
expected of so fine a gentleman, and never tolerated visitors,
male or female, whose presence would have disturbed her
peaceful, spinsterish world. A monastic stillness reigned in their
home; the blinds were drawn, and everything was spotlessly
clean, as in an operating room.

On Sunday mornings Victor Ippolitovich, accompanied by
his bulldog, usually took a leisurely walk down the Petrovka
and along Kuznetsky Most, and at one of the street corners they
were joined by the actor and gambler Constantine Illarionovich
Satanidi.

They walked together along Kuznetsky Most, telling each
other dirty stories, snorting with contempt, and laughing
shamelessly in deep, loud voices that filled the air with sounds
no more significant than the howling of a dog.

12

The weather was on the mend. Plop-plop-plop went the water
drops on the metal of the drainpipes and the cornices, roof
tapping messages to roof as if it were spring. It was thawing.

Lara walked all the way in a daze and realized what had
happened to her only when she reached home.

Everyone was asleep. She fell back into her trance and in this
abstracted state sat down at her mother's dressing table, still in
her pale mauve, almost white, lace-trimmed dress and long veil
borrowed for the evening from the workshop, like a costume.
She sat before her reflection in the mirror, and saw nothing.
Then, folding her arms, she put them on the dressing table and
buried her head in them.

If Mother learned about it she would kill her. She would kill her and then she would kill herself.

How had it happened? How could it possibly have happened? It was too late now, she should have thought of it earlier.

Now she was—what was it called?—a fallen woman. She was a woman out of a French novel, and tomorrow she would go to school and sit side by side with those other girls who were like little children compared with her. O God, O God, how did it happen?

Someday, many, many years later, when it would be possible, Lara would tell Olia Demina, and Olia would hug her and burst into tears.

Outside the window the water drops plopped on and on, the thaw muttered its spells. Down the road someone was banging on a neighbor's door. Lara did not raise her head. Her shoulders quivered. She was weeping.

13

"Ah, Emma Ernestovna, that's unimportant. I'm sick and tired of it." He kept opening and shutting drawers, turning things out, throwing cuffs and collars all over the rug and the sofa, without knowing what he was looking for.

He needed her desperately, and there was no way of seeing her that Sunday. He paced up and down the room frantically like a caged animal.

Nothing equalled her spiritual beauty. Her hands were stunning like a sublime idea. Her shadow on the wall of the hotel room was like the outline of her innocence. Her slip was stretched over her breast, as firmly and simply as linen on an embroidery frame.

His fingers drummed on the windowpane in time to the unhurried thud of horses' hoofs on the asphalt pavement below. "Lara," he whispered, shutting his eyes, and he had a vision of her head resting on his hands; her eyes were closed, she was asleep, unconscious that he watched her sleeplessly for hours on end. Her dark hair was scattered and its beauty stung his eyes like smoke and ate into his heart.

His Sunday walk was not being a success. He strolled a few paces with Jack, stopped, thought of Kuznetsky Most, of

Satanidi's jokes, of the acquaintances he met on the street—no, it was more than he could bear. He turned back. The dog, startled, looked up disapprovingly and waddled after him reluctantly.

"What can it all mean?" thought Komarovsky. "What has come over me?" Could it be his conscience, a feeling of pity, or repentance? Or was he worried about her? No, he knew she was safe at home. Then why couldn't he get her out of his head?

He walked back to his house, up the stairs, and past the first landing. The stained-glass ornamental coats of arms at the corners of the window threw colored patches of light at his feet. Halfway up the second flight he stopped.

He must not give in to this exhausting, nagging, anxious mood. He was not a schoolboy, after all. He must realize what would happen if instead of being just a toy this girl—a mere child, the daughter of his dead friend—turned into an obsession. He must come to his senses. He must be true to himself and to his habits. Otherwise everything would go up in smoke.

Komarovsky gripped the oak railing until it hurt his hand, shut his eyes a moment, then turned back resolutely and went down. On the landing, with its patches of light, the dog was waiting for him. It lifted its head like a slobbering old dwarf with hanging jowls and looked up at him adoringly.

The dog hated the girl, tore her stockings, growled at her, bared its teeth. It was jealous of her as if fearing that she would infect its master with something human.

"Ah, I see! You have decided that everything is going to be just as before—Satanidi, mean tricks, dirty jokes? All right then, take this, and this, and this." He struck the bulldog with his stick and kicked it. Jack squealed, howled, waddled up the stairs shaking his behind, and scratched at the door to complain to Emma Ernestovna.

Days and weeks went by.

14

What an inescapable spell it was! If Komarovsky's intrusion into Lara's life had merely filled her with disgust, she would have rebelled and broken free. But it was not so simple as that.

The girl was flattered that a handsome man whose hair was turning gray, a man old enough to be her father, a man who was applauded at meetings and written up in the newspapers, should spend his time and money on her, should take her out to concerts and plays, and tell her that he worshipped her, and should, as they say, "improve her mind."

After all, she was still a girl in a brown uniform who enjoyed harmless plots and pranks at school. Komarovsky's lovemaking in a carriage behind the coachman's back or in an opera box in full view of the audience fascinated her by its daring and aroused the little devil slumbering in her to imitate him.

But this mischievous, girlish infatuation was short-lived. A nagging depression and horror at herself were taking permanent hold of her. And all the time she wanted to sleep—because (she told herself) she did not get enough sleep at night, because she cried so much, because she had constant headaches, because she worked hard at school, and because she was physically exhausted.

15

He was the curse of her life; she hated him. Every day she returned to these thoughts.

She has become his slave for life. How has he subjugated her? How does he force her to submit, why does she surrender, why does she gratify his wishes and delight him with her quivering unconcealed shame? Because of his age, her mother's financial dependence on him, his cleverness in frightening her, Lara? No, no, no! That is all nonsense.

It is she who has a hold on him. Doesn't she see how much he needs her? She has nothing to be afraid of, her conscience is clear. It is he who should be ashamed, and terrified of her giving him away. But that is just what she will never do. To do this she does not have the necessary ruthlessness—Komarovsky's chief asset in dealing with subordinates and weaklings.

This is precisely the difference between them. And it is this that makes the whole of life so terrifying. Does it crush you by thunder and lightning? No, by oblique glances and whispered calumny. It is all treachery and ambiguity. Any single thread is as fragile as a cobweb, but just try to pull yourself out of the net, you only become more entangled.

And the strong are dominated by the weak and the ignoble.

16

What if she were married, she asked herself, what difference would it make? She entered the path of sophistry. But at times she was overtaken by a hopeless anguish.

How can he not be ashamed to grovel at her feet and plead with her? "We can't go on like this. Think what I have done to you! You will end up in the gutter. We must tell your mother. I'll marry you." He wept and insisted as though she were arguing and refusing. But all this was just words, and Lara did not even listen to these tragic, hollow protestations.

And he continued taking her, veiled, to dinner in the private rooms of that ghastly restaurant where the waiters and the clients undressed her with their eyes as she came in. And she merely wondered: "Does one always humiliate those one loves?"

Once she had a dream. She was buried, and there was nothing left of her except her left shoulder and her right foot. A tuft of grass sprouted from her left breast and above the ground people were singing "Black eyes and white breast" and "Masha must not go to the river."

17

Lara was not religious. She did not believe in ritual. But sometimes, to be able to bear life, she needed the accompaniment of an inner music. She could not always compose such a music for herself. That music was God's word of life, and it was to weep over it that she went to church.

Once, early in December, she went to pray with such a heavy heart that she felt as if at any moment the earth might open at her feet and the vaulted ceiling of the church cave in. It would serve her right, it would put an end to the whole thing. She only regretted that she had taken that chatterbox, Olia Demina, with her.

"There's Prov Afanasievich," whispered Olia.

"Sh-sh. Leave me alone. What Prov Afanasievich?"

"Prov Afanasievich Sokolov. The one who's chanting. He's our cousin twice removed."

"Oh, the psalmist. Tiverzin's relative. Sh-sh. Stop talking. Don't disturb me, please."

They had come in at the beginning of the service. They were singing the psalm "Bless the Lord, O my soul: and all that is within me, bless His holy name."

The church was half empty, and every sound in it echoed hollowly. Only in front was there a crowd of worshippers standing close together. The building was new. The plain glass of the window added no color to the gray, snowbound, busy street outside and the people who walked or drove through it. Near that window stood a church warden paying no attention to the service and loudly reproving a deaf, half-witted beggar-woman in a voice as flat and commonplace as the window and the street.

In the time it took Lara, clutching her pennies in her fist, to make her way to the door past the worshippers without disturbing them, buy two candles for herself and Olia, and turn back, Prov Afanasievich had rattled off nine of the beatitudes at a pace suggesting that they were well enough known without him.

Blessed are the poor in spirit. . . . Blessed are they that mourn. . . . Blessed are they which do hunger and thirst after righteousness. . . .

Lara started and stood still. This was about her. He was saying: Happy are the downtrodden. They have something to tell about themselves. They have everything before them. That was what He thought. That was Christ's judgment.

18

It was the time of the Presnia uprising. The Guishars' flat was in the rebel area. A barricade was being built on Tver Street a few yards from their house. People carried buckets of water from their yards in order to cement the stones and scrap iron with ice.

The neighboring yard was used by the workers' militia as an assembly point, something between a Red Cross post and a soup kitchen.

Lara knew two of the boys who went to it. One was Nika Dudorov, a friend of her school friend Nadia. He was proud, straightforward, taciturn. He was like Lara and did not interest her.

The other was Pasha Antipov, the gymnasium student, who lived with old Tiverzina, Olia Demina's grandmother. Lara noticed the effect she had on the boy when she met him at the Tiverzins'. He was so childishly simple that he did not conceal his joy at seeing her, as if she were some summer landscape of birch trees, grass, and clouds, and could freely express his enthusiasm about her without any risk of being laughed at.

As soon as she realized the kind of influence she had on him, she began unconsciously to make use of it. However, it was not until several years later and at a much further stage in their relationship that she took his malleable, easygoing character seriously in hand. By then Pasha knew that he was head over heels in love with her and that it was for life.

The two boys were playing the most terrible and adult of games, war; moreover, participation in this particular war was punishable by deportation and hanging. Yet the way their woollen caps were tied at the back suggested that they were children, that they still had fathers and mothers who looked after them. Lara thought of them as a grown-up thinks of children. Their dangerous amusements had a bloom of innocence that they communicated to everything—to the evening, so shaggy with hoarfrost that it seemed more black than white, to the dark blue shadows in the yard, to the house across the road where the boys were hiding, and, above all, to the continual revolver shots which came from it. "The boys are shooting," thought Lara. This was how she thought not only of Nika and Pasha but of the whole fighting city. "Good, decent boys," she thought. "It's because they are good that they are shooting."

19

They learned that the barricade might be shelled and that their house would be in danger. It was too late to think of going to stay with friends in some other part of Moscow, the quarter was surrounded; they had to find shelter in the neighborhood, within the ring. They thought of the Montenegro.

It turned out that they were not the first to think of it. The hotel was full. There were many others who shared their predicament. For old times' sake the proprietor promised to put them up in the linen room.

Not to attract attention by carrying suitcases, they packed the most necessary things into three bundles; then they put off moving from day to day.

Because the employees of the workshop were treated rather like family members, they had continued to work despite the strike. But one dull, cold afternoon there was a ring at the door. Someone had come to complain and to argue. The owner was asked for. Fetisova went instead to pour oil on the troubled waters. A few moments later she called the seamstresses into the hall and introduced them to the visitor. He shook hands all round, clumsily and with emotion, and went away having apparently reached an agreement with Fetisova.

The seamstresses came back into the workroom and began tying on their shawls and putting on their shabby winter coats.

"What has happened?" asked Madame Guishar, hurrying in.

"They're calling us out, Madam, we're on strike."

"But . . . Have I ever wronged you?" Madame Guishar burst into tears.

"Don't be upset, Amalia Karlovna. We've got nothing against you. We're very grateful to you. It's not just you and us. Everybody's doing the same, the whole world. You can't go against everybody, can you?"

They all went away, even Olia Demina and Fetisova, who whispered to Madame Guishar in parting that she had agreed to the strike for the good of the owner and the establishment. But Amalia Karlovna was inconsolable.

"What black ingratitude! To think that I was so mistaken in

these people! The kindness I've lavished on that brat! Well, admittedly she's only a child, but that old witch!"

"They can't make an exception just for you, Mother, don't you see?" Lara said soothingly. "No one bears you any malice. On the contrary. All that's being done now is done in the name of humanity, in defense of the weak, for the good of women and children. Yes, it is. Don't shake your head so skeptically. You'll see, one day you and I will be better off because of it."

But her mother could not understand. "It's always like this," she sobbed. "Just when I can't think straight you come out with something that simply astounds me. People play a dirty trick on me, and you say it's all for my good. No, really, I must be out of my mind."

Rodia was at school. Lara and her mother wandered about aimlessly, alone in the empty house. The unlit street stared emptily into the rooms, and the rooms returned its stare.

"Let's go to the hotel, Mother, before it gets dark," Lara begged. "Do come, Mother. Don't put it off, let's go now."

"Filat, Filat," they called the janitor. "Take us to the Montenegro, be a good boy."

"Very good, Madam."

"Take the bundles over. And keep an eye on the house, Filat, until things sort themselves out. And please don't forget the bird seed for Kirill Modestovich, and to change his water. And keep everything locked up. That's all, I think, and please keep in touch with us."

"Very well, Madam."

"Thank you, Filat. God keep you. Well, let's sit down* and then we must be off."

When they went out the fresh air seemed as unfamiliar as after weeks of illness. Noises, rounded, as if turned on a lathe, rolled echoing lightly through the crisp, frosty, nut-clean space. Shots and salvoes smacked, thudded, and plopped, flattening the distances into a pancake.

However much Filat tried to convince them to the contrary, Lara and Amalia Karlovna insisted that the shots were blanks.

"Don't be silly, Filat. Think it out for yourself. How could they be anything but blanks when you can't see anyone shooting? Who d'you think is shooting, the Holy Ghost or what? Of course they're blanks."

At one of the crossroads they were stopped by a patrol of

---

*A superstitious Russian custom: before a move or a journey people sit down a few moments for luck.

grinning Cossacks who searched them, insolently running their
hands over them from head to foot. Their visorless caps with
chin straps were tilted jauntily over one ear; it made all of them
look one-eyed.

"Wonderful," thought Lara as she walked on. She would not
see Komarovsky for as long as the district was cut off from the
rest of the town. Because of her mother it was impossible for
her to break with him. She could not say: "Mother, please stop
seeing him." If she did that, it would all come out. And what if
it did? Why should that frighten her? Oh, God! Anything,
anything, if only it would end! God! God! She would fall down
in a faint with disgust. What was it she had just remembered?
What was the name of that frightful picture? There was a fat
Roman in it. It hung in the first of those private rooms, the one
where it all began. "The Woman or the Vase"—yes, that was it.
Of course. It was a famous picture. The woman or the vase.
When she first saw it she was not yet a woman, she was not yet
comparable to an expensive work of art. That came later. The
table was splendidly set for a feast.

"Where do you think you are running like that? I can't keep
up with you," panted Madame Guishar. Lara walked swiftly,
some unknown force swept her on as though she were striding
on air, carried along by this proud, quickening strength.

"How splendid," she thought, listening to the gun shots.
"Blessed are the downtrodden. Blessed are the deceived. God
speed you, bullets. You and I are of one mind."

20

The brothers Gromeko had a house at the corner of Sivtsev
Vrazhok and another small street. Alexander Alexandrovich and
Nikolai Alexandrovich Gromeko were professors of chemistry,
the one at the Petrov Academy, the other at the University.
Nikolai was unmarried. Alexander had a wife, Anna Ivanovna,
née Krueger. Her father was an ironmaster; he owned an
enormous estate in the Urals, near Yuriatin, on which there
were several abandoned, unprofitable mines.

The Gromekos' house had two stories. On the top floor were
the bedrooms, the schoolroom, Alexander Alexandrovich's
study and his library, Anna Ivanovna's boudoir, and Tonia's and

Yura's rooms. The ground floor was used for receptions. Its pistachio-colored curtains, gleaming piano top, aquarium, olive-green upholstery, and potted plants resembling seaweed made it look like a green, sleepily swaying sea bed.

The Gromekos were cultivated, hospitable, and great connoisseurs and lovers of music. They often held receptions and evenings of chamber music at which piano trios, violin sonatas, and string quartets were performed.

Such a musical evening was to be held in January, 1906. There was to be a first performance of a violin sonata by a young composer, a pupil of Taneiev's, and a trio by Tchaikovsky.

The preparations were begun the day before. The furniture was moved around in the ballroom. In one corner the piano tuner struck the same chord dozens of times and scattered arpeggios like handfuls of beads. In the kitchen, chickens were being plucked, vegetables cleaned, and mustard mixed with olive oil for sauces and salad dressings.

Shura Shlesinger, Anna's bosom friend and confidante, had come first thing in the morning, making a nuisance of herself.

She was a tall thin woman with regular features and a rather masculine face which recalled the Emperor's, especially when she wore her gray astrakhan hat set at an angle; she kept it on in the house, only slightly raising the veil pinned to it.

In times of sorrow or anxiety the two friends lightened each other's burdens. They did this by saying unpleasant things to each other, their conversation becoming increasingly caustic until an emotional storm burst and soon ended in tears and a reconciliation. These periodic quarrels had a tranquillizing effect on both, like the application of leeches for high blood pressure.

Shura Shlesinger had been married several times, but she forgot her husbands as soon as she divorced them, and despite her many marriages there was a certain coldness, like that of a spinster, about her.

She was a theosophist, but she was also an expert on the ritual of the Orthodox Church, and even when she was *toute transportée,* in a state of utter ecstasy, could not refrain from prompting the officiating clergy. "Hear, O Lord," "Now and ever shall be," "glorious cherubim" she muttered ceaselessly in her hoarse, staccato patter.

Shura Shlesinger knew mathematics, esoteric Indian doctrine, the addresses of the best-known teachers at the Moscow Conservatory, who was living with whom, and God only knows what else. For this reason she was called in, as arbiter and organizer, on all important occasions in life.

At the appointed time the guests began to arrive. There came Adelaida Filippovna, Gints, the Fufkovs, Mr. and Mrs. Basurman, the Verzhitskis, Colonel Kavkaztsev. It was snowing, and whenever the front door was opened you could see the swirling air rush past, as though tangled in a thousand knots by the flickering snow. The men came in out of the cold in high clumsy snow boots, and every one of them, without exception, did his best to look like a country bumpkin; but their wives, on the contrary, their faces glowing from the frost, coats unbuttoned, shawls pushed back and hair spangled with rime, looked like hardened coquettes, cunning itself. "Cui's nephew," the whisper went round as the new pianist came in.

Beyond the open side doors of the ballroom the supper table gleamed, white and long as a winter road. The play of light on frosted bottles of red rowanberry cordial caught the eye. The crystal cruets on silver stands and the picturesque arrangement of game and zakuski* captured the imagination. The napkins folded into stiff pyramids and the baskets of mauve cineraria smelling of almonds seemed to whet the appetite.

Not to delay the pleasure of earthly food too long, the company got down hastily to their spiritual repast. They sat down in rows. "Cui's nephew," they whispered again as the musician took his place at the piano. The concert began.

The sonata was known to be dry, labored, and boring. The performance confirmed this belief, and the work turned out to be terribly long as well.

During the interval the critic Kerimbekov and Alexander Gromeko had an argument about it, Kerimbekov running it down and Gromeko defending it. All around them people smoked, talked, and moved their chairs, till the glittering tablecloth in the adjoining room once again attracted attention. All proposed that the concert be resumed without delay.

The pianist cast a sideways glance at the audience, and signalled his partners to begin. The violinist and Tyshkevich flourished their bows. The music rose plaintively.

Yura, Tonia, and Misha Gordon, who spent half his time at the Gromekos', were sitting in the third row.

"Egorovna is making signs at you," Yura whispered to Alexander Alexandrovich, who sat directly in front of him.

Egorovna, the Gromekos' white-haired old servant, stood in

*Hors d'oeuvres, including various kinds of cold meat and fish.

the doorway and by staring desperately at Yura and nodding with equal energy at Alexander Alexandrovich tried to make Yura understand that she needed urgently to speak to the master.

Alexander Alexandrovich turned, gave her a reproachful look, and shrugged his shoulders, but she stood her ground. Soon they were talking across the room by signs, like a couple of deaf-mutes. People were looking. Anna Ivanovna cast devastating glances at her husband. He got up. Something had to be done. Blushing, he tiptoed around the edge of the room.

"How can you do such a thing, Egorovna! Really now, what's all the fuss? Well, hurry up, what is it?"

Egorovna whispered in his ear.

"What Montenegro?"

"The hotel."

"Well, what about it?"

"They're asking for him to go back at once. There's a relative of his dying."

"So now they're dying! I can imagine. . . . It can't be done, Egorovna. When they've finished this piece I'll tell them. Until then I can't."

"They've sent the hotel waiter with a cab. They're waiting. Somebody's dying, I tell you, can't you understand? It's a lady."

"And I tell you it's impossible. As if a few minutes could make all that difference." He tiptoed back to his place with a worried frown, rubbing the bridge of his nose.

At the end of the first movement, before the applause had died down, he went up to the musicians and told Tyshkevich that he was needed at home, there had been some accident, they would have to stop playing. Then he turned to the audience and held up his hands for silence:

"Ladies and gentlemen, I am afraid the trio has to be interrupted. The cellist has just received some bad news. All our sympathy is with him. He has to leave us. I wouldn't like him to go by himself at such a moment. He may need help. I'll go with him. Be a good boy, Yurochka, go and tell Semion to bring the carriage around, he's had it ready for some time. Ladies and gentlemen, I won't say goodbye—I beg you all to stay—I won't be long."

The boys asked to go with him for the sake of the drive through the frosty night.

21

Although the normal flow of life had been restored since December, shooting could still be heard, and the houses burned down as the result of ordinary fires looked like the smoldering ruins of those destroyed during the uprising.

The boys had never been for such a long drive before. In reality the Montenegro was a stone's throw away—down the Smolensky Boulevard, along the Novinsky, and halfway up Sadovaia Street—but the savage frost and fog separated space into disconnected fragments, as if space were not homogeneous the world over. The shaggy, ragged smoke of bonfires,* the crunch of footsteps and the whine of sleigh runners, contributed to give the impression that they had been travelling for God knows how long and had arrived at some terrifyingly remote place.

Outside the hotel entrance stood a narrow, elegant-looking sleigh; the horse was covered with a cloth and had bandaged fetlocks. The driver sat hunched up in the passengers' seat, trying to keep warm, his swathed head buried in his huge gloved paws.

It was warm in the hotel lobby. Behind the cloakroom counter the porter dozed, lulled by the hum of the ventilator, the roar of the blazing stove, and the whistle of the boiling samovar, to be wakened occasionally by one of his own snores.

A thickly made-up woman with a face like a dumpling stood by the looking glass on the left. Her fur jacket was too light for the weather. She was waiting for someone to come down; her back to the glass, she turned her head over each shoulder to make sure that she looked attractive behind.

The frozen cab driver came in. His bulging coat made him look like a twisted bun on a baker's sign, and the clouds of steam he gave off increased the likeness. "How much longer will you be, Mam'zel?" he asked the woman by the looking glass. "Why I ever got mixed up with your sort, I don't know. I don't want my horse to freeze to death."

The incident in No. 23 was only one more nuisance added to the daily vexations of the hotel staff. Every minute the bells

---

*Fires are lit at crossroads in very cold weather.

shrilled and numbers popped up inside the long glass box on the wall showing which guest in which room was going frantic and pestering the servants without knowing what he wanted.

At the moment the doctor was giving an emetic to that old fool Guisharova and washing out her guts. Glasha, the maid, was run off her feet mopping up the floor and carrying dirty buckets out and clean ones in. But the storm now raging in the service room had started well before this hullabaloo, before Tirashka had been sent in a cab to fetch the doctor and that wretched fiddler, before Komarovsky had arrived and so many people had cluttered up the corridor outside the door.

The trouble had started that afternoon, when someone had turned clumsily in the narrow passage leading from the pantry to the landing and had accidentally pushed the waiter Sysoi just as he was rushing out, bending slightly with a fully loaded tray balanced on his right hand. The tray clattered to the floor, the soup was spilled, and two soup plates and one meat plate were smashed.

Sysoi insisted that it had been the dishwasher, she was answerable and she should pay for the damage. By now it was nearly eleven o'clock and half the staff were due to go off duty shortly, but the row was still going on.

"He's got the shakes, can't keep his hands and feet steady. All he cares about is sitting with a bottle, you'd think it was his wife, getting pickled like a herring, and then he asks who pushed him, who spilled his soup, who smashed his crockery. Now who do you think pushed you, you devil, you Astrakhan pest, you shameless creature?"

"I have told you already, Matriona Stepanovna, watch your language."

"And who's the one that all the fuss is about now, I ask you? You'd think it was somebody worth smashing crockery for. But it's that slut, that streetwalker giving herself airs, that damned madam, innocence in retirement, done so well for herself she's swigging arsenic. Of course, living at the Montenegro, she wouldn't know an alley cat if she met one."

Misha and Yura walked up and down the corridor outside Madame Guishar's room. It had all turned out quite differently from anything Alexander Alexandrovich had expected. He had imagined a clean and dignified tragedy in a musician's life. But this was sordid and scandalous, and certainly not for children.

The boys were waiting in the corridor.

"Go in to your auntie now, young gentlemen." The valet

came up to them and for the second time tried to persuade them in his soft unhurried voice. "You go in, don't worry. The lady's all right, you needn't be afraid. She's quite recovered. You can't stand here. There was an accident here this afternoon, valuable china was smashed. You can see we have to run up and down serving meals, and it's a bit narrow. You go in there."

The boys complied.

Inside the room, a lighted kerosene lamp which ordinarily hung over the table had been taken out of its bracket and carried behind the wooden screen, where it stank of bedbugs. This was a sleeping alcove separated from the rest of the room and strangers' eyes by a dusty curtain, but the curtain had been flung over the screen and in the confusion no one had thought of drawing it. The lamp stood on a bench and lit the alcove harshly from below as though by a footlight.

Madame Guishar had tried to poison herself not with arsenic, as the dishwasher thought, but with iodine. The room had the tart, astringent smell of green walnuts when their husks are still soft and blacken at a touch.

Behind the screen the maid was mopping up the floor, and lying on the bed was a half-naked woman; drenched with water, tears, and sweat, her hair stuck together, she was holding her head over a bucket and crying loudly.

The boys turned away at once, so embarrassing and unmannerly did they feel it was to look in her direction. But Yura had seen enough to be struck by the fact that in certain clumsy, tense positions, in moments of strain and exertion, a woman ceases to be such as she is represented in sculpture and looks more like a wrestler with bulging muscles, stripped down to his shorts and ready for the match.

At last someone behind the screen had the sense to draw the curtain.

"Fadei Kazimirovich, my dear, where's your hand? Give me your hand," the woman was saying, choking with tears and nausea. "Oh, I have been through such horrors. I had such terrible suspicions. . . . Fadei Kazimirovich . . . I imagined . . . but happily it has all turned out to be nonsense, just my disordered imagination. . . . Just think what a relief. And the upshot of it all . . . here I am . . . here I am alive. . . ."

"Calm yourself, Amalia Karlovna, I beg you. . . . How awkward all this is, I must say, how very awkward."

"We'll be off home now," said Alexander Alexandrovich gruffly to the children. Excruciatingly embarrassed, they stood in the doorway, and as they did not know where to look they stared straight in front of them into the shadowy depth of the main room, from which the lamp had been removed. The walls were hung with photographs, there was a bookshelf filled with music scores, a desk piled with papers and albums, and beyond the dining table with a crocheted cover a girl was asleep in an armchair, clasping its back and pressing her cheek against it. She must have been dead tired to be able to sleep in spite of all the noise and excitement.

"We'll be off now," Alexander Alexandrovich said again. There had been no sense in their coming, and to stay any longer would be indecent. "As soon as Fadei Kazimirovich comes out . . . I must say goodbye to him."

It was not Tyshkevich who came out from behind the screen, but a thickset, portly, self-confident man. Carrying the lamp above his head, he went over to the table and replaced it in its bracket. The light woke up the girl. She smiled at him, squinting her eyes and stretching.

At sight of the stranger, Misha gave a start and stared at him intently. He pulled Yura's sleeve and tried to whisper to him, but Yura would not have it. "You can't whisper in front of people. What will they think of you?"

Meanwhile a silent scene took place between the girl and the man. Not a word passed their lips, only their eyes met. But the understanding between them had a terrifying quality of magic, as if he were the master of a puppet show and she were a puppet obedient to his every gesture.

A tired smile puckered her eyes and loosened her lips, but in answer to his sneering glance she gave him a sly wink of complicity. Both of them were pleased that it had all ended so well—their secret was safe and Madame Guishar's attempted suicide had failed.

Yura devoured them with his eyes. Unseen in the half darkness, he kept staring into the circle of lamplight. The scene between the captive girl and her master was both ineffably mysterious and shamelessly frank. His heart was torn by contradictory feelings of a strength he had never experienced before.

Here was the very thing which he, Tonia, and Misha had endlessly discussed as "vulgar," the force which so frightened and attracted them and which they controlled so easily from a safe distance by words. And now here it was, this force, in front of Yura's very eyes, utterly real, and yet troubled and haunting, pitilessly destructive, and complaining and calling for help—and what had become of their childish philosophy and what was Yura to do now?

"Do you know who that man was?" said Misha when they went out into the street. Yura, absorbed in his thoughts, did not reply.

"He's the one who encouraged your father to drink and drove him to his death. In the train—you remember—I told you."

Yura was thinking about the girl and the future, not about his father and the past. At first he could not even understand what Misha was saying. It was too cold to talk.

"You must be frozen, Semion," Alexander Alexandrovich said to the coachman. They drove home.

CHAPTER THREE

The Sventitskys' Christmas Party

1

One winter Alexander Alexandrovich gave Anna Ivanovna an antique wardrobe, which he had picked up somewhere or other. It was made of ebony and was so enormous that it would not go through any door in one piece. It was taken into the house in sections; the problem then was where to put it. It would not do for the reception rooms because of its function nor for the bedrooms because of its size. In the end, a part of the landing was cleared for it outside the master bedroom.

Markel, the porter, came to put it together. He brought with him his six-year-old daughter Marinka. She was given a stick of barley sugar. Sniffling, and sucking the candy and her moist fingers, she stood intently watching her father.

At first everything went smoothly. The wardrobe grew in front of Anna Ivanovna's eyes; when only the top remained to be put on, she took it into her head to help Markel. She climbed onto the raised floor of the wardrobe, slipped, and fell against the sides, which were held in place only by tenons. The rope that Markel had tied loosely around them came undone. Anna Ivanovna fell on her back together with the boards as they clattered to the ground, and bruised herself painfully.

Markel rushed to her. "Oh, Madam, mistress," he said. "What made you do that, my dear? You haven't broken any bones? Feel your bones. It's the bones that matter, the soft part doesn't matter at all, the soft parts mend in God's good time, and, as the saying goes, they're only for pleasure anyway.— Don't bawl, you stupid!" he reprimanded the crying Marinka. "Wipe your nose and go to your mother.—Ah, Madam, couldn't you trust me to set up that clothes chest without you? Of course, to you I'm only a porter, you can't think otherwise, but the fact is, I was a cabinetmaker, yes, Ma'am, cabinetmaking was my trade. You wouldn't believe how many cupboards and sideboards of all kinds, lacquer and walnut and mahogany, passed through my hands. Or, for that matter, how many well-to-do young ladies passed me by, and vanished from under my nose, if you'll forgive the expression. And it all comes from drink, strong liquor."

Markel pushed over an armchair, and with his help Anna Ivanovna sank into it groaning and rubbing her bruises. Then he set about restoring the wardrobe. When he put the top on he said, "Now the doors, and it'll be fit for an exhibition."

Anna Ivanovna did not like the wardrobe. Its appearance and size reminded her of a catafalque or a royal tomb and filled her with a superstitious dread. She nicknamed it the tomb of Askold;* she meant the horse of Prince Oleg,† which had caused its master's death. She had read a great deal, but haphazardly, and she tended to confuse related ideas.

After that accident Anna Ivanovna developed a pulmonary weakness.

2

Throughout November, 1911, Anna Ivanovna stayed in bed with pneumonia.

Yura, Misha Gordon, and Tonia were due to graduate the following spring, Yura in medicine, Tonia in law, and Misha, who studied at the Faculty of Philosophy, in philology.

Everything in Yura's mind was still helter-skelter, but his

---

*Askold, one of the founders of the Russian state, was buried in Kiev.

†Oleg, another Prince of Kiev, was killed by a snake that came out of the skull of his favorite horse.

views, his habits, and his inclinations were all distinctly his own. He was unusually impressionable, and the originality of his vision was remarkable.

Though he was greatly drawn to art and history, he scarcely hesitated over the choice of a career. He thought that art was no more a vocation than innate cheerfulness or melancholy was a profession. He was interested in physics and natural science, and believed that a man should do something socially useful in his practical life. He settled on medicine.

In the first year of his four-year course he had spent a term in the dissecting room, situated in the cellars of the university. You went down the winding staircase. There was always a crowd of dishevelled students, some poring over their tattered textbooks surrounded by bones, or quietly dissecting, each in his corner, others fooling about, cracking jokes and chasing the rats that scurried in swarms over the stone floors. In the half darkness of the mortuary the naked bodies of unidentified young suicides and drowned women, well preserved and untouched by decay, shone like phosphorus. Injections of alum solutions rejuvenated them, giving them a deceptive roundness. The corpses were cut open, dismembered, and prepared, yet even in its smallest sections the human body kept its beauty, so that Yura's wonder before some water nymph brutally flung onto a zinc table continued before her amputated arm or hand. The cellar smelled of carbolic acid and formaldehyde, and the presence of mystery was tangible in everything, from the obscure fate of these spread-out bodies to the riddle of life and death itself—and death was dominant in the underground room as if it were its home or its headquarters.

The voice of this mystery, silencing everything else, haunted Yura, disturbing him in his anatomical work. He had become used to such distracting thoughts and took them in his stride.

Yura had a good mind and was an excellent writer. Ever since his schooldays he had dreamed of composing a book about life which would contain, like buried explosives, the most striking things he had so far seen and thought about. But he was too young to write such a book; instead, he wrote poetry. He was like a painter who was always making sketches for a big canvas he had in mind.

He was indulgent toward these immature works on account of their vigor and originality. These two qualities, vigor and originality, in his opinion gave reality to art, which he otherwise regarded as pointless, idle, unnecessary.

Yura realized the great part his uncle had played in molding his character.

Nikolai Nikolaievich now lived in Lausanne. In his books, published there in Russian and in translations, he developed his old view of history and as another universe, made by man with the help of time and memory in answer to the challenge of death. These works were inspired by a new interpretation of Christianity, and led directly to a new conception of art.

Misha Gordon was influenced by these ideas even more than Yura. They determined him to register at the Faculty of Philosophy. He attended lectures on theology, and even considered transferring later to the theological academy.

Yura advanced and became freer under the influence of his uncle's theories, but Misha was fettered by them. Yura realized that his friend's enthusiasms were partly accounted for by his origin. Being tactful and discreet, he made no attempt to talk him out of his extravagant ideas. But he often wished that Misha were a realist, more down-to-earth.

3

One night at the end of November Yura came home late from the university; he was exhausted and had eaten nothing all day. He was told that there had been a terrible alarm that afternoon. Anna Ivanovna had had convulsions. Several doctors had seen her; at one time they had advised Alexander Alexandrovich to send for the priest, but later they had changed their minds. Now she was feeling better; she was fully conscious and had asked for Yura to be sent to her the moment he got back.

Yura went up at once.

The room showed traces of the recent commotion. A nurse, moving noiselessly, was rearranging something on the night table. Towels that had been used for compresses were lying about, damp and crumpled. The water in the slop basin was pinkish with expectorated blood, and broken ampoules and swollen tufts of cotton wool floated on its surface.

Anna Ivanovna lay drenched in sweat, with parched lips. Her face had become haggard since morning.

"Can the diagnosis be wrong?" Yura wondered. "She has all the symptoms of lobar pneumonia. It looks like the crisis."

After greeting her and saying the encouraging, meaningless things that are always said on such occasions, he sent the nurse out of the room, took Anna Ivanovna's wrist to feel her pulse, and reached into his coat pocket for his stethoscope. She moved her head to indicate that this was unnecessary. He realized that she wanted him for some other reason. She spoke with effort.

"They wanted to give me the last sacraments. . . . Death is hanging over me. . . . It may come any moment. . . . When you go to have a tooth out you're frightened it'll hurt, you prepare yourself. . . . But this isn't a tooth, it's everything, the whole of you, your whole life . . . being pulled out. . . . And what is it? Nobody knows. . . . And I am sick at heart and terrified."

She fell silent. Tears were streaming down her cheeks. Yura said nothing. A moment later Anna Ivanovna went on.

"You're clever, talented. . . . That makes you different. . . . You surely know something. . . . Comfort me."

"Well, what is there for me to say?" replied Yura. He fidgeted on his chair, got up, paced the room, and sat down again. "In the first place, you'll feel better tomorrow. There are clear indications—I'd stake my life on it—that you've passed the crisis. And then—death, the survival of consciousness, faith in resurrection . . . You want to know my opinion as a scientist? Perhaps some other time? No? Right now? Well, as you wish. But it's difficult like that, all of a sudden." And there and then he delivered a whole impromptu lecture, astonished that he could do it.

"Resurrection. In the crude form in which it is preached to console the weak, it is alien to me. I have always understood Christ's words about the living and the dead in a different sense. Where could you find room for all these hordes of people accumulated over thousands of years? The universe isn't big enough for them; God, the good, and meaningful purpose would be crowded out. They'd be crushed by these throngs greedy merely for the animal life.

"But all the time, life, one, immense, identical throughout its innumerable combinations and transformations, fills the universe and is continually reborn. You are anxious about whether you will rise from the dead or not, but you rose from the dead when you were born and you didn't notice it.

"Will you feel pain? Do the tissues feel their disintegration? In other words, what will happen to your consciousness? But what is consciousness? Let's see. A conscious attempt to fall asleep is sure to produce insomnia, to try to be conscious of one's own digestion is a sure way to upset the stomach. Consciousness is a poison when we apply it to ourselves. Consciousness is a light directed outward, it lights up the way ahead of us so that we don't stumble. It's like the headlights on a locomotive—turn them inward and you'd have a crash.

"So what will happen to your consciousness? *Your* consciousness, yours, not anyone else's. Well, what are *you?* There's the point. Let's try to find out. What is it about you that you have always known as yourself? What are you conscious of in yourself? Your kidneys? Your liver? Your blood vessels? No. However far back you go in your memory, it is always in some external, active manifestation of yourself that you come across your identity—in the work of your hands, in your family, in other people. And now listen carefully. You in others—this is your soul. This is what you are. This is what your consciousness has breathed and lived on and enjoyed throughout your life—your soul, your immortality, your life in others. And what now? You have always been in others and you will remain in others. And what does it matter to you if later on that is called your memory? This will be you—the you that enters the future and becomes a part of it.

"And now one last point. There is nothing to fear. There is no such thing as death. Death has nothing to do with us. But you said something about being talented—that it makes one different. Now, that does have something to do with us. And talent in the highest and broadest sense means talent for life.

"There will be no death, says St. John. His reasoning is quite simple. There will be no death because the past is over; that's almost like saying there will be no death because it is already done with, it's old and we are bored with it. What we need is something new, and that new thing is life eternal."

He was pacing up and down the room as he was talking. Now he walked up to Anna Ivanovna's bed and putting his hand on her forehead said, "Go to sleep." After a few moments she began to fall asleep.

Yura quietly left the room and told Egorovna to send in the nurse. "What's come over me?" he thought. "I'm becoming a regular quack—muttering incantations, laying on the hands. . . ."

Next day Anna Ivanovna was better.

4

Anna Ivanovna continued to improve. In the middle of December she tried to get up but she was still weak. The doctors told her to stay in bed and have a really good rest.

She often sent for Yura and Tonia and for hours on end talked to them of her childhood, spent on her grandfather's estate, Varykino, on the river Rynva, in the Urals. Neither Yura nor Tonia had ever been there, but listening to her, Yura could easily imagine those ten thousand acres of impenetrable virgin forest as black as night, and, thrusting into it like a curved knife, the bends of the swift stream with its rocky bed and steep cliffs on the Krueger side.

For the first time in their lives Yura and Tonia were getting evening clothes, Yura a dinner jacket and Tonia a pale satin party dress with a suitably modest neckline.

They were going to wear them at the traditional Christmas party at the Sventitskys' on the twenty-seventh. When the tailor and the seamstress delivered the clothes, Yura and Tonia tried them on, were delighted, and had not yet taken them off when Egorovna came in asking them to go to Anna Ivanovna.

They went to her room in their new clothes. On seeing them, she raised herself on her elbow, looked them over, and told them to turn around.

"Very nice," she said. "Charming. I had no idea they were ready. Let me have another look, Tonia. No, it's all right, I thought the yoke puckered a bit. Do you know why I've called you? But first I want a word with you, Yura."

"I know, Anna Ivanovna, I know you've seen the letter, I had it sent to you myself. I know you agree with Nikolai Nikolaievich. You both think I should not have refused the legacy. But wait a moment. It's bad for you to talk. Just let me explain—though you know most of it already.

"Well, then, in the first place, it suits the lawyers that there should be a Zhivago case because there is enough money in Father's estate to cover the costs and to pay the lawyers' fees. Apart from that there is no legacy—nothing but debts and muddle—and a lot of dirty linen to be washed. If there really had been anything that could be turned into money, do you think I'd have made a present of it to the court and not used it myself? But that's just the point—the whole case is trumped up. So rather than rake up all that dirt it was better to give up my right to a nonexistent property and let it go to all that bunch of false rivals and pretenders who were after it. One claimant, as you know, is a certain Madame Alice, who calls herself Zhivago and lives with her children in Paris—I've known about her for a long time. But now there are various new claims—I don't know about you, but I was told of them quite recently.

"It appears that while Mother was still alive, Father became infatuated with a certain eccentric Princess Stolbunova-Enrici. This lady has a son by him, Evgraf; he is ten years old.

"The Princess is a recluse. She lives—God knows on what— in her house just outside Omsk, and she never goes out. I've seen a photograph of the house. It's very handsome, with five French windows and stucco medallions on the cornices. And recently I've been having the feeling that the house was staring at me nastily, out of all its five windows, right across all the thousands of miles between Siberia and Moscow, and that sooner or later it would give me the evil eye. So what do I want with all this—imaginary capital, phony claimants, malice, envy? And lawyers."

"All the same, you shouldn't have renounced it," said Anna Ivanovna. "Do you know why I called you?" she asked again and immediately went on, "His name came back to me. You remember the forest guard I was telling you about yesterday? He was called Bacchus. Extraordinary, isn't it! A real bogey-man, black as the devil, with a beard growing up to his eyebrows, and calls himself Bacchus! His face was all disfigured, a bear had mauled him but he had fought it off. And they're all like that out there. Such names—striking, sonorous! Bacchus or Lupus or Faustus. Every now and then somebody like that would be announced—perhaps Auctus or Frolus—somebody with a name like a shot from your grandfather's gun—and we would all immediately troop downstairs from the nursery to the kitchen. And there—you can't think what it was like—you'd find a charcoal dealer with a live bear cub, or a prospector from the far end of the province with a specimen of the ore. And your grandfather would always give them a credit slip for the office. Some were given money, some buckwheat, others cartridges. The forest came right up to the windows. And the snow, the snow! Higher than the roofs!" Anna Ivanovna had a coughing fit.

"That's enough, it's bad for you," Tonia and Yura urged her. "Nonsense, I'm perfectly all right. That reminds me. Egorovna told me that you two are worrying about whether you should go to the party the day after tomorrow. Don't let me hear anything so silly again, you ought to be ashamed of yourselves! And you call yourself a doctor, Yura! So that's settled, you'll go, and that's that. But to return to Bacchus. He used to be a blacksmith when he was young. He got into a fight and was disembowelled. So he made himself a set of iron guts. Now, Yura, don't be silly. Of course I know he couldn't. You mustn't take it literally! But that's what the people out there said."

She was interrupted by another coughing fit, a much longer one than the last. It went on and on; she could not get her breath.

Yura and Tonia hurried across to her simultaneously. They stood shoulder to shoulder by her bedside. Their hands touched. Still coughing, Anna Ivanovna caught their hands in hers and kept them joined awhile. When she was able to speak she said: "If I die, stay together. You're meant for each other. Get married. There now, you're engaged," she added and burst into tears.

5

As early as the spring of 1906—only a few months before she would begin her last year in the gymnasium—six months of Lara's liaison with Komarovsky had driven her beyond the limits of her endurance. He cleverly turned her wretchedness to his advantage, and when it suited him subtly reminded her of her shame. These reminders brought her to just that state of confusion that a lecher requires in a woman. As a result, Lara felt herself sinking ever deeper into a nightmare of sensuality which filled her with horror whenever she awoke from it. Her nocturnal madness was as unaccountable as black magic. Here everything was topsy-turvy and flew in the face of logic; sharp pain manifested itself by peals of silvery laughter, resistance and refusal meant consent, and grateful kisses covered the hand of the tormentor.

It seemed that there would be no end to it, but that spring, as she sat through a history lesson at the end of term, thinking of the summer when even school and homework would no longer keep her from Komarovsky, she came to a sudden decision that altered the course of her life.

It was a hot morning and a storm was brewing. Through the open classroom windows came the distant droning of the town, as monotonous as a beehive, and the shrieks of children playing in the yard. The grassy smell of earth and young leaves made her head ache, like a Shrovetide surfeit of pancakes and vodka.

The lesson was about Napoleon's Egyptian campaign. When the teacher came to the landing at Fréjus, the sky blackened and was split by lightning and thunder, and clouds of dust and sand swept into the room together with the smell of rain. Two teacher's pets rushed out obligingly to call the handyman to shut the windows, and as they opened the door, the wind sent all the blotting paper flying off the desks.

The windows were shut. A dirty city rain mingled with dust began to pour. Lara tore a page out of an exercise book, and wrote a note to her neighbor, Nadia Kologrivova:

"Nadia, I've got to live away from Mother. Help me to find a tutoring job, as well paid as possible. You know lots of rich people."

Nadia wrote back:

"We are looking for a governess for Lipa. Why not come to us—it would be wonderful! You know how fond my parents are of you."

6

Lara spent three years at the Kologrivovs' as behind stone walls. No one bothered her, and even her mother and brother, from whom she had become estranged, kept out of her way.

Lavrentii Mikhailovich Kologrivov was a big businessman, a brilliant and intelligent practitioner of the most modern methods. He hated the decaying order with a double hatred, as a man rich enough to outbid the treasury, and as a member of the lower classes who had risen to fabulous heights. In his house he sheltered revolutionaries sought by the police, and he paid the defense costs in political trials. It was a standing joke that he was so keen on subsidizing the revolution that he expropriated himself and organized strikes at his own plants. An excellent marksman and a passionate hunter, he went to the Serebriany woods and Losin Island in the winter of 1905, giving rifle training to workers' militia.

He was a remarkable man. His wife, Serafima Filippovna, was a worthy match. Lara admired and respected both of them, and the whole household loved her and treated her as a member of the family.

For more than three years Lara led a life free from worries. Then one day her brother Rodia went to see her. Swaying affectedly on his long legs and drawling self-importantly, he told her that the cadets of his class had collected money for a farewell gift to the head of the Academy and entrusted it to him, asking him to choose and buy the gift. This money he had gambled away two days ago down to the last kopek. Having told his story, he flopped full length in an armchair and burst into tears.

Lara sat frozen while Rodia went on through his sobs:

"Last night I went to see Victor Ippolitovich. He refused to talk about it with me, but he said if you wished him to . . . He said that although you no longer loved any of us, your power over him was still so great . . . Lara darling . . . One word from you would be enough. . . . You realize what this means to me, what a disgrace it is . . . the honor of my uniform is at stake. Go to see him, that's not too much to ask, speak to him . . . You can't want me to pay for this with my life."

"Your life . . . The honor of your uniform." Lara echoed him indignantly, pacing the room. "I am not a uniform. I have no honor. You can do what you like with me. Have you any idea of what you are asking? Do you realize what he is proposing to you? Year after year I slave away, and now you come along and don't care if everything goes smash. To hell with you. Go ahead, shoot yourself. What do I care? How much do you need?"

"Six hundred and ninety odd rubles. Say seven hundred in round figures," he added after a slight pause.

"Rodia! No, you're out of your mind! Do you know what you are saying? You've gambled away seven hundred rubles! Rodia! Rodia! Do you realize how long it takes an ordinary person like me to earn that much by honest work?"

She broke off and after a short silence said coldly, as if to a stranger, "All right. I'll try. Come tomorrow. And bring your revolver—the one you were going to shoot yourself with.

You'll hand it over to me, for good. And with plenty of bullets, remember."

She got the money from Kologrivov.

7

Her work at the Kologrivovs' did not prevent Lara from graduating from the gymnasium, and taking university courses. She did well, and was to obtain her diploma the following year, 1912.

In the spring of 1911 her pupil Lipa graduated from the gymnasium. She was already engaged to a young engineer, Friesendank, who came of a good, well-to-do family. Lipa's parents approved of her choice but were against her marrying so young, and urged her to wait. This led to scenes. Lipa, the spoiled and willful darling of the family, shouted at her parents and stamped her feet.

In this rich household where Lara was accepted as a member of the family, no one reminded her of her debt or indeed remembered it. She would have paid it back long before, if she had not had secret expenses.

Unknown to Pasha, she sent money to his father, who had been deported to Siberia, helped his querulous and ailing mother, and reduced his own expenses by paying part of his board and lodging directly to his landlady. It was she who had found him his room in a new building in Kamerger Street near the Art Theater.

Pasha, who was a little younger than Lara, loved her madly and obeyed her slightest wish. After graduating from the *Realgymnasium*, he had, at her urging, taken up Greek and Latin. It was her dream that after they had passed their state examinations the following year they would marry and go out as gymnasium teachers to some provincial capital in the Urals.

In the summer of 1911 Lara went for the last time with the Kologrivovs to Duplyanka. She adored the place, and was even fonder of it than its owners. They knew this, and every summer on their arrival the same scene was enacted as though by an unwritten agreement. When the hot, grimy train left them at the station, Lara, overwhelmed by the infinite silence and heady fragrance of the countryside, and speechless with emotion, was allowed to walk alone from the railroad station to the estate. Meanwhile, the luggage was loaded onto a cart, and the family climbed into their barouche and listened to the Duplyanka coachman in his scarlet shirt and sleeveless coat telling them the latest local news.

Lara walked along the tracks following a path worn by pilgrims and then turned into the fields. Here she stopped and, closing her eyes, took a deep breath of the flower-scented air of the broad expanse around her. It was dearer to her than her kin, better than a lover, wiser than a book. For a moment she rediscovered the purpose of her life. She was here on earth to grasp the meaning of its wild enchantment and to call each thing by its right name, or, if this were not within her power, to give birth out of love for life to successors who would do it in her place.

That summer she had arrived exhausted by the many duties she had undertaken. She was easily upset. Generous and understanding by nature, she developed a new suspiciousness and a tendency to nurse petty grievances.

The Kologrivovs were as fond of her as ever and wanted her to stay on with them, but now that Lipa had grown up she felt that she had become useless to them. She refused her salary. They had to press it on her. At the same time she needed the money, and it would have been embarrassing and unfeasible to earn it independently while she was their guest.

Lara felt that her position was false and unendurable. She imagined that they all found her a burden and were only putting a good face on it. She was a burden to herself. She longed to run away from herself and from the Kologrivovs—anywhere—but according to her standards, she must first repay the money she had borrowed, and at the moment she had no means of doing it. She felt that she was a hostage—all through Rodia's stupid fault—and was trapped in impotent exasperation.

She suspected slights at every turn. If the Kologrivovs' friends were attentive to her she was sure that they regarded her as a submissive "ward" and an easy prey. If they left her alone, that proved that she did not exist for them.

Her fits of moodiness did not prevent her from sharing in the amusements of the many house guests. She swam, went boating, joined in night picnics by the river, and danced and let off fireworks with the rest. She took part in amateur theatricals and with even more zest in shooting competitions. Short

Mauser rifles were used in these contests, but she preferred Rodia's light revolver and became very skillful in its use. "Pity I'm a woman," she said, laughing, "I'd have made an expert deullist." But the more she did to distract herself, the more wretched she felt and the less she knew what she wanted.

When they went back to town it was worse than ever, for to her other troubles were now added her tiffs with Pasha (she was careful not to quarrel with him seriously; she regarded him as her last refuge). Pasha was beginning to show a certain self-assurance. His tone was becoming a little didactic, and this both amused and irritated her.

Pasha, Lipa, the Kologrivovs, money—everything whirled inside her head. She was disgusted with life. She was beginning to lose her mind. She was obsessed with the idea of breaking with everything she had ever known or experienced, and starting on something new. In this state, at Christmastime in the year 1911, she arrived at a fatal decision. She would leave the Kologrivovs now, at once, and become independent, and she would get the money for this from Komarovsky. It seemed to her that after all there had been between them and the years of independence she had won for herself, he must help her chivalrously, disinterestedly, without explanations or disgraceful conditions.

With this in mind she set out for Petrovka Street on the night of the twenty-seventh. Rodia's revolver, loaded and with the safety catch off, was inside her muff. Should Komarovsky refuse or humiliate her in any way, she intended to shoot him.

She walked through the festive streets in a terrible excitement, seeing nothing. The intended revolver shot had already gone off in her heart—and it was a matter of complete indifference whom the shot was aimed at. This shot was the only thing that she was conscious of. She heard it all the way to Petrovka Street, and it was aimed at Komarovsky, at herself, at her own face, and at the wooden target on the Duplyanka oak tree.

8

"Don't touch my muff!"

Emma Ernestovna had put out her hand to help her off with her coat; she had received her with Oh's and Ah's, telling her that Victor Ippolitovich was out but she must stay and wait for him.

"I can't. I'm in a hurry. Where is he?"

He was at a Christmas party. Clutching the scrap of paper with the address on it, Lara ran down the familiar gloomy staircase with its stained-glass coats of arms and started off for the Sventitskys' house in Flour Town.

Only now, when she came out for the second time, did she take a look around her. It was winter. It was the city. It was night.

It was bitter cold. The streets were covered with a thick, black, glassy layer of ice, like the bottom of beer bottles. It hurt her to breathe. The air was dense with gray sleet and it tickled and pricked her face like the gray frozen bristles of her fur cape. Her heart thumping, she walked through the deserted streets past the steaming doors of cheap teashops and restaurants. Faces as red as sausages and horses' and dogs' heads with beards of icicles emerged from the mist. A thick crust of ice and snow covered the windows, and the colored reflections of lighted Christmas trees and the shadows of merrymakers moved across their chalk-white opaque surfaces as on magic lantern screens; it was as though shows were being given for the benefit of pedestrians.

In Kamerger Street Lara stopped. "I can't go on. I can't bear it." The words almost slipped out. "I'll go up and tell him everything." Pulling herself together, she went in through the heavy door.

9

Pasha, his face red from the effort, his tongue pushing out his cheek, stood in front of the mirror struggling with a collar, a stud, and the starched buttonhole of his shirt front. He was going to a party. So chaste and inexperienced was he that Lara embarrassed him by coming in without knocking and finding him with this minor incompleteness in his dress. He at once noticed her agitation. She could hardly keep on her feet. She advanced pushing the hem of her skirt aside at each step as if she were fording a river.

He hurried toward her. "What's the matter?" he said in alarm. "What has happened?"

"Sit down beside me. Sit down, don't bother to finish dressing. I'm in a hurry, I must go in a minute. Don't touch my muff. Wait, turn the other way for a minute."

He complied. Lara was wearing a tailored suit. She took off her coat, hung it up, and transferred Rodia's revolver from the muff to a pocket. Then she went back to the sofa.

"Now you can look," she said. "Light a candle, and turn off the electricity."

She liked to sit in the dim light of candles, and Pasha always kept a few spare ones. He replaced the stump in the candlestick with a new candle, put it on the window sill, and lit it. The flame choked and spluttered, shooting off small stars, and sharpened to an arrow. A soft light filled the room. In the sheet of ice covering the windowpane a black eyelet began to form at the level of the flame.

"Listen, Pasha," said Lara. "I am in trouble. You must help me. Don't be frightened and don't question me. But don't ever think we can be like other people. Don't take it so lightly. I am in constant danger. If you love me, if you don't want me to be destroyed, we must not put off our marriage."

"But that's what I've always wanted," broke in Pasha. "Just name the day. I'm ready when you are. Now tell me plainly what is worrying you. Don't torment me with riddles."

But Lara evaded his question, imperceptibly changing the subject. They talked a long time about a number of things that had nothing to do with her distress.

10

That winter Yura was preparing a scientific paper on the nervous elements of the retina for the University Gold Medal competition. Though he had qualified only in general medicine, he had a specialist's knowledge of the eye. His interest in the physiology of sight was in keeping with other sides of his character—his creative gifts and his preoccupation with imagery in art and the logical structure of ideas.

Tonia and Yura were driving in a hired sleigh to the Sventitskys' Christmas party. After six years of late childhood and early adolescence spent in the same house they knew everything there was to know about each other. They had habits in common, their own special way of snorting at each other's jokes. Now they drove in silence, their lips tightly closed against the cold, occasionally exchanging a word or two, and absorbed in their own thoughts.

Yura was thinking about the date of his competition and that he must work harder at his paper. Then his mind, distracted by the festive, end-of-the-year bustle in the streets, jumped to other thoughts. He had promised Gordon an article on Blok for the mimeographed student paper that he edited; young people in both capitals were mad about Blok, Yura and Gordon particularly. But not even these thoughts held his mind for long. He and Tonia rode on, their chins tucked into their collars, rubbing their frozen ears, and each of them thinking of something else. But on one point their thoughts converged.

The recent scene at Anna Ivanovna's bedside had transformed them. It was as though their eyes had opened, and they appeared to each other in a new light.

Tonia, his old friend, who had always been taken for granted and had never needed explaining, had turned out to be the most inaccessible and complicated being he could imagine. She had become a woman. By a stretch of imagination he could visualize himself as an emperor, a hero, a prophet, a conqueror, but not as a woman.

Now that Tonia had taken this supreme and most difficult task on her slender and fragile shoulders (she seemed slender and fragile to him, though she was a perfectly healthy girl), he was filled with the ardent sympathy and timid wonder that are the beginning of passion.

Tonia's attitude to Yura underwent a similar change.

It occurred to Yura that perhaps they should not, after all, have gone out. He was worried about Anna Ivanovna. They had been on the point of leaving when, hearing that she was feeling less well, they had gone to her room, but she had ordered them off to the party as sharply as before. They had gone to the window to have a look at the weather. As they came out, the net curtains had clung to Tonia's new dress, trailing after her like a wedding veil. They all noticed this and burst out laughing.

Yura looked around him and saw what Lara had seen shortly before. The moving sleigh was making an unusually loud noise, which was answered by an unusually long echo coming from the ice-bound trees in the gardens and streets. The windows, frosted and lighted from inside, reminded him of precious caskets made of smoky topaz. Behind them glowed the Christmas life of Moscow, candles burned on trees, and guests in fancy dress milled about playing hide-and-seek and hunt-the-ring.

It suddenly occurred to Yura that Blok reflected the Christmas spirit in all domains of Russian life—in this northern city and in the newest Russian literature, under the starry sky of this modern street and around the lighted tree in a twentieth-century drawing room. There was no need to write an article on Blok, he thought, all you had to do was to paint a Russian version of a Dutch Adoration of the Magi with snow in it, and wolves, and a dark fir forest.

As they drove through Kamerger Street Yura noticed that a candle had melted a patch in the icy crust on one of the windows. The light seemed to look into the street almost consciously, as if it were watching the passing carriages and waiting for someone.

"A candle burned on the table, a candle burned . . . ," he whispered to himself—the beginning of something confused, formless; he hoped that it would take shape of itself. But nothing more came to him.

11

From time immemorial the Sventitskys' Christmas parties followed the same pattern. At ten, after the children had gone home, the tree was lit a second time for the others, and the party went on till morning. The more staid people played cards all night long in the "Pompeiian" sitting room, curtained off from the ballroom by a heavy portiere on bronze rings. Before daybreak they would all have supper together.

"Why are you so late?" asked the Sventitskys' nephew, Georges, running through the entrance hall on his way to his uncle's and aunt's rooms. Yura and Tonia took off their things and looked in at the ballroom door before going to greet their hosts.

Rustling their dresses and treading on each other's toes, those who were not dancing but walking and talking moved like a black wall past the hotly breathing Christmas tree with its several tiers of lights.

In the center of the room the dancers twirled and spun dizzily. They were paired off or formed into chains by a young law school student, Koka Kornakov, son of an assistant public prosecutor who was leading the cotillion. "*Grand rond!*" he bellowed at the top of his voice across the room, or "*Chaîne chinoise!*"—and they all followed his orders. "*Une valse, s'il vous plaît,*" he shouted to the pianist as he led his partner at the head of the first round, whirling away with her and gradually slowing down in ever smaller and smaller circles until they were barely marking time in what was still the dying echo of a waltz. Everyone clapped, and ices and cool drinks were carried around the noisy, milling, shuffling crowd. Flushed boys and girls never stopped shouting and laughing as they greedily drank cold cranberry juice and lemonade, and the moment they put down their glasses on the trays the noise was ten times louder, as if they had gulped down some exhilarating mixture.

Without stopping in the ballroom, Tonia and Yura went through to their hosts' rooms in the back.

12

The living rooms of the Sventitskys were cluttered up with furniture that had been moved out of the ballroom and the drawing room. Here was the Sventitskys' magic kitchen, their Christmas workshop. The place smelled of paint and glue, and there were piles of colored wrappings and boxes of cotillion favors and spare candles.

The Sventitskys were writing names on cards for presents and for seats at the supper table and numbers on tickets for a lottery. They were helped by Georges, but he kept losing count and they grumbled at him irritably. They were overjoyed at Tonia's and Yura's coming; they had known them as children and unceremoniously set them to work.

"Feliciata Semionovna cannot understand that this should have been done in advance, not right in the middle of the party when the guests are here. Look what you've done now, Georges—the empty *bonbonnières* go on the sofa and the ones with sugared almonds on the table—now you've mixed up everything."

"I am so glad Annette is better. Pierre and I were so worried."

"Except that she's worse, not better, darling—worse, do you understand? You always get things *devant-derrière*."

Yura and Tonia spent half the evening backstage with Georges and the old couple.

13

All this time Lara was in the ballroom. She was not in evening dress and did not know anyone there, but she stayed on, either waltzing with Koka Kornakov like a sleepwalker or wandering aimlessly around the room.

Once or twice she stopped and stood hesitating outside the sitting room, in the hope that Komarovsky, who sat facing the doorway, might see her. But he did not take his eyes from his cards, which he held in his left hand and which shielded his face, and he either really did not notice her or pretended not to. She was choking with mortification. A girl whom she did not know went in from the ballroom. Komarovsky looked at her in the way Lara remembered so well. The girl was flattered and flushed and smiled with pleasure. Lara crimsoned with shame and nearly screamed. "A new victim," she thought. Lara saw, as in a mirror, herself and the whole story of her liaison. She did not give up her plan to speak to him but decided to do it later, at a more convenient moment; forcing herself to be calm, she went back to the ballroom.

Komarovsky was playing with three other men. The one on his left was Kornakov, the father of the elegant young man with whom Lara was dancing again, so she understood from the few words she exchanged with him. And the young man's mother was the tall dark woman in black with fiercely burning eyes and an unpleasantly snakelike neck who went back and forth between the ballroom and the sitting room, watching her son dancing and her husband playing cards. And finally Lara learned that the girl who had aroused such complicated feelings in her was the young man's sister and that her suspicions had been groundless.

She had not paid attention to Koka's surname when he had first introduced himself, but he repeated it as he swept her in the last gliding movement of the waltz to a chair and bowed himself off. "Kornakov. Kornakov." It reminded her of something. Of something unpleasant. Then it came back to her. Kornakov was the assistant public prosecutor at the Moscow central court who had made a fanatical speech at the trial of the group of railway men which had included Tiverzin. At Lara's wish, Kologrivov had gone to plead with him, but without success. "So that's it. . . . Well, well, well. . . . Interesting. . . . Kornakov. Kornakov."

14

It was almost two in the morning. Yura's ears were ringing. There had been an interval with tea and petits fours and now the dancing had begun again. No one bothered anymore to replace the candles on the tree as they burned down.

Yura stood uneasily in the middle of the ballroom, watching

Tonia dancing with a stranger. She swept up to him, flounced her short satin train—like a fish waving its fin—and vanished in the crowd.

She was very excited. During the interval, she had refused tea and had slaked her thirst with innumerable tangerines, peeling them and wiping her fingers and the corners of her mouth on a handkerchief the size of a fruit blossom. Laughing and talking incessantly, she kept taking the handkerchief out and unthinkingly putting it back inside her sash or her sleeve.

Now, as she brushed past the frowning Yura, spinning with her unknown partner, she caught and pressed his hand and smiled eloquently. The handkerchief she had been holding stayed in his hand. He pressed it to his lips and closed his eyes. The handkerchief smelled equally enchantingly of tangerines and of Tonia's hand. This was something new in Yura's life, something he had never felt before, something sharp that pierced him from top to toe. This naïvely childish smell was as intimate and understandable as a word whispered in the dark. He pressed the handkerchief to his eyes and lips, breathing through it. Suddenly a shot rang out inside.

Everyone turned and looked at the portiere that hung between the ballroom and the sitting room. There was a moment's silence. Then the uproar began. Some people rushed about screaming, others ran after Koka into the sitting room from which the sound of the shot had come; others came out to meet them, weeping, arguing and all talking at once.

"What has she done, what has she done!" Komarovsky kept saying in despair.

"Boria, Boria, tell me you're alive," Mrs. Kornakov was screaming hysterically. "Where is Doctor Drokov? They said he's here. Oh, but where, where is he?—How can you, how can you say it's nothing but a scratch! Oh, my poor martyr, that's what you get for exposing all those criminals! There she is, the scum, there she is, I'll scratch your eyes out, you slut, you won't get away this time! What did you say, Komarovsky? You? She shot at you? No, I can't bear it, this is a tragic moment, Komarovsky, I haven't time to listen to jokes. Koka, Kokochka! Can you believe it? She tried to kill your father. . . . Yes. . . . But Providence . . . Koka! Koka!"

The crowd poured out of the sitting room into the ballroom. At the head of it came Kornakov, laughingly assuring everyone that he was quite all right and dabbing with a napkin at a scratch on his left hand. Another group, somewhat apart, was leading Lara by the arms.

Yura was dumbfounded. This girl again! And again in such extraordinary circumstances! And again that gray-haired man. But this time Yura knew who he was—the prominent lawyer, Komarovsky, who had had something to do with his father's estate. No need to greet him. They both pretended not to know each other. And the girl . . . So it was the girl who had fired the shot? At the prosecutor? Must be for political reasons. Poor thing. She was in for a bad time. How haughtily beautiful she was! And those louts, twisting her arms, as if she were a common thief!

But at once he realized that he was mistaken. Lara's legs gave way under her, they were holding her up and almost carrying her to the nearest armchair, where she collapsed.

Yura was about to rush up to her to bring her around but thought it proper first to show some interest in the victim. He walked up to Kornakov.

"I am a doctor," he said. "Let me see your hand. Well, you've been lucky. It's not even worth bandaging. A drop of iodine wouldn't do any harm, though. There's Feliciata Semionovna, we'll ask her."

Mrs. Sventitskaia and Tonia, who were coming toward him, were white-faced. They told him to leave everything and quickly get his coat. There had been a message from home, they were to go back at once.

Yura, imagining the worst, forgot everything else and ran for his things.

15

They did not find Anna Ivanovna alive. When they ran up the stairs to her room she had been dead for ten minutes. The cause of death had been an attack of suffocation resulting from acute edema of the lungs; this had not been diagnosed in time. For the first few hours Tonia screamed, sobbed convulsively, and recognized no one. On the following day she calmed down but could only nod in answer to anything that Yura and her father said to her; each time she tried to speak, her grief overpowered her and she began to scream again as if she were possessed.

In the intervals between the services she knelt for hours beside the dead woman, her large, fine hands clasping a corner of the coffin standing on its dais, covered with wreaths. She was oblivious of the people around her. But whenever her eyes met those of her friends she would quickly get up and hurry from the room and up the stairs, repressing her sobs until she fell on the bed and buried her bursts of despair in the pillow.

Sorrow, standing for many hours on end, lack of sleep, the deep-toned singing and the dazzling candles by night and day as well as the cold he had caught, filled Yura's soul with a sweet confusion, a fever of grief and ecstasy.

When his mother had died ten years earlier he had been a child. He could still remember how he had cried, grief-stricken and terrified. In those days he had not been primarily concerned with himself. He could hardly even realize that such a being as Yura existed on its own or had any value or interest. What mattered then was everything outside and around him. From every side the external world pressed in on him, dense, indisputable, tangible as a forest. And the reason he had been so shaken by his mother's death was that, at her side, he had lost himself in the forest, suddenly to find her gone and himself alone in it. The forest was made up of everything in the world— clouds and shop signs and the golden balls on fire towers and the bareheaded riders who went as escort before the holy image of the Mother of God carried in a coach. Shop fronts were in it, and arcades, and the inaccessibly high star-studded sky, and the Lord God and the saints.

This inaccessibly high sky once came all the way down to his nursery, as far as his nurse's skirt when she was talking to him about God; it was close and within reach like the tops of hazel trees in the gullies when you pulled down their branches and picked the nuts. It was as if it dipped into the gilt nursery washbasin and, having bathed in fire and gold, re-emerged as the morning service or mass at the tiny church where he went with his nurse. There the heavenly stars became the lights before the icons, and the Lord God was a kindly Father, and everything more or less fell into its right place. But the main thing was the real world of the grown-ups and the city that loomed up all around him like a forest. At that time, with the whole of his half-animal faith, Yura believed in God, who was the keeper of that forest.

Now it was quite different. In his twelve years at gymnasium and university, Yura had studied the classics and Scripture, legends and poets, history and natural science, which had become to him the chronicles of his house, his family tree. Now he was afraid of nothing, neither of life nor of death; everything in the world, all the things in it were words in his vocabulary. He felt he was on an equal footing with the universe. And he was affected by the services for Anna Ivanovna differently than he had been by the services for his mother. Then he had prayed in confusion, fear, and pain. Now he listened to the services as if they were a message addressed to him and concerning him directly. He listened intently to the words, expecting them, like any other words, to have a clear meaning. There was no religiosity in his reverence for the supreme powers of heaven and earth, which he worshipped as his progenitors.

16

"Holy God, holy and mighty, holy and deathless, have mercy on us." What was it? Where was he? They must be taking out the coffin. He must wake up. He had fallen asleep in his clothes on the sofa at six in the morning. Now they were hunting for him all over the house, but no one thought of looking in the far corner of the library behind the bookshelves.

"Yura! Yura!" Markel was calling him. They were taking out the coffin. Markel would have to carry the wreaths, and nowhere could he find Yura to help him; to make matters worse he had got stuck in the bedroom where the wreaths were piled up, because the door of the wardrobe on the landing had swung open and blocked that of the bedroom.

"Markel! Markel! Yura!" people were shouting from downstairs. Markel kicked open the door and ran downstairs carrying several wreaths.

"Holy God, holy and mighty, holy and deathless," the words drifted softly down the street and stayed there; as if a feather duster had softly brushed the air, everything was swaying— wreaths, passersby, plumed horses' heads, the censer swinging on its chain from the priest's hand, and the white earth underfoot.

"Yura! My God! At last." Shura Shlesinger was shaking his

shoulder. "What's the matter with you? They're carrying out the coffin. Are you coming with us?"

"Yes, of course."

17

The funeral service was over. The beggars, shuffling their feet in the cold, closed up in two ranks. The hearse, the gig with wreaths on it, and the Kruegers' carriage stirred and swayed slightly. The cabs drew up closer to the church. Out of it came Shura Shlesinger, crying; lifting her veil, damp with tears, she cast a searching glance at the crowd, spotted the pallbearers, beckoned to them, and went back into the church. More and more people were pouring out.

"Well, so now it's Anna Ivanovna's turn. She sends her best regards. She took a ticket to a far place, poor soul."

"Yes, her dance is over, poor cricket, she's gone to her rest."

"Have you got a cab or are you going to walk?"

"I need to stretch my legs after all that standing. Let's walk a bit and then we'll take a cab."

"Did you see how upset Fufkov was? Looking at her, tears pouring down his face, blowing his nose, staring at her face. Standing next to her husband at that."

"He always had his eye on her."

They slowly made their way to the cemetery at the other end of town. That day the hard frost had broken. It was a still, heavy day; the cold had gone and the life had gone too—it was a day as though made for a funeral. The dirty snow looked as if it shone through crêpe, and the firs behind the churchyard railings, wet and dark like tarnished silver, seemed to be in deep mourning.

It was in this same churchyard that Yura's mother lay buried. He had not been to her grave in recent years. He glanced in its direction and whispered, "Mother," almost as he might have done years before.

They dispersed solemnly, in picturesque groups, along the cleared paths, whose meanderings did not harmonize with the sorrowful deliberation of their step. Alexander Alexandrovich led Tonia by the arm. They were followed by the Kruegers. Black was very becoming to Tonia.

Hoarfrost, bearded like mold, sprouted on the chains with crosses hanging from the domes and on the pink monastery walls. In the far corner of the monastery yard, washing hung on lines stretching from wall to wall—shirts with heavy sodden sleeves, peach-colored tablecloths, badly wrung out and crookedly fastened sheets. Yura realized that this, altered in appearance by the new buildings, was the part of the monastery grounds where the blizzard had raged that night.

He walked on alone, ahead of the others, stopping occasionally to let them catch up with him. In answer to the desolation brought by death to the people slowly pacing after him, he was drawn, as irresistibly as water funnelling downward, to dream, to think, to work out new forms, to create beauty. More vividly than ever before he realized that art has two constant, two unending concerns: it always meditates on death and thus always creates life. All great, genuine art resembles and continues the Revelation of St. John.

With joyful anticipation he thought of the day or two which he would set aside and spend alone, away from the university and from his home, to write a poem in memory of Anna Ivanovna. He would include all those random things that life had sent his way, a few descriptions of Anna Ivanovna's best characteristics, Tonia in mourning, street incidents on the way back from the funeral, and the washing hanging in the place where, many years ago, the blizzard had raged in the night and he had wept as a child.

CHAPTER FOUR

The Hour of the Inevitable

1

Lara lay feverish and half conscious in Feliciata Semionovna's bed; the Sventitskys, the servants, and Dr. Drokov were talking in whispers around her.

The rest of the house was dark and empty. Only in one small sitting room did a lamp on a bracket cast its dim light up and down the long suite of rooms.

Here Komarovsky strode with angry, resolute steps, as if he were at home and not a visitor. He would look into the bedroom for news and tear back to the other end of the house, past the tree with its tinsel, and through the dining room where the table stood laden with untasted dishes and the greenish crystal wineglasses tinkled every time a cab drove past the windows or a mouse scurried over the tablecloth among the china.

Komarovsky thrashed about in a fury. Conflicting feelings crowded in his breast. The scandal! The disgrace! He was beside himself. His position was threatened, his reputation would suffer from the incident. At whatever cost he must prevent the gossip or, if the news had already spread, stop the rumors, nip them in the bud.

Another reason for his agitation was that he had once again experienced the irresistible attraction of this crazy, desperate girl. He had always known that she was different. There had always been something unique about her. But how deeply, painfully, irreparably had he wounded her and upset her life, and how rebellious and violent she was in her determination to reshape her destiny and start afresh!

It was clear that he must help her in every way. Take a room for her, perhaps. But in no circumstances must he come near her; on the contrary, he must keep away, stand aside so as not to be in her way, or with her violent nature there was no knowing what she might do.

And what a lot of trouble ahead! This wasn't the sort of thing for which they patted you on the head! The law didn't wink at it. It was not yet morning, and hardly two hours had passed since it happened but already the police had been twice and he, Komarovsky, had had to go to the kitchen and see the inspector and smooth things over.

And the further it went the more complications there would be. They would have to have proof that Lara had meant to shoot at him and not at Kornakov. And even that wouldn't be the end of it; she would only be cleared of one part of the charge, but she would still be liable to prosecution.

Naturally, he would do everything to prevent it. If the case came to court he would get expert evidence from a psychiatrist that she had not been responsible for her actions at the moment when she fired the shot and would see to it that the proceedings were dropped.

With these reflections he began to calm down. The night was over. Streaks of light probed from room to room and dived under the chairs and tables like thieves or appraisers.

After a last look in the bedroom, where he was told that Lara was no better, Komarovsky left and went to see a friend of his, Ruffina Onissimovna Voit-Voitkovsky, a woman lawyer who was the wife of a political émigré. Her eight-room apartment was now too large for her, she could not afford to keep it all up, so she let two of the rooms. One of them had recently become vacant, and Komarovsky took it for Lara. There she was taken a few hours later, only half conscious with brain fever.

2

Ruffina Onissimovna was a woman of advanced views, entirely unprejudiced, and well disposed toward everything that she called "positive and vital."

On top of her chest of drawers she kept a copy of the Erfurt Program with a dedication by the author. One of the photographs on the wall showed her husband, "her good Voit," in a popular park in Switzerland, together with Plekhanov, both in alpaca jackets and panama hats.

Ruffina Onissimovna took a dislike to her sick lodger the moment she saw her. She considered Lara a malingerer. The girl's feverish ravings seemed to her nothing but play-acting. She was ready to swear that Lara was impersonating Gretchen gone mad in her dungeon.

She expressed her contempt for Lara by being brisker than usual. She banged doors, sang in a loud voice, tore through her part of the apartment like a hurricane, and kept the windows open all day long.

The apartment was on the top floor of a building in the Arbat. After the winter solstice its windows filled to overflowing with blue sky as wide as a river in flood. Through half the winter it was full of the early signs of the coming spring.

A warm wind from the south blew in through the casements. Locomotives at their distant stations roared like sea lions. Lara, lying ill in bed, filled her leisure with recollections.

She often thought of the night of her arrival in Moscow from the Urals, seven or eight years before. She was riding in a cab from the station through gloomy alleys to the hotel at the other end of town. One by one the street lamps threw the humpbacked shadow of the coachman on the walls. The shadow grew and grew till it became gigantic and stretched across the roofs, and was cut off. Then it all began again from the beginning.

The bells of Moscow's countless churches clanged in the darkness overhead, and the trolleys rang as they scurried through the streets, but Lara was also deafened by the gaudy window displays and glaring lights, as if they too emitted sounds of their own, like the bells and wheels.

In their hotel room she was staggered at the sight of a

watermelon of incredible size. It was Komarovsky's house-warming gift, and to her it was a symbol of his power and wealth. When he thrust a knife into this marvel, and the dark green globe split in half, revealing its icy, sugary heart, she was frightened, but she dared not refuse a slice. The fragrant pink mouthfuls stuck in her throat, but she forced herself to swallow them.

Just as she was intimidated by expensive food and by the night life of the capital, so she was later intimidated by Komarovsky himself—this was the real explanation of everything.

But now he had changed beyond recognition. He made no demands, never reminded her of the past, and never even came. And all that time he kept at a distance from her, and most nobly offered to help her.

Kologrivov's visit was something entirely different. She was overjoyed when he came. Not because he was tall and hand-some, but because of his overflowing vitality, her visitor with his shining eyes and intelligent smile filled half the space in her room, making it seem crowded.

He sat by her bed rubbing his hands. On the occasions when he was summoned to attend a ministerial meeting in Petersburg he spoke to the old dignitaries as if they were schoolboys; but now he saw before him a girl who till recently had been part of his household, something like a daughter to him, with whom, as with all other members of his family, he had exchanged words and glances only casually (this constituted the character-istic charm of their closeness, and both he and his family were aware of this). He could not treat Lara as an adult, with gravity and indifference. He did not know how to speak to her without offending her. "What's the big idea?" he said smilingly, as if she were a child. "Who wants these melodramas?"

He paused, and glanced at the damp stains on the walls and ceiling. Then, shaking his head reproachfully, he went on:

"There's an international exhibition opening at Düsseldorf—painting, sculpture, gardening. I'm going. You know, it's a bit damp here. And how long do you think you're going to wander about from pillar to post without a proper place to live in? This Voit woman, between ourselves, is no good, I know her. Why don't you move out? You've been ill in bed long enough—time you got up. Change your room, take up something, finish your studies. There's a painter, a friend of mine, who's going to Turkestan for two years. He's got partitions up in his studio—

it's more like a small flat. I think he'd turn it over furnished to somebody who'd look after it. How about my fixing it up? And there's another thing. I've been meaning to do it for a long time, it's a sacred duty . . . since Lipa . . . Here's a small sum, a bonus for her graduation. No, please . . . No, I beg you, don't be stubborn . . . no, really you'll have to . . ."

And in spite of her protests, her tears, and her struggles, he forced her, before he left, to accept a check for ten thousand rubles.

When she recovered, Lara moved to the lodgings Kologrivov had recommended, near the Smolensky Market. The flat was at the top of an old-fashioned two-story house. There were teamsters living in the other part of it, and there was a warehouse on the ground floor. The cobbled yard was always littered with spilled oats and hay. Pigeons strutted about cooing and fluttered up noisily to the level of Lara's window whenever a drove of rats scurried down the stone gutter.

3

Lara was greatly troubled about Pasha. So long as she was seriously ill he had not been allowed to see her, and what could he be expected to think? Lara had tried to kill a man who, as he saw it, was no more than an acquaintance of hers, and this same man, the object of her unsuccessful attempt at murder, had afterwards shielded her from its consequences. And all that after their memorable conversation at Christmas, by candlelight. If it had not been for this man, Lara would have been arrested and tried. He had warded off the punishment that hung over her. Thanks to him she was able to continue her studies, safe and unharmed. Pasha was puzzled and tormented.

When she was better Lara sent for him and said: "I am a bad woman. You don't know me, someday I'll tell you. I can't talk about it now, you can see for yourself, every time I try I start crying. But enough, forget me, I'm not worthy of you."

There followed heartrending scenes, each more unbearable than the last. All this went on while Lara was still living on Arbat Street, and Voitkovskaia, meeting Pasha in the corridor with his tear-stained face, would rush off to her room and collapse on her sofa laughing herself sick. "Oh, I can't, I can't, it's too much!" she exclaimed. "Really! The hero! Ha, ha, ha!"

To deliver Pasha from a disgraceful attachment, to tear out his love for her by the roots and put an end to his torment, Lara told him that she had decided to give him up because she did not love him, but in making this renunciation she sobbed so much that it was impossible to believe her. Pasha suspected her of all the deadly sins, disbelieved every word she said, was ready to curse and hate her, but he loved her to distraction and was jealous of her very thoughts, and of the mug she drank from and of the pillow on which she lay. If they were not to go insane they must act quickly and firmly. They made up their minds to get married at once, before graduation. The idea was to have the wedding on the Monday after Low Sunday. At Lara's wish it was again put off.

They were married on Whit Monday; by then it was quite clear that they had passed their examinations. All the arrangements were made by Liudmila Kapitonovna Chepurko, the mother of Lara's fellow student Tusia. Liudmila was a handsome woman with a high bosom, a fine low-pitched singing voice, and a head full of innumerable superstitions, some of them picked up and others invented by herself.

The day Lara was to be "led to the altar" (as Liudmila purred in her gypsy voice while helping her to dress) it was terribly hot. The golden domes of churches and the freshly sanded paths in the town gardens were a glaring yellow. The green birch saplings cut on Whitsun Eve hung over the church railings, dusty, their leaves rolled up into little scrolls and as though scorched. There was hardly a breath of air, and the sunshine made spots before your eyes. It was as though a thousand weddings were to be held that day, for all the girls were in white dresses like brides and had curled their hair and all the young men were pomaded and wore tight-fitting black suits. Everyone was excited and everyone was hot.

As Lara stepped on the carpet leading to the altar, Lagodina, the mother of another friend, threw a handful of small silver coins at her feet to ensure the future prosperity of the couple; and with the same intention Liudmila told her that, when the wedding crown was held over her head, she must not make the sign of the cross with her bare fingers but cover them with the edge of her veil or a lace frill. She also told Lara to hold her candle high in order to have the upper hand in her house. Lara, sacrificing her future to Pasha's, held her candle as low as she could, but all in vain, because however low she held it Pasha held his lower still.

Straight from the church they drove to the wedding breakfast at the studio to which the couple moved. The guests shouted, "It's bitter!" and others responded unanimously from the end of the room, "Make it sweet!" and the bride and bridegroom smiled shyly and kissed. Liudmila sang "The Vineyard" in their honor, with the double refrain "God give you love and counsel," and a song that began "Undo the braid, scatter the fair hair."

When all the guests had gone and they were left alone, Pasha felt uneasy in the sudden silence. A street lamp shone from across the road, and however tightly Lara drew the curtains, a streak of light, narrow as a board, reached into the room. This light gave Pasha no rest, he felt as if they were being watched. He discovered to his horror that he was thinking more of the street lamp than of Lara or of himself or of his love for her.

During this night, which lasted an eternity, Antipov ("Stepanida," or "the fair maiden," as he was called by his fellow students) reached the heights of joy and the lowest depths of despair. His suspicious guesses alternated with Lara's confessions. He questioned her, and with each of her answers his spirit sank as though he were hurtling down a void. His wounded imagination could not keep up with her revelations.

They talked till morning. In all Pasha's life there had not been a change in him so decisive and abrupt as in the course of this night. He got up a different man, almost astonished that he was still called Pasha Antipov.

4

Nine days later their friends arranged a farewell party for them, in that same room. Both Pasha and Lara had graduated with flying colors, and both had been offered jobs in the same town in the Urals. They were setting out for it next day.

Again they drank and sang and were boisterous, but this time there were only young people present.

Behind the partition that separated the living quarters from the studio, there stood a big wicker hamper and another, smaller one of Lara's, a suitcase, a box of crockery, and several sacks.

There was a lot of luggage. Part of it was being sent next day by freight. Almost everything was packed, but there was still a little room left in the box and in the hampers. Every now and then Lara thought of something else she meant to take and put it into one of the hampers, rearranging things to make it tidy.

Pasha was at home entertaining guests by the time Lara got back from the university office where she had gone for her birth certificate and other papers. She came up followed by the janitor with a bundle of sacking and a thick rope for those pieces that were going by freight. After he left, Lara made the round of the guests, shaking hands with some and kissing others, and went behind the partition to change. When she came back, they greeted her with applause, sat down, and a noisy party began, like the one a few days earlier. The more enterprising poured vodka for their neighbors; hands armed with forks stretched toward the center of the table where bread, appetizers, and cooked dishes were set out. There were speeches, toasts, and constant joking. Some got drunk.

"I'm dead tired," said Lara, who was sitting next to her husband. "Did you manage to get everything done?"

"Yes."

"All the same, I'm feeling wonderful. I'm so happy. Are you?"

"I too. I feel fine. But there's a lot to talk about."

As an exception Komarovsky had been allowed to join the young people's party. At the end of the evening he started to say how bereaved he would feel when his two young friends left Moscow—the town would be like a desert, a Sahara; but he became so sentimental that he began to sob, and he had to start all over from the beginning.

He asked the Antipovs' permission to write to them and to visit them at Yuriatin, if he missed them too much.

"That's quite unnecessary," Lara said loudly and nonchalantly. "And in general it's all quite pointless—writing, Sahara, and all that. As for coming, don't think of it. With God's help you'll manage without us, we aren't as important as all that. Don't you think so, Pasha? I'm sure you'll find other young friends."

Then suddenly forgetting with whom she was talking and what she was saying she hurried off to the kitchen. There she took the meat grinder apart and packed the parts into the corners of the crockery case, padding them with tufts of straw.

In doing this she scratched herself on the edge of the box and nearly ran a splinter into her hand.

She was suddenly reminded of her guests by a particularly loud outburst of laughter on the other side of the partition. It occurred to her that when people were drunk they always tried to impersonate drunkards, and the drunker they were the more they overacted.

At this moment she became aware of another peculiar sound, coming from the yard, through the open window. She pulled the curtains and leaned out.

A hobbled horse was moving across the yard with short, limping jumps. Lara did not know whose it was or how it had strayed into the yard. It was completely light though a long way to sunrise. The sleeping city seemed dead. It was bathed in the gray-blue coolness of the early hours. Lara closed her eyes. The characteristic sound of the hobbled horse's steps, so unlike anything else, transported her to some wonderful, remote village.

There was a ring at the door. Lara pricked up her ears. Someone got up from the table to open. It was Nadia! Lara ran to meet her. Nadia had come straight from the train, so fresh and enchanting that it seemed as if she brought with her the scent of the lilies of the valley of Duplyanka. The two friends stood speechless with emotion and, hugging each other, could only cry.

Nadia had brought Lara the congratulations and good wishes of the whole family and a present from her parents. She took a jewel case out of her travelling bag, snapped it open, and held out a very beautiful necklace.

There were gasps of delight and astonishment. A guest who had been drunk but had recovered a little said:

"It's pink hyacinth. Yes, yes, pink, believe it or not. That's what it is. It's just as valuable as diamonds."

But Nadia said that the stones were yellow sapphires.

Lara put Nadia next to her at table and made her eat and drink. The necklace lay beside her plate, and she could not stop looking at it. The stones had rolled into a hollow on the mauve-cushioned lining of the case and looked now like dew and now like a cluster of small grapes.

Meanwhile those of the guests who had sobered up were again drinking to keep company with Nadia, whom they soon made tipsy.

Soon everyone in the flat was fast asleep. Most of them,

planning to go to the station with Lara and Pasha in the morning, stayed the night. A good many had been snoring before Nadia came, and Lara herself never knew afterwards how she came to be lying fully dressed on the sofa next to Ira Lagodina.

She was wakened by the sound of loud voices nearby. They were the voices of strangers who had come into the yard to recover their horse. As she opened her eyes she said to herself: "What on earth can Pasha be doing pottering about in the middle of the room?" But when the man she had taken for Pasha turned his head she saw a pock-marked scarecrow whose face was cut by a deep scar from brow to chin. She realized it was a burglar and tried to shout but could not utter a sound. She remembered her necklace and raising herself cautiously on her elbow looked where she had left it on the table.

The necklace was still there among the bread crumbs and unfinished pieces of caramel; the thief hadn't noticed it among the litter. He was only rummaging in the suitcase she had packed so carefully and making a mess of her work. That was all she could think of at the moment, half asleep and still tipsy as she was. Indignant, she tried to shout and again found she couldn't. Then she dug her knee into Ira's stomach, and when Ira yelped with pain she too began to scream. The thief dropped everything and ran. Some of the men jumped up and tried to chase him without quite knowing what it was all about, but by the time they got outside the door he had vanished.

The commotion woke everyone up, and Lara, whose tipsiness had suddenly gone, did not allow them to go back to sleep. She made them coffee and packed them off home until it was time to go to the station.

Then she set to work feverishly stuffing the bed linen into the hampers, strapping up the luggage and tying it with ropes, and begging Pasha and the janitor's wife just not to bother her by trying to help.

Everything got done in time. The Antipovs did not miss their train. It started smoothly, as though wafted away by the hats their friends were waving after them. When they stopped waving and bellowed something three times—probably "Hurrah!"—the train put on speed.

5

For the third day the weather was wretched. It was the second autumn of the war. The successes of the first year had been followed by reverses. Brusilov's Eighth Army, which had been concentrated in the Carpathians ready to pour down the slopes into Hungary, was instead drawing back, caught by the ebb of the general retreat. The Russians were evacuating Galicia, which they had occupied in the first months of the fighting.

Dr. Zhivago, until recently known as Yura but now addressed more and more often as Yurii Andreievich, stood in the corridor of the gynecological section of the hospital, outside the door of the maternity ward to which he had just brought his wife Tonia—Antonina Alexandrovna. He had said goodbye to her and was waiting for the midwife, to tell her where she could reach him in case of need and to ask her how he could get in touch with her.

He was in a hurry: he had to visit two patients and get back to his hospital as soon as possible, and there he was, wasting precious time, staring out of the window at the slanting streaks of rain buffeted by the autumn wind like a cornfield in a storm.

It was not yet very dark. He could see the back yards of the hospital, the glassed-in verandas of the private houses in Devichie Pole, and the branch trolley line leading to one of the hospital blocks.

The rain poured with a dreary steadiness, neither hurrying nor slowing down for all the fury of the wind, which seemed enraged by the indifference of the water. Gusts of wind shook the creeper on one of the houses as if intending to tear it up by the roots, swung it up into the air, and dropped it in disgust like a discarded rag.

A truck with two trailers drove past the veranda to the hospital entrance. Wounded men were carried in.

The Moscow hospitals were desperately overcrowded, especially since the battle of Lutsk. The wounded were put in the passages and on landings. The general overcrowding was beginning to affect the women's wards.

Yurii Andreievich turned away from the window yawning with fatigue. He had nothing to think about. Suddenly he remembered an incident at the Hospital of the Holy Cross, where he worked. A woman had died a few days earlier in the surgical ward. Yurii Andreievich had diagnosed echinococcus of the liver, but everyone thought he was wrong. An autopsy was to be made today, but their prosector was a habitual drunkard and you never could tell how careful he would be.

Night fell suddenly. Nothing more was visible outside. As at the waving of a magic wand, lights sprang up in all the windows.

The head gynecologist came out of Tonia's ward through the narrow lobby separating it from the corridor. He was of mammoth size, and always responded to questions by shrugging his shoulders and staring at the ceiling. These silent gestures were meant to suggest that, whatever the advances of science, there were more things in heaven and earth, friend Horatio, than science ever dreamt on.

He passed Yurii Andreievich with a nod and a smile, flipped his podgy hands a few times to intimate that there was nothing for it but patience, and went off down the corridor to have a smoke in the waiting room.

After him came his assistant, who was as garrulous as her superior was taciturn.

"If I were you I'd go home," she told Yurii Andreievich. "I'll call you up tomorrow at the Holy Cross. It's most unlikely that anything will happen between now and then. There's every reason to expect a natural birth; there shouldn't be any need for surgical intervention. But of course the pelvis is narrow, the child's head is in the occipito-posterior position, there are no pains, and the contractions are slight. All this gives grounds for anxiety. However, it's too soon to say. It all depends on how the pains develop once labor begins. Then we'll know."

When he telephoned the following day, the hospital porter who took the call told him to wait while he made inquiries; after keeping him in misery for a good ten minutes he came back with the following inadequate and crudely worded information: "They say, tell him he's brought his wife too soon, he's to take her back."

Infuriated, Yurii Andreievich told him to get the nurse on the telephone. "The symptoms may be misleading," the nurse said. "We'll know more in a day or two."

On the third day he was told that labor had begun the night before, the water had broken at dawn, and there had been strong pains with short intervals since the early morning.

He rushed headlong to the hospital. As he walked down the passage to the door, which by mistake had been left half open, he heard Tonia's heartrending screams; she screamed like the victims of an accident dragged with crushed limbs from under the wheels of a train.

He was not allowed to see her. Biting his knuckle until he drew blood, he went over to the window; the same slanting rain was pouring down as on the two preceding days.

A nurse came out of the ward, and he heard the squealing of a newborn child. "She's safe, she's safe," Yurii Andreievich muttered joyfully to himself.

"It's a son. A little boy. Congratulations on a safe delivery," said the nurse in a singsong. "You can't go in yet. When they're ready we'll show you. Then you'll have to give her a nice present. She's had a bad time. It's the first one. There's always trouble with the first."

"She's safe, she's safe." Yurii Andreievich was happy. He did not understand what the nurse was telling him, and why she was including him in her congratulations as if he had played a part in what had happened. For what had he actually had to do with it? Father—son; he did not see why he should be proud of this unearned fatherhood, he felt that this son was a gift out of the blue. He was scarcely aware of all this. The main thing was that Tonia—Tonia, who had been in mortal danger—was now fortunately safe.

He had a patient living near the hospital. He went to see him and was back in half an hour. Both the door of the lobby and that of the ward were again ajar. Without knowing what he was doing, Yurii Andreievich slipped into the lobby.

The huge gynecologist, in his white coat, rose as though from under the ground in front of him, barring the way.

"Where do you think you're going?" he whispered breathlessly so that the new mother should not hear. "Are you out of your mind? After she lost all that blood, risk of sepsis, not to speak of psychological shock! And you call yourself a doctor!"

"I didn't mean to . . . Do let me have just a glance. Just from here, through the crack."

"Oh, well, that's different. All right, if you must. But don't let me catch you . . . If she sees you, I'll wring your neck."

Inside the ward two women in white uniforms stood with their backs to the door; they were the midwife and the nurse. Squirming on the palm of the nurse's hand lay a tender, squealing, tiny human creature, stretching and contracting like a

dark red piece of rubber. The midwife was putting a ligature on
the navel before cutting the cord. Tonia lay on a surgical bed of
adjustable height in the middle of the room. She lay fairly high.
Yurii Andreievich, exaggerating everything in his excitement,
thought that she was lying, say, at the level of one of those desks
at which you write standing up.

Raised higher, closer to the ceiling than ordinary mortals
usually are, Tonia lay exhausted in the cloud of her spent pain.
To Yurii Andreievich she seemed like a barque lying at rest in
the middle of a harbor after putting in and being unloaded, a
barque that plied between an unknown country and the
continent of life across the waters of death with a cargo of
immigrant new souls. One such soul had just been landed, and
the ship now lay at anchor, relaxed, its flanks unburdened and
empty. The whole of her was resting, her strained masts and
hull, and her memory washed clean of the image of the other
shore, the crossing and the landing.

And as no one had explored the country where she was
registered, no one knew the language in which to speak to her.

At Yurii Andreievich's hospital everyone congratulated him.
He was astonished to see how fast the news had travelled.

He went into the staff room, known as the Rubbish Dump.
With so little space in the overcrowded hospital, it was used as a
cloakroom; people came in from outside wearing their snow
boots, they forgot their parcels and littered the floor with papers
and cigarette ends.

Standing by the window, the flabby elderly prosector was
holding up a jar with some opaque liquid against the light and
examining it over the top of his glasses.

"Congratulations," he said, without looking around.

"Thank you. How kind of you."

"Don't thank me. I've had nothing to do with it. Pichuzhkin
did the autopsy. But everyone is impressed—echinococcus it
was. That's a real diagnostician, they're all saying. That's all
everyone is talking about."

Just then the medical director came in, greeted them both,
and said: "What the devil is happening to this place? What a
filthy mess it is! By the way, Zhivago, it was echinococcus after
all! We were wrong. Congratulations. There's another thing.
It's a nuisance. They've been reviewing the lists of exemptions
again. I can't stop them this time. There's a terrible shortage of
medical personnel. You'll be smelling gunpowder before long."

6

The Antipovs had done much better in Yuriatin than they had hoped to. The Guishars were remembered well. This had helped Lara over the difficulties of setting up house in a new place.

Lara had her hands full and plenty to think about. She took care of the house and of their three-year-old daughter, Katenka. Marfutka, their red-haired maid, did her best but could not get all the work done. Larisa Feodorovna shared all her husband's interests. She herself taught at the girls' gymnasium. She worked without respite and was happy. This was exactly the kind of life she had dreamed of.

She liked Yuriatin. It was her native town. It stood on the big river Rynva, navigable except in its upper reaches, and one of the Ural railways passed through it.

The approach of winter in Yuriatin was always heralded by the owners of boats, when they took them from the river and transported them on carts to the town, to be stored in back yards. There they lay in the open air waiting for the spring. The boats with their light upturned bottoms in the yards meant in Yuriatin what the migration of storks or the first snow meant in other places. Such a boat lay in the yard of the house rented by the Antipovs. Katenka played in the shelter of its white hull as in a summerhouse.

Larisa Feodorovna liked Yuriatin's provincial ways, the long vowels of its northern accent, and the naïve trustfulness of its intelligentsia, who wore felt boots and gray flannel sleeveless coats. She was drawn to the land and to the common people.

Paradoxically, it was her husband, Pavel Pavlovich, the son of a Moscow railway worker, who turned out to be an incorrigible urbanite. He judged the people of Yuriatin much more harshly than she. Their crudeness and ignorance irritated him.

He had an extraordinary capacity, it now appeared, for reading quickly and storing up the knowledge he picked up. He had read a great deal in the past, partly thanks to Lara. During the years of his provincial seclusion, he became so well-read that even Lara no longer seemed to him well-informed. He towered high above his fellow teachers and complained that he felt stifled among them. Now in wartime, their standard, commonplace, and somewhat stale patriotism was out of tune with his own, more complicated feelings about his country.

Pavel Pavlovich had graduated in classics. He taught Latin and ancient history. But from his earlier *Realgymnasium* days he had kept a half-forgotten passion for the exact sciences, physics and mathematics, and it had now suddenly revived in him. Teaching himself at home, he had reached university standard in these subjects, and dreamed of taking his degree, specializing in some branch of mathematics, and moving with his family to Petersburg. Studying late into the night had affected his health. He began to suffer from insomnia.

His relations with his wife were good but lacked simplicity. Her kindness and her fussing over him oppressed him, but he would not criticize her for fear that she might take some quite innocent word of his for a reproach—a hint, perhaps, that her blood was bluer than his, or that she had once belonged to someone else. His anxiety lest she suspect him of having some absurdly unfair idea about her introduced an element of artificiality into their life. Each tried to behave more nobly than the other, and this complicated everything.

One night they had guests—the headmistress of Lara's school, several fellow teachers of her husband's, the member of an arbitration court on which Pavel Pavlovich too had recently served, and a few others. They were all, from Pavel Pavlovich's point of view, complete fools. He was amazed at Lara's amiability toward them, and he could not believe that she sincerely liked any of them.

After the visitors had gone, Lara took a long time airing and tidying the rooms and washing dishes in the kitchen with Marfutka. Then she made sure that Katenka was properly tucked up and Pasha asleep, quickly undressed, turned off the light, and lay down next to him as naturally as a child getting into bed with its mother.

But Antipov was only pretending that he was asleep. As so often recently, he had insomnia. He knew that he would lie awake for three or four hours. To walk himself to sleep, and to escape from the still smoky air of the room, he got up quietly, put on his fur coat and cap over his night clothes, and went outside.

It was a clear, frosty autumn night. Thin sheets of ice crumbled under his steps. The sky, shining with stars, threw a pale blue flicker like the flame of burning alcohol over the black earth with its clumps of frozen mud.

The Antipovs lived at the other end of town from the river harbor. The house was the last in the street, and beyond it lay a field cut by a railway with a grade crossing and a guard's shelter.

Antipov sat down on the overturned boat and looked at the stars. The thoughts to which he had become accustomed in the past few years assailed him with alarming strength. It seemed to him that sooner or later they would have to be thought out to the end, and that it might as well be done now.

This can't go on, he thought. He could have foreseen it long ago, before they were married. He had caught on late. Even as a child he had been fascinated by her, and she could make him do whatever she liked. Why hadn't he had the sense to renounce her in time, that winter before their marriage, when she herself had insisted on it? Wasn't it clear that it was not he whom she loved, but the noble task she had set herself in relation to him, and that for her he was the embodiment of her own heroism? But what had her mission, however meritorious or inspired, to do with real family life? The worst of it was that he loved her as much as ever. She was stunningly beautiful. And yet—was he sure that it was love even on his side? Or was it a bewildered gratitude for her beauty and magnanimity? Who could possibly sort it all out! The devil himself would be stumped.

So what was he to do? He must set his wife and daughter free from this counterfeit life. This was even more important than to liberate himself. Yes, but how? Divorce? Drown himself? What disgusting rubbish! He rebelled against the very thought. "As if I'd ever do anything of the sort! So why rehearse this melodrama even in my mind?"

He looked up at the stars as if asking them for advice. They flickered on, small or large, quick or slow, some blue and some in all the hues of the rainbow. Suddenly they were blotted out, and the house, the yard, and Antipov sitting on his boat were thrown into relief by a harsh, darting light, as though someone were running from the field toward the gate waving a torch. An army train, puffing clouds of yellow, flame-shot smoke into the sky, rolled over the grade crossing going westward, as countless others had rolled by, night and day, for the past year.

Pavel Pavlovich smiled, got up, and went to bed. He had found a way out of his dilemma.

7

When Larisa Feodorovna learned of Pasha's decision, she was stunned and at first would not believe her ears. "It's absurd," she thought, "a whim. I won't take any notice, and he'll forget it."

But it appeared that he had been getting ready for the past two weeks. He had sent in his papers to the recruiting office, the gymnasium had found a substitute teacher, and he had been notified that he was admitted to the military school at Omsk.

Lara wailed like a peasant woman and, grabbing Pasha's hands, threw herself at his feet. "Pasha, Pashenka," she screamed, "don't leave us. Don't do it, don't. It isn't too late, I'll see to everything. You haven't even had a proper medical examination, and with your heart . . . You're ashamed to change your mind? And aren't you ashamed to sacrifice your family to some crazy notion? You, a volunteer! All your life you've laughed at Rodia, and now you're jealous of him. You have to swagger about in an officer's uniform too, you have to do your own bit of saber-rattling. Pasha, what's come over you? I don't recognize you. What's changed you like this? Tell me honestly, for the love of Christ, without any fine phrases, is this really what Russia needs?"

Suddenly she realized that it wasn't that at all. Though she could not understand all of it, she grasped the main thing. Pasha misunderstood her attitude to him. He rebelled against the motherly feeling that all her life had been a part of her affection for him and could not see that such a love was something more, not less, than the ordinary feeling of a woman for a man.

She bit her lip and, shrinking as if she had been beaten, and swallowing her tears, set about silently packing his things.

After he had left, it seemed to her that the whole town was silent, and even that there were fewer crows flying about in the sky. "Madam, madam," Marfutka would say reproachfully, trying to call her back to herself. "Mama, Mama," Katenka babbled, pulling at her sleeve. This was the greatest defeat of her life. Her best, brightest hopes had collapsed.

Her husband's letters from Siberia told her all about his moods. He had seen his mistake. He badly missed his wife and daughter. After a few months he was commissioned lieutenant before term and then, just as unexpectedly, was sent to the front. His journey took him nowhere near Yuriatin, and he was not in Moscow long enough to see anyone there.

His letters from the front were less depressed than those from the Omsk school had been. He wanted to distinguish himself so that, as a reward for some military exploit or as a result of some light wound, he could go home on leave and see his family. Soon his opportunity was within sight. Brusilov's forces had broken through and were attacking. Antipov's letters stopped coming. At first Lara was not worried. She put down his silence to the military operations: he could not write when his regiment was on the move. But in the autumn the advance slowed down, the troops were digging themselves in, and there was still no word from him. His wife began to be worried, and to make inquiries, at first locally, in Yuriatin, then by mail in Moscow and at his old field address. There was no reply; nobody seemed to know anything.

Like other local ladies, Larisa Feodorovna had been giving a hand at the military ward attached to the town hospital. Now she trained seriously and qualified as a nurse, got leave of absence from her school for six months, and, putting the house in Marfutka's care, took Katenka to Moscow. She left her with Lipa, whose husband, Friesendank, was a German subject and had been interned with other enemy civilians at Ufa.

Convinced of the futility of trying to get any news by mail, she had decided to go and look for Pasha. With this in mind, she got a job as a nurse on a hospital train going to Mezo-Laborch, on the Hungarian border, the last address Pasha had given her.

8

A Red Cross train, equipped through voluntary contributions collected by the Tatiana Committee for Aid to the Wounded, arrived at divisional headquarters. It was a long train mostly made up of shabby, short freight cars; the only first-class coach carried prominent people from Moscow with presents for the troops. Among them was Gordon. He knew that his childhood friend Zhivago was attached to the divisional hospital; hearing that it was in a nearby village, he obtained the necessary permit to travel in the area just behind the lines, and got a lift in a carriage going to the village.

The driver was a Byelorussian or a Lithuanian who spoke broken Russian. The current spy scare reduced his conversation to a stale official patter. Discouraged by his ostentatious loyalty, Gordon travelled most of the way in silence.

At headquarters, where they were used to moving armies and measured distances in hundred-mile stages, he had been told that the village was quite near—within fifteen miles at most; in reality, it was more like fifty.

All along the way, an unfriendly grunting and grumbling came from the horizon on their left. Gordon had never been in an earthquake, but he decided (quite rightly) that the sullen, scarcely distinguishable, distant sound of enemy artillery could best be compared to volcanic tremors and rumblings. Toward evening, a pink glow flared up over the skyline on that side and went on flickering until dawn.

They passed ruined villages. Some were abandoned; in others people were living in cellars deep underground. Piles of refuse and rubble were aligned as the houses had been. These gutted settlements could be encompassed in a glance, like barren desert. Old women scratched about in the ashes, each on the ruins of her own home, now and then digging something up and putting it away, apparently feeling as sheltered from the eyes of strangers as if their walls were still around them. They looked up at Gordon and gazed after him as he drove past, seeming to ask him how soon the world would come to its senses and peace and order be restored to their lives.

After dark the carriage ran into a patrol and was ordered off the main road. The driver did not know the new by-pass. They drove about in circles for a couple of hours without getting anywhere. At dawn they came to a village that had the name they were looking for, but nobody knew anything about a hospital. It turned out that there were two villages of the same name. At last, in the morning, they found the right one. As they drove down the village road, which smelled of camomile and iodoform, Gordon decided not to stay the night but to spend the day with Zhivago and go back that evening to the railway station where he had left his other friends. But circumstances kept him there for more than a week.

9

During those days the front line began to move. To the south of the village where Gordon found himself, Russian forces succeeded in breaking through the enemy positions. Supporting units followed, widening the gap, but they fell behind and the advance units were cut off and captured. Among the prisoners was Lieutenant Antipov, who was obliged to give himself up when his platoon surrendered.

There were false rumors about him. He was believed to have been killed by a shell and buried by the explosion. This was told on the authority of his friend, Lieutenant Galiullin, who had been watching through field glasses from an observation post when Antipov led the attack.

What Galiullin had seen was the usual picture of an attacking unit. The men advanced quickly, almost at a run, across the no man's land, an autumn field with dry broom swaying in the wind and motionless, spiky gorse. Their object was either to flush the Austrians out of their trenches and engage them with bayonets or to destroy them with hand grenades. To the running men the field was endless. The ground seemed to slip under their feet like a bog. Their lieutenant was running, first in front of them, then beside them, waving his revolver above his head, his mouth split from ear to ear with hurrahs which neither he nor they could hear. At intervals they threw themselves onto the ground, got up all together, and ran on shouting. Each time one or two who had been hit fell with the rest but in a different way, toppling like trees chopped down in a wood, and did not get up again.

"They're shooting long! Get the battery," Galiullin said anxiously to the artillery officer who stood next to him. "No, wait. It's all right."

The attackers were on the point of engaging the enemy. The artillery barrage stopped. In the sudden silence the observers heard their own hearts pounding as if they were in Antipov's place, had brought their men to the edge of the enemy trench, and were expected within the next few minutes to perform wonders of resourcefulness and courage. At that moment two German sixteen-inch shells burst in front of the attackers. Black clouds of dust and smoke hid what followed. "Ya Allah! Finished. They're done for," whispered Galiullin, white-lipped, believing that the lieutenant and his men had been killed. Another shell came down close to the observation post. Bent double, the observers hurried to a safer distance.

Galiullin had shared Antipov's dugout. After Antipov's comrades resigned themselves to the idea that he was dead, Galiullin, who had known him well, was asked to take charge of his belongings and keep them for his widow, a large number of whose photographs had been found among his things.

An enlisted man recently promoted to lieutenant, the mechanic Galiullin, son of Gimazetdin, the janitor of Tiverzin's tenement, was that very Yusupka whom, as an apprentice in the distant past, the foreman Khudoleiev had beaten up. It was to his old tormentor that he was now indebted for his promotion.

On getting his commission, he had found himself, against his will and for no reason that he knew of, in a soft job in a small-town garrison behind the lines. There he commanded a troop of semi-invalids whom instructors as decrepit as themselves took every morning through the drill they had forgotten. Galiullin supervised the changing of the guard in front of the commissary. Nothing else was expected of him. He did not have a care in the world when, among the replacements consisting of older reservists sent from Moscow and put under his orders, there turned up the all too familiar figure of Piotr Khudoleiev.

"Well, well, an old friend," said Galiullin, grinning sourly.

"Yes, sir," said Khudoleiev, standing at attention and saluting.

It was impossible that this should be the end of it. The very first time the lieutenant caught the private in a fault at drill he bawled him out, and when it seemed to him that his subordinate was not looking him straight in the eye but somehow sideways, he hit him in the jaw and put him on bread and water in the guardhouse for two days.

From now on every move of Galiullin's smacked of revenge. But this game, in their respective positions and with rules enforced by the stick, struck Galiullin as unsporting and mean. What was to be done? Both of them could not be in the same place. But what pretext could an officer find for transferring a private from his unit, and where, if it were not for disciplinary reasons, could he transfer him? On the other hand, what grounds could Galiullin think of to apply for his own transfer? Giving the boredom and uselessness of garrison duty as his reasons, he asked to be sent to the front. This earned him a good mark, and when, at the first engagement, he showed his other qualities it turned out that he had the makings of an excellent officer and he was quickly promoted to first lieutenant.

Galiullin had met Antipov in 1905, when Pasha Antipov spent six months with the Tiverzins and Yusupka went to play with him on Sundays. There too he had once or twice met Lara. He had heard nothing of either of them since. When Antipov came from Yuriatin and joined the regiment, Galiullin was struck by the change in his old friend. The shy, mischievous, and girlish child had turned into an arrogant, know-it-all misanthrope. He was intelligent, very brave, taciturn, and sarcastic. Sometimes, looking at him, Galiullin could have sworn that he saw in his gloomy eyes, as inside a window, something beyond, an idea that had taken firm hold of him: a longing for his daughter or for the face of his wife. Antipov seemed like one bewitched, as in a fairy tale. And now Antipov was gone, and Galiullin was left with his papers, his photographs, and the unsolved secret of his transformation on his hands.

As was bound to happen sooner or later, Lara's inquiries for her husband reached Galiullin. He meant to write to her, but he was busy, he had no time to write properly, yet he wished to prepare her for the blow. He kept postponing a long, detailed letter to her until he heard that she was somewhere at the front as a nurse. And he did not know where to address his letter to her now.

10

"Will there be horses today?" Gordon asked every time Dr. Zhivago came home to his midday meal. They were living in a Galician peasant house.

"Not a chance. Anyway, where would you go? You can't go anywhere. There's a terrible muddle. Nobody knows what's what. To the south we have outflanked or broken through the German lines in several places, and I am told some of our overextended units were encircled. To the north, the Germans have crossed the Sventa, at a point that was supposed to be impassable. That is their cavalry, about a corps in strength.

They are blowing up railways, destroying supply stores, and in my opinion trying to surround us. That's the picture, and you talk about horses. Come on, Karpenko," he said, turning to his orderly, "set the table, and make it quick. What are we having for dinner? Calves' feet? Good!"

The Medical Unit, with its hospital and its dependencies, was scattered all over the village, which by a miracle was still unharmed. The houses glittered with Western-style lattice windows stretching from wall to wall, and not so much as a pane was damaged.

The end of a hot, golden autumn had turned into an Indian summer. In the daytime the doctors and officers opened windows, swatted at the black swarms of flies along the sills and the low white ceilings, unbuttoned their tunics and hospital coats, and, dripping with sweat, sipped scalding-hot soup or tea. At night they squatted in front of the open stove, blew on the damp logs which kept going out, their eyes smarting with smoke, and cursed the orderlies for not knowing how to build a fire.

It was a still night. Gordon and Zhivago lay on two bunks facing each other. Between them were the dinner table and the low window running the whole length of the wall. The room was overheated and filled with tobacco smoke. They had opened the two end lattices to get a breath of the fresh autumn night air, which made the panes sweat. They were talking, as they had done all these nights and days, and as usual the horizon in the direction of the front was flickering with a pink glow. When the even, incessant chatter of gunfire was occasionally interrupted by a deep bang that shook the ground as though a heavy steel-bound trunk were being dragged across the floor, scraping the paint, Zhivago interrupted the conversation as if out of respect for the sound, paused for a while, and said, "That's a Bertha, a German sixteen-inch. A little fellow that weighs twenty-four hundred pounds." And then, resuming the conversation, he would forget what they had been talking about.

"What's that smell that hangs over the whole village?" asked Gordon. "I noticed it as soon as I arrived. It's a nauseatingly sweet, cloying smell, rather like mice."

"I know what you mean. That's hemp—they grow a lot of it here. The plant itself has that nagging, clinging, carrion smell. And then in the battle zone, the dead often remain undiscovered in the hemp fields for a long time and begin to decay. Of course the smell of corpses is everywhere. That's only natural. Hear that? It's the Bertha again."

In the past few days they had talked of everything in the world. Gordon had learned his friend's ideas about the war and its effect on people's thinking. Zhivago had told him how hard he found it to accept the ruthless logic of mutual extermination, to get used to the sight of the wounded, especially to the horror of certain wounds of a new sort, to the mutilation of survivors whom the technique of modern fighting had turned into lumps of disfigured flesh.

Going about with him day after day, Gordon too had seen terrible sights. Needless to say, he was aware of the immorality of being an idle spectator of other men's courage, of how they mastered, by an inhuman effort, their fear of death, of the sacrifices they made and the risks they ran. But he did not think that merely crying over them was any less immoral. He believed in behaving simply and honestly according to the circumstances in which life placed him.

That it was possible to faint at the sight of wounds he learned from his own experience when they visited a first-aid station run by a mobile Red Cross unit just behind the front line.

They drove to a clearing in a wood that had been badly damaged by artillery fire. Twisted gun carriages lay upside down in the broken and trampled undergrowth. A riding horse was tethered to a tree. A little farther in the wood was the frame structure of the forester's house; half its roof had been blown away. The first-aid station was in the house and in two big gray tents across the way.

"I shouldn't have brought you," said Zhivago. "The trenches are within half a mile and our batteries are just over there, behind the wood. You can hear what's going on. So don't play the hero, I wouldn't believe you if you did. You're bound to be scared stiff, it's only natural. Any moment the situation may change, and shells will be dropping here."

Tired young soldiers in enormous boots and dusty tunics which were black with sweat on the chest and shoulderblades sprawled on their backs or on their stomachs by the side of the road. They were the survivors of a decimated unit that had been taken out of the front line after four days of heavy fighting and was being sent to the rear for a short rest. They lay as if they were of stone, without the strength to smile or to swear, and no one turned his head when several carts came rumbling swiftly down the road. They were ammunition carts, without springs, loaded with wounded men whom they jolted, cracking their bones and twisting their guts, as they jogged along at a trot to the first-aid station. There the wounded would be hastily bandaged and the most urgent cases operated on. They had been picked up in appalling numbers on the battlefield in front of the trenches half an hour ago during a short lull in the artillery fire. A good half of them were unconscious.

When the carts stopped in front of the porch, orderlies came down the steps with stretchers and unloaded them. A nurse raised the flap of one of the tents and stood looking out; she was off duty. Two men who had been arguing loudly in the wood behind the tents, their voices echoing among the tall young trees, but their words indistinguishable, came out and walked along the road toward the house. One of them, an excited young lieutenant, was shouting at the Medical Officer of the mobile unit: there had been an artillery park in the clearing and he wanted to know where it had been moved. The doctor did not know, it was not his business; he asked the lieutenant to leave him alone and to stop shouting—there were wounded men here and he was busy. But the little lieutenant went on cursing the Red Cross, the artillery command, and everybody else. Zhivago walked up to the doctor; they greeted each other and went into the house. The lieutenant, still swearing loudly with a slight Tartar accent, untied his horse, vaulted into the saddle, and galloped down the road into the woods. The nurse was still looking on.

Suddenly her face was distorted with horror. "What are you doing? You're out of your minds!" she shouted at two lightly wounded soldiers who were walking without assistance between the stretchers. She ran out toward them.

On one stretcher lay a man who had been mutilated in a particularly monstrous way. A large splinter from the shell that had mangled his face, turning his tongue and lips into a red gruel without killing him, had lodged in the bone structure of his jaw, where the cheek had been torn out. He uttered short groans in a thin inhuman voice; no one could take these sounds for anything but an appeal to finish him off quickly, to put an end to his inconceivable torment.

The nurse had gotten the impression that the two lightly wounded men who were walking beside the stretcher had been so moved by his cries that they were about to pull out the terrible piece of iron with their bare hands.

"What's the matter with you? You can't do that. The surgeon

will do it, he has special instruments . . . if it has to be done."
(O God, O God, take him away, don't let me doubt that You
exist.)

Next moment, as he was carried up the steps, the man
screamed, and with one great shudder he gave up the ghost.

The man who had just died was Private Gimazetdin; the
excited officer who had been shouting in the wood was his son,
Lieutenant Galiullin; the nurse was Lara. Gordon and Zhivago
were the witnesses. All these people were there together, in one
place. But some of them had never known each other, while
others failed to recognize each other now. And there were
things about them which were never to be known for certain,
while others were not to be revealed until a future time, a later
meeting.

11

In this area the villages had been miraculously preserved. They
constituted an inexplicably intact island in the midst of a sea of
ruins. One day at sunset Gordon and Zhivago were driving
home. In one village they saw a young Cossack surrounded by a
crowd laughing boisterously, as the Cossack tossed a copper
coin into the air, forcing an old Jew with a gray beard and a long
caftan to catch it. The old man missed every time. The coin flew
past his pitifully spread-out hands and dropped into the mud.
When the old man bent to pick it up, the Cossack slapped his
bottom, and the onlookers held their sides, groaning with
laughter: this was the point of the entertainment. For the
moment it was harmless enough, but no one could say for
certain that it would not take a more serious turn. Every now
and then, the old man's wife ran out of the house across the
road, screaming and stretching out her arms to him, and ran
back again in terror. Two little girls were watching their
grandfather out of the window and crying.

The driver, who found all this extremely comical, slowed
down so that the passengers could enjoy the spectacle. But
Zhivago called the Cossack, bawled him out, and ordered him
to stop baiting the old man.

"Yes, sir," he said readily. "We meant no harm, we were only
doing it for fun."

Gordon and Zhivago drove on in silence.

"It's terrible," said Yurii Andreievich when they were in sight of their own village. "You can't imagine what the wretched Jewish population is going through in this war. The fighting happens to be in their Pale. And as if punitive taxation, the destruction of their property, and all their other sufferings were not enough, they are subjected to pogroms, insults, and accusations that they lack patriotism. And why should they be patriotic? Under enemy rule, they enjoy equal rights, and we do nothing but persecute them. This hatred for them, the basis of it, is irrational. It is stimulated by the very things that should arouse sympathy—their poverty, their overcrowding, their weakness, and this inability to fight back. I can't understand it. It's like an inescapable fate."

Gordon did not reply.

12

Once again they were lying on their bunks on either side of the long low window, it was night, and they were talking.

Zhivago was telling Gordon how he had once seen the Tsar at the front. He told his story well.

It was his first spring at the front. The headquarters of his regiment was in the Carpathians, in a deep valley, access to which from the Hungarian plain was blocked by this army unit.

At the bottom of the valley was a railway station. Zhivago described the landscape, the mountains overgrown with mighty firs and pines, with tufts of clouds catching in their tops, and sheer cliffs of gray slate and graphite showing through the forest like worn patches in a thick fur. It was a damp, dark April morning, as gray as the slate, locked in by the mountains on all sides and therefore still and sultry. Mist hung over the valley, and everything in it steamed, everything rose slowly—engine smoke from the railway station, gray vapors from the fields, the gray mountains, the dark woods, the dark clouds.

At that time the sovereign was making a tour of inspection in Galicia. It was learned suddenly that he would visit Zhivago's unit, of which he was the honorary Colonel. He might arrive at any moment. A guard of honor was drawn up on the station platform. They waited for about two oppressive hours, then two trains with the imperial retinue went by quickly one after the other. A little later the Tsar's train drew in.

Accompanied by the Grand Duke Nicholas, the Tsar inspected the grenadiers. Every syllable of his quietly spoken greeting produced an explosion of thunderous hurrahs whose echoes were sent back and forth like water from swinging buckets.

The Tsar, smiling and ill at ease, looked older and more tired than on the rubles and medals. His face was listless, a little flabby. He kept glancing apologetically at the Grand Duke, not knowing what was expected of him, and the Grand Duke, bending down respectfully, helped him in his embarrassment not so much by words as by moving an eyebrow or a shoulder.

On that warm gray morning in the mountains, Zhivago felt sorry for the Tsar, was disturbed at the thought that such diffident reserve and shyness could be the essential characteristics of an oppressor, that a man so weak could imprison, hang, or pardon.

"He should have made a speech—'I, my sword, and my people'—like the Kaiser. Something about 'the people'—that was essential. But you know he was natural, in the Russian way, tragically above these banalities. After all, that kind of theatricalism is unthinkable in Russia. For such gestures are theatrical, aren't they? I suppose that there were such things as 'peoples' under the Caesars—Gauls or Scythians or Illyrians and so on. But ever since, they have been mere fiction, which served only as subjects for speeches by kings and politicians: 'The people, my people.'

"Now the front is flooded with correspondents and journalists. They record their 'observations' and gems of popular wisdom, they visit the wounded and construct new theories about the people's soul. It's a new version of Dahl★ and just as bogus—linguistic graphomania, verbal incontinence. That's one type—and then there's the other: clipped speech, 'sketches and short scenes,' skepticism and misanthropy. I read a piece like that the other day: 'A gray day, like yesterday. Rain since morning, slush. I look out of the window and see the road. Prisoners in an endless line. Wounded. A gun is firing. It fires today as yesterday, tomorrow as today and every day and every hour.' Isn't that subtle and witty! But what has he got against the gun? How odd to expect variety from a gun! Why doesn't he look at himself, shooting off the same sentences, commas, lists

---

★Vladimir Ivanovich Dahl, author of a *Dictionary of the Living Russian Tongues.*

of facts day in, day out, keeping up his barrage of journalistic philanthropy as nimble as the jumping of a flea? Why can't he get it into his head that it's for him to stop repeating himself—not for the gun—that you can never say something meaningful by accumulating absurdities in your notebook, that facts don't exist until man puts into them something of his own, a bit of free human genius—of myth."

"You've hit the nail on the head," broke in Gordon. "And now I'll tell you what I think about that incident we saw today. That Cossack tormenting the poor patriarch—and there are thousands of incidents like it—of course it's an ignominy—but there's no point in philosophizing, you just hit out. But the Jewish question as a whole—there philosophy does come in—and then we discover something unexpected. Not that I'm going to tell you anything new—we both got our ideas from your uncle.

"You were saying, what is a nation? . . . And who does more for a nation—the one who makes a fuss about it or the one who, without thinking of it, raises it to universality by the beauty and greatness of his actions, and gives it fame and immortality? Well, the answer is obvious. And what are the nations now, in the Christian era? They aren't just nations, but converted, transformed nations, and what matters is this transformation, not loyalty to ancient principles. And what does the Gospel say on this subject? To begin with, it does not make assertions: 'It's like this and like that.' It is a proposal, naïve and timid: 'Do you want to live in a completely new way? Do you want spiritual happiness?' And everybody accepted, they were carried away by it for thousands of years. . . .

"When the Gospel says that in the Kingdom of God there are neither Jews nor Gentiles, does it merely mean that all are equal in the sight of God? No—the Gospel wasn't needed for that—the Greek philosophers, the Roman moralists, and the Hebrew prophets had known this long before. But it said: In that new way of living and new form of society, which is born of the heart, and which is called the Kingdom of Heaven, there are no nations, there are only individuals.

"You said that facts are meaningless, unless meanings are put into them. Well, Christianity, the mystery of the individual, is precisely what must be put into the facts to make them meaningful.

"We also talked about mediocre publicists who have nothing to say to life and the world as a whole, of petty second-raters who are only too happy when some nation, preferably a small and wretched one, is constantly discussed—this gives them a chance to show off their competence and cleverness, and to thrive on their compassion for the persecuted. Well now, what more perfect example can you have of the victims of this mentality than the Jews? Their national idea has forced them, century after century, to be a nation and nothing but a nation— and they have been chained to this deadening task all through the centuries when all the rest of the world was being delivered from it by a new force which had come out of their own midst! Isn't that extraordinary? How can you account for it? Just think! This glorious holiday, this liberation from the curse of mediocrity, this soaring flight above the dullness of a humdrum existence, was first achieved in their land, proclaimed in their language, and belonged to their race! And they actually saw and heard it and let it go! How could they allow a spirit of such overwhelming power and beauty to leave them, how could they think that after it triumphed and established its reign, they would remain as the empty husk of that miracle they had repudiated? What use is it to anyone, this voluntary martyrdom? Whom does it profit? For what purpose are these innocent old men and women and children, all these subtle, kind, humane people, mocked and beaten up throughout the centuries? And why is it that all these literary friends of 'the people' of all nations are always so untalented? Why didn't the intellectual leaders of the Jewish people ever go beyond facile *Weltschmerz* and ironical wisdom? Why have they not—even if at the risk of bursting like boilers with the pressure of their duty—disbanded this army which keeps on fighting and being massacred nobody knows for what? Why don't they say to them: 'Come to your senses, stop. Don't hold on to your identity. Don't stick together, disperse. Be with all the rest. You are the first and best Christians in the world. You are the very thing against which you have been turned by the worst and weakest among you.'"

13

The following day when Zhivago came home to dinner, he said: "Well, you were so anxious to leave, now your wish has come true. I won't say 'Just your luck' because it isn't lucky that we are being hard-pressed and beaten again. The way east is open; the pressure is from the west. All the medical units are under orders to get out. We'll be going tomorrow or the next day. Where to, I don't know. And I suppose, Karpenko, Mikhail Grigorievich's linen still hasn't been washed. It's always the same thing. Karpenko will tell you he has given it to his girl to wash, but if you ask him who and where she is, he doesn't know, the idiot."

He paid no attention to Karpenko's excuses nor to Gordon's apologies for borrowing his host's shirts.

"That's army life for you," he went on. "As soon as you get used to one place you're moved to another. I didn't like anything here when we came. It was dirty, stuffy, the stove was in the wrong place, the ceiling was too low. And now, even if you killed me I couldn't remember what it was like where we came from. I feel as if I wouldn't mind spending my life in this place, staring at that corner of the stove with the sunshine on the tiles and the shadow of that tree moving across."

They packed without haste.

During the night they were roused by shouts, gunfire, and running footsteps. There was a sinister glow over the village. Shadows flickered past the window. The landlord and his wife were getting up behind the partition. Yurii Andreievich sent the orderly to ask what the commotion was about.

He was told that the Germans had broken through. Zhivago hurried off to the hospital and found that it was true. The village was under fire. The hospital was being moved at once, without waiting for the evacuation order.

"We'll all be off before dawn," Zhivago told Gordon. "You're going in the first party, the carriage is ready now, but I've told them to wait for you. Well, good luck. I'll see you off and make sure you get your seat."

They ran down the village street, ducking and hugging the walls. Bullets whizzed past them, and from the crossroads they could see shrapnel explosions like umbrellas of fire opening over the fields.

"And what about you?" asked Gordon as they ran.

"I'll follow with the second party. I have to go back and collect my things."

They separated at the edge of the village. The carriage and several carts that made up the convoy started, bumping into one another and gradually spacing out. Yurii Andreievich waved to his friend, who saw him for a few moments longer by the light of a burning barn.

Again keeping to the shelter of the houses, Yurii Andreievich hurried back. A few yards from his house he was knocked off his feet by the blast of an explosion and hit by a shell splinter. He fell in the middle of the road, bleeding and unconscious.

14

The hospital where Yurii Andreievich was recovering in the officers' ward had been evacuated to an obscure, small town on a railway line close to the G.H.Q. It was a warm day at the end of February. The window near his bed was open at his request.

The patients were killing time before dinner as best they could. They had been told that a new nurse had joined the hospital staff and would be doing her first round that day. In the bed opposite Zhivago's, Galiullin was looking at the newspapers that had just arrived and exclaiming indignantly at the blanks left by the censorship. Yurii Andreievich was reading Tonia's letters, which had accumulated in one great batch. The breeze rustled the letters and the papers. At the sound of light footsteps he looked up. Lara came into the ward.

Zhivago and Galiullin each recognized her without realizing that the other knew her. She knew neither of them. She said: "Hello. Why is the window open? Aren't you cold?" Going up to Galiullin, she asked him how he felt and took his wrist to feel his pulse, but immediately let go of it and sat down by his bed, looking at him with a puzzled expression.

"This is indeed unexpected, Larisa Feodorovna," he said. "I knew your husband. We were in the same regiment. I've kept his things for you."

"It isn't possible," she kept saying, "it isn't possible. You knew him! What an extraordinary coincidence. Please tell me quickly how it happened. He was killed by a shell, wasn't he, and buried by the explosion? You see I know, please don't be afraid of telling me."

Galiullin's courage failed him. He decided to tell her a comforting lie.

"Antipov was taken prisoner," he said. "He advanced too far with his unit. They were surrounded and cut off. He was forced to surrender."

But she did not believe him. Shaken by the unexpectedness of the meeting and not wishing to break down in front of strangers, she hurried out into the corridor.

A few moments later she came back, outwardly collected; afraid of crying again if she spoke to Galiullin, she deliberately avoided looking at him and went over to Yurii Andreievich. "Hello," she said absentmindedly and mechanically. "What's the trouble with you?"

Yurii Andreievich had seen her agitation and her tears. He wanted to ask her why she was so upset and to tell her that he had seen her twice before in his life, once as a schoolboy and once as a university student, but it occurred to him that he would sound too familiar and she would misinterpret his meaning. Then he suddenly remembered the coffin with Anna Ivanovna's body in it and Tonia's screams, and said instead:

"Thank you. I am a doctor. I am looking after myself. I don't need anything."

"How have I offended him?" Lara wondered. She looked in surprise at the stranger with his snub nose and unremarkable face.

For several days the weather was variable, uncertain, with a warm, constantly murmuring wind in the night, smelling of damp earth.

During those days there came strange reports from G.H.Q., and there were alarming rumors from the interior. Telegraphic communications with Petersburg were cut off time and again. Everywhere, at every corner, people were talking politics.

Nurse Antipova did her rounds morning and evening, exchanging a few words with each patient, including Galiullin and Zhivago. "What a curious creature," she thought. "Young and gruff. You couldn't call him handsome with his turned-up nose. But he is intelligent in the best sense of the word, alive and with an attractive mind. However, that's unimportant. What is important is to finish my job here as soon as possible and get

transferred to Moscow to be near Katenka, and then to apply for
my discharge and go home to Yuriatin, back to the gymnasium.
It's quite clear now what happened to poor Pasha, there isn't any
hope, so the sooner I stop playing the heroine the better. I
wouldn't be here if I hadn't come to look for Pasha."

How was Katenka getting on out there, she wondered, poor
orphan, and this always made her cry.

She had noticed a sharp change around her recently. Before,
there had been obligations of all kinds, sacred duties—your duty
to your country, to the army, to society. But now that the war
was lost (and that was the misfortune at the bottom of all the
rest) nothing was sacred anymore.

Everything had changed suddenly—the tone, the moral
climate; you didn't know what to think, whom to listen to. As if
all your life you had been led by the hand like a small child and
suddenly you were on your own, you had to learn to walk by
yourself. There was no one around, neither family nor people
whose judgment you respected. At such a time you felt the need
of committing yourself to something absolute—life or truth or
beauty—of being ruled by it in place of the man-made rules that
had been discarded. You needed to surrender to some such
ultimate purpose more fully, more unreservedly than you had
ever done in the old familiar, peaceful days, in the old life that
was now abolished and gone for good. But in her own case,
Lara reminded herself, she had Katenka to fulfill her need for an
absolute, her need of a purpose. Now that she no longer had
Pasha, Lara would be nothing but a mother, devoting all her
strength to her poor orphaned child.

Yurii Andreievich heard from Moscow that Gordon and
Dudorov had published his book without his permission, and
that it was praised and regarded as showing great literary
promise; that Moscow was going through a disturbed, exciting
time and was on the eve of something important, that there was
growing discontent among the masses, and that grave political
events were imminent.

It was late at night. Yurii Andreievich was terribly sleepy. He
dozed intermittently and imagined that the excitement of the
past days was keeping him awake. A drowsy, sleepily breathing
wind yawned and stirred outside the window. The wind wept
and complained, "Tonia, Sasha, I miss you, I want to go home,
I want to go back to work." And to the muttering of the wind
Yurii Andreievich slept and woke and slept again in a quick,
troubled alternation of joy and suffering, as fleeting and
disturbing as the changing weather, as the restless night.

It occurred to Lara that after all the devotion Galiullin had shown to Pasha's memory, the pains he had taken to look after his things, she had not so much as asked him who he was and where he came from.

To make up for her omission and not seem ungrateful she asked him all about himself when she made her next morning round.

"Merciful heaven," she wondered aloud. Twenty-eight Brest Street, the Tiverzins, the revolution of 1905, that winter! Yusupka? No, she couldn't remember having met him, he must forgive her. But that year, that year, and that house! That's true, there had really been such a house and such a year! How vividly it all came back to her! The gunfire and—what was it she had called it then?—"Christ's judgment"! How strong, how piercingly sharp were the feelings you experienced for the first time as a child! "Forgive me, do forgive me, Lieutenant, what did you say your name is? Yes, yes, you did tell me once. Thank you, Osip Gimazetdinovich, I can't thank you enough for reminding me, for bringing it all back to my mind."

All day long she went about thinking of "that house" and kept talking to herself.

To think of it, Brest Street, No. 28! And now they were shooting again, but how much more frightening it was now! You couldn't say, "The boys are shooting" this time. The children had all grown up, the boys were all here, in the army, all those humble people who had lived in that house and in others like it and in villages that also were like it. Extraordinary, extraordinary!

All the patients who were not bedridden rushed in from the other rooms, hobbling noisily on crutches or running, or walking with canes, and shouted vying with each other:

"Big news! Street fighting in Petersburg! The Petersburg garrison has joined the insurgents! The revolution!"

PART TWO

CHAPTER FIVE

Farewell to the Old

1

The small town was called Meliuzeievo and lay in the fertile, black-soil country. Black dust hung over its roofs like a cloud of locusts. It was raised by the troops and convoys passing through the town; they moved in both directions, some going to the front and others away from it, and it was impossible to tell whether the war were still going on or had ceased.

Every day newly created offices sprang up like mushrooms. And they were elected to everything—Zhivago, Lieutenant Galiullin, and Nurse Antipova, as well as a few others from their group, all of them people from the big cities, well-informed and experienced.

They served as temporary town officials and as minor commissars in the army and the health department, and they looked upon this succession of tasks as an outdoor sport, a diversion, a game of blindman's buff. But more and more they felt that it was time to stop and to get back to their ordinary occupations and their homes.

Zhivago and Antipova were often brought together by their work.

2

The rain turned the black dust into coffee-colored mud and the mud spread over the streets, most of them unpaved.

The town was small. At the end of almost every street you could see the steppe, gloomy under the dark sky, all the vastness of the war, the vastness of the revolution.

Yurii Andreievich wrote to his wife:

"The disintegration and anarchy in the army continue. Measures are being taken to improve discipline and morale. I have toured units stationed in the neighborhood.

"By way of a postscript, though I might have mentioned it much earlier, I must tell that I do a lot of my work with a certain Antipova, a nurse from Moscow who was born in the Urals.

"You remember the girl student who shot at the public prosecutor on that terrible night of your mother's death? I believe she was tried later. I remember telling you that Misha and I had once seen her, when she was still a schoolgirl, at some sordid hotel where your father took us. I can't remember why we went, only that it was a bitterly cold night. I think it was at the time of the Presnia uprising. Well, that girl was Antipova.

"I have made several attempts to go home, but it is not so simple. It is not so much the work—we could hand that over easily enough—the trouble is the trip. Either there are no trains at all or else they are so overcrowded that there is no way of finding a seat.

"But of course it can't go on like this forever, and some of us, who have resigned or been discharged, including Antipova, Galiullin, and myself, have made up our minds that whatever happens we shall leave next week. We'll go separately; it gives us a better chance.

"So I may turn up any day out of the blue, though I'll try to send a telegram."

Before he left, however, he received his wife's reply. In sentences broken by sobs and with tear stains and ink spots for punctuation, she begged him not to come back to Moscow but to go straight to the Urals with that wonderful nurse whose progress through life was marked by portents and coincidences so miraculous that her own, Tonia's, modest life could not possibly compete with it.

"Don't worry about Sasha's future," she wrote. "You will never need to be ashamed of him. I promise you to bring him up in those principles which as a child you saw practiced in our house."

Yurii Andreievich wrote back at once: "You must be out of your mind, Tonia! How could you imagine such a thing? Don't you know, don't you know well enough, that if it were not for you, if it were not for my constant, faithful thoughts of you and of our home, I would never have survived these two terrible, devastating years of war? But why am I writing this—soon we'll be together, our life will begin again, everything will be cleared up.

"What frightens me about your letter is something else. If I really gave you cause to write in such a way, my behavior must have been ambiguous and I am at fault not only before you but before that other woman whom I am misleading. I'll apologize to her as soon as she is back. She is away in the country. Local councils, which formerly existed only in provincial capitals and county seats, are being set up in the villages, and she has gone to help a friend of hers who is acting as instructor in connection with these legislative changes.

"It may interest you to know that although we live in the same house I don't know to this day which is Antipova's room. I've never bothered to find out."

3

Two main roads ran from Meliuzeievo, one going east, the other west. One was a mud track leading through the woods to Zybushino, a small grain center that was administratively a subdivision of Meliuzeievo although it was ahead of it in every way. The other was gravelled and went through fields, boggy in winter but dry in summer, to Biriuchi, the nearest railway junction.

In June Zybushino became an independent republic. It was set up by the local miller Blazheiko and supported by deserters from the 212th Infantry who had left the front at the time of the upheavals, kept their arms, and come to Zybushino through Biriuchi.

The republic refused to recognize the Provisional Government and split off from the rest of Russia. Blazheiko, a religious dissenter who had once corresponded with Tolstoy, proclaimed a new millennial Zybushino kingdom where all work and property were to be collectivized, and referred to the local administration as an Apostolic Seat.

Zybushino had always been a source of legends and exaggerations. It is mentioned in documents dating from the Times of Troubles* and the thick forests surrounding it teemed with robbers even later. The prosperity of its merchants and the fabulous fertility of its soil were proverbial. Many popular beliefs, customs, and oddities of speech that distinguished this whole western region near the front originated in Zybushino.

Now amazing stories were told about Blazheiko's chief assistant. It was said that he was deaf and dumb, that he acquired the gift of speech at moments of inspiration, and then lost it again.

The republic lasted two weeks. In July a unit loyal to the Provisional Government entered the town. The deserters fell back on Biriuchi. Several miles of forest had once been cleared along the railway line on both sides of the junction, and there, among the old tree stumps overgrown with wild strawberries, the piles of timber depleted by pilfering, and the tumble-down mud huts of the seasonal laborers who had cut the trees, the deserters set up their camp.

4

The hospital in which Zhivago convalesced and later served as a doctor, and which he was now preparing to leave, was housed in the former residence of Countess Zhabrinskaia. She had offered it to the Red Cross at the beginning of the war.

It was a two-story house on one of the best sites of the town, at the corner of the main street and the square, known as the *Platz*, where soldiers had drilled in the old days and where meetings were held now.

Its position gave it a good view of the neighborhood; in addition to the square and the street it overlooked the adjoining

---

*Period of interregnum and civil war in the seventeenth century.

farm (owned by a poor, provincial family who lived almost like peasants) as well as the Countess's old garden at the back.

The Countess had a large estate in the district, Razdolnoie, and had used the house only for occasional business visits to the town and as a rallying point for the guests who came from near and far to stay at Razdolnoie in summer.

Now the house was a hospital, and its owner was in prison in Petersburg, where she had lived.

Of the large staff, only two women were left, Ustinia, the head cook, and Mademoiselle Fleury, the former governess of the Countess's daughters, who were now married.

Gray-haired, pink-cheeked, and dishevelled, Mademoiselle Fleury shuffled about in bedroom slippers and a floppy, worn-out housecoat, apparently as much at home in the hospital as she had been in the Zhabrinsky family. She told long stories in her broken Russian, swallowing the ends of her words in the French manner, gesticulated, struck dramatic poses, and burst into hoarse peals of laughter that ended in coughing fits.

She believed that she knew Nurse Antipova inside out and thought that the nurse and the doctor were bound to be attracted to each other. Succumbing to her passion for match-making, so deep-rooted in the Latin heart, she was delighted when she found them in each other's company, and would shake her finger and wink slyly at them. This puzzled Antipova and angered the doctor; but, like all eccentrics, Mademoiselle cherished her illusions and would not be parted from them at any price.

Ustinia was an even stranger character. Her clumsy, pear-shaped figure gave her the look of a brood hen. She was dry and sober to the point of maliciousness, but her sober-mindedness went hand in hand with an imagination unbridled in everything to do with superstition. Born in Zybushino and said to be the daughter of the local sorcerer, she knew countless spells and would never go out without first muttering over the stove and the keyhole to protect the house in her absence from fire and the Evil One. She could keep quiet for years, but once she was roused nothing would stop her. Her passion was to defend the truth.

After the fall of the Zybushino republic, the Meliuzeievo Executive Committee launched a campaign against the local anarchistic tendencies. Every night peaceful meetings were held at the *Platz*, attended by small numbers of citizens who had nothing better to do and who, in the old days, used to gather for gossip outside the fire station. The Meliuzeievo cultural soviet encouraged them and invited local and visiting speakers to guide the discussions. The visitors believed the tales about the talking deaf-mute to be utter nonsense and were anxious to say so. But the small craftsmen, the soldiers' wives, and former servants of Meliuzeievo did not regard these stories as absurd and stood up in his defense.

One of the most outspoken of his defenders was Ustinia. At first held back by womanly reserve, she had gradually become bolder in heckling orators whose views were unacceptable in Meliuzeievo. In the end she developed into an expert public speaker.

The humming of the voices in the square could be heard through the open windows of the hospital, and on quiet nights even fragments of speeches. When Ustinia took the floor, Mademoiselle often rushed into any room where people were sitting and urged them to listen, imitating her without malice in her broken accent: "Disorder . . . Disorder . . . Tsarist, bandit . . . Zybushi- . . . deaf-mute . . . traitor! traitor!"

Mademoiselle was secretly proud of the spirited and sharp-tongued cook. The two women were fond of each other although they never stopped bickering.

5

Yurii Andreievich prepared to leave, visiting homes and offices where he had friends, and applying for the necessary documents.

At that time the new commissar of the local sector of the front stopped at Meliuzeievo on his way to the army. Everybody said he was completely inexperienced, a mere boy.

A new offensive was being planned and a great effort was made to improve the morale of the army masses. Revolutionary courts-martial were instituted, and the death penalty, which had recently been abolished, was restored.

Before leaving, the doctor had to obtain a paper from the local commandant.

Usually crowds filled his office, overflowing far out into the street. It was impossible to elbow one's way to the desks and no one could hear anything in the roar caused by hundreds of voices.

But this was not one of the reception days. The clerks sat writing silently in the peaceful office, disgruntled at the growing complication of their work, and exchanging ironic glances. Cheerful voices came from the commandant's room; it sounded as if, in there, people had unbuttoned their tunics and were having refreshments.

Galiullin came out of the inner room, saw Zhivago, and vigorously beckoned to him.

Since the doctor had in any case to see the commandant, he went in. He found the room in a state of artistic disorder.

The center of the stage was held by the new commissar, the hero of the day and the sensation of the town, who, instead of being at his post, was addressing the rulers of this paper kingdom quite unconnected with staff and operational matters.

"Here's another of our stars," said the commandant, introducing the doctor. The commissar, completely self-absorbed, did not look around, and the commandant turned to sign the paper that the doctor put in front of him and waved him politely to a low ottoman in the center of the room.

The doctor was the only person in the room who sat normally. All the rest were lolling eccentrically with an air of exaggerated and assumed ease. The commandant almost lay across his desk, his cheek on his fist, in a thoughtful, Byronic pose. His aide, a massive, stout man, perched on the arm of the sofa, his legs tucked on the seat as if he were riding side saddle. Galiullin sat astride a chair, his arms folded on its back and his head resting on his arms, and the commissar kept hoisting himself up by his wrists onto the window sill and jumping off and running up and down the room with small quick steps, buzzing about like a wound-up top, never still or silent for a moment. He talked continuously; the subject of the conversation was the problem of the deserters at Biriuchi.

The commissar was exactly as he had been described to Zhivago. He was thin and graceful, barely out of his teens, aflame with the highest ideals. He was said to come of a good family (the son of a senator, some people thought) and to have been one of the first to march his company to the Duma in February. He was called Gints or Gintse—the doctor had not quite caught the name—and spoke very distinctly, with a correct Petersburg accent and a slight Baltic intonation.

He wore a tight-fitting tunic. It probably embarrassed him to be so young, and in order to seem older he assumed a sneer and an artificial stoop, hunching his shoulders with their stiff epaulettes and keeping his hands deep in his pockets; this did in fact give him a cavalryman's silhouette which could be drawn in two straight lines converging downward from the angle of his shoulders to his feet.

"There is a Cossack regiment stationed a short distance down the railway," the commandant informed him. "It's Red, it's loyal. It will be called out, the rebels will be surrounded, and that will be the end of the business. The corps commander is anxious that they should be disarmed without delay."

"Cossacks? Out of the question!" flared the commissar. "This is not 1905. We're not going back to prerevolutionary methods. On this point we don't see eye to eye. Your generals have outsmarted themselves."

"Nothing has been done yet. This is only a plan, a suggestion."

"We have an agreement with the High Command not to interfere with operational matters. I am not cancelling the order to call out the Cossacks. Let them come. But I, for my part, will take such steps as are dictated by common sense. I suppose they have a bivouac out there?"

"I guess so. A camp, at any rate. Fortified."

"So much the better. I want to go there. I want to see this menace, this nest of robbers. They may be rebels, gentlemen, they may even be deserters, but remember, they are the people. And the people are children, you have to know them, you have to know their psychology. To get the best out of them, you must have the right approach, you have to play on their best, most sensitive chords.

"I'll go, and I'll have a heart-to-heart talk with them. You'll see, they'll go back to the positions they have deserted. You don't believe me? Want to bet?"

"I wonder. But I hope you're right."

"I'll say to them, 'Take my own case, I am an only son, the hope of my parents, yet I haven't spared myself. I've given up everything—name, family, position. I have done this to fight for your freedom, such freedom as is not enjoyed by any other people in the world. This I did, and so did many other young men like myself, not to speak of the old guard of our glorious predecessors, the champions of the people's rights who were sent to hard labor in Siberia or locked up in the Schlüsselburg Fortress. Did we do this for ourselves? Did we have to do it? And you, you who are no longer ordinary privates but the warriors of the first revolutionary army in the world, ask yourselves honestly: Have you lived up to your proud calling? At this moment when our country is being bled white and is making a supreme effort to shake off the encircling hydra of the enemy, you have allowed yourselves to be fooled by a gang of nobodies, you have become a rabble, politically unconscious, surfeited with freedom, hooligans for whom nothing is enough. You're like the proverbial pig that was allowed in the dining room and at once jumped onto the table.' Oh, I'll touch them to the quick, I'll make them feel ashamed of themselves."

"No, that would be risky," the commandant objected half-heartedly, exchanging quick, meaningful glances with his aide.

Galiullin did his best to dissuade the commissar from his insane idea. He knew the reckless men of the 212th, they had been in his division at the front. But the commissar refused to listen.

Yurii Andreievich kept trying to get up and go. The commissar's naïveté embarrassed him, but the sly sophistication of the commandant and his aide—two sneering and dissembling opportunists—was no better. The foolishness of the one was matched by the slyness of the others. And all this expressed itself in a torrent of words, superfluous, utterly false, murky, profoundly alien to life itself.

Oh, how one wishes sometimes to escape from the meaningless dullness of human eloquence, from all those sublime phrases, to take refuge in nature, apparently so inarticulate, or in the wordlessness of long, grinding labor, of sound sleep, of true music, or of a human understanding rendered speechless by emotion!

The doctor remembered his coming talk with Antipova. Though it was bound to be unpleasant, he was glad of the necessity of seeing her, even at such a price. She was unlikely to be back. But he got up as soon as he could and went out, unnoticed by the others.

6

She was back. Mademoiselle, who gave him the news, added that she was tired, she had had a quick meal and had gone up to her room saying she was not to be disturbed. "But I should go up and knock if I were you," Mademoiselle suggested. "I am

sure she is not asleep yet."—"Which is her room?" the doctor
asked. Mademoiselle was surprised beyond words by his
question. Antipova lived at the end of the passage on the top
floor, just beyond several rooms in which all of the Countess's
furniture was kept locked, and where the doctor had never
been.

It was getting dark. Outside, the houses and fences huddled
closer together in the dusk. The trees advanced out of the depth
of the garden into the light of the lamps shining from the
windows. The night was hot and sticky. At the slightest effort
one was drenched with sweat. The light of the kerosene lamps
streaking into the yard went down the trees in a dirty, vaporous
flow.

The doctor stopped at the head of the stairs. It occurred to
him that even to knock on Antipova's door when she was only
just back and tired from her journey would be discourteous and
embarrassing. Better leave the talk for tomorrow. Feeling at a
loss as one does when one changes one's mind, he walked to the
other end of the passage, where a window overlooked the
neighboring yard, and leaned out.

The night was full of quiet, mysterious sounds. Next to him,
inside the passage, water dripped from the washbasin regularly
and slowly. Somewhere outside the window people were
whispering. Somewhere in the vegetable patch they were
watering cucumber beds, clanking the chain of the well as they
drew the water and poured it from pail to pail.

All the flowers smelled at once; it was as if the earth,
unconscious all day long, were now waking to their fragrance.
And from the Countess's centuries-old garden, so littered with
fallen branches that it was impenetrable, the dusty aroma of old
linden trees coming into bloom drifted in a huge wave as tall as a
house.

Noises came from the street beyond the fence on the right—
snatches of a song, a drunken soldier, doors banging.

An enormous crimson moon rose behind the crows' nests in
the Countess's garden. At first it was the color of the new brick
mill in Zybushino, then it turned yellow like the water tower at
Biriuchi.

And just under the window, the smell of new-mown hay, as
perfumed as jasmine tea, mixed with that of belladonna. Below
there a cow was tethered; she had been brought from a distant
village, she had walked all day, she was tired and homesick for
the herd and would not yet accept food from her new mistress.

"Now, now, whoa there, I'll show you how to butt," her
mistress coaxed her in a whisper, but the cow crossly shook her
head and craned her neck, mooing plaintively, and beyond the
black barns of Meliuzeievo the stars twinkled, and invisible
threads of sympathy stretched between them and the cow as if
there were cattle sheds in other worlds where she was pitied.

Everything was fermenting, growing, rising with the magic
yeast of life. The joy of living, like a gentle wind, swept in a
broad surge indiscriminately through fields and towns, through
walls and fences, through wood and flesh. Not to be overwhelmed by this tidal wave, Yurii Andreievich went out into
the square to listen to the speeches.

7

By now the moon stood high. Its light covered everything as
with a thick layer of white paint. The broad shadows thrown by
the pillared government buildings that surrounded the square in
a semicircle spread on the ground like black rugs.

The meeting was being held across the square. Straining one's
ears, one could hear every word. But the doctor was stunned by
the beauty of the spectacle; he sat down on the bench outside the
fire station and instead of listening looked about him.

Narrow dead-end streets ran off the square, as deep in mud as
country lanes and lined with crooked little houses. Fences of
plaited willows stuck out of the mud like bow nets in a pond, or
lobster pots. You could see the weak glint of open windows. In
the small front gardens, sweaty red heads of corn with oily
whiskers reached out toward the rooms, and single pale thin
hollyhocks looked out over the fences, like women in night
clothes whom the heat had driven out of their stuffy houses for a
breath of air.

The moonlit night was extraordinary, like merciful love or
the gift of clairvoyance. Suddenly, into this radiant, legendary
stillness, there dropped the measured, rhythmic sound of a
familiar, recently heard voice. It was a fine ardent voice and it
rang with conviction. The doctor listened and recognized it at
once. Commissar Gints was addressing the meeting on the
square.

Apparently the municipality had asked him to lend them the

support of his authority. With great feeling he chided the people of Meliuzeievo for their disorganized ways and for giving in to the disintegrating influence of the Bolsheviks, who, he said, were the real instigators of the Zybushino disorders. Speaking in the same spirit as at the Commandant's, he reminded them of the powerful and ruthless enemy, and of their country's hour of trial. Then the crowd began to heckle.

Calls of protest alternated with demands for silence. The interruptions grew louder and more frequent. A man who had come with Gints, and who now assumed the role of chairman, shouted that speeches from the floor were not allowed and called the audience to order. Some insisted that a citizeness who wished to speak should be given leave.

A woman made her way through the crowd to the wooden box that served as a platform. She did not attempt to climb on the box but stood beside it. The woman was known to the crowd. Its attention was caught. There was a silence. This was Ustinia.

"Now you were saying, Comrade Commissar, about Zybushino," she began, "and about looking sharp—you told us to look sharp and not to be deceived—but actually, you yourself, I heard you, all you do is to play about with words like 'Bolsheviks, Mensheviks,' that's all you talk about— Bolsheviks, Mensheviks. Now all that about no more fighting and all being brothers, I call that being godly, not Menshevik, and about the works and factories going to the poor, that isn't Bolshevik, that's just human decency. And about that deaf-mute, we're fed up hearing about him. Everybody goes on and on about the deaf-mute. And what have you got against him? Just that he was dumb all that time and then he suddenly started to talk and didn't ask your permission? As if that were so marvellous! Much stranger things than that have been known to happen. Take the famous she-ass, for instance. 'Balaam, Balaam,' she says, 'listen to me, don't go that way, I beg you, you'll be sorry.' Well, naturally, he wouldn't listen, he went on. Like you saying, 'A deaf-mute,' he thought, 'a she-ass, a dumb beast, what's the good of listening to her.' He scorned her. And look how sorry he was afterwards. You all know what the end of it was."

"What?" someone asked curiously.

"That's enough," snapped Ustinia. "If you ask too many questions you'll grow old before your time."

"That's no good. You tell us," insisted the heckler.

"All right, all right, I'll tell you, you pest. He was turned into a pillar of salt."

"You've got it wrong, that was Lot. That was Lot's wife," people shouted. Everyone laughed. The chairman called the meeting to order. The doctor went to bed.

8

He saw Antipova the following evening. He found her in the pantry with a pile of linen, straight out of the wringer; she was ironing.

The pantry was one of the back rooms at the top, looking out over the garden. There the samovars were got ready, food was dished out, and the used plates were stacked in the dumbwaiter to be sent down to the kitchen. There too the lists of china, silver, and glass were kept and checked, and there people spent their moments of leisure, using it as a meeting place.

The windows were open. In the room, the scent of linden blossoms mingled, as in an old park, with the caraway-bitter smell of dry twigs and the charcoal fumes of the two flatirons that Antipova used alternately, putting them each in turn in the flue to keep them hot.

"Well, why didn't you knock last night? Mademoiselle told me. But it's a good thing you didn't. I was already in bed. I couldn't have let you in. Well, how are you? Look out for the charcoal, don't get it on your suit."

"You look as if you've been doing the laundry for the whole hospital."

"No, there's a lot of mine in there. You see? You keep on teasing me about getting stuck in Meliuzeievo. Well, this time I mean it, I'm going. I'm getting my things together, I'm packing. When I've finished I'll be off. I'll be in the Urals and you'll be in Moscow. Then one day somebody will ask you: 'Do you happen to know a little town called Meliuzeievo?' and you'll say: 'I don't seem to call it to mind.'—'And who is Antipova?'—'Never heard of her.'"

"That's unlikely. Did you have a good trip? What was it like in the country?"

"That's a long story. How quickly these irons cool! Do hand

me the other, do you mind? It's over there, look, just inside the
flue. And could you put this one back? Thanks. Every village is
different, it depends on the villagers. In some the people are
industrious, they work hard, then it isn't bad. And in others I
suppose all the men are drunks. Then it's desolate. A terrible
sight."

"Nonsense! Drunks? A lot you understand! It's just that there
is no one there, all the men are in the army. What about the new
councils?"

"You're wrong about the drunks, I don't agree with you at
all. The councils? There's going to be a lot of trouble with the
councils. The instructions can't be applied, there's nobody to
work with. All the peasants care about at the moment is the land
question. . . . I stopped at Razdolnoie. What a lovely place,
you should go and see it. . . . It was burned a bit and looted
last spring, the barn is burned down, the orchards are charred,
and there are smoke stains on some of the houses. Zybushino I
didn't see, I didn't get there. But they all tell you the deaf-mute
really exists. They describe what he looks like, they say he's
young and educated."

"Last night Ustinia stood up for him on the square."

"The moment I got back there was another lot of old
furniture from Razdolnoie. I've asked them a hundred times to
leave it alone. As if we didn't have enough of our own. And this
morning the guard from the commandant's office comes over
with a note—they must have the silver tea set and the crystal
glasses, it's a matter of life and death, just for one night, they'll
send it back. Half of it we'll never see again. It's always a loan—I
know these loans. They're having a party—in honor of some
visitor or something."

"I can guess who that is. The new commissar has arrived, the
one who's appointed to our sector of the front. They want to
tackle the deserters, have them surrounded and disarmed. The
commissar is a greenhorn, a babe in arms. The local authorities
want to call out the Cossacks, but not he—he's planning to
speak to their hearts. The people, he says, are like children, and
so on; he thinks it's a kind of game. Galiullin tried to argue with
him, he told him to leave the jungle alone, not to rouse the wild
beast. 'Leave us to deal with it,' he said. But you can't do
anything with a fellow like that once he's got a thing in his head.
I do wish you'd listen to me. Do stop ironing a minute. There
will be an unimaginable mess here soon; it's beyond our power
to avert it. I do wish you'd leave before it happens."

"Nothing will happen, you're exaggerating. And anyway, I am leaving. But I can't just snap my fingers and say goodbye. I have to hand in a properly checked inventory. I don't want it to look as if I've stolen something and run away. And who is to take over? That's the problem, I can't tell you what I've been through with that miserable inventory, and all I get is abuse. I listed Zhabrinskaia's things as hospital property, because that was the sense of the decree. Now they say I did it on purpose to keep them for the owner! What a dirty trick!"

"Do stop worrying about pots and rugs. To hell with them. What a thing to fuss about at a time like this! Oh, I wish I'd seen you yesterday. I was in such good form that I could have told you all about everything, explained the whole celestial mechanics, answered any accursed question! It's true, you know, I'm not joking, I really did want to get it all off my chest. And I wanted to tell you about my wife, and my son, and myself.
. . . Why the hell can't a grown-up man talk to a grown-up woman without being at once suspected of some ulterior motive? Damn all motives—ulterior ones and others.

"Please, go on with your ironing, make the linen nice and smooth, don't bother about me, I'll go on talking. I'll talk a long time.

"Just think what's going on around us! And that you and I should be living at such a time. Such a thing happens only once in an eternity. Just think of it, the whole of Russia has had its roof torn off, and you and I and everyone else are out in the open! And there's nobody to spy on us. Freedom! Real freedom, not just talk about it, freedom, dropped out of the sky, freedom beyond our expectations, freedom by accident, through a misunderstanding.

"And how great everyone is, and completely at sea! Have you noticed? As if crushed by his own weight, by the discovery of his greatness.

"Go on ironing, I tell you. Don't talk. You aren't bored. Let me change your iron for you.

"Last night I was watching the meeting in the square. An extraordinary sight! Mother Russia is on the move, she can't stand still, she's restless and she can't find rest, she's talking and she can't stop. And it isn't as if only people were talking. Stars and trees meet and converse, flowers talk philosophy at night, stone houses hold meetings. It makes you think of the Gospel, doesn't it? The days of the apostles. Remember St. Paul? You will speak with tongues and you will prophesy. Pray for the gift of understanding."

"I know what you mean about stars and trees holding meetings. I understand that. It's happened to me too."

"It was partly the war, the revolution did the rest. The war was an artificial break in life—as if life could be put off for a time—what nonsense! The revolution broke out willy-nilly, like a sigh suppressed too long. Everyone was revived, reborn, changed, transformed. You might say that everyone has been through two revolutions—his own personal revolution as well as the general one. It seems to me that socialism is the sea, and all these separate streams, these private, individual revolutions, are flowing into it—the sea of life, the sea of spontaneity. I said life, but I mean life as you see it in a great picture, transformed by genius, creatively enriched. Only now people have decided to experience it not in books and pictures but in themselves, not as an abstraction but in practice."

The sudden trembling of his voice betrayed his rising agitation. Antipova stopped ironing and gave him a grave, astonished look. It confused him and he forgot what he was saying. After a moment of embarrassed silence he rushed on, blurting out whatever came into his head.

"These days I have such a longing to live honestly, to be productive. I so much want to be a part of all this awakening. And then, in the middle of all this general rejoicing, I catch your mysterious, sad glance, wandering God knows where, far away. How I wish it were not there! How I wish your face to say that you are happy with your fate and that you need nothing from anyone. If only someone who is really close to you, your friend or your husband—best of all if he were a soldier—would take me by the hand and tell me to stop worrying about your fate and not to weary you with my attentions. But I'd wrest my hand free and take a swing. . . . Ah, I have forgotten myself. Please forgive me."

Once again the doctor's voice betrayed him. He gave up struggling and, feeling hopelessly awkward, got up and went to the window. Leaning on the sill, his cheek on his hand, he stared into the dark garden with absent, unseeing eyes, trying to collect himself.

Antipova walked round the ironing board, propped between the table and the other window, and stopped in the middle of the room a few steps behind him. "That's what I've always been afraid of," she said softly, as if to herself. "I shouldn't have . . . Don't, Yurii Andreievich, you mustn't. Oh, now

just look at what you've made me do!" she exclaimed. She ran
back to the board, where a thin stream of acrid smoke came
from under the iron that had burned through a blouse.

She thumped it down crossly on its stand. "Yurii Andreievich," she went on, "do be sensible, go off to Mademoiselle for a minute, have a drink of water and come back, please,
as I've always known you till now and as I want you to be. Do
you hear, Yurii Andreievich? I know you can do it. Please do it,
I beg you."

They had no more talks of this kind, and a week later Larisa
Feodorovna left.

9

Some time later, Zhivago too set out for home. The night
before he left there was a terrible storm. The roar of the gale
merged with that of the downpour, which sometimes crashed
straight onto the roofs and at other times drove down the street
with the changing wind as if lashing its way step by step.

The peels of thunder followed each other uninterruptedly,
producing a steady rumble. In the blaze of continual flashes of
lightning the street vanished into the distance, and the bent trees
seemed to be running in the same direction.

Mademoiselle Fleury was waked up in the night by an urgent
knocking at the front door. She sat up in alarm and listened. The
knocking went on.

Could it be, she thought, that there wasn't a soul left in the
hospital to get up and open the door? Did she always have to do
everything, poor old woman, just because nature had made her
reliable and endowed her with a sense of duty?

Well, admittedly, the house had belonged to rich aristocrats,
but what about the hospital—didn't that belong to the people,
wasn't it their own? Whom did they expect to look after it?
Where, for instance, had the male nurses got to, she'd like to
know. Everyone had fled—no more orderlies, no more nurses,
no doctors, no one in authority. Yet there were still wounded in
the house, two legless men in the surgical ward where the
drawing room used to be, and downstairs next to the laundry
the storeroom full of dysentery cases. And that devil Ustinia
had gone out visiting. She knew perfectly well that there was a

storm coming, but did that stop her? Now she had a good excuse to spend the night out.

Well, thank God the knocking had stopped, they realized that nobody would answer, they'd given it up. Why anybody should want to be out in the weather . . . Or could it be Ustinia? No, she had her key. Oh God, how terrible, they've started again.

What pigs, just the same! Not that you could expect Zhivago to hear anything, he was off tomorrow, his thoughts were already in Moscow or on the journey. But what about Galiullin? How could he sleep soundly or lie calmly through all this noise, expecting that in the end she, a weak, defenseless old woman, would go down and open for God knows whom, on this frightening night in this frightening country.

Galiullin!—she remembered suddenly. No, such nonsense could occur to her only because she was half asleep, Galiullin wasn't there, he should be a long way off by now. Hadn't she herself, with Zhivago, hidden him, and disguised him as a civilian, and then told him about every road and village in the district to help him to escape after that horrible lynching at the station when they killed Commissar Gints and chased Galiullin all the way from Biriuchi to Meliuzeievo, shooting at him and then hunting for him all over the town!

If it hadn't been for those automobiles, not a stone would have been left standing in the town. An armored division happened to be passing through, and stopped those evil men.

The storm was subsiding, moving away. The thunder was less continuous, duller, more distant. The rain stopped occasionally, when the water could be heard splashing softly off the leaves and down the gutters. Noiseless reflections of distant lightning lit up Mademoiselle's room, lingering as though looking for something.

Suddenly the knocking at the front door, which had long since stopped, was resumed. Someone was in urgent need of help and was knocking repeatedly, in desperation. The wind rose again and the rain came down.

"Coming," shouted Mademoiselle to whoever it was, and the sound of her own voice frightened her.

It had suddenly occurred to her who it might be. Putting down her feet and pushing them into slippers, she threw her dressing gown over her shoulders and hurried to wake up Zhivago, it would be less frightening if he came down with her. But he had heard the knocking and was already coming down with a lighted candle. The same idea had occurred to both of them.

"Zhivago, Zhivago, they're knocking on the front door, I'm afraid to go down alone," she called out in French, adding in Russian: "You will see, it's either Lara or Lieutenant Gaiul."

Roused by the knocking, Yurii Andreievich had also felt certain that it was someone he knew—either Galiullin, who had been stopped in his flight and was coming back for refuge, or Nurse Antipova, prevented from continuing her journey for some reason.

In the hallway the doctor gave the candle to Mademoiselle, drew the bolts, and turned the key. A gust of wind burst the door open, putting out the candle and showering them with cold raindrops.

"Who is it? Who is it? Anybody there?"

Mademoiselle and the doctor shouted in turn into the darkness but there was no reply. Suddenly the knocking started again in another place—was it at the back door, or, as they now thought, at the French window into the garden?

"Must be the wind," said the doctor. "But just to make sure, perhaps you'd have a look at the back. I'll stay here in case there really is someone."

Mademoiselle disappeared into the house while the doctor went out and stood under the entrance roof. His eyes had become accustomed to the darkness, and he could make out the first signs of dawn.

Above the town, clouds raced dementedly as if pursued, so low that their tatters almost caught the tops of the trees, which bent in the same direction so that they looked like brooms sweeping the sky. The rain lashed the wooden wall of the house, turning it from gray to black.

Mademoiselle came back. "Well?" said the doctor.

"You were right. There's no one." She had been all around the house; a branch knocking on the pantry window had broken one of the panes and there were huge puddles on the floor, and the same thing in what used to be Lara's room—there was a sea, a real sea, an ocean. "And on this side, look, there's a broken shutter knocking on the casement, do you see it? That's all it was."

They talked a little, locked the door, and went back to their rooms, both regretting that the alarm had been a false one.

They had been sure that when they opened the door Antipova would come in, chilled through and soaked to the skin, and they would ask her dozens of questions while she took off her things, and she would go and change and come down and dry herself in front of the kitchen stove, still warm from last night, and would tell them her adventures, pushing back her hair and laughing.

They had been so sure of it that after locking the front door they imagined that she was outside the house in the form of a watery wraith, and her image continued to haunt them.

10

It was said that the Biriuchi telegrapher, Kolia Frolenko, was indirectly responsible for the trouble at the station.

Kolia, the son of a well-known Meliuzeievo clockmaker, had been a familiar figure in Meliuzeievo from his earliest childhood. As a small boy he had stayed with some of the servants at Razdolnoie and had played with the Countess's daughters. It was then that he learned to understand French. Mademoiselle Fleury knew him well.

Everyone in Meliuzeievo was used to seeing him on his bicycle, coatless, hatless, and in canvas summer shoes in any weather. Arms crossed on his chest, he free-wheeled down the road, glancing up at the poles and wires to check the condition of the network.

Some of the houses in Meliuzeievo were connected by a branch line with the exchange at the station. The calls were handled by Kolia at the station switchboard. There he was up to his ears in work, for not only the telephone and telegraph were in his charge, but, if the stationmaster Povarikhin was absent for a few moments, also the railway signals, which were operated from the same control room.

Having to look after several mechanical instruments at once, Kolia had evolved a special style of speech, obscure, abrupt, and puzzling, which enabled him, if he chose, to avoid answering questions or getting involved in a conversation. He was said to have abused the advantage this gave him on the day of the disorders.

It is true that, by suppressing information, he had defeated Galiullin's good intentions and, perhaps unwittingly, had given a fatal turn to the events.

Galiullin had called up from town and asked for Commissar Gints, who was somewhere at the station or in its vicinity, in

order to tell him that he was on his way to join him and to ask
him to wait for him and do nothing until he arrived. Kolia, on
the pretext that he was busy signalling an approaching train,
refused to call the commissar. At the same time he did his
utmost to delay the train, which was bringing up the Cossacks
summoned to Biriuchi.

When the troops arrived nevertheless he did not conceal his
dismay.

The engine, crawling slowly under the dark roof of the
platform, stopped in front of the huge window of the control
room. Kolia drew the green serge curtain with the initials of the
Company woven in yellow into the border, picked up the
enormous water jug standing on the tray on the window ledge,
poured some water into the plain, thick, straight-sided glass,
drank a few mouthfuls, and looked out.

The engineer saw him from his cab and gave him a friendly
nod.

"The stinker, the louse," Kolia thought with hatred. He stuck
out his tongue and shook his fist. The engineer not only
understood him but managed to convey by a shrug of the
shoulders and a nod in the direction of the train: "What was I to
do? I'd like to know what you'd have done in my place. He's the
boss."—"You're a filthy brute all the same," Kolia replied by
gestures.

The horses were taken, balking, out of the freight cars. The
thud of their hoofs on the wooden gangways was followed by
the ring of their shoes on the stone platform. They were led,
rearing, across the tracks.

At the end of the tracks were two rows of derelict wooden
coaches. The rain had washed them clean of paint, and worms
and damp had rotted them from inside, so that now they were
reverting to their original kinship with the wood of the forest,
which began just beyond the rolling stock, with its lichen, its
birches, and the clouds towering above it.

At the word of command, the Cossacks mounted their horses
and galloped to the clearing.

The rebels of the 212th were surrounded. In woods, horsemen always seem taller and more formidable than in an open
field. They impressed the infantrymen, although they had rifles
in their mud huts. The Cossacks drew their swords.

Within the ring formed by the horses, some timber was piled
up. Gints mounted it and addressed the surrounded men.

As usual, he spoke of soldierly duty, of the fatherland, and many other lofty subjects. But these ideas found no sympathy among his listeners. There were too many of them. They had suffered a great deal in the war, they were thick-skinned and exhausted. They had long been fed up with the phrases Gints was giving them. Four months of wooing by the Left and Right had corrupted these unsophisticated men, who, moreover, were alienated by the speaker's foreign-sounding name and Baltic accent.

Gints felt that his speech was too long and was annoyed at himself, but he thought that he had to make himself clear to his listeners, who instead of being grateful rewarded him with expressions of indifference or hostile boredom. Gradually losing his temper, he decided to speak straight from the shoulder and to bring up the threats he had so far held in reserve. Heedless of the rising murmurs, he reminded the deserters that revolutionary courts-martial had been set up, and called on them, on pain of death, to disarm and give up their ringleaders. If they refused, he said, they would prove that they were common traitors, an irresponsible swollen-headed rabble. The men had become unused to being talked to in such a tone.

Several hundred voices rose in an uproar. Some were low-pitched and almost without anger: "All right, all right. Pipe down. That's enough." But hate-filled, hysterical trebles predominated:

"The nerve! Just like in the old days! These officers still treat us like dirt. So we're traitors, are we? And what about you yourself, Excellency? Why bother with him? Obviously he's a German, an infiltrator. Show us your papers, blueblood. And what are you gaping at, pacifiers?" They turned to the Cossacks. "You've come to restore order, go on, tie us up, have your fun."

But the Cossacks, too, liked Gints's unfortunate speech less and less. "They are all swine to him," they muttered. "Thinks himself the lord and master!" At first singly, and then in ever-growing numbers, they began to sheathe their swords. One after another they got off their horses. When most of them had dismounted, they moved in a disorderly crowd toward the center of the clearing, mixed with the men of the 212th, and fraternized.

"You must vanish quietly," the worried Cossack officers told Gints. "Your car is at the station, we'll send for it to meet you. Hurry."

Gints went, but he felt that to steal away was beneath his

dignity; so he turned quite openly toward the station. He was terribly agitated but out of pride forced himself to walk calmly and unhurriedly.

He was close to the station. At the edge of the woods, within sight of the tracks, he looked back for the first time. Soldiers with rifles had followed him. "What do they want?" he wondered. He quickened his pace.

So did his pursuers. The distance between them remained unchanged. He saw the double wall of derelict coaches, stepped behind them, and ran. The train that had brought the Cossacks had been shunted. The lines were clear. He crossed them at a run and leapt onto the steep platform. At the same moment the soldiers ran out from behind the old coaches. Povarikhin and Kolia were shouting and waving to him to get into the station building, where they could save him.

But once again the sense of honor bred in him for generations, a city-bred sense of honor, which impelled him to self-sacrifice and was out of place here, barred his way to safety. His heart pounding wildly, he made a supreme effort to control himself. He told himself: "I must shout to them, 'Come to your senses, men, you know I'm not a spy.' A really heartfelt word or two will bring them to their senses."

In the course of the past months his feeling for a courageous exploit or a heartfelt speech had unconsciously become associated with stages, speakers' platforms, or just chairs onto which you jumped to fling an appeal or ardent call to the crowds.

At the very doors of the station, under the station bell, there stood a water butt for use in case of fire. It was tightly covered. Gints jumped up on the lid and addressed the approaching soldiers with an incoherent but gripping speech. His unnatural voice and the insane boldness of his gesture, two steps from the door where he could so easily have taken shelter, amazed them and stopped them in their tracks. They lowered their rifles.

But Gints, who was standing on the edge of the lid, suddenly pushed it in. One of his legs slipped into the water and the other hung over the edge of the butt.

Seeing him sitting clumsily astride the edge of the butt, the soldiers burst into laughter and the one in front shot Gints in the neck. He was dead by the time the others ran up and thrust their bayonets into his body.

11

Mademoiselle called up Kolia and told him to find Dr. Zhivago a good seat in the train to Moscow, threatening him with exposure if he did not.

Kolia was as usual conducting another conversation and, judging by the decimal fractions that punctuated his speech, transmitting a message in code over a third instrument. "Pskov, Pskov, can you hear me? What rebels? What help? What are you talking about, Mademoiselle? Ring off, please. Pskov, Pskov, thirty-six point zero one five. Oh hell, they've cut me off. Hello, hello, I can't hear. Is that you again, Mademoiselle? I've told you, I can't. Ask Povarikhin. All lies, fictions. Thirty-six . . . Oh hell . . . Get off the line, Mademoiselle."

And Mademoiselle was saying:

"Don't you throw dust in my eyes, Pskov, Pskov, you liar. I can see right through you, tomorrow you'll put the doctor on the train, and I won't listen to another word from any murdering little Judases."

12

The day Yurii Andreievich left, it was sultry. A storm like the one that had broken two days earlier was brewing. Near the station, at the outskirts of the town, littered with the shells of sunflower seeds, the clay huts and the geese looked white and frightened under the still menace of the black sky.

The grass on the wide field in front of the station and stretching to both sides of it was trampled and entirely covered by a countless multitude who had for weeks been waiting for trains.

Old men in coarse gray woollen coats wandered about in the hot sun from group to group in search of news and rumors. Glum fourteen-year-old boys lay on their elbows twirling peeled twigs, as if they were tending cattle, while their small brothers and sisters scuttled about with flying shirts and pink bottoms. Their legs stretched straight in front of them, their mothers sat on the ground with babies packed into the tight shapeless bosoms of their brown peasants' coats.

"All scattered like sheep as soon as the shooting began. They didn't like it," the stationmaster told the doctor unsympathetically as they walked between the rows of bodies lying on the ground in front of the entrance and on the floors inside the station. "In a twinkling everybody cleared off the grass. You could see the ground again; we hadn't seen it in four months with all this gypsy camp going on, we'd forgotten what it looked like. This is where he lay. It's a strange thing, I've seen all sorts of horror in the war, you'd think I'd be used to anything. But I felt so sorry somehow. It was the senselessness of it. What had he done to them? But then they aren't human beings. They say he was the favorite son. And now to the right, if you please, into my office. There isn't a chance on this train, I'm afraid, they'd crush you to death. I'm putting you on a local one. We are making it up now. But not a word about it until you're ready to get on it, they'd tear it apart before it was made up. You change at Sukhinichi tonight."

13

When the "secret" train backed into the station from behind the railway sheds, the whole crowd poured onto the tracks. People rolled down the hills like marbles, scrambled onto the embankment, and, pushing each other, jumped onto the steps and buffers or climbed in through the windows and onto the roofs. The train filled in an instant, while it was still moving, and by the time it stood by the platform, not only was it crammed but passengers hung all over it, from top to bottom. By a miracle, the doctor managed to get onto a platform and from there, still more unaccountably, into the corridor.

There he stayed, sitting on his luggage, all the way to Sukhinichi.

The stormy sky had cleared. In the hot, sunny fields, crickets chirped loudly, muffling the clatter of the train.

Those passengers who stood by the windows shaded the rest

from the light. Their double and triple shadows streaked across the floor and benches. Indeed, these shadows went beyond the cars. They were crowded out through the opposite windows, and accompanied the moving shadow of the train itself.

All around people were shouting, bawling songs, quarrelling, and playing cards. Whenever the train stopped, the noise of the besieging crowds outside was added to this turmoil. The roar of the voices was deafening, like a storm at sea, and, as at sea, there would be a sudden lull. In the inexplicable stillness you could hear footsteps hurrying down the platform, the bustle and arguments outside the freight car, isolated words from people, farewells spoken in the distance, and the quiet clucking of hens and rustling of trees in the station garden.

Then, like a telegram delivered on the train, or like greetings from Meliuzeievo addressed to Yurii Andreievich, there drifted in through the windows a familiar fragrance. It came from somewhere to one side and higher than the level of either garden or wild flowers, and it quietly asserted its excellence over everything else.

Kept from the windows by the crowd, the doctor could not see the trees; but he imagined them growing somewhere very near, calmly stretching out their heavy branches to the carriage roofs, and their foliage, covered with dust from the passing trains and thick as night, was sprinkled with constellations of small, glittering waxen flowers.

This happened time and again throughout the trip. There were roaring crowds at every station. And everywhere the linden trees were in blossom.

This ubiquitous fragrance seemed to be preceding the train on its journey north as if it were some sort of rumor that had reached even the smallest, local stations, and which the passengers always found waiting for them on arrival, heard and confirmed by everyone.

14

That night at Sukhinichi a porter who had preserved his pre-war obligingness took the doctor over the unlit tracks to the back of some unscheduled train that had just arrived, and put him in a second-class carriage.

Hardly had he unlocked it with the conductor's key and heaved the doctor's luggage inside when the conductor came and tried to throw it out. He was finally appeased by Yurii Andreievich and withdrew and vanished without a trace.

The mysterious train was a "special" and went fairly fast, stopping only briefly at stations, and had some kind of armed guard. The carriage was almost empty.

Zhivago's compartment was lit by a guttering candle that stood on the small table, its flame wavering in the stream of air from the half-open window.

The candle belonged to the only other occupant of the compartment, a fair-haired youth who, judging by the size of his arms and legs, was very tall. His limbs seemed to be attached too loosely at the joints. He had been sprawling nonchalantly in a corner seat by the window, but when Zhivago came in he politely rose and sat up in a more seemly manner.

Something that looked like a floor cloth lay under his seat. One corner of it stirred and a flop-eared setter scrambled out. It sniffed Yurii Andreievich over and ran up and down the compartment throwing out its paws as loosely as its lanky master crossed his legs. Soon, at his command, it scrambled back under the seat and resumed its former likeness to a floor rag.

It was only then that Yurii Andreievich noticed the double-barrelled gun in its case, the leather cartridge belt, and the hunter's bag tightly packed with game that hung on a hook in the compartment.

The young man had been out shooting.

He was extremely talkative, and, smiling amiably, at once engaged the doctor in conversation, looking, as he did so, fixedly at his mouth.

He had an unpleasant, high-pitched voice that now and then rose to a tinny falsetto. Another oddity of his speech was that, while he was plainly Russian, he pronounced one vowel, *u*, in a most outlandish manner, like the French *u*. To utter even this garbled *u*, he had to make a great effort, and he pronounced it louder than any other sound, accompanying it each time with a slight squeal. At moments, apparently by concentrating, he managed to correct this defect but it always came back.

"What is this?" Zhivago wondered. "I'm sure I've read about it, as a doctor I ought to know, but I can't think what it is. It must be some brain trouble that causes defective speech." The squeal struck him as so funny that he could hardly keep a straight face. "Better go to bed," he told himself.

He climbed up onto the rack which was used as a berth. The young man offered to blow out the candle lest it keep him awake. The doctor accepted, thanking him, and the compartment was plunged into darkness.

"Shall I close the window?" Yurii Andreievich asked. "You are not afraid of thieves?"

There was no reply. He repeated his question louder, but there was still no answer.

He struck a match to see if his neighbor had gone out during the brief interval. That he had dropped off to sleep in so short a time seemed even more improbable.

He was there, however, sitting in his place with his eyes open. He smiled at the doctor, leaning over him from his berth.

The match went out. Yurii Andreievich struck another, and while it was alight repeated his question for the third time.

"Do as you wish," the young man replied at once. "I've got nothing a thief would want. But perhaps leave it open. It's stuffy."

"What an extraordinary character!" thought Zhivago. "An eccentric, evidently. Doesn't talk in the dark. And how distinctly he pronounced everything now, without any slur. It's beyond me."

15

Tired out by the events of the past week, the preparations for the trip, and the early start, the doctor expected to go to sleep the moment he had stretched comfortably, but he was mistaken. His exhaustion made him sleepless. Only at daybreak did he fall asleep.

His thoughts swarmed and whirled in the dark. But they all fell clearly into two distinct groups, as it were, two main threads that kept getting tangled and untangled.

One group of thoughts centered around Tonia, their home, and their former, settled life where everything, down to the smallest detail, had an aura of poetry and was permeated with affection and warmth. The doctor was concerned about this life, he wanted it safe and whole and in his night express was impatient to get back to it after two years of separation.

In the same group were his loyalty to the revolution and his admiration for it. This was the revolution in the sense in which it was accepted by the middle classes and in which it had been understood by the students, followers of Blok, in 1905.

These familiar, long-held ideas also included the anticipations and promises of a new order which had appeared on the horizon before the war, between 1912 and 1914, which had emerged in Russian thinking, in Russian art, in Russian life, and which had a bearing on Russia as a whole and on his own future.

It would be good to go back to that climate, once the war was over, to see its renewal and continuation, just as it was good to be going home.

New things were also in the other group of his thoughts, but how different, how unlike the first! These new things were not familiar, not led up to by the old, they were unchosen, determined by an ineluctable reality, and as sudden as an earthquake.

Among these new things was the war with its bloodshed and its horrors, its homelessness and savagery, its ordeals and the practical wisdom that it taught. So, too, were the lonely little towns to which the war washed you up, and the people you met in them. And among these new things too was the revolution— not the idealized intellectuals' revolution of 1905, but this new upheaval, today's, born of the war, bloody, ruthless, elemental, the soldiers' revolution led by those professional revolution- aries, the Bolsheviks.

And among the new thoughts, too, was Nurse Antipova, stranded by the war God knows where, about whose past he knew nothing, who never blamed anyone but whose very silence seemed to be a complaint, who was mysteriously reserved and so strong in her reserve. And so was Yurii Andreievich's honest endeavor not to love her, as wholehearted as his striving throughout his life until now to love everyone, not only his family and his friends, but everyone else as well.

The train rushed on at full speed. The head wind, coming through the open window, ruffled and blew dust on Yurii Andreievich's hair. At every station, by night as by day, the crowds stormed and the linden trees rustled.

Sometimes carts or gigs rattled up to the station out of the darkness, and voices and rumbling wheels mingled with the rustling of trees.

At such moments Yurii Andreievich felt he understood what it was that made these night shadows rustle and put their heads together, and what it was they whispered to each other, lazily stirring their leaves heavy with sleep, like faltering, lisping tongues. It was the very thing he was thinking of, turning restlessly in his berth—the tidings of the ever-widening circles of unrest and excitement in Russia, the tidings of the revolution, of its difficult and fateful hour and its probable ultimate greatness.

16

The doctor did not wake up until after eleven. "Prince, Prince," his neighbor was calling softly to his growling dog. To Yurii Andreievich's astonishment, they still had the compartment to themselves; no other passenger had got in.

The names of the stations were familiar to him from childhood. They were out of the province of Kaluga and well into that of Moscow.

He washed and shaved in prewar comfort and came back to the compartment in time for breakfast, to which his strange companion had invited him. Now he had a better look at him.

What struck him most were his extreme garrulousness and restlessness. He liked to talk, and what mattered to him was not communicating and exchanging ideas but the function of speech itself, pronouncing words and uttering sounds. As he spoke he kept jumping up as if he were on springs; he laughed deafeningly for no reason, briskly rubbing his hands with contentment, and, when all this seemed inadequate to express his delight, he slapped his knees hard, laughing to the point of tears.

His conversation had the same peculiarities as the night before. He was curiously inconsistent, now indulging in uninvited confidences, now leaving the most innocent questions unanswered. He poured out incredible and disconnected facts about himself. Perhaps he lied a little; he obviously was out to impress by his extremism and by his rejection of all commonly accepted opinions.

It all reminded Zhivago of something long familiar to him. Similar radical views were advanced by the nihilists of the last century, and a little later by some of Dostoievsky's heroes, and still more recently by their direct descendants, the provincial educated classes, who were often ahead of the capitals because they still were in the habit of going to the root of things while in the capitals such an approach was regarded as obsolete and unfashionable.

The young man told him that he was the nephew of a well-known revolutionary, but that his parents were incorrigible reactionaries, real dodoes, as he called them. They had a fairly large estate in a place near the front, where he had been brought up. His parents had been at swords' points with his uncle all their lives, but the uncle did not bear them a grudge and now used his influence to save them a good deal of unpleasantness.

His own views were like his uncle's, the talkative man informed Zhivago; he was an extremist in everything, whether in life, politics, or art. This too reminded the doctor of Piotr Verkhovensky*—not so much the leftism as the frivolity and the shallowness. "He'll be telling me he's a futurist next," thought Yurii Andreievich, and indeed they spoke of modern art. "Now it'll be sport—race horses, skating rinks, or French wrestling." And the conversation turned to shooting.

The young man had been shooting in his native region. He was a crack shot, he boasted, and if it had not been for the physical defect that had kept him out of the army he would have distinguished himself by his marksmanship. Catching Zhivago's questioning glance, he exclaimed: "What? Haven't you noticed anything? I thought you had guessed what was the matter with me."

He took two cards out of his pocket and handed them to Yurii Andreievich. One was his visiting card. He had a double name; he was called Maxim Aristarkhovich Klintsov-Pogorevshikh—or just Pogorevshikh, as he asked Zhivago to call him, in honor of his uncle who bore his name.

The other card showed a table with squares, each containing a drawing of two hands variously joined and with fingers differently folded. It was an alphabet for deaf-mutes. Suddenly everything became clear. Pogorevshikh was a phenomenally gifted pupil of the school of either Hartman or Ostrogradov, a deaf-mute who had reached an incredible facility in speaking

---

*Character in Dostoievsky's *The Possessed.*

and understanding speech by observing the throat muscles of his teachers.

Putting together what he had told him of the part of the country he came from and of his shooting expedition, the doctor said:

"Forgive me if this is indiscreet; you needn't tell me. Did you have anything to do with setting up the Zybushino republic?"

"But how did you guess . . . Do you know Blazheiko? Did I have anything to do with it? Of course I did!" Pogorevshikh burst forth joyfully, laughing, rocking from side to side, and frenziedly slapping his knees. And once again he launched on a long and fantastic discourse.

He said that Blazheiko had provided the opportunity and Zybushino the place for the application of his own theories. Yurii Andreievich found it hard to follow his exposition of them. Pogorevshikh's philosophy was a mixture of the principles of anarchism and hunters' tall stories.

Imperturbable as an oracle, he prophesied disastrous upheavals in the near future. Yurii Andreievich inwardly agreed that this was not unlikely, but the calm, authoritative tone in which this unpleasant boy was making his forecasts angered him.

"Just a moment," he said hesitantly. "True, all this may happen. But it seems to me that with all that's going on—the chaos, the disintegration, the pressure from the enemy—this is not the moment to start dangerous experiments. The country must be allowed to recover from one upheaval before plunging into another. We must wait till at least relative peace and order are restored."

"That's naïve," said Pogorevshikh. "What you call disorder is just as normal a state of things as the order you're so keen about. All this destruction—it's a natural and preliminary stage of a broad creative plan. Society has not yet disintegrated sufficiently. It must fall to pieces completely, then a genuinely revolutionary government will put the pieces together and build on completely new foundations."

Yurii Andreievich felt disturbed. He went out into the corridor.

The train, gathering speed, was approaching Moscow. It ran through birch woods dotted with summer houses. Small roofless suburban stations with crowds of vacationers flew by and were left far behind in the cloud of dust raised by the train, and seemed to turn like a carousel. The engine hooted repeatedly, and the sound filled the surrounding woods and came back in long, hollow echoes from far away.

All at once, for the first time in the last few days, Yurii Andreievich understood quite clearly where he was, what was happening to him, and what awaited him in an hour or so.

Three years of changes, moves, uncertainties, upheavals; the war, the revolution; scenes of destruction, scenes of death, shelling, blown-up bridges, fires, ruins—all this turned suddenly into a huge, empty, meaningless space. The first real event since the long interruption was this trip in the fast-moving train, the fact that he was approaching his home, which was intact, which still existed, and in which every stone was dear to him. This was real life, meaningful experience, the actual goal of all quests, this was what art aimed at—homecoming, return to one's family, to oneself, to true existence.

The woods had been left behind. The train broke out of the leafy tunnels into the open. A sloping field rose from a hollow to a wide mound. It was striped horizontally with dark green potato beds; beyond them, at the top of the mound, were cold frames. Opposite the field, beyond the curving tail of the train, a dark purple cloud covered half the sky. Sunbeams were breaking through it, spreading like wheel spokes and reflected by the glass of the frames in a blinding glare.

Suddenly, warm, heavy rain, sparkling in the sun, fell out of the cloud. The drops fell hurriedly and their drumming matched the clatter of the speeding train, as though the rain were afraid of being left behind and were trying to catch up.

Hardly had the doctor noticed this when the Church of Christ the Savior showed over the rim of the hill, and a minute later the domes, chimneys, roofs, and houses of the city.

"Moscow," he said, returning to the compartment. "Time to get ready."

Pogorevshikh jumped up, rummaged in his hunter's bag, and took out a fat duck. "Take it," he said. "As a souvenir. I have rarely spent a day in such pleasant company."

Zhivago's protests were unavailing. In the end he said: "All right, I'll take it as a present from you to my wife."

"Splendid, splendid, your wife," Pogorevshikh kept repeating delightedly, as though he had heard the word for the first time, jerking and laughing so much that Prince jumped out and took part in the rejoicing.

The train drew into the station. The compartment was plunged into darkness. The deaf-mute held out the wild duck, wrapped in a torn piece of some printed poster.

CHAPTER SIX

The Moscow Encampment

1

In the train it had seemed to Zhivago that only the train was moving but that time stood still and it was not later than noon.

But the sun was already low by the time his cab had finally made its way through the dense crowd in Smolensky Square.

In later years, when the doctor recalled this day, it seemed to him—he did not know whether this was his original impression or whether it had been altered by subsequent experiences—that even then the crowd hung about the market only by habit, that there was no reason for it to be there, for the empty stalls were shut and not even padlocked and there was nothing to buy or sell in the littered square, which was no longer swept.

And it seemed to him that even then he saw, like a silent reproach to the passersby, thin, decently dressed old men and women shrinking against the walls, wordlessly offering for sale things no one bought and no one needed—artificial flowers, round coffee pots with glass lids and whistles, black net evening dresses, uniforms of abolished offices.

Humbler people traded in more useful things—crusts of stale rationed black bread, damp, dirty chunks of sugar, and ounce packages of coarse tobacco cut in half right through the wrapping.

And all sorts of nondescript odds and ends were sold all over the market, going up in price as they changed hands.

The cab turned into one of the narrow streets opening from the square. Behind them, the setting sun warmed their backs. In front of them a draft horse clattered along, pulling an empty, bouncing cart. It raised pillars of dust, glowing like bronze in the rays of the low sun. At last they passed the cart which had blocked their way. They drove faster. The doctor was struck by the piles of old newspapers and posters, torn down from the walls and fences, littering the sidewalks and streets. The wind pulled them one way and hoofs, wheels, and feet shoved them the other.

They passed several intersections, and soon the doctor's house appeared at a corner. The cab stopped.

Yurii Andreievich gasped for breath and his heart hammered loudly as he got out, walked up to the front door, and rang the bell. Nothing happened. He rang again. As there was still no reply, he went on ringing at short, anxious intervals. He was still ringing when he saw that the door had been opened by Antonina Alexandrovna and that she stood holding it wide open. The unexpectedness of it so dumbfounded them both that neither of them heard the other cry out. But as the door held wide open by Tonia was in itself a welcome and almost an embrace, they soon recovered and rushed into each other's arms. A moment later they were both talking at once, interrupting each other.

"First of all, is everybody well?"

"Yes, yes, don't worry. Everything is all right. I wrote you a lot of silly nonsense, forgive me. But we'll talk about that later. Why didn't you send a telegram? Markel will take your things up. I suppose you got worried when Egorovna didn't let you in! She is in the country."

"You're thinner. But how young you look, and so pretty! Wait a minute, I'll pay the driver."

"Egorovna has gone to get some flour. The other servants have been discharged. There's only one girl now, Niusha, you don't know her, she's looking after Sashenka, there's no one else. Everybody has been told you're coming, they're all longing to see you—Gordon, Dudorov, everyone."

"How is Sashenka?"

"All right, thank God. He's just waked up. If you weren't still dirty from the train we could go to him at once."

"Is Father at home?"

"Didn't anyone write to you? He's at the borough council from morning till night, he's the chairman. Yes, can you believe it! Have you settled with the driver? Markel! Markel!"

They were standing in the middle of the street with wicker hamper and suitcase blocking the way, and the passersby, as they walked around them, looked them over from head to foot, and stared at the cab as it pulled away from the curb and at the wide-open front door, to see what would happen next.

But Markel was already running up from the gate to welcome the young master, his waistcoat over his cotton shirt and his porter's cap in his hand, shouting as he ran:

"Heavenly powers, if it isn't Yurochka! It's our little falcon in person! Yurii Andreievich, light of our eyes, so you haven't forgotten us and our prayers, you've come home! And what do you want?" he snapped at the curious. "Be off with you. What's there to goggle at?"

"How are you, Markel? Let's embrace. Put your cap on, you eccentric. Well, what's new? How's your wife? How are the girls?"

"How should they be? They're growing, thanks be to God. As for news, you can see for yourself, while you were busy at the front we were not idle either. Such a mess they made, such bedlam, the devil couldn't sort it out! The streets unswept, roofs unrepaired, houses unpainted, bellies empty as in Lent. Real peace there—no annexations and no reparations, as they say."

"I'll tell on you, Markel. He's always like that, Yurochka. I can't stand that foolishness. He's talking like that only because he thinks you like it, but he's a sly one. All right, all right, Markel, don't argue with me, I know you. You're a deep one, Markel. Time you were sensible. After all, you know what kind of people we are."

They went in. Markel carried the doctor's things inside, shut the front door behind him, and went on confidentially:

"Antonina Alexandrovna is cross, you heard what she said. It's always like that. She says, You're all black inside, Markel, she says, like that stovepipe. Nowadays, she says, every little child, maybe even every spaniel or any other lap dog knows what's what. That, of course, is true, but all the same, Yurochka, believe it or not, those who know have seen the book, the Mason's prophecies, one hundred and forty years it's been lying under a stone, and now, it's my considered opinion, Yurochka, we've been sold down the river, sold for a song. But can I say a word? See for yourself, Antonina Alexandrovna is making signs to me, she wants me to go."

"Do you wonder? That's enough, Markel, put the things down, and that will be all, thank you. If Yurii Andreievich wants anything, he'll call you."

2

"At last we've got rid of him! All right, all right, you can listen to him if you like, but I can tell you, it's all make-believe. You talk to him and you think he's the village idiot, butter wouldn't melt in his mouth, and all the time he's secretly sharpening his knife—only he hasn't quite decided yet whom he'll use it on, the charming fellow."

"Isn't that a bit far-fetched? I expect he's just drunk, that's all."

"And when is he sober, I'd like to know. Anyway, I've had enough of him. What worries me is, Sasha might go to sleep again before you've seen him. If it weren't for typhus on trains . . . You haven't any lice on you?"

"I don't think so. I travelled comfortably—the same as before the war. I'd better have a quick wash, though; I'll wash more thoroughly afterwards. Which way are you going? Don't we go through the drawing room anymore?"

"Oh, of course, you don't know. Father and I thought and thought and we decided to give up a part of the ground floor to the Agricultural Academy. It's too much to heat in winter, anyway. Even the top floor is too big. So we've offered it to them. They haven't taken it over yet, but they've moved in their libraries and their herbariums and their specimens of seed. I only hope we don't get rats—it's grain, after all. But at the moment they're keeping the rooms spick-and-span. By the way, we don't say 'rooms' anymore, it's called 'living space' now. Come on, this way. Aren't you slow to catch on! We go up the back stairs. Understand? Follow me, I'll show you."

"I'm very glad you've given up those rooms. The hospital I've been in was also in a private house. Endless suites of rooms, here and there the parquet flooring still left. Potted palms sticking out their paws like ghosts over the beds—some of the wounded from the battle zone used to wake up screaming— they weren't quite normal, of course—shell-shocked—we had

to remove the plants. What I mean is, there really was something unhealthy in the way rich people used to live. Masses of
superfluous things. Too much furniture, too much room, too
much emotional refinement, too many circumlocutions. I'm
very glad we're using fewer rooms. We should give up still
more."

"What's that parcel you've got? There's something sticking
out of it, it looks like a bird's beak. It's a duck! How lovely! A
wild drake! Where did you get it? I can't believe my eyes. It's
worth a fortune these days."

"Somebody made me a present of it on the train. I'll tell you
later, it's a long story. What shall I do? Shall I leave it in the
kitchen?"

"Yes, of course. I'll send Niusha down at once to pluck and
clean it. They say there will be all sorts of horrors this winter,
famine, cold."

"Yes, that's what they are saying everywhere. Just now, I was
looking out of the window in the train—I thought, what is there
in the whole world worth more than a peaceful family life and
work? The rest isn't in our hands. It does look as if there is a bad
time coming for a lot of people. Some are trying to get out, they
talk of going south, to the Caucasus, or farther still. I wouldn't
want to do that, myself. A grown-up man should share his
country's fate. To me it's obvious. But for you it's different. I
wish you didn't have to go through it all. I'd like to send you
away to some safe place—to Finland, perhaps. But if we stand
gossiping half an hour on every step we'll never get upstairs."

"Wait a minute. I forgot to tell you. I've got news for you—
and what news! Nikolai Nikolaievich is back."

"What Nikolai Nikolaievich?"

"Uncle Kolia."

"Tonia! It can't be! Is it really true?"

"It is true. He was in Switzerland. He came all the way
around through London and Finland."

"Tonia! You're not joking? Have you seen him? Where is he?
Can't we get him now, at once?"

"Don't be so impatient. He's staying with someone in the
country. He promised to be back the day after tomorrow. He's
changed a lot. You'll be disappointed. He stopped in Petersburg
on the way, he's got Bolshevized. Father gets quite hoarse
arguing with him. But why do we stop on every step. Let's go.
So you too have heard there's a bad time ahead—hardships,
dangers, anything might happen."

"I think so myself. Well, what of it? We'll manage, it can't be the end of everything. We'll wait and see, the same as other people."

"They say there won't be any firewood, or water, or light. They'll abolish money. No supplies will be coming in. Now we've stopped again! Come along. Listen, they say there are wonderful iron stoves for sale in the Arbat. Small ones. You can burn a newspaper and cook a meal. I've got the address. We must get one before they're all gone."

"That's right. We'll get one. Good idea. But just think of it, Uncle Kolia! I can't get over it."

"Let me tell you what I want to do. We'll set aside a corner somewhere on the top floor, say two or three rooms, communicating ones, and we'll keep those for ourselves and Father and Sashenka and Niusha, and we'll give up all the rest of the house. We'll put up a partition and have our own door, and it will be like a separate apartment. We'll put one of those iron stoves in the middle room, with a pipe through the window, and we'll do all our laundry, and our cooking, and our entertaining, all in this one room. That way we'll get the most out of the fuel, and who knows, with God's help, we'll get through the winter."

"Of course we'll get through it. There's no question. That's a fine idea. And you know what? We'll have a housewarming. We'll cook the duck and we'll invite Uncle Kolia."

"Lovely. And I'll ask Gordon to bring some drink. He can get it from some laboratory or other. Now look, this is the room I was thinking of. All right? Put your suitcase down and go get your hamper. We could ask Dudorov and Shura Shlesinger to the housewarming as well. You don't mind? You haven't forgotten where the washroom is? Spray yourself with some disinfectant. In the meantime I'll go in to Sashenka, and send Niusha down, and when we're ready I'll call you."

3

The most important thing for him in Moscow was his little boy. He had been mobilized almost as soon as Sashenka was born. He hardly knew him.

One day, while Tonia was still in the hospital, he went to see her; he was already in uniform and was about to leave Moscow. He arrived at the babies' feeding time and was not allowed in.

He sat down in the waiting room. From the nursery, at the end of the passage beyond the maternity ward, came the squealing chorus of ten or twelve babies' voices. Several nurses came down the corridor, hurrying so that the newborn babies should not catch cold, taking them to their mothers, bundled up like shopping parcels, one under each arm.

"Wa, wa," yelled the babies all on one note, almost impassively, without feeling, as if it were all in the day's work. Only one voice stood out from the others. It was also yelling "wa, wa," and it did not express any more suffering than the rest, but it was deeper and seemed to shout less out of duty than with a deliberate, sullen hostility.

Yurii Andreievich had already decided that his child was to be called Alexander in honor of his father-in-law. For some reason he imagined that the voice he had singled out was that of his son; perhaps it was because this particular cry had its own character and seemed to foreshadow the future personality and destiny of a particular human being; it had its own sound-coloring, which included the child's name, Alexander, so Yurii Andreievich imagined.

He was not mistaken. It turned out later that this had in fact been Sashenka's voice. It was the first thing he had known about his son.

The next thing was the photographs Tonia sent to him at the front. They showed a cheerful, handsome, chubby little fellow with a cupid's-bow mouth, standing up on a blanket, bandy-legged and with its fist up as if it were doing a peasant dance. Sashenka had been a year old at the time and trying to take his first steps; now he was two and was beginning to talk.

Yurii Andreievich picked up his suitcase, put it onto the card table by the window, and began to unpack. What had the room been used for in the past, he wondered. He could not recognize it. Tonia must have changed the furniture or the wallpaper or redecorated it in some way.

He took out his shaving kit. A bright full moon rose between the pillars of the church tower exactly opposite the window. When it lit up the top layer of clothes and books inside the suitcase, the light in the room changed and he realized where he was.

It had been Anna Ivanovna's storeroom, where she used to put broken chairs and tables and old papers. Here she had kept her family archives and, in the summer, the trunks of winter clothes. During her lifetime the corners were cluttered up to the ceiling with junk, and the children were not allowed in. Only at Christmas or Easter, when huge crowds of children came to parties and the whole of the top floor was thrown open to them, was it unlocked and they played bandit in it, hiding under the tables, dressing up, and blackening their faces with cork.

The doctor stood thinking of all this, then he went down the back stairs to get his wicker hamper from the hall.

In the kitchen Niusha squatted in front of the stove, plucking the duck on a piece of newspaper. When he came in carrying his hamper she jumped up with a shy, graceful movement, blushing crimson, shook the feathers from her apron, and, after greeting him respectfully, offered to help him. He thanked her, saying he could manage, and went up. His wife called him from a couple of rooms farther on: "You can come in now, Yura."

He went into the room, which was Tonia's and his old classroom. The boy in the crib was not nearly so handsome as in his photograph, but he was the exact same image of Yurii Andreievich's mother, Maria Nikolaievna Zhivago, a more striking likeness than any of her portraits.

"Here's Daddy, here's your Daddy, wave your hand like a good boy," Antonina Alexandrovna was saying. She lowered the net of the crib to make it easier for the father to kiss the boy and pick him up.

Sashenka, though doubtless frightened and repelled, let the unshaven stranger get quite close and bend over him, then he jerked himself upright, clutching the front of his mother's dress with one hand, and angrily swung the other arm and slapped him in the face. Terrified by his own daring, he then threw himself into his mother's arms and burst into bitter tears.

"No, no," Tonia scolded him. "You mustn't do that, Sashenka. What will Daddy think? He'll think Sasha is a bad boy. Now, show how you can kiss, kiss Daddy. Don't cry, silly, it's all right."

"Let him be, Tonia," the doctor said. "Don't bother him, and don't upset yourself. I know the kind of nonsense you are thinking—that it's not accidental, it's a bad sign—but that's all rubbish. It's only natural. The boy has never seen me. Tomorrow he'll have a good look at me and we'll become inseparable."

Yet he went out of the room depressed and with a feeling of foreboding.

4

Within the next few days he realized how alone he was. He did not blame anyone. He had merely got what he had asked for.

His friends had become strangely dim and colorless. Not one of them had preserved his own outlook, his own world. They had been much more vivid in his memory. He must have overestimated them in the past. Under the old order, which enabled those whose lives were secure to play the fools and eccentrics at the expense of the others while the majority led a wretched existence, it had been only too easy to mistake the foolishness and idleness of a privileged minority for genuine character and originality. But the moment the lower classes had risen, and the privileges of those on top had been abolished, how quickly had those people faded, how unregretfully had they renounced independent ideas—apparently no one had ever had such ideas!

The only people to whom Yurii Andreievich now felt close were his wife, her father, and two or three of his colleagues, modest rank-and-file workers, who did not indulge in grandiloquent phrases.

The party with duck and vodka was given as planned, a few days after his return. By then he had seen all those who came to it, so that the dinner was not in fact the occasion of their reunion.

The large duck was an unheard-of luxury in those already hungry days, but there was no bread with it, and because of this its splendor was somehow pointless—it even got on one's nerves.

The alcohol (a favorite black-market currency) had been brought by Gordon in a medicine bottle with a glass stopper. Antonina Alexandrovna never let go of the bottle, and now and then diluted a small portion of the alcohol with more or less water, according to her inspiration. It was discovered that it is easier to hold a number of consistently strong drinks than ones of varying strength. This, too, was annoying.

But the saddest thing of all was that their party was a kind of betrayal. You could not imagine anyone in the houses across the street eating or drinking in the same way at the same time. Beyond the windows lay silent, dark, hungry Moscow. Its shops were empty, and as for game and vodka, people had even forgotten to think about such things.

And so it turned out that only a life similar to the life of those around us, merging with it without a ripple, is genuine life, and that an unshared happiness is not happiness, so that duck and vodka, when they seem to be the only ones in town, are not even duck and vodka. And this was most vexing of all.

The guests too inspired unhappy reflections. Gordon had been all right in the days when he was given to gloomy thoughts and expressed them sullenly and clumsily. He was Zhivago's best friend, and in the gymnasium many people had liked him.

But now he had decided to give himself a new personality, and the results of his efforts were unfortunate. He played the merry fellow, he was jovial, cracked jokes, and often exclaimed, "What fun!" and "How amusing!"—expressions that did not belong to his vocabulary, for Gordon had never looked upon life as an entertainment.

While they were waiting for Dudorov he told the story of Dudorov's marriage, which he thought was comical, and which was circulating among his friends. Yurii Andreievich had not yet heard it.

It turned out that Dudorov had been married for about a year and then divorced his wife. The improbable gist of this story consisted in the following:

Dudorov had been drafted into the army by mistake. While he was serving and his case was being investigated, he was constantly punished for absent-mindedly forgetting to salute officers in the street. For a long time after his discharge he would raise his arm impulsively whenever an officer came in sight, and often he imagined epaulettes where there were none.

In this latter period his behavior was erratic in other ways as well. At one point—so the rumor went—while waiting for a steamer at a Volga port, he made the acquaintance of two young women, sisters, who were waiting for the same steamer. Confused by the presence of a large number of army men and the memories of his misadventures as a soldier, he fell in love with the younger sister, and proposed to her on the spot. "Amusing, isn't it?" Gordon said. But he had to interrupt his story when its hero was heard at the door. Dudorov entered the room.

Like Gordon, he had become the opposite of what he had been. He had always been flippant and featherbrained: now he was a serious scholar. As a schoolboy he had been expelled for helping political prisoners escape; he had then tried several art schools, but in the end had become a student of the humanities. During the war he graduated from the university a few years behind his schoolmates. Now he held two chairs—those of Russian history and of general history. He was even the author of two books, one on the land policies of Ivan the Terrible, the other a study of Saint-Just.

Here at the party he spoke amiably about everyone and everything, in a voice that was muffled as though by a cold, staring dreamily at a certain fixed point in the distance like a man delivering a lecture.

Toward the end of the evening, when Shura Shlesinger burst in and added to the general noise and excitement, Dudorov, who had been Zhivago's childhood friend, asked him several times, addressing him with the formal "you" rather than the usual "thou," whether he had read Mayakovsky's *War and the World* and *Flute-Spine*.

Missing Yurii Andreievich's reply in all the noise, he asked him again a little later: "Have you read *Flute-Spine* and *Man?*"

"I told you, Innokentii. It's not my fault that you don't listen. Well, all right, I'll say it again. I've always liked Mayakovsky. He is a sort of continuation of Dostoievsky. Or rather, he's a Dostoievsky character writing lyrical poems—one of his young rebels, the 'Raw Youth' or Hippolyte or Raskolnikov. What an all-devouring poetic energy! And his way of saying a thing once and for all, uncompromisingly, straight from the shoulder! And above all, with what daring he flings all this in the face of society and beyond, into space!"

But the main attraction of the evening was, of course, Uncle Kolia. Antonina Alexandrovna had been mistaken in thinking that he was out of town; he had come back the day of his nephew's return. They had met a couple of times already and had got over their initial exclamations and had talked and laughed together to their heart's content.

The first time had been on a dull, gray night with a drizzle, fine as watery dust. Yurii Andreievich went to see him at his hotel. The hotels were already refusing to take people in except at the recommendation of the town authorities, but Nikolai Nikolaievich was well known and had kept some of his old connections.

The hotel looked like a lunatic asylum abandoned by its staff—the stairways and corridors empty, everything in a state of chaos.

Through the large window of his unswept room the huge square of those mad days looked in, deserted and frightening, more like a square in a nightmare than the one plainly to be seen in front of the hotel.

For Yurii Andreievich the encounter was a tremendous, unforgettable event. He was seeing the idol of his childhood, the teacher who had dominated his mind as a boy.

His gray hair was becoming to him, and his loose foreign suit fitted him well. He was very young and handsome for his years.

Admittedly, he was overshadowed by the grandeur of the events; seen beside them, he lost in stature. But it never occurred to Yurii Andreievich to measure him by such a yardstick.

He was surprised at Nikolai Nikolaievich's calm, at his light and detached tone in speaking of politics. He was more self-possessed than most Russians could be at that time. It marked him as a new arrival, and it seemed old-fashioned and a little embarrassing.

But it was something very different from politics that filled those first few hours of their reunion, that made them laugh and cry and throw their arms around each other's neck, and punctuated their first feverish conversation with frequent moments of silence.

Theirs was a meeting of two artists, and although they were close relatives, and the past arose and lived again between them and memories surged up and they informed each other of all that had happened during their separation, the moment they began to speak of the things that really matter to creative minds, all other ties between them vanished, their kinship and difference of age were forgotten, all that was left was the confrontation of elemental forces, of energies and principles.

For the last ten years Nikolai Nikolaievich had had no opportunity to speak about the problems of creative writing as freely and intimately as now. Nor had Yurii Andreievich ever heard views as penetrating, apt, and inspiring as on that occasion.

Their talk was full of exclamations, they paced excitedly up and down the room, marvelling at each other's perspicacity, or stood in silence by the window drumming on the glass, deeply moved by the exalting discovery of how completely they understood each other.

Such was their first meeting, but later the doctor had seen his uncle a few times in company, and then Nikolai Nikolaievich was completely different, unrecognizable.

He felt that he was a visitor in Moscow and persisted in acting like one. Whether it was Petersburg that he regarded as his home, or some other place, remained uncertain. He enjoyed his role of a social star and political oracle, and possibly he imagined that Moscow would have political salons in the style of Madame Roland's in Paris on the eve of the Convention.

Calling on his women friends at their hospitable apartments in quiet Moscow back streets, he amiably teased them and their husbands on their backwardness and parochialism. He showed off his familiarity with newspapers, as he had done formerly with books forbidden by the Church, and Orphic texts.

It was said that he had left a new young love, much unfinished business, and a half-written book in Switzerland, and had only come for a dip into the stormy waters of his homeland, expecting, if he came out safe and sound, to hasten back to his Alps.

He was pro-Bolshevik, and often mentioned two left-wing Social Revolutionaries who shared his views, a journalist who wrote under the pseudonym of Miroshka Pomor and a pamphleteer, Sylvia Koteri.

"It's frightful, what you've come down to, Nikolai Nikolaievich," Alexander Alexandrovich chided him. "You and your Miroshkas! What a cesspool! And then that Lydia Pokori."

"Koteri," corrected Nikolai Nikolaievich, "and Sylvia."

"Pokori or Potpourri, who cares. Names won't change anything."

"All the same, it happens to be Koteri," Nikolai Nikolaievich insisted patiently. They had dialogues of this sort:

"What are we arguing about? It's so obvious that it makes you blush to have to prove it. It's elementary. For centuries the mass of the people have lived impossible lives. Take any history textbook. Whatever it was called—feudalism and serfdom or capitalism and industrial workers, it was unnatural and unjust. This has been known for a long time, and the world has been preparing for an upheaval that would bring enlightenment to the people and put everything in its proper place.

"You know perfectly well that it's quite useless tinkering with the old structure, you have to dig right down to the foundations. I don't say the whole building mayn't collapse as a result. What of it? The fact that it's frightening doesn't mean it won't happen. It's a question of time. How can you dispute it?"

"That's not the point, that's not what I was talking about," Alexander Alexandrovich said angrily, and the argument flared up. "Your Potpourris and Miroshkas are people without a conscience. They say one thing and do another. Anyway, where's your logic? It's a complete non sequitur. No, wait a minute, I'll show you something," and he would begin hunting for some newspaper with a controversial article, banging the drawers of his desk and stimulating his eloquence with this noisy fuss.

Alexander Alexandrovich liked something to get in his way when he was talking; the distraction served as an excuse for his mumbling and his hems and haws. His fits of talkativeness came on him when he was looking for something he had lost—say, hunting for a matching snow boot in the dimly lighted cloakroom—or when he stood at the bathroom door with a towel over his arm, or when he was passing a heavy serving dish or pouring wine into the glasses of his friends.

Yurii Andreievich enjoyed listening to his father-in-law. He adored the familiar, old-Moscow singsong and the soft, purring Gromeko r's.

Alexander Alexandrovich's upper lip with its little cropped mustache protruded above the lower lip in just the same way as his butterfly tie stuck out from his neck. There was something in common between the lip and the tie, and it somehow gave him a touching, childishly trusting look.

On the night of the party Shura Shlesinger appeared very late. She had come straight from a meeting and was wearing a suit and a worker's cap. She strode into the room and, shaking everyone's hand in turn, at once burst into complaints and accusations.

"How are you, Tonia? Hello, Alexander. You must admit it's disgusting. The whole of Moscow knows he's back, everyone is talking about it, and I am the last to be told. Well, I suppose I'm not good enough. Where is he, anyway? Let me get at him, you surround him like a wall. Well, how are you? I've read it, I don't understand a word, but it's brilliant, you can tell at once. How are you, Nikolai Nikolaievich? I'll be back in a moment, Yurochka, I've got to talk to you. Hello, young men. You're here too, Gogochka, Goosey-Goosey-Gander" (this to a distant relative of the Gromekos', an enthusiastic admirer of all rising talents, known as Goosey because of his idiot laugh and as the Tapeworm on account of his lankiness). "So you're eating and drinking? I'll soon catch up with you. Well, my friends, you've simply no idea what you're missing. You don't know anything, you haven't seen a thing. If you only knew what's going on! You go and have a look at a real mass meeting, with real workers, real soldiers, not out of books. Just try to let out a squeak to them about fighting the war to a victorious end! They'll give you a victorious end! I've just been listening to a sailor—Yurochka, you'd simply rave! What passion! What single-mindedness!"

Shura was interrupted time and again. Everyone shouted. She sat next to Yurii Andreievich, took his hand in hers, and, moving her face close to his, shouted like a megaphone above the din:

"Let me take you along someday, Yurochka. I'll show you real people. You must, you simply must get your feet on the ground, like Antaeus. Why are you staring at me like that? I'm an old war horse, didn't you know? An old Bestuzhevist.* I've seen the inside of a prison, I've fought on the barricades.—Well of course, what did you think? Oh, we don't know the people at all. I've just come from there, I was right in the thick of it. I'm collecting a library for them."

She had had a drink and was obviously getting tipsy. But Yurii Andreievich's head was also spinning. He never noticed how it happened that Shura was now at one end of the room and he at the other; he was standing at the head of the table and apparently, quite unexpectedly to himself, making a speech. It took him some time to get silence.

"Ladies and gentlemen . . . I should like . . . Misha! Gogochka! Tonia, what am I to do, they won't listen! Ladies and gentlemen, let me say a word or two. Unprecedented, extra-ordinary events are approaching. Before they burst upon us, here is what I wish you: May God grant us not to lose each other and not to lose our souls. Gogochka, you can cheer afterwards, I haven't finished. Stop talking in the corners and listen carefully.

"In this third year of the war the people have become convinced that the difference between those on the front line and those at the rear will sooner or later vanish. The sea of blood will rise until it reaches every one of us and submerge all who stayed out of the war. The revolution is this flood.

"During the revolution it will seem to you, as it seemed to us at the front, that life has stopped, that there is nothing personal left, that there is nothing going on in the world except killing

---

*A student taking the Bestuzhev university courses for women. Many of the students were left-wing.

and dying. If we live long enough to read the chronicles and memoirs of this period, we shall realize that in these five or ten years we have experienced more than other people do in a century. I don't know whether the people will rise of themselves and advance spontaneously like a tide, or whether everything will be done in the name of the people. Such a tremendous event requires no dramatic proof of its existence. I'll be convinced without proof. It's petty to explore causes of titanic events. They haven't any. It's only in a family quarrel that you look for beginnings—after people have pulled each other's hair and smashed the dishes they rack their brains trying to figure out who started it. What is truly great is without beginning, like the universe. It confronts us as suddenly as if it had always been there or had dropped out of the blue.

"I too think that Russia is destined to become the first socialist state since the beginning of the world. When this comes to pass, the event will stun us for a long time, and after awakening we shall have lost half our memories forever. We'll have forgotten what came first and what followed, and we won't look for causes. The new order of things will be all around us and as familiar to us as the woods on the horizon or the clouds over our heads. There will be nothing else left."

He said a few more things, and by then he had sobered up completely. As before, he could not hear clearly what people were saying, and answered them pointlessly. He saw that they liked him, but could not rid himself of the sadness that oppressed him. He said:

"Thank you, thank you. I appreciate your feelings, but I don't deserve them. It's wrong to bestow love in a hurry, as though otherwise one would later have to give much more of it."

They all laughed and clapped, taking it for a deliberate witticism, while he did not know where to escape from his forebodings of disaster and his feeling that despite his striving for the good and his capacity for happiness, he had no power over the future.

The guests began to leave. They had long, tired faces. Their yawns, snapping and unsnapping their jaws, made them look like horses.

Before going, they drew the curtains and pushed the windows open. There was a yellowish dawn in the wet sky filled with dirty, pea-colored clouds. "Looks as if there's been a storm while we were chattering," said someone. "I was caught in the rain on my way here, I only just made it," Shura confirmed.

In the deserted street it was still dark and the drip-drip of the water from the trees alternated with the insistent chirruping of drenched sparrows.

There was a roll of thunder, as if a plow had been dragged right across the sky. Then silence. Then four loud, delayed thuds, like overgrown potatoes in autumn being flung out with a shovel from the soft ground.

The thunder cleared the dusty, smoke-filled room. Suddenly the element of life became distinguishable, as apprehensible as electric currents, air and water, desire for happiness, earth, sky.

The street filled with the voices of the departing guests. They had begun a heated argument in the house and continued arguing just as hotly in the street. Gradually the voices grew fainter in the distance and died out.

"How late it is," said Yurii Andreievich. "Let's go to bed. The only people I love in the world are you and Father."

5

August had gone by and now September was almost over. The inevitable was approaching. Winter was near and, in the human world, something like a state of suspended animation, which was in the air, and which everyone was talking about.

This was the time to prepare for the cold weather, to store up food and wood. But in those days of the triumph of materialism, matter had become a disembodied idea, and the problems of alimentation and fuel supply took the place of food and firewood.

The people in the cities were as helpless as children in the face of the unknown—that unknown which swept every established habit aside and left nothing but desolation in its wake, although it was itself the offspring of the city and the creation of city-dwellers.

All around, people continued to deceive themselves, to talk endlessly. Everyday life struggled on, by force of habit, limping and shuffling. But the doctor saw life as it was. It was clear to him that it was under sentence. He looked upon himself and his milieu as doomed. Ordeals were ahead, perhaps death. Their days were counted and running out before his eyes.

He would have gone insane had he not been kept busy by the

details of daily life. His wife, his child, the necessity to earn money, the humble daily ritual of his practice—these were his salvation.

He realized that he was a pygmy before the monstrous machine of the future; he was anxious about this future, and loved it and was secretly proud of it, and as though for the last time, as if in farewell, he avidly looked at the trees and clouds and the people walking in the streets, the great Russian city struggling through misfortune—and was ready to sacrifice himself for the general good, and could do nothing.

He most often saw the sky and the people from the middle of the street when he crossed the Arbat at the corner of Old Coachyard Row, near the pharmacy of the Russian Medical Society.

He resumed his duties at his old hospital. It was still called the Hospital of the Holy Cross, although the society of that name had been dissolved. So far no one had thought of a new name for the hospital.

The staff had already divided up into camps. To the moderates, whose obtuseness made the doctor indignant, he seemed dangerous; to those whose politics were advanced, not Red enough. Thus he belonged to neither group, having moved away from the former and lagging behind the latter.

In addition to his normal duties, the medical chief had put him in charge of general statistics. Endless questionnaires and forms went through his hands. Death rate, sickness rate, the earnings of the staff, the degree of their political consciousness and of their participation in the elections, the perpetual shortage of fuel, food, medicines, everything had to be checked and reported.

Zhivago worked at his old table by the staff-room window, stacked with charts and forms of every size and shape. He had pushed them to one side; occasionally, in addition to taking notes for his medical works, he wrote in snatches his "Playing at People, a Gloomy Diary or Journal Consisting of Prose, Verse, and What-have-you, Inspired by the Realization that Half the People Have Stopped Being Themselves and Are Acting Unknown Parts."

The light, sunny room with its white painted walls was filled with the creamy light of the golden autumn days that follow the Feast of the Assumption, when the mornings begin to be frosty and titmice and magpies dart into the bright-leaved, thinning woods. On such days the sky is incredibly high, and through the transparent pillar of air between it and the earth there moves an icy, dark-blue radiance coming from the north. Everything in the world becomes more visible and more audible. Distant sounds reach us in a state of frozen resonance, separately and clearly. The horizons open, as if to show the whole of life for years ahead. This rarefied light would be unbearable if it were not so short-lived, coming at the end of the brief autumn day just before the early dusk.

Such was now the light in the staff room, the light of an early autumn sunset, as succulent, glassy, juicy as a certain variety of Russian apple.

The doctor sat at his desk writing, pausing to think and to dip his pen while some unusually quiet birds flew silently past the tall windows, throwing shadows on his moving hands, on the table with its forms, and on the floor and the walls, and just as silently vanished from sight.

The prosector came in; he was a stout man who had lost so much weight that his skin hung on him in bags. "The maple leaves are nearly all gone," he said. "When you think how they stood up to all the rain and wind, and now a single morning frost has done it."

The doctor looked up. The mysterious birds darting past the window had in fact been wine-red maple leaves. They flew away from the trees, gliding through the air, and covered the hospital lawn, looking like bent orange stars.

"Have the windows been puttied up?" the prosector asked.

"No," Yurii Andreievich said, and went on writing.

"Isn't it time they were?"

Yurii Andreievich, absorbed in his work, did not answer.

"Pity Taraska's gone," went on the prosector. "He was worth his weight in gold. Patch your boots or repair your watch—he'd do anything. And he could get you anything in the world. Now we'll have to do the windows ourselves."

"There's no putty."

"You can make some. I'll give you the recipe." He explained how you made putty with linseed oil and chalk. "Well, I'll leave you now. I suppose you want to get on with your work."

He went off to the other window and busied himself with his bottles and specimens. "You'll ruin your eyes," he said a minute later. "It's getting dark. And they won't give you any light. Let's go home."

"I'll work another twenty minutes or so."

"His wife is a nurse here."

"Whose wife?"

"Taraska's."

"I know."

"Nobody knows where he is himself. He prowls about all over the country. Last summer he came twice to see his wife, now he's in some village. He's building the new life. He's one of those soldier-Bolsheviks, you see them everywhere, walking about in the streets, travelling in trains. And do you know what makes them tick? Take Taraska. He can turn his hand to anything. Whatever he does, he has to do it well. That's what happened to him in the army—he learned to fight, just like any other trade. He became a crack rifleman. His eyes and hands—first-class! All his decorations were awarded him, not for courage, but for always hitting the mark. Well, anything he takes up becomes a passion with him, so he took to fighting in a big way. He could see what a rifle does for a man—it gives him power, it brings him distinction. He wanted to be a power himself. An armed man isn't just a man like any other. In the old days such men turned from soldiers into brigands. You just try to take Taraska's rifle away from him now! Well, then came the slogan 'Turn your bayonets against your masters,' so Taraska turned. That's the whole story. There's Marxism for you."

"That's the most genuine kind—straight from life. Didn't you know?"

The prosector went back to his test tubes.

"How did you make out with the stove specialist?" he asked after a while.

"I'm most grateful to you for sending him. A most interesting man. We spent hours talking about Hegel and Croce."

"Naturally! Took his doctorate in philosophy at Heidelberg. What about the stove?"

"That's not so good."

"Still smoking?"

"Never stops."

"He can't have fixed the stovepipe right. It ought to be connected with a flue. Did he let it out through the window?"

"No, the flue, but it still smokes."

"Then he can't have found the right air vent. If only we had Taraska! But you'll get it right in the end. Moscow wasn't built in a day. Getting a stove to work isn't like playing the piano, it takes skill. Have you laid in your firewood?"

"Where am I to get it from?"

"I'll send you the church janitor. He's an expert at stealing wood. Takes fences to pieces and turns them into firewood. But you'll have to bargain with him. No, better get the exterminator."

They went down to the cloakroom, put their coats on, and went out.

"Why the exterminator? We don't have bedbugs."

"That's got nothing to do with it. I'm talking about wood. The exterminator is an old woman who is doing a big business in wood. She's got it all set up on a proper business footing— buys up whole houses for fuel. It's dark, watch your step. In the old days I could have taken you blindfold anywhere in this district. I knew every stone. I was born near here. But since they've started pulling down the fences I can hardly find my way about, even by day. It's like being in a strange town. On the other hand, some extraordinary places have come to light. Little Empire houses you never knew were there, with round garden tables and half-rotten benches. The other day I passed a place like that, a sort of little wilderness at an intersection of three streets, and there was an old lady poking about with a stick—she must have been about a hundred. 'Hello, Granny,' I said, 'are you looking for worms to go fishing?' I was joking, of course, but she took it quite seriously. 'No, not worms,' she said, 'mushrooms.' And it's true, you know, the town is getting to be like the woods. There's a smell of decaying leaves and mushrooms."

"I think I know where you mean—between Serebriany and Molchanovka, isn't it? The strangest things are always happening to me there—either I meet someone I haven't seen in twenty years, or I find something. They say it's dangerous, and no wonder, there's a whole network of alleys leading to the old thieves' dens near Smolensky. Before you know where you are, they've stripped you to the skin and vanished."

"And look at those street lamps—they don't shine at all. No wonder they call bruises shiners. Be careful you don't bump yourself."

6

All sorts of things did indeed happen to the doctor at that place. One cold dark night, shortly before the October fighting, he came across a man lying unconscious on the sidewalk, his arms flung out, his head against a curbstone, and his feet in the gutter. Occasionally he uttered weak groans. When the doctor tried to rouse him he muttered a few words, something about a wallet. He had been attacked and robbed. His head was battered and covered with blood, but a casual examination revealed that the skull was intact.

Zhivago went to the pharmacy in the Arbat, telephoned for the cab that the hospital used in emergencies, and took the patient to the emergency ward.

The wounded man proved to be a prominent political leader. The doctor treated him till he recovered, and for years afterwards this man acted as his protector, getting him out of trouble several times in those days that were so heavy with suspicion.

7

Antonina Alexandrovna's plan had been adopted and the family had settled for the winter in three rooms on the top floor.

It was a cold, windy Sunday, dark with heavy snow clouds. The doctor was off duty.

The fire was lit in the morning, and the stove began to smoke. Niusha struggled with the damp wood. Antonina Alexandrovna, who knew nothing about stoves, kept giving her absurd and bad advice. The doctor, who did know, tried to interfere, but his wife took him gently by the shoulders and pushed him out of the room, saying: "Don't you meddle in this. You'll only pour oil on the fire."

"Oil wouldn't be so bad, Toniechka, the stove would be ablaze at once! The trouble is, there is neither oil nor fire."

"This is no time for jokes. There are moments when they are out of place."

The trouble with the stove upset everyone's plans. They had all hoped to get their chores done before dark and have a free evening, but now dinner would be late, there was no hot water, and various other plans might have to be dropped.

The fire smoked more and more. The strong wind blew the smoke back into the room. A cloud of black soot stood in it like a fairy-tale monster in a thick wood.

Finally Yurii Andreievich drove everyone out into the two other rooms, and opened the top pane of the window. He removed half the wood from the stove, and spaced out the rest with chips and birchwood shavings between them.

Fresh air rushed in through the window. The curtain swayed and flew up. Papers blew off the desk. A door banged somewhere down the hall, and the wind began a cat-and-mouse game with what was left of the smoke.

The logs flared up and crackled. The stove was ablaze. Its iron body was covered with red-hot spots like a consumptive flush. The smoke in the room thinned out and soon vanished.

The room grew lighter. The windows, which Yurii Andreievich had recently fixed according to the prosector's recipe, gave off the warm, greasy smell of putty. An acrid smell of charred fir bark and the fresh, toilet-water scent of aspen came from the wood drying by the stove.

Nikolai Nikolaievich burst into the room as impetuously as the wind coming through the open window.

"They're fighting in the street," he reported. "There is a regular battle between the cadets who support the Provisional Government and the garrison soldiers who support the Bolsheviks. There is skirmishing all over the city. I got into trouble coming here—once at the corner of Bolshaia Dmitrovka and once at the Nikitsky Gate. Now you can't get through directly, you have to go around. Hurry up, Yura! Put your coat on, let's go. You've got to see it. This is history. This happens once in a lifetime."

But he stayed talking for a couple of hours. Then they had dinner, and by the time he was ready to go home and was dragging the doctor out, Gordon burst in, in exactly the same way as Nikolai Nikolaievich and with much the same news.

Things had progressed, however. There were new details. Gordon spoke of increasing rifle fire and of passersby killed by stray bullets. According to him, all traffic had stopped. He had got through by a miracle, but now the street was cut off.

Nikolai Nikolaievich refused to believe him and dashed out but was back in a minute. He said bullets whistled down the street knocking chips of brick and plaster off the corners. There was not a soul outside. All traffic had stopped.

That week Sashenka caught a cold.

"I've told you a hundred times, he's not to play near the stove," Yurii Andreievich scolded. "It's much worse to let him get too hot than cold."

Sashenka had a sore throat and a fever. He had a special, overwhelming terror of vomiting, and when Yurii Andreievich tried to examine his throat he pushed away his hand, clenching his teeth, yelling and choking. Neither arguments nor threats had the slightest effect on him. At one moment, however, he inadvertently yawned, and the doctor quickly took advantage of this to insert a spoon into his son's mouth and hold down his tongue for long enough to get a look at his raspberry-colored larynx and swollen tonsils covered with alarming white spots.

A little later, by means of a similar maneuver, he got a specimen and, as he had a microscope at home, was able to examine it. Fortunately, it was not diphtheria.

But on the third night Sashenka had an attack of nervous croup. His temperature shot up and he could not breathe. Yurii Andreievich was helpless to ease his suffering and could not bear to watch it. Antonina Alexandrovna thought the child was dying. They carried him about the room in turn, and this seemed to make him feel better.

They needed milk, mineral water, or soda water for him. But the street fighting was at its height. Gun and rifle fire never ceased for a moment. Even if Yurii Andreievich had crossed the battle zone at the risk of his life, he would not have found anyone about in the streets beyond it. All life in the city was suspended until the situation would be definitively clarified.

Yet there could be no doubt about the outcome. Rumors came from all sides that the workers were getting the upper hand. Small groups of cadets were fighting on, but they were cut off from each other and from their command.

The Sivtzev quarter was held by soldiers' units who were pressing on toward the center. Soldiers who had fought against Germany and young working boys sat in a trench they had dug down the street; they were already getting to know the people who lived in the neighborhood and joked with them as they came and stood outside their gates. Traffic in this part of the town was being restored.

Gordon and Nikolai Nikolaievich, who had got stuck at the Zhivagos', were released from their three days' captivity. Zhivago had been glad of their presence during Sashenka's illness, and his wife forgave them for adding to the general disorder. But they had felt obliged to repay the kindness of their hosts by entertaining them with ceaseless talk. Yurii Andreievich was so exhausted by three days of pointless chatter that he was happy to see them go.

8

They learned that their guests had got home safely. But military operations continued, several streets were still closed, and the doctor could not yet go to his hospital. He was impatient to return to his work and the manuscript he had left in the drawer of the staff-room desk.

Only here and there did people come out in the morning and walk a short distance to buy bread. When they saw a passerby carrying a milk bottle, they would surround him trying to find out where he had got it.

Occasionally the firing resumed all over the town, and the streets were cleared again. It was said that the two sides were engaged in negotiations, whose course, favorable or unfavorable, was reflected in the varying intensity of the firing.

At about 10 P.M. one evening in late October (Old Style) Yurii Andreievich went without any particular necessity to call on one of his colleagues. The streets he passed were deserted. He walked quickly. The first thin powdery snow was coming down, scattered by a rising wind.

He had turned down so many side streets that he had almost lost count of them when the snow thickened and the wind turned into a blizzard, the kind of blizzard that whistles in a field covering it with a blanket of snow, but which in town tosses about as if it had lost its way.

There was something in common between the disturbances in the moral and in the physical world, near and far on the ground and in the air. Here and there resounded the last salvoes of islands of resistance. Bubbles of dying fires rose and broke on the horizon. And the snow swirled and eddied and smoked at Yurii's feet, on the wet streets and pavements.

A newsboy running with a thick batch of freshly printed papers under his arm and shouting "Latest news!" overtook him at an intersection.

"Keep the change," said the doctor. The boy peeled a damp sheet off the batch, thrust it into his hand, and a minute later was engulfed in the snowstorm.

The doctor stopped under a street light to read the headlines. The paper was a late extra printed on one side only; it gave the official announcement from Petersburg that a Soviet of People's Commissars had been formed and that Soviet power and the dictatorship of the proletariat were established in Russia. There followed the first decrees of the new government and various brief news dispatches received by telegraph and telephone.

The blizzard lashed at the doctor's eyes and covered the printed page with gray, rustling pellets of snow. But it was not the snowstorm that prevented him from reading. The historic greatness of the moment moved him so deeply that it took him some time to collect himself.

To read the rest of the news he looked around for a better lit, sheltered place. He found that he was standing once again at that charmed spot, the intersection of Serebriany and Molchanovka, in front of a tall, five-story building with a glass door and a spacious, well-lit lobby.

He went in and stood under the electric light, next to the staircase, reading the news.

Footsteps sounded above him. Someone was coming down the stairs, stopping frequently, as though hesitating. At one point, he actually changed his mind and ran up again. A door opened somewhere and two voices welled out, so distorted by echoes that it was impossible to tell whether men or women were speaking. Then the door banged and the same steps ran down, this time resolutely.

Yurii Andreievich was absorbed in his paper and had not meant to look up, but the stranger stopped so suddenly at the foot of the stairs that he raised his head.

Before him stood a boy of about eighteen in a reindeer cap and a stiff reindeer coat worn, as in Siberia, fur side out. He was dark and had narrow Kirghiz eyes. His face had an aristocratic quality, the fugitive spark and reticent delicacy that give an impression of remoteness and are sometimes found in people of a complex, mixed parentage.

The boy obviously mistook Yurii Andreievich for someone else. He looked at him, puzzled and shy, as if he knew him but could not make up his mind to speak. To put an end to the misunderstanding Yurii Andreievich measured him with a cold, discouraging glance.

The boy turned away confused and walked to the entrance. There he looked back once again before going out and banging the heavy glass door shut behind him.

Yurii Andreievich left a few minutes after him. His mind was full of the news; he forgot the boy and the colleague he had meant to visit, and set out straight for home. But he was distracted on the way by another incident, one of those details of everyday life that assumed an inordinate importance in those days.

Not far from his house he stumbled in the dark over an enormous pile of timber near the curb. There was an institution of some sort in the street, to which the government had probably supplied fuel in the form of boards from a dismantled house in the outskirts of the town. Not all of it would go into the yard, and the rest had been left outside. A sentry with a rifle was on duty by this pile; he paced up and down the yard and occasionally went out into the street.

Without thinking twice, Yurii Andreievich took advantage of a moment when the sentry's back was turned and the wind had raised a cloud of snow into the air to creep up on the dark side, avoiding the lamplight, carefully loosen a heavy beam from the very bottom, and pull it out. He loaded it with difficulty on his back, immediately ceasing to feel its weight (your own load is not a burden), and, hugging the shadow of the walls, took the wood safely home.

Its arrival was timely; they had run out of firewood. The beam was chopped up, and the pieces were stacked. Yurii Andreievich lit the stove and squatted in front of it in silence, while Alexander Alexandrovich moved up his armchair and sat warming himself.

Yurii Andreievich took the newspaper out of the side pocket of his coat and held it out to him.

"Seen that? Have a look."

Still squatting on his heels and poking the fire, he talked to himself.

"What splendid surgery! You take a knife and with one masterful stroke you cut out all the old stinking ulcers. Quite simply, without any nonsense, you take the old monster of injustice, which has been accustomed for centuries to being bowed and scraped and curtsied to, and you sentence it to death.

"This fearlessness, this way of seeing the thing through to the end, has a familiar national look about it. It has something of Pushkin's uncompromising clarity and of Tolstoy's unwavering faithfulness to the facts."

"Pushkin, you said? Wait a second. Let me finish. I can't read and listen at the same time," said Alexander Alexandrovich under the mistaken impression that his son-in-law was addressing him.

"And the real stroke of genius is this. If you charged someone with the task of creating a new world, of starting a new era, he would ask you first to clear the ground. He would wait for the old centuries to finish before undertaking to build the new ones, he'd want to begin a new paragraph, a new page.

"But here, they don't bother with anything like that. This new thing, this marvel of history, this revelation, is exploded right into the very thick of daily life without the slightest consideration for its course. It doesn't start at the beginning, it starts in the middle, without any schedule, on the first weekday that comes along, while the traffic in the street is at its height. That's real genius. Only real greatness can be so unconcerned with timing and opportunity."

9

Winter came, just the kind of winter that had been foretold. It was not as terrifying as the two winters that followed it, but it was already of the same sort, dark, hungry, and cold, entirely given to the breaking up of the familiar and the reconstruction of all the foundations of existence, and to inhuman efforts to cling to life as it slipped out of your grasp.

There were three of them, one after the other, three such terrible winters, and not all that now seems to have happened in 1917 and 1918 really happened then—some of it may have been later. These three successive winters have merged into one and it is difficult to tell them apart.

The old life and the new order had not yet come in contact. They were not yet openly hostile to each other, as when the civil war broke out a year later, but there was no connection between the two. They stood apart, confronting each other, incompatible.

There were new elections everywhere—in administration of buildings, organizations of all kinds, government offices, public services. Commissars invested with dictatorial powers were appointed to each, men of iron will in black leather jackets, armed with means of intimidation and guns, who shaved rarely and slept even more rarely.

They knew the slinking bourgeois breed, the ordinary holders of cheap government bonds, and they spoke to them without the slightest pity and with Mephistophelean smiles, as to petty thieves caught in the act.

These were the people who reorganized everything in accordance with the plan, and company after company, enterprise after enterprise became Bolshevized.

The Hospital of the Holy Cross was now known as the Second Reformed. Many things had changed in it. Part of the staff had been dismissed and others had resigned because they did not find the work sufficiently rewarding. These were doctors with a fashionable practice and high fees, and glib talkers. They left out of self-interest but asserted that they had made a civic gesture of protest and looked down on those who had stayed on, almost boycotting them. Zhivago had stayed.

In the evenings husband and wife had conversations of this sort:

"Don't forget Wednesday, at the Doctors' Union; they'll have two sacks of frozen potatoes for us in the basement. I'll let you know what time I can get away. We'll have to go together and take the sled."

"All right, Yurochka, there's plenty of time. Why don't you go to bed now, it's late. I wish you'd rest, you can't do everything."

"There's an epidemic. Exhaustion is lowering resistance. You and Father look terrible. We must do something. If only I knew what. We don't take enough care of ourselves. Listen. You aren't asleep?"

"No."

"I'm not worried about myself, I've got nine lives, but if by any chance I should get ill, you will be sensible, won't you, you mustn't keep me at home. Get me into the hospital at once."

"Don't talk like that. Pray God you'll keep well. Why play Cassandra?"

"Remember, there aren't any honest people left, or any friends. Still less any experts. If anything should happen don't trust anyone except Pichuzhkin. That is if he's still there, of course. You aren't asleep?"

"No."

"The pay wasn't good enough, so off they went; now it turns out they had principles and civic sentiments. You meet them in the street, they hardly shake hands, just raise an eyebrow: 'So you're working for *them?*'—'I am,' I said, 'and if you don't mind, I am proud of our privations and I respect those who honor us by imposing them on us.'"

10

For a long time most people's daily food consisted of thin millet boiled in water and soup made of herring heads; the herring itself was used as a second course. A sort of kasha was also made of unground wheat or rye.

A woman professor who was a friend of Antonina Alexandrovna's taught her to bake bread in an improvised Dutch oven. The idea was to sell some of the bread and so cover the cost of heating the tile stove as in the old days, instead of using the iron stove, which continued to smoke and gave almost no heat.

Antonina Alexandrovna's bread was good but nothing came of her commercial plans. They had to go back to the wretched iron stove. The Zhivagos were hard up.

One morning, after Yurii Andreievich had gone to work, Antonina Alexandrovna put on her shabby winter coat—she was so run down that she shivered in it even in warm weather— and went out "hunting." There were only two logs left. For about half an hour she wandered through the alleys in the neighborhood where you could sometimes catch a peasant from one of the villages outside Moscow selling vegetables and potatoes. In the main streets, peasants with loads were liable to be arrested. Soon she found what she was looking for. A sturdy young fellow in a peasant's coat walked back with her, pulling a sleigh that looked as light as a toy, and followed her cautiously into the yard.

Covered up by sacking inside the sleigh was a load of birch logs no thicker than the balusters of an old-fashioned country house in a nineteenth-century photograph. Antonina Alexandrovna knew their worth—birch only in name, the wood was of the poorest sort and too freshly cut to be suitable for burning. But as there was no choice, it was pointless to argue.

The young peasant carried five or six armloads up to the living room and took in exchange Tonia's small mirror wardrobe. He carried it down and packed it in his sleigh to take away as a present for his bride. In discussing a future deal in potatoes, he asked the price of the piano.

When Yurii Andreievich came home he said nothing about his wife's purchase. It would have been more sensible to chop up the wardrobe, but they could never have brought themselves to do it.

"There's a note for you on the table, did you see it?" she said.

"The one sent on from the hospital? Yes, I've had the message already. It's a sick call. I'll certainly go. I'll just have a little rest first. But it's pretty far. It's somewhere near the Triumphal Arch, I've got the address."

"Have you seen the fee they are offering you? You'd better read it. A bottle of German cognac or a pair of stockings! What sort of people are they, do you imagine? Vulgar. They don't seem to have any idea of how we live nowadays. *Nouveaux riches*, I suppose."

"Yes, that's from a supplier."

Suppliers, concessionnaires, and authorized agents were names then given to small businessmen to whom the government, which had abolished private trade, occasionally made concessions at moments of economic difficulties, charging them with the procurement of various goods.

They were not former men of substance or dismissed heads of old firms—such people did not recover from the blow they had received. They were a new category of businessmen, people without roots who had been scooped up from the bottom by the war and the revolution.

Zhivago had a drink of hot water and saccharin whitened with milk and went off to see his patient.

Deep snow covered the street from wall to wall, in places up to the level of the ground-floor windows. Silent half-dead shadows moved all over this expanse carrying a little food or pulling it along on sleds. There was almost no other traffic.

Old shop signs still hung here and there. They had no relation to the small new consumer shops and co-operatives, which were all empty and locked, their windows barred or boarded up.

The reason they were locked and empty was not only that

there were no goods but that the reorganization of all aspects of life, including trade, had so far remained largely on paper and had not yet affected such trifling details as the boarded-up shops.

11

The house to which the doctor went was at the end of Brest Street near the Tver Gate.

It was an old barracklike stone building with an inside courtyard, and three wooden staircases rose along the courtyard walls.

That day the tenants were at their general meeting, in which a woman delegate from the borough council participated, when a military commission suddenly turned up to check arms licenses and to confiscate unlicensed weapons. The tenants had to go back to their flats, but the head of the commission asked the delegate not to leave, assuring her that the search would not take long and the meeting could be resumed within a short time.

When the doctor arrived, the commission had almost finished but the flat where he was going had not yet been searched. Zhivago was stopped on the landing by a soldier with a rifle, but the head of the commission heard them arguing and ordered the search to be put off until after the doctor had examined his patient.

The door was opened by the master of the house, a polite young man with a sallow complexion and dark, melancholy eyes. He was flustered by a number of things—because of his wife's illness, the impending search, and his profound reverence for medical science and its representatives.

To save the doctor time and trouble he tried to be as brief as possible, but his very haste made his speech long and incoherent.

The flat was cluttered with a mixture of expensive and cheap furniture, hastily bought as an investment against the rapid inflation. Sets were supplemented by odd pieces.

The young man thought his wife's illness had been caused by nervous shock. He explained with many digressions that they had recently bought an antique clock. It was a broken-down chiming clock, and they had bought it for a song merely as a remarkable example of the clockmaker's art (he took the doctor into the next room to see it). They had even doubted whether it could be repaired. Then, one day, suddenly the clock, which had not been wound for years, had started of itself, played its complicated minuet of chimes, and stopped. His wife was terrified, the young man said; she was convinced that her last hour had struck, and now there she was delirious, refused all food, and did not recognize him.

"So you think it's nervous shock," Yurii Andreievich said doubtfully. "May I see her now?"

They went into another room, which had a porcelain chandelier, a wide double bed, and two mahogany bedside tables. A small woman with big black eyes lay near the edge of the bed, the blanket pulled up above her chin. When she saw them she freed one arm from under the bedclothes and waved them back, the loose sleeve of her dressing gown falling back to her armpit. She did not recognize her husband, and as if she were alone in the room, she began to sing something sad in a low voice, which upset her so much that she cried, whimpering like a child and begging to "go home." When the doctor went up to the bed she turned her back on him and refused to let him touch her.

"I ought to examine her," he said, "but it doesn't really matter. It's quite clear that she's got typhus—a severe case, poor thing; she must be feeling pretty wretched. My advice to you is to put her in a hospital. I know you'd see to it that she had everything she needed at home, but it's most important that she should have constant medical supervision in the first few weeks. Could you get hold of any sort of transportation—a cab or even a cart? Of course she'll have to be well wrapped up. I'll give you an admission order."

"I'll try, but wait a moment. Is it really typhus? How horrible!"

"I'm afraid so."

"Look, I know I'll lose her if I let her go—couldn't you possibly look after her here? Come as often as you possibly can—I'll be only too happy to pay you anything you like."

"I am sorry—I've told you: what she needs is constant supervision. Do as I say—I really am advising you for her good. Now, get a cab at any cost and I'll write out the order. I'd better do it in your house committee room. The order has to have the house stamp on it, and there are a few other formalities."

12

One by one the tenants, in shawls and fur coats, had returned to the unheated basement, which had once been a wholesale egg store and was now used by the house committee.

An office desk and several chairs stood at one end of it. As there were not enough chairs, old empty egg crates turned upside down had been placed in a row to form a bench. A pile of them as high as the ceiling towered at the far end of the room; in a corner was a heap of shavings stuck into lumps with frozen yolk that had dripped from broken eggs. Rats scurried noisily inside the heap, making an occasional sortie into the middle of the stone floor and darting back.

Each time this happened a fat woman climbed squealing onto a crate and, holding up her skirt daintily and tapping her fashionable high shoes, shouted in a deliberately hoarse, drunken voice:

"Olia, Olia, you've got rats all over the place. Get away, you filthy brute. Ai-ai-ai! look at it, it understands, it's mad at me. Ai-ai-ai! it's trying to climb up, it'll get under my skirt, I'm so frightened! Look the other way, gentlemen. Sorry, I forgot, you're comrade citizens now, not gentlemen."

Her astrakhan cape hung open over the three quaking layers of her double chin and rich, silk-swathed bosom and stomach. She had once been the belle of her circle of small tradesmen and salesmen, but now her little pig eyes with their swollen lids could scarcely open. A rival had once tried to splash her with vitriol but had missed and only a drop or two had plowed traces on her cheek and at the corner of her mouth, so slight as to be almost becoming.

"Stop yelling, Khrapugina. How can we get on with our work?" said the delegate of the borough council, who had been elected chairman and was sitting behind the desk.

The delegate had known the house and many of the tenants all her life. Before the meeting she had had an unofficial talk with Aunt Fatima, the old janitress who had once lived with her husband and children in a corner of the filthy basement but had now only her daughter with her and had been moved into two light rooms on the first floor.

"Well, Fatima, how are things going?" the delegate asked.

Fatima complained that she could not cope with such a big house and so many tenants all by herself and that she got no help because, although each family was supposed to take turns cleaning the yard and the sidewalks, not one of them did it.

"Don't worry, Fatima, we'll show them. What kind of committee is this, anyway? They're hopeless. Criminal elements are given shelter, people of doubtful morals stay on without registration. We'll get rid of them and elect another. I'll make you house-manageress, only don't make a fuss."

The janitress begged to be let off, but the delegate refused to listen.

Looking around the room and deciding that enough people were present, she called for quiet and opened the meeting with a short introductory speech. She condemned the committee for slackness, proposed that candidates should be put up for the election of a new one, and went on to other business.

In conclusion she said:

"So that's how it is, comrades. Frankly speaking, this is a big house, it's suitable for a hostel. Look at all the delegates who come to town to attend conferences, and we don't know where to put them. It's been decided to take over the building for a district soviet hostel for visitors from the country and to call it the Tiverzin Hostel, in honor of Comrade Tiverzin, who lived here before he was deported, as everyone knows. No objections? Now, as to dates. There's no hurry, you've got a whole year. Working people will be rehoused; others must find accommodations for themselves and are given a year's notice."

"We're all working people! Every one of us! We're all workers," people shouted from every side, and one voice sobbed out: "It's Great-Russian chauvinism! All the nations are equal now! I know what you're hinting at."

"Not all at once, please. Whom am I to answer first? What have nations got to do with it, Citizen Valdyrkin? Look at Khrapugina, you can't think there's a question of nationality involved in her case, and we are certainly evicting her."

"You are, are you! Just you try and evict me, we'll see about that! You crushed sofa! You crumpled bedsheet!" Khrapugina screamed, calling the delegate every meaningless name she could think of in the heat of the quarrel.

"What a she-devil!" The janitress was indignant. "Haven't you any shame?"

"Don't you meddle in this, Fatima, I can look after myself," said the delegate. "Stop it, Khrapugina, I know all about you. Shut up, I tell you, or I'll hand you over at once to the authorities before they catch you brewing vodka and running an illegal bar."

The uproar was at its height when the doctor came into the room. He asked the first man he ran into at the door to point out to him a member of the house committee. The other held up his hands like a trumpet in front of his mouth and shouted above the noise:

"Ga-li-ul-li-na! Come here. You're wanted."

The doctor could not believe his ears. A thin elderly woman with a slight stoop, the janitress, came up to him. He was struck by her likeness to her son. He did not, however, identify himself at once, but said: "One of your tenants has got typhus" (he told her the name). "There are various precautions that have to be taken to prevent its spreading. Moreover, the patient must go to the hospital. I'll make out an admission order, which the house committee has to certify. How and where can we get that done?"

She thought he meant "How is the patient to get to the hospital?" and replied: "There's a cab coming from the soviet for Comrade Demina, that's the delegate. She's very kind, Comrade Demina, I'll tell her, she's sure to let your patient have the cab. Don't worry, Comrade Doctor, we'll get her there all right."

"That's wonderful. Actually, I only meant where could I write out the order. But if there's a cab as well . . . May I ask you, are you the mother of Lieutenant Galiullin? We were in the same unit at the front."

Galiullina started violently and grew pale. She grasped the doctor's hand. "Come outside," she said. "We'll talk in the yard."

As soon as they were outside the door she said quickly: "Talk softly, for God's sake. Don't ruin me. Yusupka's gone wrong. Judge for yourself—what is he? He was an apprentice, a worker. He ought to understand—simple people are much better off now, a blind man can see that, nobody can deny it. I don't know what you feel yourself, maybe it would be all right for you, but it's a sin for Yusupka, God won't forgive him. Yusupka's father was a private, he was killed, they say his face was shot off, and his arms and legs."

Her voice broke, she waited till she was more calm, then she went on: "Come. I'll get you the cab. I know who you are. He was here for a couple of days. He told me. He said you knew Lara Guishar. She was a good girl, I remember her, she used to come and see us. What she's like now, I don't know—who can tell with you people? After all, it's natural for the masters to stick together. But for Yusupka it's a sin. Come, let's ask for the cab. I'm sure Comrade Demina will let you have it. You know who Comrade Demina is? She's Olia Demina, a seamstress she was, worked for Lara's mother, that's who she is, and she's from this house. Come along."

<h1 style="text-align:center">13</h1>

Night had fallen. All around them was darkness. Only the small round patch of light from Demina's pocket flashlight jumped from snowdrift to snowdrift four or five paces ahead, confusing more than lighting the way. The darkness was all around them, and they had left behind them the house where so many people had known Lara, where she had often come as a girl, and where, they said, Antipov, her husband, had grown up.

"Will you really find your way without a flashlight, Comrade Doctor?" Demina was facetiously patronizing. "If not, I'll lend you mine. It's a fact, you know, I had a real crush on her when we were little girls. They had a dressmaking establishment, I was an apprentice in the workshop. I've seen her this year. She stopped on her way through Moscow. I said, 'Where are you off to, silly? Stay here. Come and live with us. We'll find you a job.' But it wasn't any good, she wouldn't. Well, it's her business. She married Pasha with her head, not with her heart, she's been crazy ever since. Off she went."

"What do you think of her?"

"Careful—it's slippery. I don't know how many times I've told them not to throw the slops out of the door—might as well talk to a wall. What do I think of her? How do you mean, think? What should I think? I haven't any time to think. Here's where I live. One thing I didn't tell her—her brother, who was in the army, I think they've shot him. As for her mother, my mistress she used to be—I'll save her, I'm seeing to it. Well, I've got to go in, goodbye."

They parted. The light of Demina's little flashlight shot into the narrow stone entrance and ran on, lighting up the stained walls and the dirty stairs while the doctor was left surrounded by the darkness. On his right lay Sadovaia Triumphalnaia Street, on his left Sadovaia Karetnaia Street. Running into the black snowy distance, they were no longer streets but cuttings in the jungle of stone buildings, like cuttings through the impassable forests of Siberia or the Urals.

At home it was light and warm.

"Why are you so late?" asked Antonina Alexandrovna. "An extraordinary thing happened while you were out," she went on before he could reply. "Really quite unaccountable. Yesterday Father broke the alarm clock—I forgot to tell you—he was terribly upset, it was our only clock. He tried to repair it, he tinkered and tinkered with it, but he got nowhere. The clockmaker around the corner wanted a ridiculous price—three pounds of bread. I didn't know what to do and Father was completely dejected. Well, about an hour ago—can you believe it—there was a sudden ringing—such a piercing, deafening noise, we were all frightened out of our wits. It was the alarm clock! Can you imagine such a thing? It had started up again, all by itself."

"My hour for typhus has struck," said Yurii Andreievich, laughing. He told her about his patient and the chiming clock.

14

But he did not get typhus until much later. In the meantime the Zhivagos were tried to the limits of endurance. They had nothing and they were starving. The doctor went to see the Party member he had once saved, the one who had been the victim of a robbery. This man did everything he could for the doctor, but the civil war was just beginning and he was hardly ever in Moscow; moreover, he regarded the privations people had to suffer in those days as only natural, and he himself went hungry, though he concealed it.

Yurii Andreievich tried to get in touch with the supplier in Brest Street. But in the intervening months the young man had disappeared and nothing was known about his wife, who had recovered. Galiullina was out when Yurii Andreievich called, most of the tenants were new, and Demina was at the front.

One day he received an allocation of wood at the official price. He had to bring it from the Vindava Station. Walking home along the endless stretches of Meshchanskaia Street— keeping an eye on the cart loaded with his unexpected treasure—he noticed that the street looked quite different; he found that he was swaying from side to side, his legs refusing to carry him. He realized that he was in for a bad time, that he had typhus. The driver picked him up when he fell down and slung him on top of the wood. The doctor never knew how he got home.

15

He was delirious off and on for two weeks. He dreamed that Tonia had put two streets on his desk, Sadovaia Karetnaia on his left and Sadovaia Triumphalnaia on his right, and had lit the table lamp; its warm orange glow lit up the streets and now he could write. So he was writing.

He was writing what he should have written long ago and had always wished to write but never could. Now it came to him quite easily, he wrote eagerly and said exactly what he wanted to say. Only now and then a boy got in his way, a boy with narrow Kirghiz eyes, in an unbuttoned reindeer coat worn fur side out, as in the Urals or Siberia.

He knew for certain that this boy was the spirit of his death or, to put it quite plainly, that he was his death. Yet how could he be his death if he was helping him to write a poem? How could death be useful, how was it possible for death to be a help?

The subject of his poem was neither the entombment nor the resurrection but the days between; the title was "Turmoil."

He had always wanted to describe how for three days the black, raging, worm-filled earth had assailed the deathless incarnation of love, storming it with rocks and rubble—as waves fly and leap at a seacoast, cover and submerge it—how for three days the black hurricane of earth raged, advancing and retreating.

Two lines kept coming into his head:

"We are glad to be near you," and "Time to wake up."

Near him, touching him, were hell, dissolution, corruption, death, and equally near him were the spring and Mary Magdalene and life. And it was time to awake. Time to wake up and to get up. Time to arise, time for the resurrection.

16

He began to get better. At first he took everything for granted, like a halfwit. He remembered nothing, he could see no connection between one thing and another and was not surprised at anything. His wife fed him on white bread and butter and sugared tea; she gave him coffee. He had forgotten that such things did not exist, and he enjoyed their taste like poetry or like fairy tales, as something right and proper for a convalescent. Soon, however, he began to think and wonder.

"How did you get all this?" he asked his wife.

"Your Grania got it for us."

"What Grania?"

"Grania Zhivago."

"Grania Zhivago?"

"Well, yes, your brother Evgraf, from Omsk. Your half brother. He came every day while you were ill."

"Does he wear a reindeer coat?"

"That's right. So you did see him. You were unconscious nearly all the time. He said he had run into you on the stairs in some house or other. He knew you—he meant to speak to you, but apparently you frightened him to death! He worships you, he reads every word you write. The things he got for us! Rice, raisins, sugar! He's gone back now. He wants us to go there too. He's a strange boy, a bit mysterious. I think he must have some sort of connection with the government out there. He says we ought to get away for a year or two, get away from the big towns, 'go back to the land' for a bit, he says. I thought of the Krueger place and he said it was a very good idea. We could grow vegetables and there's the forest all around. There isn't any point in dying without a struggle, like sheep."

In April that year Zhivago set out with his whole family for the former Varykino estate, near the town of Yuriatin, far away in the Urals.

CHAPTER SEVEN

Train to the Urals

1

The end of March brought the first warm days of the year, false heralds of spring which were always followed by a severe cold spell.

The Zhivagos were hurriedly getting ready to leave. To disguise the bustle, the tenants—there were more of them now than sparrows in the street—were told that the apartment was having a spring cleaning for Easter.

Yurii Andreievich had opposed the move. So far, he had thought that it would come to nothing and had not interfered with the preparations, but they had advanced and were about to be completed. The time had come to discuss the matter seriously.

He reiterated his doubts at a family council made up of himself, his wife, and his father-in-law. "Do you think I'm wrong?" he asked them after stating his objections. "Do you still insist on going?"

"You say that we must manage as best we can for the next couple of years," said his wife, "until land conditions are settled, then we might get a vegetable garden near Moscow. But how are we to endure until then? That's the crucial point, and you haven't told us."

"It's sheer madness to count on such things," her father backed her up.

"Very well then, you win," Yurii Andreievich said. "What bothers me is that we are going blindfold, to a place we know nothing about. Of the three people who lived at Varykino, Mother and Grandmother are dead, and Grandfather Krueger is being held as a hostage—that is, if he is still alive.

"You know he made a fictitious sale in the last year of the war, sold the forests and the factories or else put the title deeds in the name of someone else, a bank or a private person, I don't know. We don't know anything, in fact. To whom does the estate belong now? I don't mean whose property it is, I don't care if we lose it, but who is in charge there? Who runs it? Is the timber being cut? Are the factories working? And above all, who is in power in that part of the country, or rather, who will be by the time we get there?

"You are relying on the old manager, Mikulitsyn, to see us through, but who is to tell us if he is still there? Or whether he is still alive? Anyway what do we know about him except his name—and that we only remember because Grandfather had such difficulty in pronouncing it.

"However, what is there to argue about? You have made up your minds, and I've agreed. Now we must find out exactly what one does about travelling these days. There is no point in putting it off."

2

Yurii Andreievich went to the Yaroslavsky Station to make inquiries.

Endless queues of passengers moved along raised gangways between wooden handrails. On the stone floors lay people in gray army coats who coughed, spat, shifted about, and spoke in voices that resounded incongruously loudly under the vaulted ceilings.

Most of these people had recently had typhus and been discharged from the overcrowded hospitals as soon as they were off the critical list. Yurii Andreievich, as a doctor, knew the necessity for this, but he had had no idea that there could be so many of these unfortunates or that they were forced to seek refuge in railway stations.

"You must get a priority," a porter in a white apron told him. "Then you must come every day to ask if there is a train. Trains are rare nowadays, it's a question of luck. And of course" (he rubbed two fingers with his thumb) "a little flour or something . . . Wheels don't run without oil, you know, and what's more" (he tapped his Adam's apple) "you won't get far without a little vodka."

3

About that time Alexander Alexandrovich was asked several times to act as consultant to the Higher Economic Council, and Yurii Andreievich to treat a member of the government who was dangerously ill. Both were paid in what was then the highest currency—credit slips for an allotment of articles from the first of the newly opened distribution centers.

The center was an old army warehouse next to the Simonov Monastery. The doctor and his father-in-law went through the monastery and the barrack yard and straight through a low stone door into a vaulted cellar. It sloped down and widened at its farther end, where a counter ran across from wall to wall; behind it stood an attendant, weighing, measuring, and handing out goods with calm unhurried movements, crossing off the items on the list with broad pencil strokes and occasionally replenishing his stock from the back of the store.

There were not many customers. "Containers," said the storekeeper, glancing at the slips. The professor and the doctor held out several large and small pillowcases and, with bulging eyes, watched them being filled with flour, cereals, macaroni, sugar, suet, soap, matches, and something wrapped in paper that was later found to be Caucasian cheese.

Overwhelmed by the storekeeper's generosity and anxious not to waste his time, they hurriedly stuffed their bundles into big sacks and slung them over their shoulders.

They came out of the vault intoxicated not by the mere thought of food but by the realization that they too were of use in the world and did not live in vain and had deserved the praise and thanks that Tonia would shower on them at home.

4

While the men disappeared for whole days into government offices, seeking travel documents and registering the apartment so that they should be able to go back to it on their return to Moscow, Antonina Alexandrovna sorted the family belongings.

Walking up and down the three rooms now officially assigned to the Zhivagos, she weighed even the smallest article twenty times in her hand before deciding whether to put it into the pile of things they were taking with them. Only a small part of their luggage was intended for their personal use; the rest would serve as currency on the way and in the first weeks after their arrival.

The spring breeze came in through the partly open window, tasting faintly of newly cut white bread. Cocks were crowing and children playing and shouting in the yard. The more the room was aired the more noticeable became the smell of mothballs from the open trunks in which the winter clothes had been packed.

As for the choice of things to be taken or left behind, there existed a whole theory, developed by those who had left earlier and communicated their observations to friends at home. The simple, indisputable rules of this theory were so distinctly present in Antonina Alexandrovna's mind that she imagined hearing them repeated by some secret voice coming from outside with the chirruping of sparrows and the cries of playing children.

"Lengths for dresses," she pondered, "but luggage is checked on the way, so this is dangerous unless they are tacked up to look like clothes. Materials and fabrics, clothes, preferably coats if they're not too worn. No trunks or hampers (there won't be any porters); be sure to take nothing useless and tie up everything in bundles small enough for a woman or a child to carry. Salt and tobacco have been found very useful but risky. Money in Kerenkas.* Documents are the hardest thing to carry safely." And so on and so on.

---

*Kerenkas: paper money introduced by the Kerensky government and still in circulation at that time.

5

On the day before they left there was a snowstorm. Gray clouds of spinning snow swept into the sky and came back to earth as a white whirlwind, which ran off into the black depths of the street and covered it with a white shroud.

All the luggage was packed. The apartment, with such things as remained in it, was being left in the care of an elderly former salesclerk and his wife, relatives of Egorovna's who, the preceding winter, had helped Antonina Alexandrovna to trade old clothes and furniture for potatoes and wood.

Markel could not be trusted. At the militia post which he had selected as his political club he did not actually say that his former masters sucked his blood, but he accused them, instead, of having kept him in ignorance all these years and deliberately concealed from him that man is descended from apes.

Antonina Alexandrovna took the couple on a final survey of the house, fitting keys to locks, opening and shutting drawers and cupboards, and giving them last-minute instructions.

The chairs and tables had been pushed against the walls, the curtains taken down, and there was a pile of bundles in the corner. The snowstorm, seen through the bare windows of the rooms stripped of their winter comfort, reminded each of them of past sorrows. Yurii Andreievich thought of his childhood and his mother's death, and Antonina Alexandrovna and her father of the death and funeral of Anna Ivanovna. They felt that this was their last night in the house, that they would never see it again. They were mistaken on this point, but under the influence of their thoughts, which they kept to themselves in order not to upset each other, they looked back over the years spent under this roof, struggling against the tears that came to their eyes.

In spite of all this, Antonina Alexandrovna kept within the rules of propriety in the presence of strangers. She talked endlessly with the woman in whose care she was leaving everything. She overestimated the favor the couple were doing her. Anxious not to seem ungrateful, she kept apologizing, going next door and coming back with presents for the woman—blouses and lengths of cotton and silk prints. And the dark materials, with their white check or polka-dot patterns, were like the dark snow-bound street checkered with bricks and covered with white dots which, that farewell night, looked in through the uncurtained windows.

6

They left for the station at dawn. The other tenants were usually asleep at this hour, but one of them, Zevorotnina, incurably fond of organizing any social occasion, roused them all shouting: "Attention! Attention! Comrades! Hurry up! The Gromeko people are going. Come and say goodbye!"

They all poured out onto the back porch (the front door was kept boarded up) and stood in a semicircle as though for a photograph. They yawned and shivered and tugged at the shabby coats they had thrown over their shoulders and stamped about in the huge felt boots they had hastily pulled on over their bare feet.

Markel had already managed to get drunk on some murderous brew he had succeeded in obtaining even in those dry days, and he hung like a corpse over the worn porch railings, which threatened to collapse under him. He insisted on carrying the luggage to the station and was offended when his offer was refused. At last they got rid of him.

It was still dark. The wind had fallen and the snow fell thicker than the night before. Large, fluffy flakes drifted down lazily and hung over the ground, as though hesitating to settle.

By the time they had left the street and reached the Arbat it was lighter. Here the snow came down like a white, slowly descending stage curtain as wide as the street, its fringe swinging around the legs of the passersby so that they lost the sense of moving forward and felt they were marking time.

There was not a soul about except the travellers, but soon they were overtaken by a cab with a snow-white nag and a driver who looked as if he had been rolled in dough. For a fabulous sum (worth less than a kopek in those days) he took them to the station with their luggage, except for Yurii Andreievich, who at his own request was allowed to walk.

7

He found Antonina Alexandrovna and her father standing in one of the endless queues squeezed between the wooden handrails. Niusha and Sashenka were walking about outside and occasionally looking in to see if it were time to join the grown-ups. They gave off a strong smell of kerosene, which had been thickly smeared on their necks, wrists, and ankles as a protection against lice.

The queues went up to the gates of the platforms, but in fact the passengers had to board the train a good half mile farther down the line. With not enough cleaners, the station was filthy and the tracks in front of the platforms were unusable because of dirt and ice. The trains stopped farther out.

Antonina Alexandrovna waved to her husband and when he was close enough shouted instructions as to where he was to get their travel papers stamped.

"Show me what they've put," she said when he came back. He held out a batch of papers across the handrail.

"That's for the special coach," said the man behind her in the queue, reading over her shoulder.

The man in front of her was more explicit. He was one of those sticklers for form who seem to be familiar with and accept without question every regulation in the world.

"This stamp," he explained, "gives you the right to claim seats in a classified coach, that is to say a passenger coach, if there is a passenger coach on the train."

The whole queue joined in at once.

"Passenger coach indeed! If you can get a seat on the buffers you must be thankful nowadays!"

"Don't listen to them," said the other. "I'll explain, it's quite simple. Today there is only one type of train, and it always includes army, convict, cattle, and passenger cars. Why mislead the man?" he said, turning to the crowd. "Words don't cost anything, you can say what you like, but you should say it clearly so that he can understand."

"A lot you've explained." He was shouted down. "A lot you've said when you've told him he's got stamps for the special coach! You should look at a man first, before you start explaining. How can anyone with such a face go in the special coach? The special coach is full of sailors. A sailor has a trained eye and a gun. He takes a look at him and what does he see? A member of the propertied classes—worse than that: a doctor, former quality. He pulls out his gun—and goodbye."

There is no knowing to what lengths the sympathy aroused by the doctor's case would have gone if the crowd had not turned its attention to something else.

For some time people had been looking curiously through the enormous plate-glass windows at the tracks, which were roofed in for several hundred yards. The falling snow could be seen only beyond the far end of the roofs; seen so far away, it looked almost still, sinking to the ground as slowly as bread crumbs thrown to fishes sink through water.

For some time, figures had been strolling into the distance along the tracks, singly or in groups. At first they were taken for railwaymen attending to their duties, but now a whole mob rushed out, and from the direction in which they were running there appeared a small cloud of smoke.

"Open up the gates, you scoundrels," yelled voices in the queue. The crowd stirred and swung against the gates, those at the back pushing those in front.

"Look what's going on! They've locked us in here and through there some people have found a way around and jumped the queue. Open up, you bastards, or we'll smash the gates. Come on, let's give it a push."

"They needn't envy that lot, the fools," said the know-it-all stickler for form. "Those men are conscripts, called up for forced labor from Petrograd. They were supposed to be sent to Vologda, but now they're being taken to the eastern front. They're not travelling of their own choice. They're under escort. They'll be digging trenches."

8

They had been travelling three days but had not got far from Moscow. The landscape was wintry. Tracks, fields, woods, and village roofs—everything was covered with snow.

The Zhivagos had been lucky enough to get a corner to themselves on the upper bunks, right up against the long bleary window close under the ceiling.

Antonina Alexandrovna had never travelled in a freight car before. The first time they got in Yurii Andreievich lifted her up to the high floor and pushed open the heavy sliding doors for her, but later she learned to climb in and out by herself.

The car looked to Antonina Alexandrovna no better than a pigsty on wheels, and she had expected it to fall apart at the first jar. But for three days now they had been jolted back and forth and from side to side as the train had changed speed or direction, for three days the wheels had rattled underneath them like the sticks on a mechanical toy drum, and there had been no accident. Her fears had been groundless.

The train had twenty-three cars (the Zhivagos were in the fourteenth). When it stopped at country stations, only a few front, middle, or end cars stood beside the short platform.

Sailors were in front, civilian passengers in the middle, and the labor conscripts in eight cars at the back. There were about five hundred of the latter, people of all ages, conditions, and professions.

They were a remarkable sight—rich, smart lawyers and stockbrokers from Petrograd side by side with cab drivers, floor polishers, bath attendants, Tartar ragpickers, escaped lunatics, shopkeepers, and monks, all lumped in with the exploiting classes.

The lawyers and stockbrokers sat on short thick logs in their shirt sleeves around red-hot iron stoves, told endless stories, joked, and laughed. They were not worried, they had connections, influential relatives were pulling strings for them at home, and at the worst they could buy themselves off later on.

The others, in boots and unbuttoned caftans, or barefoot and in long shirts worn outside their trousers, with or without beards, stood at the half-open doors of the airless cars, holding on to the sides or to the boards nailed across the openings, and gazed sullenly at the peasants and villages by the wayside, speaking to no one. These had no influential friends. They had nothing to hope for.

There were too many conscripts for the cars allotted to them, and the overflow had been put among the civilian passengers, including those of the fourteenth car.

9

Whenever the train stopped, Antonina Alexandrovna sat up cautiously to avoid knocking her head on the ceiling and looked down through the slightly open door to see if it were worthwhile to go out. This depended on the size of the station, the probable length of the halt, and the consequent likelihood of profitable barter.

So it was on this occasion. The train had wakened her from a doze by slowing down. The number of switches over which it bumped and rattled suggested that the station was fairly large, and that they would stop for a long time.

She rubbed her eyes, tidied her hair, and after rummaging at the bottom of a bundle pulled out a towel embroidered with cockerels, oxbows, and wheels.

The doctor, who had waked up in the meantime, jumped down first from his bunk, and helped his wife to get to the floor. Guards' shelters and lampposts drifted past the door, followed by trees bending under heavy piles of snow, which they held out toward the train as though in sign of welcome. Long before it had stopped, sailors jumped off into the untrodden snow and raced around the corner of the station building where peasant women were usually to be found trading illegally in food.

Their black uniforms with bell-bottom trousers and ribbons fluttering from their visorless caps gave an air of reckless speed to their advance and made other people give way as before the onrush of racing skiers or skaters.

Around the corner, girls and women from nearby villages, as excited as if they were at the fortuneteller's, stood one behind the other in single file in the shelter of the station wall selling cucumbers, cottage cheese, and platters of boiled beef and rye pancakes kept hot and tasty by quilted napkins. Muffled up in shawls tucked inside their sheepskins, the women blushed a fiery red at the sailors' jokes but at the same time were terrified of them, for it was generally sailors who formed the units organized to fight against speculation and the forbidden free market.

The apprehensions of the peasant women were soon dispelled. When the train stopped and civilian passengers joined the crowd, trade became brisk.

Antonina Alexandrovna walked down the line inspecting the wares, her towel flung over her shoulder as if she were going to the back of the station to wash in the snow. Several women had called out: "Hey, what do you want for your towel?" but she continued on her way, escorted by her husband.

At the end of the row there was a woman in a black shawl with a scarlet pattern. She saw the towel and her bold eyes lit up. Glancing around cautiously, she sidled up to Antonina Alexandrovna and, uncovering her wares, whispered eagerly: "Look at this. Bet you haven't seen that in a long while. Tempting, isn't it? Don't think about it too long or it will be gone. Like to give me your towel for a half?"

Antonina Alexandrovna missed the last word.

"What do you mean, my good woman?"

The woman meant half a hare, roasted whole from head to tail and cut in two. She held it up. "I'm telling you, I'll give you a half for your towel. What are you staring at? It isn't dog meat. My husband is a hunter. It's hare, all right."

They exchanged their goods. Each believed that she had had the best of the bargain. Antonina Alexandrovna felt as ashamed as if she had swindled the peasant woman, while she, delighted with her deal, called a friend who had also sold out her wares and made off with her, home to their village, striding down the snowy path into the distance.

At this moment there was an uproar in the crowd. An old woman was screaming: "Hey, you! Where are you off to? Where's my money? When did you pay me, you cheat? Look at him, greedy pig, you call him and he doesn't even bother to turn around. Stop! Stop, I tell you, Mister Comrade! I've been robbed! Stop, thief! There he goes, that's him, catch him!"

"Which one?"

"That one, the one who's clean-shaven and grinning."

"Is that the one with the hole in his sleeve?"

"Yes, yes, catch him, the heathen!"

"The one with the patched elbow?"

"Yes, yes. Oh, I've been robbed."

"What's going on here?"

"Fellow over there bought some milk and pies, stuffed himself, and went off without paying, so the old woman is crying."

"That shouldn't be allowed. Why don't they go after him?"

"Go after him! He's got straps and cartridge belts all over him. He'll go after you."

10

There were several labor conscripts in car fourteen. With them was their guard, Private Voroniuk. Three of the men stood out from the rest. They were Prokhor Kharitonovich Prituliev, who had been cashier in a government liquor store in Petrograd—the cashier, as he was called in the car; Vasia Brykin, a sixteen-year-old boy apprenticed to an ironmonger; and Kostoied-Amursky, a gray-haired revolutionary co-operativist, who had been in all the forced-labor camps of the old regime and was now discovering those of the new.

The conscripts, who had all been strangers when they were impressed, were gradually getting to know each other. It turned out that the cashier and Vasia, the apprentice, came from the same part of the country, the Viatka government, and also that the train would be going through their native villages.

Prituliev came from Malmyzh. His hair was cropped and he was pockmarked, squat, and hideous. His gray sweater, black with sweat under the arms, fitted him snugly like a fleshy woman's blouse. He would sit for hours as silent as a statue, lost in thought, scratching the warts on his freckled hands until they bled and suppurated.

One day last autumn, he was going down the Nevsky when he walked into a militia roundup at the corner of Liteiny Street. He had to show his papers and was found to hold a fourth-class ration book, the kind issued to nonworkers, on which nothing could ever be bought. He was consequently detained, with many others who were arrested for the same reason, and taken under escort to barracks. His group was to be sent, like the one preceding it, to dig trenches on the Archangel front, but was diverted on its way and sent east through Moscow.

Prituliev had a wife in Luga, where he had worked before the war. She heard indirectly of his misfortune and rushed off to Vologda (the junction for Archangel) to look for him and obtain his release. But the unit had not gone there, her labors had been in vain, and she lost track of him.

In Petrograd Prituliev lived with a certain Pelagia Nilovna

Tiagunova. At the time he was arrested he had just said goodbye to her, preparing to go in a different direction to keep an appointment, and looking down Liteiny Street he could still see her back disappearing among the crowd.

She was a plump woman with a stately carriage, beautiful hands, and a thick braid which she tossed from time to time, with deep sighs, over her shoulder. She was now with the convoy, having volunteered to accompany Prituliev.

It was difficult to know what it was that attracted women to such an ugly man, but certainly they clung to him. In a car farther forward there was another woman friend of his, Ogryzkova, a bony girl with white eyelashes who had somehow made her way onto the train and whom Tiagunova called "the squirt," "the nozzle," and many other insulting names. The rivals were at swords' points and took good care to avoid each other. Ogryzkova never went to the other's car. It was a mystery to know how she ever met the object of her passion. Perhaps she contented herself with seeing him from afar, when the engine was being refuelled with the help of all the passengers.

11

Vasia's story was quite different. His father had been killed in the war and his mother had sent him to Petrograd to be apprenticed to his uncle.

The uncle kept a private shop in Apraksin Yard. One day last winter he had been summoned by the local soviet to answer a few questions. He mistook the door and walked into the office of the labor corps selection board. The room was full of conscripts; after a while soldiers came in, surrounded the men, and took them to the Semenov barracks for the night, and escorted them to the Vologda train in the morning.

The news of so many arrests spread and the prisoners' families came to say goodbye to them at the station. Among them were Vasia and his aunt. His uncle begged the guard (Voroniuk, who was now in car fourteen) to let him out for a minute to see his wife. The guard refused without a guarantee that he would return. The uncle and aunt offered Vasia as a hostage. Voroniuk agreed. Vasia was brought in and his uncle was let out. This was the last he ever saw of his aunt or uncle.

When the fraud was discovered, Vasia, who had suspected nothing, burst into tears. He threw himself at Voroniuk's feet, kissed his hands, and begged him to let him go, but to no avail. The guard was inexorable not because he was cruel, but discipline was very strict in those troubled times. The guard answered for the number of his charges with his life, and the numbers were checked by roll call. That was how Vasia came to be in the labor corps.

The co-operativist, Kostoied-Amursky, who had enjoyed the respect of his jailors under both Tsarism and the present government and who was always on good terms with them, repeatedly spoke to the head of the convoy about Vasia's predicament. The officer admitted that it was a terrible misunderstanding but said there were formal difficulties in the way of examining the case until they arrived; he promised to do his best at that moment.

Vasia was an attractive boy with regular features who looked like a royal page or an angel of God in a picture. He was unusually innocent and unspoiled. His favorite occupation was to sit on the floor at the feet of his elders, looking up at them, his hands clasped around his knees, and listen to their discussions and stories. By watching the muscles of his face, as he just barely restrained himself from tears or choked with laughter, you could almost follow the conversation.

12

The Zhivagos had invited the co-operativist Kostoied to dinner. He sat in their corner sucking a leg of hare with a loud wheezing noise. He dreaded drafts and chills, and changed his place several times, looking for a sheltered spot. At last he found a place where he did not feel the draft. "That's better," he said. He finished his bone, sucked his fingers clean, wiped them on his handkerchief, thanked his hosts, and said: "It's your window. It has to be cemented. But to go back to our discussion: You're mistaken, Doctor. Roast hare is an excellent thing, but to conclude that the peasants are prosperous is rash, to say the least, if you'll forgive my saying so."

"Oh, come," said Yurii Andreievich. "Look at all these stations. The trees aren't cut, the fences are intact. And these markets! These women! Think how wonderful! Somewhere life is still going on, some people are happy. Not everyone is wretched. This justifies everything."

"It would be good if that were true. But it isn't. Where did you get all those ideas? Take a trip to any place that is fifty miles from the railway. You'll find that there are peasant rebellions everywhere. Against whom? you'll ask. Well, they're against the Reds or against the Whites, whoever happens to be in power. You'll say, Aha, that's because the peasants are enemies of all authority, they don't know what they want. Allow me to differ. The peasant knows very well what he wants, better than you or I do, but he wants something quite different.

"When the revolution woke him up, he decided that his century-old dream was coming true—his dream of living on his own land by the work of his hands, in complete independence and with no obligations to anyone. Instead, he found he had only exchanged the oppression of the former state for the new, much harsher yoke of the revolutionary superstate. Can you wonder that the villages are restless and can't settle down? And you say they are prosperous! No, there are a lot of things you don't know, my dear fellow, and as far as I can see you don't want to know them."

"All right, it's true, I don't. Why on earth should I know and worry myself sick over every blessed thing? History hasn't consulted me. I have to put up with whatever happens, so why shouldn't I ignore the facts? You tell me my ideas don't correspond to reality. But where is reality in Russia today? As I see it, reality has been so terrorized that it is hiding. I want to believe that the peasants are better off and flourishing. If it is an illusion, what am I to do? What am I to live by; whom am I to believe? And I have to go on living, I've got a family."

He made a despairing gesture and, leaving the argument to his father-in-law, moved away, and hung his head over the edge of the bunk to look at what was going on below.

Prituliev, Tiagunova, Vasia, and Voroniuk were talking together. As the train was approaching his native province, Prituliev recalled the way to his village, the station, and the road you took according to whether you went by horse or on foot, and at the mention of familiar village names, Vasia repeated them with shining eyes, as if they were a marvellous fairy tale.

"You get off at Dry Ford?" he asked, choking with excitement. "Our station! Of course! And then you go on to Buisky, right?"

"That's right, you take the Buisky road."

"That's what I say—Buisky—Buisky village. Of course I know it, that's where you get off the main road, you turn right and right again. That's to get to us, to Veretenniki. And your way must be left, away from the river, isn't it? You know the river Pelga? Well, of course! That's our river. You keep following the river, on and on, and away up on the cliff on the right, overhanging that same river Pelga, there's our village, Veretenniki! It's right up on the edge, and it's stee-eep! It makes you giddy, honest to God it does. There's a quarry down below, for millstones. That's where my mother lives, in Veretenniki, and my two little sisters. Alenka and Arishka . . . Mother is a bit like you, Aunt Pelagia, she's young and fair. Uncle Voroniuk! Please, Uncle Voroniuk, for the love of Christ, please, I beg you, for God's sake . . . Uncle Voroniuk!"

"Well, what? Uncle, uncle, I know I'm not your aunt. What do you expect me to do? Am I mad? If I let you go that would be the end of me, amen, they'd put me up against a wall."

Pelagia Tiagunova sat looking thoughtfully out of the window, stroking Vasia's reddish hair. Now and then she bent down to him and smiled as if she were telling him: "Don't be silly. This isn't something to talk to Voroniuk about in front of everyone. Don't worry, have patience, it will be all right."

13

Peculiar things began to happen when they left Central Russia behind on their way east. They were going through a restless region infested with armed bands, past villages where uprisings had recently been put down.

The train stopped frequently in the middle of nowhere and security patrols checked the passengers' papers and luggage.

Once they stopped at night, but no one came in and no one was disturbed. Yurii Andreievich wondered if there had been an accident and went out to see.

It was dark. For no apparent reason the train had stopped between two stations, in a field, with a row of firs on either side of the track. Other passengers who had come out and were stamping their feet in the snow told Yurii Andreievich that there was nothing wrong, but that the engineer refused to go on, saying that this stretch was dangerous and should first be inspected by handcar. Spokesmen of the passengers had gone to reason with him and if necessary to grease his palm. It was said that sailors were also taking a hand in it and would undoubtedly get their way.

The snow at the head of the train was lit up at intervals, as from a bonfire, by fiery flashes from the smokestack or the glowing coals in the firebox. By this light several dark figures were now seen running to the front of the engine.

The first of them, presumably the engineer, reached the far end of the running board, leapt over the buffers, and vanished as if the earth had swallowed him. The sailors who were chasing him did exactly the same thing: they too flashed for a moment through the air and vanished.

Curious about what was going on, several passengers including Yurii Andreievich went to see.

Beyond the buffers, where the track opened out before them, they were met with an astonishing sight. The engineer stood in the snow up to his waist. His pursuers surrounded him in a semicircle, like hunters around their quarry; like him, they were buried in snow up to the waist.

"Thank you, comrades, fine stormy petrels you are,"* the engineer was shouting. "A fine sight, sailors chasing a fellow worker with guns! All because I said the train must stop. You be my witnesses, comrade passengers, you can see what kind of place this is. Anybody might be roaming around unscrewing the bolts. Do you think I'm worrying about myself, you God-damned bastards? To hell with you. It's for you I was doing it, so that nothing should happen to you, and that's all the thanks I get for my trouble! Go on, go on, why don't you shoot? Here I am. You be my witnesses, comrade passengers, I'm not running away."

Bewildered voices rose from the group. "Pipe down, old man . . . They don't mean it . . . Nobody would let them . . . They don't really mean it . . ." Others urged him on: "That's right, Gavrilka, stand up for yourself! Don't let them bully you!"

The first sailor to scramble out of the snow was a red-haired giant with a head so huge that it made his face look flat. He turned to the passengers and spoke in a deep, quiet, unhurried

---

*Stormy petrels: The reference is to the sailors in the *Potemkin* mutiny and is also an allusion to Gorky's story of that name.

voice with a Ukrainian accent, like Voroniuk's, his composure oddly out of keeping with the scene.

"Beg pardon, what's all this uproar about? Be careful you don't catch a chill in this cold, citizens. It's windy. Why not go back to your seats and keep warm?"

The crowd gradually dispersed. The giant went to the engineer, who was still worked up, and said:

"Enough hysterics, comrade engineer. Get out of the snow, and let's get going."

14

Next day the train, creeping at a snail's pace lest it run off the tracks, powdered by the wind with unswept snow, pulled up beside a lifeless, burned-out ruin. This was all that was left of the station, Nizhni Kelmes, its name still faintly legible on its blackened façade.

Beyond it lay a deserted village blanketed in snow. This too was damaged by fire. The end house was charred, the one next to it sagged where its corner timbers had fallen in; broken sleighs, fences, rusty pieces of metal, and smashed furniture were scattered all over the street; the snow was dirty with soot, and black patches of earth showed through the frozen puddles with half-burnt logs sticking out of them—all evidence of the fire and of the efforts to put it out.

The place was not in fact as dead as it looked; there were a few people still about. The stationmaster rose out of the ruins and the guard jumped down from the train and commiserated with him. "The whole place was burned down?"

"Good day to you, and welcome. Yes, we certainly had a fire, but it was worse than that."

"I don't follow."

"Better not try."

"You don't mean Strelnikov!"

"I do."

"Why? What had you done?"

"We didn't do anything, it was our neighbors; we got it too for good measure. You see that village over there? Nizhni Kelmes is in the Ust-Nemdinsk county—it was all because of them."

"And what crime had they committed?"

"Just about all the seven deadly sins: Dissolved their Poor Peasants' Committee, that's one; refused to supply horses to the Red Army, that's two (and they're all Tartars, mind you, horsemen); resisted the mobilization decree, that makes three. Well, there you are."

"Yes, I see. I quite see. So they were shelled?"

"Naturally."

"From the armored train?"

"Of course."

"That's bad. All our sympathy. Still, it's none of our business."

"Besides, it's an old story. And the news I have isn't very good either. You'll have to stop here for a couple of days."

"You're joking! I'm taking replacements to the front. This is an urgent matter."

"I'm not joking at all. We've had a blizzard for a solid week—snowdrifts all along the line, and no one to clear it. Half the village has run away. I'll put the rest of them on the job, but it won't be enough."

"Damn. What am I to do?"

"We'll get it cleared, somehow."

"How deep is the snow?"

"Not too bad. It varies. The worst patch is in the middle—about two miles long; we'll certainly have trouble there. Farther on the forest has kept the worst of the snow off the tracks. And on this side it's open country, so the wind has blown away some of it."

"Hell, what a pain in the neck! I'll mobilize all the passengers."

"That's what I was thinking."

"We mustn't use the sailors and Red Army men. But there's a whole corps of labor conscripts—including the other passengers, there are about seven hundred in all."

"That's more than enough. We'll start the moment we get the shovels. We're a bit short of them, so we've sent to the nearby villages for more. We'll manage."

"God, what a blow! Do you think we can do it?"

"Of course we can. With plenty of troops you can take a city, they say, and this is only a bit of tracks. Don't worry."

15

Clearing the line took three days, and all the Zhivagos, even Niusha, took part in it. They were the best three days of their journey.

The landscape had a withdrawn, secretive quality. It made one think of Pushkin's story about the Pugachev uprising and of some places described by Aksakov. The ruins added to the air of mystery; so did the wariness of the remaining villagers, who, afraid of informers, avoided the passengers and were silent even among themselves.

The workers were divided into gangs, with the labor conscripts and the civilians kept apart. Armed soldiers guarded each working group.

The tracks were cleared in several places at the same time by separate gangs. Mounds of snow between the sections hid the gangs from one another and were left untouched until the last.

The workers spent all day in the open, going back only to sleep. The days were clear and frosty, and the shifts were short because there were not enough shovels. It was sheer pleasure.

Zhivago's section of the track had a fine view. The country to the east dipped down into a valley and rose in gentle hills as far as the horizon.

On the top of a hill there was a house exposed to all the winds; its park must have been luxuriant in summer but could not give it any shelter now with its frosty lacework.

The snow smoothed and rounded all contours. It could not quite conceal the winding bed of a stream which in spring would rush down to the viaduct below the railway bank but at present was tucked up in the snow like a child in its cot with its head under the eiderdown.

Was anyone living in the house on the hill, Zhivago wondered, or was it standing empty and falling into ruins, held by some land committee? What had happened to the people who had once lived there? Had they fled abroad? Or been killed by the peasants? Or had they been popular and were they allowed to settle in the district as technical specialists? If they had stayed, had they been spared by Strelnikov or shared the fate of the kulaks?

The house teased his curiosity but kept its sorrowful silence. Questions were not in order in these days, and no one ever answered them. But the sun sparkled on the pure whiteness with a glare that was almost blinding. How cleanly his shovel cut into its smooth surface! How dry, how iridescent, like diamonds, was each shovelful. He was reminded of the days when, as a child in their yard at home, dressed in a braided hood and a black sheepskin fastened with hooks and eyes sewn in the curly fleece, he cut the dazzling snow into cubes and pyramids and cream puffs and fortresses and the cities of cave dwellers. Life had had zest in those far-off days, everything was a feast for the eyes and the stomach!

But these three days in the air, too, gave the impression of a feast. And no wonder! At night the workers received loaves of hot fresh bread, which was brought no one knew from where or by whose orders. The bread had a tasty crisp crust, shiny on top, cracked at the side, and with bits of charcoal baked into it underneath.

16

They became fond of the ruined station, as one becomes attached to a shelter used for a few days on a climbing trip in a snow-bound mountain. Its shape, its site, the details of its damage, remained imprinted in their memory.

They returned to it every evening just as the sun, as if out of loyalty to the past, set at its usual place behind an old birch tree outside the telegrapher's window.

At that spot the wall had caved into the room, but the corner facing the window had remained intact, with its coffee-colored wallpaper, the tiled stove with the round vent and the copper lid closed with a chain, and the inventory of the office furniture hanging on the wall in a black frame. As before the collapse, the setting sun brushed the tiles, brought out the warm brown glow on the wallpaper, and hung the shadow of the birch on the wall as if it were a woman's scarf.

At the rear of the building, on the nailed door to the ruins of the waiting room, there was still an announcement, put up in the first days of the February revolution, or shortly before it, which said:

"Sick passengers are temporarily requested not to bother about medicines and bandages. For obvious reasons, am sealing door, of which am giving notice hereby."

"Medical Assistant"
"Ust-Nemdinsk District"

When finally the last piles of snow between the cleared tracks were levelled, the entire line of rails came into view, flying into the distance like an arrow. On each side stretched white mountains of shovelled snow, bordered all along by the black walls of the forest.

As far as the eye could reach, groups of people with shovels in hand stood at intervals along the line. Seeing themselves for the first time in full force, they were astonished at their numbers.

17

It was learned that the train would leave shortly, despite the lateness of the hour and the approaching night. Yurii Andreievich and Antonina Alexandrovna went out to enjoy the sight of the cleared line once again. No one else was on the tracks. The doctor and his wife stood a while, gazing into the distance, exchanged a few words, and turned back to their car.

On the way they heard the angry voices of two quarrelling women. They recognized them at once as those of Ogryzkova and Tiagunova, who were walking in the same direction as they were, from the head to the end of the train, but on the station side, while the doctor and his wife walked on the wooded side. The endless line of cars screened the two couples from each other. The women seemed hardly ever to be abreast of the doctor and Antonina Alexandrovna, but always to be ahead of them or falling behind.

They seemed to be in a state of great agitation, and it was as though their strength failed them. Judging from the way their voices rose to a shriek or died down to a whisper, either their legs refused to carry them or else they kept stumbling and falling into snowdrifts. Tiagunova seemed to be chasing Ogryzkova, perhaps belaboring her with her fists whenever she caught up with her. She showered her rival with choice abuse, and her genteel, melodious voice made the insults sound infinitely more obscene than the coarse and unmusical swearing of men.

"You slut, you drag-tailed whore," Tiagunova screamed. "I can't move an inch without seeing you flouncing up and down, and ogling. Isn't my old fool enough for you without your having to make eyes at a babe in arms, to seduce a minor?"

"So Vasia too is your legal husband?"

"I'll give you legal husband, you filthy plague! One more word from you, and I'll kill you, don't tempt me."

"Now, now, keep your hands to yourself. What do you want of me?"

"I want to see you dead, you lecherous louse, you cat in heat, you shameless bitch!"

"That's what I am, is it? Naturally, I'm nothing but a cat, a bitch, compared with such a grand lady as you! Born in the gutter, married in a ditch, a rat in your belly, and a hedgehog for a brat! . . . Help! Help! She'll kill me! Help a poor orphan, help a poor defenseless girl!"

"Come along," Antonina Alexandrovna urged her husband. "I can't bear to listen to it, it's too disgusting. It will end badly."

18

Suddenly everything changed—the weather and the landscape. The plains ended, and the track wound up hills through mountain country. The north wind that had been blowing all the time dropped, and a warm breath came from the south, as from an oven.

Here the woods grew on escarpments projecting from the mountain slopes, and when the track crossed them, the train had to climb sharply uphill until it reached the middle of the wood, and then go steeply down again.

The train creaked and puffed on its way into the wood, hardly able to drag itself along, as if it were an aged forest guard walking in front and leading the passengers, who turned their heads from side to side and observed whatever was to be seen.

But there was nothing yet to see. The woods were still deep in their winter sleep and peace. Only here and there a branch would rustle and shake itself free of the remaining snow, as though throwing off a choker.

Yurii Andreievich was overcome with drowsiness. All these days he lay in his bunk and slept and woke and thought and listened. But there was nothing yet to hear.

19

While Yurii Andreievich slept his fill, the spring was heating and melting the masses of snow that had fallen all over Russia, first in Moscow on the day they had left and since then all along the way—all that snow they had spent three days clearing off the line at Ust-Nemdinsk, all that thick, deep layer of snow that had settled over the immense distances.

At first the snow thawed quietly and secretly from within. But by the time half the gigantic labor was done it could not be hidden any longer and the miracle became visible. Waters came rushing out from below with a roar. The forest stirred in its impenetrable depth, and everything in it awoke.

There was plenty of room for the water to play. It flung itself down the rocks, filled every pool to overflowing, and spread. It roared and smoked and steamed in the forest. It streaked through the woods, bogging down in the snow that tried to hinder its movement, it ran hissing on level ground or hurtled down and scattered into a fine spray. The earth was saturated. Ancient pine trees perched on dizzy heights drank the moisture almost from the clouds, and it foamed and dried a rusty white at their roots like beer foam on a mustache.

The sky, drunk with spring and giddy with its fumes, thickened with clouds. Low clouds, drooping at the edges like felt, sailed over the woods and rain leapt from them, warm, smelling of soil and sweat, and washing the last of the black armor-plating of ice from the earth.

Yurii Andreievich woke up, stretched, raised himself on one elbow, and looked and began to listen.

20

As they approached the mining region, there were more and more settlements, the runs were shorter, the stations more frequent. More people got on and off at the small stations. Instead of settling down and going to sleep, those who had only a short way to go found seats anywhere—near the door or in the middle of the car—and sat up arguing in low voices about local matters intelligible only to themselves.

From the hints dropped by such local passengers in the past three days Yurii Andreievich gathered that in the north the Whites were getting the upper hand and had seized or were about to occupy Yuriatin. Moreover, unless he had misheard the name or his old friend had a namesake, the White forces were led by Galiullin, whom he had last seen in Meliuzeievo.

Not to worry his family, he said nothing to them about these unconfirmed rumors.

21

Yurii Andreievich woke up shortly after midnight brimming with a vague feeling of happiness, which was, however, strong enough to have aroused him. The train was standing still. The station bathed in the glassy dusk of a white night. Something subtle and powerful in this luminous darkness suggested a vast and open landscape and that the station was situated high up.

People walked along the platform past the carriage speaking softly and treading as silently as shadows. Zhivago was touched by this evidence of a prewar consideration for the sleeping passengers.

The doctor was mistaken. There was the same din of shouting voices and stamping boots on this platform as on any other. But there was a waterfall nearby. It widened the expanse of the white night by a breath of freshness and freedom; that was what had filled him with happiness in his sleep. Its incessant noise dominated all other sounds and gave an illusion of stillness.

Knowing nothing of its existence but soothed and braced by it, the doctor fell fast asleep.

Two men were talking underneath his bunk.

"Well, have they had their tails twisted yet? Are they keeping quiet now?"

"The shopkeepers, you mean?"

"That's right. The grain merchants."

"Feed out of your hand! As soon as a few were bumped off by way of example, all the others piped down. A fine has been imposed on the district."

"How much?"

"Forty thousand."

"You're lying!"

"Why should I lie?"

"Forty thousand—that isn't even chicken feed!"

"Not forty thousand rubles, of course—forty thousand bushels."

"That was smart!"

"Forty thousand of the finest ground."

"Well, that's not such a miracle, after all. It's rich soil. Right in the thick of the corn belt. From here on, along the Rynva till you get to Yuriatin, it's village to village, harbor to harbor, one wholesaler after another."

"Don't shout. You'll wake people up."

"All right." He yawned.

"How about going to sleep? Looks as if we're moving."

The train, however, stayed where it was. But the rumble of another train came from behind, bursting into a deafening thunder and obliterating the sound of the waterfall as it approached, and an old-fashioned express rushed past at full speed on the parallel track, roared, hooted, winked its tail lights, and vanished into the distance ahead.

The conversation was resumed.

"Well, we're in for it. Now we'll never go."

"Yes. It won't be soon."

"It's an armored express—must be Strelnikov."

"Must be him."

"He's a wild beast when it comes to counterrevolutionaries."

"He's after Galeiev."

"Who's that?"

"Hetman Galeiev. They say he's outside Yuriatin with a Czech covering force. He's seized the harbors, the pest, and he's hanging on. Hetman Galeiev."

"Never heard of him."

"Or it may be Prince Galileiev. I can't quite remember the name."

"There aren't any such princes. Must be Ali Kurban. You've mixed them up."

"May be Kurban."

"That's more like it."

22

Toward morning Yurii Andreievich woke up a second time. He had had a pleasant dream. The feeling of bliss and liberation was still with him. Again the train was standing still, perhaps at the same station as before, possibly at another. Once more there was the sound of the waterfall, perhaps a different waterfall but more probably the same one.

He went back to sleep almost at once, and as he was dozing off he dimly heard the sound of running feet and of some commotion. Kostoied was quarrelling with the commander of the convoy and they were shouting at each other. The air was even more pleasant than before. It had a breath of something new in it, something that had not been there earlier—something magical, springlike, white, blackish, thin and insubstantial, like a snow flurry in May when the wet, melting flakes falling on the earth make it seem black rather than white. It was something transparent, blackish-white, sweet-smelling—"Wild cherry," Yurii Andreievich decided in his sleep.

23

Next morning Antonina Alexandrovna said:

"Really, Yura, you're extraordinary, you're a mass of contradictions. Sometimes a fly will wake you up and you can't get back to sleep till morning, and here you slept through all this row and I simply couldn't get you to wake up. Prituliev and Vasia have escaped, just think of it! And so have Tiagunova and Ogryzkova! Can you imagine such a thing! Wait, that isn't all.

Voroniuk as well. It's true, I tell you, he's run away. Now listen. How they managed it, together or separately, and in what order—it's all a complete mystery. Voroniuk, of course, I understand—once he found the others had gone, he would have to try to save his skin. But what about the rest? Did they really all vanish of their own free will, or was somebody done away with? For instance, if the women are to be suspected, did Tiagunova kill Ogryzkova or was it the other way around? Nobody knows. The commander of the escort has been running up and down the train like a lunatic. 'You're not to start the train. I order you in the name of the law not to move till I've caught my prisoners.' And the commanding officer shouts back: 'I'm taking replacements up to the front, I'm not waiting for your lousy crew. What an idea!' Then they both went for Kostoied. 'You, a syndicalist, an educated man, how could you sit by and let a simple soldier, an ignorant child of nature, act in such a reckless manner! And you a populist!'* And Kostoied gave them as good as he got. 'That's interesting,' he says. 'The prisoner has to look after his guard, does he? Well, really, the day that happens the hens will start to crow.' I was shaking you as hard as I could. 'Yura,' I cried, 'get up, there's been an escape.' But nothing doing. If a gun had gone off in your ear you wouldn't have heard it. . . . But I'll tell you more later. . . . Look! Father, Yura, look, isn't the view superb!"

Through the opening in the window they could see the country covered with spring floods as far as the eye could reach. Somewhere a river had overflowed its banks and the water had come right up to the embankment. In the foreshortened view from the bunk it looked as if the train were actually gliding on the water.

Only here and there was its smoothness broken by streaks of a metallic blue, but over all the rest of its surface the hot morning sun was chasing glassy patches of light as smooth and oily as melted butter that a cook brushes with a feather on a pie crust.

In this shoreless flood were sunk the shafts of the white clouds, their pediments submerged together with the fields, the hollows, and the bushes.

And somewhere in the middle of the flood there was a narrow strip of land with a row of doubled trees going up and down and suspended between earth and sky.

*Left-wing idealists who devoted themselves to work among the people.

"Look, a family of ducks!" Alexander Alexandrovich cried out.

"Where?"

"Near the island. More to the right. Damn, they've flown. We've frightened them."

"Yes, I see them now," said Yurii Andreievich. "I must have a talk with you, Alexander Alexandrovich. Some other time. . . . As for our labor conscripts and the women, good for them. And I'm sure there wasn't any murder. They just broke free like the water."

24

The white northern night was ending. Everything could be seen clearly—the mountain, the thicket, and the ravine—but seemed unreal, as though made up.

The wood, which had several blossoming wild cherries in it, was just coming into leaf. It grew under an overhanging cliff, on a narrow ledge above another precipice.

The waterfall, though not far away, could be seen only from the edge of the ravine beyond the thicket. Vasia was tired from walking to see it, to experience the joy and terror of the spectacle.

The waterfall had no equal anywhere around, nothing that could match it. This uniqueness endowed it with an awesome quality; it was like a living and conscious creature, a local dragon or winged serpent who levied tribute and preyed upon the countryside.

Halfway down, it broke on a sharp rock and divided in two. The top was almost motionless, but the two lower columns weaved slightly from side to side as if the water were continually slipping and righting itself, shaken but always recovering.

Vasia had spread his sheepskin on the ground and was lying at the edge of the thicket. When it grew lighter, a large bird with heavy wings flew down from the mountain, soared in a smooth circle around the wood, and settled on a pine close to where he lay. He looked up enchanted at its dark blue throat and gray-blue breast and whispered its Urals name, *ronzha*. Then he got up, picked up his sheepskin, flung it over his shoulders, and crossed the clearing to speak to his companion.

"Come on, Auntie Polia. Goodness, how cold you are! I can hear your teeth chattering. Well, what are you staring at, why are you so frightened? We've got to go, I'm telling you, we must get to a village. They'll hide us, they won't harm their own kind. If we go on like this we'll die of starvation. We've had nothing to eat for two days. Uncle Voroniuk must have raised a terrible hullabaloo, they must all be out looking for us. We have to go, Auntie; to put it plainly, we've got to run. I don't know what to do with you, Auntie, not a word out of you for two whole days. You worry too much, honest to God, you do. What are you so unhappy about? It isn't as if you'd meant to push Auntie Katia Ogryzkova off the train, you just caught her sideways, by accident, I saw you. She picked herself up off the grass—I saw her with my own eyes—and she got up and ran away. She and Uncle Prokhor, Prokhor Kharitonovich, are sure to catch up with us, we'll all be together again. The main thing is to stop worrying, then you'll find your tongue again."

Tiagunova got up, took Vasia's hand, and said softly: "All right, let's go, lamb."

25

Their timbers creaking, the cars climbed up the steep hill. Below the bank there was a thicket, its top not quite reaching the level of the track. Lower still were fields. The floods had just withdrawn and the grass was strewn with sand and pieces of timber. The boards must have been washed down from somewhere higher up the hill where they had been stacked preparatory to floating them downstream.

The young wood below the embankment was still almost as bare as in winter. Only in the buds that spotted it all over like drops of candle grease there was something not in accord with the rest, something superfluous, some disturbance, perhaps dirt or an inflammation causing them to swell, and the disturbance, superfluity, and dirt were the signs of life, which had already set the most forward of the trees on fire with its green leafy flame.

Here and there a birch stretched itself like a martyr pierced by the barbs and arrows of its opening shoots, and you knew its smell by just looking at it, the smell of its glistening resin, which is used for making varnish.

Soon the tracks drew level with the place where the logs washed down by the flood might have come from. A cutting through the wood showed at a bend of the tracks; it was littered all over with chips and shavings, and there was a pile of timber in the middle. The engine braked and the train shuddered and stopped on the curve of the hill, bending slightly in a wide arc.

A few short barking hoots and shouts came from the engine, but the passengers did not need these signals to know that the engineer had stopped to take on a supply of fuel.

The freight-car doors rolled open, and a crowd the size of the population of a small town poured out. Only the sailors stayed in the front cars; they were excused from all chores.

There was not enough small firewood in the clearing to fill the tender, and some of the large timber had to be cut down to the right size. The engine crew had saws as part of their equipment and these were issued to volunteers, one to each pair, the doctor and his father-in-law among them.

Grinning sailors stuck their heads out of their doors. They were a curious mixture of middle-aged workingmen, straight from their emergency training, and boys just out of naval college who looked as if they had got in by mistake among the staid fathers of families and who joked and played the fool with the older sailors to keep themselves from thinking. All of them felt that their hour of trial was at hand.

Jokes and guffaws followed the work parties.

"Hey, Grandfather! I'm not shirking, I'm too young to work, my nanny won't let me." "Hey, Marva, don't saw off your skirt, you'll catch cold!" "Hey, young one, don't go to the wood, come and be my wife instead!"

26

There were several trestles in the clearing. Yurii Andreievich and Alexander Alexandrovich went up to one of them and began to saw.

This was the moment of spring when the earth emerges from the snow looking much as when the snow had trapped it six months earlier. The wood smelled of damp and was heaped with last year's leaves like an unswept room where people have been tearing up letters, bills, and receipts for years.

"Don't go so fast, you'll tire yourself," said the doctor, giving a slower and more even movement to the saw. "What about a rest?"

The wood echoed to the hoarse ringing of other saws; somewhere, very far away, a nightingale was trying out its voice, and at longer intervals a blackbird whistled as if blowing dust out of a flute. Even the engine steam rose into the sky warbling like milk boiling up on a nursery alcohol stove.

"What did you want to speak to me about?" asked Alexander Alexandrovich. "Do you remember? We were going past the island, the ducks flew away, and you said you wanted to speak to me."

"Oh, yes. . . . Well, I don't quite know how to put it briefly. I was thinking that we are going farther and farther. The whole of this region is in ferment. We don't know what we'll find when we get there. Perhaps we ought to talk things over just in case . . . I don't mean about our convictions—it would be absurd to try to define them in five minutes in a spring wood. Besides, we know each other well. You and I and Tonia and many others like us, we make up our own world these days, the only difference between us is in the degree of our awareness of it. But that's not what I want to talk about. What I meant was that perhaps we ought to agree in advance on how to behave under certain circumstances, so that we need never blush for one another or make each other feel ashamed."

"I know what you mean. I like the way you put it. Now this is what I'll tell you. Do you remember that night you brought me the paper with the first government decrees in the winter, in a snowstorm? You remember how unbelievably uncompromising they were? It was that single-mindedness that carried us away. But such things retain their original purity only in the minds of those who have conceived them, and then only on the day they are first made public. Next day, the casuistry of politics has turned them inside out. What can I say to you? Their philosophy is alien to me, their regime is hostile to us, I have not been asked if I consent to all this change. But I have been trusted, and my own actions, even if they were not freely chosen, put me under a certain obligation.

"Tonia keeps asking if we'll arrive in time to plant our vegetables. I don't know. I don't know the soil or the climate in the Urals; the summer is so short I can't imagine how anything ever ripens in time.

"But after all, it is not for the sake of gardening that we are going all this enormous distance. No, we had better face things honestly, our object is quite different. We are going to try to subsist in the modern fashion, taking our share in the squandering of old Krueger's properties, his factories and machines. We are not going to rebuild his fortune, but like everyone else and in the same incredibly chaotic way we'll fritter it away and lend a hand in the collective squandering of thousands for the sake of earning a kopek's worth of living. Not that I would take back the estate on the old terms, even if you showered me with gold. That would be as foolish as to start running about naked or trying to forget the alphabet. No, the age of private property in Russia is over, and anyway, we Gromekos lost our acquisitive passion a generation ago."

27

It was too hot and stuffy in the car to sleep. The doctor's pillow was soaked in sweat. Carefully, so as not to wake the others, he got down from his bunk and pushed open the car doors.

Sticky damp heat struck him in the face as if he had walked into a cobweb in a cellar. "Mist," he guessed. "Tomorrow will be scorching hot. That's why it is so airless and so heavy and oppressive now."

It was a big station, possibly a junction. Besides the mist and the stillness, there was a feeling of emptiness, of neglect, as if the train had been lost and forgotten. It must be standing at the farthest end of the station, and so great was the maze of tracks separating it from the station buildings that if, at the other end of the yard, the earth were to open and swallow up the station, no one in the train would have noticed it.

Two faint sounds could be heard in the distance.

Behind him, where they had come from, there was a rhythmic splashing, as if clothes were being rinsed or the wind were flapping a heavy, damp flag against a pole.

From ahead there came an even rumbling, which made the doctor, who had been at the front, prick up his ears. "Long-range guns," he decided after listening to the calmly echoing, low, susstained note.

"That's it, we're right at the front." He shook his head and jumped down from the car. He walked a few steps forward. Two cars farther up, the train ended; the rest had been uncoupled and had gone away with the engine.

"So that was why they were so keyed up yesterday," the doctor thought. "They had a feeling they would be thrown in as soon as we arrived."

He walked around the front car, meaning to cross the rails and look for the main part of the station, but a sentry with a rifle rose in his path.

"Where're you going? Got a pass?"

"What is this station?"

"Never mind. Who are you?"

"I am a doctor from Moscow. My family and I are passengers on this train. Here are my papers."

"To hell with your papers. I'm not such a fool as to try to read in the dark. There's a mist—can't you see? I don't need any papers to know what kind of doctor you are. Those are more of your doctors shooting twelve-inch guns at us. Put an end to you, I would, but it's too soon for that. Get back now, while you're still in one piece."

"He's taking me for someone else," thought Zhivago. Clearly, it was no use arguing, better follow his advice before it was too late. He turned and walked the other way.

The gunfire was now at his back. There, behind him, was the east. There the sun had risen in a drift of mist and was peering dully through floating shadows, like a naked man through clouds of steam at the baths.

Zhivago walked down the length of the train and passed the end car. His feet sank deeper and deeper into soft sand.

The even sound of splashing came nearer. The ground sloped down steeply. He stopped, trying to make out the indistinct shapes in front of him; the mist made them unnaturally large. One more step, and the hulls of beached boats came up out of the dark. Before him was a wide river, its lazy ripples splashing slowly, wearily against the sides of the fishing smacks and the planks of landing stages along the shore.

A figure rose from the beach.

"Who gave you permission to prowl around?" asked another sentry with a rifle.

"What is this river?" shot out Yurii Andreievich, though he had firmly resolved not to ask any more questions.

By way of answer the sentry put his whistle to his mouth, but he was saved the trouble, for the first sentry, whom it was meant to summon, had evidently been following the doctor without a sound, and now joined his comrade. They stood talking.

"There's no doubt about it. You can tell this kind of bird at a glance. 'What's this station?' 'What's this river?' There's dust in your eyes! What do you say? Shall we take him straight to the jetty or to the train first?"

"I say to the train. See what the boss says.—Your documents," he barked. Grabbing the bunch of papers in his fist and calling back to someone: "Keep an eye on him," he strode away with the first sentry toward the station.

The third figure, whom Zhivago had not so far made out, was evidently a fisherman. He had been lying on the beach, but he now grunted, stirred, and set about enlightening the doctor on his position.

"It's lucky for you they're taking you to the boss. That may save your skin. But you mustn't blame them. They're only doing their duty. The people are on top nowadays. Perhaps it's even for the best in the long run, though there isn't much to be said for it now. They've made a mistake, you see. They've been hunting, hunting all the time, for a certain man. So they thought it was you. That's him, they thought, that's the enemy of the workers' state, we've got him. A mistake, that's all it is. If anything happens, insist on seeing the boss. Don't you let those two get away with anything. They're politically conscious, it's a misfortune, God help us. They'd think nothing of doing away with you. So, if they say 'Come along,' see you don't go. Say you must see the boss."

From the fisherman Yurii Andreievich learned that the river was the famous waterway, the Rynva, and that the station by the river served Razvilie, an industrial suburb of the town of Yuriatin. He also learned that Yuriatin, which lay a couple of miles upstream, seemed now to have been recaptured from the Whites. And that there had been troubles in Razvilie and that they too seemed to have been put down, the reason for the great stillness all around being that the station area had been cleared of civilians and strictly cordoned off. He learned finally that among the trains at the station which were used as military offices was the special train of Army Commissar Strelnikov, to whom the two sentries had gone to report.

A third sentry now came from the direction in which the two others had gone; he was distinguished from them chiefly by the fact that he pulled his rifle after him, the butt trailing on the ground, or propped it up in front of him like a tipsy friend who needed his support. This guard took the doctor to the commissar.

28

Sounds of laughter and movement came from one of the two coupled parlor cars to which the guard, after giving the password to the sentry, took the doctor, but they ceased the moment the two men went in.

The guard led the doctor down a narrow passage to a wide central compartment. It was a clean, comfortable room where tidy, well-dressed people worked in complete silence. The doctor had had a very different idea of the background of Strelnikov, the famous non-Party military expert who was the pride and terror of the region.

But undoubtedly the real center of his activities lay elsewhere, closer to the staff H.Q. and to the field of military operations. This could only be his personal suite, his private office and sleeping quarters.

Hence the stillness, rather like that in a steam bath with cork floors and attendants in soft slippers.

The office was in the former dining car, carpeted and with several desks in it.

"One moment," said a young officer whose desk was by the door. He nodded absent-mindedly, dismissing the guard who left, rattling his rifle butt on the metal strips nailed across the floor of the passage. After this, everyone felt free to forget the doctor and paid no more attention to him.

From where he stood at the entrance he could see his papers lying on a desk at the far end of the room. The desk was occupied by a man who was older than the rest and who looked like an old-style colonel. He was an army statistician of some sort. Mumbling to himself, he consulted reference books, studied field maps, checked, compared, cut out, and pasted things in. After looking around at every window in the room he announced: "It's going to be hot," as though forced to this conclusion only by the examination of all the windows.

An army electrician was crawling about on the floor mending a broken wire. When he reached the desk by the door the young officer got up to make room for him. At the next table a typist in an army leather jacket was struggling with her typewriter; its carriage had slipped and got stuck. The young officer stood over her and examined the cause of the mishap from above while the electrician crawled in under her desk and examined it from below. The old-style colonel got up and joined them, and all four busied themselves with the typewriter.

This made Yurii Andreievich feel better. These people must know his fate better than he did; it was hardly likely that they would be so unconcerned and so busy with trifles in the presence of a man whom they considered doomed.

"And yet who knows?" he reflected. "Why are they so unconcerned? Guns are going off and people are dying, and they calmly prognosticate heat—not the heat of the battle but of the weather. Perhaps, after all, they have seen so much that they have no sensibility left."

To occupy himself, he stared across the room through the window opposite.

29

He could see the edge of the tracks and higher up the hill the station and the suburb of Razvilie.

Three flights of unpainted wooden steps led from the platforms to the station building.

At the end of the tracks there was a large graveyard for old engines. Locomotives without tenders, with smokestacks shaped like the tops of knee boots or like beakers, stood smokestack to smokestack amid piles of scrap.

The engine graveyard below and the human graveyard above, the crumpled iron on the tracks and the rusty iron of the roofs and shop signs of the suburb, composed a single picture of neglect and age under the white sky scalded by the early morning heat.

Living in Moscow, Yurii Andreievich had forgotten how many shop signs there still were in other towns and how much of the façades they covered. Some of those he was seeing now were so large that he could read them easily from where he stood, and they came down so low over the crooked windows of the sagging one-story buildings that the squat little houses were almost hidden by them like the faces of village children in their fathers' caps.

The mist had gone from the west, and now what remained of it in the east stirred, swayed, and parted like the curtain of a stage.

And there, on a hill above Razvilie and a mile or two beyond it, stood a large town, the size of a provincial capital. The sun warmed its colors and the distance simplified its lines. It clung to the summit of the hill in tiers, house by house and street by street, with a big church in the middle on the top, as in a cheap color print of a desert monastery or of Mount Athos.

"Yuriatin," the doctor thought excitedly. "The town I used to hear about so often from Anna Ivanovna and from Nurse Antipova. How strange that I should see it in these circumstances!"

At the moment the attention of the military was diverted from the typewriter to something they could see from one of the other windows, and the doctor looked around.

A group of prisoners was being taken under guard up the station steps. Among them was a boy in a school uniform who was wounded in the head. He had received first aid, but a trickle of blood seeped through the bandage and he kept smudging it with his hand over his dark sweaty face. Walking between two Red Army men at the tail of the procession, he attracted notice not only by his resolute air, his good looks, and the pathos of so young a rebel's plight, but by the utter absurdity of his own and his two companions' gestures. They were doing exactly the opposite of what they should have done.

He was still wearing his school cap. It slithered continually from his bandaged head, and instead of taking it off and carrying it in his hand he rammed it back each time, disturbing the bandage and the wound, and in this his two guards assisted him readily.

In this absurdity, so contrary to common sense, the doctor saw a profound symbol. He longed to rush out and address the boy in words that were impatiently welling up inside him. He longed to shout to him and to the people in the railway coach that salvation lay not in loyalty to forms but in throwing them off.

He turned away. Strelnikov came in with long, vigorous strides and stood in the middle of the room.

How was it possible that he, a doctor, with his countless acquaintances, had never until this day come across anything so definite as this man's personality? How was it that they had never been thrown together, that their paths had not crossed?

In some inexplicable way it was clear at once that this man was entirely a manifestation of the will. So completely was he the self he resolved to be that everything about him seemed inevitable, exact, perfect—his well-proportioned, handsomely set head, his impetuous step, his long legs, his knee boots which may well have been muddy but looked polished, and his gray serge tunic which may have been creased but looked as if it were made of the best linen and had just been pressed.

Such was the irresistible effect of his brilliance, his unaffected ease, and his sense of being at home in any conceivable situation on earth.

He must certainly, Yurii Andreievich thought, be possessed of a remarkable gift, but it was not necessarily the gift of originality. This talent, which showed itself in his every movement, might well be the talent of imitation. In those days everyone modelled himself on someone else—they imitated heroes of history, or the men who had struck their imagination by winning fame in the fighting at the front or in the streets, or those who had great prestige with the people, or this or that comrade who had won distinction, or simply one another.

Strelnikov politely concealed any surprise or annoyance he may have felt at the presence of a stranger. He addressed his staff, treating him as if he belonged among them.

He said: "Congratulations. We have driven them back. It all seems more like playing at war than serious business, because they are as Russian as we are, only stuffed with nonsense—they won't give it up, so we have to beat it out of them. Their commander was my friend. His origin is even more proletarian than mine. We grew up in the same house. He has done a great deal for me in my life and I am deeply indebted to him. And here I am rejoicing that we have thrown them back beyond the river and perhaps even farther. Hurry up with that connection, Gurian, we need the telephone, we can't possibly manage with only messengers and the telegraph. Have you noticed how hot it is? I managed to get in an hour's sleep, just the same. Oh, yes!" He turned to the doctor, remembering that he had been waked up to deal with some nonsense in connection with this man.

"This man?" Strelnikov thought, looking him over sharply. "Nonsense! He's nothing like him. Fools!" He laughed, and said to Yurii Andreievich:

"My apologies, comrade. They mistook you for someone else. My sentries got mixed up. You are free to go. Where are the comrade's work papers? Ah, here are your documents. May I just have a glance . . . Zhivago . . . Zhivago . . . Doctor Zhivago . . . Moscow . . . How about going to my place for a moment? This is the secretariat, I'm in the next car. This way, I won't keep you long."

30

Who, in fact, was Strelnikov?

That he should have reached and held his position was remarkable, for he was a non-Party man. He had been totally unknown because, though born in Moscow, he had gone straight from the university to the provinces as a teacher, and in the war had been taken prisoner, reported missing, believed killed, and had only recently come back from German captivity.

He was recommended and vouched for by Tiverzin, a railway worker of advanced political views in whose family he had lived as a child. Those who controlled appointments were impressed by him: in those days of inordinate rhetoric and political extremism his revolutionary fervor, equally unbridled, was remarkable for its genuineness. His fanaticism was not an imitation but was his own, a natural consequence of all his previous life.

Strelnikov justified the confidence of the authorities.

His fighting record over the past few months included the actions at Nizhni Kelmes and Ust-Nemdinsk, the suppression of the Gubysov peasants who had put up armed resistance to food levies, and of the men of the 14th Infantry who had plundered a food convoy. He had also dealt with Stenka Razin soldiers, who had started an uprising in the town of Turkatui and gone over to the Whites, and with the mutiny at Chirkin Us, where a loyal commander had been killed.

In each case, he had taken his enemies by surprise and had investigated, tried, sentenced, and enforced his sentence with speed, severity, and resolution.

He had brought the epidemic of desertions in this whole region under control and had successfully reorganized the recruiting bodies. As a result, conscription went ahead and the Red Army reception centers were working overtime.

Finally, when the White pressure from the north increased and the position became admittedly grave, Strelnikov was entrusted with new responsibilities, military, strategic, and operational. His interventions produced immediate results.

Strelnikov ("the shooter") knew that rumor had nicknamed him Razstrelnikov, the Executioner. He took this in his stride; he was disturbed by nothing.

He was a native of Moscow, and his father was a worker who had been sent to prison for taking part in the revolution of 1905. He did not participate in the revolutionary movement in those years, first because he was too young, and at the university because young men who come from a poor background value higher education more and work harder than the children of the rich. The ferment among other students left him uninvolved. He absorbed an immense amount of information and after taking his degree in the humanities trained himself later in science and mathematics.

Exempted from the army, he enlisted voluntarily, was commissioned, sent to the front, and captured, and on hearing of the revolution in Russia he escaped in 1917 and came home. He had two charcteristic features, two passions: an unusual power of clear and logical reasoning, and a great moral purity and sense of justice; he was ardent and honorable.

But he would not have made a scientist of the sort who breaks new ground. His intelligence lacked the capacity for bold leaps into the unknown, the sudden flashes of insight that transcend barren, logical deductions.

And if he were really to do good, he would have needed, in addition to his principles, a heart capable of violating them—a heart which knows only of particular, not of general, cases, and which achieves greatness in little actions.

Filled with the loftiest aspirations from his childhood, he had looked upon the world as a vast arena where everyone competed for perfection, keeping scrupulously to the rules. When he found that this was not so, it did not occur to him that his conception of the world order might have been over-simplified. He nursed his grievance and with it the ambition to judge between life and the dark forces that distorted it, and to be life's champion and avenger.

Embittered by his disappointment, he was armed by the revolution.

31

"Zhivago," repeated Strelnikov when they were settled in his room. "Zhivago . . . Trade, I think. Or upper class . . . Well, of course, a Moscow doctor . . . Going to Varykino. That's strange, why should you leave Moscow for such a provincial hole?"

"That's just the idea. In search of quiet, seclusion, and obscurity."

"Well, well, how romantic! Varykino? I know most of the places around here. That used to be Krueger's estate. You aren't related to him, by any chance? You don't happen to be his heir?"

"Why the irony? Being his 'heir' has nothing to do with it. Though it is true that my wife . . ."

"Ah, so you see! But if you're feeling nostalgic for the Whites I'm going to disappoint you. You're too late. We've cleared the district."

"You're still making fun of me?"

"And then, a doctor. An army medical officer. And we're at war. That really is my business. You're a deserter. The Greens★ are also seeking refuge in the woods. Your reasons?"

"I have been wounded twice and discharged as an invalid."

"Next you'll be handing me a reference from the People's Commissariat of Education or Health to prove that you are a Soviet citizen, a 'sympathizer,' 'entirely loyal.' These are

---

★Greens: Anarchistic elements, chiefly peasants, who fought both Reds and Whites.

apocalyptic times, my dear sir, this is the Last Judgment. This is a time for angels with flaming swords and winged beasts from the abyss, not for sympathizers and loyal doctors. However, I told you you were free, and I won't go back on my word. But remember, it's for this once. I have a feeling that we'll meet again, and then our conversation will be quite different. Watch out."

Neither the threat nor the challenge disturbed Yurii Andreievich. He said: "I know what you think of me. From your point of view you are right. But the issue you wish me to discuss with you is one I have been arguing with an imaginary accuser all my life, and it would be odd if I had not by now reached some conclusion. Only I could not put it into a couple of words. So if I am really free, permit me to leave without having it out with you. If I am not, then you must decide what to do with me. I have no excuses to make to you."

They were interrupted by the telephone. The line was repaired. Strelnikov picked up the receiver.

"Thanks, Gurian. Now be a good fellow and send somebody along to see Comrade Zhivago to his train; I don't want any more accidents. And give me the Razvilie Cheka Transport Department."

When Zhivago had gone, Strelnikov telephoned the railway station.

"There's a schoolboy they've brought in, keeps pulling his cap over his ears and he's got a bandaged head, it's disgraceful.—That's right.—He's to have medical aid if he needs it.—Certainly.—Yes, like the apple of your eye, you'll be responsible to me personally.—Food, too, if necessary. That's right. Now, let's get down to business. . . . I'm still talking, don't cut me off. Damn, there's somebody else on the line. Gurian! Gurian! They've cut me off."

He gave up trying to finish his conversation for the time being. "It could be one of my former pupils," he thought. "Fighting us, now he's big." He counted up the years since he had stopped teaching to see if the boy could have been his pupil. Then he looked out of the window toward the panorama of the horizon, and searched for the part of Yuriatin where they had lived. Suppose his wife and daughter were still there! Couldn't he go to them? Why not now, this very minute? Yes, but how could he? They belonged to another life. First he must see this one through, this new life, then he could go back to the one that had been interrupted. Someday he would do it. Someday. But when, when?

CHAPTER EIGHT

Arrival

1

The train that had brought the Zhivago family was still on a siding behind several other trains that screened it from the station, yet they had a feeling that their connection with Moscow—which till now had remained unbroken—snapped that morning, that it had come to an end. Here began another territory, a different, provincial world, which had a center of gravity of its own.

Here people were closer together than in the capitals. Although the station area was cleared of civilians and surrounded by Red Army units, passengers for the local trains managed in some unaccountable way to get to the tracks, to "infiltrate," as we would say today. They had already crammed the cars, thronging in the open sliding doors, and they walked back and forth along the train and stood in small groups on the embankment.

All of them, without exception, were acquainted; they waved and called out as soon as they caught sight of each other, and they exchanged greetings as they passed. Their speech and dress, their food and manners, were all a little different from those of people in the capitals.

"How do they earn their living?" the doctor wondered. What were their interests and their material resources, how did they cope with the difficulties of the times, how did they evade the laws?

All these questions were soon answered in the most vivid way.

2

Escorted by the sentry who dragged his rifle after him or used it as a walking stick, the doctor went back to his carriage. It was a sultry day. The hot sun beat down on the rails and the roofs of the cars. The black puddles of oil on the ground blazed with a yellow shimmer, like gold leaf.

The sentry's rifle butt plowed a furrow in the sand. It clinked against the ties.

"The weather has settled," he was saying. "Time for the spring sowing—oats, wheat, millet—it's the best time. It's too early for the buckwheat, though. Where I come from we sow the buckwheat on the Feast of Akulina. I'm not from these parts, I come from Morshansk, in the Tambov government. Eh, Comrade Doctor, if it wasn't for this here civil war and this plague of a counterrevolution, do you think I'd be wasting my time in strange parts at this season? The class war has run between us like the black cat of discord, and just look at what it's doing."

3

Hands stretched out of the carriage to help him up.

"Thanks, I can manage."

Yurii Andreievich hoisted himself into the car, and after regaining his balance embraced his wife.

"At last! Thank God, it's ended well," she said. "Actually, we knew you were all right."

"What do you mean, you knew?"

"We knew everything."

"How?"

"The sentries told us. How could we have stood it otherwise? As it is, Father and I nearly went out of our minds. There he is, he's fast asleep, you can't wake him, sleeping like a log after all the excitement. There are several new passengers, I'll introduce you in a moment, but listen to what everybody's talking about—they are all congratulating you on your lucky escape. Here he is," she said suddenly, turning and introducing her husband over her shoulder to one of the new passengers who was hemmed in by the crowd at the back of the freight car.

"Samdeviatov," the stranger introduced himself, raising his soft hat over other people's heads and pushing his way forward through the press of bodies.

"Samdeviatov," thought the doctor. "With a name like that he ought to have come straight out of an old Russian ballad, complete with a bushy beard, a smock, and a studded belt. But he makes you think of the local Arts Club, with his graying curls, mustache, goatee . . ."

"Well, did Strelnikov give you a fright?" said Samdeviatov. "Tell the truth."

"No, why? We had an interesting talk. Certainly he has a powerful personality."

"I should think so. I've got some idea of what he's like. He's not from these parts. He's one of you Moscow people. Like all our newfangled things. They too are imported from the capital. We wouldn't have thought of them ourselves."

"Yurochka, this is Anfim Efimovich, he knows everything," Antonina Alexandrovna said. "He's heard about you and about your father, and he knew my grandfather—he knows everyone, absolutely everyone!—I suppose you must have met the schoolteacher, Antipova?" she slipped in casually, and Samdeviatov replied just as casually: "What about Antipova?" Yurii Andreievich heard this exchange but did not say anything, and his wife went on: "Anfim Efimovich is a Bolshevik. Be on your guard, Yurochka. You must watch your tongue when he is around."

"Really? I'd never have thought so. I'd have taken him for an artist of some sort."

"My father kept an inn," said Samdeviatov. "He had seven troikas on the road. But I went to the university, and it's true that I'm a Social Democrat."

"Listen to what Anfim Efimovich told me, Yurochka, and by the way, if you don't mind my saying so, Anfim Efimovich, your name is a real tongue-twister!—So, listen, Yurochka, we've been terribly lucky. We can't change at Yuriatin—part of the town is on fire and the bridge has been blown up, you can't get through. Our train will be switched to another line, and that line happens to be just the one we need to get to Torfianaia. Isn't it wonderful! We don't have to change and lug all our stuff from one station to another. On the other hand, we'll be shunted back and forth for hours before we really start off. Anfim Efimovich told me all that."

4

Antonina Alexandrovna was right. Cars were coupled and uncoupled, and the train was shifted endlessly from one congested line to another where other trains blocked its way into the open country.

The town lay in the distance partly hidden by the rolling countryside. Only now and then did its roofs, the chimneys of its factories, and the crosses on its belfries emerge above the horizon. One of its suburbs was on fire. The smoke drifted across the sky looking like a gigantic horse's mane blowing in the wind.

The doctor and Samdeviatov sat on the floor of the freight car, their legs dangling over the side. Samdeviatov kept pointing into the distance and explaining what they saw to Yurii Andreievich. Every now and then the train would jerk noisily and drown his voice, and he would lean across bringing his mouth close to the doctor's ear and repeat what he had said, shouting himself hoarse.

"That's a movie house, the 'Giant,' they've set on fire. The cadets were holding it, though they'd surrendered earlier. Otherwise, the fighting isn't over yet. You see those black dots on the belfry? Those are our people, sniping at the Czechs."

"I can't see a thing. How can you see them at such a distance?"

"That's the artisans' quarter, Khokhriki, burning over there. Kholodeievo, the shopping center, is farther on. I'm interested because our inn is there. Luckily, it's only a small fire, it hasn't spread. So far the center has remained intact."

"What did you say? I can't hear you."

"I said the center, the center of the town—the cathedral, the library . . . Our name, Samdeviatov, is a garbled Russian form of San Donato. We're supposed to be descended from the Demidovs."

"I still can't hear."

"I said Samdeviatov is a form of San Donato. They say we are a branch of the Demidov family, the Princess Demidov San Donato. But it may be just a family legend. This place here is called Spirka's Dell. It's full of summer houses and amusement parks. Strange name, isn't it?"

Before them extended a field crisscrossed by branch tracks. Telegraph poles strode away to the horizon like giants in seven-league boots, and the broad winding ribbon of a highway competed in beauty with the tracks. It vanished beyond the horizon, reappeared in a broad arc at a turn, and again vanished.

"That's our famous highway. It runs right across Siberia. The convicts used to sing songs about it. Now it's the operational base of the partisans. . . . You'll like it here, you know, it's not at all bad. You'll get used to it. You'll get to like the curiosities of the town. Our water pumps, for instance. The women queue up for water at the intersections, it's their open-air club through the winter."

"We are not going to live in town. We're going to Varykino."

"I know. Your wife told me. Still, you'll be coming in to town on business. I guessed who your wife was the moment I saw her. She's the living image of Krueger—eyes, nose, forehead—just like her grandfather. Everyone here remembers him."

There were round red oil tanks in the field, and large advertisements on wooden billboards. One of them caught the doctor's eye twice. It bore the inscription: "Moreau & Vetchink-in. Mechanical seeders. Threshing machines."

"That was a good firm. Their agricultural machinery was first-rate."

"I can't hear. What did you say?"

"A good firm, I said. Can you hear? A good firm. They made agricultural machinery. It was a corporation. My father was a stockholder."

"I thought you said he kept an inn."

"He did. That didn't mean he couldn't have stock. Very shrewd investments he made, too. He had money in the 'Giant.'"

"You sound as if you were proud of it."

"Of my father being shrewd? Of course I am."

"But what about your socialism?"

"Good Lord, what has that got to do with it? Why on earth should a man, because he is a Marxist, be a drivelling idiot? Marxism is a positive science, a theory of reality, a philosophy of history."

"Marxism a science? Well, it's taking a risk, to say the least, to argue about that with a man one hardly knows. However— Marxism is too uncertain of its ground to be a science. Sciences are more balanced, more objective. I don't know a movement more self-centered and further removed from the facts than Marxism. Everyone is worried only about proving himself in practical matters, and as for the men in power, they are so anxious to establish the myth of their infallibility that they do their utmost to ignore the truth. Politics doesn't appeal to me. I don't like people who don't care about the truth."

Samdeviatov took the doctor's words for the fooling of a witty eccentric. He listened with a smile, and did not contradict him.

The train was still being shunted. Every time it reached the "go" signal, an elderly woman with a milk can tied to her belt, who was on duty at the switch, shifted her knitting, bent down, and moved the lever, sending the train back. As it slowly rolled away she sat up and shook her fist at it.

Samdeviatov took this personally. "Why does she do that?" he wondered. "Her face is familiar. Can it be Tuntseva? No, I don't think it can be Glasha. She looks too old. Anyway, what has she got against me? I suppose, what with Mother Russia in the throes of her upheavals and the railways in a muddle, the poor old thing is having a bad time, so she is taking it out on me. Oh, to hell with her!—Why should I rack my brains about her?"

At long last the woman waved her flag, shouted something to the engineer, and let the train past the signals, out into the open; but as the fourteenth car sped by she stuck her tongue out at the two men chatting on the floor, who had got on her nerves. Once again Samdeviatov wondered.

5

When the outskirts of the burning town, the round oil tanks, telegraph poles, and advertisements had vanished in the distance, giving way to a landscape of woods and low hills with occasional glimpses of the winding road, Samdeviatov said:

"Let's go back to our seats. I have to get off soon and your station is the one after the next. Be careful you don't miss it."

"I suppose you know all this area very well?"

"Like my own back yard. Up to a hundred-mile radius. I'm a lawyer, you know. Twenty years of practice. I'm always travelling about on business."

"Even now?"

"Certainly."

"But what kind of business can there be, these days?"

"Anything you please. Old unfinished deals, business operations, breaches of contract. I'm up to my ears in it."

"But haven't all such activities been abolished?"

"Of course they have, nominally. But in practice people are asked to do all sorts of things, sometimes mutually exclusive. There's the nationalization of all enterprises, but the municipal soviet needs fuel, and the Provincial Economic Council wants transportation. And everyone wants to live. This is a transitional period, when there is still a gap between theory and practice. At a time like this you need shrewd, resourceful people like myself. Blessed is the man who doesn't see too much. Also an occasional punch on the jaw doesn't come amiss, as my father used to say. Half the province depends on me for its livelihood. I'll be dropping in at Varykino about timber one of these days. Not just yet, though. You can't get there except by horse, and my horse is lame. Otherwise you wouldn't catch me jolting along on this pile of scrap. Look at the way it crawls. Calls itself a train! I might be useful to you in Varykino. I know those Mikulitsyns of yours inside out."

"Do you know why we are going there, what we want to do?"

"More or less. I have an idea. Man's eternal longing to go back to the land. The dream of living by the sweat of your brow."

"What's wrong with it? You sound disapproving."

"It's naïve and idyllic, but why not? Good luck to you. Only I don't believe in it. It's utopian. Arts and craftsy!"

"How do you think Mikulitsyn will receive us?"

"He won't let you in, he'll drive you out with a broomstick, and he'll be quite right! He's in a fine pickle as it is. Idle factories, workers gone, no means of livelihood, no food, and then you turn up. If he murders you, I won't blame him!"

"There you are. You are a Bolshevik, and yet you yourself don't deny that what's going on isn't life—it's madness, an absurd nightmare."

"Of course it is. But it's historically inevitable. It has to be gone through."

"Why is it inevitable?"

"Are you a baby, or are you just pretending? Have you dropped from the moon? Gluttons and parasites sat on the backs of the starving workers and drove them to death, and you imagine things could stay like that? Not to mention all the other forms of outrage and tyranny. Don't you understand the rightness of the people's anger, of their desire for justice, for truth? Or do you think a radical change was possible through the Duma, by parliamentary methods, and that we can do without dictatorship?"

"We are talking at cross-purposes, and even if we argued for a hundred years we'd never see eye to eye. I used to be very revolutionary, but now I think that nothing can be gained by brute force. People must be drawn to good by goodness. But let's drop the subject. To return to Mikulitsyn—if that's what is in store for us, then why are we going? We should turn back."

"Nonsense. To begin with, Mikulitsyn is not the only pebble on the beach. And second, Mikulitsyn is kind to excess, almost criminally kind. He'll make a fuss and refuse and resist, and then he'll relent. He'll give you the shirt off his back and share his last crust of bread with you." And Samdeviatov told Yurii Andreievich Mikulitsyn's story.

6

"Mikulitsyn arrived here twenty-five years ago from Petersburg. He had been a student at the Technological Institute. He was deported and put under police supervision. He came here, got a job as manager at Krueger's, and married. There were four sisters here in those days—one more than in Chekhov's play—the Tuntsevas, Agrippina, Avdotia, Glafira, and Serafima. All the young men were after them. Mikulitsyn married the eldest.

"Before long they had a son. His fool of a father, who worshipped freedom, gave him the unusual name Liberius. Liberius—Livka, for short—grew up a bit wild but he had all sorts of unusual talents. When the war came he was fifteen. He faked the date on his birth certificate and made off to the front as a volunteer. His mother, a sickly woman, couldn't stand the shock. She took to her bed and didn't get up again. She died the year before last, just before the revolution.

"At the end of the war Liberius came back as a lieutenant hero with three medals, and of course he was a thoroughly indoctrinated Bolshevik delegate from the front. Have you heard about the 'Forest Brotherhood'?"

"No, I'm afraid not."

"In that case there's no sense in telling you the story, half the point would be lost. And there isn't any point in your staring out of the window at the highway either. What's so remarkable about the highways these days? The partisans. And what are the partisans? They are the backbone of the revolutionary army in the civil war. Two things account for the power of this army: the political organization that has taken over the leadership of the revolution, and the common soldier who after the last war refused to obey the old authorities. The partisan army was born of the union of the two. Most of them are middle peasants, but you find all sorts of people—poor peasants, unfrocked monks, sons of kulaks up in arms against their fathers. There are ideological anarchists, riffraff without identity papers, and highschool boys expelled for precocious skirt chasing. And then there are German and Austrian prisoners of war lured by the promise of freedom and repatriation. Well, one of the units of this great people's army is called the Forest Brotherhood, and the Forest Brotherhood is commanded by Comrade Forester, and Comrade Forester is Livka, Liberius Averkievich, the son of Averkii Stepanovich Mikulitsyn."

"You don't mean it!"

"I do indeed. But to go on with my story. After his wife's death, Averkii Stepanovich married again. His second wife, Elena Proklovna, went straight from school to the altar. Naïve by nature, she also affects naïveté; and although she is still quite young, she already pretends to be younger still, prattles, twitters, plays the ingénue, the little foolish girl, the pure field lily. The moment she sees you, she puts you through an exam: 'When was Suvorov born? Enumerate the conditions of equality of triangles.' And if she can trip you, she's overjoyed. But you'll see for yourself in a few hours.

"The old man has his own peculiarities. He was going to be a sailor. He studied marine engineering. He's clean-shaven, never takes his pipe out of his mouth, talks through his teeth in a slow, friendly voice, has the pipe smoker's jutting lower jaw, and cold gray eyes. Oh, and a detail I almost forgot—he's a Social Revolutionary and was elected regional deputy to the Constituent Assembly."

"That is surely very important! So father and son are at swords' points? Political enemies?"

"In theory, of course they are. But in practice the Forest Brotherhood doesn't make war against Varykino. However, to go on with the story. The three remaining Tuntsevas—Mikulitsyn's sisters-in-law by his first marriage—live in Yuriatin to this day, all confirmed spinsters—but times have changed and so have the girls.

"The oldest, Avdotia, is librarian at the public library. Dark, pretty, desperately shy, blushes scarlet at the slightest provocation. She has a terrible time at the library. It's as quiet as a tomb, and the poor girl has a chronic cold—gets sneezing fits and looks as if she'd like to drop through the floor. All nerves.

"The next one, Glafira Severinovna, is the family's blessing. Terrific drive, a wonderful worker, doesn't mind what she does. Livka, Comrade Forester, is supposed to take after her. One day she's a seamstress or she's working in a stocking factory, then before you know where you are she's turned herself into a hairdresser. You saw the woman at the switch, who shook her fist at us? Bless me, I thought, if it isn't Glafira gone to work on the railway. But I don't think it was Glafira, she looked too old.

"And then there's the youngest, Simushka. She's their cross, she gives them no end of trouble. She's an educated girl, well read, used to go in for poetry and philosophy. But since the revolution, what with all the general uplift, speeches, demonstrations, she's become a bit touched in the head, she's got a religious mania. The sisters lock her up when they go to work, but she gets out of the window and off she goes down the street, collecting crowds, preaching the Second Coming and the end of the world. Well, it's time I stopped talking, we're nearly there. This is my station. Yours is next. You'd better get ready."

After Samdeviatov had gone Antonina Alexandrovna said: "I don't know about you but I feel he's a godsend. I think he'll play some good sort of part in our lives."

"Very possible, Toniechka. But it worries me that everybody recognizes you as Krueger's granddaughter and that Krueger is so well remembered here. Even Strelnikov, the moment I said 'Varykino,' asked me sarcastically if we were Krueger's heirs.

"I am afraid that after leaving Moscow to escape notice, we are going to be even more conspicuous here. Not that there is anything to be done about it, and there certainly isn't any sense in crying over spilt milk. But we'd better stay in the background and keep quiet. Generally speaking, I'm not too happy about the whole thing. . . . But we must be nearly there. Let's wake up the others and get ready."

7

Antonina Alexandrovna stood on the platform at the Torfianaia station counting her family and her luggage over and over to make sure that nothing had been left on the train. The well-trodden sand of the platform was firm under her feet, but the anxiety lest they miss the station remained with her and the clatter of the wheels was still in her ears although the train was standing motionless before her eyes. This prevented her from seeing, hearing, or thinking properly.

Passengers who were continuing their journey were calling out goodbye and waving to her from the car but she never noticed them. Nor did she notice that the train was leaving and realized that it had gone only when she found herself looking at the green fields and the blue sky across the empty track.

The station was built of stone and had benches on either side of the entrance. The Zhivagos were the only travellers who had got out at Torfianaia. They put their luggage down and sat on one of the benches.

They were struck by the silence, emptiness, and tidiness of the station. It seemed strange not to be surrounded by a milling, cursing mob. History had not caught up with this remote provincial life. It had not yet relapsed into savagery, as at the capitals.

The station nestled in a birch wood. When the train drew in, the cars were plunged into darkness. Now the shadows of the scarcely stirring trees moved lightly over their hands and faces, over the ground and the station walls and roofs, and over the platform with its clean, damp, yellow sand. It was cool in the grove, and the singing of the birds in it had an equally cool sound. Candid and pure as innocence, it pierced and carried through the wood from end to end. Two roads cut through the grove—the railroad and a country road—and both were shaded by branches, which swayed like long sleeves.

Suddenly Antonina Alexandrovna's eyes and ears opened. She became aware of everything at once—the ringing bird calls, the pure woodland solitude, and the flowing, unruffled stillness. She had prepared a speech in her mind: "I couldn't believe that we would really get here safely. Your Strelnikov, you know, could quite easily have made a display of magnanimity, and then sent a telegram telling them to arrest all of us as soon as we got off the train. I don't believe in their noble sentiments, my dear, it's all a sham." But quite different words broke from her at sight of the enchanting scene before her. "How lovely!" she cried out. She could not say any more. Tears choked her, and she began to weep.

At the sound of her crying a little old man in a station-master's uniform came out and shuffled across to them. Touching the peak of his red-topped cap, he asked politely:

"Would the young lady like a sedative? We have some in the station medicine chest."

"It's nothing. Thank you. She'll be all right in a moment," said Alexander Alexandrovich.

"It's the anxiety and the worry of the journey that does it, it's well known. And then this African heat, which is so rare in this latitude. Not to mention the events in Yuriatin."

"We saw the fire from the train as we went by."

"You're from Central Russia, if I'm not mistaken?"

"From the very heart of it."

"From Moscow! Little wonder, then, that the lady's nerves are upset. They say there isn't a stone left standing."

"Not quite as bad as that. People exaggerate. But we've certainly seen plenty. This is my daughter, and that's her husband, and that's their little boy. And this is his nurse, Niusha."

"How do you do. How do you do. Delighted. I was rather expecting you. Anfim Efimovich Samdeviatov telephoned from Sakma. Dr. Zhivago is coming with his family from Moscow, he said, and would I please give them every possible assistance. So that's who you are, am I right?"

"No, Dr. Zhivago is my son-in-law, there he is. I'm a professor of agronomy and my name is Gromeko."

"Pardon me. My mistake. I am very glad to make your acquaintance."

"So you know Samdeviatov?"

"Who doesn't know him, the wonder-worker! I don't know what we would have done without him—we'd have all been dead long ago. Give them every possible assistance, he said. Very good, I said. I promised I would. So if you need a horse or anything . . . ? Where are you bound for?"

"We want to get to Varykino. Is it far from here?"

"Varykino! That's why I've kept wondering whom your daughter reminds me of! So it's Varykino you want! That explains everything! Old man Krueger and I built this road together. I'll see to the horse right away, I'll call one of the men and we'll see about a cart.—Donat! Donat! Take these things into the waiting room for the time being. And how about a horse? Run over to the tearoom and see what can be done. Bacchus was hanging around here this morning. See if he's still there. Tell them four passengers for Varykino. They're new arrivals. They've got hardly any luggage, tell them. And make it snappy. And now, lady, may I give you a piece of fatherly advice? I purposely didn't ask you how closely you were related to Ivan Ernestovich. Be very careful what you say about it. You can't talk too much with everyone in times like these."

At the mention of Bacchus the travellers looked at each other in amazement. They remembered Anna Ivanovna's tales about the fabulous blacksmith who had made himself an indestructible set of iron guts and the many other local legends she had told them.

8

The horse was a white mare that had recently foaled, and their driver was a lop-eared old man with dishevelled white hair. For some reason everything about him was white: his new birchbark shoes had not had time to grow dark, and his linen shirt and trousers had faded with age.

The foal, with a short, curly mane, and black as night, like a painted toy, ran after its mother kicking out its soft-boned legs.

The travellers clung to the sides of the cart as it jolted over the ruts. Their hearts were at peace. Their dream was coming true, they were almost at the end of their journey. The last hours of the clear day lingered generously, as though eager to prolong its splendor.

Their way led sometimes through woods and sometimes across open fields. Driving through the forest, each time they were jolted violently when the cart wheel hit a root, they scowled, hunched their shoulders, and pressed close to each other. Every time they came out into the open, where the space seemed exuberantly to toss its cap into the air, they sat up straight and more comfortably, and breathed sighs of relief.

It was hilly country. The hills, as always, had their own expression. They rose huge and dark in the distance, like proud shadows, silently scrutinizing the travellers. A comfortingly rosy light followed them across the fields, soothing them and giving them hope.

They liked and they marvelled at everything, most of all at the unceasing chatter of their quaint old driver, in whose speech archaic Russian forms, Tartar idioms, and local oddities of diction were punctuated with obscurities of his own invention.

Whenever the foal lagged behind, the mare stopped and waited. The foal would catch up with her in graceful, wavelike bounds, and then, walking up to the cart clumsily on its long legs set too close together, it would stretch its long neck and push its tiny head under the shaft to nurse.

"But I don't understand," Antonina Alexandrovna shouted to her husband, slowly, for fear that her teeth, which chattered with the shaking of the cart, should bite off the tip of her tongue at some sudden jolt. "Can this be the same Bacchus that Mother used to tell us about? You remember all that stuff about the blacksmith who was disembowelled in a fight and made himself a set of new bowels? Bacchus Iron-Belly. Of course I know it's only a story, but can it have been told about him? Is he the same Bacchus?"

"No, of course not. To begin with, as you say, it's only a story, a legend, and then Mother told us that even the legend was over a hundred years old when she heard it. But don't talk so loud. You don't want to hurt the old man's feelings."

"He won't hear anything, he's deaf. And if he did, he wouldn't understand—he's not quite right in the head."

"Hey, Feodor Nefeodich!" the old man shouted to his horse, addressing it for some reason by a male name and patronymic, although he knew as well as his passengers did that it was a mare. "Curse this heat! Like unto the children of Abraham in the Persian furnace! Gee-up, you unredeemed devil! It's you I'm talking to, you bungler."

Sometimes, he would suddenly burst into snatches of old songs composed in the former Krueger factories.

> *"Goodbye, main office,*
> *Goodbye, shaft and mine.*
> *The master's bread is stale to me*
> *And I am sick of drinking water.*
> *A swan is swimming past the shores,*
> *He makes furrows in the water.*
> *It isn't wine that makes me sway*
> *It is because Vania is going into the army.*
> *But I, Masha, I won't blunder.*
> *But I, Masha, am not a fool,*
> *I'll go to the town of Seliaba,*
> *And work for Sentetiurikha."*

"Eh, you Godforsaken beast. Look at that carrion. I give her the whip and she gives me the lip! Eh, Fedia Nefedia, are you making up your mind to go?—That forest, it's called the taiga, there's no end to it. And there's no end of peasant folk inside it, the Forest Brotherhood is there.—Eh, Fedia Nefedia, have you stopped again, you devil?"

All at once he turned and looked Antonina Alexandrovna straight in the eye.

"Do you really think, young woman, that I didn't know who you were? You're simple-minded, young lady, that I can see.

May I fall dead if I didn't recognize you! Certainly I recognized you! Couldn't believe my eyes—you're the living image of Grigov." (This was his version of Krueger's name.) "You wouldn't be his granddaughter, would you? Who could tell a Grigov if not me! I've spent my life working for him. Did every kind of job for him—worked in the mines as a woodman, and at the winch above ground, and in the stables.—Gee-up, get a move on! Stopped again, like she had no legs! Angels in China! Can't you hear I'm talking to you?

"Well now, you were asking if I'm that same blacksmith Bacchus. What a simpleton you are, little mother, such big eyes and a lady, but a fool. Your Bacchus—he was called Post-anogov, Postanogov Iron-Belly—he went to his grave more than fifty years ago. But my name is Mekhonoshin. Our Christian names are the same but our surnames are different."

Little by little, the old man told them in his own words what they had already heard from Samdeviatov about the Mikulit-syns. He called them Mikulich and Mikulichna. He spoke of the latter as the manager's second wife and of his first wife as an "angel," a "white cherub." When he came to the partisan leader, Liberius, and learned that his fame had not yet reached Moscow and that the Forest Brotherhood was unknown there, he could hardly believe it.

"They haven't heard? They haven't heard of Comrade Forester? Angels in China, then what has Moscow got ears for?"

Evening was coming on. Their shadows, growing longer and longer, ran ahead of them. They were driving through a flat, treeless stretch. Here and there, in lonely clusters, stood tall stringy stalks of goosefoot, of willow herb and thistle tipped with flowering tufts. Their ghostlike contours, widely spaced, loomed like mounted guards keeping watch over the plain.

Far ahead of them, the plain abutted a tall range of hills. They stood across the road like a wall, beyond which there was perhaps a ravine or a stream. It was as though the sky over there were enclosed by a rampart, and the road were leading to its gate.

A long, one-story white house emerged at the top of the ridge.

"See the lookout up on the hill?" said Bacchus. "That's where your Mikulich and Mikulichna live. And down below there's a gully, Shutma it's called."

Two rifle shots rang out from the hills, followed by rolling echoes.

"What's that? It wouldn't be partisans shooting at us, would it, little grandfather?"

"Bless you, no! Partisans! That's Stepanych scaring the wolves away in the Shutma."

9

Their first meeting with the Mikulitsyns took place in the yard of the manager's house. It was a painful scene that began in silence and became noisily confused.

Elena Proklovna was coming home across the yard from a walk in the woods. The rays of the setting sun, as golden as her golden hair, trailed behind her from tree to tree through the wood. She wore a light summer dress. She was hot from her walk and was wiping her face with her handkerchief. Her straw hat hung at her back from an elastic around her bare throat.

Her husband was coming to meet her from the ravine; he had just climbed up from it with his gun, which he meant to clean because he had noticed that there was something wrong with it.

Suddenly, into this peaceful setting Bacchus rolled up smartly with a loud clatter of cart wheels over the cobbles, bringing his surprise.

The passengers got out, and Alexander Alexandrovich, hemming and hawing and taking off and putting on his hat, began to explain.

Their hosts were struck dumb with amazement. Their genuine speechlessness lasted for several minutes; so did the sincere and appalled confusion of their miserable guests, who were burning with shame. The situation could not have been plainer, whatever might have been said, not only to those directly involved but also to Sashenka, Niusha, and Bacchus. Their painful embarrassment seemed to communicate itself even to the mare, the foal, the golden rays of the setting sun, and the gnats that swarmed around Elena Proklovna and settled on her face and neck.

The silence was finally broken by Mikulitsyn. "I don't understand. I don't understand a thing and I never will. What do you think this is? The south, where the Whites are, and plenty of bread? Why did you pick on us? What on earth has brought you here—here, of all places?"

"Has it occurred to you, I wonder, what a responsibility this is for Averkii Stepanovich?"

"Don't interrupt, Lenochka. Yes, she's quite right. Did you stop to think what a burden you would be imposing on us?"

"But heavens above! You misunderstand us. There is no question of intruding on you, of upsetting your peaceful existence. All we want is a very small thing, a corner in any old empty, tumble-down building and a strip of land that happens to be going to waste because nobody wants it, so that we can grow vegetables. And a cartload of firewood from the forest when there's no one to see us take it. Is this really asking so much, is it such an imposition?"

"True, but the world is a big place. What does this have to do with us? Why should we be chosen for this honor, rather than anyone else?"

"Because we've heard of you and we hoped that you'd have heard of us, so that we would not be coming to complete strangers."

"Ah! So it's because of Krueger! Because you are related to him! But how can you even bring yourselves to admit such a thing at a time like this?"

"I wonder, do you understand? Precisely because you're related to Krueger you should have spared us the pleasure of your acquaintance."

"Lenochka, don't meddle. My wife is absolutely right. Precisely because you're related."

Yurii Andreievich had had no time to compare Samdeviatov's portrait with the original. During the awkward scene the doctor forgot Samdeviatov's description. Later, after things had calmed down, he was struck by the likeness and the aptness of the portrait. However, Anfim Efimovich's characterization of the manager was incomplete. Yurii Andreievich supplemented it later.

Averkii Stepanovich pronounced the sound *l* in the Polish manner, like a *w*. He actually never was separated from his pipe, which was an integral part of his face and which contributed to his style of speech, because he composed his words and ideas while relighting it and making it draw.

He had regular features. He tossed his hair back and took great strides, planting his feet squarely on the ground. In summer he wore a Russian shirt tied with a silk tasselled cord. He was the kind of man who, in the old days, might have become a pirate on the Volga. In more recent times such people have created the type of the eternal student, the dreamer turned schoolmaster.

Mikulitsyn had devoted his youth to the movement for emancipation, to the revolution, and his only fear had been that he would not live to see it or that when it came it would be too moderate, not bloody enough for him. Now it had come, surpassing his wildest dreams, but he, the born and faithful champion of the proletariat who had been among the first to set up a Factory Committee in the Sviatogor Bogatyr, and to hand the place over to the workers, had been left high and dry; instead of being in the thick of things, he was in a remote village from which the workers—some of whom were Mensheviks— had fled! And now what was this ridiculous nonsense on top of everything? These uninvited remnants of Krueger's family seemed to him fate's crowning joke, a deliberate trick, which was more than he could bear.

"This is beyond all reason. Do you realize the danger you will put me in? I suppose I must be mad. I don't understand. I don't understand a thing and never will."

"I wonder if you realize what a volcano we are sitting on even without you here?"

"Just a moment, Lenochka. My wife is quite right. Things are bad enough without you. It's a dog's life, a madhouse. I am caught between two fires. Between those who make my life a misery because my son is a Red, a Bolshevik, the people's favorite, and those who want to know why I was elected to the Constituent Assembly. Nobody is pleased, I have no one to turn to. And now you! A nice thought, to have to face a firing squad on your account!"

"Oh, come! Be sensible. What's the matter with you!"

A little later he relented.

"Well, there isn't any point in squabbling in the yard. We can go inside. Not, of course, that I can see any good coming of it, but 'we see as in a glass darkly.' Still, we aren't Janizaries, we aren't heathens, we won't drive you out into the forest to be eaten by bears. I think, Lenochka, we'd better put them in the palm room for the moment, next to the study. We'll see later where they can settle down, we might find them some place in the park. Do come inside. Bring their things in, Bacchus, give the guests a hand."

Bacchus did as he was told, muttering: "Mother of God! They've got no more stuff than pilgrims! Nothing but little bundles, not a single trunk."

10

The night was cold. They washed, and the women got the room ready for the night. Sashenka, who from long custom expected to have his childish utterances greeted with raptures and therefore prattled obligingly, was upset because for once he had no success, no one took any notice of him. He was disappointed that the black foal had not been brought into the house, and when he was told sharply to be quiet he burst into tears, afraid that he might be sent back to the baby shop where, he believed, his parents had bought him. His fear was genuine, and he wanted to share it with everyone around him, but his charming absurdities on this occasion failed to produce the usual effect. Ill at ease in a strange house, the grown-ups seemed to him to be in more than their usual hurry as they went about silently absorbed in their tasks. Sashenka was offended, and he sulked. He was made to eat and put to bed with difficulty. When at last he was asleep, Ustinia, the Mikulitsyns' maid, took Niusha to her room to give her supper and initiated her into the secrets of the household. Antonina Alexandrovna and the men were invited to tea with the Mikulitsyns.

Alexander Alexandrovich and Yurii Andreievich first went out on the veranda for a breath of air.

"What a lot of stars!" said Alexander Alexandrovich.

It was very dark. Standing only a few steps apart, the two men could not see each other. Lamplight streamed from a window behind them into the ravine. In its shaft shrubs, trees, and other vague shapes rose cloudily in the cold mist. But the two men were outside this light, which only thickened the darkness around them.

"First thing tomorrow we must have a look at the annex he's got in mind for us, and if it's any good we must start repairing it at once. Then, by the time we've got it fitted up the ground will have thawed out and we can start digging the beds without losing any time. Didn't he say he'd let us have some seed potatoes?"

"He certainly did. He promised us other seed as well. I heard him say so with my own ears. As for the place he offers us, we saw it as we were crossing the park. You know where it is? It's the annex behind the main house, you can hardly see it for the thistles. It's wooden, though the house is of stone. I pointed it out to you, do you remember? I thought it would be a good place for the seedbeds. It looked to me as if there might have been a flower garden once, at least it looked like that from a distance, but I may have been mistaken. The soil in the old flower beds must have been well manured; I imagine it might still be pretty good."

"I don't know, we'll have a look tomorrow. I should think it's rank with weeds and hard as stone by now. There must have been a kitchen garden somewhere for the house. Possibly we can use it. We'll find out tomorrow. Probably there's still frost in the mornings. There's sure to be a frost tonight. Anyway, what bliss to be here at last—that's something to be thankful for. It's a good place. I like it."

"They are nice people. He especially. She's a bit affected. There is something she doesn't like about herself. That's why she talks such a lot and why she makes herself sillier than she is. It's as if she were in a hurry to distract your attention from her looks, before you've had time to get a bad impression. And her forgetting to take off her hat and wearing it around her neck isn't absent-mindedness either—it really is becoming to her."

"Well, we'd better go back or they'll think we're rude."

On their way to the dining room, where their hosts and Antonina Alexandrovna were having tea at the round table under the hanging lamp, they went through Mikulitsyn's dark study.

It had an enormous window the length of the wall, overlooking the ravine. Earlier, while it was still light, the doctor had noticed the view from it over the gully and the plain beyond, which they had crossed with Bacchus. At the window stood a draftsman's table which also took up the width of the wall. A gun lying lengthways on it and leaving plenty of room at either end further emphasized the great width of the table.

Now, as they went through, Yurii Andreievich once more thought with envy of the window with its vast view, the size and position of the table, and the spaciousness of the well-furnished room, and it was the first thing he spoke of to his hosts as he entered the dining room.

"What a wonderful place you have! What a splendid study, it must be a perfect place to work in, a real inspiration."

"A glass or a cup? And do you like it strong or weak?"

"Yurochka, do look at this. It's a stereoscope, Averkii Stepanovich's son made it when he was a child."

"He still hasn't grown up and settled down, even though he has captured district after district for the Soviets from Komuch."

"What's Komuch?"

"It's the army of the Siberian Government; it's fighting to restore the Constituent Assembly."

"We've been hearing praise of your son all day long. You must be very proud of him."

"Those stereoscopic photographs of the Urals—they are his work too, and he took them with a homemade camera."

"Wonderful cookies! Are they made with saccharin?"

"Good gracious, no! Where would we get saccharin in our wilderness? It's honest to God sugar. Didn't you see me putting sugar in your tea?"

"Of course it is! I was looking at the photographs. And it's real tea, isn't it?"

"Certainly! It's jasmine tea."

"How on earth do you get it?"

"We have a sort of magician. A friend of ours. He's a public figure of the new sort. Very left-wing. He's the official representative of the Provincial Economic Council. He takes our timber to town and gets us flour and butter through his friends. Pass me the sugar bowl, Siverka" (that was what she called Averkii). "And now, I wonder, can you tell me the year of Griboiedov's death?"

"He was born in 1795, I think. But just when he was killed, I don't remember."

"More tea?"

"No, thank you."

"Now here's something for you. Tell me the date of the Treaty of Nimwegen and which countries signed it."

"Don't torment them, darling. They've hardly recovered from their journey."

"And now this is what I'd like to know. How many kinds of lenses are there, and when are the images real, reversed, natural, or inverted?"

"How do you come to know so much about physics?"

"We had an excellent science teacher in Yuriatin, he taught both in the boys' school and in ours. I can't tell you how good he was. He was a wonder. It was all so clear when he explained it to you! His name was Antipov. He was married to a teacher too. All the girls were mad about him, they all fell in love with him. He went off to the war as a volunteer and was killed. Some people say this scourge of ours, Commissar Strelnikov, is Antipov risen from the dead. But that's only a silly rumor, of course. It's most unlikely. Though, who can tell, anything is possible. Another cup?"

CHAPTER NINE

Varykino

1

In the winter, when Yurii Andreievich had more time, he began a notebook. He wrote: "How often, last summer, I felt like saying with Tiutchev:

> *'What a summer, what a summer!*
> *This is magic indeed.*
> *And how, I ask you, did it come*
> *Just like that, out of the blue?'*

What happiness, to work from dawn to dusk for your family and for yourself, to build a roof over their heads, to till the soil to feed them, to create your own world, like Robinson Crusoe, in imitation of the Creator of the universe, and, as your own mother did, to give birth to yourself, time and again.

"So many new thoughts come into your head when your hands are busy with hard physical work, when your mind has set you a task that can be achieved by physical effort and that brings its reward in joy and success, when for six hours on end you dig or hammer, scorched by the life-giving breath of the sky. And it isn't a loss but a gain that these transient thoughts, intuitions, analogies are not put down on paper but forgotten. The town recluse whipping up his nerves and his imagination with strong black coffee and tobacco doesn't know the strongest drug of all—good health and real necessity.

"I am not going further than this. I am not preaching Tolstoyan austerity and the return to the land, I am not trying to improve on socialism and its solution to the agrarian problem. I am merely stating a fact, I am not building a system on the basis of our own accidental experience. Our example is debatable and unsuitable for deductions. Our economy is too mixed. What we produce ourselves—potatoes and vegetables—is only a small part of what we need; the rest comes from other sources.

"Our use of the land is illegal. We have taken the law into our own hands, and we conceal what we are doing from the state. The wood we cut is stolen, and it is no excuse that we steal from the state or that the property once belonged to Krueger. We can do all this thanks to Mikulitsyn's tolerant attitude (he lives in much the same way as we do), and we can do it safely because we are far from the town, where, fortunately, nothing is known, for the time being, about our illegal activities.

"I have given up practicing medicine, and I don't tell anyone that I am a physician, because I don't want to restrict my freedom. But there are always some good souls who get wind of the fact that there is a doctor in Varykino. So they trudge twenty miles to consult me, and bring a chicken or eggs, or butter, or something. And there is no way to persuade them that I don't want to be paid, because people don't believe in the effectiveness of free medical advice. So my practice brings in a little. But our chief mainstay, Mikulitsyn's and ours, is Samdeviatov.

"He is a fantastically complicated character. I can't make him out. He is a genuine supporter of the revolution and he fully deserves the confidence that the Yuriatin Soviet has in him. With all the powers they have given him he could requisition the Varykino timber without so much as telling Mikulitsyn or us, and he knows that we wouldn't protest. On the other hand, if he felt like robbing the state, he could fill his pocket and again no one would say a word. He has no need to bribe or share with anybody. What, then, is it that makes him take care of us; help the Mikulitsyns, and everyone in the district, for instance, the stationmaster at Torfianaia? All the time he is on the road, getting hold of something to bring us. He is just as familiar with Dostoievsky's *Possessed* as with the Communist Manifesto, and he talks about them equally well. I have the impression that if he didn't complicate his life so needlessly, he would die of boredom."

2

A little later the doctor wrote:

"We are living in two rooms in a wooden annex at the back of the old house. When Anna Ivanovna was a child Krueger used it for special servants—the dressmaker, the housekeeper, and the retired nurse.

"It was pretty dilapidated when we came, but we repaired it fairly quickly. With the help of experts we rebuilt the stove, which serves both rooms. We have rearranged the flues and it gives more heat.

"In this part of the grounds the old garden has vanished, obliterated by new growth. But now, in winter, when everything is inanimate, living nature no longer covers the dead; in snowy outline the past can be read more clearly.

"We have been lucky. The autumn was dry and warm. It gave us time to dig up the potatoes before the rains and the cold weather. Not counting those we gave back to Mikulitsyn, we had twenty sacks. We put them in the biggest bin in the cellar and covered them with old blankets and hay. We also put down two barrels of salted cucumbers and two of sauerkraut prepared by Tonia. Fresh cabbages hang in pairs from the beams. There are carrots buried in dry sand, and radishes and beets and turnips, and plenty of peas and beans are stored in the loft. There is enough firewood in the shed to last us till spring.

"I love the warm, dry winter breath of the cellar, the smell of earth, roots, and snow that hits you the moment you raise the trap door as you go down in the early hours before the winter dawn, a weak, flickering light in your hand.

"You come out; it is still dark. The door creaks or perhaps you sneeze or the snow crunches under your foot, and hares start up from the far cabbage patch and hop away, leaving the snow crisscrossed with tracks. In the distance dogs begin to bark and it is a long time before they quiet down. The cocks have finished their crowing and have nothing left to say. Then dawn breaks.

"Besides the tracks of hares, the endless snowy plain is patterned by those of lynxes, stretching across it neatly, like strings of beads. The lynx walks like a cat, putting one paw down in front of the other, and they say it travels many miles in a night.

"Traps are set for them, but instead of the lynxes the wretched hares get caught, half buried in the snow, and are taken out, frozen stiff.

"At the beginning, during spring and summer, we had a very hard time. We drove ourselves to the utmost. But now we can relax in the winter evenings. Thanks to Samdeviatov, who supplies us with kerosene, we sit around a lamp. The women sew or knit, Alexander Alexandrovich or I read aloud. The stove is hot, and I, as the appointed stoker, watch it for the right moment to close the damper so as not to waste any heat. If a charred log prevents the fire from drawing properly, I remove it and run out with it smoking and fling it as far as possible into the snow. It flies through the air like a torch, throwing off sparks and lighting up the white rectangular lawns of the sleeping park and then buries itself, hissing, in a snowdrift.

"We read and reread *War and Peace*, *Evgenii Onegin* and Pushkin's other poems, and Russian translations of Stendhal's *The Red and the Black*, Dickens's *Tale of Two Cities*, and Kleist's short stories."

3

As spring approached, the doctor wrote:

"I believe Tonia is pregnant. I told her and she doesn't believe it, but I feel sure of it. The early symptoms are unmistakable to me, I don't have to wait for the later, more certain ones.

"A woman's face changes at such a time. It isn't that she becomes less attractive, but her appearance is no longer quite under her control. She is now ruled by the future which she carries within her, she is no longer alone. Her loss of control over her appearance makes her seem physically at a loss; her face dims, her skin coarsens, her eyes shine in a different way, not as she wants them to, it is as if she couldn't quite cope with all these things and has neglected herself.

"Tonia and I have never drifted apart, but this year of work has brought us even closer together. I have noticed how efficient, strong, and tireless she is, how cleverly she plans her work, so as to waste as little time as possible between one job and another.

"It has always seemed to me that every conception is immaculate and that this dogma, concerning the Mother of God, expresses the idea of all motherhood.

"At childbirth, every woman has the same aura of isolation, as though she were abandoned, alone. At this vital moment the man's part is as irrelevant as if he had never had anything to do with it, as though the whole thing had dropped from heaven.

"It is the woman, by herself, who brings forth her progeny, and carries it off to some remote corner of existence, a quiet, safe place for a crib. Alone, in silence and humility, she feeds and rears the child.

"The Mother of God is asked to 'pray zealously to her Son and her God,' and the words of the psalm are put into her mouth: 'My soul doth magnify the Lord, and my spirit hath rejoiced in God my Savior. For He hath regarded the low estate of his handmaiden: for, behold, from henceforth all generations shall call me blessed.' It is because of her child that she says this, He will magnify her ('For He that is mighty hath done to me great things'): He is her glory. Any woman could say it. For every one of them, God is in her child. Mothers of great men must have been familiar with this feeling, but then, all women are mothers of great men—it isn't their fault if life disappoints them later."

4

"We go on endlessly rereading *Evgenii Onegin* and the poems. Samdeviatov came yesterday and brought presents—nice things to eat and kerosene for the lamps. We have endless discussions about art.

"I have always thought that art is not a category, not a realm covering innumerable concepts and derivative phenomena, but that, on the contrary, it is something concentrated, strictly limited. It is a principle that is present in every work of art, a force applied to it and a truth worked out in it. And I have never seen art as form but rather as a hidden, secret part of content. All this is as clear to me as daylight. I feel it in every bone of my body, but it's terribly difficult to express or to define this idea.

"A literary creation can appeal to us in all sorts of ways—by its theme, subject, situations, characters. But above all it appeals to us by the presence in it of art. It is the presence of art in *Crime and Punishment* that moves us deeply rather than the story of Raskolnikov's crime.

"Primitive art, the art of Egypt, Greece, our own—it is all, I think, one and the same art through thousands of years. You can call it an idea, a statement about life, so all-embracing that it can't be split up into separate words; and if there is so much as a particle of it in any work that includes other things as well, it outweighs all the other ingredients in significance and turns out to be the essence, the heart and soul of the work."

5

"A slight chill, a cough, probably a bit of temperature. Gasping all day long, the feeling of a lump in my throat. I am in a bad way. It is my heart. The first symptoms that I have inherited my poor mother's heart—she suffered from it all her life. Can it really be that? So soon? If so, my tenure in this world is short.

"A faint smell of charcoal in the room. A smell of ironing. Tonia is ironing, every now and then she gets a coal out of the stove and puts it in the iron, and the lid of the iron snaps over it like a set of teeth. It reminds me of something, but I can't think of what. Must be my condition.

"To celebrate Samdeviatov's gift of soap we have had two washing days and Sashenka has been running wild. As I write he sits astride the crosspiece under the table and, imitating Samdeviatov, who takes him out in his sleigh whenever he comes, pretends that he is giving me a ride.

"As soon as I feel better I must go to the town library and read up on the ethnography and history of the region. They say the library has had several important donations and is exceptionally good. I have an urge to write. But I'll have to hurry. It will be spring before we know where we are—and then there'll be no time for reading or writing.

"My headache gets worse and worse. I slept badly. Had a muddled dream of the kind you forget as you wake up. All that remained in my memory was the part that woke me up. It was a woman's voice, I heard it in my dream, sounding in the air. I remembered it and kept hearing it in my mind and going through the list of our women friends—I tried to think of someone who spoke in that deep, soft, husky voice. It didn't belong to any of them. I thought it might be Tonia's, and that I had become so used to her that I no longer heard the tone of her voice. I tried to forget that she was my wife and to become sufficiently detached to find out. But it wasn't her voice either. It remains a mystery.

"About dreams. It is usually taken for granted that you dream of something that has made a particularly strong impression on you during the day, but it seems to me it's just the contrary.

"Often it's something you paid no attention to at the time—a vague thought that you didn't bother to think out to the end, words spoken without feeling and which passed unnoticed—these are the things that return at night, clothed in flesh and blood, and they become the subjects of dreams, as if to make up for having been ignored during waking hours."

6

"A clear, frosty night. Unusual brilliance and perfection of everything visible. Earth, sky, moon, and stars, all seem cemented, riveted together by the frost. Shadows of trees lie across the paths, so sharp that they seem carved in relief. You keep thinking you see dark figures endlessly cross the road at various places. Big stars hang in the woods between branches like blue lanterns. Small ones are strewn all over the sky like daisies in a summer field.

"We go on discussing Pushkin. The other night we talked about the early poems he wrote as a schoolboy. How much depended on his choice of meter!

"In the poems with long lines, his ambition did not extend beyond the Arzamas Literary Circle; he wanted to keep up with the grown-ups, impress his uncle with mythologism, bombast, faked epicureanism and sophistication, and affected a precocious worldly wisdom.

"But as soon as he stopped imitating Ossian and Parny and changed from 'Recollections of Tsarskoie Selo' to 'A Small

Town' or 'Letter to My Sister' or 'To My Inkwell' (written later in Kishinev), or 'To Yudin,' the future Pushkin was already there.

"Air, light, the noise of life, reality burst into his poetry from the street as through an open window. The outside world, everyday things, nouns, crowded in and took possession of his lines, driving out the vaguer parts of speech. Things and more things lined up in rhymed columns on the page.

"As if this, Pushkin's tetrameter, which later became so famous, were a measuring unit of Russian life, a yardstick, as if it had been patterned after the whole of Russia's existence, as you draw the outline of a foot or give the size of a hand to make sure that the glove or the shoe will fit.

"Later in much the same way, the rhythm of spoken Russian, the intonations of ordinary speech were expressed in Nekrassov's trimeters and dactyls."

7

"I should like to be of use as a doctor or a farmer and at the same time to be gestating something lasting, something fundamental, to be writing some scientific paper or a literary work.

"Every man is born a Faust, with a longing to grasp and experience and express everything in the world. Faust became a scientist thanks to the mistakes of his predecessors and contemporaries. Progress in science is governed by the laws of repulsion, every step forward is made by refutation of prevalent errors and false theories. Faust was an artist thanks to the inspiring example of his teachers. Forward steps in art are governed by the law of attraction, are the result of the imitation of and admiration for beloved predecessors.

"What is it that prevents me from being a doctor and a writer? I think it is not our privations or our wanderings or our unsettled lives, but the prevalent spirit of high-flown rhetoric, which has spread everywhere—phrases such as 'the dawn of the future,' 'the building of a new world,' 'the torch-bearers of mankind.' The first time you hear such talk you think 'What breadth of imagination, what richness!' But in fact it's so pompous just because it is so unimaginative and second-rate.

"Only the familiar transformed by genius is truly great. The best object lesson in this is Pushkin. His works are one great hymn to honest labor, duty, everyday life! Today, 'bourgeois' and 'petty bourgeois' have become terms of abuse, but Pushkin forestalled the implied criticism in his 'Family Tree,' where he says proudly that he belongs to the middle class, and in 'Onegin's Travels' we read:

> 'Now my ideal is the housewife,
> My greatest wish, a quiet life
> And a big bowl of cabbage soup.'

"What I have come to like best in the whole of Russian literature is the childlike Russian quality of Pushkin and Chekhov, their modest reticence in such high-sounding matters as the ultimate purpose of mankind or their own salvation. It isn't that they didn't think about these things, and to good effect, but to talk about such things seemed to them pretentious, presumptuous. Gogol, Tolstoy, Dostoievsky looked restlessly for the meaning of life, and prepared for death and balanced accounts. Pushkin and Chekhov, right up to the end of their lives, were absorbed in the current, specific tasks imposed on them by their vocation as writers, and in the course of fulfilling these tasks they lived their lives, quietly, treating both their lives and their work as private, individual matters, of no concern to anyone else. And these individual things have since become of concern to all, and their works, like apples picked while they are green, have ripened of themselves, mellowing gradually and growing richer in meaning."

8

"First signs of spring. Thaw. The air smells of buttered pancakes and vodka, as at Shrovetide. A sleepy, oily sun blinking in the forest, sleepy pines blinking their needles like eyelashes, oily puddles glistening at noon. The countryside yawns, stretches, turns over, and goes back to sleep.

"Chapter Seven of *Evgenii Onegin* describes the spring, Onegin's house deserted in his absence, Lensky's grave by the stream at the foot of the hill.

> *'The nightingale, spring's lover,*
> *Sings all night. The wild rose blooms.'*

Why 'lover'? The fact is, the epithet is natural, apt: the
nightingale *is* spring's lover. Moreover, he needed it for the
rhyme. I wonder whether the nickname Nightingale, for the
brigand son of Odikmantii, in the well-known Russian folk
epic, is not a metaphor based on similarity of sound. How well
the song characterizes him!

> *'At his nightingale whistle,*
> *At his wild forest call,*
> *The grass is all a-tremble,*
> *The flowers shed their petals,*
> *The dark forest bows down to the ground,*
> *And all good people fall down dead.'*

We came to Varykino in early spring. Soon the trees grew
green—alder and nut trees and wild cherry—especially in the
Shutma, the ravine below Mikulitsyn's house. And soon after
that the nightingales began to sing.

"Once again, as though hearing them for the first time, I
wondered at the difference between their song and that of all
other birds, at the sudden jump, without transitions, that nature
makes to the richness and uniqueness of their trills. Such variety
and power and resonance! Turgenev somewhere describes these
whistling, fluting modulations. There were two phrases that
stood out particularly. One was a luxurious, greedily repetitive
tiokh-tiokh-tiokh, in response to which the vegetation, all
covered with dew, trembled with delight. The other was in two
syllables, grave, imploring, an appeal or a warning: 'Wake up!
Wake up!'"

9

"Spring. We are preparing for the spring sowing. No time for a
diary. It was pleasant to write. I'll have to stop until next winter.

"The other day—and now it really was Shrovetide—right in
the middle of the spring floods, a sick peasant drove his sleigh
into the yard through the mud and slush. I refused to examine

him. 'I've given up practicing,' I said. 'I have neither medicines nor equipment.' But he persisted. 'Help me. My skin is bad. Have pity on me. I'm sick.' What could I do? I don't have a heart of stone. I told him to undress. He had lupus. As I was examining him I glanced at the bottle of carbolic acid on the window sill (don't ask me where it comes from—that and a few other things I couldn't do without—everything comes from Samdeviatov). Then I saw there was another sleigh in the yard. I thought at first it was another patient. But it was my brother, Evgraf, who had dropped in on us out of the blue. The family took charge of him—Tonia, Sashenka, Alexander Alexandrovich. Later I went out and joined them. We showered him with questions. Where had he come from? How had he come? As usual, he was evasive, he smiled, shrugged, spoke in riddles.

"He stayed about two weeks, went often to Yuriatin, and then vanished suddenly as if the earth had swallowed him. I realized while he was staying with us that he had even more influence than Samdeviatov and that his work and his connections were even more mysterious. What is he? What does he do? Why is he so powerful? He promised to make things easier for us so that Tonia should have more time for Sashenka and I for practicing medicine and writing. We asked him how he proposed to do this. He merely smiled. But he has been as good as his word. There are signs that our living conditions are really going to change.

"It is truly extraordinary. He is my half brother. We bear the same name. And yet I know virtually nothing about him.

"For the second time he has burst into my life as my good genius, my rescuer, resolving all my difficulties. Perhaps in every life there has to be, in addition to the other protagonists, a secret, unknown force, an almost symbolic figure who comes unsummoned to the rescue, and perhaps in mine Evgraf, my brother, plays the part of this hidden benefactor?"

At this point Yurii Andreievich's diary breaks off. He never went on with it.

10

Yurii Andreievich looked through the books he had ordered at the reading room of the Yuriatin public library. The reading room had several windows and could seat about a hundred people. Long tables stood in rows that ended by the windows. The library closed at sunset; in the spring the town had no lighting. Zhivago always left before dark, however, and never stayed in town later than the dinner hour. He would leave the horse that Mikulitsyn lent him at Samdeviatov's inn, read all morning, and ride back to Varykino in the afternoon.

Before he began visiting the library Yurii Andreievich had only rarely been to Yuriatin; he had nothing in particular to do there, and he hardly knew it. Now, as the reading room gradually filled with local people, some sitting down near to him and others farther away, he felt as if he were getting to know the town by standing at one of its bustling intersections, and as if not only the people but also the houses and the streets in which they lived were coming into the room.

However, from the windows one could also see the actual Yuriatin, real and not imagined. In front of the central, largest window was a tank of boiled water. Readers who wanted a break went out to the landing to smoke or gathered around the tank for a drink and, after emptying the cup into the basin, stood at the window, admiring the view over the town.

The readers were of two kinds. The majority were elderly members of the local intelligentsia; the rest were of more humble origin.

The former, mostly women, were poorly dressed and had a neglected, hangdog look and long, sickly faces which for one reason or another—whether through hunger, jaundice, or dropsy—were puffy. They were habitués of the library, and knew the attendants personally and felt at home here.

The common people looked well and handsome and were neatly dressed in their best clothes; they came in timidly as though they were entering a church; they made more noise than the others, not because they did not know the rules but because in their anxiety not to make a sound they could not control their vigorous steps and voices.

The librarian and his two assistants sat on a dais in a recess in the wall opposite the window, separated from the rest of the room by a high counter. One of the assistants was a cross-looking woman who wore a woollen shawl and kept putting on her pince-nez and taking it off, apparently in accordance with mood rather than need. The other, in a black silk blouse, seemed to have a weak chest, for she breathed and spoke through her handkerchief and never took it away from her nose and mouth.

The staff had the same long, puffy, flabby faces as most of the readers, and the same loose skin, earthy and greenish like pickled cucumbers or gray mold. The three of them took turns explaining the rules in whispers to new readers, sorted the order slips, handed out books and took them back, and in the intervals worked on some report or other.

Through an unaccountable association of ideas started by the sight of the real town outside the window and the imagined one inside the room, as well as by the swollen faces around him, which made it seem as though everyone had goiter and somehow recalled the face of the sulky woman in charge of the Yuriatin railway switch on the morning of his arrival, Yurii Andreievich remembered the distant panorama of the town and Samdeviatov beside him on the floor of the car, and his comments and explanations. He tried to connect these explanations, given him so far outside the town, with his immediate surroundings now that he was at the center of the picture. But he did not remember what Samdeviatov had told him, and he did not get anywhere.

11

Yurii Andreievich sat at the far end of the room. In front of him were several reports on local land statistics and some reference books on the ethnography of the region. He had also asked for two books on the history of the Pugachev rebellion, but the librarian in the silk blouse had whispered through her handkerchief that no one reader could have so many volumes at the same time and that he would have to give back some of the journals and reference books before taking out the others that interested him.

So he applied himself to his unsorted pile of books with more haste and industry than before in order to set aside those that he really needed and exchange the rest for the historical books he wanted. He was leafing through the manuals and going over the chapter headings, wholly concentrated on his work and not looking about him. The crowd of readers did not distract him. He had had a good look at his neighbors; those on his left and right were fixed in his mind, he knew they were there without raising his eyes and he had the feeling that they would not leave before him, just as the houses and churches outside the window would not move from their places.

The sun, however, did move. It had shifted from the east corner of the room and was now shining through the windows in the south wall straight into the eyes of the nearest readers.

The librarian who had a cold came down from her dais and went over to the windows. They had pleated white curtains that softened the light pleasantly. She drew them all except at the last window, which was still in the shade. Coming to it, she pulled the cord to open the transom and had a fit of sneezing.

After she had sneezed ten or twelve times Yurii Andreievich realized that she was Mikulitsyn's sister-in-law, one of the Tuntseva girls mentioned by Samdeviatov. Like other readers, he raised his head and looked in her direction.

Now he noticed a change in the room. At its farther end there was a new reader. Yurii Andreievich recognized Antipova at once. She was sitting with her back to him, speaking in a low voice with the sneezing librarian, who stood leaning over her. The conversation seemed to have a good effect on the librarian. It cured her instantly, not only of her annoying cold but of her nervous tenseness. With a warm, grateful glance at Antipova, she took the handkerchief she had been ceaselessly pressing to her mouth away from her face, put it in her pocket, and went back to her place behind the partition, happy, self-confident, and smiling.

The incident marked by this touching detail was noticed by several people in different parts of the room; they too smiled, looking at Antipova with approval. From these trivial signs Yurii Andreievich gathered that Antipova was known and liked in the town.

12

His first impulse was to get up and speak to her. But a shyness and lack of simplicity, entirely alien to his nature, had, in the past, crept into his relationship with her and now held him back. He decided not to disturb her and not to interrupt his work. To keep away from the temptation of looking at her he turned his chair sideways, so that its back was almost against his table; he tried to concentrate on his books, holding one in his hand and another on his knees.

But his thoughts had wandered far from his studies. Suddenly he realized that the voice he had once heard in a dream on a winter night in Varykino had been Antipova's. The discovery dumbfounded him, and startling his neighbors he jerked his chair back to be able to see Antipova. He began to look at her.

He saw her in a quarter view from the rear. She wore a light checked blouse with a belt and read with complete absorption, like a child, her head bent slightly over her right shoulder. Occasionally she stopped to think, looked up at the ceiling or straight in front of her, then again propped her cheek on her hand and copied excerpts from the volume she was reading, writing with a swift, sweeping movement of her pencil in her notebook.

Yurii Andreievich noticed again what he had observed long ago in Meliuzeievo. "She does not want to please or to look beautiful," he thought. "She despises all that aspect of a woman's nature; it's as though she were punishing herself for being lovely. But this proud hostility to herself makes her ten times more irresistible.

"How well she does everything! She reads not as if reading were the highest human activity, but as if it were the simplest possible thing, a thing that even animals could do. As if she were carrying water from a well, or peeling potatoes."

These reflections calmed him. A rare peace descended upon his soul. His mind stopped darting from subject to subject. He could not help smiling; Antipova's presence affected him the same way as it had affected the nervous librarian.

No longer worrying about the angle of his chair nor afraid of distractions, he worked for an hour or so with even greater concentration than before her arrival. He went through the whole pile of books in front of him, setting aside those he needed most, and even had time to read two important articles he found in them. Then, deciding that he had done enough for the day, he collected his books and took them back to the desk. With an easy conscience and without any ulterior motive, he reflected that after his hard morning's work he deserved to take time off to see an old friend and that he could legitimately allow himself this pleasure. But when he stood up and looked around the room, Antipova was no longer there.

The books she had just returned were still lying on the counter where he had put his own. They were textbooks of Marxism. She must be re-educating herself politically before going back to her teaching job.

On her order slips, which stuck out from between the pages of the books, was her address. Yurii Andreievich took it down, surprised by its oddity: "Merchant Street, opposite the house with sculptures." He asked another reader what this meant and was told that the expression "house with sculptures" was as familiar in Yuriatin as in Moscow the designation of a street by the name of its parish church, or the phrase "the Five Corners" in Petersburg.

The name referred to a dark, steel-gray house decorated with Caryatides and statues of the Muses holding cymbals, lyres, and masks. A merchant had built it in the last century as his private theater. His heirs had sold it to the Merchants' Guild, which gave its name to the street, and the whole neighborhood was known by the name of the house. It was now used by the Party's Town Committee, and the lower part of its façade, where posters and programs had been displayed in the old days, was now covered with government proclamations and decrees.

13

It was a cold, windy afternoon at the beginning of May. Yurii Andreievich, having finished what he had to do in town and having looked in at the library, suddenly changed his plans and decided to go see Antipova.

The wind often held him up, barring his way with clouds of dust and sand. He averted his head, closed his eyes, waited for the dust to stop blowing, and continued on his way.

Antipova lived at the corner of Merchant Street opposite the dark, blue-gray house with sculptures, which he now saw for the first time. It did indeed live up to its name, and there was something strange and disturbing about it.

Its entire top floor was surrounded by female mythological figures half as big again as human beings. Between two gusts of the dust storm it seemed to him as if all the women in the house had come out on the balcony and were looking down at him over the balustrade.

There were two doors into Antipova's house, one from Merchant Street, the other around the corner from the alley. Not having noticed the front entrance, Yurii Andreievich went in from the side street.

As he turned in at the gate the wind whirled scraps and trash up into the sky, screening the yard from the doctor. Through this black curtain, hens, chased by a cock, fled clucking from under his feet.

When the dust settled the doctor saw Antipova by the well. She had filled two buckets and hung them on a yoke across her left shoulder. Her hair was hastily tied in a kerchief knotted in front to protect it from the dust, and she was holding her billowing skirt down between her knees. She started for the house, but was stopped by another gust that tore the kerchief from her head and carried it off to the far end of the fence where the hens were still cackling.

Yurii Andreievich ran after it, picked it up, and took it back to her at the well. Preserving her usual natural air, she did not, even by an exclamation, betray her amazement or embarrassment. All she said was: "Zhivago!"

"Larisa Feodorovna!"

"What on earth are you doing here?"

"Put your buckets down. I'll carry them for you."

"I never stop halfway, I never leave what I do unfinished. If it's me you've come to see, let's go."

"Who else?"

"How should I know?"

"Anyway, let me take those buckets. I can't just stand by while you work."

"You call that work? Leave them alone. You'd only splash the stairs. Better tell me what brought you here. You've been around more than a year and you never found a moment to come till now."

"How do you know?"

"Things get around. Moreover, I saw you in the reading room."

"Why didn't you speak to me?"

"Don't tell me you didn't see me."

Swaying a little under the weight of the lightly swinging buckets, she walked in front of him through the low arch of the entrance. Here she squatted quickly, setting the pails on the earth floor, took the yoke off her shoulder, straightened up, and dried her hands with a small handkerchief.

"Come, I'll take you through the inside passage to the front hall. It's lighter. You'll have to wait there a moment. I'll take the buckets up the back stairs and tidy up a bit. I won't be long. Look at our smart stairs—cast-iron steps with an open-work pattern. You can see everything through them from the top. It's an old house. The shelling has shaken it up a bit, you can see where the masonry has come loose. See this crack in the brick-work? That's where Katenka and I leave the key to the flat when we go out. Keep it in mind. You might come someday when I'm out—you can open the door and make yourself at home till I come back. You see, there it is, but I don't need to use it now. I'll go in the back way and open the door from inside. Our only trouble is rats. There are swarms and swarms of them, and you can't get rid of them. It's these old walls. Cracks and crevices all over the place. I stop up all the ratholes I can, but it doesn't do much good. Perhaps you'd come one day and help me? The cracks between the skirting and the floor boards need stopping up. Yes? Well, you stay here in the hall and think about something. I won't be long, I'll call you in a minute."

While waiting, he looked around at the peeling walls and the cast-iron steps. He told himself: "In the reading room I thought she was absorbed in her reading with the ardor she would give to a real, hard physical task. Now I see that the reverse is also true: she carries water from the well as lightly and effortlessly as if she were reading. There is the same gracefulness in everything she does, as if she had taken a flying start early in life, way back in her childhood, and now everything she does follows this momentum, easily, naturally. This quality is in the line of her back when she bends down and in her smile as it parts her lips and rounds her chin, and in her words and thoughts."

"Zhivago!" Antipova called down from the top landing.

He went up.

14

"Give me your hand and do as I tell you. We have to go through two dark rooms piled with furniture. You might bump into something and hurt yourself."

"True. It is like a labyrinth. I'd never have found my way. Why is it like this? Is the flat being redecorated?"

"Oh no, nothing like that. It belongs to someone else, I don't even know who it is. I had my own flat in the school building. When the school was taken over by the Town Housing Department, Katenka and I were given part of this house. The owners had gone away, leaving all their furniture. There was an awful lot of it. I don't want other people's things, so I put it all into these two rooms and whitewashed the windows to keep out the sun. Don't let go of my hand or you'll get lost. Here we are, we turn right, now we're out of the maze, here's my door. It will be lighter in a second. Watch the step."

As he followed her into the room he was struck by the view from the window facing the door. It looked out on the yard and over the low roofs of the houses beyond it to the vacant lots by the river. Goats and sheep grazed there, and their long woolly coats swept the ground like long skirts. There too was the familiar billboard: "Moreau & Vetchinkin. Mechanical seeders. Threshing machines."

Reminded by it of the day of his arrival from Moscow, the doctor proceeded to describe it to Larisa Feodorovna. Forgetting there was a rumor that Strelnikov was her husband, he told her of his meeting with the commissar in the train. This part of his story made a deep impression on her.

"You saw Strelnikov?" she asked eagerly. "I won't tell you now, but really it is extraordinary. It's as if you were predestined to meet. I'll tell you all about it sometime, you'll be amazed. If I'm not mistaken, he made a good rather than a bad impression on you?"

"Yes, on the whole. He ought to have repelled me. We had actually passed through the country where he had brought death and destruction. I expected to see a brutal soldier or a revolutionary Jack-the-Ripper, but he was neither. It's a good thing when a man is different from your image of him. It shows

he isn't a type. If he were, it would be the end of him as a man.
But if you can't place him in a category, it means that at least a
part of him is what a human being ought to be. He has risen
above himself, he has a grain of immortality."

"They say he is not a Party member."

"Yes, I think that's true. What is it that makes one like him?
He is a doomed man. I believe that he'll come to a bad end. He
will atone for the evil he has done. Revolutionaries who take the
law into their own hands are horrifying not because they are
criminals, but because they are like machines that have got out
of control, like runaway trains. Strelnikov is as mad as the
others, only his madness does not spring from theories, but
from the ordeals he has gone through. I don't know his secret,
but I am sure he has one. His alliance with the Bolsheviks is
accidental. So long as they need him, they put up with him, and
he happens to be going their way. The moment they don't need
him they'll throw him overboard with no regret, and crush
him, as they have done with other military experts."

"You think so?"

"I am sure of it."

"Is there no escape for him? Couldn't he run away?"

"Where could he run, Larisa Feodorovna? You could do that
in the old days, under the Tsars. But just you try nowadays!"

"Too bad. You've made me feel sorry for him. You've
changed, you know. You used to speak more calmly about the
revolution, you were less harsh about it."

"That's just the point, Larisa Feodorovna. There are limits to
everything. In all this time something definite should have been
achieved. But it turns out that those who inspired the revolution
aren't at home in anything except change and turmoil, they
aren't happy with anything that's on less than a world scale. For
them transitional periods, worlds in the making, are an end in
themselves. They aren't trained for anything else, they don't
know anything except that. And do you know why these never-
ending preparations are so futile? It's because these men haven't
any real capacities, they are incompetent. Man is born to live,
not to prepare for life. Life itself, the phenomenon of life, the
gift of life, is so breath-takingly serious! So why substitute this
childish harlequinade of immature fantasies, these schoolboy
escapades? But enough of this. It's my turn to ask questions. We
arrived on the morning of the local upheaval. Were you in it?"

"I should say I was! There were fires all around us, it's a
wonder the house didn't burn down. It was pretty badly shaken,

as I told you. To this day there's an unexploded shell in the yard just inside the gate. Looting, bombardment, all kinds of horrors—as at every change of government. But by then we were used to it, it wasn't the first time. And the things that went on under the Whites! Murders to settle old accounts, extortions, blackmail—a real orgy! But I haven't told you the most extraordinary thing. Our Galiullin! He turned up with the Czechs as a most important personage—a sort of Governor-General."

"I know. I heard about it. Did you see him?"

"Very often. You can't think how many people I managed to save, thanks to him, how many I hid. In all fairness, he behaved perfectly, chivalrously, not like all those small fry—little Cossack captains, policemen, and what not. Unfortunately, it was the small fry who set the tone, not the decent people. Galiullin helped me a lot, bless him. We are old friends, you know. When I was a little girl I often went to the house where he grew up. Most of the tenants were railway workers. I saw a lot of poverty as a child. That's why my attitude to the revolution is different from yours. It's closer to me. There's a lot of it I understand from the inside. But that Galiullin, that the son of a janitor should become a White Colonel—perhaps even a General! There aren't any soldiers in my family, I don't know much about army ranks. And by profession I am a history teacher. . . . Anyway, that's how it was. Between us, we managed to help quite a lot of people. I used to go and see him. We talked about you. I've always had friends and connections in every government—and also sorrows and disappointment from all of them. It's only in mediocre books that people are divided into two camps and have nothing to do with each other. In real life everything gets mixed up! Don't you think you'd have to be a hopeless nonentity to play only one role all your life, to have only one place in society, always to stand for the same thing?— Ah, there you are!"

A little girl of about eight came in, her hair done up in finely braided pigtails. Her narrow eyes had a sly, mischievous look and went up at the corners when she laughed. She knew her mother had a visitor, having heard his voice outside the door, but she thought it necessary to put on an air of surprise. She curtsied and looked at the doctor with the fearless, unblinking stare of a lonely child who had begun to think early in life.

"My daughter, Katenka. I hope you'll be friends!"

"You showed me her photograph in Meliuzeievo. How she's grown and changed since then!"

"I thought you were out. I didn't hear you come in."

"I took the key out of the crack and there was an enormous rat in it—as big as this! You should have seen me jump! I nearly died of fright."

She made an absurd face, opening her eyes wide and rounding her mouth like a fish out of water.

"Off you go now. I'll get Uncle to stay to dinner, and call you when the kasha is ready."

"Thank you, I wish I could stay. But we have dinner at six since I've started coming to town and I try not to be late. It takes me over three hours to get home—nearly four. That is why I came so early. I'm afraid I'll have to go soon."

"You can stay another half hour."

"I'd love to."

15

"And now, since you have been so frank with me, I'll be frank with you. The Strelnikov you met is my husband, Pasha, Pavel Pavlovich Antipov, whom I went to look for at the front and in whose death I so rightly refused to believe."

"What you say does not come as a surprise. I was prepared for something of the sort. I heard that rumor, but I didn't believe it for a moment. That's why I spoke about him to you so freely, ignoring the rumor, which is sheer nonsense. I've seen this man. How could anyone connect him with you? What do you have in common with him?"

"And yet it's true. Strelnikov is Antipov, my husband. I share the general belief. Katenka knows it and is proud of her father. Strelnikov is his pseudonym—he has an assumed name, like all active revolutionaries. For some reason he must live and act under an alias.

"It was he who took Yuriatin, and shelled us, knowing that we were here, and never once tried to find out if we were alive, in order not to reveal his identity. Of course it was his duty. If he had asked me I would have told him to do just that. You might say that my being safe and the Town Soviet's giving me a reasonable place to live in shows that he is secretly looking after us. But that he should actually have been here and resisted the temptation to have a look at us—it's inconceivable! It's beyond me, it isn't natural, it's like the ancient Roman virtue, one of those newfangled ideas. But I mustn't let myself be influenced by your way of looking at things. You and I don't really think alike. When it comes to the intangible, the marginal choices, we understand each other. But when it comes to the big issues, to one's outlook on life, we don't see eye to eye. But to go back to Strelnikov. . . .

"Now he's in Siberia, and you are right—I have heard him accused of things that make my blood run cold. He is out there, in command of one of our most advanced positions, and he is fighting and beating poor old Galiullin, his childhood friend and his comrade in arms in the German war. Galiullin knows who he is, and he knows that I am his wife, but he has had the delicacy—I can't value it too highly—never to refer to it, though goodness knows he goes mad with rage at the sound of Strelnikov's name.

"Yes, that's where he is now, in Siberia. But he was here for a long time, living in that railway car where you saw him. I kept hoping I'd run into him by accident. Sometimes he went to the staff headquarters, which were in the building where Komuch—the Constituent Assembly Army—used to have its headquarters. And by an odd coincidence, the entrance was through the wing where Galiullin used to see me. I was always going there to ask him to help somebody or to stop some horrible business or other. For instance, there was that affair at the military academy, which made a lot of noise at the time. If an instructor was unpopular the cadets ambushed him and shot him, saying he was a Bolshevik sympathizer. And then there was the time when they started beating up the Jews. Incidentally, if you do intellectual work of any kind and live in a town, as we do, half of your friends are bound to be Jews. Yet in times when there are pogroms, when all these terrible, despicable things are done, we don't only feel sorry and indignant and ashamed, we feel wretchedly divided, as if our sympathy came more from the head than from the heart and had an aftertaste of insincerity.

"It's so strange that these people who once liberated mankind from the yoke of idolatry, and so many of whom now devote themselves to its liberation from injustice, should be incapable of liberating themselves from their loyalty to an obsolete, antediluvian identity that has lost all meaning, that they should not rise above themselves and dissolve among all the rest whose religion they have founded and who would be so close to them, if they knew them better.

"Of course it's true that persecution forces them into this futile and disastrous attitude, this shamefaced, self-denying isolation that brings them nothing but misfortune. But I think some of it also comes from a kind of inner senility, a historical centuries-long weariness. I don't like their ironical whistling in the dark, their prosaic, limited outlook, the timidity of their imagination. It's as irritating as old men talking of old age or sick people about sickness. Don't you think so?"

"I haven't thought about it much. I have a friend, Misha Gordon, who thinks as you do."

"Well, I used to go to this place hoping to catch Pasha on his way in or out. In Tsarist times the Governor-General used to have his office in that part of the building. Now there is a notice on the door: 'Complaints.' Have you seen it? It's the prettiest place in town. The square in front of it is paved with wooden blocks, and across the square there is the town park, full of maples, hawthorn, honeysuckle. There was always a line in the street outside the door. I used to stand there and wait. Of course I didn't try to crash the door, I didn't say I was his wife. After all, our names are different. And don't think that an appeal to sentiment would move them! Their ways are quite different. Do you know, his own father, Pavel Ferapontovich Antipov, a former political exile, an old worker, is quite near here, in a settlement along the highway, where he lived as an exile. And his friend Tiverzin is there too. They are both members of the local revolutionary court. Well, can you believe it, Pasha hasn't been to see his father and he hasn't told him who he is. And his father takes it for granted, he isn't a bit hurt. If his son wants to remain incognito, then that's as it should be, he can't see him and that's all there is to it. They are made of stone, these people, they aren't human, with all their discipline and principles.

"Even if I had managed to prove that I was his wife, it wouldn't have done me any good! What do wives matter to them at a time like this? The workers of the world, the remaking of the universe—that's something! But a wife, just an individual biped, is of no more importance than a flea or a louse!

"His aide-de-camp used to come out and ask people what they wanted to see him for and let some of them in. But I never told him my name and when he asked me what my business was I always said it was personal. Of course, I knew I was wasting my time. The aide would shrug his shoulders and give me a suspicious look. I never once saw him.

"I suppose you think he can't be bothered with us, he doesn't love us, he's forgotten us? Well, you are wrong. I know him too well. I know just what he wants, and it's just because he loves us. He can't bear to come back to us empty-handed. He wants to come back as a conqueror, full of honor and glory, and lay his laurels at our feet. To immortalize us, to dazzle us! Just like a child."

Katenka came in again. Larisa Feodorovna snatched her up and, to the girl's astonishment, started swinging her around and tickling and hugging her.

16

Yurii Andreievich was riding back to Varykino. He had been over this stretch of country countless times. He was so used to the road that he was no longer aware of it, he hardly saw it.

Soon he would come to the crossroad in the forest where the way ahead led to Varykino and another path turned off to the fishing village of Vasilievskoie on the river Sakma. Here stood yet a third billboard advertising agricultural machinery. As usual he reached the crossroad at dusk.

Two months had now elapsed since the day when, instead of going home from Yuriatin, he spent the night at Larisa Feodorovna's and told his family that he had been kept on business and had stayed at Samdeviatov's inn. He had long been calling her Lara and addressing her as "thou," though she still called him Zhivago. Yurii Andreievich was betraying Tonia, and his involvement was becoming ever more serious. This was shocking, impossible.

He loved Tonia, he worshipped her. Her peace of mind meant more to him than anything in the world. He would defend her honor more devotedly than her father or herself. He would have torn apart with his own hands anyone who would hurt her pride. And yet he himself was now the offender.

At home he felt like a criminal. His family's ignorance of the truth and their unchanged affection were a mortal torment to him. In the middle of a conversation he would suddenly be numbed by the recollection of his guilt and cease hearing a word of what was being said around him.

If this happened during a meal, his food stuck in his throat and he put down his spoon and pushed away his plate. He choked, repressing his tears. "What is wrong with you?" Tonia would ask, puzzled. "You must have had some bad news when you were in town. Has anyone been arrested? Or shot? Do tell me. Don't be afraid of upsetting me. You'll feel better when you've told me."

Had he been unfaithful because he preferred another woman? No, he had made no comparison, no choice. The idea of "free love," terms like "the legitimate demands of love," were alien to him. To think or speak in such terms seemed to him degrading. He had never "sown wild oats," nor did he regard himself as a superman with special rights and privileges. Now he was crushed by the weight of his guilty conscience.

"What next?" he had sometimes wondered, and hoped wretchedly for some impossible, unexpected circumstance to solve his problem for him.

But now he no longer wondered. He had decided to cut the knot, and he was going home with a solution. He would confess everything to Tonia, beg her to forgive him, and never see Lara again.

Not that everything was quite as it should be. He felt now that he had not made it clear enough to Lara that he was breaking with her for good, forever. He had announced to her that morning that he wished to make a clean breast of it with Tonia and that they must stop seeing each other, but now he had the feeling that he had softened it all down and not made it sufficiently definite.

Larisa Feodorovna had realized how unhappy he felt and had no wish to upset him further by painful scenes. She tried to hear him out as calmly as she could. They were talking in one of the empty front rooms. Tears were running down her cheeks, but she was no more conscious of them than the stone statues on the house across the road were of the rain running down their faces. She kept saying softly: "Do as you think best, don't worry about me. I'll get over it." She was saying it sincerely, without any false magnanimity, and as she did not know that she was crying she did not wipe away her tears.

At the thought that Lara might have misunderstood him, and that he had left her with a wrong impression and false hopes, he nearly turned and galloped straight back, to say what he had left unsaid and above all to take leave of her much more warmly, more tenderly, in a manner more suitable to a last farewell. Controlling himself with difficulty, he continued on his way.

As the sun went down, the forest was filled with cold and darkness. It smelled of damp leaves. Swarms of mosquitoes hung in the air as still as buoys, humming sadly on a constant, high-pitched note. They settled on his sweating face and neck, and he kept swatting them, his noisy slaps keeping time with the sounds of riding—the creaking of the saddle, the heavy thud of hoofs on the squelching mud, and the dry, crackling salvoes as the horse broke wind. In the distance, where the sunset glow seemed to endure forever, a nightingale began to sing.

"Wake up! Wake up!" it called persuasively; it sounded almost like the summons on the eve of Easter Sunday: "Awake, O my soul, why dost thou slumber?"

Suddenly Yurii Andreievich was struck by a very simple thought. What was the hurry? He would not go back on his promise to himself; the confession would be made, but who had said that it must be made that day? He had not said anything to Tonia yet, it was not too late to put it off till his next trip to town. He would finish his conversation with Lara, with such warmth and depth of feeling that it would make up for all their suffering. How splendid, how wonderful! How strange that it had not occurred to him before!

At the thought of seeing Lara once more his heart leapt for joy. In anticipation he lived through his meeting with her.

The wooden houses and pavements on the outskirts of the town . . . He is on his way to her. In a moment he will leave the wooden sidewalks and vacant lots for the paved streets. The small suburban houses flash by like the pages of a book, not as when you turn them over one by one with your forefinger but as when you hold your thumb on the edge of the book and let them all swish past at once. The speed is breath-taking. And over there is her house at the far end of the street, under the white gap in the rain clouds where the sky is clearing, toward the evening. How he loves the little houses in the street that lead to her! He could pick them up and kiss them! Those one-eyed attics with their roofs pulled down like caps. And the lamps and icon lights reflected in the puddles and shining like berries! And her house under the white rift of the sky! There he will again receive the dazzling, God-made gift of beauty from the hands of its Creator. A dark muffled figure will open the door, and the promise of her nearness, unowned by anyone in the world and guarded and cold as a white northern night, will reach him like the first wave of the sea as you run down over the sandy beach in the dark.

Yurii Andreievich dropped his reins, leaned forward in his saddle, flung his arms around the horse's neck, and buried his face in its mane. Taking this display of affection for an appeal to its strength, the horse broke into a gallop.

As it bounded smoothly, its hoofs barely touching the ground, it seemed to Yurii Andreievich that, besides the joyful thudding of his own heart, he heard shouts, but he thought he was imagining it.

Suddenly a deafening shot was fired very close to him. He sat up, snatched at the reins, and pulled. Checked in full flight, the horse side-stepped, backed, and went down on its haunches ready to rear.

In front of him was the crossroad. The sign, "Moreau & Vetchinkin. Mechanical seeders. Threshing machines," glowed in the rays of the setting sun. Three armed horsemen blocked his way: a boy in a school cap and a tunic with two cartridge belts, a cavalryman in an officer's overcoat and fur cap, and a fat man oddly clothed as for a fancy-dress ball in quilted trousers and a wide-brimmed clerical hat pulled low over his forehead.

"Don't move, Comrade Doctor," said the cavalryman in the fur cap, who was the oldest of the three. "If you obey orders, we guarantee that you will not be harmed. If you don't—no offense meant—we'll shoot you. The surgeon attached to our unit has been killed and we are conscripting you as a medical worker. Get down from your horse and hand the reins over to this young man. And let me remind you: if you try to escape we'll give you short shrift."

"Are you Comrade Forester, Mikulitsyn's son Liberius?"

"No, I am his chief liaison officer."

CHAPTER TEN

The Highway

1

There were towns, villages, and Cossack settlements along the highway. It was the ancient post road, the oldest highway in Siberia. It cut through the towns like a knife, slicing them like a loaf of bread along the line of their main streets. As for the villages, it swept through them without a backward glance, scattering them right and left, leaving the rows of houses far behind it, or going around them in a broad arc or a sharp turn.

In the distant past, before the railway came to Khodatskoie, the mail was rushed along the highway by troikas. Caravans of tea, bread, and pig iron travelled one way, and convicts under guard, on foot, were driven the other. They walked in step, jangling their fetters—lost souls, desperadoes who filled one's heart with terror. And around them the forests rustled, dark, impenetrable.

Those who lived along the highway were as one family. Friendships and marriages linked village to village and town to town. Khodatskoie stood at a crossing of the road and the railway; it had engine repair shops and other workshops connected with the upkeep of the line, and there, crowded into barracks, the poorest of the poor lived and wasted away and

died. Political exiles who had technical qualifications and had
served their term of hard labor came to work as skilled
mechanics, and settled here.

The original Soviets, which had been set up all along the line,
had long since been overthrown. For some time the region had
been under the Siberian Provisional Government, but now it
had fallen to Admiral Kolchak, who had given himself the title
of "Supreme Ruler."

2

At one stretch the road had a long uphill climb disclosing an
ever broader panorama. It seemed as if there would be no end to
the slow ascent and to the widening of the horizon, but when
the tired horses and passengers stopped for a rest they found that
they had reached the summit of the hill. The road went on over
a bridge and the river Kezhma swirled beneath it.

Beyond the river, on an even steeper rise, they could see the
brick walls of the Vozdvizhensky Monastery. The road circled
the hill of the monastery and zigzagged on through the outskirts
of the town.

When it reached the center of the town it skirted the
monastery grounds once again, for the green-painted iron door
of the monastery gave on to the main square. The icon over the
arched gate was framed by the legend in gold letters: "Rejoice,
life-giving Cross, unconquerable victory of piety."

It was Holy Week, the end of Lent, and winter was almost
over. The snow on the roads was turning black, betraying the
beginning thaw, but on the roofs it was still white, and covered
them as with tall hats.

To the boys who had climbed up to the belfry to watch the
bell ringers, the houses below looked like small caskets and
boxes jumbled close together. Little black people, hardly bigger
than dots, walked toward the houses. Some could be recognized
from the belfry by the way they moved. They stopped to read
the decree of the Supreme Ruler, posted on the walls, announc-
ing that three age groups were drafted.

3

Many unexpected things had happened in the night. It had turned unusually warm for the time of year. A drizzle was coming down, so fine and airy that it seemed to drift away in mist before it reached the earth. But this was an illusion. In reality there was enough rain water to stream, warm and swift, along the ground—which had turned black all over and glistened as if it sweated—and to wash it clean of the remaining snow.

Stunted apple trees, covered with buds, reached miraculously across the garden fences. Drops of water fell from them, and their arhythmic drumming on the wooden pavements could be heard throughout the town.

Tomik, the puppy, chained up for the night in the photographer's yard, squealed and yelped, and in the Galuzins' garden the crow, perhaps irritated by the noise, cawed loud enough to keep the whole town awake.

In the lower part of the town, three cartloads of goods had been taken to the merchant, Liubeznov, who refused to accept delivery, saying it was a mistake, he had never ordered the stuff. The draymen, arguing the lateness of the hour, begged him to put them up for the night, but he cursed and sent them to the devil and refused to open the gate. This row, too, could be heard from one end of the town to the other.

At the seventh canonical hour, at one in the morning by the clock, a dark low sweet humming drifted from the deepest of the monastery bells, which hardly stirred. It mixed with the dark drizzle in the air. It drifted from the bell, sinking and dissolving in the air, as a clump of earth, torn from the riverbank, sinks and dissolves in the water of the spring floods.

It was the night of Maundy Thursday. Almost indistinguishable in the distance, behind the network of rain, candles, lighting a face here, a forehead or a nose there, stirred and moved across the monastery yard. The fasting congregation was going to Mass.

A quarter of an hour later, steps sounded on the wooden sidewalk coming from the church. This was Galuzina, the grocer's wife, going home, although the service had only begun. She went at an uneven pace, now running, now slowing down and stopping, her kerchief over her head and her fur coat unbuttoned. She had felt faint in the stuffy church and had come out into the fresh air, but now she was ashamed and sorry that she had not stayed to the end, and because, for the second year now, she was not fasting in Lent. But this was not the chief cause of her worry. The mobilization order posted that day affected her poor, silly boy, Terioshka. She tried to drive the thought of it from her head, but the white patches in the darkness were there to remind her at every turn.

Her house was just around the corner, but she felt better out of doors and was not in a hurry to go back into the airless rooms.

She was upset by gloomy thoughts. Had she tried to think them all out aloud, one by one, she would not have had sufficient words or time enough till dawn. But out here, in the street, these comfortless reflections flew at her in clusters, and she could deal with all of them together, in the short while it took her to walk a few times from the monastery gate to the corner of the square and back.

It was almost Easter and there was not a soul in the house; they had all gone away, leaving her alone. Well, wasn't she alone? Of course she was. Her ward Ksiusha didn't count. Who was she, anyway? Could you ever know anyone's heart? Perhaps she was a friend, or perhaps she was an enemy or a secret rival. She was supposed to be the daughter of her husband's first wife by another marriage. Her husband, Vlas, said that he had adopted her. But suppose she was his natural daughter? Or suppose she wasn't his daughter but something else? Could you ever see into a man's heart? Though, to give Ksiusha her due, there was nothing wrong with her. She had brains, looks, manners—much more brains than either poor stupid Terioshka or her adoptive father!

So here she was, deserted for Holy Week. They had all scattered, everyone had gone his way.

Her husband was travelling up and down the highway making speeches to the new recruits, exhorting them to mighty feats of arms. Instead of looking after his own son, the fool, and saving him from his mortal peril!

And Terioshka too had dashed away from home on the eve of the great feast. He had gone to their relatives in Kuteiny village to amuse himself and forget his troubles. The poor boy had been expelled from school. They had kept him back an extra year in almost every other grade, and now that he was in the eighth they had to kick him out!

Oh, how depressing it all was! Oh, Lord! Why had everything gone so wrong? It was so disheartening, she felt like giving up, she had no wish to live. What had caused all this misery? Was it the revolution? No, oh no! It was the war. The war had killed off the flower of Russia's manhood, now there was nothing but rotten, good-for-nothing rubbish left.

How different it had been in her father's time! Her father had been a contractor. Sober, literate. They had lived off the fat of the land. She and her two sisters, Polia and Olia, as fine a pair of girls as you could hope to meet and as well matched as their names. And master carpenters had called on their father, every one a fine, upstanding man, and a good match. At one time, she and her sisters—the things they would think of!—had got it into their heads to knit scarves in wool of six colors. And believe it or not, such good knitters were they that their scarves had become famous all over the province! And everything in those days had been fine and rich and seemly—church services and dances and people and manners—everything had rejoiced her heart, for all that her own family were simple people who came of peasant and worker stock. And Russia too had been a marriageable girl in those days, courted by real men, men who would stand up for her, not to be compared with this rabble nowadays. Now everything had lost its glamour, nothing but civilians left, lawyers and Yids clacking their tongues day and night. Poor old Vlas and his friends thought they could bring back those golden days by toasts and speeches and good wishes! But was this the way to win back a lost love? For that you had to move mountains!

4

By now she had crossed the square and walked as far as the marketplace more than once. From there her house was down the street on the left, but every time she came to it she changed her mind about going in and turned back into the maze of alleys adjoining the monastery.

The marketplace of Krestovozdvizhensk was as big as a field. In times gone by, it had been crowded on market days with peasants' carts. At one end of it was Eleninskaia Street; the other formed a sharp arc lined with one- or two-story buildings used for warehouses, offices, and workshops.

There, she remembered, in more peaceful times, Brukhianov, a boorish misogynist in spectacles, and a long frock coat, who dealt in leather, oats and hay, cart wheels and harness, would read the penny paper as he sat importantly on a chair outside his great, four-panelled iron door.

And there, in a small dim window, a few pairs of beribboned wedding candles and posies in cardboard boxes gathered dust for years, while in the small room at the back, empty of either furniture or goods except for a pile of large round cakes of wax, thousand-ruble deals were made by the unknown agents of a millionaire candle manufacturer who lived nobody knew where.

There, in the middle of the row of shops, was the Galuzins' large grocery store with its three windows. Its bare, splintery floor was swept morning, noon, and night with used tea leaves: Galuzin and his assistants drank tea all day long. And here Galuzina as a young married woman had often and willingly sat at the cash box. Her favorite color was a violet mauve, the color of church vestments on certain solemn days, the color of lilac in bud, the color of her best velvet dress and of her set of crystal wine glasses. It was the color of happiness and of her memories, and Russia too, in her prerevolutionary virginity, seemed to her to have been the color of lilac. She had enjoyed sitting at the cash box because the violet dusk in the shop, fragrant with starch, sugar, and purple black-currant caramels in glass jars, had matched her favorite color.

Here at the corner, beside the timber yard, stood an old, gray frame house which had settled on all four sides like a dilapidated coach. It had two stories and two entrances, one at either end. Each floor was divided in two; downstairs were Zalkind's pharmacy on the right and a notary's office on the left. Above the pharmacist lived old Shmulevich, a ladies' tailor, with his big family. The flat across the landing from Shmulevich, and above the notary, was crammed with lodgers whose trades and professions were stated on cards and signs covering the whole of the door. Here watches were mended and shoes cobbled; here Kaminsky, the engraver, had his workroom and two photographers, Zhuk and Shtrodakh, worked in partnership.

As the first-floor premises were overcrowded, the photographers' young assistants, Blazheïn, a student, and Magidson, who retouched the photographs, had fixed up a darkroom at one end of the large woodshed in the yard. To judge by the angry red eye of the lamp winking blearily in the darkroom window, they were working there now. It was underneath this window that the puppy, Tomik, sat on his chain and yelped, so that you could hear him all along Eleninskaia Street.

"There they all are in a pack, the whole Kehillah," thought Galuzina as she passed the gray house. "It's a den of filthy beggars." And yet, she reflected at once, her husband carried his Jew-hating too far. After all, these people were not important enough to affect Russia's destinies. Though, if you asked old Shmulevich why he thought the country was in such turmoil and disorder, he would twist and turn and contort his ugly face into a grin and say: "That's Leibochka up to his tricks."

Oh, but what nonsense was she wasting her time thinking about! Did they matter? Were they Russia's misfortune? Her misfortune was the towns. Not that the country stood or fell by the towns. But the towns were educated, and the country people had had their heads turned, they envied the education of the towns and tried to copy their ways and could not catch up with them, so now they were neither one thing nor the other.

Or perhaps it was the other way around, perhaps ignorance was the trouble? An educated man can see through walls, he knows everything in advance, while the rest of us are like people in a dark wood. We only miss our hats when our heads have been chopped off. Not that the educated people were having an easy time now. Look at the way the famine was driving them out of the towns! How confusing all this was! Even the devil couldn't make head or tail of it!

And yet, it was the country people who knew how to live. Look at her relatives, the Selitvins, Shelaburins, Pamphil Palykh, the brothers Nestor and Pankrat Modykh. They relied on their own hands and their own heads, they were their own masters. The new farmsteads along the highway were a lovely sight. Forty acres of arable land, with sheep, horses, pigs, cows, and enough corn in the barns for three years ahead! And their farming machines! They even had harvesters! Kolchak was buttering them up, trying to get them on his side, and so were the commissars, to get them into the forest army. They had come back from the war with St. George Crosses and everyone was after them, wanting to employ them as instructors. Epaulettes or no epaulettes, if you knew your job you were always in demand. You would always land on your feet.

But it was time she went home. It wasn't decent for a woman to be wandering about the streets so late. It wouldn't have mattered so much if she had been in her own garden. But it was so muddy, it was like a bog. Anyway, she thought, she felt a little better now.

Thus entangled in her reflections and having quite lost the thread of them, Galuzina went home. But before she went inside, she stood for a moment in front of the porch, going over a few more things in her mind.

She thought of the people who were lording it in Khodatskoie now; she knew more or less what they were like, they were former political exiles from the capitals, Tiverzin, Antipov, the anarchist "Black Banner" Vdovichenko, the local locksmith "Mad Dog" Gorsheny. They were cunning and they knew their own minds, they had stirred up plenty of trouble in their day, they were sure to be plotting something again now. They couldn't live unless they were up to something. They spent their lives dealing with machines, and they were cold and merciless as machines. They went about in sweaters under their jackets, they smoked through bone cigarette holders, and they drank boiled water for fear of catching something. Poor Vlas was wasting his time, these men would turn everything upside down, they would always get their way.

Then she thought about herself. She knew she was a fine woman, with a mind of her own, intelligent and well preserved; all in all, she was not a bad person. But none of her qualities was appreciated in this Godforsaken hole—nor anywhere else, for all she knew. The indecent song about the silly old woman Sentetiurikha, which was well known throughout the Urals, came into her mind, but only the first two lines could be quoted:

> "*Sentetiurikha sold her cart*
> *And bought a balalaika. . . .*"

After this came nothing but obscenities. They sang it in Krestovozdvizhensk, aiming it, she suspected, at herself.

She sighed bitterly and went into the house.

5

She went straight to her bedroom, without stopping in the hall to take off her coat. The room looked out into the garden. Now, at night, the massed shadows on this side of the window and outside it almost repeated each other. The limp, drooping shapes of the curtains were like the limp, drooping shapes of the bare, dark trees in the garden with their uncertain outlines. The velvety darkness in the garden, where the winter was almost over, was being warmed by the dark purple heat of the coming spring bursting out of the ground. And there was a similar interaction of two elements inside the room with its dusty curtains, where the airless darkness was softened by the warm dark violet tones of the coming Feast.

The Virgin in the icon, freeing her dark, narrow hands from the silver covering, held them up, seeming to hold in each the first and last letters of her Greek name, Μήτηρ Θεοῦ, Mother of God. The garnet-colored icon lamp, dark as an inkwell in its gold bracket, scattered its star-shaped light, splintered by the cut glass, on the bedroom carpet.

Taking off her coat and kerchief, Galuzina made an awkward movement and felt her old pain, a stitch in the side under her shoulder blade. She gave a frightened cry and murmured: "Mighty protectress of the sorrowful, chaste Mother of God, help of the afflicted, shelter of the universe . . ." Halfway through the prayer she burst into tears. When the pain died down, she began to undo her dress, but the hooks at the back slipped through her fingers and got lost in the soft crinkled stuff. She had difficulty in finding them.

Her ward Ksiusha woke up and came into the room.

"Why are you in the dark, Mother? Shall I bring a lamp?"

"No, don't. There's enough light."

"Let me undo your dress, Mother. Don't tire yourself."

"My fingers are all thumbs, I could cry. And that tailor didn't have the sense to sew the hooks on so that you can get at them. I've got a notion to rip them all off and throw them at his ugly face."

"How well they sang at the monastery! It's so still, you could hear it from the house."

"The singing was all right, but I'm not feeling so well, my girl. I've got that stitch again—here and here. Everywhere. . . . It's such a nuisance, I don't know what to do."

"The homeopath, Stydobsky, helped you the last time."

"He's always telling you to do something impossible. He's a quack, your homeopath. That's one thing. And the other thing is that he's gone away. He's gone, I tell you, he's left town. And he isn't the only one, they've all rushed off just before the holiday—as if they expected an earthquake or something."

"Well, then, what about that Hungarian doctor, the one who is a prisoner of war? His treatment did you good."

"That's no use either. I tell you, there isn't a soul left. Kerenyi Lajos is with the other Hungarians beyond the demarcation line. They've conscripted him for the Red Army."

"But you know, Mother, you're imagining a lot of it. A nervous heart. In a case like yours suggestion can do wonders; it's what the peasants do, after all. Do you remember that soldier's wife who conjured away your pain? What was her name?"

"Well, really! You take me for an ignorant fool! It wouldn't surprise me if you sang 'Sentetiurikha' behind my back."

"Mother! How can you say such a thing! It's a sin. You ought to be ashamed of yourself. You'd do much better to help me remember that woman's name. It's on the tip of my tongue. I won't have any peace till it comes back to me."

"She has more names than petticoats. I don't know which is the one you're thinking of. They call her Kubarikha and Medvedikha and Zlydarikha and I don't know how many other names besides. She isn't around here anymore. No more guest appearances. She's gone. Vanished. They locked her up in the Kezhemsk jail for practicing abortion and making pills and powders of some sort. But sooner than be bored in jail she escaped and got away somewhere to the Far East. I tell you, everyone has run away—Vlas and Terioshka and your Aunt Polia—Aunt Polia of the loving heart. Apart from the two of us, fools that we are, there isn't an honest woman left in town, I'm not joking. And no medical help of any sort. If anything happened, you couldn't get a doctor. They say there's one in Yuriatin, some famous professor from Moscow, the son of a Siberian merchant who committed suicide. But just when I was thinking of sending for him, the Reds cut the road in twelve places. . . . Now, off to bed with you, and I'll try to get some sleep too. By the way, that student of yours, Blazhein, he's turned your head. What's the good of saying no?—you're getting red as a beet. He'll be sweating all night long over some photographs I gave him to develop, poor boy. They don't sleep in that house, and they keep everyone else awake as well. Their Tomik is barking, you can hear him all over town, and our wretched crow is cawing its head off up in the apple tree. Looks as if I'll have another sleepless night. . . . Now what are you so cross about? Don't be so touchy. What are students for if not for girls to fall in love with!"

6

"What's that dog howling for? Go and see what's the matter with it, it can't be making all that noise for nothing. Wait a minute, Lidochka, quiet, hold it! We've got to find out what's what or we'll have the police on us before we know it. Stay here, Ustin, and you, Sivobluy. They'll manage without you."

Lidochka, the representative of the Central Committee, did not hear the partisan leader asking him to stop and continued his tired patter:

"By its policy of looting, requisitioning, violence, shooting, and torture the bourgeois militarist regime in Siberia is bound to open the eyes of the gullible. It is hostile not only to the working class but, in fact, to the whole of the toiling peasantry. The toiling peasantry of Siberia and the Urals must understand that only in alliance with the city proletariat and the soldiers, only in alliance with the poor Kirghiz and Buriat peasants . . ."

At last he became aware of the interruptions, stopped, wiped his sweaty face with his handkerchief, and wearily shut his puffy eyes.

"Have a rest. Have a drink of water," whispered those who were standing closest to him.

The worried partisan leader was reassured.

"What's all the fuss about? Everything is in order. The signal lamp is in the window and the lookout, if I may use a picturesque expression, has his eyes glued to space. I don't see why we shouldn't go on with the discussion of the report. Go on, Comrade Lidochka."

The wood kept in the large barn in the photographers' yard

had been moved aside, and the illegal meeting was being held in the cleared space screened from the small darkroom at the entrance by a wall of logs as high as the ceiling. In case of emergency there was a way of escape through a trap door to an underground passage that came out in a lonely alley at the back of the monastery.

The speaker, who had a sallow complexion, a beard from ear to ear, and a black cotton cap on his bald head, suffered from nervous perspiration and sweated profusely. He kept relighting the stump of his cigarette in the stream of hot air over the kerosene lamp, puffing greedily. Bending low over his scattered papers, he looked them over nervously with his near-sighted eyes, as if he were sniffing them, and continued in his flat, tired voice:

"Only through the Soviets can this alliance of the poor in town and country be achieved. Willy-nilly, the Siberian peasant will now pursue the end for which the workers of Siberia began to fight long ago. Their common goal is the overthrow of the hateful autocracy of hetmans and admirals, and the establishment, by means of an armed uprising, of the power of the peasants' and soldiers' Soviets. In fighting the officer and Cossack hirelings of the bourgeoisie, who are armed to the teeth, the insurgents will have to wage a full-fledged war. The struggle will be long and stubborn."

Once again he stopped, wiped his face, and shut his eyes. In defiance of the rules, someone in the audience got up and raised his hand, signifying his intention to make a comment.

The partisan leader, or, to be more exact, the commander of the Kezhemsk group of the trans-Ural partisan units, sat in a provocatively nonchalant attitude under the speaker's very nose; he kept interrupting him rudely and disrespectfully. It was hard to believe that so young a soldier—little more than a boy— could be in charge of whole armies and that his men obeyed him and looked up to him with veneration. He sat with his hands and feet wrapped in the skirts of his cavalry overcoat; its top, thrown back over his chair, showed his ensign's tunic with dark patches on the shoulders where the epaulettes had been removed.

On either side of him stood a silent bodyguard of his own age, in a white sheepskin grown a little gray, with a curly lamb's-wool edging. Their handsome, stony faces revealed nothing except blind loyalty to their chief and readiness to do anything for him. Taking no part in the discussion and unmoved by any of the issues raised in it, they neither spoke nor smiled.

There were a dozen or so other people in the room. Some were standing, others sitting on the floor; they leaned against the walls of calked logs, their legs stretched out in front of them or their knees drawn up under their chins.

Three or four were guests of honor and sat on chairs. They were old workers, veterans of the revolution of 1905. Among them were Tiverzin, morose and greatly changed since his Moscow days, and his friend, old Antipov, who always agreed with every word he said. Counted among the gods at whose feet the revolution laid its gifts and its burnt offerings, they sat silent and grim as idols. They had become dehumanized by political conceit.

There were other noteworthy figures in the shed, such as that pillar of Russian anarchism, "Black Banner" Vdovichenko, who, never resting a moment, kept sitting down on the floor and getting up again or pacing back and forth and stopping in the middle of the shed. A fat giant of a man, with a big head, a big mouth, and a lion's mane of hair, who had been an officer in the war with Japan if not in the one with Turkey, he was a dreamer eternally absorbed in his fantasies.

Because of his excessive good nature and colossal size, which kept him from noticing anything smaller than himself, he did not pay sufficient attention to what was going on, misunderstood everything, and, mistaking the views of his opponents for his own, agreed with everything they said.

Next to him on the floor sat his friend Svirid, a trapper. Although he was not a tiller of the soil, his earthy nature showed through the collar of his opened dark cloth shirt, which he bunched in his hand together with the cross he wore around his neck, pulling it about and scratching his chest with it. He was half Buriat, warm-hearted and illiterate; his hair was plaited in thin braids, and he had a sparse mustache and a still sparser beard. His Mongol features aged his face, which was always creased in a sympathetic smile.

The speaker, who was touring Siberia on a military mission from the Central Committee, mentally surveyed the vast expanses he had still to cover. He was uninterested in most of the men he was addressing. But as an old revolutionary and from childhood a champion of the people, he gazed with adoration at the young commander who sat facing him. Not only did he forgive him his lack of manners, which he regarded as the expression of a genuinely revolutionary temperament, but he delighted in his insolence as an infatuated woman may be pleased by the arrogant ways of a masterful lover.

The partisan commander was Mikulitsyn's son, Liberius. The speaker was a former member of the co-operative labor movement, Kostoied-Amursky, who had once been a Social Revolutionary. He had recently revised his views, admitted his past errors, and recanted them in several detailed statements, and he had not only been received into the Communist Party but had soon afterwards been entrusted with his present responsible task.

He was chosen for it—though he was anything but a soldier—partly as a tribute to his long years of revolutionary service and his ordeals in Tsarist prisons, and partly on the assumption that, as a former member of the co-operative movement, he knew the mood of the peasant masses in insurgent western Siberia. For the purpose of his mission his knowledge was regarded as more important than military training.

His change of political convictions had altered his looks and manners beyond recognition. No one could remember him as either bald or bearded in the old days. But then, perhaps it was all merely a disguise. He was under strict orders from the Party not to reveal his former identity. His underground names were Berendey and Comrade Lidochka.

There was a moment of commotion when Vdovichenko prematurely said that he agreed with the instructions just read. When calm was restored, Kostoied went on:

"In order to keep up with the growing movement of the peasant masses, it is essential to establish contact at once with all the partisan units operating in the territory of the Party Provincial Committee."

He then spoke of arrangements for secret meeting places, passwords, codes, and means of communication and went over the whole ground in detail.

"The units must be informed of the location of the stores of arms, food, and equipment belonging to the Whites and of the places where they keep large sums of money, as well as of their means of safeguarding it.

"It is essential to work out to the last detail all questions concerning the organization of partisan detachments, their commanders, proletarian discipline, conspiratorial work, contact with the outside world, behavior toward the local population, revolutionary courts-martial, and sabotage in enemy territory—for example, the destruction of bridges, railway lines, steamships, barges, stations, workshops with all their technical equipment, telegraph offices, mines, and food supplies."

Liberius could bear it no longer. All that had been said seemed to him to be irrelevant and amateurish.

"A very fine lecture," he said. "I shall take it to heart. I suppose we must accept all this without a word of protest, lest we lose the support of the Red Army?"

"Of course you must."

"And what am I to do with your childish recitation, my wonderful Lidochka, when my forces, damn it—three regiments, including artillery and cavalry—have been campaigning for months and routing the enemy?"

"What a marvel! What strength!" thought Kostoied.

The argument was interrupted by Tiverzin, who disliked Liberius's impertinent tone.

"Pardon me, Comrade Speaker, there is something that I don't understand. I may have put down one of the points in the instructions incorrectly. May I read it out—I should like to be sure. 'It is most desirable that war veterans who were at the front and belonged to soldiers' organizations at the time of the revolution should be drawn into the committee. It is desirable that the membership of the committee should include one or two N.C.O.'s and one military technician.' Have I put it down correctly, Comrade Speaker?"

"Perfectly. Word for word."

"Then allow me to say this. I find the point concerning military specialists disquieting. We workers who took part in the revolution of 1905 are not used to trusting army people. There are always counterrevolutionary elements among them."

There were cries of "That's enough! The resolution! Let's have a resolution! It's time to go home, it's late."

"I am in agreement with the majority," said Vdovichenko in a deep rumbling voice. "To put it poetically, civic institutions should be founded on democracy, they should grow up from below, like seedlings that are planted and take root in the soil. You can't hammer them in from above like stakes for a fence. This was precisely the mistake of the Jacobin dictatorship and the reason why the Convention was crushed by the Thermidorians."

"It's as clear as daylight," Svirid, his friend and fellow vagabond, backed him up. "Any child can see it. We should

have thought of it earlier, now it's too late. Now our business is
just to fight and to push on for all we're worth. How can we
turn back, now we've started? We've cooked our soup, so now
we must eat it. We've jumped into the water, and we mustn't
complain."

"The resolution! The resolution!" people were repeating on
all sides. They talked on a little longer, but what they said made
less and less sense, and finally, at dawn, the meeting broke up.
They went home one by one, taking the usual precautions.

7

There was a picturesque place along the highway, where the
swift little river Pazhinka divided the two villages of Kuteiny
Posad and Maly Ermolaï, the one extending down a steep hill
and the other spread in the valley below it. In Kuteiny a farewell
party was being given for the new recruits, and in Ermolaï the
medical board under Colonel Strese had resumed, after the
Easter break, its examination of the draftees of that area.
Mounted militia and Cossacks were stationed in the village for
the occasion.

It was the third day of an unusually late Easter and an
unusually early spring, warm and without a breath of wind.
Tables spread with food and drink for the recruits stood in a
street in Kuteiny, some distance from the highway. Placed end
to end but not quite in a straight line and covered with white
cloths hanging to the ground, they stretched down the street
like a long hose.

The villagers had pooled their resources to provide the treat.
The main dishes were the remnants of the Easter food, two
smoked hams, several *kulich* buns, two or three large paskha
cakes. Spread over the tables were bowls of pickled mushrooms, cucumbers, and sauerkraut, plates of home-baked bread
cut into thick slices, and dishes piled with Easter eggs; most of
them were colored pink or light blue.

Broken eggshells, pink and light blue with white insides,
littered the new grass around the tables. Pink and light blue
were the shirts of the young men and the dresses of the girls.
And pink clouds sailed in the blue sky, slowly and gracefully,
and it seemed as if the sky were sailing with them.

Wearing a pink shirt with a silk sash and pointing his toes right and left, Vlas Pakhomovich Galuzin clattered down the steps of Pafnutkin's house on the slope above the highway and the tables, ran down to the tables, and began his speech:

"For want of champagne, I drink to you, my boys, in our own home-brewed vodka. A long life and happy years to you young men who are setting forth today. I should like to make you many other toasts. Gentlemen recruits! May I have your attention! The cavalry that stretches out before you is the road of defense of our motherland against the ravishers who flood her fields with fratricidal blood. The people cherished the hope of enjoying the conquests of the revolution in peace, but the party of the Bolsheviks, in the pay of foreign capital, dispersed the Constituent Assembly, which was the people's highest hope, by brute force of bayonets, and now the blood of the defenseless flows in rivers. Young men who are setting forth today, to you is entrusted the outraged honor of Russian arms! We have covered ourselves with shame and we are in debt to our gallant Allies. For not only the Reds but also Germany and Austria are raising their brazen heads once again. God is with us, boys. . . ." He was still speaking when his voice was drowned in a roar of hurrahs. He raised the glass of weak, poorly distilled vodka to his lips and sipped. It gave him no pleasure. He was used to vintage wines. But the thought that he was making a sacrifice to the public good filled him with satisfaction.

"He's a fine one for speeches, your old man! Deputy Miliukov is nothing to him," said Goshka Riabikh to his friend Terentii Galuzin, who sat next to him, in a tipsy voice amidst the loud, drunken voices at the table. "He certainly is a fine fellow! But I suppose it's not for nothing he's working so hard. I expect he'll earn you an exemption from the draft with his speeches."

"Shame on you, Goshka! How can you think such a thing! Get me exempted indeed. I'd like to see him try! I'll get my notification the same day you get yours, and that'll be that. We'll serve in the same unit. They've kicked me out of school, the bastards. Mother's eating her heart out. I suppose I won't get a commission now. . . . As for Father, he certainly knows how to make a speech. He hits it off every time. And the extraordinary thing is, it's a natural gift he has. He's had no formal education."

"Have you heard about Sanka Pafnutkin?"

"Yes. Is it really such a terrible disease?"

"Incurable. He'll end up with it in his spine. It's his own fault. We warned him not to go. You have to be very careful whom you get mixed up with."

"What will happen to him now?"

"It's tragic. He wanted to shoot himself. He's been called up, he's having his medical now in Ermolaï. I suppose they'll take him. He said he'd join the partisans—'to avenge the ills of society,' he said."

"You know, Goshka, you talk about infectious diseases, but if you don't go to them you might get another disease."

"I know what you mean. I suppose you know it from personal experience. But that isn't a disease, it's a secret vice."

"I'll punch your nose for saying things like that, Goshka. That's a nice way to talk to a friend, you rotten liar!"

"Calm down, it was only a joke. What I wanted to tell you was this—I went to Pazhinsk for Easter, and there was a visiting lecturer there, an anarchist, very interesting he was. He talked about the Liberation of the Personality. I liked that, it was good stuff. I'll join the anarchists, damned if I won't. There's an inner force in us, he said. Sex, he said, and character are the manifestations of animal electricity. How do you like that? A genius, he said. . . . But I'm pretty loaded. People bawling their heads off all around, it's enough to deafen a man. I can't stand it any longer, so shut up, Terioshka, dry up, I tell you."

"What you were saying about that electric force—I've heard about that. I was thinking of ordering an electric truss from Petersburg—cash on delivery—I saw it in an advertisement. 'To increase your vigor,' it said. But then there was another revolution, so there were other things to think about."

Terentii did not finish his sentence. The roar of drunken voices was drowned by a loud, rumbling explosion not far away. For a moment the din at the table stopped. Then it broke out much louder and more confused. Some people jumped up from their seats, and those who were least unsteady remained on their feet. Others tried to stagger away but slumped under the table and at once began to snore. Women screamed. There was a general uproar.

Vlas Pakhomovich stood looking around for the culprit. At first he thought that the rumble had come from somewhere in the village, perhaps even from somewhere quite close to the tables. The veins in his neck stood out, his face went purple, and he bawled: "Who is the Judas in our ranks? Who has committed

this outrage? Who's been throwing hand grenades around? I'll
throttle him with my own hands, the reptile, even if it's my
own son. Citizens, we will not allow anyone to play such jokes
on us. We must cordon off the village. We'll find the provocateur, we won't let him get away."

At first they listened to him, then their attention was
distracted by a pillar of black smoke slowly rising up into the
sky from the county office building in Maly Ermolaï, and they
all rushed to the edge of the ravine to see what was happening in
the valley.

The building was on fire. Several recruits—one of them
barefoot and naked except for his trousers—ran out of the
building with Colonel Strese and the other officers of the draft
board. Mounted Cossacks and militiamen, leaning low out of
their saddles and swinging their nagaikas, their horses writhing
under them like snakes, galloped back and forth through the
village, hunting for someone. Many people were running up the
road to Kuteiny, pursued by the urgent flurry of the church bells
ringing the alarm.

Event followed event with terrifying speed. At dusk Colonel
Strese, apparently convinced that his quarry had left Ermolaï,
rode up with his Cossacks to Kuteiny, surrounded the village
with guards, and began to search every house and every farm.

Half the recruits were by now dead drunk. They had stayed
on at the party and were snoring slumped on the ground or with
their heads on the tables. By the time it became known that the
militia were in the village it was already dark.

Several young men took to their heels, made their way
through back yards to the nearest barn, and, kicking and
jostling each other, crawled underneath the floor through a
narrow opening at the bottom of the wall. In the dark and the
commotion they had not been able to make out whose barn it
was, but now, judging by the smell of fish and kerosene, it
seemed to be one used as a warehouse by the village shop.

The young men had nothing on their conscience and it was
foolish of them to hide; most of them had merely run away on
the spur of the moment, because they were drunk and had lost
their heads. A few, however, had kept company that now
seemed to them compromising and might, they were afraid,
lead to their undoing if it were known. It was true that their
friends were nothing worse than hooligans, but you never
knew. They knew that everything had a political angle in those
days. Hooliganism was considered a sign of black reaction in the

Soviet zone, while in the White zone it was regarded as Bolshevism.

They found that they were not alone in the barn; others had got in before them. The space between the ground and the floor was crammed with people from both villages. Those from Kuteiny were dead drunk. Some were snoring and grinding their teeth and moaning in their sleep, and others were being sick. It was pitch-dark and airless, and the stench was terrible. To conceal their hide-out, those who had come last had plugged the opening through which they had crowded with stones and earth. After a time the snores and grunts ceased. There was complete silence. The drunks had settled down to sleep quietly. Only in one corner was there an urgent, persistent whispering, where Terentii and Goshka huddled in panic with Koska Nekhvalenykh, a quarrelsome, heavy-handed bully from Ermolaï.

"Not so loud," Koska was saying. "You'll give us all away, you devil. Can't you hear—Strese's crowd are prowling up and down. They've been to the end of the street, now they're coming back. There they are. Don't breathe or I'll strangle you. . . . Lucky for you they've gone by. . . . What the devil did you have to come here for? What did you have to hide for, blockhead? Who on earth would have laid a finger on you?"

"I heard Goshka yelling 'Hide,' so I crawled in here."

"Goshka's got good reason to hide. His whole family is in trouble, they're all under suspicion. They've got relatives working at the railway yards in Khodatskoie, that's why. . . . Don't fidget, keep still, you fool. People have been throwing up and crapping all over the place; if you move you'll get the mess all over us. Can't you smell the stink? Do you know why Strese is racing around the village? He's looking for people from outside, from Pazhinsk, that's what he's doing."

"How did all this happen, Koska? How did it all begin?"

"Sanka started it—Sanka Pafnutkin. We were all at the recruiting office, lined up naked waiting for the doctor. When Sanka's turn came he wouldn't get undressed. He was a bit drunk when he came into the office. The clerk told him politely to take his clothes off, even saying 'you' to him. Sanka snapped his head off. 'I won't undress,' he says, 'I won't show my private parts to everybody.' As if he were ashamed. And then he sidles up to the clerk and hits him in the jaw. And then, believe it or not, before you could so much as blink, Sanka bends down, grabs the office table by the leg, and turns it over. Bang it goes on the floor with everything that's on it, inkstand and army lists and all! Then Strese comes in shouting: 'I'm not putting up with hooligans. I'm not having any bloodless revolution here. I'll teach you to be disrespectful to the law in an official place. Who's the ringleader?' "

"Sanka yells: 'Grab your things, comrades. We're in for it,' and he goes to the window and puts his fist through it. I pick up my things and run after him, putting them on as I run. Out he runs into the street and goes like the wind. I went after him, and so did one or two others. We all ran as fast as our legs would carry us, and they came after us yelling and shouting. But if you ask me what it's all about—nobody can make head or tail of it."

"But what about the bomb?"

"What about it?"

"Well, who threw it? The bomb or the grenade or whatever it was."

"My God! You don't think we did?"

"Who did, then?"

"How should I know? It must have been someone else. Somebody sees all this hullabaloo going on and says to himself: 'Why shouldn't I blow the place up while the racket is going on—they'll suspect the others.' It must have been someone political, one of those politicals from Pazhinsk, the place is full of them. . . . Quiet! Shut up! Can't you hear—Strese's men are coming back. That'll be the end of us. Keep quiet, I tell you."

Voices could be heard approaching from down the street; boots creaked, spurs clanked.

"Don't argue. You can't fool me," came the crisp commanding voice of the Colonel speaking with Petrograd distinctness. "I am certain that there was somebody talking over there."

The Mayor of the village of Ermolaï, an old fisherman, Otviazhistin, said:

"You might have imagined it, Your Excellency. And why should people not be talking in a village? It isn't a churchyard. Maybe they were talking. People aren't dumb animals. Or perhaps the devil was shaking someone in his sleep."

"Come, come! Stop playing the village idiot! The devil indeed! You've all been getting too big for your boots here. You'll get so clever you'll talk yourselves into Bolshevism next."

"Merciful goodness, how can you say that, Your Excellency,

Mr. Colonel! Our village yokels are so ignorant, they can't read the prayerbook, what would they want with Bolshevism!"

"That's how you all talk, until you're caught. Have the shop searched from top to bottom. Turn everything inside out, and see that you look under the counters."

"Yes, Your Excellency."

"I want Pafnutkin, Riabikh, and Nekhvalenykh, dead or alive. I don't care if you have to dredge them up from the bottom of the sea. And that Galuzin puppy as well. I don't care how many patriotic speeches his Papa makes. He can talk the hind leg off a donkey, but he won't catch us napping. There's bound to be something fishy when a shopkeeper goes around making speeches. It's suspicious. It's unnatural. We have information that the Galuzins hide political criminals and hold illegal meetings in their house in Krestovozdvizhensk. Get me the brat. I haven't yet decided what to do with him, but if there's anything against him, I won't think twice about stringing him up as a lesson to the others."

The searchers moved away. When they were quite far away, Koska whispered to Terioshka, who was nearly dead with fright:

"Hear that?"

"Yes," he whispered in a changed voice.

"Well, there's only one place for me and you and Sanka and Goshka now; that's the forest. I don't mean we'll have to stay there for good—just until they calm down. Then we'll see, we might come back."

CHAPTER ELEVEN

The Forest Brotherhood

1

It was more than a year since Yurii Andreievich had been taken prisoner by the partisans. The limits of his freedom were very ill defined. The place of his captivity was not surrounded by walls; he was not under guard, and no one watched his movements. The partisan force was constantly on the move, and Yurii Andreievich moved with it. It did not remain apart from the local population through whose lands and settlements it passed; it mixed and indeed dissolved in it.

On the surface, this captivity, this dependence, seemed to be nonexistent, as though the doctor were free and merely failed to take advantage of his freedom. His captivity, his dependence, were not different from other forms of compulsion in life, which are often equally invisible and intangible, and seem to be non-existent and merely a figment of the imagination, a chimera. But although he was not fettered, chained, or watched, the doctor had to submit to his unfreedom, imaginary though it appeared.

Each of his three attempts at escaping from the partisans had ended in capture. He did not suffer any penalties, but he was playing with fire, and he did not try again.

He was favored by the partisan chief, Liberius Mikulitsyn, who liked his company and made him sleep in his tent. Yurii Andreievich found this enforced companionship irksome.

2

During this period, the partisans were constantly moving eastward. At times this movement was part of the general campaign to drive Kolchak from western Siberia; at other times, when the Whites struck from the rear, threatening to encircle the partisans, the same eastward marches turned into retreats. For a long time the doctor could not understand these subtleties.

The partisans moved parallel to the highway and occasionally they made use of it. The villages and small towns along it were Red or White according to the fortunes of war. It was difficult to tell from their outward appearance in whose power they were at any particular moment.

While the peasant army was passing through the villages or small towns, everything else in them sank into insignificance. The houses on both sides of the road seemed to shrink into the ground, and the riders, horses, guns, and big jostling riflemen splashing through the mud loomed higher than the houses.

One day, in one such small town, the doctor was ordered to take over a stock of British medical supplies abandoned by the White officers' unit under General Kappel and now seized by the partisans.

It was a bleak, rainy afternoon with only two colors: wherever the light fell it was white, everywhere else it was black; and the doctor's mood was of the same bleak simplification unsoftened by transitions and half-tones.

The road, completely destroyed by the frequent movements of troops, was nothing but a river of black mud. It could be forded in only a few places, which could be reached by hugging the houses for hundreds of yards. It was in these circumstances, at Pazhinsk, that the doctor met Pelagia Tiagunova, who had been his fellow passenger in the train from Moscow.

She recognized him first. It took him some moments to remember the woman who kept looking at him from across the street, as from the opposite bank of a canal, with an expression suggesting a readiness to greet him if he knew her or to remain anonymous if he did not.

Finally he did remember her, and, together with the picture of the overcrowded freight car, the labor conscripts and their guards, and the woman with a braid over her shoulder, there flashed into his mind an image of his family. Sharp details of the journey crowded in on him, and the faces of his dear ones, whom he missed desperately, rose vividly in his memory.

He nodded to her to go farther up the street to a place where it could be crossed on stones protruding from the mud and, walking in the same direction, went over and greeted her.

She told him many things about the past two years. Reminding him of Vasia, the boy with the handsome, unspoiled face, who had been unlawfully conscripted and who had shared their car, she described her stay with his mother in their village, Veretenniki. She had been very happy among them, but the village treated her as an outsider. She had been falsely accused of having a love affair with Vasia and in the end had had to leave if she were not to be pecked to death. She had settled with her married sister, Olga Galuzina, in Krestovozdvizhensk. Rumors that Prituliev had been seen in the neighborhood had brought her to Pazhinsk. The rumors had proved false and she had found herself stranded in the little town, where she had later got work.

In the meanwhile, misfortune had overtaken her friends. Veretenniki had been raided in reprisal for withholding food supplies. It was said that Vasia's house had been burned down and that a member of his family had perished. And at Krestovozdvizhensk, Pelagia's brother-in-law, Vlas Galuzin, had either been put in jail or been shot, and her nephew had vanished without a trace. Her sister had starved for some time but was now working for her keep in the village of Zvonarskaia as a servant in a family of peasants who were related to her.

It so happened that Tiagunova had a job as assistant at the Pazhinsk pharmacy, whose stock the doctor was about to requisition. All the pharmacist's dependents, including herself, were faced with ruin by this measure. But the doctor was powerless to call it off. Tiagunova was present at the taking over of the stock.

The doctor's cart pulled up at the back of the shop. Sacks, cases, and bottles packed in wickerware were carried out.

The employees watched the operation dejectedly, and their feelings seemed to infect the pharmacist's thin, mangy mare watching sadly from her stable. The rainy day was drawing to its close. The sky cleared a little. Hemmed in by the clouds, the setting sun peered out and splashed the yard with dark bronze rays, casting a sinister glow on the puddles of liquid manure. The wind did not stir them; the muddy slops were too heavy. But the rain water on the road rippled and glistened with cinnabar reflections.

The troops moved on along the street, walking or riding around the deeper pools. The requisitioned supplies were found to contain a whole jar of cocaine, to which the partisan chief had recently become addicted.

3

The doctor was up to his neck in work. In winter there was typhus and in summer dysentery, and on top of all that there were the wounded, whose numbers kept increasing now that the fighting was renewed.

In spite of setbacks and frequent retreats, the ranks of the partisans were continually swollen by new insurgents from the settlements through which the peasant hordes passed and by deserters from the enemy. In the eighteen months the doctor had spent with the partisans, their army had increased tenfold, actually reaching the number of which Liberius Averkievich had boasted at the underground meeting at Krestovozdvizhensk.

Yurii Andreievich had several newly appointed medics and two chief assistants, both former prisoners of war—Kerenyi Lajos, a Hungarian Communist who had been a doctor in the Austrian army, and the Croat, Angelar, who had had some medical training. With the former, Yurii Andreievich spoke in German; the latter more or less understood Russian.

4

According to the Red Cross International Convention, the army medical personnel must not take part in the military operations of the belligerents. But on one occasion the doctor was forced to break this rule. He was in the field when an engagement began and he had to share the fate of the combatants and shoot in self-defense.

The front line, where he was caught by enemy fire, was at the edge of a forest. He threw himself down on the ground next to the unit's telephonist. The forest was at their back, in front of them was a field, and across this open, undefended space the Whites were attacking.

The Whites were now close enough for the doctor to see their faces. They were boys, recent volunteers from the civilian population of the capitals, and older men mobilized from the reserve. The tone was set by the youngsters, first-year students from the universities and last-year students from gymnasiums.

None of them were known to the doctor, yet half the faces looked familiar. Some of them reminded him of former classmates and he wondered if they were their younger brothers; others he felt he had noticed in a theater crowd or in the street in years gone by. Their expressive, handsome faces seemed to belong to people of his own kind.

Responding to duty as they understood it, they displayed enthusiasm and a reckless courage that was entirely out of place. Advancing in extended formation and excelling the parade ground smartness of the Imperial Guards, they walked defiantly upright, neither running nor throwing themselves to the ground, ignoring the irregularities of the terrain behind which they might easily have taken cover. The bullets of the partisans mowed them down.

In the middle of the wide, bare field there was a dead tree, blasted by lightning or charred by fire, or scorched and splintered in the course of some earlier battles. Each of the advancing volunteers glanced at it, fighting the temptation to stop behind it for shelter and a surer aim, then, casting the thought aside, walked on.

The partisans had a limited supply of cartridges and were under orders to fire only at short range and at clearly visible targets.

Yurii Andreievich had no rifle; he lay on the grass watching the course of the engagement. All his sympathies were on the side of these heroically dying children. With all his heart he wished them success. They belonged to families who were probably akin to him in spirit, in education, in moral discipline and values.

It occurred to him to run out into the field and give himself up, thus obtaining his release. But that was dangerous, too dangerous. While he was running with his arms raised above his head he could be shot down from both sides, struck in the breast and in the back—by the partisans in punishment for his betrayal and by the Whites in misunderstanding of his motives. He knew this kind of situation, he had been in it before, he had considered all the possibilities of such escape plans and had rejected them as unfeasible. So resigning himself to his divided feelings, he lay on his belly on the grass, his face toward the clearing, and watched, unarmed, the course of the battle.

But to look on inactively while the mortal struggle raged all around was impossible, it was beyond human strength. It was not a question of loyalty to the side that held him captive or of defending his own life, but of submitting to the order of events, to the laws governing what went on around him. To remain an outsider was against the rules. You had to do what everyone was doing. A battle was going on. He and his comrades were being shot at. He had to shoot back.

So when the telephonist at his side jerked convulsively and then lay still, he crept over to him, took his cartridge bag and rifle, and, going back to his place, emptied the gun, shot after shot.

But as pity prevented him from aiming at the young men whom he admired and with whom he sympathized, and simply to shoot into the air would be too silly, he fired at the blasted tree, choosing those moments when there was no one between his sights and his target. He followed his own technique.

Setting the sights and gradually improving his aim as he pressed the trigger slowly and not all the way down, as if not in fact intending to release the bullet, so that in the end the shot went off of itself and as it were unexpectedly, he fired with the precision of old habit at the dead wood of the lower branches, lopping them off and scattering them around the tree.

But alas!—however carefully he tried to avoid hitting anyone, every now and then a young attacker would move into his firing line at the crucial moment. Two of them he wounded, and one who fell near the tree seemed to have lost his life.

At last the White command, convinced of the futility of the attack, ordered a retreat.

The partisans were few. Part of their main force was on a march and others had engaged a larger enemy detachment some way off. Not to disclose their weakness, they refrained from pursuing the retreating Whites.

Angelar joined the doctor in the clearing with two medics

carrying stretchers. Telling him to attend to the wounded, the doctor bent over the telephonist in the vague hope that he might still be breathing and could be revived. But when he undid his shirt and felt his heart, he found that it had stopped.

An amulet hung by a silk cord from the dead man's neck. The doctor took it off. It contained a sheet of paper, worn and rotted at the folds, sewn into a piece of cloth.

Written on the paper, which almost fell apart in the doctor's fingers when he unfolded it, were excerpts from the Ninety-first Psalm with such changes in the wording as often creep into popular prayers through much repetition, making them deviate increasingly from the original. The Church Slavonic text was transliterated into Russian script.

The words of the psalm, "He that dwelleth in the secret place of the Most High," had become the title, "Dwell High." The verse "Thou shalt not be afraid for the terror by night nor for the arrow that flieth by day" was changed into the exhortation: "Do not be afraid of the arrows of flying war." Where the psalm says: "He hath known my name," the paper said: "He postpones my name," and "I will be with him in trouble: I will deliver him" was garbled into "I will relieve him from darkness."

The text was believed to be miraculous and a protection against bullets. It had been worn as a talisman by soldiers in the last imperialist war. Decades later prisoners were to sew it into their clothes and mutter its words in jail when they were summoned at night for interrogation.

Leaving the telephonist, Yurii Andreievich went out into the field to the young White Guardsman whom he had killed. The boy's handsome face bore the marks of innocence and of all-forgiving suffering. "Why did I kill him?" thought the doctor.

He undid the boy's coat and opened it. Some careful hand—probably his mother's—had embroidered his name and sur-name, Seriozha Rantsevich, in carefully traced cursive letters on the lining. From the opening of Seriozha's shirt there slipped out and hung suspended by a chain a cross, a locket, and some other small flat gold case, rather like a snuffbox, dented as if a nail had been driven into it. A paper fell out. The doctor unfolded it and could not believe his eyes. It was the same Ninety-first Psalm but this time printed in its full and original Slavonic text.

At this moment Seriozha groaned and stirred. He was alive. It appeared afterward that he had only been stunned as the result of a slight internal injury. The bullet had been stopped by his mother's amulet and this had saved him. But what was to be done with this unconscious man now?

It was a time when savagery was at its height. Prisoners did not reach headquarters alive and enemy wounded were knifed in the field.

In the existing state of the partisan force, with its high turnover of deserters to and from the enemy, it was possible, if the strictest secrecy were kept, to pass Rantsevich off as a recently enlisted ally.

Yurii Andreievich took off the outer clothing of the dead telephonist and, with the help of Angelar, in whom he confided, exchanged it for that of the boy.

He and Angelar nursed Seriozha back to health. When he was well they released him, although he did not conceal from them that he meant to go back to Kolchak's army and continue fighting the Reds.

5

In the autumn the partisans took up quarters in Fox's Thicket, a small wood on a steep hill with a swift stream foaming around three sides of it and biting into the shores.

The Whites had wintered in it the year before and had dug themselves in with the help of the neighboring villagers, but they had left in the spring without destroying their fortifications. Now their dugouts and communication trenches were used by the partisans.

The doctor shared a dugout with Liberius Mikulitsyn, who had kept him awake by chattering for two nights running.

"I wonder what my esteemed parent, my respected Papa, is doing at this moment."

"God, how I hate this buffoonery," the doctor thought, with a sigh. "And yet he's the living image of his father."

"Judging from our previous talks, you got to know him quite well. You seem to have formed a not unfavorable opinion of him. What can you say on the subject, my dear sir?"

"Liberius Averkievich, tomorrow we have the pre-election meeting. And there is the trial of the medics who have been brewing vodka coming up—Lajos and I have still got to go through the evidence. I have to see him tomorrow for that purpose. And I haven't slept for two nights. Can't we put this conversation off? I'm dead tired."

"Well, anyway, just tell me what you think of the old bird."

"To begin with, your father is quite young. I don't know why you refer to him that way. Well, all right, I'll tell you. As I've often said to you, I am very bad at sorting out the various shades of socialism, and I can't see much difference between Bolsheviks and other socialists. Your father is one of those to whom Russia owes its recent disorders and disturbances. He is a revolutionary type, a revolutionary character. Like yourself, he represents the principle of ferment in Russian life."

"Is that meant as praise or blame?"

"Once again, I beg you to put off this discussion to a more convenient time. And I must really draw your attention to your excessive consumption of cocaine. You have been willfully depleting the stock of which I am in charge. You know perfectly well that it is needed for other purposes, as well as that it is a poison and I am responsible for your health."

"You cut the study group again last night. You have an atrophied social sense, just like an illiterate peasant woman or a bourgeois diehard. And yet you are a doctor, you are well read, I believe you even write. How do you explain it?"

"I don't. Apparently it can't be helped. You should be sorry for me."

"Why the mock modesty? If instead of using that sarcastic tone you took the trouble to find out what we do in our classes, you wouldn't be so supercilious."

"Heavens, Liberius Averkievich. I'm not being supercilious. I have the utmost respect for your educational work. I've read the discussion notes you circulate. I know your ideas on the moral improvement of the soldier, they're quite excellent. All you say about what the soldier's attitude should be to the people's army, to his fellows, to the weak, the helpless, to women, and about honor and chastity—it's almost the teaching of the Dukhobors. All that kind of Tolstoyism I know by heart. My own adolescence was full of those aspirations toward a better life. How could I laugh at such things?

"But, first, the idea of social betterment as it is understood since the October revolution doesn't fill me with enthusiasm. Second, it is so far from being put into practice, and the mere talk about it has cost such a sea of blood, that I'm not sure that the end justifies the means. And last—and this is the main thing—when I hear people speak of reshaping life it makes me lose my self-control and I fall into despair.

"Reshaping life! People who can say that have never understood a thing about life—they have never felt its breath, its heartbeat—however much they have seen or done. They look on it as a lump of raw material that needs to be processed by them, to be ennobled by their touch. But life is never a material, a substance to be molded. If you want to know, life is the principle of self-renewal, it is constantly renewing and remaking and changing and transfiguring itself, it is infinitely beyond your or my obtuse theories about it."

"And yet, you know, if you came to our meetings, if you kept in touch with our splendid, our magnificent people, you wouldn't feel half so low. You wouldn't suffer from this melancholia. I know what it comes from. You see us being beaten and you can't see a ray of hope ahead. But one should never panic, my friend. I could tell you much worse things—to do with me personally, not to be made public for the moment—and yet I don't lose my head. Our setbacks are purely temporary, Kolchak is bound to lose in the end. You mark my words. You'll see, we'll win in the long run. So cheer up!"

"It's unspeakable," thought the doctor. "How can anyone be so dense, so childish! I spend my time dinning into him that our ideas are diametrically opposed, he has captured me by force, he is keeping me against my will, and yet he imagines that his setbacks fill me with dismay and that his hopes can cheer me up! How can anyone be as blind as this? For him the fate of the universe is less important than the victory of the revolution."

Yurii Andreievich said nothing, merely shrugging his shoulders and making no secret of his almost uncontrollable exasperation at Liberius's naïveté. Nor did this escape Liberius's notice.

"You are angry, Jupiter, therefore you must be wrong," he said.

"Do, for God's sake, understand once and for all that none of this means anything to me. 'Jupiter' and 'Never panic' and 'Anyone who says A must say B' and 'The Moor has done his work, the Moor can go'—none of these clichés, these vulgar commonplaces, appeal to me. I'll say A but I won't say B—whatever you do. I'll admit that you are Russia's liberators, the shining lights, that without you it would be lost, sunk in misery and ignorance, and I still don't give a damn for any of you, I don't like you and you can all go to the devil.

"The people you worship go in for proverbs, but they've

forgotten one proverb—'You can lead a horse to water but you can't make it drink'—and they've got into the habit of liberating and of showering benefits on just those people who haven't asked for them. I suppose you think I can't imagine anything in the world more pleasant than your camp and your company. I suppose I have to bless you for keeping me a prisoner and thank you for liberating me from my wife, my son, my home, my work, from everything I hold dear and that makes life worth living for me!

"There is a rumor going around that some unknown force— not Russian—has raided and sacked Varykino. Kamennodvorsky doesn't deny it. They say your people and mine managed to escape. Apparently some sort of mythical slit-eyed warriors in padded coats and fur hats crossed the Rynva in a terrible frost, and calmly shot every living soul in the place and vanished as mysteriously as they had come. Do you know anything about it? Is it true?"

"Nonsense. All lies. Groundless rumors."

"If you are as kind and generous as you claim to be when you lecture on the moral improvement of the soldiers, then let me go. I'll go and look for my family—I don't know where they are, I don't even know whether they are alive or dead. And if you won't do that, then shut up, for heaven's sake, and leave me alone, because I am not interested in anything else and I won't answer for myself if you go on. Anyway, the devil take it, haven't I the right to go to sleep?"

Yurii Andreievich lay down flat on his bunk, his face in his pillow, doing his utmost not to listen to Liberius justifying himself and comforting him once more with the prospect of a final victory over the Whites by the spring. The civil war would be over, there would be peace, liberty, and prosperity, and no one would dare to detain the doctor a moment longer. But until then he must be patient. After all they had gone through, and all the sacrifices they had made, and all that time they had been waiting, a few months mattered little, and anyhow, where could the doctor go at present? For his own good he must be prevented from going anywhere alone.

"Just like a phonograph record, the devil!" Yurii Andreievich raged in silent indignation. "He can't stop. Why isn't he ashamed of chewing on the same cud all these years? How can he go on listening to the sound of his own voice, the wretched dope-fiend? Day and night he goes on. God, how I hate him! As God is my witness, I'll murder him someday!

"Tonia, my darling, my poor child! Where are you? Are you alive? Dear Lord, she was to have her baby long ago. How did she get through the confinement? Have we got a son or a daughter? My dear ones, what is happening to all of you? Tonia, you are my everlasting reproach. Lara, I daren't speak your name for fear of gasping out my life. O God! God!—And that loathsome, unfeeling brute is still talking! One day he'll go too far and I'll kill him, I'll kill him."

6

The Indian summer was over. It was a clear, golden autumn day. At the western end of Fox's Thicket the wooden turret of a blockhouse built by the Whites showed above the ground. Here Yurii Andreievich had arranged to meet Dr. Lajos, to discuss various service matters. He arrived on time and, waiting for his friend, strolled along the edge of the crumbling earthworks, climbed into the watchtower, and looked out of the slits in front of the now empty machine-gun nests at the wooded distance beyond the river.

The autumn had already clearly marked the frontiers between the coniferous and the deciduous trees. Between the gloomy, bristling walls of almost black pines the leafy thickets shone flame- and wine-colored like medieval towns with painted and gold-roofed palaces built of the timber cut down in the thickness of the forest.

The earth at the doctor's feet, inside the trench and in the ruts of the forest road, was hard with ground frost and heaped with small dry willow leaves, curled up in little scrolls. The autumn smelled of these brown, bitter leaves and of many other things. Greedily he breathed in the mixed peppery smell of frostbitten apples, bitter dry twigs, sweetish damp earth, and the blue September mist that smoked like the fumes of a recently extinguished fire.

He did not hear Lajos come up behind him.

"How are you, colleague?" Lajos said in German. They discussed their business.

"There are three points. First, the court-martial of the vodka brewers; second, the reorganization of the field ambulance and the pharmacy; and third, my proposal for the treatment of mental illnesses. I don't know whether you agree with me, my dear Lajos, but from what I observe we are going mad, and modern forms of insanity spread like an epidemic.

"It's a very interesting question. I'll come to it in a moment. But first I'd like to mention something else. There is unrest in the camp. There is sympathy with the vodka brewers. Moreover, the men are worried about their families who are fleeing from the Whites. As you know, there's a convoy coming, with wives, children, and old people, and many of the partisans have refused to leave the camp until it comes."

"I know. We'll have to wait for them."

"And all this on the eve of the election of a joint commander for our unit and several others, so far independent of us. I think the only candidate is Comrade Liberius. But some of the young people are putting Vdovichenko forward. He is supported by a group, alien to us in spirit, connected with the vodka brewers— sons of shopkeepers and kulaks, deserters from Kolchak. They are particularly restless."

"What do you think will happen to the vodka brewers?"

"I think they will be sentenced to be shot and be reprieved."

"Well, let's get down to business. First, the field ambulance."

"All right. But I must tell you that I am not surprised at your suggestion for preventive psychiatry. I believe in it myself. We are faced with the rise and spread of a form of psychic illness that is typical of our time and is directly related to the contemporary upheavals. We have a case of it in the camp— Pamphil Palykh, a former private in the Tsarist army with a highly developed class instinct and devoted to the revolution. The cause of his trouble is precisely his anxiety for his family in the event of his being killed and of their falling into the hands of the Whites and being made to answer for him. It's a very complex case. I believe his family is one of those who are coming in the convoy. I don't know enough Russian to question him properly. You could find out from Angelar or Kamennod-vorsky. He ought to be examined."

"I know Palykh very well. At one time we often came across each other in the army soviet. Swarthy and cruel with a low forehead. I can't think what good you find in him. He was always for extreme measures, harshness, execution. I've always found him repellent. All right, I'll see what I can do about it."

7

It was a clear, sunny day; the weather had been still and dry for a whole week.

The usual rumble of noise hung over the large camp, like the distant roar of the sea. There were footsteps, voices, axes chopping wood, the ringing of anvils, the neighing of horses, the barking of dogs, the crowing of cocks. Crowds of sun-burned, smiling men with shining white teeth moved through the forest. Those who knew the doctor nodded to him, others passed him by without a greeting.

The men had refused to leave Fox's Thicket until their families had caught up with them, but now the fugitives were expected shortly and preparations for the move were being made. Things were being cleaned and mended, crates nailed down, carts counted and checked over.

There was a large clearing in the middle of the wood where meetings were often held. It was a sort of mound or barrow on which the grass had been trodden down. A general meeting had been called that day for an important announcement.

Many of the trees in the forest had not yet turned; in its depths they were still fresh and green. The afternoon sun was setting behind the forest, piercing it with its rays, and the leaves, letting them through, glowed green like transparent bottle glass.

In an open space outside his tent Kamennodvorsky, the chief liaison officer, was burning papers, discarded rubbish from General Kappel's records that had fallen into his hands, as well as papers from his own partisan files. The fire with the setting sun behind it was as transparent as the leaves; the flames were invisible and only the waves of shimmering heat showed that something was burning.

Here and there the woods were brilliant with ripe berries—bright tassels of lady's smock, brick-red alderberries, and clusters of viburnum, shimmering from white to purple. Whirring their glassy wings, dragonflies as transparent as the flames and the leaves sailed slowly through the air.

Ever since his childhood Yurii Andreievich had been fond of woods seen at evening against the setting sun. At such moments he felt as if he too were being pierced by shafts of light. It was as though the gift of the living spirit were streaming into his breast, piercing his being and coming out at his shoulders like a pair of wings. The archetype that is formed in every child for life and seems for ever after to be his inward face, his personality, awoke in him in its full primordial strength, and compelled nature, the forest, the afterglow, and everything else visible to be transfigured into a similarly primordial and all-embracing likeness of a girl. Closing his eyes, "Lara," he whispered and thought, addressing the whole of his life, all God's earth, all the sunlit space spread out before him.

But everyday, current reality was still there, Russia was going through the October revolution, and he was a prisoner of the partisans. Absent-mindedly he went up to Kamennodvorsky's bonfire.

"Burning your records? Not finished yet?"

"There's enough of this stuff to burn for days."

The doctor kicked a heap of papers with his foot. It was the White staff headquarters' correspondence. It occurred to him that he might come across some mention of Rantsevich. But all he saw were boring, out-of-date communiqués in code. He kicked another heap. It proved to be an equally dull collection of minutes of partisan meetings. A paper on top of the pile said: "Extra urgent. Re furloughs. Re-election of members of draft board. Current business. In view of the fact that the charges against the schoolmistress of the village Ignatodvortsy have not been substantiated, the army soviet proposes . . ."

Kamennodvorsky took a piece of paper from his pocket and handed it to the doctor.

"Here are your marching orders for the medical unit. The convoy with the partisans' families is quite near and the dissensions inside the camp will be settled by this evening, so we can expect to move any day now."

The doctor glanced at the paper and groaned:

"But you're giving me less transportation than last time and there are all those extra wounded. Those who can will have to walk; there are only a few of these. What am I to do with the stretcher cases? And the stores and the bedding and the equipment?"

"You'll have to manage somehow. We must adjust ourselves to circumstances. Now another thing. It's a request from all of us. Will you have a look at a comrade of ours—tried, tested, devoted to the cause and a splendid soldier. There's something wrong with him."

"Palykh? Lajos told me."

"Yes. Go to see him. Examine him."

"He's a mental case?"

"I suppose so. He says he sees will-o'-the-wisps. Hallucinations, evidently. Insomnia. Headaches."

"All right. I might as well go and see him now, since I'm free at the moment. When does the meeting begin?"

"I think they're coming now. But why bother? As you see, I'm not going either. They'll manage without us."

"Then I'll go and see Pamphil. Though I can hardly keep my eyes open, I'm so sleepy. Liberius Averkievich likes to philosophize at night, and he's worn me out with his talk. Where do I find Pamphil?"

"You know the birch grove behind the rubbish pit?"

"Yes, I think I know it."

"You'll find some commanders' tents in a clearing. We've put one of them at Pamphil's disposal. He's got his family coming, they're in the convoy. That's where you'll find him—in one of the tents—he's got battalion commander status as a reward for revolutionary merit."

8

On his way to see Pamphil, the doctor was overcome with fatigue. It was the cumulative effect of several sleepless nights. He could go back to his dugout and lie down, but he was afraid of staying there, for at any moment Liberius might come in and disturb him. He stopped in a glade scattered with golden leaves from the surrounding woods. They lay in a checkerboard pattern, and so did the low rays of the sun falling on their golden carpet. This double, crisscross brightness made your head spin and sent you to sleep like small print or a monotonous murmur.

The doctor lay down on the silkily rustling leaves, his head on his arm and his arm on a pillow of moss at the foot of a tree. He dozed off at once. The dazzle of light and shadow that had put him to sleep now covered him with its patchwork so that his body, stretched on the ground, was indistinguishable from the kaleidoscopic brilliance of the rays and leaves, invisible as if he had put on a magic cap.

But soon the very force of his desire and need for sleep aroused him. Direct causes operate only within certain limits; beyond them they produce the opposite effect. His wakeful consciousness, not finding any rest, worked feverishly of its own momentum. Thoughts whirled and wheeled inside his head, his mind was knocking like a faulty engine. This inner confusion worried and exasperated him. "That swine Liberius," he thought indignantly. "As if there weren't enough things in the world to drive people mad, he has to take a sane man and turn him deliberately into a neurotic by keeping him a prisoner and boring him with his friendship and chatter. Someday I'll kill him."

Folding and unfolding like a scrap of colored stuff, a brown speckled butterfly flew across the sunny side of the clearing. The doctor watched it sleepily. Choosing a background with a color like its own, it settled on the brown speckled bark of a pine and became indistinguishable from it, vanishing as completely as Yurii Andreievich, hidden by the play of light and shadow, had vanished.

His mind turned to its accustomed round of thoughts—he had touched on them indirectly in many medical works—concerning will and purposefulness as superior forms of adaptation; mimicry and protective coloring; the survival of the fittest; and the hypothesis that the path of natural selection is the very path leading to the formation and emergence of consciousness. And what was subject? What was object? How was their identity to be defined? In the doctor's reflections, Darwin was next to Schelling, the butterfly that had just flown by next to modern painting and Impressionist art. He thought of creation, the creature, creativeness, the instincts of creation and simulation.

Once again he fell asleep but woke up a moment later. A soft, muffled conversation nearby had disturbed him. The few words he overheard were enough to tell him that it concerned some secret and illicit plan. He had not been seen, the conspirators had no suspicion of his presence. The slightest movement that would betray it now might cost him his life. Yurii Andreievich remained quiet and listened.

Some of the voices he recognized. They were those of the scum of the partisans, hangers-on such as Goshka, Sanka, Koska, and their usual follower Terentii Galuzin, young good-for-nothings who were at the bottom of every kind of outrage and disorder. Zakhar Gorazdykh was also there, an even more

sinister personality who was mixed up in the affair of the vodka
brewing but was not being prosecuted just now because he had
denounced the chief offenders. What surprised Yurii Andreievich was the presence of Sivobluy, a partisan of the crack
"Silver Company" who was one of the commander's body-
guards. In keeping with a tradition going back to Stenka Razin
and Pugachev, this favorite, known to be in the confidence of
the chief, was nicknamed "The Hetman's Ear." And yet he too
seemed to be in the conspiracy.

The plotters were negotiating with delegates from the
advanced positions of the enemy. The delegates were inaudible,
so softly did they speak to the traitors, and Yurii Andreievich
could only guess that they were speaking when an occasional
silence seemed to interrupt the whispering.

Zakhar Gorazdykh, the drunkard, was doing most of the
talking, cursing every other moment in his hoarse, wheezing
voice. He seemed to be the ringleader.

"Now, you others, listen. The chief thing is, we've got to
keep it quiet. If anybody talks—you see this knife?—I'll rip his
guts. Is that clear? Now you know as well as I do—we're stuck.
There's no way out for us. We've got to earn our pardon. We've
got to work such a trick as nobody's seen before. They want
him taken alive. Now they say their boss Gulevoy is coming."
(They corrected him—"Galiullin"—but he did not catch the
name and said "General Galeiev.") "That's our chance. There
won't be another like it. Here're their delegates. They'll tell you
all about it. They say we've got to take him alive. Now you tell
them, you others."

Now the others, the delegates, began to speak. Yurii Andreievich could not catch a word, but from the length of the
pause he judged that they explained the proposal in detail. Then
Gorazdykh spoke again.

"Hear that, boys? You see what a nice fellow he is. Why
should we pay for him? He isn't even a man—he's a halfwit of
some sort, a monk or a hermit. You stop grinning, Terioshka.
I'll give you something to grin about, you stupid ass. I wasn't
talking about you. I'm telling you—he's a hermit, that's what he
is. Let him have his way and he'll turn you all into monks—
eunuchs. What does he tell you? No cursing, no getting drunk,
all this stuff about women. How can you live like that? Tonight
we'll get him down to the ford. I'll see that he comes. Then
we'll all fall on him together. It won't be hard. That's nothing.
What's difficult is that they want him alive. Tie him up, they

say. Well, if it doesn't work out that way I'll deal with him
myself, I'll finish him off with my own hands. They'll send
their people along to help."

He went on explaining the plan, but gradually they moved
away and the doctor ceased to hear them.

"That's Liberius they're plotting to hand over to the Whites
or to kill, the swine," he thought with horror and indignation,
forgetting how often he had himself wished his tormentor dead.
How was it to be prevented? He decided to go back to
Kamennodvorsky and tell him of the plot without mentioning
any names, and also to warn Liberius.

But when he got back, Kamennodvorsky had gone; only his
assistant was keeping an eye on the smoldering fire to prevent
its spreading.

The crime did not take place. It was forestalled. The
conspiracy, as it turned out, was known. That day the details
were disclosed and the plotters seized. Sivobluy had played the
role of *agent provocateur*. Yurii Andreievich felt even more
disgusted.

9

It was learned that the partisans' families were now within two
days' journey of the camp. The partisans were getting ready to
welcome them and soon afterwards to move on. Yurii Andreievich went to Pamphil Palykh.

He found him at the entrance to his tent, an ax in his hand. In
front of him was a tall heap of birch saplings; he had cut them
down but had not yet stripped them. Some had fallen where
they stood and, toppling with their whole weight, had dug the
sharp ends of their broken branches into the damp ground.
Others he had dragged from a short distance and piled on top of
the rest. Shuddering and swaying on their springy branches,
these trees lay neither on the ground nor close together. It
seemed as though with outstretched arms they were fending off
Pamphil, who had cut them down, and that their tangled green
foliage was barring his way to his tent.

"It's for my dear guests," explained Pamphil. "My wife and
children. The tent is too low. And the rain comes through. I've
cut these down for joints to make a roof."

"I shouldn't count on their allowing you to have them in your tent, Pamphil. Who has ever heard of civilians, women and children, being allowed to live inside a camp? They'll stay with the wagons somewhere just outside, you'll be able to see them as much as you like in your spare time, but I shouldn't think they'd be allowed to live in your tent. But that isn't what I've come about. They tell me you're getting thin, you can't eat or sleep. Is that true? I must say you look all right. Though you could do with a haircut."

Pamphil was a huge man with black tousled hair and beard and a bumpy forehead that looked double; a thickening of the frontal bone, like a ring or a steel band pressed over his temples, gave him a beetling, glowering look.

When at the beginning of the revolution it had been feared that, as in 1905, the upheaval would be a short-lived episode in the history of the educated upper classes and leave the deeper layers of society untouched, everything possible had been done to spread revolutionary propaganda among the people to upset them, to stir them up and lash them into fury.

In those early days, men like Pamphil Palykh, who needed no encouragement to hate intellectuals, officers, and gentry with a savage hatred, were regarded by enthusiastic left-wing intellectuals as a rare find and greatly valued. Their inhumanity seemed a marvel of class-consciousness, their barbarism a model of proletarian firmness and revolutionary instinct. By such qualities Pamphil had established his fame, and he was held in great esteem by partisan chiefs and Party leaders.

To Yurii Andreievich this gloomy and unsociable giant, soulless and narrow-minded, seemed subnormal, almost a degenerate.

"Come into the tent," said Pamphil.

"No, why? It's pleasanter out in the open. Anyway, I couldn't get in."

"All right. Have it your own way. After all, it is a stinking hole. We can sit on the trees."

They sat down on the springy birch saplings, and Pamphil told the doctor the story of his life. "They say a tale is soon told. But mine is a long story. I couldn't tell it in three years. I don't know where to begin.

"Well, I'll try. My wife and I, we were young. She looked after the house. I worked in the fields. It wasn't a bad life. We had children. They drafted me into the army. They sent me to the war. Well, the war. What should I tell you about the war?

You've seen it, Comrade Doctor. Then the revolution. I saw the
light. The soldiers' eyes were opened. Not the Fritzes, who are
Germans, were the enemies, but some of our own people.
'Soldiers of the world revolution, down your rifles, go home,
get the bourgeois!' And so on. You know it all yourself,
Comrade Army Doctor. Well, to go on. Then came the civil
war. I joined the partisans. Now I'll have to leave out a lot or I'll
never end. After all that, what do I see now, at the present
moment? That parasite, he's brought up the two Stavropolsky
regiments from the Russian front, and the first Orenburg
Cossack as well. I'm not a child am I? Don't I understand?
Haven't I served in the army? We're in trouble, Doctor, it's all
up with us. What he wants to do, the swine, is to fall on us with
all that scum. He wants to surround us.

"But I've got a wife and children. If he comes out on top,
how will they get away? They're innocent, of course, they have
nothing to do with it, but this won't stop him. He'll tie up my
wife with a rope and he'll torture her to death on my account,
my wife and my children, he'll break every bone in their bodies,
he'll tear them apart. And you ask, why don't I sleep. A man
could be made of iron, but a thing like that is to make you lose
your mind."

"What an odd fellow you are, Pamphil. I can't make you out.
For years you've been away from them, you didn't even know
where they were and you didn't worry. Now you're going to
see them in a day or two, and instead of being happy about it
you act as though it were their funeral."

"That was before, now it's different. He's beating us, the
White bastard. Anyway, it isn't me we're talking about. I'll soon
be dead. But I can't take my little ones with me into the next
world, can I? They'll stay and they'll fall into his dirty paws.
He'll squeeze the blood out of them, drop by drop."

"Is that why you see will-o'-the-wisps? I was told you keep
seeing things."

"Well, Doctor, I haven't told you everything. I've kept back
the most important thing. Now, I'll tell you the whole truth if
you want it, I'll say it to your face, but you mustn't hold it
against me.

"I've done away with a lot of your kind, there's a lot of
officers' blood on my hands. Officers, bourgeois. And it's never
worried me. Spilled it like water. Names and numbers all gone
out of my head. But there's one little fellow I can't get out of my
mind. I killed that youngster and I can't forget it. Why did I

have to kill him? He made me laugh, and I killed him for a joke, for nothing, like a fool.

"During the February revolution that was. Under Kerensky. We were having a mutiny. We were near a railway station. We'd left the front. They sent a young fellow, an agitator, to talk us into going back. To fight on to victory. Well, that little cadet came to talk us into being good. Just like a chicken, he was. 'Fight on to victory'—that was his slogan. He got up on a water butt shouting that slogan, the water butt was on the railway platform. He got up there, you see, so as to make his call to battle come from higher up, and suddenly the lid turned upside down under him and he fell right in. Right into the water. You can't think how funny he looked. Made me split my sides laughing! I was holding a rifle. And I was laughing my head off. Couldn't stop. It was just as if he was tickling me. And then, I aimed and fired and killed him on the spot. I can't think how it happened. Just as though somebody had pushed me.

"Well, that's my will-o'-the-wisp. I see that station at night. At the time it was funny, but now I'm sorry."

"Was that at Biriuchi station near the town of Meliuzeievo?"

"Can't remember."

"Were you in the Zybushino rebellion?"

"Can't remember."

"Which front were you at? Was it the western front? Were you in the west?"

"Somewhere like that. It could have been in the west. I can't remember."

CHAPTER TWELVE

The Rowan Tree

1

The convoy with the partisans' families, complete with children and belongings, had long been following the main partisan force. After it, behind the wagons, came vast herds of cattle, mainly cows—several thousand of them.

With the arrival of the womenfolk a new figure appeared in the camp. This was Zlydarikha or Kubarikha, a soldier's wife who was a cattle healer, a veterinarian, and also, secretly, a witch. She went about in a little pancake hat cocked on her head and a pea-green Royal Scots Fusiliers overcoat, which formed part of the British equipment supplied to the Supreme Ruler, and she assured everyone that she had made them out of a prisoner's cap and uniform. She said that the Reds had liberated her from the Kezhemsk jail where for some unknown reason Kolchak had kept her.

The partisans had now moved to a new campground. They were supposed to stay there only until the neighborhood had been reconnoitered and suitable winter quarters found. But as a result of unforeseen developments they were to spend the winter there.

This new camp was quite unlike the old one. The forest

around it was a dense, impenetrable taiga. On one side, away from the camp and the highway, there was no end to it. In the early days, while the tents were being pitched and Yurii Andreievich had more leisure, he had explored the forest in several directions and found that one could easily get lost in it. Two places had struck him in the course of these excursions and remained in his memory.

One was at the edge of the taiga, just outside the camp. The forest was autumnally bare, so that you could see into it as through an open gate; here a splendid, solitary, rust-colored rowan tree had alone kept its leaves. Growing on a mound that rose above the low, squelchy, hummocky marsh, it reached into the sky holding up the flat round shields of its hard crimson berries against the leaden, late-autumn sky. Small birds with feathers as bright as frosty dawns—bullfinches and tomtits— settled on the rowan tree and picked the largest berries, stretching out their necks and throwing back their heads to swallow them.

There seemed to be a living intimacy between the birds and the tree, as if it had watched them for a long time refusing to do anything, but in the end had had pity on them and given in and fed them like a nurse unbuttoning her blouse to give breast to a baby. "Well, all right, all right," it seemed to be saying with a smile, "eat me, have your fill."

The other place was even more remarkable. This was on a height that fell off steeply on one side. Looking down, you felt that at the bottom of the escarpment there should be something different from what was on top—a stream or a hollow or a wild field overgrown with seedy, uncut grass. But in fact it was a repetition of the same thing, only at a giddy depth, as if the forest had simply sunk to a lower level with all its trees, so that the treetops were now underfoot. There must have been a landslide there at some time.

It was as if the grim, gigantic forest, marching at cloud level, had stumbled, lost its footing, and hurtled down, all in one piece, and would have dropped right through the earth if it had not, by a miracle, saved itself at the last moment—so that there it was now, safe and sound, rustling below.

But what made the high place in the forest remarkable was something else. All along its edge it was locked in by granite boulders standing on end, looking like the flat stones of prehistoric dolmens. When Yurii Andreievich came across this stony platform for the first time, he was ready to swear that it was not of natural origin, that it bore the mark of human hands. It might well have been the site of an ancient pagan shrine, where prayers and sacrifices had once been offered by unknown worshippers.

It was here that the death sentence against eleven ringleaders of the conspiracy and two male nurses condemned for brewing vodka was executed one cold, sullen morning.

Twenty of the most loyal partisans, including a core of the commander's bodyguard, brought the condemned men to the spot. Then the escort closed around them in a semicircle, rifle in hand, and advancing at a quick, jostling pace drove them to the edge of the platform, where there was no way out except over the precipice.

As a result of questioning, long imprisonment, and maltreatment they had lost their human appearance. Black, hairy, and haggard, they were as terrible as ghosts.

They had been disarmed when they were arrested, and it had not even occurred to anyone to search them again before the execution. Such a search would have seemed superfluous and vile, a cruel mockery of men so close to death.

But now, suddenly, Rzhanitsky, a friend of Vdovichenko, who walked beside him and who, like him, was an old anarchist, fired three shots at the guards, aiming at Sivobluy. He was an excellent marksman but his hand shook in his excitement and he missed. Once again, tactfulness and pity for their former comrades kept the guards from falling on him or shooting him down at once for his attempt. Rzhanitsky had three unspent bullets left in his revolver, but maddened by his failure and perhaps, in his agitation, forgetting that they were there, he flung his Browning against the rocks. It went off a fourth time, wounding one of the condemned men, Pachkolia, in the foot.

Pachkolia cried out, clutched his foot, and fell, screaming with pain. The two men nearest him, Pafnutkin and Gorazdykh, raised him and dragged him by the arms, so that he should not be trampled to death by his comrades, who no longer knew what they were doing. Unable to put down his wounded foot, Pachkolia hopped and limped toward the rocky ledge where the doomed men were being driven, and he screamed without stopping. His inhuman shrieks were infectious. As though at a given signal, everyone lost his self-control. An indescribable scene followed. The men swore loudly, begged for mercy, prayed and cursed.

The young Galuzin, who still wore his yellow-braided school

cap, removed it, fell on his knees, and, still kneeling, edged backward following the rest of the crowd toward the terrible stones. Bowing repeatedly to the ground before the guards and crying loudly, he chanted, quite beside himself:

"Forgive me, comrades, I'm sorry, I won't do it again, please let me off. Don't kill me. I haven't lived yet. I want to live a little longer, I want to see my mother just once more. Please let me off, comrades, please forgive me. I'll do anything for you. I'll kiss the ground under your feet. Oh, help, help, Mother, I'm done for!"

Someone else, hidden in the crowd, chanted:

"Good comrades, kind comrades! Is this possible? In two wars we fought together! We stood up and fought for the same things! Let us off, comrades, have pity on us. We'll repay your kindness, we'll be grateful to you all our lives, we will prove it to you. Are you deaf, or what? Why don't you answer? Aren't you Christians?"

Others screamed at Sivobluy:

"Judas! Christ-killer! If we are traitors, you are a traitor three times over, you dog, may you be strangled. You killed your lawful Tsar, to whom you took your oath, you swore loyalty to us and you betrayed us. Go ahead, kiss your Forester, that devil, before you betray him! You'll betray him too!"

Even at the edge of the grave Vdovichenko remained true to himself. His head high, his gray hair streaming in the wind, he spoke to Rzhanitsky as one fellow anarchist to another, in a voice loud enough to be heard by all:

"Don't humble yourself! Your protest will not reach them. These new *oprichniki*,* these master executioners of the new torture chambers, will never understand you! But don't lose heart. History will tell the truth. Posterity will pillory the Bourbons of the commissarocracy together with their dirty deeds. We die as martyrs for our ideals at the dawn of the world revolution. Long live the revolution of the spirit! Long live world anarchy!"

A volley of twenty shots, discharged at some inaudible command caught only by the riflemen, mowed down half the condemned men, killing most of them outright. The rest were shot down by another salvo. The boy, Terioshka Galuzin, twitched longest, but finally he too lay still.

Oprichniki—security troops of Ivan the Terrible.

2

The idea of moving to another place, farther east, for the winter was not given up easily. Patrols were sent out to survey the country beyond the highway, along the Vytsk-Kezhemsk watershed. Liberius was often absent, leaving the doctor to himself.

But it was too late for the partisans to move and they had nowhere to go to. This was the time of their worst setbacks. Shortly before they were finally crushed, the Whites, resolving to destroy the irregular forest units once and for all, had encircled them and were pressing them from every side. The position would have been catastrophic for the partisans had the radius of the encirclement been smaller. They were saved by its size, for the approaching winter made the taiga impenetrable and prevented the enemy from pulling his ring tighter.

To move, however, had become impossible. They could, indeed, have broken through to new positions had any plan offered specific military advantages. But no such definite plan had been worked out. The men were at the end of their tether. The junior officers lost heart and with it their influence over their subordinates. Senior commanders met nightly in council and proposed conflicting solutions. The idea of shifting camp had finally to be abandoned in favor of fortifying the present positions in the heart of the taiga. Their advantage was that the deep snow made them inaccessible, particularly because the Whites were ill supplied with skis. The immediate task was to dig in and lay in large supplies.

Bisiurin, the camp quartermaster, reported an acute shortage of flour and potatoes. Cattle, however, were plentiful and he foresaw that the staple food in winter would be milk and meat.

There was a shortage of winter clothing; many of the partisans went about half dressed. All the dogs in the camp were strangled, and people with experience as furriers were set to making dogskin jackets, to be worn fur side out.

The doctor was denied the use of transportation. The carts were kept for more important needs. The last time the partisans had moved camp the wounded were carried thirty miles on stretchers.

The only medicines he had left were quinine, Glauber's salts, and iodine. The iodine was in the form of crystals and had to be dissolved in alcohol before it could be used for dressings or operations. The destruction of the vodka still was now regretted, and those of the brewers who had been acquitted at the trial as less guilty than the rest were told to mend it or construct a new one. The manufacture of alcohol was resumed for medical purposes. When this became known in the camp, people exchanged meaningful glances and shook their heads. Drunkenness broke out again, and contributed to the general demoralization.

The alcohol produced was almost 100 proof. At this strength it was suitable for dissolving crystals and also for preparing tincture of quinine, which was used in the treatment of typhus when it reappeared at the onset of the cold weather.

3

At this time the doctor went to see Pamphil and his family. His wife and children had spent the whole of the past summer as fugitives on dusty roads under the open sky. They were thoroughly frightened by the horrors they had gone through, and they anticipated new ones. Their endless wanderings had marked them indelibly. Pamphil's wife, two daughters, and little son had light hair, faded to a flaxen color by the sun, and bristling eyebrows, white against their tanned and weather-beaten faces. But while the children were too young to bear the marks of their experiences, the mother's face had become lifeless. Strain and fear had narrowed her lips to a thread and frozen her dry, regular features in a rigid expression of suffering and defensiveness.

Pamphil was devoted to all of them and loved his children to distraction. He surprised the doctor by his skill in carving toy rabbits, cocks, and bears for them, using a corner of his finely sharpened ax blade.

With the arrival of his family he had cheered up and begun to recover. But now the news had got about that the presence of the families was considered bad for discipline, and they were going to be sent, under proper escort, to winter quarters at some distance from the camp, which would thus be relieved of its burden of civilian refugees. There was more talk about this plan than actual preparation, and the doctor thought it would never be carried out, but Pamphil's spirits fell and his hallucinations came back.

4

Before winter finally set in, the camp went through a period of disturbances—anxieties, uncertainties, confused, threatening situations, and a number of weird incidents.

The Whites had completed the encirclement according to plan. They were headed by Generals Vitsyn, Quadri, and Bassalygo, who were known far and wide for their harshness and unyielding resolution, and whose names alone terrified the refugees inside the camp as well as the peaceful population remaining in its native villages at the rear of the encircling troops.

As we have said, the enemy had no means of tightening his grip, so the partisans had no reason to worry on this account; on the other hand, it was impossible for them to remain inactive. They realized that passive acceptance of their plight would strengthen enemy morale. However safe they were inside their trap, they had to attempt a sortie, even if only as a military demonstration.

A strong force was set aside for this purpose and concentrated against the western arc of the circle. After several days' hard fighting, the partisans defeated the Whites and broke through to their rear.

This breach opened a way to the camp in the taiga, and through it poured a stream of new refugees. Not all of these were related to the partisans. Terrified by the punitive measures of the Whites, all the peasants of the surrounding countryside had fled from their homes and now sought to join the partisans, whom they regarded as their natural protectors.

But the camp, anxious to get rid of its own dependents, had no place for newcomers and strangers. Men were sent to meet the fugitives and to divert them to a village on the river Chilimka. The village was called Dvory ("farms") because of the farmsteads that had grown up around its mill. There it was proposed to settle the refugees for the winter and to send the supplies that were allotted to them.

While these steps were being taken, however, events followed their own course and the camp command could not always cope with them.

The enemy had closed the breach in his positions and the partisan unit that had broken through was now unable to get back into the taiga.

Also, the women refugees were getting out of hand. It was easy to lose one's way in the taiga. The men sent out to turn back the refugees often missed them, and the women flooded into the forest, chopping down trees, building roads and bridges, and achieving prodigies of resourcefulness.

All this was counter to the intentions of the partisan command, working havoc with the plan made by Liberius.

5

That was why he was in such a temper as he stood talking to the trapper, Svirid, near the highway, which came close to the edge of the taiga at this point. Several of his officers stood on the highway, arguing about whether to cut the telegraph line that ran along the road. Liberius would have the final word, but he was deep in conversation with the trapper and kept signalling to the others to wait for him.

Svirid had been deeply shocked by the shooting of Vdovichenko, whose only crime had been that his influence rivalled that of Liberius and brought dissension into the camp. Svirid wished he could leave the partisans and go back to his old, private, independent life. But this was out of the question. He had made his choice, and were he to leave his Forest Brothers now he would be executed as a deserter.

The weather was the worst imaginable. A sharp, scudding wind swept torn, low clouds as black as flying soot before it. Snow would suddenly fall from them with a convulsive, insane haste. In a moment the broad expanse of the earth was covered with a white blanket. The next minute, the white blanket was consumed, melted completely, and the earth emerged as black as coal under the black sky splashed with slanting streaks of distant showers. The earth could not absorb any more water. Then the clouds would part like windows, as though to air the sky, which shimmered with a cold, glassy white brilliance. The stagnant, unabsorbed water on the ground responded by opening the windows of its pools and puddles, shimmering with the same brilliance. The vapors skidded like smoke over the pine woods; their resinous needles were as waterproof as oilcloth. Raindrops were strung on the telegraph wires like beads one next to the other without ever falling.

Svirid was one of those who had been sent to meet the women refugees. He wanted to tell his chief about the things he had seen, about the confusion resulting from conflicting orders, none of which could be carried out, and about the atrocities committed by the weakest elements of the female hordes, the first to succumb to despair. Trudging on foot, loaded with sacks, bundles, and babies, young mothers who had lost their milk, driven out of their minds by the horrors of the journey, abandoned their children, shook the corn out of their sacks onto the ground, and turned back. A quick death, they had decided, was preferable to a slow death by starvation. Better to fall into the clutches of the enemy than to be torn to pieces by some beast in the forest.

Other women, the strongest, were models of courage and self-control, unsurpassed by men. Svirid had many other things to tell his chief. He wanted to warn him of an impending new rebellion, more dangerous than the one that had been put down, but Liberius, by hurrying him, deprived him of the power of speech. Liberius kept interrupting Svirid not only because his friends were calling and waving to him from the highway, but because during the past two weeks he had been given similar warnings time and again, and by now he knew them by heart.

"Give me time, Comrade Chief. I am no good at finding words. They stick in my throat, they choke me. What I say is this, go to the refugee camp and tell those women to stop their nonsense. Otherwise, I ask you, what is this supposed to be— 'All against Kolchak!' or a civil war among the women?"

"Get on with it, Svirid. You see I'm wanted. Don't spin it out."

"And now there's that she-devil, Zlydarikha, God only knows what she is. She says: 'Put me down as a woman ventilator to look after the cattle. . . .'"

"Veterinary, you mean."

"That's what I say—a woman ventilator to cure cattle of wind. But she's not looking after cattle now, such a heretic, devil's reverend mother she has turned out to be, she says cows' masses, and turns young refugee wives from their duty. 'You've only yourselves to blame for your miseries,' she says to them. 'That's what comes of hitching up your skirts and running after the Red flag. Don't do it again.'"

"What refugees are you talking about—ours, from the camp, or some other kind?"

"The others, of course. The new ones, the strangers."

"But they had orders to go to Dvory. How have they got here?"

"Dvory! That's a good one. Your Dvory's burned out, mill and all, nothing left of it but cinders. That's what they saw when they came by—not a living thing. Half of them went crazy, yelled and howled and turned straight back to the Whites, and the other half turned this way."

"But how do they get through the taiga, through the swamps?"

"What are saws and axes for? Some of our men, who were sent to guard them, helped them a bit. Twenty miles of road they've cut, they say. Bridges and all, the brutes! Talk about women! They've done things that would take us a month of Sundays!"

"That's a fine thing, twenty miles of road! And what are you looking so pleased about, you jackass? That's just what the Whites want, a highway into the taiga! Now all they have to do is to roll in their artillery!"

"Send a force to guard the road."

"I can do my own thinking, thank you."

6

The days were getting shorter; it was dark by five. Toward dusk Yurii Andreievich crossed the highway at the very place where Liberius had stood talking to Svirid a few days earlier. He was on his way back to the camp. Near the clearing where the mound and the rowan tree marked the camp boundary, he heard the bold, challenging voice of Kubarikha, his "rival" as he jokingly called the cattle healer. She was singing a gay jingle and her voice had a raucous, boisterous screech in it. Judging by the peals of approving laughter that kept interrupting her, there was a crowd of men and women listening. Then came silence. The people must have dispersed.

Thinking herself alone, Kubarikha sang a different song, softly, as if to herself. Yurii Andreievich, who was cautiously making his way in the dusk along the footpath that skirted the swamp in front of the rowan tree, stopped in his tracks. Kubarikha was singing an old Russian song, but he did not know it. Or was she improvising it?

An old Russian folk song is like water held back by a dam. It looks as if it were still and were no longer flowing, but in its depths it is ceaselessly rushing through the sluice gates and the stillness of its surface is deceptive. By every possible means, by repetitions and similes, the song slows down the gradual unfolding of its theme. Then at some point it suddenly reveals itself and astounds us. That is how the song's sorrowing spirit comes to expression. The song is an insane attempt to stop time by means of its words.

Kubarikha half sang and half recited:

> "As a hare was running about the wide world,
> About the wide world, over the white snow,
> He ran, the lop-eared hare, past a rowan tree,
> Past a rowan tree, and complained to it:
> Have I not, he said, a timorous heart,
> A timorous heart, so faint and weak?
> I am frightened, he said, of the wild beast's tracks,
> Wild beast's tracks, the wolf's hungry belly.
> Pity me, O rowan bush! O fair rowan tree!
> Do not give thy beauty to the wicked enemy,
> The wicked enemy, the wicked raven.
> Scatter thy red berries to the wind,
> To the wind, over the wide world, over the white snow.
> Fling them, roll them to my native town,
> To the far end of the street, the last house,
> The last house in the street, the last window, the room
> Where she has shut herself in,
> My beloved, my longed-for love.
> Whisper to my grieving love, my bride,
> A warm, an ardent word.
> I, a soldier, languish in captivity,

Homesick, I am, poor soldier, kept in foreign parts.
I'll break from durance bitter,
I'll go to my red berry, to my lovely bride."

7

Agafia Fotievna, Pamphil's wife, had brought her sick cow to
Kubarikha. The cow had been separated from the herd and
tethered to a tree by a rope tied to her horns. Her mistress sat on
a tree stump by the cow's forelegs and Kubarikha, on a milking
stool, by her hind legs.

The rest of the countless herd was crammed into a glade,
hemmed in all around by the dark forest of triangular firs, as tall
as hills and rising from their spreading lower branches as if they
were squatting on fat bottoms on the ground.

The cows were mostly black with white spots and belonged
to some Swiss breed popular in Siberia. They were exhausted,
no less exhausted than their owners by privations, endless
wandering, and intolerable crowding. Rubbing flank to flank
and maddened by the lack of space, they forgot their sex and
reared and climbed on top of one another, pulling up their heavy
udders with an effort and roaring like bulls. The heifers who
were covered by them broke away from underneath and rushed
off into the forest, tails in the air and trampling shrubs and
branches. Their herdsmen—old men and children—ran shrieking after them.

And as if they too were hemmed in by the tight circle of
treetops in the winter sky above the glade, the black and white
clouds reared and piled and toppled as chaotically as the cows.

The knot of curious onlookers who stood at a distance
annoyed the witch, and she measured them from top to toe with
a hostile look. But, vain as an artist, she felt that it was beneath
her dignity to admit that they embarrassed her. She pretended
not to notice them. The doctor watched her from the back of
the crowd, where she could not see him.

This was the first time he took a good look at her. She wore
her usual English cap and pea-green overcoat with its crumpled
collar. But the haughty and passionate expression that gave a
youthful fire and darkness to this aging woman's eyes showed

plainly that she did not care in the least what she was wearing or not wearing.

What astonished Yurii Andreievich was the change in Pamphil's wife. He could scarcely recognize her. In the last few days she had aged terribly. Her goggling eyes were almost ready to pop out of their sockets and her neck was as thin and long as a cart shaft. Such was the effect upon her of her secret fears.

"She doesn't give any milk, my dear," she was saying. "I thought she might be in calf, but then she would have had milk by now and she still hasn't any."

"Why should she be in calf? You can see the scab of anthrax on her udder. I'll give you some herb ointment to rub it with. And of course I'll cast a spell on her."

"My other trouble is my husband."

"I'll charm him back, so he won't stray. That's easy. He'll stick to you so you won't be able to get rid of him. What's your third trouble?"

"It isn't that he strays. That would be nothing. The misfortune is that he clings to me and the children with all his might, and that breaks his heart. I know what he thinks. He thinks they'll separate the camps, that they will send us one way and him another. And that we'll fall into the hands of Bassalygo's men and he won't be there and we won't have anyone to stand up for us. And that they'll torture us, they'll rejoice in our torments. I know his thoughts. I'm afraid he'll do away with himself."

"I'll think about it. I'll find a way to end your grief. What's your third trouble?"

"I haven't a third one. That's all there is—my cow and my husband."

"Well, you are poor in sorrows, my dear. See how merciful God has been to you! Such as you are hard to find. Only two sorrows in your poor heart, and one of them a fond husband! Well, let's begin. What will you give me for the cow?"

"What will you take?"

"I'll have a loaf of bread and your husband."

The onlookers burst out laughing.

"Are you joking?"

"Too much, is it? All right, I'll do without the loaf. We'll settle for your husband."

The laughter grew louder.

"What's the name? Not your husband's, your cow's."

"Beauty."

"Half the herd is called that. All right. We'll start with God's blessing."

She recited the spell for the cow. At first she was indeed concerned with the cow, but after a while she got carried away and gave Agafia a whole set of instructions on witchcraft. Yurii Andreievich listened spellbound, just as, when he first arrived in Siberia from European Russia, he had listened to the florid chatter of the driver, Bacchus.

The woman was saying:

"Aunt Margesta, come and be our guest. Come on Wednesday, take away the pest, take away the spell, take away the scab. Ringworm, leave the heifer's udder. Stand still, Beauty, do your duty, don't upset the pail. Stand still as a hill, let milk run and rill. Terror, terror, show your mettle, take the scab, throw it in the nettle. Strong as a lord is the sorcerer's word.

"You see, Agafia, you have to know everything—bidding and forbidding, the word for escaping and the word for safekeeping. Now you, for example, you look over there and you say to yourself: 'There's a forest.' But what there is over there is the forces of evil fighting the angelic hosts—they're at war like your men with Bassalygo's.

"Or take another example, look over there where I'm pointing. You're looking the wrong way, my dear, use your eyes, not the back of your head, look where my finger is pointing. That's right! Now, what do you think that is? You think it's two twigs that the wind has tangled together? Or a bird building its nest? Well, it isn't either. That thing is a real devil's work, a garland the water spirit started weaving for her daughter. She heard people coming by, that frightened her, so she left it half done, but she'll finish it one of these nights, you will see.

"Or again, take your red banner. You think it's a flag, isn't that what you think? Well, it isn't a flag. It's the purple kerchief of the death woman, she uses it for luring. And why for luring? She waves it and she nods and winks and lures young men to come and be killed, then she sends famine and plague. That's what it is. And you went and believed her. You thought it was a flag. You thought it was: 'Come to me, all ye poor and proletarians of the world.'

"You have to know everything these days, Agafia my girl, every single thing. What every bird is and every stone and every herb. That bird, for example, that's a starling. And that beast is a badger.

"Now, another thing, suppose you take a fancy to someone, you just tell me. I'll make him pine for you, whoever he is— your Forester, the one who is your chief, if you like, or Kolchak or Ivan Tsarevich—anyone. You think I'm boasting? I am not. Now look, I'll tell you. When winter comes with blizzards and whirlwinds and snowspouts chasing each other in the fields, I will stick a knife into such a pillar of snow, right up to the hilt, and when I take it out of the snow, it will be red with blood. Have you ever heard of such a thing? Well, there you are! And you thought I was boasting. Now, how can it be, you tell me, that blood should come out of a snowspout that is made only of wind and snow? That's just it, my dear, that whirlwind isn't just wind and snow, it's a werewolf, a changeling that's lost its little bewitched child and is looking for it, it goes about the fields crying and looking for it. That is what I struck with my knife, that is why there is blood on it. Now, with that knife I can cut away the footprint of any man, and I can sew it with a silk thread to your skirt, and that man—whoever he is, Kolchak, or Strelnikov, or any new Tsar they set up—will follow you step by step wherever you go. And you thought I was telling lies! You thought it was: 'Come to me, all ye poor and proletarians of the world.'

"And many other things there are, such as stones raining from heaven, so that a man may go forth out of his house and the stones rain upon him. Or, as some have seen, horsemen riding through the sky, the horses' hoofs hitting the tops of the houses. Or as sorcerers prophesied of old, saying: 'In this woman there is corn, in that one honey, in a third marten fur.' And the knight opened the shoulder of the woman, as if it were a casket, and with his sword took out of her shoulder blade a measure of corn or a squirrel or a honeycomb."

Occasionally we experience a deep and strong feeling. Such a feeling always includes an element of pity. The more we love, the more the object of our love seems to us to be a victim. In the case of some men, compassion for a woman exceeds all measure and transports her to an unreal, entirely imaginary world. Such men are jealous of the very air she breathes, of the laws of nature, of everything that happened in the world before she was born.

Yurii Andreievich was sufficiently well read to suspect that Kubarikha's last words repeated the opening passage of an ancient chronicle, either of Novgorod or Epatievo, but so distorted by copyists and the sorcerers and bards who had transmitted them orally for centuries that its original meaning had been lost. Why, then, had he succumbed so completely to the tyranny of the legend? Why did this gibberish, this absurd talk, impress him as if it were describing real events?

Lara's left shoulder had been cut open. Like a key turning in the lock of a secret safe, the sword unlocked her shoulder blade and the secrets she had kept in the depths of her soul came to light. Unfamiliar towns, streets, rooms, countrysides unrolled like a film, whole reels of film, unfolding, discharging their contents.

How he loved her! How beautiful she was! In exactly the way he had always thought and dreamed and wanted! Yet what was it that made her so lovely? Was it something that could be named and analyzed? No, a thousand times no! She was lovely by virtue of the matchlessly simple and swift line that the Creator had, at a single stroke, drawn all around her, and in this divine form she had been handed over, like a child tightly wrapped in a sheet after its bath, into the keeping of his soul.

And what had happened to him now, where was he? In a Siberian forest with the partisans, who were encircled and whose fate he was to share. What an unbelievable, absurd predicament! Once again everything in his head and before his eyes became confused, blurred. At that moment, instead of snowing as had been expected, it began to drizzle. Like a huge banner stretching across a city street, there hung before him in the air, from one side of the forest glade to the other, a blurred, greatly magnified image of a single, astonishing, idolized head. The apparition wept, and the rain, now more intense, kissed and watered it.

"Go along now," said the witch to Agafia. "I have charmed your cow, she will get well. Pray to the Mother of God, who is the abode of light and the book of the living word."

8

There was fighting on the western border of the taiga. But the taiga was so immense that the battles were like border warfare on the edges of a great kingdom, and the camp hidden in its heart was so full of people that however many went away to fight, there seemed always to be more people left.

The rumble of the distant battle hardly ever reached the camp. Suddenly, several shots rang out in the forest. They followed one another at very close intervals, and all at once turned into a quick, ragged fusillade. People started up and ran quickly to their tents or wagons, and a general commotion began. Everyone got ready for battle.

It proved to be a false alarm. But then a growing crowd streamed toward the place where the shots had been fired.

They stood around a bleeding stump of a man lying on the ground. His right arm and left leg had been chopped off. It was inconceivable how, with his remaining arm and leg, he had crawled to the camp. The chopped-off arm and leg were tied in terrible bleeding chunks onto his back with a small wooden board attached to them; a long inscription on it said, with many words of abuse, that the atrocity was in reprisal for similar atrocities perpetrated by such and such a Red unit—a unit that had no connection with the Forest Brotherhood. It also said that the same treatment would be meted out to all the partisans unless, by a given date, they submitted and gave up their arms to the representatives of General Vitsyn's army corps.

Fainting repeatedly from loss of blood, the dying man told them in a faltering voice of the tortures and atrocities perpetrated by Vitsyn's investigating and punitive squads. His own sentence of death had been allegedly commuted; instead of hanging him, they had cut off his arm and leg in order to send him into the camp and strike terror among the partisans. They had carried him as far as the outposts of the camp, where they had put him down and ordered him to crawl, urging him on by shooting into the air.

He could barely move his lips. To make out his almost unintelligible stammering, the crowd around him bent low. He was saying: "Be on your guard, comrades. He has broken through."

"Patrols have gone out in strength. There's a big battle going on. We'll hold him."

"There's a gap. He wants to surprise you. I know. . . . I can't go on, men. I am spitting blood. I'll die in a moment."

"Rest a bit. Keep quiet.—Can't you see it's bad for him, you heartless beasts!"

The man started again: "He went to work on me, the devil. He said: You will bathe in your own blood until you tell me who you are. And how was I to tell him, a deserter is just what I am? I was running from him to you."

"You keep saying 'he.' Who is it that got to work on you?"

"Let me just get my breath. . . . I'll tell you. Hetman, Bekeshin. Colonel, Strese. Vitsyn's men. You don't know out here what it's like. The whole town is groaning. They boil people alive. They cuts strips out of them. They take you by the scruff of the neck and push you inside, you don't know where you are, it's pitch black. You grope about—you are in a cage, inside a freight car. There are more than forty people in the cage, all in their underclothes. From time to time they open the door and grab whoever comes first—out he goes. As you grab a chicken to cut its throat. I swear to God. Some they hang, some they shoot, some they question. They beat you to shreds, they put salt on the wounds, they pour boiling water on you. When you vomit or relieve yourself they make you eat it. As for children and women—O God!"

The unfortunate was at his last gasp. He cried out and died without finishing the sentence. Somehow they all knew it at once and took off their caps and crossed themselves.

That night, the news of a far more terrible incident flew around the camp.

Pamphil had been in the crowd surrounding the dying man. He had seen him, heard his words, and read the threatening inscription on the board.

His constant fear for his family in the event of his own death rose to a new climax. In his imagination he saw them handed over to slow torture, watched their faces distorted by pain, and heard their groans and cries for help. In his desperate anguish— to forestall their future sufferings and to end his own—he killed them himself, felling his wife and three children with that same, razor-sharp ax that he had used to carve toys for the two small girls and the boy, who had been his favorite.

The astonishing thing was that he did not kill himself immediately afterward. What could he be thinking of? What could he look forward to? What intentions could he have, what plans? It was a clear case of insanity, and nothing could save him now.

While Liberius, the doctor, and the members of the army soviet debated what to do with him, he roamed freely about the camp, his head hung low over his chest, his dirty-yellow eyes glowering unseeingly. An obtuse vague grimace of inhuman, unconquerable suffering never left his face.

No one was sorry for him. Everyone avoided him. Some people said he should be lynched, but they were not heeded.

There was nothing in the world left for him to do. At dawn he vanished from the camp, fleeing from himself like a dog with rabies.

9

High winter came with its severe frosts. Torn, seemingly disconnected sounds and shapes rose out of the icy mist, stood still, moved, and vanished. The sun was not the sun to which the earth was used, it was a changeling. Its crimson ball hung in the forest and from it, stiffly and slowly as in a dream or in a fairy tale, amber-yellow rays of light as thick as honey spread and, catching in the trees, froze to them in midair.

Invisible feet in felt boots, touching the ground softly with padded soles, yet making the snow screech angrily at each step, moved in all directions, while the hooded and fur-jacketed torsos belonging to them sailed separately through the upper air, like heavenly bodies.

Friends stopped and talked, their faces close together, flushed as at the steam baths, with beards bristling like iced loofahs. Clouds of dense, clammy steam puffed out of their mouths, too large for the clipped, frost-bitten words they accompanied.

Walking along the footpath, the doctor ran into Liberius.

"Hello, stranger! Come to my dugout this evening. Spend the night. We'll have a good talk. There is news."

"Is the courier back? Any news from Varykino?"

"Not a word about your people or mine. This, however, leads me to the comforting conclusion that they must have got away in time, otherwise we would be sure to have heard something. We'll talk about it tonight. I'll expect you."

Going into the dugout that evening, the doctor repeated his question: "What have you heard about our families? Just tell me that."

"You never want to see further than your nose. So far as I know, they are safe and sound. But the point is that the news is first-rate. Have some cold veal."

"No, thanks. Come on now, don't change the subject."

"Are you sure you won't? Well, I'll have a bite. Though bread and vegetables are what we really need. There's a lot of scurvy about. We should have got in more nuts and berries last autumn when the women were there to pick them. Well, as I was saying, our affairs are in excellent shape. What I've always prophesied is coming true. The worst is over. Kolchak's forces are retreating all along the line. It's a complete rout. Now do you see? What did I always tell you? Do you remember how you used to moan?"

"When did I moan?"

"All the time. Especially when we were being pressed by Vitsyn."

The doctor recalled the autumn, the shooting of the rebels, Pamphil's killing of his wife and children, the whole senseless murderous mess to which there seemed to be no end. White and Red atrocities rivalled each other in savagery, outrage breeding outrage. The smell of blood was in his nose and throat, it choked him, it nauseated him, it mounted to his head, it made his eyes swim. That wasn't moaning, that was something entirely different, but how could he explain it to Liberius?

The dugout was lit by torches made of sticks stuck into a metal holder. They gave off an aromatic smell of charcoal. As a stick burned down, the cinder dropped into a bowl of water standing underneath, and Liberius lit a fresh one.

"See what I have to burn? There's no more oil. And the wood is too dry, it burns too quickly. Sure you won't have some veal? About the scurvy. What are you waiting for to call a staff meeting and give us a lecture on scurvy and the means of dealing with it?"

"Stop tormenting me, for God's sake. What exactly do you know about our people?"

"I've told you. There is nothing certain in the report. But I didn't finish telling you what I've learned from the latest communiqués. The civil war is over. Kolchak's forces are smashed. The main part of the Red Army is in pursuit, it is driving him eastward, along the railway, into the sea. Another part of it is hurrying over this way, and we are joining forces to mop up the considerable scattered numbers of Whites in the rear. The whole of southern Russia is clear of the enemy. Well, why aren't you glad? Isn't that enough for you?"

"I am glad. But where are our families?"

"Not in Varykino, and that's a very lucky thing. Not that there is any confirmation of that crazy business Kamennodvorsky told you about—you remember that rumor last summer about mysterious strangers raiding Varykino? I always thought it was nonsense. But the village is deserted. So it looks as if something did happen after all, and it's a very good thing they got out in time, as they evidently did. That is what the few remaining inhabitants think, according to my source."

"And Yuriatin? What happened there? Who is holding it?"

"That's another absurdity. It can't possibly be true."

"What's that?"

"They say the Whites are still there, but that's a sheer impossibility. I'll prove it to you, you'll see for yourself."

He put another stick in the holder and, getting out a tattered map and folding it so that the district he was talking about was on top, explained the position, pencil in hand.

"Look. All these are sectors where the Whites have been thrown back—here, and here, and here, all over this region. Do you follow?"

"Yes."

"So they can't possibly be anywhere near Yuriatin, because if they were, with their communications cut, they couldn't avoid being captured. Even their commanders must realize this, however incompetent they may be. Why are you putting on your coat? Where are you going?"

"I'll be back in a moment. There's a lot of smoke here, and I've got a headache. I'll just go out for a breath of air."

When he was outside, the doctor swept the snow off the wooden block that served as a seat at the entrance to the dugout and sat down, his elbows on his knees and his head propped on his fists.

The taiga, the camp, his eighteen months among the partisans, went right out of his head. He forgot all about them. Memories of his dear ones filled his mind and crowded out all else. He tried to guess their fate, and images rose before him, each more frightening than the last.

Here is Tonia walking through a field in a blizzard with Sasha in her arms. She keeps wrapping him up in a blanket, her feet sinking into the deep snow. She can barely drag along, using all her strength, but the blizzard knocks her down, she stumbles and falls and gets up, too weak to stand on her feet, the wind buffeting her and the snow covering her up. Oh, but he is forgetting. She has two children with her, and she nurses the little one. Both her hands are busy, like the fugitives at Chilimka who broke down and went mad with grief and strain.

She has both her hands full and there is no one near to help her. Sasha's father has vanished, no one knows where he is. He is away, he has always been away, all his life he has remained

apart from them. What kind of father is he? Is it possible for a
real father always to be away? And what about her own father?
Where is Alexander Alexandrovich? And Niusha? And the
others? Better not ask, better not think about it.

The doctor got up and turned to go back into the dugout.
Suddenly his thoughts took a different direction and he changed
his mind about returning to Liberius.

Long ago he had cached a pair of skis, a bag of biscuits, and
other things he would need if a chance to make his escape should
ever come. He had buried them in the snow just outside the
camp, at the foot of a tall pine. To make double sure of finding it
he had marked the tree with a notch. Now he turned and
walked along the footpath trodden between the snowdrifts in
the direction of his buried treasure. It was a clear night with a
full moon. He knew where the sentries were posted and at first
avoided them successfully. But when he came to the clearing
with the mound and rowan tree a sentry hailed him from a
distance, took a run on his skis, and standing straight up on
them glided swiftly toward him.

"Halt or I shoot! Who are you? Password."

"What's come over you, man? Don't you know me? I'm the
camp doctor, Zhivago."

"Sorry, Comrade Zhelvak. I didn't recognize you, no offense
meant. All the same, Zhelvak or not, I'm not letting you go any
farther. Orders are orders."

"As you wish. The password is 'Red Siberia,' and the reply,
'Down with the Interventionists.'"

"That's better. Go ahead. What are you chasing after at this
time of night? Anyone sick?"

"I was thirsty and I couldn't sleep. I thought I'd go out for a
breath of air and eat some snow. Then I saw the rowan tree with
iced berries on it. I want to go and pick a few."

"If that isn't just like a gentleman's notion! Who's ever heard
of picking berries in winter! Three years we've been beating the
nonsense out of you others but you're still the same. All right,
go and pick your berries, you lunatic. What do I care."

And as swiftly as he had come, the sentry took a run, stood
straight up on his long skis, and whistled over the untrodden
snow into the distance beyond the bare winter shrubs as thin as
thinning hair.

The footpath brought the doctor to the foot of the rowan
tree, whose name he had just spoken. It was half in snow, half in
frozen leaves and berries, and it held out two white branches

toward him. He remembered Lara's strong white arms and seized the branches and pulled them to him. As if in answer, the tree shook snow all over him. He muttered without realizing what he was saying, and completely beside himself: "I'll find you, my beauty, my love, my rowan tree, my own flesh and blood."

It was a clear night with a full moon. He made his way farther into the taiga, to the marked tree, unearthed his things, and left the camp.

CHAPTER THIRTEEN

Opposite the House of Sculptures

1

Merchant Street rambled crookedly downhill, overlooked by the houses and churches of the upper part of Yuriatin.

At the corner there was the dark gray house with sculptures. The huge square stones of the lower part of its façade were covered with freshly posted sheets of government newspapers and proclamations. Small groups of people stood on the sidewalk, reading in silence.

After the recent thaw it was dry and frosty. Now it was light at a time of day when only a few weeks before it had been dark. The winter had just gone, and the emptiness it had left was filled by the light that lingered on into the evenings. The light made one restless, it was like a call from afar that was disturbing, it put one on one's guard.

The Whites had recently left the town, surrendering it to the Reds. The bombardment, bloodshed, and wartime anxieties had ceased. This too was disturbing, and put one on one's guard, like the going of the winter and the lengthening of the spring days.

One of the proclamations pasted on the wall and still readable by the light of the longer day announced:

"Workbooks are obtainable by those qualified at the cost of 50 rubles each, at the Food Office, Yuriatin Soviet, 5 October Street (formerly Governor Street), Room 137.

"Anyone without a workbook, or filling it in incorrectly, or (still worse) fraudulently, will be prosecuted with the utmost rigor of the wartime regulations. Detailed instructions for the correct use of workbooks are printed in I.Y.I.K. No. 86 (1013) for the current year and are posted at the Yuriatin Food Office, Room 137."

Another proclamation stated that the town had ample food supplies. These, it said, were merely being hoarded by the bourgeoisie with the object of disorganizing distribution and creating chaos. It ended with the words:

"Anyone found hoarding food will be shot on the spot."

A third announcement read:

"Those who do not belong to the exploiting class are admitted to membership in Consumer Associations. Details are obtainable at the Food Office, Yuriatin Soviet, 5 October Street (formerly Governor Street), Room 137."

Former members of the military were warned:

"Anyone who fails to surrender his arms or who continues carrying them without having the appropriate new permit will be prosecuted with the utmost severity of the law. New permits are obtainable at the Office of the Yuriatin Revolutionary-Military Committee, 6 October Street, Room 63."

2

The group in front of the building was joined by a wild-looking, emaciated man, black with grime, with a bag flung over his shoulder, and carrying a stick. There was not yet any white in his long, shaggy hair, but his bristly, dark-blond beard was graying. This was Yurii Andreievich. His fur coat must have been taken from him on the road or perhaps he had bartered it for food. His thin, tattered, short-sleeved coat, which did not keep him warm, was the result of an exchange.

All he had left in his bag was the remnant of a crust of bread that someone had given him out of charity, in a village near the town, and a piece of suet. He had reached Yuriatin somewhat earlier, but it had taken him a whole hour to trudge from the outskirts through which the railway ran to this corner of Merchant Street, so great was his weakness and so much had the last few days of the journey exhausted him. He had often stopped, and he had barely restrained an impulse to fall to his knees and kiss the stones of the town, which he had despaired of ever seeing again, and the sight of which filled him with happiness, like the sight of a friend.

For almost half his journey on foot he had followed the railway track. All of it was out of use, neglected and covered with snow. He had passed train after train abandoned by the Whites; they stood idle, stopped by the defeat of Kolchak, by lack of fuel, and by snowdrifts. Immobilized and buried in the snow, they stretched almost uninterruptedly for miles on end. Some of them served as strongholds for armed bands of highwaymen or as hideouts for escaping criminals or political fugitives—the involuntary vagrants of those days—but most of them had become mortuaries and mass graves for the victims of the cold and of the typhus raging all along the line and mowing down whole villages.

That period confirmed the ancient proverb, "Man is a wolf to man." Traveller turned off the road at the sight of traveller, stranger meeting stranger killed for fear of being killed. There were isolated cases of cannibalism. The laws of human civilization were suspended. The jungle law was in force. Man dreamed the prehistoric dreams of the cave dweller.

Every now and then Yurii Andreievich would see lonely shadows stealing along the ditch or scurrying across the road ahead of him. He avoided them carefully whenever he could, but many of them seemed familiar. He imagined that he had seen them all at the partisan camp. In most cases he was mistaken, but once his eyes did not deceive him. The boy who darted out of a snowdrift that concealed a train of *wagons-lits,* relieved himself, and darted back had indeed been a member of the Forest Brotherhood. It was Terentii Galuzin, who was believed to have been shot dead. In reality he had only been wounded and had lost consciousness. When he came to he had crawled away from the place of execution, hidden in the forest until he recovered from his wounds, and was now making his way home to Krestovozdvizhensk under an assumed name, hiding in the buried trains and running at the sight of human beings.

These scenes and incidents had the strangeness of the transcendental, as if they were snatches torn from lives on other planets that had somehow drifted to the earth. Only nature had remained true to history and appeared in the guise it assumed in modern art.

Now and then there was a quiet, pale gray, dark rose evening, with birches, black and fine as script against the afterglow, and black streams faintly clouded over with gray ice flowing between steep white banks of snow blackened at the edges where the running water had eroded them. Such, in an hour or two, would be the evening in Yuriatin: frosty, gray, transparent, and as soft as pussy willows.

The doctor meant to read the notices posted on the house of sculptures, but his eyes kept wandering to the third-floor windows of the house across the street. These were the windows of the rooms in which the furniture left by the previous occupants had been stored. Now, although the frost had filmed them at the edges, it was clear that the glass was transparent; the whitewash had evidently been removed. What did this mean? Had the former occupants returned? Or had Lara moved out and new tenants moved in, rearranging everything?

The uncertainty was unbearable. The doctor crossed the street, went in, and climbed the front staircase he knew so well and which was so dear to him. How often at the camp he had recalled the openwork pattern of the cast-iron steps down to the last scroll. In one place you could look through into the lumber room in the basement where broken chairs and old pails and tin tubs had been stacked. They were still there; nothing had changed. The doctor was almost grateful to the staircase for its loyalty to the past.

There had been a doorbell once, but it had broken and stopped ringing even before the doctor had been captured by the partisans. He was about to knock when he noticed that there was now a padlock on the door, hanging from two rings roughly screwed into the old oak panels with their fine carving, which in places had come away. Such destructiveness would have been inconceivable in the old days. There would have been a fitted lock, and if it had been out of order there were locksmiths to repair it. This trifling detail was eloquent of the general deterioration of things, which had gone a great deal further in his absence.

The doctor was sure that Lara and Katenka were not at home.

Perhaps they were not even in Yuriatin, and perhaps they were not even alive. He was prepared for the worst. It was only in order not to leave a stone unturned that he decided to look for the key in the hollow between the bricks, where a rat had so greatly frightened Katenka. He kicked at the wall, to make sure of not putting his hand on one now. He had not the slightest hope of finding anything. The hollow was closed by a brick. He removed it and felt inside. Oh, miracle! A key and a note! It was a long note covering a large sheet of paper. He took it to the window on the landing. Another miracle, even more unbelievable! The note was addressed to him! He read it quickly:

"Lord, what happiness! They say you are alive and have turned up. Someone saw you near the town and rushed over to tell me. I take it you'll go straight to Varykino, so I'm going there with Katenka. But just in case, I'm leaving the key in the usual place. Wait for me, don't move. You'll see I am using the front rooms now. The flat is rather empty, I've had to sell some of the furniture. I've left a little food, boiled potatoes mostly. Put the lid back on the saucepan with a weight on it, to keep the rats out. I'm mad with joy."

He read to the bottom of the page, and did not notice that the letter continued on the back. He pressed it to his lips, folded it, and put it into his pocket with the key. Mixed with his immense joy, he felt a sharp, stabbing pain. Since Lara was going to Varykino, and not even bothering to explain, it must be that his family were not there. He felt not only anxious because of this, but unbearably aggrieved and sad about them. Why hadn't she said a single word of how and where they were?—as if they didn't exist at all!

But it was getting darker, and he had still many things to do while it was light. One of the most urgent was to read the texts of the decrees posted in the street. It was no trifling matter in those days to be ignorant of the regulations; it might cost you your life. Without going into the flat or taking off his bag, he went down and crossed the street, to the wall thickly covered with various announcements.

3

There were newspaper articles, texts of speeches at meetings, and decrees. Yurii Andreievich glanced at the headings. "Requisitioning, assessment, and taxation of members of the propertied classes." "Establishment of workers' control." "Factory and plant committees." These were the regulations the new authorities had issued on entering the town in place of those that had been in force. No doubt, Yurii Andreievich thought, they were intended as a reminder of the uncompromising nature of the new regime, in case it had been forgotten under the Whites. But these monotonous, endless repetitions made his head go around. What period did they belong to? That of the first upheaval, or of some later re-establishment of the regime after a White rebellion? Had they been composed last year? The year before? Only once in his life had this uncompromising language and single-mindedness filled him with enthusiasm. Was it possible that he must pay for that rash enthusiasm all his life by never hearing, year after year, anything but these unchanging, shrill, crazy exclamations and demands, which became progressively more impractical, meaningless, and unfulfillable as time went by? Was it possible that because of one moment of over-generous response he had been enslaved forever?

His eyes lit on a fragment of a speech:

"The reports on the famine disclose the unbelievable inactivity of the local organizations. There are glaring abuses, there is speculation on a gigantic scale, but what are our regional and municipal factory committees doing? Only mass searches in the commercial districts of Yuriatin and Razvilie, only terror applied in all its harshness, down to the shooting of speculators on the spot, can deliver us from famine."

"What an enviable blindness!" thought the doctor. "To be able to talk of bread when it has long since vanished from the face of the earth! Of propertied classes and speculators when they have long since been abolished by earlier decrees! Of peasants and villages that no longer exist! Don't they remember their own plans and measures, which long since turned life upside down? What kind of people are they, to go on raving with this never-cooling, feverish ardor, year in, year out, on nonexistent, long-vanished subjects, and to know nothing, to see nothing around them?"

The doctor's head was spinning. He fainted and fell down unconscious on the sidewalk. When he came to and people helped him to get up and offered to take him where he wished to go, he thanked them and refused, saying he had only to cross the street.

4

He went up again, and this time he unlocked the door of Lara's flat. It was still light on the landing, no darker than before he had gone out. He was glad that the sun was not hurrying him.

The creaking of the door touched off a commotion inside. The uninhabited flat greeted him with the clang and rattle of falling tin pans. Rats, scuttling off the shelves, plopped onto the floor and scattered. They must have bred here by the thousands. The doctor felt sick and helpless to deal with this abomination and decided to barricade himself for the night in one room with a closely fitting door, where he could stop the ratholes with broken glass.

He turned left to the part of the flat that he did not know, crossed a dark passage, and came into a light room with two windows facing the street. Directly opposite the window was the gray building with the statues; groups of people stood with their back to him, reading the announcements.

The light in the room was of the same quality as outside, it was the same new, fresh evening light of early spring. This seemed to make the room a part of the street; the only difference was that Lara's bedroom, where he was standing, was colder than the street.

His sudden weakness earlier that afternoon as he approached the town and walked through it an hour or two ago had made Yurii Andreievich think that he was ill, and had filled him with fears. Now, the sameness of the light in the house and in the street exhilarated him. Bathed in the same chilled air as the passersby, he felt a kinship with them, an identity with the mood of the town, with life in the world. This dispelled his fears. He no longer thought he would be ill. The transparency of the spring evening, the all-penetrating light were a good omen, a promise of generous fulfillment of distant and far-reaching hopes. All would be well, he would achieve all he wanted in life, he would find and reunite and reconcile them all, he would think everything out and find all the right words. He waited for the joy of seeing Lara as an immediate proof that all the rest would follow.

A wild excitement and an uncontrollable restlessness supplanted his earlier fatigue. In reality this animation was an even surer symptom of approaching illness than his recent weakness. Yurii Andreievich could not sit still. Once again he felt the urge to go out.

He wanted, before he settled down, to have a haircut and get rid of his beard. He had looked for a barber earlier, on his way through town. But some of the barbershops he had known before stood empty, others had changed hands and were used for other purposes, and those still in business were locked. He had no razor of his own. Scissors would have done the job, but though he turned everything upside down on Lara's dressing table, in his haste he did not find any.

Now it occurred to him that there had once been a tailor's workshop in Spassky Street; if it still existed and he got to it before closing time, he might borrow a pair of scissors. He walked out.

5

His memory had not failed him. The workshop was still there, with its entrance from the street and a window running the width of the front. The seamstresses worked in full view of the passersby. You could see right into the back of the room.

It was packed with sewing women. In addition to the seamstresses there were probably aging local ladies who knew how to sew and had obtained jobs in order to become entitled to the workbooks mentioned in the proclamation on the wall of the gray building.

It was easy to tell them from the professionals. The workshop made nothing but army clothes, padded trousers and jackets and parti-colored fur coats, made of the skins of dogs of different breeds, such as Yurii Andreievich had seen on the partisans. This work, more suitable for furriers, was particularly hard on the amateurs, whose fingers looked all thumbs as they pushed the stiffly folded hems through the sewing machines.

Yurii Andreievich knocked on the window and made signs that he wished to be let in. The women replied by signs that no private orders were accepted. He persisted. The women motioned him to go away and leave them alone, they had urgent work to do. One of them made a puzzled face, held up her hand, palm out, like a little boat, in a gesture of annoyance, and questioned with her eyes what on earth he wanted. He snipped two fingers like scissor blades. This was not understood. They decided it was some impertinence, that he was mimicking them and making fun of them. Standing out there, torn and tattered and behaving so oddly, he looked like a madman. The girls giggled and waved him on. At last he thought of going around the house, through the yard, and knocking on the back door.

6

It was opened by a dark, elderly, stern woman in a dark dress who might have been the head seamstress.

"What a pest you are. Can't you leave us alone? Well, get on with it, what is it you want?"

"I want scissors. Don't be so surprised. I'd like to borrow a pair of scissors to cut my hair and my beard. I could do it here and give them back to you at once, it wouldn't take a minute. I'd be terribly grateful."

The woman looked astonished and mistrustful. She clearly doubted his sanity.

"I've just arrived from a long journey. I wanted to get a haircut but there isn't a single barbershop open. So I thought I'd do it myself, but I haven't any scissors. Would you kindly lend me some?"

"All right. I'll give you a haircut. But I warn you. If you've got something else in mind—any tricks such as changing your appearance to disguise yourself for political reasons—don't blame us if we report you. We are not risking our lives for you."

"For heaven's sake! What an idea!"

She let him in and took him into a side room little bigger than a closet; next moment he was sitting in a chair with a sheet wrapped around him and tucked under his chin as at the barber's. The seamstress went out of the room and came back with a pair of scissors, a comb, clippers, a strap, and a razor.

"I've done every kind of job in my life," she explained, noticing her client's astonishment. "At one time I was a hairdresser. I learned haircutting and shaving when I was a nurse in the other war. Now we'll snip off that beard and then we'll have a shave."

"Could you cut my hair very short, please?"

"I'll do my best. Why are you pretending to be so ignorant, an educated man like you? As if you didn't know that we now count time by the decade and not by the week, and today is the seventeenth of the month and the barbers have their day off on every date with a seven in it."

"Honestly I didn't know. I've told you, I've just come from a long way off. Why should I pretend anything?"

"Don't fidget or you'll get cut. So you've just arrived. How did you come?"

"On my feet."

"Along the highway?"

"Partly that, partly along the railway track. I don't know how many trains I've seen, all buried in the snow. Luxury trains, special trains, every kind of train you can think of."

"There, just this little bit to snip off and it's finished. Family business?"

"Heavens, no! I worked for a former union of credit co-operatives as their travelling inspector. They sent me on an inspection tour to eastern Siberia and there I got stuck. No chance of a train, as you know. There was nothing for it but to walk. Six weeks, it took me. I can't begin to tell you all I've seen on the way."

"If I were you, I wouldn't begin. I see I'll have to teach you a thing or two. Have a look at yourself first. Here's a mirror. Get your hand out from under the sheet and hold it. All right?"

"I don't think it's quite short enough. Couldn't you take off a bit more?"

"It won't stay tidy if it's any shorter. As I was saying, don't start telling anything at all. It's better to keep your mouth shut. Credit co-operatives, luxury trains, inspection tours—forget all about such things. It isn't the moment for them. You could get into no end of trouble. Better pretend you are a doctor or a schoolteacher. There now—beard cut off, now we'll shave it clean. Just a spot of lather and you'll be ten years younger. I'll go and boil the kettle."

"Whoever can she be?" Yurii Andreievich wondered. He had a feeling he had some connection with her—something he had seen or heard, someone she reminded him of—but he could not think who it was.

She came back with the hot water.

"Now we'll have a shave. As I was telling you, it's much better not to say a word. Speech is of silver, silence is gold. That has always been true. And your special trains and credit co-operatives—better think of something else, say you are a doctor or a teacher. As for seeing sights, keep that to yourself. Whom are you going to impress these days? Am I hurting you?"

"A little."

"It scrapes a bit, I know, it can't be helped. Just a little bit of patience, my dear man. Your skin isn't used to the razor and your beard is very coarse. It won't take a minute. Yes. There's nothing people haven't seen. They've been through everything. We've had our troubles, too. The things that went on under the Whites! Murder, rape, abduction, manhunts. There was one little lordling who took a dislike to an ensign. He sent soldiers to ambush him in a wood outside the town, near Krapulsky's house. They got him and disarmed him and took him under guard to Razvilie. In those days Razvilie was the same as the regional Cheka is nowadays—a place of execution. Why are you jerking your head like that? It scrapes, does it? I know, my dear, I know. It can't be helped. Your hair is just like bristles. There's just this one tough place. Well, the ensign's wife was in hysterics. 'Kolia! Kolia! What will become of my Kolia!' Off she went, straight to the top, to General Galiullin. That's in a manner of speaking, of course. She couldn't get straight to him. You had to pull strings. There was somebody in the next street over there who knew how to reach him, an exceptionally kind person, very sensitive, not like anyone else, always stood up for people. You can't think what went on all over the place, lynchings, atrocities, dramas of jealousy. Just as in Spanish novels."

"That's Lara she's talking about," thought Yurii Andreievich. But he kept prudently silent and did not ask for details. Her

absurd remark about the Spanish novels again oddly reminded
him of something—precisely by its absurdity and irrelevance—
but he still couldn't think what it was.

"Now, of course, it's all quite different. Admittedly there's
any amount of investigations, informing, shooting, and so on.
But the idea is quite different. To begin with, it's a new
government, it's only just come into power, it hasn't got into its
stride yet. And then, whatever you say, they are on the side of
the common people, that's their strength. In our family we are
four sisters, counting myself, all working women. It's natural
that we should be drawn to them. One sister died. Her husband
was a political exile, worked as manager at one of the local
factories. Their son—my nephew, that is—he's at the head of
the peasant forces—he's quite a celebrity."

"So that's who she is," Yurii Andreievich realized. "Liberius's
aunt, Mikulitsyn's sister-in-law, the one who is a local legend,
barber—seamstress—signal woman—Jack of all trades!" But he
decided to say nothing so as not to give himself away.

"My nephew was always drawn to the people, ever since his
childhood. He grew up among the workers at the factory.
Perhaps you've heard of the Varykino factories? Now look at
what I've done, fool that I am. Half your chin is smooth and the
other half is bristly. That's what comes of talking. Why didn't
you stop me? Now the lather's dry and the water is cold. I'll go
and warm it up."

When she came back, Yurii Andreievich asked: "Varykino,
that's somewhere miles out in the country, isn't it? That should
have been safe enough in all these upheavals."

"Well, it wasn't exactly safe. They had it worse than we did in
some ways. They had some sort of armed bands out there,
nobody quite knows what they were. They didn't speak our
language. They went through the place, house by house, shot
everyone they found and went off again, without a by-your-
leave. The corpses just stayed in the snow. That was in the
winter, of course. Do stop jerking your head, I nearly cut you."

"You were saying your brother-in-law lived in Varykino.
Was he there when all this happened?"

"No. God is merciful. He and his wife got out in time—that's
his second wife. Where they are, nobody knows, but it's certain
that they escaped. There were some new people there as well,
strangers from Moscow. They left even earlier. The younger of
the two men, a doctor, the head of the family, he's missing.

That's in a manner of speaking, of course; it was called 'missing'
to spare their feelings. Actually he must be dead—sure to have
been killed. They kept looking and looking for him, but he
never turned up. In the meantime the other one, the older of the
two, he was called back home. A professor he was, an
agronomist. The government called him back, I was told. They
all stopped in Yuriatin on their way to Moscow, just before the
Whites came back. Now you're at it again, twisting and jerking.
You'll really make me cut your throat. You get your money's
worth out of your barber, my dear man."

So they were in Moscow!

7

"In Moscow! In Moscow!" The words echoed in his heart at
every step of the cast-iron stairs, as he climbed them for the
third time. The empty flat again met him with the hellish din of
scampering, flopping, racing rats. It was clear to Yurii Andreievich that, however tired he was, he would never get to
sleep unless he could keep this abomination away from him.
The first thing before settling down for the night was to stop the
ratholes. Fortunately, there were fewer of them in the bedroom
than in the rest of the flat, where the floor boards and skirtings
were in a worse state. But he had to hurry. It was getting dark.
It was true that a lamp stood on the kitchen table—perhaps in
expectation of his coming it had been taken down from its
bracket and half filled with kerosene, and a match box with a
few matches in it had been left out. But it was better to save
both the matches and the kerosene. In the bedroom he found a
small oil lamp; the rats had been at the oil but a little was left.

In some places the skirting had come away from the floor. It
took him a little over an hour to pack the cracks with broken
glass. The door fitted well, and once it was closed the bedroom
should be ratproof.

There was a Dutch stove in a corner of the room, with a tiled
cornice not quite reaching the ceiling. In the kitchen there was a
stack of logs. Yurii Andreievich decided to rob Lara of a couple
of armfuls and, getting down on one knee, he gathered them up
and balanced them on his left arm. Carrying them into the

bedroom, he stacked them near the stove and had a look inside to see how it worked and in what condition it was. He had meant to lock the door but the latch was broken; he wedged it firmly with paper; then he laid the fire at his leisure and lit it.

As he put in more logs, he noticed that the cross section of one of them was marked with the letters "K.D." He recognized them with surprise. In the old Krueger days when timber rejected by the factories was sold for fuel, the boles were stamped before they were cut up into sections to show where they came from. "K.D." stood for Kulabish Division in Varykino.

The discovery upset him. These logs in Lara's house must mean that she was in touch with Samdeviatov and that he provided for her as he had once supplied the doctor and his household with all their needs. He had always found it irksome to accept his help. Now his embarrassment at being in his debt was complicated by other feelings.

It was hardly likely that Samdeviatov helped Lara out of sheer goodness of heart. He thought of Samdeviatov's free and easy ways and of Lara's rashness as a woman. There must surely be something between them.

The dry Kulabish logs crackled merrily and stormed into a blaze, and, as they caught, Yurii Andreievich's blind jealousy turned from the merest suppositions into certainty.

But so tormented was he on every side that one anxiety drove out another. He could not get rid of his suspicions, but his mind leapt from subject to subject, and the thought of his family, flooding it again, submerged for a time his jealous fantasies.

"So you are in Moscow, my dear ones?" It seemed to him now that the seamstress had given him an assurance of their safe arrival. "So you made all that long journey once again, and this time without me. How did you manage on the way? Why was Alexander Alexandrovich called back? Was it to return to his chair at the Academy? How did you find the house? How silly of me! I don't even know whether the house is still standing. Lord, how hard and painful it all is! If only I could stop thinking. I can't think straight. What's the matter with me, Tonia? I think I'm ill. What will become of us? What will become of you, Tonia, Tonia darling, Tonia? And Sashenka? And Alexander Alexandrovich? And myself? Why hast Thou cast me off? O Light everlasting! Why are we always separated, my dear ones? Why are you always being swept away from me?

But we'll be together again, we'll be reunited, won't we, darling? I'll find you, even if I have to walk all the way to get to you. We'll see each other, we'll be together, we'll be all right again, won't we?

"Why doesn't the earth swallow me up, why am I such a monster that I keep forgetting that Tonia was to have another child, and that she has surely had it? This isn't the first time I've forgotten it. How did she get through her confinement? To think that they all stopped in Yuriatin on their way to Moscow! It's true that Lara didn't know them, but here is a complete stranger, a seamstress, a hairdresser who has heard all about them, and Lara says nothing about them in her note. How could she be so careless, so indifferent? It's as strange as her saying nothing about knowing Samdeviatov."

Yurii Andreievich now looked around the room with a new discernment. All its furnishings belonged to the unknown tenants who had long been absent and in hiding. There was nothing of Lara's among them, and they could tell him nothing of her tastes. The photographs on the walls were of strangers. However that might be, he suddenly felt uncomfortable under the eyes of all these men and women. The clumsy furniture breathed hostility. He felt alien and unwanted in this bedroom.

What a fool he had been to keep remembering this house and missing it, what a fool to have come into this room not as into an ordinary room but as if into the heart of his longing for Lara! How silly his way of feeling would seem to anyone outside! How different was the way strong, practical, efficient, handsome males, such as Samdeviatov, lived and spoke and acted! And why should Lara be expected to prefer his weakness and the dark, obscure, unrealistic language of his love? Did she need this confusion? Did she herself want to be what she was to him?

And what was she to him, as he had just put it? Oh, that question he could always answer.

A spring evening. The air punctuated with scattered sounds. The voices of children playing in the streets coming from varying distances as if to show that the whole expanse is alive. And this vast expanse is Russia, his incomparable mother; famed far and wide, martyred, stubborn, extravagant, crazy, irresponsible, adored, Russia with her eternally splendid, and disastrous, and unpredictable adventures. Oh, how sweet to be alive! How good to be alive and to love life! Oh, the ever-present longing to thank life, thank existence itself, to thank them as one being to another being.

This was exactly what Lara was. You could not communicate with life and existence, but she was their representative, their expression, in her the inarticulate principle of existence became sensitive and capable of speech.

And all that he had just reproached her with in a moment of doubt was untrue, a thousand times untrue! Everything about her was perfect, flawless.

Tears of admiration and repentance filled his eyes. Opening the stove door, he poked the fire; he pushed the logs that were ablaze and had turned into pure heat to the back and brought forward into the draft those that were less incandescent. Leaving the door open, he sat before the open flames, delighting in the play of light and the warmth on his face and hands. The warmth and light brought him completely to his senses. He missed Lara unbearably and he longed for something that could bring him into touch with her at that very moment.

He drew her crumpled letter from his pocket. It was folded so that the back of the page he had read earlier was outside, and now he saw that there was something written on it. Smoothing it out, he read it by the dancing firelight:

"You surely know what's happened to your family. They are in Moscow. Tonia has had a little girl." After that several lines were crossed out, then: "I've crossed it out because it's silly to write about it. We'll talk our fill when we meet. I'm rushing out, I must get hold of a horse. I don't know what I'll do if I can't. It's so difficult with Katenka. . . . " The rest of the sentence was smudged and illegible.

"She got the horse from Samdeviatov," Yurii Andreievich reflected calmly. "If she had anything to conceal, she wouldn't have mentioned it."

8

When the stove was hot Yurii Andreievich closed the flue and had something to eat. After that he felt so sleepy that he lay down on the sofa without undressing and at once fell fast asleep. The loud, insolent noise of the rats behind the walls and the door did not reach him. He had two bad dreams, one after the other.

He was in Moscow in a room with a glass door. The door was locked. For greater safety he was keeping hold of it by the handle and pulling it toward himself. From the other side, his little boy, Sashenka, dressed in a sailor suit and cap, was knocking, crying and begging to be let in. Behind the child, splashing him and the door with its spray, there was a waterfall. It was making a tremendous noise. Either the water was pouring from a burst pipe (a usual occurrence in those days) or else the door was a barrier against some wild countryside, a mountain gorge filled with the sound of its raging torrent and the millennial cold and darkness of its caves.

The noise of the tumbling water terrified the boy. It drowned his cries, but Yurii Andreievich could see him trying, over and over again, to form the word "Daddy" with his lips.

Heartbroken, Yurii Andreievich longed with all his being to take the boy in his arms, press him to his chest, and run away with him as fast as his feet would carry him.

Yet, with tears pouring down his face he kept hold of the handle of the locked door, shutting out the child, sacrificing him to a false notion of honor, in the name of his alleged duty to another woman, who was not the child's mother and who might at any moment come into the room from another door.

He woke up drenched in sweat and tears. "I've got a fever, I am sick," he thought. "This isn't typhus. This is some sort of exhaustion that is taking the form of a dangerous illness—an illness with a crisis, it will be just like any serious infection, and the only question is which is going to win, life or death. But I'm too sleepy to think." He dropped off to sleep again.

He dreamed of a dark winter morning in a bustling Moscow street. Judging by the early morning traffic, the trolleys ringing their bells, and the yellow pools of lamplight on the gray snow-covered street, it was before the revolution.

He dreamed of a big apartment with many windows, all on the same side of the house, probably no higher than the third story, with drawn curtains reaching to the floor.

Inside, people were lying about asleep in their clothes like travellers, and the rooms were untidy like a railway car, with half-eaten legs and wings of roast chicken and other remnants of food scattered about on greasy bits of newspaper. The shoes that the many friends, relatives, callers, and homeless people, all sheltering in the apartment, had removed for the night, were standing in pairs on the floor. The hostess, Lara, in a dressing gown tied hastily around her waist, moved swiftly and silently from room to room, hurrying about her chores, and he was following her step by step, muttering clumsy irrelevant explanations and generally making a nuisance of himself. But she no longer had a moment to give him and took no notice of his mutterings except for turning to him now and then with a tranquil, puzzled look or bursting into her inimitable, candid, silvery laughter. This was the only form of intimacy that remained between them. And how distant, cold, and compellingly attractive was this woman to whom he had sacrificed all he had, whom he had preferred to everything, and in comparison with whom everything seemed to him worthless!

9

It was not he but something greater than himself that wept and sobbed in him, and shone in the darkness with bright, phosphorescent words. And with weeping soul, he too wept. He felt pity for himself.

"I am ill," he realized in intervals of clarity between sleep, and delirium, and unconsciousness. "I must have some form of typhus that isn't described in textbooks, that we didn't study at school. I ought to get myself something to eat or I'll die of starvation."

But the moment he tried to raise himself on his elbow he found that he was incapable of moving, and fainted or fell asleep.

"How long have I been lying here?" he wondered during one such interval of clarity. "How many hours? How many days? When I lay down it was early spring. But now the windows are so thick with hoarfrost that the room is dark."

In the kitchen, rats were rattling the plates, scurrying up the walls, and heavily flopping down and squealing in their disgusting contralto voices.

And he again fell asleep, and on awakening discovered that the snowy windows had filled with a pink light, glowing like red wine in crystal glasses. And he wondered whether it was dawn or dusk.

Once he thought he heard voices near him and was terrified, imagining that he was going mad. Crying with self-pity, he complained in a soundless whisper that Heaven had abandoned him. "Why hast Thou cast me off, O Light everlasting, and cast me down into the darkness of hell?"

Suddenly he realized that he was not delirious, that he no longer had his clothes on, that he had been washed and was in a clean shirt, lying not on the sofa but in a freshly made bed, and that sitting beside him, leaning over him, her hair mingling with his and her tears falling with his own, was Lara. He fainted with joy.

10

He had complained that Heaven had cast him off, but now the whole breadth of heaven leaned low over his bed, holding out two strong, white, woman's arms to him. His head swimming with joy, he fell into a bottomless depth of bliss as one who drops unconscious.

All his life he had been active, doing things about the house, looking after patients, thinking, studying, writing. How good it was to stop doing, struggling, thinking, to leave it all for a time to nature, to become her thing, her concern, the work of her merciful, wonderful, beauty-lavishing hands.

His recovery was rapid. Lara fed him, nursed him, surrounded him with her care, and her dazzling loveliness, her questions and answers, whispered in a warm, gentle voice, were always present.

Their subdued conversations, however casual, were as full of meaning as the dialogues of Plato.

Even more than by what they had in common, they were united by what separated them from the rest of the world. They were both equally repelled by what was tragically typical of modern man, his textbook admirations, his shrill enthusiasms, and the deadly dullness conscientiously preached and practiced by countless workers in the field of art and science in order that genius should remain in a great rarity.

Their love was great. Most people experience love without

becoming aware of the extraordinary nature of this emotion. But to them—and this made them exceptional—the moments when passion visited their doomed human existence like a breath of eternity were moments of revelation, of continually new discoveries about themselves and life.

11

"Of course you must go back to your family. I won't keep you a day more than necessary. But just look at what is going on. As soon as we became part of Soviet Russia we were sucked into its ruin. To keep going, they take everything from us. You have no idea of how much Yuriatin has changed while you were ill. Our supplies are sent to Moscow—for them it's a drop in the ocean, all these shipments simply vanish down a bottomless pit—and in the meantime nothing is left to us. There are no mails, there is no passenger service, all the trains are used for bread. There's a lot of grumbling going on in town, as there was before the Haida uprising, and once again, the Cheka is savagely putting down the slightest sign of discontent.

"How could you travel, weak as you are, nothing but skin and bones? Do you really imagine you could go on foot? You would never get there. When you are stronger, it will be different.

"I won't presume to give you advice, but in your place I would take a job for the time being. Work at your own profession—they'd like that. You might get something in the regional health service.

"You'll have to do something. Your father was a Siberian millionaire who committed suicide, your wife is the daughter of a local landowner and industrialist, you were with the partisans and you ran away. You can't get around it—you left the ranks of the revolutionary army, you're a deserter. Under no circumstances must you remain idle. I am not in a much better position myself. I'll have to do something too. I'm living on a volcano as it is."

"How do you mean? What about Strelnikov?"

"It's precisely because of him. I told you before that he has many enemies. Now that the Red Army is victorious those non-Party soldiers who got too near the top and knew too much are done for. Lucky if they're only thrown out and not killed so as to leave no trace. Pasha is particularly vulnerable; he is in very great danger. You know he was out in the East. I've heard he's run away. He's in hiding. They're hunting for him. But don't let's talk about it. I hate crying, and if I say another word about him I know I'll howl."

"You were very much in love with him? You still are?"

"I married him, he's my husband, Yurochka. He has a wonderful, upright, shining personality. I am very much at fault. It isn't that I ever did him any harm, it wouldn't be true to say that. But he is so outstanding, so big, he has such immense integrity—and I'm no good at all, I'm nothing in comparison. That's where my fault lies. But please let's not talk about it now. I'll tell you more some other time, I promise you I will.

"How lovely your Tonia is. Just like a Botticelli. I was there when she had her baby. We got on terribly well. But let's not talk about that either just at the moment!

"As I was saying, let's both get jobs. We'll go out to work every morning, and at the end of the month we'll collect our salaries in billions of rubles. You know, until quite recently the old Siberian bank notes were still valid. Then they were declared invalid and for a long time, all the time you were ill, we had no currency at all! Just imagine! Well, we managed somehow. Now they say a whole trainload of new bank notes has arrived, at least forty carfuls! They are printed on big sheets in two colors, red and blue, and divided into little squares like postage stamps. The blue squares are worth five million rubles each and the red ones ten. They are badly printed, they fade and the colors are smudged."

"Yes, I've seen that kind of money. It was put into circulation in Moscow just before we left."

12

"Why were you so long in Varykino? Is there anybody there? I thought there wasn't a soul, it was deserted. What kept you so long?"

"I was cleaning your house with Katenka. I thought you'd go

there first thing and I didn't want you to see it in the state it was in."

"Why, what kind of state is it in? Is it so bad?"

"It was untidy, dirty, and we put it straight."

"How evasively terse! I feel there's something you are not telling me. But just as you like, I won't try to get it out of you. Tell me about Tonia. What did they call the little girl?"

"Masha, in memory of your mother."

"Tell me all about them."

"Please, not now. I've told you, I still can't talk about it without crying."

"That Samdeviatov who lent you the horse, he's an interesting character, don't you think?"

"Very."

"I know him quite well, you know. He was in and out of the house when we lived there. It was all new to us and he helped us to settle in."

"I know, he told me."

"You must be great friends. Is he trying to help you, too?"

"He positively showers me with kindness! I don't know what I should do without him."

"I can imagine! I suppose you're on informal, comradely terms. Does he run after you much?"

"All the time! Naturally!"

"And you like him? Sorry. I shouldn't have asked you that. I've got no business to question you. That was going too far! I apologize."

"Oh, that's all right! I suppose what you really mean is, what kind of terms are we on? Is there anything more between us than friendship? Of course there isn't! He has done a tremendous amount for me, I am enormously in his debt, but if he gave me my weight in gold, if he gave his life for me, it wouldn't bring me a step nearer to him. I have always disliked men of that kind, I have nothing whatever in common with them. These resourceful, self-confident, masterful characters—in practical things they are invaluable, but in matters of feeling I can think of nothing more horrible than all this impertinent, male complacency! It certainly isn't my idea of life and love! More than that, morally Anfim reminds me of someone else, of someone infinitely more repulsive. It's his fault that I've become what I am."

"I don't understand. What do you think you are? What have you got in mind? Explain to me. You are the best person in the world."

"How can you, Yurochka! I am talking seriously, and you pay me compliments as though we were in a drawing room. What am I like? There's something broken in me, there's something broken in my whole life. I discovered life much too early, I was made to discover it, and I was made to see it from the very worst side—a cheap, distorted version of it—through the eyes of a self-assured, elderly parasite, who took advantage of everything and allowed himself whatever he fancied."

"I think I understand. I thought there was something. But wait a moment. I can imagine your suffering as a child, a suffering much beyond your years, the shock to your inexperience, a very young girl's sense of outrage. But all that is in the past. What I mean is that it isn't for you to make yourself unhappy about it now, it's for people who love you, people like myself. It's I who should be tearing my hair because I wasn't with you to prevent it, if it really makes you unhappy. It's a curious thing. I think I can be really jealous—deadly, passionately jealous—only of my inferiors, people with whom I have nothing in common. A rival whom I look up to arouses entirely different feelings in me. I think if a man whom I understood and liked were in love with the same woman as I am I wouldn't feel a grievance, or want to quarrel with him, I would feel a sort of tragic brotherhood with him. Naturally, I wouldn't dream of sharing the woman I loved. But I would give her up and my suffering would be something different from jealousy—less raw and angry. It would be the same if I came across an artist who was doing the same sort of thing as I do and doing it better. I would probably give up my own efforts, I wouldn't want to duplicate his, and there would be no point in going on if his were better.

"But that wasn't what we were talking about. I don't think I could love you so much if you had nothing to complain of and nothing to regret. I don't like people who have never fallen or stumbled. Their virtue is lifeless and of little value. Life hasn't revealed its beauty to them."

"It's this beauty I'm thinking of. I think that to see it your imagination has to be intact, your vision has to be childlike. That is what I was deprived of. I might have developed my own view of life if I hadn't, right from the beginning, seen it stamped in someone else's vulgar distortion. And that isn't all. It's because of the intrusion into my life, right at the start, of this immoral, selfish nonentity that when later on I married a man who was really big and remarkable, and who loved me and whom I loved, my marriage was destroyed."

"Wait a moment before you tell me about your husband. I am not jealous of him. I told you I can be jealous only of my inferiors, not of my equals. Tell me first about this other man."

"Which man?"

"This wrecker who spoiled your life. Who was he?"

"A fairly well-known Moscow lawyer. A friend of my father's. When Father died and we were very badly off he gave my mother financial help. He was unmarried, rich. I've probably made him sound a lot more interesting than he is by painting him so black. He couldn't be more ordinary. I'll tell you his name if you like."

"You needn't. I know it. I saw him once."

"Really?"

"In a hotel room, when your mother took poison. It was late at night. You and I were both still at school."

"Oh, I remember. You came with someone else. You stood in the shadow, in the hallway. I don't know if I would have remembered by myself, but I think you reminded me of it once, it must have been in Meliuzeievo."

"Komarovsky was there."

"Was he? Quite possible. It wasn't unusual for us to be in the same place. We often saw each other."

"Why are you blushing?"

"At the sound of Komarovsky's name coming from you. I'm no longer used to hearing it, I was taken by surprise."

"There was a school friend of mine who went with me that night, and this is what he told me there in the hotel. He recognized Komarovsky as a man he had happened to see once before. As a child, during a journey, this boy, Misha Gordon, witnessed the suicide of my father—the millionaire industrialist. They were in the same train. Father jumped deliberately from the moving train and was killed. He was accompanied on this journey by Komarovsky, who was his lawyer. He made Father drink, he got his business into a muddle, he brought him to the point of bankruptcy, and he drove him to suicide. It was his fault that my father killed himself and that I was left an orphan."

"It isn't possible! It's extraordinary! Can it really be true? So
he was your evil genius, too! It brings us even closer! It must be
predestination!"

"He is the man of whom I shall always be incurably, insanely
jealous."

"How can you say such a thing? It isn't just that I don't love
him—I despise him."

"Can you know yourself as well as that? Human nature, and
particularly woman's, is so mysterious and so full of contradictions. Perhaps there is something in your loathing that keeps
you in subjection to him more than to any man whom you love
of your own free will, without compulsion."

"What a terrible thing to say! And as usual, the way you put it
makes me feel that this thing, unnatural as it is, seems to be true.
But how horrible if it is!"

"Don't be upset. Don't listen to me. I only meant that I am
jealous of a dark, unconscious element, something irrational,
unfathomable. I am jealous of your toilet articles, of the drops of
sweat on your skin, of the germs in the air you breathe which
could get into your blood and poison you. And I am jealous of
Komarovsky, as if he were an infectious disease. Someday he
will take you away, just as certainly as death will someday
separate us. I know this must seem obscure and confused, but I
can't say it more clearly. I love you madly, irrationally,
infinitely."

13

"Tell me more about your husband—'One writ with me in sour
misfortune's book,' as Shakespeare says."

"Where did he say that?"

"In *Romeo and Juliet*."

"I told you a lot in Meliuzeievo when I was looking for him,
and then here, when I heard how his men arrested you and took
you to his train. I may have told you—or perhaps I only thought
I did—how I once saw him from a distance when he was getting
into his car. But you can imagine how many guards there were
around him! I found him almost unchanged. The same hand-

some, honest, resolute face, the most honest face I've ever seen in my life. The same manly, straightforward character, not a shadow of affectation or make-believe. And yet I did notice a difference, and it alarmed me.

"It was as if something abstract had crept into his face and made it colorless. As if a living human face had become an embodiment of a principle, the image of an idea. My heart sank when I noticed it. I realized that this had happened to him because he had handed himself over to a superior force, but a force that is deadening and pitiless and will not spare him in the end. It seemed to me that he was a marked man and that this was the seal of his doom. But perhaps I'm confused about it. Perhaps I'm influenced by what you said when you described your meeting with him. After all, in addition to what we feel for each other, I am influenced by you in so many ways!"

"Tell me about your life with him before the revolution."

"Very early, when I was still a child, purity became my ideal. He was the embodiment of it. You know we grew up almost in the same house. He, Galiullin, and I. As a little boy he was infatuated with me. He used almost to faint whenever he saw me. I probably shouldn't be talking this way. But it would be worse to pretend I didn't know. It was the kind of all-absorbing childish passion that a child conceals because his pride won't let him show it, but one look at his face is enough to tell you all about it. We saw a lot of each other. He and I were as different as you and I are alike. I chose him then and there in my heart. I decided that as soon as we were old enough I would marry this wonderful boy, and in my own mind I became engaged to him.

"You know it's extraordinary how gifted he is! His father was a signal man, or a crossing guard, I don't know which, and by sheer brains and hard work he reached, I was going to say the level, but it's more like the summit, of present academic knowledge in two fields—classics and mathematics! After all, that's something!"

"But then what spoiled your marriage, if you loved each other so much?"

"Ah, that's hard to answer. I'll try to tell you. But it's strange that I, an ordinary woman, should explain to you, who are so wise, what is happening to human life in general and to life in Russia and why families get broken up, including yours and mine. Ah, it isn't a matter of individuals, of being alike or different in temperament, of loving or not loving! All customs and traditions, all our way of life, everything to do with home and order, has crumbled into dust in the general upheaval and reorganization of society. The whole human way of life has been destroyed and ruined. All that's left is the naked human soul stripped to the last shred, for which nothing has changed because it was always cold and shivering and reaching out to its nearest neighbor, as cold and lonely as itself. You and I are like Adam and Eve, the first two people on earth who at the beginning of the world had nothing to cover themselves with—and now at the end of it we are just as naked and homeless. And you and I are the last remembrance of all that immeasurable greatness which has been created in the world in all the thousands of years between them and us, and it is in memory of all those vanished marvels that we live and love and weep and cling to one another."

14

She was silent for a while, then she went on more calmly:

"I'll tell you. If Strelnikov became Pashenga again, if he stopped his raging and rebelling; if time turned back; if by some miracle, somewhere, I could see the window of our house shining, the lamplight on Pasha's desk and his books, even if it were at the end of the earth—I would crawl to it on my knees. Everything in me would respond. I could never hold out against the call of the past, of loyalty. There is nothing I wouldn't sacrifice, however precious. Even you. Even our love, so carefree, so spontaneous, so natural. Oh, forgive me! I don't mean that. It isn't true!"

She threw herself into his arms, sobbing. But very soon she controlled herself and, wiping away her tears, said:

"Isn't it the same call of duty that drives you back to Tonia? Oh, God, how miserable we are! What will become of us? What are we to do?"

When she had recovered she went on:

"But I haven't answered your question about what it was that spoiled our happiness. I came to understand it very clearly afterward. I'll tell you. It isn't only our story. It has become the fate of many others."

"Tell me, my love, you who are so wise."

"We were married two years before the war. We were just beginning to make a life for ourselves, we had just set up our home, when the war broke out. I believe now that the war is to blame for everything, for all the misfortunes that followed and that hound our generation to this day. I remember my childhood well. I can still remember a time when we all accepted the peaceful outlook of the last century. It was taken for granted that you listened to reason, that it was right and natural to do what your conscience told you to do. For a man to die by the hand of another was a rare, an exceptional event, something quite out of the ordinary. Murders happened in plays, newspapers, and detective stories, not in everyday life.

"And then there was the jump from this peaceful, naïve moderation to blood and tears, to mass insanity, and to the savagery of daily, hourly, legalized, rewarded slaughter.

"I suppose one must always pay for such things. You must remember better than I do the beginning of disintegration, how everything began to break down all at once—trains and food supplies in towns, and the foundations of the family, and moral standards."

"Go on. I know what you'll say next. How well you see all these things. What a joy to listen to you!"

"It was then that untruth came down on our land of Russia. The main misfortune, the root of all the evil to come, was the loss of confidence in the value of one's own opinion. People imagined that it was out of date to follow their own moral sense, that they must all sing in chorus, and live by other people's notions, notions that were being crammed down everybody's throat. And then there arose the power of the glittering phrase, first the Tsarist, then the revolutionary.

"This social evil became an epidemic. It was catching. And it affected everything, nothing was left untouched by it. Our home, too, became infected. Something went wrong in it. Instead of being natural and spontaneous as we had always been, we began to be idiotically pompous with each other. Something showy, artificial, forced, crept into our conversation—you felt you had to be clever in a certain way about certain world-important themes. How could Pasha, who was so discriminat-

ing, so exacting with himself, who distinguished so unerringly
between reality and appearance, how could he fail to notice the
falsehood that had crept into our lives?

"And at this point he made his fatal, terrible mistake. He
mistook the spirit of the times, the social, universal evil, for a
private and domestic one. He listened to our clichés, to our
unnatural official tone, and he thought it was because he was
second-rate, a nonentity, that we talked like this. I suppose you
find it incredible that such trivial things could matter so much in
our married life. You can't imagine how important this was,
what foolish things this childish nonsense made him do.

"Nobody asked him to go to the war, he went because he
imagined himself a burden to us, so that we should be free of
him. That was the beginning of all his madness. Out of a sort of
misdirected, adolescent vanity he took offense at things at
which one doesn't take offense. He sulked at the course of
events. He quarrelled with history. To this day he is trying to
get even with it. That's what makes him so insanely defiant. It's
this stupid ambition that's driving him to his death. God, if I
could only save him!"

"How immensely pure and strong is your love for him! Go
on, go on loving him. I'm not jealous of him. I won't stand in
your way."

15

Summer came and went almost unnoticed. The doctor recovered. While planning to go to Moscow he took not one but
three temporary jobs. The rapid devaluation of money made it
difficult to make ends meet.

Every morning he got up at daybreak, left the house, and
walked down Merchant Street, past the "Giant" movie house as
far as the former printing shop of the Urals Cossack Army, now
renamed the Red Compositor. At the corner of City Street the
door of the town hall bore the notice "Complaints." He crossed
the square, turned into Buianovka Street, and coming to the
hospital went in through the back door to the out-patient
department of the Army Hospital, where he worked. This was
his main job.

Most of his way from Lara's to the hospital lay in the shadow of spreading trees, past curious little frame houses with steep roofs, decorated doors, and carved and painted patterns around the windows. The house next to the hospital, standing in its own garden, had belonged to Goregliadova, a merchant's wife. It was faced with glazed, diamond-cut tiles, like the ancient boyar houses in Moscow.

Three or four times a week Yurii Andreievich attended the board meetings of the Yuriatin Health Service in Miassky Street.

At the other end of town stood the former Institute of Gynecology, founded by Samdeviatov's father in memory of his wife, who had died in childbirth, now renamed the Rosa Luxemburg Institute, where Yurii Andreievich lectured on general pathology and one or two optional subjects as part of the new, shortened course of medicine and surgery.

Coming home at night, hungry and tired, he found Lara busy at her domestic chores, cooking or washing. In this prosaic, weekday aspect of her being, dishevelled, with her sleeves rolled and her skirts tucked up, she almost frightened him by her regal attractiveness, more breathtaking than if he had found her on the point of going to a ball, taller in high-heeled shoes and in a long, low-cut gown with a sweeping, rustling skirt.

She cooked or washed and used the soapy water to scrub the floors, or more quietly, less flushed, pressed and mended linen for the three of them. Or when the cooking, washing, and cleaning had all been got out of the way, she gave lessons to Katenka; or with her nose in her textbooks worked at her own political re-education, in order to qualify as a teacher at the new, reorganized school.

The closer this woman and her daughter became to him, the less he dared to think of them as family and the stricter was the control imposed on his thoughts by his duty to his own family and the pain of his broken faith. There was nothing offensive to Lara or Katenka in this limitation. On the contrary, this attitude on his part contained a world of deference that excluded every trace of vulgarity.

But the division in him was a sorrow and a torment, and he became accustomed to it only as one gets used to an unhealed and frequently reopened wound.

16

Two or three months went by. One day in October Yurii Andreievich said to Larisa Feodorovna:

"You know, it looks as if I'll be forced to resign from my jobs. It's always the same thing—it happens again and again. At first everything is splendid. 'Come along. We welcome good, honest work, we welcome ideas, especially new ideas. What could please us better? Do your work, struggle, carry on.'

"Then you find in practice that what they mean by ideas is nothing but words—claptrap in praise of the revolution and the regime. I'm sick and tired of it. And it's not the kind of thing I'm good at.

"I suppose they are right, from their point of view. Of course, I'm not on their side. Only I find it hard to reconcile myself to the idea that they are radiant heroes and that I am a mean wretch who sides with tyranny and obscurantism. Have you ever heard of Nikolai Vedeniapin?"

"Well, of course! Both before I met you and from what you've told me yourself. Sima Tuntseva often speaks of him, she's a follower of his. To my shame, I haven't read his books. I don't like purely philosophical works. I think a little philosophy should be added to life and art by way of seasoning, but to make it one's specialty seems to me as strange as eating nothing but horseradish. But I'm sorry, I've distracted you with my nonsense."

"No, actually it's very much what I think myself. Well, about my uncle, I'm supposed to be corrupted by his influence. One of my sins is a belief in intuition. And yet see how ridiculous: they all shout that I'm a marvellous diagnostician, and as a matter of fact it's true that I don't often make mistakes in diagnosing a disease. Well, what is this immediate grasp of a situation as a whole supposed to be if not the intuition they find so detestable?

"Another thing is that I am obsessed by the problem of mimicry, the outward adaptation of an organism to the color of its environment. I think this biological phenomenon can cast light on the problem of the relationship between the inward and the outward world.

"I dared to touch on this problem in my lectures. Immediately there was a chorus: 'Idealism, mysticism, Goethe's *Naturphilosophie*, neo-Schellingism.'

"It's time I got out. I'll stay on at the hospital until they throw me out, but I'll resign from the Institute and the Health Service. I don't want to worry you, but occasionally I have the feeling that they might arrest me any day."

"God forbid, Yurochka. It hasn't come to that yet, fortunately. But you are right. It wouldn't do any harm to be more careful. I've noticed that whenever a regime comes to power it goes through certain regular stages. In the first stage it's the triumph of reason, of the spirit of criticism, the fight against prejudice and so on.

"Then comes the second stage. The accent is all on the shady activities of the pretended sympathizers, the hangers-on. There is more and more suspicion—informers, intrigues, hatreds. And you are right—we are at the beginning of the second stage.

"We don't have to go far to find evidence of it. The local revolutionary court has had two new members transferred to it from Khodatskoie—two old political convicts from among the workers, Tiverzin and Antipov.

"They both know me perfectly well—in fact, one of them is my father-in-law. And yet it's only since their arrival, quite recently, that I've begun really to tremble for Katenka's and my life. They are capable of anything. Antipov doesn't like me. It would be quite like them to destroy me and even Pasha one of these days in the name of higher revolutionary justice."

The sequel to this conversation took place very soon. A search had been carried out by night at the widow Goregliadova's, at 48 Buianovka Street, next door to the hospital. A cache of arms had been found and a counterrevolutionary organization uncovered. Many people were arrested and the wave of searches and arrests continued. It was whispered that some of the suspects had escaped across the river. "Though what good will it do them?" people said. "There are rivers and rivers. Now the Amur, for instance, at Blagoveshchensk—you jump in and swim across and you are in China! That really is a river. That's quite a different matter."

"The air is full of threats," said Lara. "Our time of safety is over. They are sure to arrest us, you and me. And then what will become of Katenka? I am a mother, I can't let this misfortune happen, I must think of something. I must have a plan. It's driving me out of my mind."

"Let's try to think. Though what is there that we can do? Is it in our power to avert this blow? Isn't it a matter of fate?"

"We certainly can't escape, there's nowhere to go. But we could withdraw into the shadow, into the background. Go to Varykino, for instance. I keep thinking of the house there. It's very lonely and neglected, but we would be less in the way than here, we wouldn't attract so much attention. Winter is coming on. I wouldn't at all mind spending it there. By the time they got around to us we'd have gained a year of life; that's always something. Samdeviatov would be a link between us and the town. Perhaps he'd help us to go into hiding. What do you think? It's true, there isn't a soul, it's empty and desolate, at least it was when I was there in March. And they say there are wolves. It's rather frightening. But then people, anyway people like Tiverzin and Antipov, are more frightening than wolves."

"I don't know what to say. Haven't you been urging me to go to Moscow all this time, telling me not to put it off? That's easier now. I made inquiries at the station. Apparently they've stopped worrying about black-marketeers. Not everyone whose papers aren't in order gets taken off the train. They shoot less, they've got tired.

"It worries me that I've had no reply to my letters to Moscow. I ought to go there and see what's happening to them—you keep telling me so yourself. But then how am I to take what you say about Varykino? You surely wouldn't go to such an out-of-the-way place by yourself?"

"No, of course, without you it would be impossible."

"And yet you tell me to go to Moscow?"

"Yes, you should go."

"Listen. I'll tell you what, I've got a wonderful idea—let's go to Moscow, all three of us."

"To Moscow? You're mad! What should I do in Moscow? No, I have to stay, I must be near here. It's here that Pasha's fate will be decided. I must wait here and be within reach if he needs me."

"Well then, let's think about Katenka."

"I was talking about her with Sima—Sima Tuntseva, she comes to see me sometimes."

"Yes, I know, I've often seen her."

"I'm surprised at you. In your place I'd have fallen in love with her at once. I don't know where you men keep your eyes! She's such a marvel! Pretty, graceful, intelligent, well read, kind, clear-headed."

"Her sister gave me a haircut the day I arrived—Glafira, the seamstress."

"I know. They both live with their oldest sister, Avdotia, the one who's a librarian. They are a good honest working family. I thought of asking them—if it comes to the worst, if you and I are arrested—if they would look after Katenka. I haven't made up my mind yet."

"Only if there really isn't any other way out. Pray God, it won't come to that."

"They say Sima is a bit odd—not quite right in the head. It's true she is not quite normal, but that's only because she's so profound and original. She's not an intellectual, but she's phenomenally educated. You and she are extraordinarily alike in your views. I think I should be quite happy about Katenka if she brought her up."

17

Once again he had been to the station and had again come back without having accomplished anything. Everything was still undecided. He and Lara were faced with the unknown. The weather was cold and dark as before the first snow. The sky, particularly where large patches of it could be seen, as at intersections, had a wintry look.

When Yurii Andreievich came home, he found that Lara had a visitor, Sima. They were having a conversation that was more like a lecture Sima was delivering to her hostess. Yurii Andreievich did not want to be in their way. He also wanted to be alone a little. The women were talking in the next room. The door between the two rooms was open; through the curtain that hung to the floor he could hear all they were saying.

"I'll go on with my sewing but don't take any notice of it, Sima dear. I'm listening. I attended lectures on history and philosophy. Your way of thinking interests me very much. Moreover, it's a great relief to listen to you. We haven't slept

much the last few nights, worrying about Katenka. I know it's
my duty as her mother to see to it that she is safe if anything
happens to us. I ought to think it out calmly and sensibly, but
I'm not very good at that. It makes me sad to realize it. I am
depressed from exhaustion and sleeplessness. It steadies me to
listen to you. And then, it's going to snow any minute. It's
lovely when it's snowing to listen to long, intelligent talk. If you
glance out of the corner of your eye at the window when it's
snowing you always feel as if someone were coming to the door
across the yard, have you noticed? Go on, Sima dear. I'm
listening."

"Where did we leave off last time?"

Yurii Andreievich did not catch Lara's reply. He listened to
what Sima was saying:

"It's possible to use words such as 'culture,' 'epochs.' But
people understand them in so many different ways. Because
their meaning is ambiguous, I won't use them. I'll replace them
with other words.

"I would say that man is made up of two parts, of God and
work. Each succeeding stage in the development of the human
spirit is marked by the achievement over many generations of
an enormously slow and lengthy work. Such a work was
Egypt. Greece was another. The theology of the Old Testament
prophets was a third. The last in time, not yet superseded by
anything else and still being accomplished by all who are
inspired, is Christianity.

"To show you the completely new thing it brought into the
world in all its freshness—not as you know it and are used to it
but more simply, more directly—I should like to go over a few
extracts from the liturgy—only a very few, and abridged at that.

"Most liturgical texts bring together the concepts of the Old
and the New Testament and put them side by side. For instance,
the burning bush, the exodus from Egypt, the youths in the
fiery furnace, Jonah and the whale are presented as parallels to
the immaculate conception and the resurrection of Christ.

"Such comparisons bring out, very strikingly, I think, the
way in which the Old Testament is old and the Gospel is new. In
a number of texts Mary's motherhood is compared to the
crossing of the Red Sea by the Jews. For instance there is one
verse that begins: 'The Red Sea is the likeness of the virgin
bride,' and goes on to say that 'as the sea was impenetrable after

its crossing by the Israelites, the Immaculate One was incorrupt after the birth of Emmanuel.' That is to say, after the Jews crossed the Red Sea it became impassable, as before, and the Virgin after giving birth to our Lord was as immaculate as before. A parallel is drawn between the two events. What kind of events are they? Both are supernatural, both are recognized as miracles. What, then, was regarded as miraculous in each epoch—the ancient, primitive epoch and the later, post-Roman epoch which was far more advanced?

"In the first miracle you have a popular leader, the patriarch Moses, dividing the waters by a magic gesture, allowing a whole nation—countless numbers, hundreds of thousands of people—to go through, and when the last man is across the sea closes up again and submerges and drowns the pursuing Egyptians. The whole picture is in the spirit of antiquity—the elements obeying the magician, great jostling multitudes like Roman armies on the march, a people and a leader. Everything is visible, audible, overpowering.

"In the second miracle you have a girl—an everyday figure who would have gone unnoticed in the ancient world—quietly, secretly bringing forth a child, bringing forth life, bringing forth the miracle of life, the 'universal life,' as He was afterwards called. The birth of her child is not only a violation of human laws as interpreted by the scribes, since it was out of wedlock; it also contradicts the laws of nature. She gives birth not by virtue of a natural process but by a miracle, by an inspiration. And from now on, the basis of life is to be that inspiration which the Gospel strives to make the foundation of life, contrasting the commonplace with the unique, the week-day with the holiday, and repudiating all compulsion.

"What an enormously significant change! How did it come about that an individual human event, insignificant by ancient standards, was regarded as equal in significance to the migration of a whole people? Why should it have this value in the eyes of heaven?—For it is through the eyes of heaven that it must be judged, it is before the face of heaven and in the sacred light of its own uniqueness that it all takes place.

"Something in the world had changed. Rome was at an end. The reign of numbers was at an end. The duty, imposed by armed force, to live unanimously as a people, as a whole nation, was abolished. Leaders and nations were relegated to the past.

"They were replaced by the doctrine of individuality and freedom. Individual human life became the life story of God, and its contents filled the vast expanses of the universe. As it says in a liturgy for the Feast of the Annunciation, Adam tried to be like God and failed, but now God was made man so that Adam should be made God.

"I'll come back to this in a minute," said Sima. "But now I'd like to digress a little. With respect to the care of the workers, the protection of the mother, the struggle against the power of money, our revolutionary era is a wonderful, unforgettable era of new, permanent achievements. But as regards its interpretation of life and the philosophy of happiness that is being propagated, it's simply impossible to believe that it is meant to be taken seriously, it's such a comic survival of the past. If all this rhetoric about leaders and peoples had the power to reverse history, it would set us back thousands of years to the Biblical times of shepherd tribes and patriarchs. But fortunately this is impossible.

"Now a few words about Christ and Mary Magdalene—this isn't from the Gospel but from the prayers for one of the days in Holy Week, I think it's Tuesday or Wednesday. You know it all, Larisa Feodorovna, without me; I only want to remind you of something, I am not trying to teach you.

"As you know, the word 'passion' in Slavonic means in the first place suffering, the passion of Christ—'Christ entering upon His passion.' The liturgy also uses it in its later Russian connotation of 'lust' and 'vice.' 'My soul is enslaved by passions, I have become like the beasts of the field,' 'Being cast out of paradise, let us become worthy to be readmitted to it by mastering our passions,' and so on. It may be wrong of me, but I don't like the Lenten texts on the curbing of the senses and the mortification of the flesh. They are curiously flat and clumsy and without the poetry of other spiritual writings. I always think they were composed by fat monks. Not that I care if they themselves broke the rules and deceived other people or if they lived according to their conscience—it's not they that I'm concerned with, but with the actual content of these passages. All these acts of contrition give too much importance to various infirmities of the flesh and to whether it is fat or famished—it's repulsive. It seems to me to raise something dirty, unimportant, inconsequential, to a dignity that does not belong to it. Forgive me for all these digressions.

"I have always wondered why Mary Magdalene is mentioned on the very eve of Easter, just before the death and resurrection of Christ. I don't know the reason for it, but this reminder of what life is seems so timely at the moment of His taking leave of it and shortly before He rises again. Now listen to how the reminder is made—what genuine passion there is in it and what an uncompromising directness.

"There is some doubt as to whether this does refer to the Magdalene or to one of the other Marys, but anyway, she begs our Lord:

"'Unbind my debt as I unbind my hair.' It means: 'As I loosen my hair, do Thou release me from my guilt.' Could any expression of repentance, of the thirst to be forgiven, be more concrete, more tangible?

"And later on in the liturgy for the same day there is another, more detailed passage, and this time it almost certainly refers to Mary Magdalene.

"Again she repents in a terribly tangible way over her past, saying that every night her flesh burns because of her old, inveterate habits. 'For the night is to me the flaring up of lust, the dark, moonless zeal of sin.' She begs Christ to accept her tears of repentance and be moved by the sincerity of her sighs, so that she may dry His most pure feet with her hair— reminding Him that in the rushing waves of her hair Eve took refuge when she was overcome with fear and shame in paradise. 'Let me kiss Thy most pure feet and water them with my tears and dry them with the hair of my head, which covered Eve and sheltered her in its rushing waves when she was afraid in the cool of the day in paradise.' And immediately after all this about her hair, she exclaims: 'Who can fathom the multitude of my sins or the depths of Thy mercy?' What familiarity, what equality between God and life, God and the individual, God and a woman!"

18

Yurii Andreievich had come home from the station tired. It was his day off, and usually he slept enough that day to last him the nine others of the ten-day week. He sat sprawling on the sofa, occasionally half reclining or stretching full length. But although he listened to Sima through a mist of oncoming drowsiness, her reflections delighted him. "Of course, she's taken it all from Uncle Nikolai," he thought. "But how intelligent she is, how talented."

He got up and went to the window. It looked out on the yard, like the window of the room next door from which only unintelligible whispers could now be heard.

The weather was getting worse, and it was growing dark in the yard. Two magpies flew in from the street and fluttered around looking for a place to settle, their feathers ruffled by the wind. They perched on the lid of the trash bin, flew up onto the fence, flew down to the ground, and walked about the yard.

"Magpies mean snow," thought the doctor. At the same moment Sima said aloud in the other room:

"Magpies mean news. You'll have guests, or else a letter."

A little later someone pulled the handle of the doorbell, which Yurii Andreievich had mended a few days earlier. Lara came out from behind the curtain and walked swiftly through to the hall to open the door. Yurii Andreievich heard her talking with Sima's sister Glafira.

"You've come for your sister? Yes, she's here."

"No, I didn't come for her, though we might as well go home together if she is ready. I've brought a letter for your friend. It's lucky for him that I once had a job at the post office. I don't know how many hands it's been through, it's from Moscow and it's been five months on the way. They couldn't find the addressee. At last they thought of asking me and I knew, of course—he once came to me for a haircut."

The long letter, written on many sheets of paper, crumpled and soiled in its tattered envelope, which had been opened at the post office, was from Tonia. The doctor found it in his hands without knowing how it had got there; he had not noticed Lara handing it to him. When he began reading it he was still conscious of being in Yuriatin, in Lara's house, but gradually, as he read on, he lost all realization of it. Sima came out, greeted him, and said goodbye; he said the right things automatically but paid no attention to her and never noticed when she left the house. Gradually he forgot more and more completely where he was or what surrounded him.

"Yura," Antonina Alexandrovna wrote, "do you know that

we have a daughter? We have christened her Masha in memory of your mother, Maria Nikolaievna.

"Now something entirely different. Several prominent people, professors who belonged to the Cadet Party and Right-wing Socialists, Miliukov, Kizevetter, Kuskov, and several others including your Uncle Nikolai, my father, and the rest of us, are being deported abroad.

"This is a misfortune, especially in your absence, but we must accept it and thank God that our exile takes so mild a form when at this terrible time things could have been so much worse for us. If you were here, you would come with us. But where are you? I am sending this letter to Antipova's address, she'll give it to you if she finds you. I am tortured by not knowing if the exit permit we are getting as a family will be extended to you later on, when, if God is willing, you are found. I have not given up believing that you are alive and that you will be found. My loving heart tells me that this is so, and I trust it. Perhaps by then, by the time you reappear, conditions in Russia will be milder and you will manage to get a separate visa for yourself and we shall all be together once again in the same place. But as I write this, I don't believe in the possibility of such happiness.

"The whole trouble is that I love you and that you don't love me. I keep trying to discover the meaning of this judgment on me, to interpret it, to justify it. I look into myself, I go over our whole life together and everything I know about myself, and I can't find the beginning, and I can't remember what it is I did or how I brought this misfortune on myself. I have a feeling that you misjudge me, that you take an unkind view of me, that you see me as in a distorting mirror.

"As for me, I love you. If only you knew how much I love you! I love all that is unusual in you, the good with the bad, and all the ordinary traits of your character, whose extraordinary combination is so dear to me, your face ennobled by your thoughts, which otherwise might not seem handsome, your great gifts and intelligence which, as it were, have taken the place of the will that is lacking. All this is dear to me, and I know no man who is better than you.

"But listen, do you know what? Even if you were not so dear to me, even if I did not like you so much, even then the distressing truth of my coldness would not have been disclosed to me, even then I would have believed that I love you. Out of sheer terror before the humiliating, destructive punishment which failure to love is, I would unconsciously have shunned the realization that I do not love you. Neither I nor you would ever have learned it. My own heart would have concealed it from me, for failure to love is almost like murder and I would have been incapable of inflicting such a blow on anyone.

"Nothing is definitely settled yet, but we are probably going to Paris. I'll be in those distant lands where you were taken as a child and where Father and my uncle were brought up. Father sends you his greetings. Sasha has grown a lot, he is not particularly good-looking but he is a big, strong boy and whenever we speak of you he cries bitterly and won't be comforted. I can't go on. I can't stop crying. Well, goodbye. Let me make the sign of the cross over you and bless you for all the years ahead, for the endless parting, the trials, the uncertainties, for all your long, long, dark way. I am not blaming you for anything. I am not reproaching you, do as you please with your life, I'll be happy if all is well with you.

"Before we left the Urals—what a terrible and fateful place it turned out to be for us—I got to know Larisa Feodorovna fairly well. I am thankful to her for being constantly at my side at a difficult time and for helping me through my confinement. I must honestly admit that she is a good person, but I don't want to be a hypocrite—she is my exact opposite. I was born to make life simple and to look for sensible solutions; she, to complicate it and create confusion.

"Farewell, I must stop. They have come for the letter, and it's time I packed. Oh, Yura, Yura, my dear, my darling, my husband, the father of my children, what is happening to us? Do you realize that we'll never, never see each other again? Now I've written it down, do you realize what it means? Do you understand, do you understand? They are hurrying me and it's as if they had come to take me to my death. Yura! Yura!"

Yurii Andreievich looked up from the letter with absent, tearless eyes, dry with grief, ravaged by suffering. He could see nothing around him, he was not conscious of anything.

Outside it was snowing. The wind swept the snow aside, ever faster and thicker, as if it were trying to catch up with something, and Yurii Andreievich stared ahead of him out of the window, as if he were not looking at the snow but were still reading Tonia's letter and as if what flickered past him were not small dry snow crystals but the spaces between the small black letters, white, white, endless, endless.

Involuntarily he groaned and clutched his breast. He felt he was going to faint, hobbled the few steps to the sofa, and fell down on it unconscious.

CHAPTER FOURTEEN

Return to Varykino

1

Winter had settled in. It was snowing hard as Yurii Andreievich walked back from the hospital. Lara met him in the hall.

"Komarovsky is here," she said in a low, hoarse voice. She stood looking bewildered as if she had been struck.

"Where? Here?"

"No, of course not. He came this morning and said he would come back tonight. He'll be here soon. He wants to have a word with you."

"Why has he come?"

"I didn't understand all he said. He said he was going to the Far East and that he had come out of his way to see us. Particularly to see you and Pasha. He talked a great deal about both of you. He insists that we are in mortal danger, all three of us, you and Pasha and I. And that he alone can save us, provided we do as he says."

"I will go out. I don't want to see him."

Lara burst into tears and tried to throw herself at his feet and clasp his knees, but he forced her to get up.

"Please don't go, for my sake," she implored him. "It isn't that I'm frightened of being alone with him, but it's so painful.

Spare me from having to see him alone. Besides, he is practical, experienced—he might really have some advice to give us. Your aversion for him is natural, but please put your feelings aside. Don't go."

"What is the matter with you, darling? Don't be so upset. What are you trying to do? Don't fall on your knees. Get up now, and cheer up. You really must get rid of this obsession— he's frightened you for life. You know I'm with you. I'll kill him if necessary, if you tell me to."

Night fell about half an hour later. It was completely dark. It was half a year now since all the ratholes had been stopped up. Yurii Andreievich watched for new ones, plugging them up in time. They also kept a big, fluffy tomcat who spent his time in immobile contemplation, looking enigmatic. The rats were still in the house, but they were now more cautious.

Waiting for Komarovsky, Larisa Feodorovna cut some slices of rationed black bread and put a plate with a few boiled potatoes on the table. They had decided to receive him in the old dining room, which they still used for their meals. The large, heavy, dark oak table and sideboard were part of its original furnishings. Standing on the table was a bottle of castor oil with a wick in it which they used as a portable lamp.

Komarovsky came in out of the dark December night covered with snow. Lumps of it fell from his hat, coat, and galoshes and melted into puddles on the floor. His mustache and beard, plastered with snow, made him look like a clown. (He had been clean-shaven in the old days.) He wore a well-preserved suit with striped, well-creased trousers. Before greeting his hosts he spent a long time combing his rumpled, glistening hair with a pocket comb and drying his mustache and eyebrows with a handkerchief. Then, silently and with a solemn expression, he stretched out both his hands—the left one to Larisa Feodorovna and the right one to Yurii Andreievich.

"We'll assume that we are old acquaintances," he said to Yurii Andreievich. "I was a great friend of your father's, as you probably know. He died in my arms. I keep looking at you to see if there is any likeness. But I don't think you take after him. He was an expansive man, spontaneous and impulsive. You must be more like your mother. She was gentle, a dreamer."

"Larisa Feodorovna asked me to see you. She said you had some business with me. I agreed, but our meeting is not of my choice, and I don't consider that we are acquainted. So shall we get on with it? What is it you want?"

"I am so happy to see you both, my dears. I understand everything, absolutely everything. Forgive my boldness, but you are wonderfully well suited to each other. A perfect match."

"I'll have to interrupt you. Kindly don't interfere in what doesn't concern you. We haven't asked for your sympathy. You forget yourself."

"Don't be so touchy, young man. Perhaps after all you do take after your father. He used to lose his temper just like that. Well, my children, with your permission I offer you my best wishes. Unfortunately, however, you really are children—not just in a manner of speaking—completely ignorant and thought-less children. In two days here I've learned more about you than you know or suspect about yourselves. Without knowing it, you are walking on the brink of a precipice. Unless you do something about it, the days of your freedom and perhaps even of your lives are numbered.

"There exists a certain Communist style, Yurii Andreievich. Few people measure up to it. But no one flouts that way of life and thought as openly as you do. Why you have to flirt with danger, I can't imagine. You are a living mockery of that whole world, a walking insult to it. If at least your past were your own secret—but there are people from Moscow who know you inside out. Neither of you are at all to the liking of the local priests of Themis. Comrades Antipov and Tiverzin are busy sharpening their claws, ready to pounce on Larisa Feodorovna and you.

"However, you are a man, Yurii Andreievich, you are your own master, and you have a perfect right to gamble with your life if you feel like it. But Larisa Feodorovna is not a free agent. She is a mother, she has a child's life in her hands, and she can't go about with her head in the clouds.

"I wasted all my morning trying to get her to take the situation seriously. She wouldn't listen to me. Will you use your influence? She has no right to play with her daughter's safety. She must not disregard my arguments."

"I've never in my life forced my views on anyone. Certainly not on those who are close to me. Larisa Feodorovna is free to listen to you or not as she thinks fit. It's her business. Apart from that, I have no idea what you are talking about. I haven't heard what you call your arguments."

"Really, you remind me more and more of your father—just

as intractable. Well, I'll tell you. But it's a fairly complicated business, so you'll have to be patient with me and not interrupt.

"Big changes are being planned at the top. Yes, really, I have it from a most reliable source and you can take it that it's true. What they have in mind is to take a more democratic line, make a concession to legality, and this will come about quite soon.

"But just because of it, the punitive organs that are to be abolished will be in all the greater hurry to settle their local accounts before the end, and they will be all the more savage. You are marked for destruction, Yurii Andreievich. Your name is on the list—I am telling you this in all seriousness, I've seen it myself. You must think of saving yourself before it is too late.

"But all this is by way of introduction. I am coming to the point.

"Those political forces that are still faithful to the Provisional Government and the disbanded Constituent Assembly are concentrating in the Maritime Province on the Pacific coast. Deputies to the Duma, the more prominent members of the old Zemstvos, and other public figures, businessmen and industrialists, are getting together. The remnants of the armies that fought against the Reds are being concentrated there.

"They intend to form a Far Eastern republic, and the Soviet Government winks at it, because at the moment it would suit it to have a buffer between Red Siberia and the outside world. The republic is to have a coalition government. More than half the seats, at the insistence of Moscow, will go to Communists. When it suits them, they will stage a *coup d'état* and bring the republic to heel. The plan is quite transparent, but it gives us a certain breathing space; and we must make the most of it.

"At one time before the revolution I used to look after the affairs of the Merkulovs, the Arkharov Brothers, and several other banks and trading firms in Vladivostok. They know me there, and an emissary came to see me on behalf of the shadow cabinet, to offer me the post of Minister of Justice in the future government. This was done secretly, but with unofficial Soviet approval. I accepted and I am on my way there now. All I've just told you is happening with the tacit consent of the Soviet Government, but not so openly that it would be wise to talk much about it.

"I can take you and Larisa Feodorovna with me. From there, you can easily get a boat and join your family overseas. You know, of course, that they have been deported. It made a lot of noise; the whole of Moscow is still talking about it.

"I have promised Larisa Feodorovna to save Strelnikov. As a member of an independent government recognized by Moscow, I can look for him in eastern Siberia and help him to cross over into our autonomous region. If he does not succeed in escaping, I'll suggest that he should be exchanged for someone who is in Allied custody and is valuable to the Moscow Government."

Larisa Feodorovna had followed Komarovsky's explanation with difficulty, but when he came to the arrangements for the safety of the doctor and of Strelnikov, she pricked up her ears. Blushing a little, she said:

"You see, Yurochka, how important all this is for you and for Pasha?"

"You are too trusting, my dear. You can't take a half-formed plan for an accomplished fact. I don't say Victor Ippolitovich is deliberately misleading us, but so far he has only told us about castles in the air. For my part," he said, turning to Komarovsky, "thank you for the interest you take in my affairs, but you surely don't imagine that I am going to let you run them? As for Strelnikov, Lara will have to think it over."

"All it comes down to," said Lara, "is whether we go with him or not. You know perfectly well I wouldn't go without you."

Komarovsky sipped the diluted alcohol that Yurii Andreievich had brought from the hospital, ate boiled potatoes, and became more and more tipsy.

2

It was getting late. Every time the wick was trimmed it spluttered and burned brightly, lighting up the room, then the flame died down and the shadows returned. The hosts were sleepy, they wanted to talk things over by themselves and go to bed, but Komarovsky stayed on. His presence was oppressive, as was the sight of the heavy oak sideboard and the December darkness outside the windows.

He was not looking at them but over their heads, his glazed eyes staring at some distant point and his drowsy, slurred voice grinding on and on, tedious and interminable. His latest hobbyhorse was the Far East. He was explaining the political importance of Mongolia. Yurii Andreievich and Larisa Feodorovna, who were not interested in the subject, had missed the point at which he had got onto it, and this made his explanations even more boring. He was saying:

"Siberia—truly a New America, as it is often called—has immense possibilities. It is the cradle of Russia's future greatness, the gauge of our progress toward democracy and political and economic health. Still more pregnant with future possibilities is our great Far Eastern neighbor—Outer Mongolia. What do you know about it? You yawn and blink shamelessly, and yet Mongolia has nearly a million square miles and untold mineral wealth; it is a virgin land that tempts the greed of China, of Japan, and of the United States. They are all ready to snatch at it to the detriment of our Russian interests—interests that have been recognized by all our rivals, whenever there has been a division of that remote quarter of the globe into spheres of influence.

"China exploits the feudal-theocratic backwardness of Mongolia through her influence over the lamas and other religious dignitaries. Japan backs the local princes—the *hoshuns*. Red Russia has found an ally in the Revolutionary Association of Insurgent Mongolian Herdsmen. I myself would like to see a really prosperous Mongolia with a freely elected government. What should interest you personally is that once you are across the Mongolian frontier, the world is at your feet—you are as free as a bird."

His wordy dissertation got on Larisa Feodorovna's nerves. Finally, bored to tears and utterly tired, she held out her hand to him and said abruptly and with undisguised hostility:

"It's late and it's time for you to go. I am sleepy."

"I hope you aren't going to be so inhospitable as to throw me out at this hour of the night! I don't believe I can find my way—I don't know the town and it's pitch dark."

"You should have thought of that earlier, instead of sitting on and on. No one asked you to stay so late."

"Why are you so sharp with me? You didn't even ask me if I have anywhere to stay."

"It doesn't interest me in the slightest. You are perfectly well able to look after yourself. If you are angling for an invitation to spend the night, I certainly won't put you in the room where we and Katenka sleep, and the other rooms are full of rats."

"I don't mind them."

"Well, have it your way."

3

"What is wrong, darling? You don't sleep for nights on end, you don't touch your food, you go about all day looking like a maniac. You are always brooding about something. What is bothering you? You mustn't let your worries get the better of you."

"Izot, the watchman from your hospital, has been around again—he is having an affair with the laundress downstairs. So he dropped in and gave me a cheerful piece of news! 'It's terribly secret,' he said. 'It's jail for your friend. Any day now. And then it'll be your turn, poor thing.' 'How do you know?' I asked him. 'Oh, it's quite certain, I heard it from a friend who works at the Comics.' Of course, what he means by that is the Executive Committee. That's what he calls the Comics." They both burst out laughing.

"He is quite right," said Yurii Andreievich. "The danger has caught up with us and it's time we vanished. The problem is where. There is no question of going to Moscow—we couldn't make the arrangements for the journey without attracting attention. We must slip away so that nobody sees us go. Do you know, my love, we'll do what you thought of in the first place, we'll go to Varykino and drop out of sight. Let's go there for a week or two or a month."

"Thank you, thank you, my dear. Oh, how glad I am! I understand how much you dislike the idea. But we wouldn't live in your house. You couldn't possibly face that—the sight of the empty rooms, the self-reproach, the comparisons with the past. How well I know what it means to build one's happiness on the sufferings of others, to trample on what is dear to one, and holy. I'd never accept such a sacrifice from you. But there is no question of that. Your house is in such a state that it would be difficult to make the rooms fit to live in, anyway. I was thinking of the house where the Mikulitsyns lived."

"All that is true enough, and I am grateful to you for being so considerate. But wait a minute. I keep meaning to ask you and forgetting. What has happened to Komarovsky? Is he still here or is he gone? Since I quarrelled with him and threw him out I've heard nothing more of him."

"I don't know anything either. But who cares! What do you want with him?"

"I have come to think that perhaps we shouldn't have rejected his proposal outright—I mean both of us. We are not in the same position. You have your daughter to think of. Even if you wanted to share my fate, you'd have no right to do it.

"But about Varykino. Of course, to go to that wilderness in winter, without food, without strength or hope—it's utter madness. But why not, my love! Let's be mad, if there is nothing except madness left to us. We'll forget our pride once more and beg Samdeviatov to lend us a horse. And we'll ask him, or not even him but the speculators who depend on him, to let us have flour and potatoes on credit, for what our credit is still worth. And we'll persuade him not to take advantage of the favor he's doing us by coming to see us at once, but to wait until later—not to come until he needs his horse. Let's be alone for a while. Let's go, my love. And we'll cut and use more logs in a week than a careful housewife would use in a year in peaceful times.

"And once again, forgive me for my confused way of speaking. How I wish I could talk with you without being so stupidly solemn! But after all, it's true that we haven't any choice. Call it what you like, death is really knocking at our door. Our days are really numbered. So at least let us take advantage of them in our own way. Let us use them up saying goodbye to life, being together for the last time before we are parted. We'll say goodbye to everything we hold dear, to the way we look at things, to the way we've dreamed of living and to what our conscience has taught us, and to our hopes and to each other. We'll speak to one another once again the secret words we speak at night, great and pacific like the name of the Asian ocean. It's not for nothing that you stand at the end of my life, my hidden, forbidden angel, under the skies of wars and turmoil, you who arose at its beginning under the peaceful skies of childhood.

"That night, as a girl in a dark brown school uniform, in the half shadow of the hotel room, you were exactly as you are now, and just as breathtakingly beautiful.

"Often since then I have tried to define and give a name to the enchantment that you communicated to me that night, that faint glow, that distant echo, which later permeated my whole being and gave me a key to the understanding of everything in the world.

"When you rose out of the darkness of that room, like a shadow in a schoolgirl's dress, I, a boy who knew nothing about you, understood who you were, with all the tormenting intensity which responded in me: I realized that this scraggy, thin little girl was charged, as with electricity, with all the femininity in the world. If I had touched you with so much as the tip of my finger, a spark would have lit up the room and either killed me on the spot or charged me for the whole of my life with magnetic waves of sorrow and longing. I was filled to the brim with tears, I cried and glowed inwardly. I was mortally sorry for myself, a boy, and still more sorry for you, a girl. My whole being was astonished and asked: If it is so painful to love and to be charged with this electric current, how much more painful must it be to be a woman and to be the current, and to inspire love.

"There—at last I've said it. Such a thing can drive you mad. It expresses my very being."

Larisa Feodorovna lay dressed at the edge of her bed. She was not feeling well, and had curled up and covered herself with a shawl. Yurii Andreievich sat on a chair beside her, speaking quietly, with long pauses. Sometimes she raised herself on her elbow, propped her chin on her hand, and gazed at him, her lips parted. At other times she buried her head in his shoulder and cried silently with joy, without noticing her tears. At last she leaned out of bed, put her arms around him, and whispered happily:

"Yurochka! Yurochka! How wise you are! You know everything, you divine everything, Yurochka, you are my strength and my refuge, God forgive me the blasphemy. Oh, I am so happy. Let's go, my darling, let's go. Out there I'll tell you something I have on my mind."

He decided that she was referring to pregnancy, probably a false pregnancy, and he said: "I know."

4

They left town on the morning of a gray winter day. It was a weekday. People in the streets were going about their business; there were many familiar faces. At the squares, women who had no wells in their yards were queueing up for water at the old pumps, their yokes and buckets on the ground beside them. The doctor drove around them carefully, checking Samdeviatov's spirited, smoky-yellow horse. The sleigh kept gliding off the slope of the street, icy with splashed water, onto the sidewalks and hitting lampposts and curbstones.

Galloping at full tilt, they caught up with Samdeviatov, who was walking down the street, and swept past him without looking back to see if he had recognized them and his horse, or whether he had anything to say to them. A little farther on they passed Komarovsky, and again swept by without a greeting.

Glafira Tuntseva shouted to them from across the street: "What lies people tell! They said you had left yesterday. Going for potatoes?" and signalling that she could not hear what they replied waved them goodbye.

They slowed down for Sima, and this was on an awkward slope where it was impossible to stop; the horse kept pulling at the reins. Sima, muffled from head to foot in several shawls and looking as stiff as a log, hobbled out into the middle of the street to say goodbye and wish them a good journey.

"When you come back we must have a talk," she said to Yurii Andreievich.

At last they left the town behind. Although the doctor had been on this road in winter, he mostly remembered it in its summer aspect and hardly recognized it now.

They had pushed their sacks of food and other bundles deep into the hay in the front of the sleigh and had tied them down with rope. Yurii Andreievich drove either kneeling upright on the floor of the sleigh like the local peasants or sitting with his legs in Samdeviatov's felt boots hanging over the side.

In the afternoon when, as usual in winter, the day seemed on the point of ending long before sunset, Yurii Andreievich began to whip the horse mercilessly. It shot forward like an arrow. The sleigh pitched and tossed on the uneven road, like a ship in a storm. Lara and Katia were bundled up in their fur coats so that they could hardly move. Swinging around corners and bumping over ruts, they rolled from side to side and down into the hay like sacks, laughing themselves sick. Sometimes the doctor drove into the snowy banks on purpose, for a joke, and harmlessly tipped them all out into the snow. After being dragged for a few yards by the reins he stopped the horse, righted the sleigh, and was pummelled by Lara and Katia, who climbed back, scolding and laughing.

"I'll show you the place where I was stopped by the partisans," the doctor told them when they were at some distance from the town, but he was unable to keep his promise because the winter bareness of the woods, the dead quiet, and the emptiness all around changed the country beyond recognition. "Here it is," he soon shouted, mistaking the first of the Moreau & Vetchinkin signs, which stood in a field, for the one in the forest where he was captured. When they galloped past the second, still in its old place in the thicket at the Sakma crossroads, it was indistinguishable from the dazzling lacework of hoarfrost that made the forest look like black and silver filigree, so that they never saw it.

It was still daylight when they swept into Varykino, and as the Zhivagos' house came first they stopped in front of it. They burst in like robbers, hurrying because it would soon be dark. But inside it was dark already, so that Yurii Andreievich never saw half the destruction and abomination. Part of the furniture he remembered was still there; Varykino was deserted and there was no one to complete the damage. He could see no personal belongings; but as he had not been there when his family left he could not tell how much they had taken with them. In the meantime Lara was saying:

"We must hurry. It will be dark in a moment. We haven't time to stand about thinking. If we are to stay here, the horse must go into the barn, the food into the hallway, and we must fix this room for ourselves. But I'm against it. We talked it all out before. It will be painful for you and therefore also for me. What was this room, your bedroom? No, the nursery. There's your son's crib. It would be too small for Katia. On the other hand, the windows are whole, there are no cracks in the walls or ceiling, and the stove is marvellous—I admired it last time I came. So if you insist on our staying here—though I am against it—I'll get out of my coat and set to work at once. The first thing is to get the stove going, and to stoke and stoke and stoke, we'll have to keep it going all the time for at least twenty-four hours. But what is it, my darling? You haven't answered."

"In a moment. I'm all right. I'm sorry. . . . No, perhaps we'd better have a look at the Mikulitsyns' house."

They drove on.

5

The Mikulitsyns' door was padlocked. Yurii Andreievich wrenched off the lock together with its screws and splintered wood, and here again they rushed in hurriedly, going straight to the inner rooms without taking off their coats, hats, and felt boots.

They were immediately struck by the tidiness of certain parts of the house, particularly of Mikulitsyn's study. Someone must have been living here until recently, but who? Had it been any of the Mikulitsyns, where had they gone, and why had they put a padlock on the door instead of using their keys? Furthermore, if the Mikulitsyns had been here continuously for long stretches, wouldn't the whole house have been tidy and not just some of the rooms? Everything spoke of an intruder, but who could it have been? Neither the doctor nor Lara worried about the mystery. They did not try to solve it. There were plenty of half-looted houses now, and plenty of fugitives. "Some White officer on the run," they told each other. "If he comes we'll make some arrangement."

Once again, as so long before, Yurii Andreievich stood spellbound in the door of the study, so spacious and comfortable with its large, convenient table by the window. And once again he thought that such austere surroundings would be conducive to patient, fruitful work.

Among the outbuildings in the yard was the stable adjoining the barn, but it was locked and Yurii Andreievich did not bother to break in, since in any case it might not be fit to use. The horse could spend the night in the barn, which opened easily. He unharnessed the horse and when it had cooled down gave it water which he had got at the well. He had meant to give it the hay he had brought along, but it had been trampled to rubbish under their feet. Luckily, there was enough of it in the large loft over the barn.

They lay down without undressing, using their fur coats for blankets, and fell into a deep, sound, blissful sleep, like children after running about and playing all day.

6

From the moment they got up, Yurii Andreievich kept glancing at the table standing so temptingly by the window. His fingers itched for paper and pen. But he put off writing until the evening, until after Lara and Katia would have gone to bed. Until then he would have his hands full, even if no more than two of the rooms were to be made habitable.

In looking forward to the evening he had no important work in mind. It was merely that the passion to write possessed him.

He had to scribble something. For a beginning, he would put down old unwritten thoughts, just to get him into trim. Later, he hoped, if he and Lara managed to stay on, there would be time for undertaking something new, important.

"Are you busy? What are you doing?"

"Stoking and stoking. What is it?"

"I want a tub to wash the linen in."

"We'll run out of logs in three days if we go on using them at this rate. I must have a look in our old woodshed, there might be some left—who knows? If there are, I'll bring them over. I'll do that tomorrow. A tub, you said. I'm sure I've seen one somewhere, I can't think where."

"So have I, and I can't think where either. It must have been somewhere it had no business to be, that's why I forgot. Well, never mind. Remember, I'm heating a lot of water for cleaning up. What's left I'll use for laundering some of Katia's and my things. You might as well give me your laundry too. We'll have baths in the evening, when we've settled in, before we go to bed."

"Thank you. I'll get my things now. I've moved all the heavy furniture away from the walls, as you wanted it."

"Good. I'll use the dish-washing basin for the laundry, since we can't find the tub. But it's greasy, I'll have to scrub it."

"As soon as the stove is properly stoked I'll go through the rest of the drawers. I keep finding more things in the desk and the chest—soap, matches, paper, pencils, pens, ink. And the lamp on the table is full of kerosene. I am sure the Mikulitsyns didn't have any, it must come from somewhere else."

"What luck! It's our mysterious lodger. Just like something out of Jules Verne. But here we are gossiping again, and my water's boiling."

They bustled and dashed about from room to room, their hands never still or empty for a moment, running into one another and stumbling over Katenka, who was always under their feet. She drifted about, getting in the way of their work and sulking when they scolded her. She shivered and complained of the cold.

"These poor modern children," thought the doctor, "victims of our gypsy life, wretched little fellow wanderers." Aloud he said:

"Cheer up, girl. You can't be cold, that's nonsense, the stove is red hot."

"The stove may be feeling warm but I'm cold."

"Well then, you'll have to be patient till this evening. I'll get a huge blaze going and you heard Mama say she'll give you a hot bath. And now you play with these—catch." He got all Liberius's old toys out of the chilly storeroom and dumped them on the floor, some whole, some broken, blocks, trains, and locomotives, boards with squares and pictures or numbers on them for games with dice and counters.

"What can you be thinking of, Yurii Andreievich?" Katia protested like a grown-up. "They aren't mine. And they are for a baby. I'm too big."

But the next moment she had made herself comfortable in the middle of the rug and all the toys had turned into bricks for a house for Ninka, the doll she had brought from town. It was a much more sensible and settled home than any of the temporary lodgings in other people's houses where she had spent most of her life.

Lara watched her from the kitchen. "Look at that instinct for domesticity. It just shows, nothing can destroy the longing for home and for order. Children are more honest, they aren't frightened of the truth, but we are so afraid of seeming to be behind the times that we are ready to betray what is most dear to us and praise what repels us and say yes to what we don't understand."

"Here's the tub," said Yurii Andreievich, coming in out of the dark hallway. "It certainly wasn't in its place. It was standing under the leak in the ceiling. I suppose it's been there since last autumn."

7

For dinner, Lara, who had started on the provisions they had brought and had cooked enough for three days, served an unprecedented feast of potato soup and roast mutton and potatoes. Katenka ate till she could eat no more, giggling and getting more and more naughty, and afterwards, warm and full, curled up in her mother's shawl on the sofa and went to sleep.

Larisa Feodorovna, hot and tired from the oven, almost as sleepy as her daughter, and pleased with the success of her cooking, was in no hurry to clear away the plates and sat down to have a rest. After making sure that Katenka was asleep, she said, leaning forward on the table, with her chin on her hand:

"I'd slave and be happy if only I knew it was getting us somewhere, if it wasn't all for nothing. You'll have to keep reminding me that we came here to be together. Keep cheering me up, don't let me think. Because strictly speaking, if you look at it honestly, what are we doing, what is all this? We've raided someone else's house, we've broken in and made ourselves at home, and now we bustle around like mad so as not to see that this isn't life, that it's a stage set, that it isn't real, that it's all 'pretend,' as children say, a child's game—just ridiculous."

"But, darling, isn't it you who insisted on our coming? Don't you remember how long I held out against it?"

"Certainly I did. I don't deny it. So now I am at fault! It's all right for you to think twice and hesitate, but I have to be logical and consistent all the time! You come in, you see your son's crib, and you nearly faint. That's your right, but I'm not allowed to be worried, to be afraid for Katenka, to think about the future, everything has to give way before my love for you."

"Larusha! Pull yourself together. Think. It's not too late to go back on your decision. I was the first to tell you to take Komarovsky's plan more seriously. We've got a horse. If you like we'll go straight back to Yuriatin tomorrow. Komarovsky is still there, we saw him—and incidentally I don't think he saw us. I'm sure we'll still find him."

"I've hardly said a word, and you sound annoyed. But tell me, am I so wrong? We might just as well have stayed in Yuriatin if we weren't going to hide better than this. If we really meant to save ourselves we should have had a sensible plan, properly thought out, and that after all is what Komarovsky offered us. Disgusting as he is, he is a well-informed and practical man. We are in greater danger here than anywhere else. Just think!—alone on a boundless, wind-swept plain! If we were snowed under in the night we couldn't dig ourselves out in the morning! Or suppose our mysterious benefactor, who visited this house, turns out to be a bandit and comes and slits our throats! Have you at least got a gun? I thought not! You see? What terrifies me is your thoughtlessness, and you've infected me with it as well. I simply can't think straight."

"But what do you want? What do you want me to do now?"

"I don't know myself what to say. Keep me under your thumb all the time. Keep reminding me that I'm your loving slave and that it's not my business to think or argue. Oh, I'll tell you what. Your Tonia and my Pasha are a thousand times better than we are, but that isn't the point. The point is that the gift of love is like any other gift. However great it is, it won't thrive without a blessing. You and I, it's as though we have been taught to kiss in heaven and sent down to earth together, to see if we know what we were taught. It's a sort of crowning harmony—no limits, no degrees, everything is of equal value, everything is a joy, everything has become spirit. But in this wild tenderness that lies in wait for us at every moment there is something childish, unrestrained, irresponsible. It's a willful, destructive element, hostile to domestic happiness, such a love. It's my duty to be afraid of it and to distrust it."

She threw her arms around his neck, struggling with tears.

"Don't you see, we are not in the same position. You were given wings to fly above the clouds, but I'm a woman, mine are given me to stay close to the ground and to shelter my young."

He was deeply moved by everything she said, but he didn't show it, lest he give way to his emotions.

"It's quite true that there is something false and strained about this camp life we lead. You are perfectly right. But it isn't we who invented it. This frantic dashing about from pillar to post is what is happening to everyone, it's in the spirit of the times.

"I've been thinking about it myself all day. I should like to do everything possible to stay here for some time. I can't tell you how I'm longing to get back to work. I don't mean farming. That's what we were doing here before, we took it on as a family and we succeeded. But I wouldn't have the strength to do it again. I've got something else in mind.

"Things are gradually settling down. Perhaps one day they'll start publishing books again.

"This is what I was thinking. Couldn't we come to an agreement with Samdeviatov—we'd have to give him profitable terms, of course—so that he should keep us here for six months at his expense, on condition that I spend this time writing a book, say a textbook on medicine, or something literary, perhaps a collection of poems. Or I might translate some famous classic. I'm good at languages. I saw an advertisement the other day, there's a big publisher in Petersburg who is doing nothing but translations. I'm pretty sure this sort of work will have a value in terms of money. I'd be very happy doing something of that kind."

"I am glad you reminded me, I was also thinking of something like that today. But I have no faith in our future here. On the contrary, I have a foreboding that we'll soon be swept away, somewhere even more distant. But so long as we still have this breathing space, I want to ask you a favor. Will you give up a few hours in the next few evenings and put down all the poems I have heard from you at different times? Half of them you've lost and the rest you've never written down, and I'm afraid you'll forget them and they'll be lost altogether as you say has often happened before."

8

At the end of the day they washed in plenty of hot water, and Lara bathed Katenka. Feeling blissfully clean, Yurii Andreievich sat down at the table before the window, his back to the room where Lara, wrapped in a bath towel and fragrant with soap, her hair twisted in a turban with another towel, was putting Katenka to bed and tucking her up. Enjoying the foretaste of concentrated work, he took in what was going on around him with a happy, diffuse attentiveness.

It was one in the morning when Lara, who had been

pretending, finally went to sleep. Her nightdress and Katenka's, like the freshly laundered linen on the beds, shone clean and lacy. Even in those days, Lara managed somehow to get starch.

The stillness that surrounded Yurii Andreievich breathed with happiness and life. The lamplight fell softly yellow on the white sheets of paper and gilded the surface of the ink inside the ink-well. Outside, the frosty winter night was pale blue. To see it better, Yurii Andreievich stepped into the next room, cold and dark, and looked out of the window. The light of the full moon on the snow-covered clearing was as viscid as white of egg or thick white paint. The splendor of the frosty night was inexpressible. His heart was at peace. He went back into the warm, well-lit room and began to write.

Careful to convey the living movement of his hand in his flowing writing, so that even outwardly it should not lose individuality and grow numb and soulless, he set down, gradually improving them and moving further and further away from the original as he made copy after copy, the poems that he remembered best and that had taken the most definite shape in his mind—"Christmas Star," "Winter Night," and a number of others of the same kind, which later were forgotten, mislaid, and never found again.

From these old, completed poems, he went on to others that he had begun and left unfinished, getting into their spirit and sketching the sequels, though without the slightest hope of finishing them now. Finally getting into his stride and carried away, he started on a new poem.

After two or three stanzas and several images by which he himself was struck, his work took possession of him and he felt the approach of what is called inspiration. At such moments the relation of the forces that determine artistic creation is, as it were, reversed. The dominant thing is no longer the state of mind the artist seeks to express but the language in which he wants to express it. Language, the home and receptacle of beauty and meaning, itself begins to think and speak for man and turns wholly into music, not in terms of sonority but in terms of the impetuousness and power of its inward flow. Then, like the current of a mighty river polishing stones and turning wheels by its very movement, the flow of speech creates in passing, by virtue of its own laws, meter and rhythm and countless other forms and formations, which are even more important, but which are as yet unexplored, insufficiently recognized, and unnamed.

At such moments Yurii Andreievich felt that the main part of the work was being done not by him but by a superior power which was above him and directed him, namely the movement of universal thought and poetry in its present historical stage and the one to come. And he felt himself to be only the occasion, the fulcrum, needed to make this movement possible.

This feeling relieved him for a time of self-reproach, of his dissatisfaction with himself, of the sense of his own insignificance. He looked up, he looked around him.

He saw the two sleeping heads on their snow-white pillows. The purity of their features and of the clean linen and the clean rooms, and of the night, the snow, the stars, the moon, surged through his heart in a single wave of meaning, moving him to a joyful sense of the triumphant purity of being.

"Lord! Lord!" he whispered, "and all this is for me? Why hast Thou given me so much? Why hast Thou admitted me to Thy presence, allowed me to stray into Thy world, among Thy treasures, under Thy stars, and to the feet of my luckless, reckless, uncomplaining love, who fills my eyes with perpetual delight?"

At three in the morning Yurii Andreievich looked up from his papers. He came back from his remote, selfless concentration, home to reality and to himself, happy, strong, peaceful. Suddenly the stillness of the open country stretching into the distance outside the window was broken by a mournful, plaintive sound.

He went into the unlit adjoining room to look through the window, but while he had been working the glass had frosted over. He dragged away the roll of carpet that had been pushed against the front door to stop the draft, threw his coat over his shoulders, and went out.

He was dazzled by the white glow playing on the shadowless, moonlit snow and could at first see nothing. Then the long, whimpering, deep-bellied howl sounded again, muffled by the distance, and he noticed four long shadows, no thicker than pencil strokes, at the edge of the clearing just beyond the gully.

The wolves stood in a row, their heads raised and their muzzles pointing at the house, baying at the moon or at its silver reflection on the windows. But scarcely had Yurii Andreievich realized that they were wolves when they turned and trotted off like dogs, almost as if they could read his thoughts. He lost sight of them before he noticed the direction in which they had vanished.

"That's the last straw!" he thought. "Is their lair quite close? Perhaps in the gully? How terrible! And Samdeviatov's horse in the barn! They must have scented it."

He decided for the time being not to tell Lara, lest he upset her. Going back, he shut all the doors between the cold rooms and the heated part of the house, pushed rugs and clothes against the cracks to keep out the draft, and went back to his desk. The lamplight was bright and welcoming as before. But he was no longer in the mood to write. He couldn't settle down. He could think of nothing but wolves and of looming dangers and complications of every kind. Moreover, he was tired.

Lara woke up. "Are you still burning, my precious bright light?" she whispered in a husky voice heavy with sleep. "Come and sit beside me for a moment. I'll tell you my dream."

He put out the light.

9

Another day of quiet madness went by. They had found a child's sled in the house. Katenka, flushed bright red and bundled up in her coat, glided, shrieking with laughter, down the unswept paths from the snow-chute Yurii Andreievich had made for her by packing the snow hard with his spade and pouring water on it. Endlessly, she climbed back to the top of the mound, pulling the sled by a string, her smile never leaving her face.

It was freezing; the air was getting noticeably colder, but it was sunny. The snow was yellow at noon, with orange seeping into its honey color like an aftertaste at sunset.

The laundering and washing that Lara had done the day before had made the house damp. The steam had covered the windows with thick hoarfrost and left black streaks of damp on the wallpaper. The rooms were dark and cheerless. Yurii Andreievich carried logs and water and went on with his inspection of the house, making more and more discoveries, and he helped Lara with her endless chores.

In the rush of some task or other their hands would meet and join, and then they set down whatever they were carrying, weak and giddy with the irresistible onslaught of their tenderness, all thought driven from their heads. And the moments went by until it was late and they both remembered, horrified, that Katenka had been left alone much too long or that the horse was unwatered and unfed, and rushed off, conscience-stricken, to make up for their omissions.

Yurii Andreievich had not slept enough; there was a pleasant haze in his head, like tipsiness, and he ached all over with a nagging blissful weakness. He waited impatiently for the night, to go back to his interrupted writing.

The preliminary part of the work was being done outside his consciousness, during the drowsiness that filled him and veiled his surroundings and his thoughts. The diffuse mistiness in which everything was enveloped marked the stage preceding the distinctness of the final embodiment. Like the confusion of a first rough draft, the wearisome inactivity of the day was a necessary preparation for the night.

Although he felt exhausted, nothing was left untouched, unchanged. Everything was being altered and transformed.

Yurii Andreievich felt that his dream of remaining in Vary-kino would not come true, that the hour of his parting with Lara was at hand; he would inevitably lose her and with her the will to live and perhaps life itself. He was sick at heart, yet his greatest torment was his impatience for the night, his longing so to express his grief that everyone should be moved to tears.

The wolves he had been remembering all day long were no longer wolves on the snowy plain under the moon, they had become a theme, they had come to symbolize a hostile force bent upon destroying him and Lara and on driving them from Varykino.

The thought of this hostility developed in him and by evening it loomed like a prehistoric beast or some fabulous monster, a dragon whose tracks had been discovered in the ravine and who thirsted for his blood and lusted after Lara.

The night came and once again the doctor lit the lamp on the table. Lara and Katenka went to bed earlier than the night before.

What he had written that night fell into two parts. Clean copies—improved versions of earlier poems—were set out in his best penmanship. New work was written in an illegible scrawl full of gaps and abbreviations.

In deciphering these scribbles, he went through the usual disappointments. Last night these rough fragments had moved him to tears, and he himself had been surprised by some felicitous passages. Now these very passages seemed to him distressingly and conspicuously strained.

It had been the dream of his life to write with an originality so discreet, so well concealed, as to be unnoticeable in its disguise of current and customary forms; all his life he had struggled for a style so restrained, so unpretentious that the reader or the hearer would fully understand the meaning without realizing how he assimilated it. He had striven constantly for an unostentatious style, and he was dismayed to find how far he still remained from his ideal.

Last night he had tried to convey, by words so simple as to be almost childish and suggesting the directness of a lullaby, his feeling of mingled love and fear and longing and courage, in such a way that it should speak for itself, almost apart from the words.

Looking over these rough sketches now, he found that they needed a connecting theme to give unity to the lines, which for lack of it fell apart. He crossed out what he had written and began to write down the legend of St. George and the dragon in the same lyrical manner. At first he used a broad, spacious pentameter. The regularity of the rhythm, independent of the meaning and inherent in the meter itself, annoyed him by its doggerel artificiality. He gave up the pompous meter and the caesura and cut down the lines to four beats, as you cut out useless words in prose. The task was now more difficult but more engaging. The result was livelier but still too verbose. He forced himself to even shorter lines. Now the words were crammed in their trimeters, and Yurii Andreievich felt wide awake, roused, excited; the right words to fill the short lines came, prompted by the measure. Things scarcely named in the lines evoked concrete images. He heard the horse's hoofs ringing on the surface of the poem, as you hear the ambling of a horse in one of Chopin's ballades. St. George was galloping over the boundless expanse of the steppe. He could watch him, as he grew smaller in the distance. He wrote in a feverish hurry, scarcely able to keep up with the words as they poured out, always to the point and tumbling into place of themselves.

He had not noticed Lara getting out of bed and coming across to the table. She seemed very thin in her long nightdress and taller than she really was. He started with surprise when she appeared beside him, pale, frightened, stretching out her hand and whispering:

"Do you hear? A dog howling. Even two of them, I think. Oh, how terrible! It's a very bad omen. We'll bear it somehow till the morning, and then we'll go, we'll go! I won't stay here any longer."

An hour later, after much persuasion, she calmed down and fell asleep. Yurii Andreievich went outside. The wolves were nearer than the night before. They vanished even more swiftly and again before he could make out in which direction they went. They had stood in a bunch and he had not had time to count them, but it seemed to him that there were more of them.

10

It was the thirteenth day of their stay at Varykino. There was nothing new or different about it. The wolves, after having disappeared for a few days, had again howled in the night. Once again, mistaking them for dogs, and frightened by the omen, Larisa Feodorovna just as before, announced that she was leaving the next day. Her usual balance was disturbed by attacks of anxiety, natural in a woman unused to pouring out her feelings all day long or to the luxury of unrestrained affection.

The same scenes were repeated again and again, so that when that morning Lara, as she had done so many times before, began to pack for the return journey, it was as if the thirteen days since their arrival had not existed at all.

It was again damp and dark in the rooms, this time because the weather was overcast. It was less cold, and judging from the look of the dark, low clouds it would snow any moment. Yurii Andreievich was exhausted by the physical and mental strain of too many sleepless nights. His legs were weak and his thoughts were in a tangle; shivering with cold and rubbing his hands, he walked about from room to room, waiting to see what Lara would decide and what he would have to do in consequence.

She did not know herself. Just then she would have given anything to exchange their chaotic freedom for a daily round, however strenuous, but laid down once and for all, for work and obligations, so that they could live a decent, honest, sensible life.

She began her day as usual by making the beds, sweeping,

dusting, and cooking breakfast. Then she began to pack and asked the doctor to harness the horse; she had firmly resolved to go.

Yurii Andreievich did not argue. It was mad to return to town, where the wave of arrests must have reached its peak, but it was equally mad to remain, alone and unarmed, in this winter desert with its own hazards.

Besides, there was hardly an armful of hay left in the barn or the sheds. Of course, had it been possible to settle down for a long stay, the doctor would have scouted around looking for new ways of getting food and fodder, but it wasn't worth it for a few uncertain days. He gave up the thought and went to harness the horse.

He wasn't good at it. Samdeviatov had taught him how to do it, but he kept forgetting. Still, he managed it, though clumsily. He strapped the yoke to the shafts, wound the slack and knotted the end of the metal-studded strap around one of them, then, one leg braced against the horse's flank, pulled the two ends of the stiff collar tight and fastened them. At last he led the horse to the porch, tied it, and went inside to call Lara.

She and Katenka had their coats on and everything was packed, but Lara was in great distress. Wringing her hands and on the verge of tears, she begged him to sit down a moment and, throwing herself into a chair and getting up again, spoke incoherently in a high-pitched plaintive sing-song, stumbling over her words and repeatedly interjecting: "What do you think?"

"I can't help it, I don't know how it's happened, but you can see for yourself, we can't possibly go now, so late, it will be dark soon, we'll be caught in the darkness in your terrible forest. What do you think? I'll do whatever you tell me to, but I simply can't make up my mind to go, something tells me not to, but do whatever you think best. What do you think? Why don't you say something? We've wasted half the day, goodness knows how. Tomorrow we'll be more sensible, more careful. What do you think? How would it be if we stayed one more night? And tomorrow we'll get up early and start at daybreak, at six or seven. What do you think? You'll light the stove and write one more evening and we'll have one more night here, wouldn't that be lovely, darling, wonderful? Oh, God, have I done something wrong again? Why don't you say something?"

"You're exaggerating. Dusk is a long way off, it's quite early.

But have it your way. We'll stay. Only calm yourself, don't be
so upset. Come now, let's take off our coats and unpack. And
Katenka says she's hungry. We'll have something to eat. You are
quite right, there would have been no point in going so
suddenly, with so little preparation. But don't be so upset, and
don't cry. I'll light the stove in a moment. But before I do that, I
might as well take the sleigh, since it's at the door, and bring
what's left of the logs in our old woodshed; we're entirely out.
Don't cry now. I'll be back soon."

11

Several sets of sleigh tracks led up to the woodshed of the
Zhivagos' house; Yurii Andreievich had made them on his
earlier trips, and the snow over the threshold was trampled and
littered from his last visit two days before.

The sky, which had been cloudy since morning, had cleared.
It was cold again. The old park came right up to the shed, as if
to peer at the doctor's face and remind him of something. The
snow was deep that winter. It was piled high over the threshold
so that the lintel seemed lower and the shed hunchbacked. Snow
hung over the edge of the roof almost down to the doctor's
head, like the rim of a gigantic mushroom. Just above it, as
though plunging a point of its crescent into the snow, stood the
new moon, glowing with a gray blaze along its edge.

Although it was early in the afternoon and full daylight, the
doctor felt as if he were standing late at night in the dark forest
of his life. Such was the darkness in his soul, such was his
dejection. The new moon shining almost at eye level was an
omen of separation and an image of solitude.

He was so tired that he could hardly stand. He threw the logs
out of the shed onto the sleigh in smaller armfuls than usual; to
handle the icy wood with snow clinging to it was painful even
though he wore gloves. The work did not make him feel any
warmer. Something within him had broken and come to a
standstill. He cursed his luckless fate and prayed God to spare
the life of the beautiful, sad, humble, and simple-hearted
woman he loved. And the new moon stood over the barn
blazing without warmth and shining without giving light.

The horse turned its head in the direction of the Mikulitsyns' house and whinnied, at first softly, timidly, then louder, with assurance.

"What's that for?" Yurii Andreievich wondered. "It can't be fright. A frightened horse wouldn't neigh, and it wouldn't be such a fool as to signal to the wolves if it had scented them, and so cheerfully, too. It must be looking forward to going home. Hold on a moment, we'll soon be off."

He added chips for kindling to the logs, and strips of bark that curled like shoe leather, covered the load with sacking, lashed it to the sleigh with a rope, and turned back, walking at the horse's head.

The horse neighed again, this time in answer to another horse neighing in the distance. "What can that be? Is it possible that Varykino is not as deserted as we thought?" It never occurred to him that they had guests or that the neighing came from the direction of Mikulitsyn's house. He took the sleigh around the farm buildings, and since the house was hidden from him by snowy folds of land he did not see its front entrance.

Taking his time—why should he hurry?—he stacked the wood and, unhitching the horse, left the sleigh in the barn. Then he took the horse to the stables, put it in the far stall where there was less draft, and stuffed the few remaining handfuls of hay into the rack of the manger.

He felt uneasy as he walked home. In front of the porch stood a roomy peasant sleigh with a sleek black foal harnessed to it, and walking up and down beside it was an equally sleek, plump stranger, who gave the horse an occasional slap and had a look at its fetlocks.

There were voices coming from the house. Neither wishing to eavesdrop nor close enough to hear more than an occasional word, Yurii Andreievich nevertheless involuntarily slowed down and suddenly stopped. He recognized the voice of Komarovsky talking to Lara and Katenka. They were apparently in the first room near the door. They were arguing, and, judging from the sound of her voice, Lara was upset and crying, now violently contradicting him and now agreeing with him.

Something made Yurii Andreievich feel that just then Komarovsky was speaking about him, saying something to the effect that he should not be trusted ("serving two masters," he thought he heard), that it was impossible to tell if he were more attached to Lara or to his family, that Lara must not rely on him, because if she did she would be "running with the hare and the hounds" and would "fall between two stools." Yurii Andreievich went in.

As he had thought, they were in the first room on the right, Komarovsky in a fur coat reaching to his heels, Lara holding Katenka by her coat collar, trying to fasten it but not finding the hooks and shouting at her not to wriggle, and Katenka protesting: "Easy, Mama, you'll choke me." All three were standing in their outdoor clothes, ready to leave. When Yurii Andreievich came in, Lara and Komarovsky rushed to meet him, speaking together:

"Where have you been all this time? We need you so badly!"

"Hello, Yurii Andreievich. As you see, in spite of the rude things we said to each other last time, I'm with you once again, though you didn't invite me."

"Hello, Victor Ippolitovich."

"Where on earth have you been?" Lara asked again. "Now listen to what he says and decide quickly for both of us. There isn't any time. We have to hurry."

"But why are we all standing? Sit down, Victor Ippolitovich. How do you mean, darling, where have I been? You know I went to get the wood, and afterwards I saw to the horse. Victor Ippolitovich, do sit down, please."

"Well, aren't you amazed to see him? How is it you don't look surprised? Here we were, regretting that he had gone away and that we hadn't jumped at his offer, and now here he is, right under your very eyes, and you don't even look surprised! But what is even more astonishing is what he has to tell us now. Tell him, Victor Ippolitovich."

"I don't know what Larisa Feodorovna has in mind. One thing I must explain is this: I deliberately spread the rumor that I had left, but I stayed on to give you and Larisa Feodorovna more time to think over what we had discussed, and perhaps come to a less rash decision."

"But we can't put it off any longer," broke in Lara. "Now is the perfect time to leave. And tomorrow morning . . . But let Victor Ippolitovich tell you himself."

"One moment, Lara dear. Forgive me, Victor Ippolitovich. Why should we all stand about in our coats? Let's take them off and sit down. After all, these are serious things we have to talk about, we can't settle them in a minute. I am afraid, Victor Ippolitovich, our discussion has touched on something personal; it would be ludicrous and embarrassing to go into it. But the fact is that while I have never considered going away with you, Lara's case is different. On the rare occasions when our concerns were not the same and we remembered that we were not one person but two, I have always told her that she ought to give your suggestion more consideration. And in fact she has never stopped thinking about it, she has come back to it again and again."

"But only on condition that you come with us," broke in Lara.

"It is as difficult for you as it is for me to think of our being separated, but perhaps we ought to put our feelings aside and make this sacrifice. Because there's no question of my going."

"But you haven't heard anything yet, you don't know . . . Listen to what Victor Ippolitovich says. . . . Tomorrow morning . . . Victor Ippolitovich."

"Larisa Feodorovna is evidently thinking of the news I brought and have already told her. In the sidings at Yuriatin, an official train of the Far Eastern Government is standing under steam. It arrived yesterday from Moscow and is leaving for the East tomorrow. It belongs to our Ministry of Communications. Half the carriages are *wagons-lits*.

"I have to go by this train. Several seats have been put at my disposal for my assistants. We could travel in great comfort. There won't ever be another chance like this again. I realize that you are not in the habit of speaking lightly, you are not the man to go back on your decisions, and you have made up your mind not to go with us. But even so, shouldn't you reconsider it for Larisa Feodorovna's sake? You heard her say that she won't go without you. Come with us, if not to Vladivostok, then at least as far as Yuriatin—and there we shall see. Only we must really hurry—there is not a moment to lose. I have a driver with me— I don't drive myself—and there isn't room for five of us in my sleigh. But I understand you have Samdeviatov's horse—didn't you say you had gone with it to get the wood? Is it still harnessed?"

"No, I have unharnessed it."

"Well then, harness it again as quickly as you possibly can. My driver will help you. . . . Though, come to think of it, why bother—let's forget about your sleigh, we'll manage with mine, we'll squeeze in somehow. Only let's hurry, for heaven's sake. You only need to pack the most essential things for the journey—whatever comes to hand first. There's no time to fuss with packing when it's a question of a child's life."

"I don't understand you, Victor Ippolitovich. You talk as if I had agreed to come. Go and good luck to you, and let Lara go with you if she wishes. You needn't worry about the house. I'll clean it up and lock it after you've gone."

"What are you talking about, Yura? What's all this nonsense you don't even believe yourself? 'Lara's wishes' indeed! As if you didn't know perfectly well that I won't go without you and I won't make any decision on my own. So what's all this talk about your locking up the house?"

"So you are quite adamant?" said Komarovsky. "In that case, with Larisa Feodorovna's permission I should like to have a couple of words with you, if possible alone."

"Certainly. We can go into the kitchen. You don't mind, darling?"

12

"Strelnikov has been captured, condemned to death, and shot."

"How horrible! Are you really sure?"

"It's what I've been told, and I am convinced it's true."

"Don't tell Lara. She would go out of her mind."

"Of course I won't. That's why I asked to speak to you alone. Now that this has happened, she and her daughter are in imminent danger. You must help me to save them. Are you quite sure you won't go with us?"

"Quite sure. I've told you already."

"But she won't go without you. I simply don't know what to do. You'll have to help me in a different way. You'll have to pretend, let her think that you might be willing to change your mind, look as if you might allow yourself to be persuaded. I can't see her saying goodbye and leaving you, either here or at the station at Yuriatin. We'll have to make her think that you are coming after all, if not now, then later, when I've arranged another opportunity for you to come. You'll have to pretend that you'll be willing to do that. You'll just have to convince her of this, even if you have to lie. Though this is no empty offer on my part—I swear to you on my honor that at the first sign you give me I'll get you out to the East and I'll arrange for you to go on from there anywhere you like. But Larisa Feodorovna must believe that you are at least coming to see us off. You'll simply have to make her believe that. For instance, you might pretend that you are going to get your sleigh ready and urge us to start at once, without waiting for you, not to waste any time—say you'll catch up with us as soon as you are ready."

"I am so shaken by the news about Strelnikov that I cannot collect my wits. I have hardly taken in all you've said. But you are right. Now that they've settled accounts with him, we must conclude, things being as they are, that Larisa Feodorovna and Katia's lives are also threatened. Either she or I will certainly be arrested, so we'll be parted anyway. It's better that it should be you who separate us and take them off, as far away as possible. I am saying this, but it doesn't make much difference—things are already going your way. Probably in the end I'll break down completely, and swallow my pride and my self-respect and crawl to you, and ask you for her, for my life, and for a sea passage to my family, and for my own salvation, and accept it all from your hands. But you must give me time to think about it. I am stunned by the news. I am so distressed that I can't think or reason properly. Perhaps, by putting myself in your hands, I am making a disastrous mistake and it will appall me all the rest of my life. But I am so dazed and overcome that all I can do at the moment is to agree with you blindly and obey you helplessly. . . . Very well, then, for her sake I'll go out now and tell her that I'll get the sleigh ready and catch up with you, but in fact I shall stay behind. . . . There's one thing, though. How can you go now, when it will soon be dark? The road runs through woods, and there are wolves. Watch out."

"I know. Don't worry. I've got a gun and a revolver. I've brought a bit of liquor too, by the way, to keep out the cold. Would you like some? I've got enough."

13

"What have I done? What have I done? I've given her up, renounced her, given her away. I must run after them. Lara! Lara!

"They can't hear. The wind is against me and they are probably shouting at each other. She has every reason to feel happy, reassured. She has no idea of the trick I've played on her.

"She is thinking: It's wonderful that things have gone so well, they couldn't be better. Her absurd, obstinate Yurochka has relented at last, thank heaven, we are going to a nice, safe place, where people are more sensible than we are, where you can be sure of law and order. Suppose even, just to be annoying, he doesn't come on tomorrow's train, Komarovsky will send another to bring him, and he'll join us in no time at all. And at the moment, of course, he's in the stable, hurrying, excited, fumbling with the harness, and he'll rush after us full tilt and catch up with us before we get into the forest.

"That's what she must be thinking. And we didn't even say goodbye properly, I just waved to her and turned back, trying to swallow my pain as if it were a piece of apple stuck in my throat, choking me."

He stood on the veranda, his coat over one shoulder. With his free hand he was clutching the slender wooden pillar just under the roof as if he meant to strangle it. His whole attention was concentrated on a point in the distance. There a short stretch of the road could be seen climbing uphill, bordered by a few sparse birches. The low rays of the setting sun fell on this open space, and there the sleigh now hidden by a shallow dip would appear at any moment.

"Farewell, farewell," he said over and over again in anticipation of that moment; his words were breathed almost soundlessly into the cold afternoon air. "Farewell, my only love, my love forever lost.

"They're coming, they're coming," he whispered through dry, blenched lips as the sleigh shot like an arrow out of the dip, swept past the birches one after another, gradually slowing down, and—oh, joy!—stopped before the last of them.

His heart thumped with such a wild excitement that his knees shook and he felt weak and faint, the whole of his body soft as cloth, like the coat slipping from his shoulder. "O God, is it Thy will to give her back to me? What can have happened? What is going on out there near the sunset? What can be the meaning of it? Why are they standing still? No. It's finished. They've moved. They're off. She must have stopped for a last look at the house. Or perhaps to make sure that I had left? That I was chasing after them? They've gone."

With luck, if the sun didn't go down first (he wouldn't see them in the dark) they would flash past once again, for the last time, on the other side of the ravine, across the field where the wolves had stood two nights before.

And now this moment also had come and gone. The dark red sun was still round as a ball above the blue snowdrifts along the horizon, flooding the plain with a juicy pineapple-colored light that the snow greedily sucked in, when the sleigh swept into sight and vanished. "Farewell, Lara, until we meet in the next world, farewell, my love, my inexhaustible, everlasting joy. I'll never see you again, I'll never, never see you again."

It was getting dark. Swiftly the bronze-red patches of sunset scattered on the snow died down and went out. The soft, ashy distance filled with a lilac dusk that turned to deep mauve, its smoky haze smudging the fine lacework of the roadside birches lightly traced on the pink sky, pale as though it had suddenly grown shallow.

Grief had sharpened Yurii Andreievich's senses and quickened his perception a hundredfold. The very air surrounding him was rare, unique. The winter evening was alive with sympathy, like a friendly witness. It was as if there had never been such a dusk before and night were falling now for the first time in order to console him in his loneliness and bereavement; as if the valley were not always girded by a panorama of wooded hills on the horizon but the trees had only taken up their places now, rising out of the ground in order to comfort him with their presence.

He almost waved away the tangible beauty of the hour, like a crowd of persistent friends, almost saying to the lingering afterglow: "Thank you, thank you, I'll be all right."

Still standing on the veranda, he turned his face to the shut door, his back to the world. "My bright sun has set," he kept repeating inwardly, as though trying to engrave these words in his memory. He did not have the strength to utter all these words aloud.

He went into the house. A double monologue was going on in his mind, two different kinds of monologue, the one dry and businesslike, the other addressed to Lara, like a river in flood.

"Now I'll go to Moscow," ran his thoughts. "The first job is to survive. I must not force myself to sleep. Instead, I must work all through the night till I drop with exhaustion. Yes, and another thing, light the stove in the bedroom at once, there is no reason why I should freeze tonight."

But there was also this other inward conversation: "I'll stay with you a little, my unforgettable delight, for as long as my

arms and my hands and my lips remember you. I'll put my grief
for you in a work that will endure and be worthy of you. I'll
write your memory into an image of aching tenderness and
sorrow. I'll stay here till this is done, then I too will go. This is
how I will portray you, I'll trace your features on paper as the
sea, after a fearful storm has churned it up, traces the form of the
greatest, farthest-reaching wave on the sand. Seaweed, shells,
cork, pebbles, the lightest, most imponderable things that it
could lift from its bed, are cast up in a broken, sinuous line on
the sand. This line endlessly stretching into the distance is the
frontier of the highest tide. That was how life's storm cast you
up on my shore, O my pride, that is how I'll portray you."

He went in, locked the door behind him, and took off his
coat. When he went into the bedroom, which Lara had tidied up
so well and so carefully that morning and which her hurried
packing had again turned inside out, when he saw the disar-
ranged bed and the things thrown about in disorder on the
chairs and floor, he knelt down like a little boy, leaned his breast
against the hard edge of the bedstead, buried his head in the
bedclothes, and wept freely and bitterly as children do. But not
for long. Soon he got up, hastily dried his face, looked around
him with tired, absent-minded surprise, got out the bottle of
vodka Komarovsky had left, drew the cork, poured half a glass,
added water and snow, and with a relish almost equal in
strength to the hopelessness of the tears he had shed drank long,
greedy gulps.

14

Something unaccountable was going on in Yurii Adreievich. He
was slowly losing his mind. Never before had he led such a
strange existence. He neglected the house, he stopped taking
proper care of himself, he turned night into day and had lost
count of time since Lara had left.

He drank vodka and he wrote about Lara; but the more he
crossed out and rewrote what he had written the more the Lara
of his poems and notebooks grew away from her living
prototype, from the Lara who was Katia's mother off on a
journey with her daughter.

The reason for his revision and rewriting was his search for strength and exactness of expression, but they also followed the promptings of an inward reticence that forbade him to disclose his personal experiences and the real events in his past with too much freedom, lest he offend or wound those who had directly taken part in them. As a result, his feeling, still pulsing and warm, was gradually eliminated from his poems, and romantic morbidity yielded to a broad and serene vision that lifted the particular to the level of the universal and familiar. He was not deliberately striving for such a goal, but this broad vision came of its own accord as a consolation, like a message sent to him by Lara from her travels, like a distant greeting from her, like her appearance in a dream or the touch of her hand on his forehead, and he loved this ennobling imprint.

At the same time that he was working on his lament for Lara he was also scribbling the end of the notes he had accumulated over the years concerning nature, man, and various other things. As had always happened to him whenever he was writing, a host of ideas about the life of the individual and of society assailed him.

He reflected again that he conceived of history, of what is called the course of history, not in the accepted way but by analogy with the vegetable kingdom. In winter, under the snow, the leafless branches of a wood are thin and poor, like the hairs on an old man's wart. But in only a few days in spring the forest is transformed, it reaches the clouds, and you can hide or lose yourself in its leafy maze. This transformation is achieved with a speed greater than in the case of animals, for animals do not grow as fast as plants, and yet we cannot directly observe the movement of growth even of plants. The forest does not change its place, we cannot lie in wait for it and catch it in the act of change. Whenever we look at it, it seems to be motionless. And such also is the immobility to our eyes of the eternally growing, ceaselessly changing history, the life of society moving invisibly in its incessant transformations.

Tolstoy thought of it in just this way, but he did not spell it out so clearly. He denied that history was set in motion by Napoleon or any other ruler or general, but he did not develop his idea to its logical conclusion. No single man makes history. History cannot be seen, just as one cannot see grass growing. Wars and revolutions, kings and Robespierres, are history's organic agents, its yeast. But revolutions are made by fanatical men of action with one-track minds, geniuses in their ability to confine themselves to a limited field. They overturn the old order in a few hours or days, the whole upheaval takes a few weeks or at most years, but the fanatical spirit that inspired the upheavals is worshipped for decades thereafter, for centuries.

Mourning for Lara, he also mourned that distant summer in Meliuzeievo when the revolution had been a god come down to earth from heaven, the god of the summer when everyone had gone crazy in his own way, and when everyone's life had existed in its own right, and not as an illustration for a thesis in support of the rightness of a superior policy.

As he scribbled his odds and ends, he made a note reaffirming his belief that art always serves beauty, and beauty is delight in form, and form is the key to organic life, since no living thing can exist without it, so that every work of art, including tragedy, expresses the joy of existence. And his own ideas and notes also brought him joy, a tragic joy, a joy full of tears that exhausted him and made his head ache.

Samdeviatov came to see him. He brought him more vodka and told him of how Antipova and her daughter had left with Komarovsky. He came by the railway handcar. He scolded the doctor for not looking after the horse properly and took it back, unwilling to leave it for three or four more days as Yurii Andreievich wished, but promising to come back within the week, and personally take him away from Varykino for good.

Sometimes, after losing himself in his work, Yurii Andreievich suddenly remembered Lara as vividly as if she were before him, and broke down from tenderness and the sharpness of his loss. As in his childhood, when after his mother's death he thought he heard her voice in the bird calls, in the summer magnificence of Kologrivov's garden, so now his hearing, accustomed to Lara's voice and expecting it as part of his life, played tricks on him and he heard her calling, "Yurochka!" from the next room.

He also had other hallucinations that week. Toward the end of it, he woke up in the night from a nonsensical nightmare about a dragon that had its lair underneath the house. He opened his eyes. A light flashed from the gully and he heard the crack and echo of a rifle shot. Strangely, a few moments after so unusual an experience, he went back to sleep, and in the morning told himself that it had been a dream.

15

This is what happened a day or two later. The doctor had at last convinced himself that he must be sensible, that if he wished to kill himself he could find a quicker and less painful method. He promised himself to leave as soon as Samdeviatov came for him.

A little before dusk, while it was still light, he heard loud crunching footsteps on the snow. Someone was calmly approaching the house with a firm, easy step.

Strange! Who could it be? Samdeviatov had his horse, he would not have come on foot, and Varykino was deserted. "They've come for me," Yurii Andreievich decided. "A summons or an order to go back to town. Or they've come to arrest me. No, there would be two of them and they would have transportation to take me back. It's Mikulitsyn," he thought joyfully, imagining that he recognized the step. The stranger, still unidentified, fumbled at the door with its broken bolt, as if he had expected the padlock to be there; then he walked in confidently, certain of his way, opening the connecting doors and closing them carefully behind him.

Yurii Andreievich had been sitting at his desk with his back to the door. As he rose and turned to face it he found the stranger already in the doorway, where he had stopped dead.

"Whom do you want to see?" The doctor mechanically blurted out these conventional words without thinking, and was not surprised when there was no reply.

The stranger was a powerful, well-built man with a handsome face. He was dressed in a fur jacket and trousers, and warm, goatskin boots, and he had a rifle slung over his shoulder on a strap.

Only the moment of his appearance took the doctor by surprise, not his arrival in itself. The traces of occupation in the house had prepared him for it. This, evidently, was the owner of the supplies he had found, which, as he knew, could not have been left by the Mikulitsyns. Something about him struck Yurii Andreievich as familiar, he felt he had seen him before. Neither did the caller look as astonished as might have been expected at the sight of Yurii Andreievich. Perhaps he had been told that the house was lived in, and even who was living in it. Perhaps he even recognized the doctor.

"Who is he? Who is he?" The doctor racked his brains. "Where have I seen him, for heaven's sake? Surely not . . . A hot morning in May, God knows in what year. The station at Razvilie. The Commissar's coach, promising nothing good. Cut-and-dried ideas, a one-track mind, harsh principles, and integrity, absolute integrity . . . Strelnikov!"

16

They had been talking for hours. They talked as only Russians in Russia can talk, particularly as they talked then, desperate and frenzied as they were in those anxious, frightened days. Night was falling, and it was getting dark.

Apart from the nervous garrulousness that was common in those days, Strelnikov had some personal reason for talking ceaselessly.

He went on and on, doing everything possible to keep the conversation going, in order to avoid being alone. Was it his conscience he was afraid of, or the sad memories that haunted him, or was he tormented by that self-dissatisfaction which makes a man so hateful and intolerable to himself that he is ready to die of shame? Or had he made some dreadful, irrevocable decision and was he unwilling to remain alone with it and anxious to delay its execution by chatting with the doctor and staying in his company?

Whatever it was, he was evidently keeping to himself some important secret that burdened him, while pouring out his heart all the more effusively on every other subject.

It was the disease, the revolutionary madness of the age, that at heart everyone was different from his outward appearance and his words. No one had a clear conscience. Everyone could justifiably feel that he was guilty, that he was a secret criminal, an undetected impostor. The slightest pretext was enough to launch the imagination on an orgy of self-torture. Carried away by their fantasy, people accused themselves falsely not only out of terror but out of a morbidly destructive impulse, of their own will, in a state of metaphysical trance, in a passion for self-condemnation which cannot be checked once you give it its head.

As an important military leader who had often presided at military courts, Strelnikov must have heard and read any number of confessions and depositions by condemned men. Now he was himself swayed by the impulse to unmask himself, to reappraise his whole life, to draw up a balance sheet, while monstrously distorting everything in his feverish excitement.

He spoke incoherently, jumping from confession to confession.

"This all happened near Chita. . . . Were you surprised at all the outlandish things you found in the drawers and cupboards? All that comes from the requisitioning we did when the Red Army occupied eastern Siberia. Naturally, I didn't bring it here all by myself. I've always had trustworthy, devoted people around me; life has been very good to me that way. These candles, matches, coffee, tea, writing materials, and so on all come from requisitioned military stores, partly Czech, partly English and Japanese. Odd, don't you think? . . . 'What do you think?' was my wife's favorite expression, I suppose you noticed. I couldn't make up my mind whether to tell you when I arrived, but I might as well admit it now—I came to see her and my daughter. The message saying that they were here didn't reach me till too late. That's how I missed them. When rumors and reports reached me of your intimacy with her and the name Dr. Zhivago was mentioned to me, for some inexplicable reason, out of the thousands of faces I'd seen in these years, I remembered a doctor of that name who had once been brought to me for questioning."

"And were you sorry you hadn't had me shot?"

Strelnikov ignored the question. Perhaps he had not even heard the interruption. Lost in his thoughts, he went on with his monologue.

"Naturally, I was jealous—I'm jealous now, for that matter. What could you expect? . . . I came to this district only a few months ago, after my other hide-outs farther east were uncovered. I was to be court-martialled on a trumped-up charge. It wasn't difficult to guess the outcome. I wasn't guilty. I thought there might be a hope of defending myself and clearing my good name at some time in the future, in more propitious circumstances. So I decided to disappear while I still could, before they arrested me, and hide for the present, lead a hermit's life, keep moving. Perhaps I would have succeeded if it hadn't been for a young scoundrel who wheedled himself into my confidence.

"It was while I was making my way westward across Siberia, on foot, keeping out of people's way and starving. I used to sleep in snowdrifts, or in trains—there were endless rows of them standing buried in the snow all along the line.

"Well, I came across this boy, a tramp, who said he had got away from a partisan shooting squad—they had lined him up with a lot of other condemned men, but he was only wounded, and he crawled out from under a pile of dead bodies and hid in the forest and recovered, and now he was moving from one hide-out to another, like me. That was his story, anyway. He was a good-for-nothing, vicious and backward; he had been kicked out of school because he was dull-witted."

The more details Strelnikov added to his description, the more certain the doctor felt that he knew the boy.

"Was his name Terentii Galuzin?"

"Yes."

"Then everything he said about the partisans and the shooting was true. He didn't invent a word."

"The only good thing about him was that he was devoted to his mother. His father had been shot as a hostage, and his mother was in prison, and the same thing was likely to happen to her. When he heard that, he made up his mind to do all he could to get her out. He went to the local Cheka, gave himself up, and offered to work for them. They agreed to give him a chance on condition he made some important betrayal. He told them where I was hiding. But fortunately I got away in time.

"By a fantastic effort and after endless adventures, I got across Siberia and reached this part of the country. I am so well known here, I thought it was the last place they'd expect to find me; they wouldn't suppose I'd have the nerve. And in fact, they went on for a long time looking for me around Chita, while I was hiding either in this house or in one or two others I knew were safe in the neighborhood. But now that's out, they're on my trail. Listen. It's getting dark and I don't like it because I haven't been able to sleep for ages. You know what a torment that is. If any of my candles are still left—good, aren't they, real tallow!—then let's go on talking for a bit. Let's go on talking for as long as you can stand it, right through the night, in luxury, by candlelight."

"The candles are all there. I've opened only one box. I've been using the kerosene, which probably you also left."

"Have you any bread?"

"No."

"Then what have you been living on? But what a silly question! Potatoes, of course."

"That's right. Any amount of those. The people who used to live here were good housekeepers, they knew how to store them, they're all safe and sound in the cellar, neither rotten nor frozen." Strelnikov suddenly switched to the revolution.

17

"None of this can mean anything to you. You couldn't understand it. You grew up quite differently. There was the world of the suburbs, of the railways, of the slums and tenements. Dirt, hunger, overcrowding, the degradation of the worker as a human being, the degradation of women. And there was the world of the mother's darlings, of smart students and rich merchants' sons; the world of impunity, of brazen, insolent vice; of rich men laughing or shrugging off the tears of the poor, the robbed, the insulted, the seduced; the reign of parasites, whose only distinction was that they never troubled themselves about anything, never gave anything to the world, and left nothing behind them.

"But for us life was a campaign. We moved mountains for those we loved, and if we brought them nothing but sorrow, they did not hold it against us because in the end we suffered more than they did.

"But before I go on, I ought to tell you something. This is the point. You've got to leave Varykino, don't put it off if you value your life. They are closing in on me, and whatever happens to me will involve you. You are implicated already by the very fact of talking to me now. And apart from everything else, there are a lot of wolves around here; I had to shoot my way out of the Shutma the other night."

"So it was you shooting."

"Yes. Of course, you heard me. I was on my way to another hide-out, but before I got there I saw by various signs that it had been discovered. The people who were there have probably been shot. I won't stay long with you. I'll spend the night and leave in the morning. . . . Well, I'll go on if I may.

"Of course, it wasn't only in Moscow or in Russia that there existed these elegant Tverskaia Yamskaia Streets with young rakes in fancy hats and spats rushing about with their girls in cabs. That street, the night life of the street, the night life of the past century, and the race horses and the rakes, existed in every city in the world. But what gave unity to the nineteenth century, what set it apart as one historical period? It was the birth of socialist thought. Revolutions, young men dying on the barricades, writers racking their brains in an effort to curb the brute insolence of money, to save the human dignity of the poor. Marxism arose, it uncovered the root of the evil and it offered the remedy, it became the great force of the century. And the elegant streets of the age were all that, as well as the dirt and the heroism, the vice and the slums, and the proclamations and the barricades.

"You can't think how lovely she was as a child, a schoolgirl. You have no idea. She had a school friend who lived in a tenement next door to us; most of the tenants were railway workers on the Brest line. It was called the Brest line in those days, it's been renamed several times since. My father—he's a member of the Yuriatin revolutionary court now—he was a track overseer. I used to go to that house and see her there. She was still a child, but even then, the alertness, the watchfulness, the restlessness of those days—it was all there, you could read it all in her face, her eyes. All the themes of the century—all the tears and the insults and the hopes, the whole accumulation of resentment and pride were written in her face and bearing, which expressed both girlish shyness and self-assured grace. She was a living indictment of the age. This is something, isn't it? It's predestination. Something nature endowed her with, something to which she had a birthright."

"How well you speak of her. I too saw her in those days, just as you have described her. A schoolgirl, and yet at the same time the secret heroine of an unchildish drama. Her shadow on the wall was the shadow of helpless, watchful self-defense. That was how I saw her, and so I still remember her. You put it perfectly."

"You saw and you remembered? And what did you do?"

"That's another story altogether."

"Yes. Well. So you see, the whole of this nineteenth

century—its revolutions in Paris, its generations of Russian exiles starting with Herzen, its assassinations of Tsars, some only plotted, others carried out, the whole of the workers' movement of the world, the whole of Marxism in the parliaments and universities of Europe, the whole of this new system of ideas with its newness, the swiftness of its conclusion, its irony, and its pitiless remedies elaborated in the name of pity— all of this was absorbed and expressed in Lenin, who fell upon the old world as the personified retribution for its misdeeds.

"And side by side with him there arose before the eyes of the world the vast figure of Russia bursting into flames like a light of redemption for all the sorrows and misfortunes of mankind. But why on earth am I telling you all this? To you it must be the tinkling of a cymbal—just words.

"For the sake of this girl I studied and became a teacher, and went to Yuriatin, which I did not know at that time. For her sake I devoured piles of books and absorbed a great mass of knowledge, to be available to her if she asked for my help. To win her back after three years of marriage, I went to war, and when the war was over and I returned from captivity, I took advantage of having been listed as dead, and under an assumed name plunged headlong into the revolution, to pay back in full all the wrongs that she had suffered, to wash her mind clean of those memories, so that it should not be possible to return to the past, so that there should be no more Tverskaia-Yamskaias. And all the time they, she and my daughter, were next door, they were here! What an effort it cost me to resist the longing to rush to them, to see them! But I wanted to finish my life's work first. Oh, what wouldn't I give now for one look at them! When she came in it was as if the window flew open and the room filled with air and light."

"I know how much you loved her. But forgive me, have you any idea of her love for you?"

"Sorry. What was that you said?"

"I asked you, had you any idea of how much she loved you— more than anyone in the world?"

"What makes you say that?"

"Because she told me so herself."

"She said that? To you?"

"Yes."

"Forgive me, I realize it's an impossible thing to ask, but if it isn't hopelessly indiscreet, if you can, will you tell me exactly what it was she said to you?"

"Gladly. She said that you were the embodiment of what a human being should be, a man whose equal she had never met, that you were unique in your genuineness, and that if she could go back to the home she had shared with you she would crawl to it on her knees from the end of the earth."

"Forgive me, but if it isn't intruding on something too intimate, can you remember the circumstances in which she said this?"

"She had been doing this room and she went outside to shake the carpet."

"Sorry, which carpet? There are two."

"That one, the larger one."

"It would have been too heavy for her. Did you help her?"
"Yes."

"Each of you held one end, and she leaned far back throwing up her arms high as on a swing and turning away her face from the blowing dust and squinted her eyes and laughed? Isn't that how it was? How well I know her ways! And then you walked toward each other folding up the heavy carpet first in two and then in four, and she joked and made faces, didn't she? Didn't she?"

They stood up and went to different windows and looked out in different directions. After a time Strelnikov walked up to Yurii Andreievich, caught hold of his hands, pressed them to his breast, and went on as hurriedly as before:

"Forgive me. I realize that I am touching on things that are dear and holy to you. But I should like to ask you more questions, if you'll let me. Only please don't go away. Don't leave me alone. I'll be going soon myself. Just think—six years of separation, six years of inconceivable self-restraint. But I kept thinking that freedom was not yet wholly won. When I'd won it, I thought, my hands would be untied and I could belong to my family. And now, all my calculations have come to nothing. They'll arrest me tomorrow. You are near and dear to her. Perhaps you'll see her one day and . . . But what am I saying! I'm mad. They'll arrest me, and they won't let me say a word in my own defense. They'll come at me with shouts and curses and gag me. Don't I know how it's done!"

18

At long last, Yurii Andreievich had a good sleep. For the first time in many nights he fell asleep the moment he lay down. Strelnikov spent the night; the doctor put him in the next room. The few times the doctor woke up and turned over or pulled the blankets to his chin, he was conscious of the strong refreshment of sleep and he dropped off happily again at once. Toward morning he had several short, kaleidoscopic dreams of his childhood, so detailed and logical that he took them for reality.

He dreamed, for instance, that his mother's watercolor showing a place on the Italian Riviera suddenly dropped from the wall, and he was aroused by a sound of breaking glass. He opened his eyes. "No, it can't be that," he thought. "It's Antipov, Lara's husband Strelnikov, scaring the wolves in the Shutma as Bacchus would say." But no, what nonsense! It was the picture. There it was, lying in pieces on the floor, he assured himself, back in his dream.

He woke up late, with a headache from having slept too long. For a time he couldn't think who or where he was.

Then he remembered: "Strelnikov is in here. It's late. I must get dressed. He must be up by now. If not, I'll wake him and make some coffee, and we'll have it together."

"Pavel Pavlovich!" he called out.

There was no answer. "He's still asleep. He's a sound sleeper, I must say." He dressed unhurriedly and went into the next room. Strelnikov's fur hat was on the table, but he was nowhere in the house. "Must have gone for a walk. And without his hat. Toughening himself up. I ought to be getting out of Varykino today, but it's too late now. Again I've overslept, it's the same thing every day."

He lit the kitchen range, picked up a bucket, and started toward the well. A few yards from the door, Strelnikov lay across the path with his head in a snowdrift. He had shot himself. The snow was a red lump under his left temple where he had bled. Drops of spurting blood that had mixed with the snow formed red beads that looked like rowanberries.

CHAPTER FIFTEEN

Conclusion

1

It remains to tell the brief story of the last eight or ten years of Zhivago's life, during which he went more and more to seed, gradually losing his knowledge and skill as a doctor and a writer, emerging from his state of depression and resuming his work only to fall back, after a short flare-up of activity, into long periods of indifference to himself and to everything in the world. During these years the heart disease which he had himself diagnosed earlier but without realizing its gravity developed to an advanced stage.

He went to Moscow at the beginning of the NEP, the most ambiguous and hypocritical of all Soviet periods. He was even thinner, more neglected, and more unkempt than when he went to Yuriatin after escaping from the partisans. In the course of his journey he had again gradually discarded those of his clothes that had some value, exchanging them for bread and a few worn old rags to cover his nakedness. So he had lived off his second fur coat and suit, and arrived in the streets of Moscow dressed in a gray sheepskin hat, puttees, and a worn-out army overcoat stripped of all its buttons like a convict's uniform. In this getup he was indistinguishable from the countless Red Army men who thronged the stations and the streets and squares of the capital.

He had not arrived alone. Following him wherever he went was a good-looking young peasant boy who was also dressed in old army clothes. They both turned up in the few surviving Moscow drawing rooms like those in which Yurii Andreievich had spent his childhood, where he was remembered and welcomed with his companion (after tactful inquiries as to whether they had been to the baths—typhus was still raging) and in which he was soon told of the circumstances of his family's departure from Russia.

Both of them shied away from people, and their unsociability made them avoid going among people separately, for fear of becoming the center of attention and having to talk. Usually, when these two lanky figures made their appearance at any gathering of friends, they retired to some corner, where they could spend the evening in silence, without having to take part in the general conversation.

Dressed in his rags and accompanied everywhere by the boy, the tall, gaunt doctor looked like a peasant Seeker after Truth, and his companion like a patient, blindly devoted, and obedient disciple. Who was his young companion?

2

Yurii Andreievich had made the last stage of his journey by train but had covered the earlier and much longer part on foot.

The villages he went through looked no better than those he had seen in Siberia and the Urals, after running away from his captivity in the woods. Only then it had been winter, while now, at the end of the summer and the beginning of a warm, dry autumn, the weather made things easier.

Half the villages he passed were deserted, the fields abandoned and unharvested as after an enemy raid. Such were the effects of war—the civil war.

For two or three days at the end of September his road followed the steep bank of a river. The river flowing toward him was on his right. On his left the wide, unharvested fields stretched from the road to the cloudbanks on the horizon. At long intervals they were interrupted by woods, for the most part oak, maple, and elm. The woods ran to the river in deep gullies, which dropped precipitously and cut across the road.

In the unharvested fields the ripe grain spilled and trickled on the ground. Yurii Andreievich gathered it in handfuls, and at the worst, if he had no means of boiling it and making gruel, he stuffed it into his mouth and chewed it with great difficulty. The raw, half-chewed grain was almost indigestible.

Never in his life had he seen such dark-looking rye, rusty, brown, the color of old gold. Usually, when it is harvested in time, its color is much lighter.

These flame-colored fields blazing without fire, these fields silently proclaiming their distress, were coldly bordered by the vast, quiet sky, its face already wintry and shadowed by ceaselessly moving, long, flaky snow-clouds with black centers and white flanks.

Everything was moving slowly, regularly—the flowing river, the road running by it, and the doctor walking along the road in the same direction as the drifting clouds. Nor were the rye fields motionless. Their surface was alive, they were astir with an incessant crawling that suggested something foul and repellent.

Never had there been such a plague of mice. They had bred in unprecedented quantities. They scurried over the doctor's face and hands and inside his sleeves and trousers at night, when he was caught by darkness and forced to sleep in the open, they raced across the road by day, gorged and teeming, and turned into squeaking pulsing slush when they were trodden underfoot.

Shaggy village curs, turned wild, followed him at a respectful distance, exchanging glances as if to decide on the best moment to fall on him and tear him to pieces. They fed on carrion, did not disdain mice, and eyed Yurii Andreievich from afar, moving after him confidently as though waiting for something. For some reason they never ventured into the wood and, whenever he came near one, gradually fell back, turned tail, and vanished.

The woods and the fields offered a complete contrast in those days. Deserted by man, the fields looked orphaned as if his absence had put them under a curse. The forest, however, well rid of him, flourished proudly in freedom as though released from captivity.

Usually the nuts are not allowed to ripen, as people, and particularly village children, pick them green, breaking off whole branches. But now the wooded sides of hills and gullies were thick with rough, golden foliage dusted and coarsened by the sun. Festive among it were bulging clusters of nuts, three or four, as if tied together, ripe and ready to fall from the branches. Yurii Andreievich cracked and crunched them in quantity. He stuffed his pockets and his bag full of them; for a whole week he fed on hazelnuts.

The fields appeared to him as something seen in the fever of a dangerous illness, and the woods, by contrast, in the lucidity of health regained. God, so it seemed to him, dwelled in the woods, while the fields echoed with the sardonic laughter of the devil.

3

At this point of his journey, Yurii Andreievich came to a deserted, burned-out village. All the houses had stood in one row on the side of the road opposite the river. The strip of land between the road and the edge of the steep riverbank had not been built on.

Only a few houses, blackened by fire, were still standing, but they too were empty, uninhabited. Nothing was left of the others but piles of charred rubble with black chimneys rising out of them.

The cliffs facing the river were honeycombed with pits where the villagers had quarried rock for millstones; this had been their means of livelihood. Three such unfinished stones were lying on the ground in front of the last house in the row, one of the few that had remained standing. Like the others, this house was uninhabited.

Yurii Andreievich went inside. It was a still afternoon, but the moment he entered it was as if a gust of wind burst into the house. Tufts of straw and hay slithered across the floors, remnants of paper flapped on the walls, and the whole place stirred and rustled. Like the countryside, it swarmed with mice which scampered off, squeaking, in all directions.

He came out. The sun was setting behind the fields in back of the village. A warm, golden glow flooded the opposite bank, and its fading brilliance was reflected by pools and on bushes, some of which reached out into the middle of the stream. Yurii Andreievich crossed the road and sat down on one of the millstones that lay on the grass.

A fair, shaggy head came up over the edge of the bank, then shoulders, then arms. Someone was climbing up the cliff path with a bucket of water. Seeing the doctor, he stopped, still visible only from the waist up.

"Would you like a drink of water? If you won't hurt me, I won't hurt you."

"Thank you. Yes, I'd like a drink. But come over here, don't be frightened. Why should I hurt you?"

The water carrier was a boy in his teens, barefoot, ragged, and dishevelled.

In spite of his friendly words, he pierced the doctor with a worried, suspicious stare. For some reason the boy was strangely agitated. Finally, putting down his bucket, he rushed toward the doctor but stopped halfway, muttering:

"It isn't . . . It can't be . . . I must be dreaming. Pardon me, comrade, if I ask you, but haven't I seen you before? Yes! Yes! Surely! You're the doctor, aren't you?"

"And who are you?"

"Don't you recognize me?"

"No."

"We were in the same train from Moscow, in the same car. They'd conscripted me for labor. I was in the convoy."

It was Vasia Brykin. He threw himself on the ground before the doctor, kissed his hands, and wept.

The burned ruins were those of his native village, Vereten-niki. His mother was dead. When the village was destroyed, Vasia hid in a cave in the quarries, but his mother, thinking he had been taken off to town, went mad with grief and drowned herself in the river—that very river Pelga which flowed at the foot of the cliff where they were sitting and talking. His sisters Alia and Aria were said to be in an orphanage in another district, but he knew nothing certain about them. He went on to Moscow with the doctor, and on the way told him of many terrible happenings.

4

"That's last winter's corn going to waste in the fields. We'd just finished sowing it when our troubles began. It was after Aunt Polia went away. Do you remember Aunt Polia?"

"No. I never even knew her. Who is she?"

"You never knew Aunt Polia? She was with us in the train! Tiagunova. The one who was plump and fair, and looked you straight in the eye."

"That's the one who was always braiding and undoing her hair?"

"That's it! The one with the pigtail, that's the one!"

"Yes, I remember her. Wait a moment, now I come to think of it, I met her later in a town in Siberia, we met in the street."

"You don't mean it! You met Aunt Polia!"

"What's the matter with you, Vasia? Why are you shaking my hands like a madman? If you're not careful you'll pull them off. And what are you blushing for, like a girl?"

"Well, tell me quickly, how is she? Tell me."

"She was all right when I saw her. She spoke about you and your people. Didn't she say she'd been staying with you, or have I got it wrong?"

"Of course she did, of course she did. She stayed with us. My mother loved her like her own sister. She's quiet and a good worker, very clever with her hands. We had plenty of everything in the house as long as she was living with us. But they made her life a misery in Veretenniki with all their talk.

"There was a man in the village called Rotten Kharlam. He was making up to Polia. He's a slanderer, and he had no nose. She wouldn't even look at him. He had a grudge against me for that. He spoke evil about me and Polia. In the end she left, she couldn't stand it anymore. And that was the beginning of all our troubles.

"There was a terrible murder near here. A widow who lived all by herself on a farm, up toward Buiskoie. Used to walk about in a man's shoes with elastic straps. She kept a fierce dog chained to a long wire, which ran all around the house. Gorlan, she called it. She did all the work around the house and on the farm by herself, without any help. Well, last year the winter came before anyone expected it. The snow was early, and the old woman hadn't dug up her potatoes. So she comes to Veretenniki and says, 'Help me,' she says, 'I'll pay you either in money or a share of the potatoes.'

"I said I'd do it, but when I got to the farm Kharlam was there, he'd taken the job on before me and she hadn't bothered to tell me. Well, I wasn't going to fight him about it, so we did the work together. It was wicked weather—rain and snow and mud and slush. We dug and we dug, and we burned the tops to dry the potatoes in the smoke. When we'd finished she settled with us, fair and square, and she let Kharlam go, but she gave me a wink as much as to say, I should stay on or come back later.

"So I went back again and she said: 'I don't want to give up my surplus to the state. You're a good boy,' she says, 'I know you won't give me away. You see, I'm not hiding anything from you. I would dig a pit myself, but you see what it's like outside. I've left it too late, it's winter, I can't manage by myself. If you dig it for me, you won't be sorry.'

"So I made the pit in the proper way for a hiding place, wide at the bottom and narrow at the top, like a jug, and we started a fire again and warmed and dried the pit with the smoke—all in a howling blizzard. Then we put the potatoes into the pit and the earth back on top. A very neat job it was. Of course, I didn't say a word to a living soul, not even to my mother or my sisters. God forbid!

"Well, hardly a month went by before the farm was robbed. People coming past from Buiskoie said the door was wide open, and the whole place was cleaned out. No sign of the widow, and Gorlan had broken his chain and bolted.

"A bit later still, there was a thaw just before the New Year. On St. Basil's Eve it rained, so the snow got washed off the high ground, you could see the bare soil. Then Gorlan came back to the farm and found the place where the potatoes were buried, and started rooting up the earth. He dug and dug and threw the earth back, and there were the old woman's feet sticking up out of the hole, in those shoes with elastic straps she used to wear—horrible!

"Everyone in Veretenniki was sorry for the old woman. No one suspected Kharlam, and can you blame them? It was unthinkable. He wouldn't have had the nerve. If he had done it, he would have run away, far from here.

"The kulaks, in the village, were very pleased about the murder. Here's a chance to stir up trouble, they thought. 'See what those town people are doing to you,' they said. 'They did it on purpose to frighten you, so you wouldn't hide your grain and bury your potatoes. And you think it's bandits from the woods that killed her, fools that you are! Just you go on doing what the town people tell you. They've got a lot more up their sleeves, they'll take everything, they'll starve you out. If you want to know what's good for you, then listen to us, we'll teach you some sense. When they come to take away what you've earned by the sweat of your brow, tell them, We haven't so much as a grain of rye, let alone surpluses. And in case of trouble, use your pitchforks. And anyone who's against the village had better look out!' Well, the old fellows talked and held village meetings, and that was just what Kharlam wanted. Off he went to the town with his tale. 'Fine goings-on in the village,' he says, 'and what are you doing about it? A Poor Peasants' Committee, that's what we need. Give the word and I'll have them all at each other's throats in no time.' Then he made off somewhere, and never showed up in our parts again.

"What came after happened of itself. Nobody informed. Nobody's to blame. They sent Red Army men from the town, and they set up a court. And they started on me. That was because of what Kharlam had told them. I'd dodged the labor service. I'd run away. And I'd killed the old woman and stirred up the village, they said. They locked me up, but luckily I thought to pull up one of the floor boards and got away. I hid in a cave in the old quarry. The village was burned over my head—I never saw it, and my own mother drowned herself in a hole in the ice and I never knew. It all happened by itself. They'd put the Red Army men in a house by themselves and given them liquor, and they all got dead drunk. In the night the house happened to catch fire, and the fire spread to the other houses, from one to the next. Our village people, when it started, jumped out of their houses and ran away. But the people from town—mind you, nobody set fire to them—naturally, they were all burned to death. Nobody told our people to run away or to stay away from their burned-out homes, but they were afraid that something else would happen. The kulaks spread a rumor that every tenth man would be shot. When I came out of the cave, they'd all gone. I didn't find a soul, they're wandering around somewhere."

5

The doctor and Vasia arrived in Moscow in the spring of 1922 at the beginning of the NEP. The weather was fine and warm. Sunshine glancing off the golden domes of the Church of the Savior played on the square below where grass was growing in the cracks between the paving stones.

The ban on private enterprise had been lifted and trade within certain narrow limits was allowed. Deals were made on the scale of the turnover of a rag-and-bone merchant in a flea market; their pettiness led to speculation and abuses. No new wealth was created by these transactions and they did nothing to relieve the squalor of the town, but fortunes were made out of the futile reselling of goods already sold a dozen times over.

The owners of several modest private libraries got down their books from their shelves and collected them all in one place. They notified the Town Soviet of their wish to start a co-operative bookshop. They applied for premises and obtained the use of some shoestore or florist's, which had been empty and closed down since the first days of the revolution, and there, under its spacious vaults, they sold out their small haphazard collections.

Professors' wives who, when times had been hard before, had secretly baked white rolls and sold them in defiance of the regulations, now sold them openly at some bicycle repair shop or other which had been requisitioned and left unused all these years. They changed sides, accepted the revolution, and no longer used their genteel language.

In Moscow Yurii Andreievich said:

"You'll have to work at something, Vasia."

"I'd like to study."

"That goes without saying."

"Another thing I want to do is draw my mother's picture from memory."

"That's a good idea too. But for that you'd have to know how to draw. Have you ever tried?"

"When I was apprenticed to my uncle I used to play around with charcoal when he wasn't looking."

"Well, why not? We'll see what can be done."

Vasia did not show any great talent for drawing but he had enough aptitude to enter a school of industrial design. With the help of his friends, Yurii Andreievich got him into what had been the Stroganov Institute, where he first took a course in general subjects and then specialized in printing, binding, and book design.

The doctor and Vasia combined their efforts. The doctor wrote booklets on various subjects and Vasia set them up and printed them in small editions, as part of his training at the Institute. They were then distributed through the secondhand bookshops that had been recently opened by their friends.

These booklets contained Yurii Andreievich's philosophy, his views on medicine, his definitions of health and sickness, reflections on the doctrine of evolution, his theory of individuality as the biological basis of the organism, and thoughts about religion and history (which had much in common with those of his uncle and Sima), as well as his poems, short stories, and sketches of the Pugachev country he had visited.

They were written in an easy conversational style but were anything but works of popularization, since they advanced opinions that were controversial, hypothetical, and untested, though always lively and original. The booklets found an easy sale among collectors.

In those days everything became a specialty, including versification and the art of translation; theoretical studies were written on all possible subjects, and institutes were founded right and left. There arose all sorts of Palaces of Thought, Academies of Artistic Ideas. Yurii Andreievich acted as medical consultant to half of these pseudo-cultural institutions.

For a long time he and Vasia remained friends and lived together. During that period they moved from one dilapidated place to another, each uninhabitable and uncomfortable in a different way.

Immediately on arriving in Moscow, Yurii Andreievich had revisited his old home in Sivtsev Vrazhok. He was told that his family had not stayed there when they returned to Moscow. After their deportation, the rooms registered in their name had been given to new tenants and there was not a sign of their belongings. Yurii Andreievich himself was avoided by his former neighbors, who regarded him as dangerous to know.

Markel was no longer there. He had gone up in the world and

had been appointed house manager at Flour Town. The manager's flat had been put at his disposal, but he preferred the old porter's lodge, which had floors of beaten earth but which also had running water and an enormous Russian stove. All the pipes and radiators in the buildings burst in the cold weather, but the porter's lodge was always warm and dry, and the water did not freeze.

There came a time when the friendship between Yurii Andreievich and Vasia cooled. Vasia had developed remarkably. He no longer thought or spoke like the ragged, barefoot, dishevelled boy from Veretenniki. The obviousness, the self-evidence of the truths proclaimed by the revolution attracted him increasingly, and the doctor's language, with its obscurities and its imagery, now struck him as the voice of error, doomed, conscious of its weakness and therefore evasive.

The doctor was making calls on various government departments. He was trying to obtain the political rehabilitation of his family and permission for them to return to Russia. At the same time he applied for a foreign passport for himself and permission to bring his family back from Paris.

Vasia was astonished at how lukewarm and half-hearted his efforts were. Yurii Andreievich seemed always to be in a hurry to decide that he was not getting anywhere, and he spoke with too much conviction and almost with satisfaction of the futility of undertaking anything further.

Vasia found fault with him more and more often, and although Yurii Andreievich did not take offense at being justly criticized, his relationship with Vasia gradually deteriorated. Finally their friendship broke up, and they parted company. The doctor left the room that they had shared to Vasia and moved to Flour Town, where Markel was all-powerful and had set aside for him a corner at the back of what had been the Sventitskys'. It consisted of a derelict bathroom, a room with a single window adjoining it, and the dilapidated, crumbling kitchen and back entrance. After he had moved in, Yurii Andreievich gave up medicine, neglected himself, stopped seeing his friends, and lived in great poverty.

6

It was a gray Sunday in winter. Smoke was rising in columns from the roofs and in thin black streams from the windows, which, in spite of the regulations, were still used as outlets for the metal pipes of stoves. The amenities of town life had still not been restored. The tenants of Flour Town went about unwashed and suffered from boils and colds.

As on every Sunday, Markel Shchapov and his family were all at home.

They were having dinner at a large kitchen table. At this same table in days gone by, at the time of the bread rationing, all the tenants' coupons were collected and cut, snipped, counted, sorted, and wrapped in pieces of paper or tied into bundles according to their category before being taken to the baker's at dawn; and here too, later on in the morning, the loaves were cut and broken and crumbled to make up each tenant's apportioned weight. But all this was now only a memory. Food rationing had been replaced by other forms of control, and the Shchapovs at their midday meal ate their fill and champed and chewed with relish.

Half the room was taken up by the broad Russian stove, which stood in the middle and had bedding on its flat top and quilts hanging down over the sides.

Near the entrance was a faucet, and here the pipes were not frozen. Benches ran down two sides of the room; under them were kept the family belongings in trunks and bundles. The table was on the left and had a plate rack fixed above it.

The room was very hot. The stove was going full blast. In front of it stood Markel's wife Agafia; her sleeves were rolled up above her elbows and she was using a long pair of tongs to move the pots inside the oven, crowding them together or spacing them out according to need. Her sweating face was in turn lit by the blaze in the oven and misted over by steam. Pushing the pots to one side, she pulled out from behind them a pastry on an iron sheet, flipped it over, and put it back to brown. Yurii Andreievich came in with two buckets.

"Good appetite."

"Make yourself at home. Sit down and have dinner with us."

"Thank you, I've had mine."

"We know what you call dinner. Why don't you sit down and have something hot? You needn't turn up your nose at it—it's good stuff, baked potatoes, pie with kasha."

"No thanks, really. . . . I'm sorry to keep on opening the door and letting in the cold. I want to take up as much water as I can. I've cleaned the bathtub, now I'm filling that and the wash tubs. I'll come in half a dozen times and then I won't trouble you again for a long time. Forgive me for bothering you like this, but I can't get water anywhere else."

"Help yourself. If you asked for syrup, we haven't got any, but there's plenty of water. Take as much as you like, we won't even charge you for it!"

They all laughed.

When Yurii Andreievich came for the third time to fill his fifth and sixth buckets, the tone had changed.

"My sons-in-law have been asking me who you are. I told them but they don't believe me. You go on running the water, don't mind me. Only don't slop it on the floor, clumsy! Don't you see, you've splashed some in the doorway. If it freezes over I can't see you coming to hack it up with a crowbar. And shut the door properly, you oaf, there's a draft coming in. Yes, so I was telling them who you are but they won't believe it. The money that was spent on you! All that learning, and where has it got you, I'd like to know?"

When Yurii Andreievich came in for the fifth or sixth time, Markel frowned.

"Just once more and that's that. There's a limit to everything, old man. If our little Marina didn't keep sticking up for you, I'd lock the door, no matter how high-born you are. You remember our Marina, don't you? There she is, the dark one at the end of the table. She's gone all red, look. 'Don't hurt his feelings, Dad,' she keeps telling me. As if anybody wants to hurt your feelings. She's a telegrapher at the Central Post Office—she knows foreign languages. 'He's unfortunate,' she says. She's so sorry for you, she'd go through fire and water for you! As if I'm to blame that you're a poor fish! You shouldn't have run away to Siberia, leaving your house at a bad time. It's your own fault. Look at us here—we sat it out through the famine and the White blockade, we didn't flinch—so here we are, safe and sound. Blame yourself. If you'd taken proper care of Tonia, she wouldn't be traipsing abroad now. Well, it's your business, what do I care. Only what I'd like to know, begging your pardon, is what do you want with all this water? Hired yourself out to make a skating rink or something? You and your water! I can't even get mad at you, you're such a wet rag!"

Again they all laughed. Marina, however, looked around angrily, flared up, and began to chide them. Yurii Andreievich was astonished by the sound of her voice, though he could not as yet have said why.

"There's a lot of cleaning to be done in the house, Markel. I've got to scrub the floors and wash some of my things as well."

The Shchapovs were amazed.

"Aren't you ashamed of yourself, saying such things, let alone doing them? You'll be starting a Chinese laundry next."

"Let me send my daughter up," said Agafia. "She'll do your washing and scrubbing, and your mending, if there is any. You don't need to be afraid of him, my dear. You can see how well brought up he is, he wouldn't hurt a fly."

"What an idea, Agafia Tikhonovna! I wouldn't dream of letting Marina do my scrubbing. Why on earth should she dirty her hands for me? I'll manage all right."

"You can dirty your hands and I can't, is that it?" Marina broke in. "Why are you so difficult, Yurii Andreievich? Would you really drive me out if I came up to see you?"

Marina could have been a singer. She had a pure, well-modulated voice of great range and strength. She did not speak loudly, but her voice gave the impression of being stronger than was needed for ordinary conversation; it seemed to have a life of its own, as though it did not belong to her. It seemed to come from behind her back or from the next room. This voice was her protection, her guardian angel; no one could wish to hurt or distress a woman with such a voice.

It was from this water-carrying on a Sunday that a friendship sprang up between the doctor and Marina. She would often come and help him with his housework. One day she stayed with him and did not again go back to the lodge. Thus she became Yurii Andreievich's third wife, though he was not divorced from the first, and they did not register their marriage. They had children. Markel and Agafia spoke of their daughter, not without pride, as the doctor's wife. Her father grumbled that there had never been a proper wedding either in church or at the registry, but his wife said: "Are you out of your mind? With Tonia still alive, that would be bigamy."—"It's you that's stupid," said Markel. "What's Tonia got to do with it? It's just the same as if she were dead. There's no law to protect her."

Yurii Andreievich sometimes said jokingly that theirs was a romance in twenty buckets, as you might have a novel in twenty chapters.

Marina forgave the doctor his eccentricities, the dirt and disorder he made in the house, his moods and his fancies; they were those of a man who was letting himself go and knew it. She bore with his grumbling, his tempers, and his nerves.

Her devotion went even further. At times they were destitute through his fault, and in order not to leave him alone at such moments she would give up her own job at the post office, where her work was so highly thought of that she was always taken back after her enforced absence. In obedience to Yurii Andreievich's whim, she would go out with him, doing odd jobs from house to house. They chopped wood for a good many of the tenants on the different floors. Some of them, particularly speculators who had made fortunes at the beginning of the NEP and artists and scholars who were close to the government, were setting up house on a comfortable scale. One day Yurii Andreievich and Marina, stepping carefully in their felt boots so as not to dirty the carpet with sawdust, were carrying wood into the study of a tenant who remained insultingly engrossed in something he was reading and did not honor them with so much as a glance. It was his wife who gave the orders and who paid them.

"What has the pig got his nose in?" the doctor wondered. The scholar was scribbling furiously in the margins of his book. As he passed him with a bundle of logs, Yurii Andreievich glanced over his shoulder. On the desk lay a pile of the early editions of the booklets that he had written and Vasia had printed.

7

Yurii Andreievich and Marina were now living in Spiridonovka Street, and Gordon had a room in Malaia Bronnaia Street nearby. Marina and the doctor had two daughters, Kapka (Capitolina), who was five years old, and the baby Klazhka (Claudia), who was only six months.

The early summer of 1929 was very hot. People who lived in the same neighborhood would go to see each other, hatless and in their shirtsleeves.

Gordon's room was part of a curious structure, which had once been the premises of a fashionable tailor. The shop had been on two floors, connected by a spiral staircase, and both looking out onto the street through one large plate-glass window, on which the tailor's name and occupation were traced in gold letters.

The premises were now divided into three. By means of floor boards an extra room had been fitted into the space between the lower and the upper levels. It had what was, for a living room, a curious window, about three feet high, starting at floor level and with part of the gold letters remaining. From outside through the gaps in the lettering, anyone in the room could be seen up to the knees. This was Gordon's room. With him at the moment were Zhivago, Dudorov, Marina, and the children, who, unlike the grown-ups, were entirely visible through the glass. Marina soon left with the little girls, and the three men remained alone.

They were having one of those unhurried, lazy summer conversations that go on between men who were at school together and have many years of friendship behind them.

To carry on a conversation naturally and intelligently, a man must have an adequate supply of words. Of the three, only Yurii Andreievich answered this requirement.

The other two were always at a loss for an expression. They did not possess the gift of eloquence. At a loss for words, they paced up and down, puffed at their cigarettes, gesticulated, and repeated themselves. ("That, plainly, is dishonest, old man! Dishonest, yes, yes, that's what it is, dishonest.")

They were unaware that such dramatic excesses, far from showing their warmth and breadth of character, expressed intellectual poverty.

Both Gordon and Dudorov moved among cultured academicians, they spent their lives among good books, good thinkers, good composers and good music, which was as good yesterday as today (but always good!), and they did not know that the misfortune of having average taste is a great deal worse than the misfortune of having no taste at all.

Neither Dudorov nor Gordon realized that even their admonitions to Zhivago were prompted less by a friendly wish to influence his conduct than by their inability to think with freedom and to guide the conversation at will. Like a runaway cart, the conversation took them where they did not want to go. Unable to steer it, they were bound, sooner or later, to bump into something, and to be hit. And so, in their sermonizing, time and again they got off their tracks.

To Zhivago, their unconscious motives, their artificial emotionalism, and their strained reasoning were transparent. But he could hardly say to them: "Dear friends, how desperately commonplace you are—you and your circle, the names and the authorities you always quote, their glamour and art which you so much admire! The only bright and vital thing about you is that you are my contemporaries and friends!" How could anyone confess to such a thought? So, in order to spare their feelings, he listened meekly.

Dudorov had recently come back from his first deportation. His civil rights had been restored, and he had been allowed to resume his regular work at the university.

Now he was telling his friends about his experiences as a deportee. He spoke sincerely and without hypocrisy. He was not motivated by fear; he really believed in what he was saying.

He said that the arguments of the prosecution, his treatment in prison and after he came out, and particularly his private talks with the examining judge had "aired" his brains, re-educated him politically, opened his eyes to many things he had not seen before, and made him more mature as a person.

These reflections appealed to Gordon just because they were so hackneyed. He nodded his head with sympathy and agreed with Dudorov in everything. It was the very triteness of the feelings and expressions that moved him most; he mistook Dudorov's reflection of prescribed feeling for a genuine expression of humanity.

Dudorov's pious platitudes were in the spirit of the times. But it was precisely their conformism, their transparent sanctimoniousness, that exasperated Yurii Andreievich. Men who are not free, he thought, always idealize their bondage. So it was in the Middle Ages, and later the Jesuits always exploited this human trait. Zhivago could not bear the political mysticism of the Soviet intelligentsia, though it was the very thing they regarded as their highest achievement, or as it would have been called in those days, "the spiritual ceiling of the age." But this he also kept to himself in order not to hurt the feelings of his friends.

What did interest him in Dudorov's story was his account of a cellmate of his, Bonifatii Orletsov, a follower of Tikhon, the Patriarch of Moscow. Orletsov had a six-year-old daughter, Christina. The arrest and subsequent fate of her beloved father had been a terrible blow to her. Terms such as "obscurantist priest" and "disenfranchised" seemed to her the stigma of dishonor. Dudorov felt that in her childish ardor she had vowed someday to remove that stigma from her family name. This goal, conceived at such an early age and nursed with burning resolution, made of her even now an enthusiastic champion of Communist ideals.

"I must go," said Yurii Andreievich. "Don't be cross with me, Misha. It's hot and stuffy in here. I need to get some air."

"But the window is open, look, down there on the floor. . . . I'm sorry, we've been smoking too much. We keep forgetting that we shouldn't smoke with you here. It isn't my fault that it gets so stuffy, it's the idiotic way the window is made. You should find me another room."

"I must be off, Misha. We've talked enough. Thank you both for your concern. . . . I'm not pretending, you know. It's an illness I've got, sclerosis of the heart. The walls of the heart muscle wear out and get thin, and one fine day they may burst. I'm not yet forty, you know, and it isn't as if I were a drunkard, or burned the candle at both ends!"

"Nonsense! We aren't playing your funeral march yet. You'll last us out."

"Microscopic forms of cardiac hemorrhages have become very frequent in recent years. They are not always fatal. Some people get over them. It's a typical modern disease. I think its causes are of a moral order. The great majority of us are required to live a life of constant, systematic duplicity. Your health is bound to be affected if, day after day, you say the opposite of what you feel, if you grovel before what you dislike and rejoice at what brings you nothing but misfortune. Our nervous system isn't just a fiction, it's a part of our physical body, and our soul exists in space and is inside us, like the teeth in our mouth. It can't be forever violated with impunity. I found it painful to listen to you, Innokentii, when you told us how you were re-educated and became mature in jail. It was like listening to a circus horse describing how it broke itself in."

"I must stand up for Dudorov," said Gordon. "You've got unused to simple human words, they don't reach you anymore."

"It may very well be, Misha. But in any case, you must let me go now. I can hardly breathe. I swear, I'm not exaggerating."

"Wait a moment, you're just looking for excuses. We won't let you go until you've given us an honest, straightforward answer. Do you or don't you agree that it's time you changed your ways and reformed? What are you going to do about it? To start with, you must clarify your situation with Tonia and Marina. They are human beings, women who feel and suffer, not disembodied ideas existing only in your head. And second, it's a scandal that a man like you should go to waste. You've got to wake up and shake off your inertia, pull yourself together and look at things without this impermissible arrogance, yes, yes, without this inexcusable haughtiness in regard to everyone, you must go back to work and take up your practice."

"All right, I'll give you my answer. I've been thinking something of this sort myself recently, so I can really promise you that there's going to be a change. I think everything will come out all right. And quite soon, at that. You'll see. I really mean it. It's already begun. I have an incredible, passionate desire to live, and to live always means to strive to move higher, toward perfection, and to achieve it.

"I am glad that you stand up for Marina, Misha, just as you always stood up for Tonia. But after all, I have no quarrel with either of them, I am not at war with them, or with anyone else for that matter. You used to reproach me at first because Marina said 'you' to me and called me Yurii Andreievich, while I said 'thou' and 'Marina' to her—as though it didn't distress me too! But you know that the deeper causes of this unnatural behavior were removed long ago, and now we treat each other as equals.

"Now I can tell you another piece of good news. I've been getting letters again from Paris. The children are growing up, they have a lot of French friends of their own age. Sasha is about to graduate from the *école primaire* and Masha is soon going to it. I've never seen her, you know. I have a feeling in spite of everything that although they've become French citizens, they'll soon be back and that everything will be straightened out in some way or other.

"It seems that Tonia and my father-in-law know about Marina and our children. I didn't tell them in my letters, but they must have heard about it from others. Naturally, Alexander Alexandrovich, as a father, feels outraged and hurt. That would explain why our correspondence was interrupted for almost five years. I used to correspond with them, you know, after I got back to Moscow, and then they suddenly stopped writing.

"Now, quite recently, they've begun writing again, all of them, even the children. They write very warmly and affectionately. For some reason they've relented. Perhaps Tonia has found someone else; I hope with all my heart she has. I don't know. I too write from time to time. . . . But I really can't stay any longer. I must go or I'll get an attack. Goodbye."

Next morning Marina came running in to Gordon, greatly distressed. There was no one she could leave the children with, so in one arm she carried the baby wrapped in a blanket and with her free hand she was pulling Kapka, who trailed behind and dragged her feet.

"Is Yura here, Misha?" she asked in a frightened voice.

"Didn't he go home last night?"

"No."

"Then he must have spent the night at Innokentii's."

"I've come from there. Innokentii is at the university, but the neighbors know Yura and they say he hasn't been there."

"Where can he be, then?"

Marina put Klazhka down on the sofa, and then she began to sob hysterically.

8

For two days Gordon and Dudorov did not dare to leave Marina alone and took turns watching her and hunting for the doctor. They called at all the places he might conceivably have gone to—Flour Town, Sivtsev Vrazhok, all the Palaces of Thought and Academies of Ideas he had ever been employed in; they looked up every friend of his they had ever heard him talk about and whose address they could discover—but with no success.

They did not report him as missing to the police. Although he was registered and had no police record, it was better not to draw the attention of the authorities to a man who, by the standards of the day, lived anything but an exemplary life. They decided not to put them on his track except as a last resort.

On the third day, letters from Yurii Andreievich came by different mails for all three of them—Gordon, Dudorov, and Marina. He was full of regret for the trouble and anxiety he had caused them, he begged them not to worry about him, and he implored them by everything that was holy to give up their search for him, saying that it would in any case be fruitless.

He told them that in order to rebuild his life as completely and rapidly as possible, he wished to spend some time by himself, concentrating on his affairs, and that as soon as he was settled in a job and reasonably certain of not falling back into his old ways he would leave his hiding place and return to Marina and the children.

He told Gordon that he was sending him a money order for Marina and asked him to get a nurse for the children, so that Marina could go back to work. He explained that he was not sending the money to her address for fear of someone seeing the receipt and her thus being exposed to the risk of robbery.

The money soon came, and the amount far exceeded the standards of Yurii and his friends. The nurse was hired. Marina went back to work at the post office. She was still greatly upset but, accustomed as she was to Yurii Andreievich's oddities, she eventually resigned herself to his latest whim. All three of them went on looking for him, but gradually they came to the conclusion that it was as futile as he had warned them it would be. They could find no trace of him.

9

Yet all the time he was living within a stone's throw, right under their eyes and noses, in the very middle of the district they were combing for him.

On the day of his disappearance he left Gordon and went out into Bronnaia Street a little before dusk. He turned straight toward home, but almost immediately, within less than a hundred yards, he ran into his half brother Evgraf, who was coming down the street toward him. He had neither seen him nor heard of him for more than three years. It turned out that

Evgraf had just arrived in Moscow; as usual, he came quite unexpectedly, and he shrugged off all questions with a smile or a joke. On the other hand, from the few questions he asked Yurii Andreievich, he gathered the gist of his troubles at once, and then and there, between one corner and another as they walked along the narrow, twisting, crowded street, he worked out a practical plan to rescue him. It was his idea that Yurii Andreievich should disappear and remain in hiding for some time.

He took a room for him in Kamerger Street, as it was still called, near the Arts Theater. He provided him with money. He took steps to get him a good position in a hospital, with plenty of opportunity for going on with his research, and assisted him by his patronage. Finally, he gave him his word that the ambiguity of his family's situation in Paris would be resolved. Either Yurii Andreievich would go to them or they would come to him. All these things Evgraf undertook to see to himself. As usual, his brother's help put new heart into Yurii Andreievich. As always before, the riddle of his power remained unsolved. Yurii Andreievich did not even try to penetrate the secret.

10

His room faced south. It almost adjoined the theater and looked out over the rooftops opposite; beyond them, the summer sun stood over Okhotny Ryad, and the street below was in shadow.

To Yurii Andreievich the room was more than a place for work, more than his study. At this time of devouring activity, when the pile of notebooks on his desk was too small to hold all his plans and ideas and the surplus floated in the air like apparitions—as unfinished pictures stand with their faces to the walls in a painter's studio—his living room was to him a banqueting room of the spirit, a cupboard of mad dreams, a storeroom of revelations.

Fortunately, Evgraf's negotiations with the hospital dragged on, and the start of Yurii Andreievich's new job was indefinitely postponed. The delay gave him time to write.

He began by trying to sort out those of his earlier poems of which he could remember snatches or of which Evgraf somehow got him the texts. (These were manuscripts, some in his own hand, some copies made by others.) But the disorderliness of the material made him squander his energy even more than he was inclined to do by nature. He soon gave it up and turned to new work.

He would make the rough draft of an article, like the notes he had kept when he first went to Varykino, or put down the middle, or the end, or the beginning of a poem as it came into his mind. There were times when he could hardly keep pace with his thoughts, even in his shorthand made up of initials and abbreviations.

He was in a hurry. Whenever his imagination flagged he whipped it up by making drawings in the margins of his notebooks. The drawings were always of forest cuttings or of street intersections marked by the sign: "*Moreau & Vetchinkin. Mechanical seeders. Threshing machines.*"

The articles and poems were all on the same theme, the city.

11

These notes were found later among his papers:

"When I came back to Moscow in 1922 I found it deserted and half destroyed. So it had come out of the ordeals of the first years after the revolution; so it remains to this day. Its population has decreased, no new houses are being built, and the old ones are left in disrepair.

"But even in this condition it is still a big modern city, and cities are the only source of inspiration for a new, truly modern art.

"The seemingly incongruous and arbitrary jumble of things and ideas in the work of the Symbolists (Blok, Verhaeren, Whitman) is not a stylistic caprice. This is a new order of impressions, taken directly from life.

"Just as they hurry their succession of images through the lines of their poems, so the street in a busy town hurries past us, with its crowds and its broughams and carriages at the end of the last century, or its streetcars and subways at the beginning of ours.

"Pastoral simplicity doesn't exist in these conditions. When it is attempted, its pseudo-artlessness is a literary fraud, not inspired by the countryside but taken from the shelves of academic archives. The living language of our time, born spontaneously and naturally in accord with its spirit, is the language of urbanism.

"I live at a busy intersection. Moscow, blinded by the sun and the white heat of its asphalt-paved yards, scattering reflections of the sun from its upper windows, breathing in the flowering of clouds and streets, is whirling around me, turning my head and telling me to turn the heads of others by writing poems in its praise. For this purpose, Moscow has brought me up and made me an artist.

"The incessant rumbling by day and night in the street outside our walls is as inseparable from the modern soul as the opening bars of an overture are inseparable from the curtain, as yet secret and dark, but already beginning to crimson in the glow of the footlights. The city, incessantly moving and roaring outside our doors and windows, is an immense introduction to the life of each of us. It is in these terms that I should like to write about the city."

There are no such poems in what has been preserved of Zhivago's work. Or does the one entitled "Hamlet" belong to this category?

12

One morning at the end of August, Yurii Andreievich took the trolley at a stop at a corner of Gazetny Street which went up along Nikita Street to the Kudrinskaia terminal. He was going for the first time to his job at the Botkin Hospital, which was then known as the Soldatenko Hospital. He had been there before only once or twice for reasons connected with his job.

He had no luck with his trolley; it had a defective motor and kept getting into trouble of every sort. Either its way was blocked by a cart in front of it with its wheels caught in the grooves of the rails, or the insulation went wrong on the roof or under the floor and the current short-circuited with a flash and a crackle.

The driver would step off the front platform, walk around the trolley with a wrench, and squat down and tinker with the machinery between the rear platform and the wheels.

The ill-fated trolley blocked the traffic all along the line. The whole street was dammed up with other trolleys that had already been stopped, and still others kept joining. The end of the line now reached as far back as the riding school and beyond. Passengers from cars in the rear moved to the front car, hoping to gain time, and got into the very car that was the cause of all the trouble. It was a hot morning, and the car was crowded and stuffy. Above the crowds running about in the street from one trolley to another, a dark lilac thundercloud was creeping higher and higher up the sky. A storm was gathering.

Yurii Andreievich sat on a single seat on the left, pressed against the window. He could see the left side of Nikita Street, where the Conservatory was situated. With the vague attention of a man thinking of something else, he watched the people walking and driving past on that side, missing no one.

A gray-haired old lady, in a light straw hat with linen daisies and cornflowers and a tight old-fashioned lilac dress, was trudging along the pavement, panting and fanning herself with a flat parcel that she was carrying in her hand. Tightly corseted, exhausted by the heat, and streaming with sweat, she kept mopping her damp lips and eyebrows with a small lace handkerchief.

Her course was parallel to that of the trolley. Yurii Andreievich had already lost sight of her several times, whenever the trolley had started up after a stop for repairs and passed her. She had again come back into his field of vision when it broke down once more and she overtook it.

Yurii Andreievich thought of the problems in school arithmetic in which you are asked how soon and in what order trains, starting at different times and going at different speeds, get to their destinations; he tried to remember the general method of solving them, but it escaped him and he went on from these school memories to others and to still more complicated speculations.

He tried to imagine several people whose lives run parallel and close together but move at different speeds, and he wondered in what circumstances some of them would overtake and survive others. Something like a theory of relativity governing the hippodrome of life occurred to him, but he became confused and gave up his analogies.

There was a flash of lightning and a roll of thunder. The ill-starred trolley was stuck for the nth time; it had stopped halfway down the hill from Kudrinskaia to the Zoo. The lady in lilac appeared in the frame of the window, passed beyond it, and moved on. The first heavy drops of rain fell on the street, the sidewalk, and the lady. A gusty wind whipped past the trees, flapped the leaves, tugged at the lady's hat, ballooned her skirt, and suddenly died down.

The doctor felt an attack of nausea coming on. Surmounting his weakness, he got up from his seat and jerked the window straps up and down trying to open the window. But he could not budge it.

People shouted to him that the window was fastened with screws, but the doctor, fighting against his attack and seized by a sort of panic, was not aware that the people were addressing him, or of the meaning of their words. He continued his attempts to open the window and again gave three sharp tugs at the strap—up, down, and toward himself. Suddenly he felt a sharp pain, greater than any he had ever experienced before; he realized that something had broken in him, he had done something irreparable, fatal, that this was the end. At this moment the trolley started, but after going only a short way down the Presnia it stopped again.

By a superhuman effort of the will, Yurii Andreievich pushed through the solid crowd down the center passage, swaying and stumbling, and came out on the rear platform; people blocked his way and snapped at him. The fresh air seemed to revive him and he thought that perhaps everything was not lost, that he was better.

He began to squeeze his way through the crush on the rear platform, provoking kicks and more abuse. Ignoring the resentful cries, he broke through the crowd, got down from the standing trolley into the street, took a step, another, a third, collapsed on the stone paving, and did not get up again.

There arose a hubbub of talk, arguments, suggestions. Several people got off the trolley and surrounded him. They soon found that he was not breathing and his heart had stopped. The group around the body was joined by others who stepped off the sidewalks, some relieved and others disappointed that the dead man had not been run over and his death had nothing to do with the trolley. The crowd grew larger. The lady in lilac came up too, stood a moment, looked at the body, listened to the talk, and went on. She was a foreigner, but she understood that some people were in favor of putting the body on the trolley and taking it to the hospital, while others said that the police should be called. She did not wait to learn the outcome.

The lady in lilac was a Swiss national; she was Mademoiselle Fleury, from Meliuzeievo, and she was now very, very old. For twelve years she had been writing to the authorities in Moscow for permission to return to her native country, and quite recently her application had been granted. She had come to Moscow for her exit visa and was now on her way to her embassy to collect it, fanning herself as she went along with her documents, which were done up in a bundle and tied with a ribbon. So she walked on, overtaking the trolley for the tenth time and quite unaware that she had overtaken Zhivago and survived him.

13

Through the open door of the passage could be seen one end of the room with the table placed at an angle in the corner. On the table the coffin, like a roughly carved canoe, pointed at the door with its lower, narrow end, which bore the feet of the corpse. It was the same table at which Yurii Andreievich had done his writing; the room had no other. The manuscripts had been put away in a drawer, and the coffin stood on the top. His head was raised on a mound of pillows, and his body lay in the coffin as on a hillside.

He was surrounded by a great many flowers, whole bushes of white lilac, hard to find at this season, cyclamen and cineraria in pots and baskets. The flowers screened the light from the windows. The light filtered thinly through the banked flowers to the waxen face and hands of the corpse and the wood and lining of the coffin. Shadows lay on the table in a pattern of leaves and branches as if they had just stopped swaying.

The custom of cremating the dead had by this time become widespread. In the hope of a pension for the children, and to ensure their education and Marina's position at the post office, it had been decided to dispense with a church service and simply have a civil cremation. The proper authorities had been notified and their representatives were expected.

In the interval the room seemed empty, like premises vacant between the going of one set of tenants and the coming of another. The stillness was broken only by the unwitting shuffling of the mourners, as they tiptoed in to take their leave of the dead. There were not many of them, but nevertheless a good many more than might have been expected. The news of the death of this almost unknown man had spread with amazing speed. Among the people were many who had known him at different times in his life, though he had afterwards lost touch with them and forgotten them. His poetry and scientific work attracted an even greater number of unknown friends who had never met the man but had been drawn to him and had now come to see him for the first and last time.

In these hours when the silence, unaccompanied by any ceremony, became oppressive as if it were an almost tangible privation, only the flowers compensated for the absence of the ritual and the chant.

They did more than blossom and smell sweet. Perhaps hastening the return to dust, they poured forth their scent as in a choir and, steeping everything in their exhalation, seemed to take over the function of the Office of the Dead.

The vegetable kingdom can easily be thought of as the nearest neighbor of the kingdom of death. Perhaps the mysteries of evolution and the riddles of life that so puzzle us are contained in the green of the earth, among the trees and the flowers of graveyards. Mary Magdalene did not recognize Jesus risen from the grave, "supposing Him to be the gardener. . . ."

14

When Yurii Andreievich's body was taken to the flat in Kamerger Street (this had been his last registered address), his friends, notified of his death and shaken by it, came in, straight from the landing through the wide-open door, bringing Marina with them. Half out of her mind with shock and grief, she threw herself down on the floor, beating her head against the edge of the long wooden chest in the hallway. The body had been left there until the coffin (which had already been ordered) was delivered and the living room was put in order. She was in a flood of tears, now whispering, now crying out, choking over her words and breaking into loud lamentations. She grieved with an abundance of speech, as peasants do, neither distracted nor embarrassed by strangers. She clung to the body and could scarcely be torn away when the time came for it to be carried into the room, washed, and placed in the coffin. All this had been the day before. Today the frenzy of her grief had abated, giving way to a weary numbness; she sat in silence, though still only half conscious of herself or her surroundings.

Here she had stayed the rest of the preceding day and all through the night, never leaving the room. Here the baby had been brought for her to feed, and Kapka and her young nurse had come and gone.

She was accompanied by her friends Gordon and Dudorov, who also were numb with grief. Markel, her father, would sit down on the bench by her side and sob and blow his nose into his handkerchief loudly. Her weeping mother and sisters came and went.

But there were two people in the gathering, a man and a woman, who stood out from all the rest. They did not claim any closer tie with the deceased than the others. They did not compete in sorrow with Marina, her daughters, or his friends. But although they made no claims, they evidently had their own special rights over the dead man, and no one questioned or disputed the undeclared authority that they had unaccountably assumed. These were the people who had apparently taken it upon themselves to arrange the funeral, and they had seen to everything from the first with unruffled calm, as if it gave them satisfaction. Their composure was remarkable and it produced a strange impression, as if they were involved not only in the funeral but also in the death, not in the sense of having directly or indirectly caused it but as people who, once it had occurred, had given their consent to it, were reconciled, and did not see it as the most important event in the story of Zhivago. Few of the mourners knew them, a few others surmised who they were, but most had no idea.

Yet whenever this man, whose narrow Kirghiz eyes both expressed and aroused curiosity, came into the room with the casually beautiful woman by his side, they all, including even Marina, at once, without protest, as if by agreement, got up from where they had been sitting on the chairs and stools placed in a row against the wall, and went out, crowding uncomfortably into the corridor and the hallway and leaving the couple alone, behind half-closed doors, like two experts who needed, quietly, unhindered, to accomplish something directly concerned with the funeral, and vitally important.

So it was now. They remained alone, sat down on two chairs near the wall, and at once began to talk.

"What have you found out, Evgraf Andreievich?"

"The cremation is to be tonight. In half an hour they'll come from the Medical Workers' Union to get the body and take it to their club. The civil ceremony is at four. Not one of his papers was in order; his workbook was out of date, he had an old union card, which he hadn't changed for the new one, and his dues hadn't been paid up for years. All that had to be put in order, that was why I took so long. Before they take him away—that's quite soon, we ought to get ready—I'll leave you here alone as you asked. . . . Sorry. That's the telephone. I'll just be a moment."

Evgraf went out into the corridor crowded with the doctor's colleagues, his school friends, junior members of the hospital staff, and people from the publishing world. Marina, her arms around both her children, sheltered them in the folds of the coat she had thrown over her shoulders (it was a cold day), and sat on the edge of the wooden bench waiting to go back into the living room, as a visitor who has gone to see a prisoner in jail waits for the guard to admit her. The corridor and hall were overcrowded. The front door was open and a great many people were standing or strolling about smoking on the landing. Others stood talking on the flight of stairs leading down to the ground floor, the louder and more freely the lower down and closer to the street they were.

Straining to hear above the sustained murmur and speaking in a decorously muffled voice, his hand over the receiver, Evgraf answered questions over the telephone about the funeral arrangements and the circumstances of the doctor's death. Then he went back into the living room and the conversation was resumed.

"Please don't vanish after the cremation, Larisa Feodorovna. I don't know where you are staying, don't disappear without letting me know. I have a great favor to ask you. I'd like as soon as possible—tomorrow or the day after—to begin sorting my brother's papers. I'll need your help. You know so much about him, probably more than anyone else. You mentioned that you had come from Irkutsk only a couple of days ago and not for long, and that you came up here for some other reason, not knowing it had been my brother's flat in recent months or what had happened to him. I didn't understand all you said and I am not asking you to explain, but please don't go away without leaving me your address. It would be best if we could spend the few days that we still need to go through these manuscripts in the same room, or at least quite near, perhaps in two other rooms in this house. It could be arranged. I know the manager."

"You say you didn't understand what I said. What is there to understand? I arrived in Moscow, checked my things at the station, and went for a walk through some old Moscow streets. Half of it I couldn't recognize, I've been away so long I'd forgotten. Well, I walked and walked, down Kuznetsky Most and up Kuznetsky Pereulok, and suddenly I saw something terribly, extraordinarily familiar—Kamerger Street. That was where my husband, Antipov, who was shot, used to live as a student—in this house and in this very room where you and I are sitting now. I'll go in, I thought; who knows, the old tenants might still be there, I'll look them up. You see, I didn't know it had all changed—no one so much as remembers their name—I didn't find that out till later, the day after and today, gradually, by asking people. But you were there, I don't know why I'm telling you. I was thunderstruck—the door wide open, people all over the place, a coffin in the room, a dead man. Who is it? I come in, I come up and look. I thought I had lost my mind. But you were there, you saw me, didn't you? Why on earth am I telling you?"

"Wait a moment, Larisa Feodorovna, I must interrupt you. I've already told you, neither my brother nor I ever suspected that there was anything extraordinary about this room—for instance, that Antipov once lived here. But even more amazing is something you said just now. I'll tell you in a moment. About Antipov, Strelnikov, at one time at the beginning of the civil war I used to hear of him very often, almost every day, and I met him two or three times, never realizing, of course, that his name would come to mean so much to me for family reasons. But forgive me, I may have misheard you, I thought you said— it could only have been a slip of the tongue—that he'd been shot. You must surely know that he shot himself?"

"Yes, I've heard that version, but I don't believe it. Pavel Pavlovich wasn't a man to commit suicide."

"But it's quite certain. Antipov shot himself in that house where, my brother said, you were living before you went to Vladivostok. It happened very soon after you left. My brother found his body. He buried him. How is it you weren't told?"

"I was told something different. . . . So it's really true, he shot himself? People said so but I didn't believe it. And in that very house? It doesn't seem possible. It's very important to me, that detail. You don't know, I suppose, whether he and Zhivago ever met, whether they got to know each other?"

"From what Yurii told me, they had a long conversation."

"Is it possible! Well, thank God, thank God, that's better." Antipova slowly crossed herself. "What an extraordinary, preordained coincidence! Will you let me come back to this and ask you more about it later? Every detail is so dear to me. But this isn't the moment, don't you think? I couldn't, I'm too upset. I'll keep quiet a little, I'll rest and collect my thoughts. What do you think?"

"Of course! Of course!"

"Don't you really think so?"

"Yes, naturally."

"Oh, yes. I nearly forgot. You asked me not to go away after the cremation. All right. I promise. I won't disappear. I'll come back here with you and stay wherever you tell me and for as long as necessary. We'll go through Yurochka's manuscripts. I'll help you. It's true, I might be useful to you. It will comfort me a great deal. I know his writing so well, every twist of it. I know it with my heart, with my life's blood. And then, you know, there's something I want to ask you, too. I'll need your help. Didn't I hear you were a lawyer? Or anyway, you know all the present customs and regulations. And another thing, I need to know what government department to apply to for information. So few people can tell one things like that. What do you think? I'll need your advice about something terrible, something really terrible. It's about a child. But we'll talk about it later, when we come back from the crematorium. All my life I've had to keep looking for people. Tell me, suppose in some quite imaginary case it was necessary to trace a child, a child who had been turned over to strangers to be brought up by them, is there any centralized source of information about all the children's homes throughout the country? And is there any record of all the waifs and strays, has anything like that ever been done or attempted? No, don't tell me now, please don't. We'll talk about it later. I'm so frightened. Life is so terrifying—what do you think? I don't know about later on, when my daughter comes and joins me, but for the moment I don't see why I shouldn't stay in this flat. Katia has a remarkable talent for music and for acting, she's marvellous at imitating people and she acts out entire scenes that she makes up herself, and she sings whole operatic arias, all by ear. She's a remarkable child. What do you think? I want her to go to the junior classes either at the drama school or the Conservatory, whichever will take her, and I must apply for a scholarship, that's really why I've come without her at the moment, to make the arrangements; when I've fixed it all I'll go back. Things are so complicated, don't you think, you can't explain everything. But we'll talk about it later. Now I'll wait a bit, I'll pull myself together, I'll keep quiet and collect my thoughts and try to forget my anxieties. Besides, we've kept Yurii's friends out of the room much too long. Twice I thought I heard someone knocking. And there's something going on outside, they've probably come from the undertaker's. I'll stay here quietly for a bit, but you'd better open the door and let them come in. It's time, don't you think? Wait, wait. There ought to be a footstool near the coffin, otherwise people can't reach up to Yurochka. I tried to on tiptoe, but it's very difficult. And Marina Markelovna and the children, they'll need it. Besides, it's prescribed in the ritual: 'And you shall kiss me with a last kiss.' Oh, I can't bear it. It's all so terrible. What do you think?"

"I'll let them in. But just one thing before I do that. You have said so many baffling things and raised so many questions that are evidently painful to you that I don't know what to tell you. But there's one thing I want you to know. Please count on my help in everything. I offer it to you willingly, with all my heart. And remember: you must never, under any circumstances, despair. To hope and to act, these are our duties in misfortune. To do nothing and to despair is to neglect our duty. Now I'm going to let the mourners in. You're right about the footstool, I'll get one."

But Antipova was no longer listening. She never heard him opening the door nor the people pouring in from the corridor, nor the directions he gave to the undertaker's men and the chief mourners; she heard neither the shuffling of the crowd nor Marina's sobs, neither the coughing of the men nor the tears and cries of the women.

The ceaseless, monotonous noise made her feel sick and giddy. It took all her strength not to faint. Her heart was bursting and her head ached. Lowering her head, she withdrew into memories, reflections, conjectures. She escaped into them, sank into them, as though carried forward for a time, for a few hours, into some future that she might not live to see, a future that aged her by several decades, a future where she was an old woman. In her thoughts she seemed to touch the very bottom of her unhappiness.

"No one is left. One has died. The other has killed himself. And only that one is left alive who should have been killed, whom I tried to kill and missed, that stranger who had nothing in common with me, that complete cipher who turned my life into a chain of crimes beyond my knowing. And that monster of mediocrity is busy dashing about in the mythical byways of Asia known only to stamp collectors, and not one of those who are near to me and whom I need is left.

"Ah, it was at Christmastime, and I had set out to shoot that caricature of vulgarity when I had that talk in this very room, lit only by a candle, with Pasha, who was still a boy, and Yura, whose body they are taking leave of now, had not yet come into my life."

She strained her memory to reconstruct that Christmas conversation with Pasha, but she could remember nothing except the candle burning on the window sill and melting a round patch in the icy crust on the glass.

Did she divine that Yurii, whose dead body was lying on the table, had seen the candle as he was driving past, and noticed it, and that from the moment of his seeing its light from the street ("A candle burned on the table, a candle burned . . .") his life took its fatal course?

Her thoughts scattered. She thought: "But what a pity he isn't having a church funeral. The burial service is so grand and solemn! It's more than most people deserve when they die, but it would have been so appropriate for Yurochka! He would have deserved all that, he would have justified and given meaning to 'the lament over the grave which is the hymn of Alleluiah.'"

Now she felt a wave of pride and relief, as always at the thought of Yurii and as in the short intervals of her life that she had spent beside him. Now, too, she was enveloped in the air of that freedom and unconcern that he had always emanated. She got up impatiently from her chair. Something incomprehensible was happening to her. She wanted, if only for a few moments, to break free with Yurii's help into the open, out of the sorrows that imprisoned her, to feel again the joy of liberation. Such a joy, it seemed to her, would be the joy of taking leave of him, of using the right and the occasion to weep her fill over him unhindered. With a passionate haste, she looked around her at the crowd, with eyes as smarting, unseeing, and tearful as if an oculist had put caustic eye-drops into them, and all the people began to move, shuffle, and walk out of the room, leaving her at last alone, behind half-closed doors. She went up to the table with the coffin on it, quickly crossing herself, got up on the footstool Evgraf had brought, made three sweeping signs of the cross over the body, and pressed her lips to the cold forehead and hands. She brushed aside the impression that the cold forehead was somehow smaller, like a hand clenched into a fist, she managed not to notice it. For a moment she stood still and silent, neither thinking nor crying, bowed over the coffin, the flowers, and the body, shielding them with her whole being, her head, her breast, her heart, and her arms, as big as her heart.

15

She was shaken by her repressed sobs. She fought her tears as long as she could, but at times it was beyond her strength and they burst from her, pouring down her cheeks and onto her dress, her hands, and the coffin, to which she clung.

She neither spoke nor thought. Sequences of ideas, notions, insights, truths drifted and sailed freely through her mind, like clouds in the sky, as happened so often before during their nighttime conversations. It was such things that had brought them happiness and liberation in those days. A spontaneous mutual understanding, warm, instinctive, immediate.

Such an understanding filled her now, a dark, indistinct knowledge of death, preparedness for death, a preparedness that removed all feeling of helplessness in its presence. It was as if she had lived twenty lives, and had lost Yurii countless times, and had accumulated such experience of the heart in this domain that everything she felt and did beside this coffin was exactly right and to the point.

Oh, what a love it was, utterly free, unique, like nothing else on earth! Their thoughts were like other people's songs.

They loved each other, not driven by necessity, by the "blaze of passion" often falsely ascribed to love. They loved each other because everything around them willed it, the trees and the clouds and the sky over their heads and the earth under their feet. Perhaps their surrounding world, the strangers they met in the street, the wide expanses they saw on their walks, the rooms in which they lived or met, took more delight in their love than they themselves did.

Ah, that was just what had united them and had made them so akin! Never, never, even in their moments of richest and wildest happiness, were they unaware of a sublime joy in the total design of the universe, a feeling that they themselves were a part of that whole, an element in the beauty of the cosmos.

This unity with the whole was the breath of life to them. And the elevation of man above the rest of nature, the modern coddling and worshipping of man, never appealed to them. A social system based on such a false premise, as well as its political application, struck them as pathetically amateurish and made no sense to them.

16

And now she took her leave of him, addressing him in the direct language of everyday life. Her speech, though lively and informal, was not down-to-earth. Like the choruses and monologues of ancient tragedies, like the language of poetry or music, or any other conventional mode of expression, its logic was not rational but emotional. The rhetorical strain in her effortless, spontaneous talk came from her grief. Her simple, unsolemn words were drenched in tears.

It was these tears that seemed to hold her words together in a tender, quick whispering like the rustling of silky leaves in a warm, windy rain.

"At last we are together again, Yurochka. And in what a terrible way God has willed our reunion. Can you conceive of such misfortune! I cannot, cannot. Oh, God! I can't stop crying. Think of it! It's again so much in our style, made to our

measure. Your going—my end. Again something big, irreparable. The riddle of life, the riddle of death, the enchantment of
genius, the enchantment of unadorned beauty—yes, yes, these
things were ours. But the small problems of practical life—
things like the reshaping of the planet—these things, no thank
you, they are not for us.

"Farewell, my great one, my own, farewell, my pride,
farewell, my swift, deep, dear river, how I loved your day-long
splashing, how I loved to plunge into your cold waves.

"Remember how we said goodbye that day out there in the
snow? How you deceived me! Would I ever have gone without
you? Oh, I know, I know, you forced yourself to do it, you
thought it was for my good. And after that everything was
ruined. Oh, God, what I suffered there, what I went through!
But of course you don't know any of that. Oh, what have I
done, Yura, what have I done? I am such a criminal, you have
no idea. But it wasn't my fault. I was in the hospital for three
months, a whole month I was unconscious. And since then my
life has been nothing but torment, Yura. My soul has no peace, I
am torn by remorse and pain. But I'm not telling you the most
important thing. I can't say it, I haven't the strength. Every time
I come to that part of my life my hair stands on end with horror.
And you know, I'm not even sure I'm in my right mind. But
you see, I haven't taken to drink as so many people do, I'm
staying away from that, because a drunken woman, that really
is the end, it's impossible, don't you think?"

She went on speaking and sobbing in her agony. Suddenly
she looked up in surprise and glanced around her. People had
come into the room and were going about their business. She
got down from the footstool and moved away from the coffin,
swaying, pressing her hand to her eyes as if to wipe away the
last of her tears.

Men came up to the coffin and lifted it on three cloths. The
funeral procession began.

17

Larisa Feodorovna stayed several days in Kamerger Street. The sorting of Zhivago's papers was begun with her help but finished without her. She also had her talk with Evgraf Andreievich and told him an important fact.

One day Larisa Feodorovna went out and did not come back. She must have been arrested in the street at that time. She vanished without a trace and probably died somewhere, forgotten as a nameless number on a list that afterwards got mislaid, in one of the innumerable mixed or women's concentration camps in the north.

CHAPTER SIXTEEN

Epilogue

1

In the summer of 1943, after the breakthrough on the Kursk bulge and the liberation of Orel, Gordon, recently promoted to Second Lieutenant, and Major Dudorov were returning to their unit, the one from a service assignment in Moscow, the other from three days' furlough.

They met on their way back and spent the night at Chern, a small town which, although in ruins, was not completely destroyed, as were most of the settlements in this "desert zone" left in the wake of the retreating invader.

Among the heaps of broken bricks and stone ground into fine dust they found an undamaged barn and settled down in it for the night.

They could not sleep, and talked for hours on end. When Dudorov finally dozed off at about three in the morning, a little before dawn, he was soon waked up again by Gordon. Awkwardly diving into the soft hay and rolling about in it as in water, he collected a few clothes into a bundle and then just as awkwardly crawled off the top of the mountain of hay, down to the door.

"Where are you going? It's early."

"I'm going down to the river. I want to wash my things."

"That's mad. We'll be back with the unit by evening. Tania, the laundry girl, will give you a change of clothes. What's the hurry?"

"I don't want to wait till then. They're sweaty, filthy. I'll rinse them quickly and wring them out well, in this heat they'll be dry in no time. I'll have a bath and change."

"Still, it won't look good. After all, you're an officer."

"It's early, there's no one about, they're all asleep. Anyway, I'll get behind a bush or something, nobody will see me. Stop talking and go back to sleep, or you'll wake yourself up for good."

"I won't sleep anymore anyway. I'll go with you."

So they went down to the river, past the white stone ruins, already hot though it was only a little after sunrise. In what had once been streets, people were sleeping on the ground in the sun, snoring, their faces red and sweaty. They were mostly natives who had lost their homes, old men, women, and children, with a sprinkling of Red Army men who had lost touch with their units and were trying to catch up with them. Gordon and Dudorov made their way carefully through them so as not to disturb their sleep.

"Keep your voice down or you'll wake up the town and then it'll be goodbye to my washing."

They continued their last night's conversation quietly.

2

"What's this river?"

"I don't know. The Zusha, probably."

"No, that isn't the Zusha."

"Then I don't know what it is."

"It's on the Zusha, you know, that it all happened—Christina, I mean."

"Yes, but that would be lower down the river. They say the Church has canonized her."

"There was an old stone building, which they called Stables. Once it actually was used as the stables of a sovkhoz stud-farm—now the name will go down in history—a very old place with huge thick walls. The Germans fortified it and made it impregnable. It was on a hill and they had the whole district under fire and were holding up our advance. It had to be captured. Christina, by a miracle of courage and ingenuity, got inside the German lines and blew it up, and was taken alive and hanged."

"Why do they call her Christina Orletsova and not Dudorova?"

"We were only engaged, you know. We decided in the summer of forty-one that we'd be married at the end of the war. After that I moved about a great deal, like everybody in the army. My unit was sent from one place to another. Because of all those endless transfers I lost touch with her. I never saw her again. I heard of her extraordinary exploit and heroic death like everyone else—from the newspapers and the regimental orders. They say they're going to put up a monument to her somewhere near here. I hear Zhivago—the General, Yurii's brother— is going around the district collecting data about her."

"I'm sorry—I shouldn't have made you talk about her. It must all be very painful for you."

"Well . . . But we've lost track of time, and I don't want to hold you up. You get undressed and into the water, and get going. I'll lie on the bank and chew a blade of grass and think. I may even sleep a bit."

A few moments later they began to talk again.

"Where did you learn to wash clothes like that?"

"From necessity. We were unlucky. We got sent to just about the worst of the penal camps. There were very few survivors. Our arrival, to begin with. We got off the train. A wilderness of snow. Forest in the distance. Guards with rifles, muzzles pointing at us, wolfhounds. About the same time, other groups were brought up. We were spread out and formed into a big polygon all over the field, facing outward, so that we wouldn't see each other. Then we were ordered down on our knees, and told to keep looking straight ahead on pain of death. Then the roll call, an endless, humiliating business going on for hours and hours. And all the time we were on our knees. Then we got up and the other groups were marched off and ours was told: 'This is your camp. Make the best of it!' An open snow field with a post in the middle and a notice on it saying: 'GULAG 92 Y.N. 90'—that's all there was."

"It wasn't nearly so bad with us; we were lucky. Of course I was doing my second stretch, which followed automatically from the first. Moreover, I was sentenced under a different article, so the conditions were quite different. When I came out, I was reinstated again as I'd been the first time and allowed to go on lecturing. And when I was mobilized I was given my full rank of Major, not put into a disciplinary battalion, like you."

"Yes, well . . . That was all there was, the post and the notice board, 'GULAG 92 Y.N. 90.' First we broke saplings with our bare hands in the bitter cold, to get wood to build huts. And in the end, believe it or not, we gradually built our whole camp. We put up our prison and our stockade and our cells and our watchtowers, all with our own hands. And then we began our job as lumberjacks. We cut trees. We harnessed ourselves, eight to a sledge, and we hauled timber and sank into the snow up to our necks. For a long time we didn't know the war had started. They kept it from us. And then suddenly there came the offer. You could volunteer for front-line service in a disciplinary battalion, and if you came out alive you were free. After that, attack after attack, mile after mile of electrified barbed wire, mines, mortars, month after month of artillery barrage. They called our company the death squad. It was practically wiped out. How and why I survived, I don't know. And yet—would you believe it—all that utter hell was nothing, it was bliss compared to the horrors of the concentration camp, and not because of the material conditions but for an entirely different reason."

"Yes, poor fellow. You've taken a lot."

"It wasn't just washing clothes you learned out there, you learned everything there is to learn."

"It's an extraordinary thing, you know. It isn't only in comparison with your life as a convict, but compared to everything in the thirties, even to my easy situation at the university in the midst of books and money and comfort, the war came as a breath of fresh air, a purifying storm, a breath of deliverance.

"I think that collectivization was an erroneous and unsuccessful measure and it was impossible to admit the error. To conceal the failure people had to be cured, by every means of terrorism, of the habit of thinking and judging for themselves, and forced to see what didn't exist, to assert the very opposite of what their eyes told them. This accounts for the unexampled cruelty of the Yezhov* period, the promulgation of a constitution that was

---

*Nikolai Ivanovich Yezhov, head of the Secret Police, 1936–38.

never meant to be applied, and the introduction of elections that violated the very principle of free choice.

"And when the war broke out, its real horrors, its real dangers, its menace of real death were a blessing compared with the inhuman reign of the lie, and they brought relief because they broke the spell of the dead letter.

"It was felt not only by men in your position, in concentration camps, but by absolutely everyone, at home and at the front, and they all took a deep breath and flung themselves into the furnace of this mortal, liberating struggle with real joy, with rapture.

"The war has its special character as a link in the chain of revolutionary decades. The forces directly unleashed by the revolution no longer operated. The indirect effects of the revolution, the fruit of its fruit, the consequences of the consequences, began to manifest themselves. Misfortune and ordeals had tempered characters, prepared them for great, desperate, heroic exploits. These fabulous, astounding qualities characterize the moral elite of this generation.

"And when I see such things I am filled with happiness, in spite of Christina's martyrdom and our losses and my wounds, in spite of the high cost in blood of the war. The light of self-sacrifice that illuminates Orletsova's death and the lives of all of us helps me to bear her loss.

"I was released just when you, poor fellow, were going through your endless torture. Soon after that, Christina came to the university as a history student. I taught her. I had noticed her before, after my first term in concentration camp, as a remarkable girl, when she was still a child. You remember, Yurii was still alive, I told you both. Well, now she was one of my students.

"That was the time when the custom of political re-education of teachers by students had come in. Orletsova flung herself into that work with passion. I had no idea why she went at me so fiercely. She was so aggressive and unjust that sometimes the other students protested and stood up for me. She had a great sense of humor and she made fun of me to her heart's content in the wall newspaper, referring to me by some invented name that everyone could see through. And then suddenly, completely by chance, I realized that this inveterate hostility was a camouflage of her love for me—a strong, enduring love she had felt for a long time, and which I had always returned.

"We spent a wonderful summer in forty-one, just before and after the beginning of the war. Christina was in a group of undergraduates, men and women, who were billeted in a Moscow suburb where my unit was also stationed. Our friendship began and ran its course against this background. At that time civilian units were being formed, Christina was being trained as a parachutist, the first German bombers were spotted from the rooftops of Moscow and driven back. That was when we became engaged, as I told you, but we were separated almost at once because my regiment was moved. I never saw her again.

"Later on, when the war took a turn for the better and the Germans were surrendering by the thousands, I was transferred after I had been wounded twice, from Anti-Aircraft to the Seventh Staff Division, where they needed people who knew languages. Then, after I fished you out of the depths, I got you assigned to my unit."

"Tania, the laundry girl, was a friend of Christina's. They got to know each other at the front. She talks a lot about her. Have you noticed the way Tania smiles, all over her face, like Yurii? You forget the snub nose and the high cheekbones, and you think she's quite pretty and attractive. It's the same type, you see it all over Russia."

"I know what you mean. No, I hadn't noticed."

"What a hideous, barbarous nickname, Tania Bezocheredeva, 'Tania Out-of-Turn.' It can't possibly be her surname. I wonder how she got it."

"She told us, you know. She was a bezprizornaia of unknown parents. Probably somewhere in the depths of Russia where the language is still pure she was called Bezotchcheia, 'Fatherless.' Then her name was distorted by city people who introduced a connotation closer to their recent experiences."

3

Shortly after this, Gordon and Dudorov were in the town of Karachev, which had been razed to the ground. There they caught up with some rear units of their army.

It was a hot autumn; the weather had been fine and still for more than a month. The black soil of Bryanshchina, the blessedly fertile region between Orel and Bryansk, shimmered a chocolate or coffee brown under the blue, cloudless sky.

The main street, which was part of the highway, cut straight across the town. On one side of it had been houses that were blown up and turned into piles of rubble by mines, and uprooted, splintered, and charred fruit trees from the blasted gardens. Nor were there any houses on the other side, but it was less ravaged by fire and explosions, probably because it had consisted largely of vacant lots and thus offered no targets for destruction.

On the side where there had once been houses, the homeless inhabitants were poking about in the still smoldering ashes, picking up odds and ends in different corners of the ruins and putting them all together in one place. Others were busy making dugouts and cutting strips of turf with which to roof them.

The vacant lots across the road were white with tents and crowded with auxiliary-service trucks and horse-drawn wagons of all kinds—field ambulances, cut off from their divisional staffs, and units of every sort of commissariat and depot, lost and mixed up and trying to sort themselves out. And here, too, weedy boys from the replacement companies, in gray caps, with heavy, rolled-up overcoats on their backs, their faces earthy, drawn, and wasted from dysentery, rested their packs and had a sleep and a snack before trudging on farther west.

Half the gutted, blown-up town was still burning and in the distance delayed-action mines kept exploding. Every now and then, people digging in their yards straightened their bent backs, leaned on their picks, and rested, turning and gazing in the direction of a blast.

There, the gray, black, brick-red clouds of smoke, flame, and rubble rose into the sky, first in jets and fountains, then more lazily, like heavily rising scum, then fanning and spreading into plumes; finally they scattered and sank back to earth. Then the diggers went on with their work.

Across the road from the ruins there was an open space bordered by a hedge and shaded by tall old trees. The trees and the hedge isolated it from the rest of the world, like a private courtyard, shaded and cool.

Here Tania, the laundry girl, together with several people from her unit, as well as others who had joined them, including

Dudorov and Gordon, had been waiting since morning for the truck that had been sent for her. The regimental laundry entrusted to her care was packed in several crates that stood piled one on top of the other on the ground. Tania kept a close eye on it, and the rest of the group remained in sight for fear of missing the chance of a lift.

They had been waiting a long time—more than five hours. With nothing to do, they listened to the incessant chatter of the garrulous girl, who had seen a great deal in her life. At the moment she was telling them of how she had met Major-General Zhivago.

"Of course. Yesterday. They took me to the General himself. Major-General Zhivago. He was passing through here, and asking everyone about Christina. He was looking for eye-witnesses, people who had known her personally. They pointed me out to him. They said we'd been friends. He told them to bring me along. So they came and got me. He didn't scare me a bit. Nothing special about him, just like everybody else. He's got slit eyes and black hair. Well, I told him what I knew. He heard me out and said thank you. And who are you? he said to me. Where do you come from? Well, naturally, I was shy. What have I got to boast about? I'm a bezprizornaia. One of the homeless children. And all that. I don't have to tell you. Reformatories, always on the move. But he kept at me. Let's have it, he said. Don't be embarrassed. There's nothing to be ashamed of. Well, at first I couldn't say much, then I told him a bit more, and he kept nodding his head, then as he went on nodding, I wasn't afraid any longer. And it's true I've got a lot to tell. You wouldn't believe it if I told you; you'd say, She's making it up. Well, it was the same with him. When I finished he got up and started walking up and down the room. That's extraordinary, he said. Really extraordinary. I'll tell you what, he said. I haven't got time now. But I'll find you again, you can be sure of that. I'll find you and send for you again. I never thought I'd hear a thing like that. I won't leave you this way, he said, I've just got to take care of a few things. And then, who can tell, I might put myself down as your uncle, you'll be promoted to being General's niece. And I'll send you to a university, he said. Anywhere you like. I swear to God, that's what he said. Probably a joke, just to tease me."

At this moment a long, empty cart with high sides, of the kind used for carting hay in Poland and West Russia, drove up.

The two horses in their shaft harness were driven by a soldier from the horse transport corps who in the old days would have been called a wagoner. He pulled up, jumped down from his seat, and began to unhitch the cart. Everyone except Tania and one or two soldiers crowded around him begging him to take them wherever they were going, telling him, of course, that they would make it worth his while. But the driver refused, saying he had no right to use the cart or the horses except as he was ordered. He led the horses away and was not seen again.

Tania and the others, who until then had been sitting on the ground, all climbed into the empty cart, which had been left standing in the field. The conversation, interrupted by its arrival and by the argument with the driver, was resumed.

"What did you tell the General?" asked Gordon. "Tell us, if you can."

"Why not? I'll tell you."

And so she told them her terrible story.

4

"Yes, it's true that I've got a lot to tell. They say I don't come from poor people. Whether strangers told me or I somehow remembered it, I don't know, but I've heard it said that my mother, Raïsa Komarova, was the wife of a Russian cabinet minister, Comrade Komarov, who was in hiding in White Mongolia. But I guess Komarov was not my real father. Well, of course, I'm not an educated girl, I grew up an orphan without a father and mother. Perhaps what I say seems funny to you, but I'm only saying what I know, you have to put yourselves in my place.

"Yes. Well now, what I'm going to tell you, it all happened beyond Krushitsy, the other end of Siberia, beyond the Cossack country, near the Chinese border. When we—the Reds, that is—moved up to the chief town of the Whites, that same Komarov, the minister, he put my mother and all those families on a special train and ordered it to take them away. My mother was frightened, you see, she didn't dare to move a step without him.

"This Komarov didn't know about me. He didn't know that I even existed. My mother had me when she had been parted from him for a long time, and she was frightened to death that somebody might tell him. He hated children terribly, and he yelled and stamped his feet. They only bring filth and worry into the house, I can't stand it, he used to yell.

"Well now, as I was saying, when the Reds began to come up to the town, my mother sent to Nagornaia Station for Marfa, the signal woman. That was three stations away from the town. I'll tell you how it was. First there was Nizovaia, and then there was Nagornaia, and then there was the Samsonov Pass. Now I think I understand it, why Mother knew this signal woman. I think this signal woman, Marfa, used to come and sell milk and vegetables in the town. That's it.

"And here is something I don't know. I think they cheated Mother, they didn't tell her the truth. The Lord only knows what sort of story they told her, I suppose they said it was just for a time, for a day or two, till things settled down. She didn't mean to give me to strangers forever. To be brought up by strangers—Mother could not have given up her own child like that.

"Well, you know how it is with a child. 'Go and talk to Auntie, she'll give you a piece of gingerbread, nice Auntie, don't be frightened of Auntie.' How I cried afterwards, how heartbroken I was, how I missed my mother—it's better not to remember that. I wanted to hang myself, I nearly went out of my mind as a small child. That was all I was at that time. I suppose Aunt Marfa got money for my keep, a lot of money.

"There was a rich farm that went with the signal job, a cow and a horse and of course all kinds of fowl, and a big place for vegetables—out there you could get as much land as you liked— and of course no rent because the house belonged to the government; it was right next to the tracks. When the train was coming from home, it could hardly get up the hill, it was so steep, but coming from your parts, from Russia, down it came so fast they had to use the brakes. Down below, in the autumn, when the woods thinned out, you could see Nagornaia as if it were set on a saucer.

"The signal man, Uncle Vasilii, I used to call just Daddy. He was a kind and cheerful man, only terribly trusting, especially when he was drunk. Everybody knew all there was to know about him all over the countryside. He'd turn his heart inside out to every stranger he met.

"But the signal woman I never could call Mother. Whether it

was because I couldn't forget my own mother or for some other reason, the fact is Aunt Marfa really was terrible. Yes. And so I called the signal woman Aunt Marfa.

"Well, time went on, years went by, how many I don't know. I was beginning to go out to the trains to wave the flag, and I could bring the cow in or unhitch the horse. Aunt Marfa taught me to spin, and as for the housework, it goes without saying I did that. Anything like sweeping or tidying or doing a bit of cooking, that was nothing to me, I did all that. Oh, yes, and I forgot to tell you, I looked after Petia. Our Petia had withered legs, he was three but he couldn't walk at all, so I carried him around. And now, after all those years, I still get shivers down my back when I think of how Auntie Marfa used to squint at my strong legs as much as to say why weren't my legs withered, it would be better if I had withered legs instead of her Petia, as if I'd put the evil eye on him. You wouldn't believe what spite and superstition there is in the world.

"But now listen to what I'm going to tell you. All that was nothing to what happened later. It'll make your hair stand on end.

"It was the time of NEP, a thousand rubles was worth a kopeck. Uncle Vasia sold a cow down below and got two sacks full of money. Kerenki it was called—no, sorry, they were called lemons then, that's what they were called. He had a drink and told everyone in Nagornaia how rich he was.

"I remember it was a windy day in autumn. The wind was tearing at the roof, it nearly knocked you off your feet, and the engines couldn't get uphill because the wind was head on. Suddenly I saw an old beggar woman coming down from the top of the hill, the wind tugging at her skirt and blowing off her kerchief.

"She was walking along and moaning and clutching her belly. She asked us to take her in, and we put her on the bench. Oh, she yelled, I can't stand it, I can't stand it, my belly is on fire, this is my end. In Christ's name, she begged, take me to the hospital, I'll pay you whatever you like. Well, Daddy hitched Udaloy, the horse, to the cart, put the old woman in the cart, and took her to the county hospital, which was eleven miles away.

"After a time we went to bed, Aunt Marfa and I, then we heard Udaloy neighing outside and the cart driving into the yard. It seemed a bit too soon for them to be back. But anyway

Aunt Marfa lit a light, put on her jacket, and undid the bolt without waiting for Daddy to knock.

"She opened the door, but it wasn't Daddy, it was a stranger, dark and frightening, and he said, Show me where the money is that you got for the cow. I've killed your old man in the wood, he said, but you being a woman I'll let you alone if you tell me where the money is. If you don't tell me you know what will happen, you'll only have yourself to blame, and better not keep me waiting, I don't have any time to hang around.

"Oh, God in heaven, need I tell you the state we were in, you can imagine, yourselves. We were shaking all over, half dead with fright and speechless with terror! First Uncle Vasia was killed, he'd said so himself, he'd killed him with an ax, and now we were alone with him, a murderer right in our house, we could see he was a murderer.

"I suppose it was just then that Aunt Marfa went out of her mind. The moment she heard her husband was dead, something snapped inside her. And she knew she mustn't show how she felt.

"First she threw herself at his feet. Have mercy on me, she said, don't kill me, I don't know a thing, I've never heard about any money, I don't know what money you are talking about. But he wasn't going to be put off with that, he wasn't such a fool, the devil. All right, then, she told him. The money is in the cellar. I'll open the trap door for you. But the devil saw right through that. No, he said, you go down, you know the way, you get it. I don't care if you go down to the cellar or up on the roof, all I want is the money. But remember—don't try to pull any tricks, he said, it doesn't pay to fool with me.

"Then she said to him: God be with you, why are you so suspicious? I'd gladly go down and get it for you myself, but my legs are bad, I can't manage the ladder. I'll stand on the top step and hold the light for you. Don't worry, I'll send my daughter down with you, she said. That was me she meant.

"Oh, God in heaven, need I tell you how I felt when I heard that? Well, that's the end of me, I thought, and everything went black in front of my eyes and my legs wouldn't hold me up, I thought I'd fall down.

"But that devil, he was no fool, he took one look at both of us and screwed up his eyes and grinned at her, showing all his teeth, as much as to say: I know your tricks, you can't fool me. He could see that I meant nothing to her, I wasn't her own flesh

and blood, so he made a grab at Petia and picked him up in one
hand and pulled up the trap door with the other. Let's have a
light, he said to her, and down he went—down the ladder into
the cellar with Petia.

"I think she was already cracked and couldn't understand
anything; her mind was gone. As soon as he had gone down
with little Petia, bang, she slammed the trap door and locked it
and began to drag a heavy trunk on top of it, nodding and
beckoning to me to help her, because it was too heavy for her.
She got it in place and sat on it, pleased with herself, the crazy
woman. No sooner had she sat down than the robber started
yelling and banging on the floor. You couldn't make out what
he was saying, the floor boards were too thick, but you could
tell from his voice what he meant: let him out or he'd murder
Petia. He roared worse than a wild beast to frighten us. Now
your Petia's in for it, he yelled, but she couldn't understand a
thing. She just sat there winking at me and laughing, as much as
to say: No matter what you do, I won't budge from the trunk
and I'll keep the keys. I did everything I could with her, I
screamed right into her ears saying she must open up the cellar
and save Petia, and I tried to push her off the trunk, but I
couldn't, she was too strong for me and she wouldn't listen.

"Well, he was banging, banging on the floor, and the time
was going by, and she just sat there rolling her eyes, not
listening to anything.

"Well, after a time—Oh, God in heaven, I've been through
many things in my life, but this I'll never forget. As long as I
live I'll hear Petia's thin little voice—little Petia cried and
groaned down below, the little angel, that devil choked him to
death.

"Now what shall I do, what shall I do with this mad old
woman and this murderer, I thought. And I had to do
something. The moment I thought this I heard Udaloy neighing
outside. He'd been standing out there in the yard and he hadn't
been unharnessed. Yes. Udaloy was neighing as much as to say:
Let's fly quickly, Tania, and find some good people and get
help. I looked out of the window and I saw that it was near
dawn. You're right, Udaloy, it's a good idea, I thought. Let's
go. But hardly had I thought this when again I heard, like a
voice calling from the wood, Wait, don't hurry, Tania, we'll do
it another way. And again I knew I wasn't alone in the wood. It
was like our own cock crowing. An engine hooted down

below. I recognized its whistle; it was from the engine that they
always kept ready at Nagornaia—a pusher, they called it—to
help freight trains up the hill. This was a mixed train going by,
it always went by at that time every night. Well, I heard this
engine I knew, calling me from below. I listened and my heart
leapt. Am I off my head, I wondered, like Auntie Marfa, that
every living beast and every dumb engine speaks to me in plain
Russian?

"Well, it was no good thinking, the train was getting near,
there was no time to think. I grabbed the lantern—there wasn't
much light yet—and I raced to the track and stood right in the
middle, between the rails, waving the light up and down.

"Well, what more is there to say? I stopped the train. Because
of the wind it was going slowly, very slowly, almost at a crawl.
I stopped it and the driver, who knew me, leaned out of the
window of the cab and called out something, I couldn't hear
what it was because of the wind. I shouted to him, the signal
house had been raided, murder and robbery, a killer in the
house, help us, Comrade Uncle, we need help right away. And
while I was saying this, Red Army men came jumping out of
the train, one after the other, it was an army train, they jumped
out on the track. What's up? they asked, they couldn't make out
why on earth the train had stopped in the wood, on a steep hill
at night, and was standing still.

"I told them everything. They dragged the murderer out of
the cellar. He was squealing in a voice thinner than Petia's, Have
mercy on me, good people, he said, don't kill me, I'll never do it
again. They took the law into their own hands. They dragged
him out onto the tracks, tied his hands and feet to the rails, and
drove the train over him.

"I never even went back for my clothes, I was so frightened. I
asked them to take me along in the train, and they put me on the
train and off I went. After this, I wandered over half our own
country and others with the bezprizornys, I don't know where I
haven't been. I'm not exaggerating. What happiness, what
freedom now, after all I suffered as a child! Though it must be
said that there was also much sin and misery. But all this came
later, I'll tell you about it some other time. . . . That night I
was telling you about, a railway official came off the train and
went to the house to take charge of the government property,
and to decide what to do about Auntie Marfa. Some say she
never recovered and died in a madhouse, but others say she got
better and came out."

For a long time after hearing Tania's story Gordon and Dudorov strolled about under the trees in silence. Then the truck came; it turned clumsily off the road into the clearing, and the crates were loaded onto it. Gordon said:

"You realize who this Tania is?"

"Yes, of course."

"Evgraf will look after her." Gordon added after a pause: "It has often happened in history that a lofty ideal has degenerated into crude materialism. Thus Greece gave way to Rome, and the Russian Enlightenment has become the Russian Revolution. There is a great difference between the two periods. Blok says somewhere: 'We, the children of Russia's terrible years.' Blok meant this in a metaphorical, figurative sense. The children were not children, but the sons, the heirs, the intelligentsia, and the terrors were not terrible but sent from above, apocalyptic; that's quite different. Now the metaphorical has become literal, children are children and the terrors are terrible, there you have the difference."

5

Five or ten years later, one quiet summer evening, Dudorov and Gordon were again together, sitting at an open window above Moscow, which extended into the dusk as far as the eye could reach. They were looking through an album of Yurii's writings that Evgraf had put together, a book they had read more than once and almost knew by heart. They read and talked and thought. By the time they came to the middle of the book it was dark and they turned on the light.

And Moscow, right below them and stretching into the distance, the author's native city, in which he had spent half his life—Moscow now struck them not as the stage of the events connected with him but as the main protagonist of a long story, the end of which they had reached that evening, book in hand.

Although victory had not brought the relief and freedom that were expected at the end of the war, nevertheless the portents of freedom filled the air throughout the postwar period, and they alone defined its historical significance.

To the two old friends, as they sat by the window, it seemed that this freedom of the soul was already there, as if that very evening the future had tangibly moved into the streets below them, that they themselves had entered it and were now part of it. Thinking of this holy city and of the entire earth, of the still-living protagonists of this story, and their children, they were filled with tenderness and peace, and they were enveloped by the unheard music of happiness that flowed all about them and into the distance. And the book they held seemed to confirm and encourage their feeling.

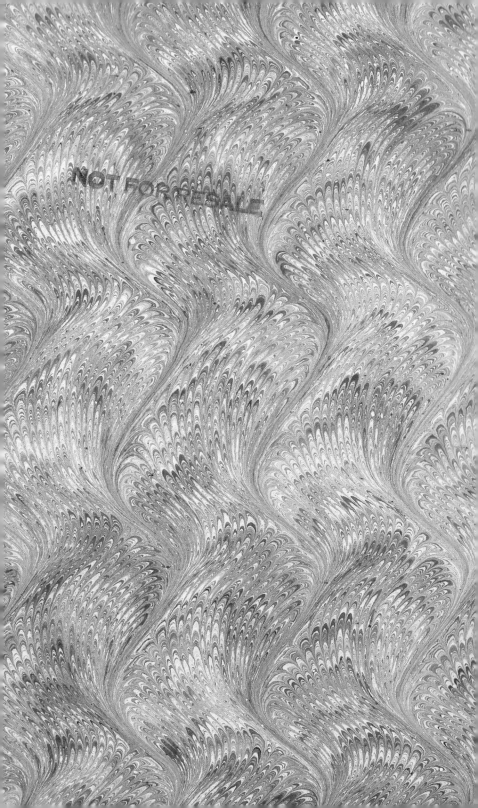